THE AETHEREALS OMNIBUS

This Omnibus Edition includes:
THE HOLLOW PLANE
THE RAVAGED DARK
and "Chevalier, First Class"

by Allison Carr Waechter

Print ISBN: 978-1-963134-16-2, 978-1-963134-28-5

Ebook ISBN: 978-1-963134-25-4

Book Cover by Averil the Artist

Editing by Kenna Kettrick

Interior Illustrations and Map by Rachael Ward of Cartography Bird

The Aethereals Omnibus collects books from *The Aethereals Duology*: *The Hollow Plane* and *The Ravaged Dark*

*for all the babes who've lived one too many lives and forgotten who they are.
relearning yourself is a journey. be gentle with yourself as you travel.*

THE PEOPLE OF SIRIN

The Oscarovi: Witches.

Elemental Spirits: Incorporeal creatures who align closely with the six elements: earth, air, water, fire, empyrae, and aether. Elemental spirits sometimes choose to pair with the Oscarovi as their familiars.

THE VILHARI

The Vilhari are a multi-racial group of fey people who came to Sirin nearly 4000 years prior to the present day of the book. They traveled the stars in a starcraft called the Avalonne that had to make an emergency landing. When the ship could not be repaired, the entire population of the enormous ship was forced to make their home on Sirin. The people on the ship included:

- **Vilhar/Vilhari:** This term most commonly refers to humanoid fey in the present-day of the book. These fey have pointed ears, and some have feathered wings.
- **Strix:** The Strix have humanoid bodies and the heads

(visages) of various owls. They also have taloned hands that they often cover with gloves.

- **Corvidae:** The Corvidae have humanoid bodies and the heads (visages) of ravens and crows. Like the Strix, they have taloned hands that they cover with gloves.
- **Sirens/Sybils:** The sirens and sybils are people with bird and animal bodies that have humanoid faces/heads.

THE VENTYR:

The Ventyr were an invading force of humanoid people that came to Sirin approximately 2000 years before the present day of the book. At that time, all the fey people from the Avalonne, the elemental spirits, and the Oscarovi aligned to defeat them and drive them out. This invasion changed the course of magic on Sirin forever.

AUTHOR'S NOTE

The Aethereals Duology is written for and marketed to adult audiences only. Please see the author's website at www.allisoncar rwaechter.com for information regarding content guidelines and glossary.

DIANTHIC RANGE
SILV
PEVKA
NORTHERN AERIES
ACHERA RIVER
KYOVKA
MONTCLAIR ESTATE
SOMERHAVEN
EASTERN AERIES
SOMERSHIRE
CABIN
PRAVHNA
CERNE
VAIA MAR

CITIES
TOWNS
NATIONAL BORDERS
TRAIN LINES

ISMIT
SATU
NIAPOLI
BREKTOS
NOVO MALA
VATRA
OZUN
ASTROS
RANGE
THE ORRERY
AERIE
PONTUS AXEINOS
SIRIN

THE HOLLOW PLANE

BOOK ONE

THE
HOLLOW
PLANE
BOOK ONE OF THE AETHEREALS
DUOLOGY

ALLISON
CARR WAECHTER

MINA

The punishment for remembering had been forgetting again—and, of course, the oubliette. Water kissed my ankles, a whispered threat. It was difficult to remember if it had done so before. But then, it was difficult to remember anything.

There was no reliable way to tell how long I'd been at the bottom of this damp, stone hole. I'd been without food or water for long enough that it should worry me, but I felt no hunger. No gnawing emptiness in my belly, only a curious void in my mind.

The cold water filling the bottom of the oubliette numbed my feet. Had water ever touched me before? I should think I would know if it had. Though, there were many things I should know that I didn't. Perhaps this was another. That was the trouble with the oubliette; time moved oddly. And not because time itself was odd. It moved in strange ways because I could not remember one moment to the next.

I am Wilhelmina Sofya Wildfang, I reminded myself, for either the first time, or the thousandth. Was that even my true name? I might never know. It was difficult to discern between memory, dream, and hallucination as they flitted in and out of my mind's eye. Here one moment, gone another. This, of course, was the purpose of the oubliette. The oubliette was made for forgetting.

The water rose higher, covering my ankles. Ice cold, it stung as angry little waves whipped my calves. So small, but fierce. Was it time to be worried now? Was any of this real? I gazed upward at the churning water high above me. The smooth, circular stone of the oubliette was dizzying in its sameness. The water was the only thing that changed.

When I could move again, I looked down. Water wasn't leaking in from above, it was rising from below. There was a struggle inside me to recognize what that meant, what the consequences might be for this change. I was frustratingly slow to catch on.

Water hissed at the underside of my ribcage now, rising faster by the moment. Could water hiss? If it could not, what made that noise? Now was probably not the best time to consider the sonic possibilities of water, but I struggled to attach myself to my present reality. Was it some part of the oubliette's magic that made me still when I should move, or was this a new unknown in the forgotten catalogue of things gone wrong?

Saltwater hit me square in the face, flooding in from above now, forcing me to focus. The sheer frigidity of the water should have been enough to knock me out of my senses, but I stayed frighteningly present. Freezing water buffeted my body about, pushing its way inside my nostrils and mouth, threatening to fill my lungs—to keep me here, on the floor of the oubliette.

Why hadn't I moved?

My feet were fixed to the stone floor.

My arms could move though, as could the rest of me. This was a new revelation, perhaps, but probably not the time to consider the implications of time moving in a linear fashion again.

What was true was all that mattered now. The oubliette had trapped me in this position for Fate knew how long, frozen in a perpetual state of forgetting anything I managed to remember. Now whatever magic governed this place failed, and I would drown.

The thought was a peaceful one at first. Whatever happened here, however long I had been here, it was too long. There was a kind of relief in this all being over. I closed my eyes against the saltwater, preparing to inhale as much water in as I could, and hurry things along. That much I remembered, I remembered how to die.

How to die, yes. But not if I *could.*

I can drown, but I will not die. The thought slammed into me, just as my mouth fell open, filling with water. I clamped it shut directly, trying to make sense of that thought. The chill in the water would dull my senses soon, but now it served to clarify things, if only a little.

I will drown, again and again, stuck to the bottom of the oubliette. Forever. It was as though the voice in my head was someone else, or at least speaking *about* someone else. I wanted to argue with the voice. The things it said couldn't possibly be true. Little bits of recent memory crept back in, haunting me. The days I'd managed to count. Weeks, even months, piling up without food or water. This was just another part of the torture: finding out I could not die, as any living creature, even an immortal, might.

For even an immortal required sustenance to survive, and I did not. While I had eaten food every day of my nearly twenty-eight years, in the oubliette, it became apparent I did not actually need to do so. And that was a terrifying thought, because what living thing could exist without food?

I knew its name, though I wished I did not: *fetch.*

Knowing did nothing for my current problems. I no longer had a choice about whether or not I drowned. Water pushed past my lips, filling my throat, and then my lungs. The sensation differed from what I'd imagined, a raging fire inside me, rather than cool suffocation. I could give into an eternity of endless drowning, or *do something.*

I tried to pull my feet free, but they were still stuck fast, though my arms flailed with the effort of trying to move my legs. Sudden panic shot into me, unfamiliar and painful after so long in numbness. The panic was unfamiliar, but the pain was an old friend—a lifelong companion—and with it, I pulled a piece of myself from the icy depths of the sea.

A self that existed before the fetch, before this place.

A self that need not stay anywhere I did not desire to be.

A self I had too long forgotten.

The shapeless memory of who I'd been before moved me. Even the essence of my true self was enough to remind me that I needed no jewel, no spirit, no magical aid to access the power the cosmos gave freely. My eyes shut in concentration, as my feet slowly loosened from the rock. There was no need to struggle upward or fight the water in my lungs. My body lifted, gliding of its own accord through the bubbling sapphire water. There was a snap of energy as I broke the seal that still topped the oubliette.

Water rolled off me in beads as I crested the rolling waves like a newborn goddess, drawing both aether and empyrae at the same time to push the sea back. Lightning crashed towards me, attracted by my pull on empyrae, the sweet smell of ozone filling my nostrils. This is what Maman and Helene had always feared. Unlike *them*, I could wield celestial fire, as well as shadowy aether. What I had remembered before the oubliette hardly mattered; this was the truth of me, and I would never deny it again.

Back and back the water went until it revealed a stone path that led back to shore. The water would have receded on its own eventually, revealing the stones for a brief window of time. I did not need to wait for such things as the tide. Wind whipped my soaked hair around me as my eyes adjusted slowly to the dim glow of the raging storm. Despite the low-hanging clouds, and the tempest brewing further out at sea, I had to squint in the pre-dawn air. Even the moon's weak light through the clouds was too much for me. The oubliette had been dark, even in the daylight hours.

I walked forward, my bare feet sensitive as they moved over the slick rock. Each step was painful after being trapped for so long, but from the memory traveling back to me now, this did not differ from how it had always been. The past twenty-eight years were marked by constant pain.

Rain lashed my body, the last pieces of my ragged chemise plastering to my skin. I scanned the rocky shoreline for people, but the beach was as desolate as my shattered mind. With each step onto shore, stones sliced into my tender feet, too damp for too long at the bottom of the oubliette.

As I stumbled towards the cliffs and the sea stairs, each step was an ode to pain that clarified my purpose. The hot spears of agony were not only the result of the oubliette. All of this was Maman's fault—the fault of this unnatural body she'd forced me into—the fetch. She would answer for all she'd done. First, my questions, and then she would take her punishment, as I had always taken mine.

The woman was an expert at divvying consequences out, and now we would find out if she could reap what she'd sown. Aether swirled around my fingers as I mounted the sea-stairs. The fury rising in me must have set my eyes alight with a telltale glow that would infuriate Maman.

Good. Let her be angry. Let Helene try to calm me. I would not be calmed now. First there would be truth, and then they would pay. No one should wield the power to craft a person as they would a machine. Each step on the stairs was unbearable. My muscles screamed, both from disuse and the cuts on the bottoms of my feet. The fetch heated, the skin flushing as I took each stair a little quicker than the last.

My skin. *My* body. My mind spoke to me as though it were bargaining. For more time, more memories, for all I'd lost of myself. All that was futile, but to survive this, I agreed with the voice in my head.

"This body is mine," I spat out as I pulled myself upward. One step and then the next, over and over, up the face of the cliff. "And forevermore, it will do as *I* say."

Never again would I be another's pawn. Never. Again. Hot tears streamed down my face. Once I reached the top of the stairs, there would be no more tears. No more frivolous anger. As I dragged my body upwards, I promised I would become a tool for truth, a weapon for so much destruction there would be nothing left of my little family.

I might not remember why I was sent to the oubliette, but with each step closer to the manor house, memories of my dark childhood flooded back. Maman's obsession with perfection. Her constant need for more attention, more money, more status, and calling it love. The oubliette was the end of any illusions I had of ever being loved.

Love was for the weak.

The words were a memory, the breaking of a spell, cutting through the obfuscation in my mind. They were an ancient senti-ment, one I'd carried for much longer than the twenty-eight years this body had carried my soul. A last tear rolled down the curve of my cheek, chilled by the fell wind tearing at my hair. Roughly, I wiped my eyes, steeling myself to meet Maman and Helene with dignity. Only three more steps. Just moments more and Somerhaven would appear—imposing and grand, decrepit and fearsome—an appropriately isolated stage for Maman's infinite cruelty.

The barest hint of warmth hit my back. My shoulder blades drew together, aching with phantom memory. My throat closed with some forgotten loss. All that I had been waited just beyond a frustrating wall in my mind. The warmth intensified; I turned as the sun crept above the horizon, sending weak rays across the roiling sea. The break in the clouds did not last long, and soon dawn was gray as a dove's feathers.

My eyes fell as I turned, resting on the dried skeletons of summer achillea swaying the wind. I had not bothered to wonder what season it was, and if Maman and Helene would even be in residence at Somerhaven.

I paused, thoughts racing for the first time in longer than I could remember. Keeping up would be an adjustment, but I latched onto the simplest of those rushing by me and let it manifest fully. *It must be well into autumn for the achillea to have dried so.*

That was helpful. I leaned against the cliff side for a moment. Rushing into this was foolish. What if my family was not alone? These were the days of endless country holidays and hunts in the lower range of the Dianthic Mountains, but not here. Not so far north as Somerhaven. The return of such mundane knowledge was a comfort. Until winter came, Maman and Helene would be in residence. They never joined the season early, as others did, preferring to move to town only when the manor house was too costly to heat.

I wavered, balking at the inevitable. There would be no autumnal holiday at Somerhaven, no house parties or hunts. Maman allowed no such gatherings here—we would be alone. Dallying longer only prolonged what must be. I spun back towards the upward slope. My resolve hardened as I took the last three steps at an excruciating pace.

At the top of the sea stairs, I stumbled, crumpling onto the ground, unable to fathom the sight before me. My heart, which had just pounded with the exertion of climbing, stopped. The stillness crushed me as much as the charred manor house. Somerhaven was gone.

CHAPTER 2

MINA

I curled into myself, staring at the hem of my chemise rather than the burned husk of the manor house. Everything dimmed for a moment, my vision black around the edges, darkness creeping in as my mouth went dry. Was I screaming? Or was that sound coming from elsewhere?

I shook, though if I shivered or convulsed, I could not say. Somerhaven was gone, and though I would not miss it, could not miss it even if I tried, there was despair in its destruction. My head swam with dizzying confusion. Memories mixed with lies, and there was no way to discern what was real. I focused on the wet lace of my chemise, a faraway afternoon filling my mind's eye.

A sun-drenched field high in the mountains replaced the charred manor house, along with the sound of laughter. Dark shadows lurked just at the edge of the merry scene, threatening to break it apart. Something about this was wrong, but I refused to know what it was.

Helene's laughter rang out as we hung laundry, night dresses with lacy edges, just like that of my chemise. Then the sound of her crystalline soprano singing folk songs. The shadows flickered at the edge of the scene, blurring it for a moment—this couldn't be a memory. Helene's hair was not red, but icy blonde, and though my sister could carry a tune, she would never sing a folk song.

I pushed my consciousness back down, deep into the impossibly sunny day. There had never been a day so clear on Sirin, but it was possible this was something more than a phantasm. It certainly could not be a genuine memory, though. If I had been on a mountainside hanging laundry, it was not with my haughty sister. The vision slipped away, leaving me bereft, to confront what was real.

Keeping my eyes down, I hauled myself off the ground with a determination I could not wholly feel. Each breath that came through my lungs was sharp with the pain of being denied the opportunity to confront Maman. If she and Helene were dead—no, I wouldn't think of that now. The first thing to do was search the house. No need to get ahead of myself.

I took stock of what lay ahead of me. The house had taken the most damage in the south wing, where the sleeping quarters were located. There was not much of the structure left, only charred stone and shattered glass. Tempted as I was to rush in and search, I knew better than to enter ruins without careful observation. My feet crushed bits of burnt wood as I circled the house, peering into the blackened remains of windows, trying to make sense out of devastation. All the furniture had been destroyed. Or, at the very least, someone had carted away anything of value after the fire, because the house was utterly empty.

When did it happen? Why hadn't I smelled the smoke? Even deep within the oubliette, a blaze this large would have been noticeable. Only a shell of the house remained, heavy stone, charred, but not destroyed. Another gust of wind sent leaves into a tailspin, and the faint scent of rotten eggs hit my nostrils. Sulphur. The odor was an unmistakable remnant of empyraen power. Someone with command of empyrae had burned the house down.

My mind churned as I rounded the east corner of the house, looking for a point of entry that might be safe. The fire had warped the glass in the dining room doors, leaving just enough room for me to squeeze through, a path free of shattered glass ahead of me.

Inside, the rooms reconstituted themselves in my mind, filling me to the brim with memories. Some good, many bad, but most somewhere in the murky between of an unhappy childhood. Unlike the confusing mountain scene, these played out before me with painful accuracy, ghoulish and real. There was no doubt in my mind that Helene had twisted my arm 'til it broke, there by where the buffet used to stand, just to see if I'd scream. Or that Maman had struck my palms with a tassel of sharp reeds until blood beaded through tiny cuts, over there by the butler's pantry.

None of this did me any good, so I forced myself to focus only on my surroundings as I slipped further into the house. I did not think, "that is the place where Maman slapped me so hard my face swelled for a week," but "the floor in the back hall is safe to walk on." I replaced each memory that threatened to break me with careful observation. The systematic dismissal of unwanted thoughts was one way I'd learned to exert control over my life as a child, and it came back to me easily.

In what had been the main entrance hall, the grand staircase had been destroyed. Searching what was left of the second and third floors would be impossible. It had been a longshot, given the state of the house. That confirmed, I picked my way through the rubble to the library, which sat directly beneath the wing where Maman and Helene's rooms had been. It was possible some clue to what had happened might have fallen through the floors. I had little hope for that, but it was necessary to be thorough.

As I climbed over fallen walls and charred pieces of the manor, the chill of the stone bothered me. To make things worse, the northern autumn air sank into my bones with each passing moment. Though the ferocious wind had nearly dried me, the chemise alone would not be enough for much longer. My teeth chattered, and the sound was more than I could bear, let alone the feeling of them touching one another.

Focus on survival first, silly—leave all these feelings *for later.* Helene's words crept into my mind, insidious and unwanted.

"I don't need your help," I muttered, uselessly. Even the mere memory of Helene had to give her superior input. Maman was cruel, but Helene had made it her life's purpose to outdo me in all ways.

And I had let her. Wanting them to love me had been my first mistake. Thinking it was possible for my family to love *anyone* had been my second. Loving them had been my third. There would not be a fourth such mistake.

When I found them, there could be no forgiveness. No reconciliation. After the oubliette, there was no doubt in my mind that it was time for us to clear the air and part ways for good. One way or another, this was the end for us.

Still, the whisper of Helene left in my memory wasn't wrong. I did need to focus on survival first. While I could not die, my pain and discomfort were all too real. I almost turned and left the house, but my need to complete the task at hand was too pressing.

When I reached the library, the crumbling, empty shelves were not a shock. There hadn't been books in Somerhaven's library for nearly a decade. Maman had sold Papa's collection of fiction long ago to fund outfitting herself and Helene for a social season. I was asked to stay at Orchid House alone while they masqueraded about Pravhna as the wealthy family we'd once been, but were no longer. Most of Somerhaven's valuables had been discreetly sold off.

The only beautiful thing left in the library was the enormous mirror above the fireplace. It was too heavy and fragile to move—a fact I resented now as I avoided my ragged, soot stained appearance. When I caught sight of myself head-on, I recoiled. I looked like a haunt, wild-eyed and vengeful, my dark heavy hair hanging in long hanks around my shoulders. I appeared as a thing more than a woman, which was a little too close to the truth for my comfort.

A weak ray of sunlight broke through the clouds. It was only for the briefest of moments, but the pinprick of light hit something on the floor that shone. A tiny prism of light spun out around the room, a hum of power emanating from its center.

Every muscle in my body froze, my heart thumping wildly against my ribcage, a wild thing trying to escape its prison. I didn't have to see the stone up close to know exactly what it was. The massive round emerald, set in a bouquet of golden oleander, was utterly familiar. Maman had never taken the ring off—would *never* have taken it off voluntarily. My body moved as though treading nearly frozen water, thick with mounting emotion.

When I reached the jewel, my ears rang with the fury building inside me. Aether and empyrae flowed off me in alternating waves of light and shadow. Inside my mind, a keening death knell screamed out from the center of the ring. The elemental spirit within had been trapped, and now wailed with some unidentifiable emotion.

It could not be sadness, for Maman's familiar bore no love for her —only the power they wielded together. The elemental's screams stoked my desperation into a fever pitch, my body heating to an unnatural temperature. It was not possible for Maman to have left her familiar behind, trapped in such a way, even if she'd wanted to. The inspirited were bound until death parted them.

Maman was dead.

Someone had used empyrae to burn Somerhaven.

There were no answers here.

These three thoughts repeated in my mind, echoing with a frustrating lack of nuance. I tried to stop the spin of them as they gained traction, but to no avail. My fingers closed around the ring, empyrae emanating from my clenched fist in a molten glow. I had to let her familiar out. If I wanted answers, this was the only place I would find them.

My knuckles turned white, gold dripping from between my fingers on to the sooty floor. Gold was nothing to the heat of empyrae. The emerald, however, was nearly impenetrable, as all elemental portals are. Oscarovi jewelers perfected the method nearly two thousand years ago, giving our kind access to as much power as the fey, and even my power could not break the jewel open so easily. My anger mounted. I would have answers, even if I had to wring them from stone. If Maman was not here, her familiar Demophon must answer for her.

The ground shook beneath my feet as I refocused my attention. My ears rang as my empyrae built, the pressure building steadily. In the distance, something fell and shattered, but I stayed focused on the emerald, on breaking its surface open. All sense disappeared in the effort, so I was surprised to find a compact figure pulling at the hem of my chemise, bidding for my attention amongst the chaos.

My vision would not focus though, as channeling the powers of limen and the cosmos at once was no small feat. *Demophon!* I cried out, within the confines of my mind. *Answer me! Demophon!*

Near my feet, something pulled on my chemise again. It spoke, though it was not the elemental spirit trapped within the jewel. *Demophon is gone, girl. Disappeared the moment you cracked the stone.*

Impossible. I only meant to release the mountain elemental, not destroy the stone. My fingers unfurled as I looked down. There was nothing but emerald dust and a pool of molten gold marring my palm. Demophon was gone. I fell to my knees, narrowly missing whatever had spoken to me, nothing more than a blur as my eyes squeezed shut.

Screams, ripped from deep inside my soul, ravaged my throat as I sobbed. Rage took over as what remained of the house shook. Again, something tugged at my chemise. I nearly lashed out with my power, but something stopped me. The thing at my feet was a rangy, lean hare, aether swirling off it in billowing clouds. As it moved, scratching at me with sharp claws, it came into focus. The hare was larger than a mundane beast, with harrowing eyes that swirled with the light of stars in deep space. Its sleek fur was an unsettling shade of indigo—the color of pure aether.

You'll bring the rest of the house down on yourself, it cautioned.

The floor shook harder now, as a slow creaking noise swelled into an anguished groan. The house was coming apart. What the hare said might make sense. My vision expanded to take in the room. Around me, there was a halo of safety, generated not by my magic, but by the nebula of power curling off the hare. Its body had been slightly incorporeal before, and now was dissolving before my eyes.

It was protecting me. But why? "Who are you? Are you related to Demophon?" I shouted above the cacophonous wind swirling around us.

The thing was obviously a wild elemental. All familiars started off as elemental spirits who desired more of an effect on the corporeal world, but mountain elementals rarely wished for such relationships with us. The hare did not answer, but loped away, toward the doors to the garden, the orb of howling winds breaking apart as it went.

Move! the hare shouted.

I did as bidden, running through the lush grass of the garden, until the forest loomed dark ahead. As I turned to look back, the remaining husk of the manor house crumbled. I winced—destruction hadn't been my intention—as my body gave out. The pain was finally too much, and my knees buckled, slamming into the ground. Only the long, soft grass kept me from further damage.

Movement in my peripheral vision caught my attention. Another hare crept down the rocky hillside behind the manor, through the dense forest of evergreens. Its movements were both erratic and far too smooth, as the edges of its form blurred and sharpened in turns.

As the second hare joined the first, I felt dozens, if not hundreds, of eyes on me from the depths of the shadowed forest. My stomach flipped in response, heart skipping a beat—my body recognizing what my mind could not catch up to. Elementals surrounded me, a band of spirits. My breath snagged on the gravity of the danger I was in, threatening to pull me down entirely.

Mountain elementals were not curious about the corporeal world. They did not pair with Oscarovi without dangerous bargains, and they were not our friends as their kin in cities and towns might be. Mountain elementals were more likely to lure souls into the forest to feed their nameless, eldritch gods, never to be seen again. Carefully, I scooted away from the pair of hares, trying my best not to appear hurried or afraid.

They could be vicious if not treated with perfect respect. They were medial creatures, striding the line between this reality and that which was between, but they *could* touch me. Those long claws and powerful legs were not wholly incorporeal. To be safer, I struggled to my feet, though there was nothing I could do against them if they attacked. Even with my power, even with empyrae, I would stand little chance against a drove of mountain elementals.

There was no use in running or trying to evade them if they wanted something from me. They could use the spirit paths, the limen, to find me. I'd accepted their help in escaping the crumbling manor, and now I was beholden to them. The first rule of dealing with mountain elementals was to accept no aid, no bargain, without first understanding the parameters. There had been no help for it though; I'd lost my grip on reality, letting my rage get the better of me.

All I could do was take a deep breath as they entered the garden, making a small bow in the hopes it might please them. "Greetings fair ones. I am honored by your presence."

As a child of Somershire, I knew the old ways, the old lore. I knew better than to believe that because the first hare had saved me, the drove wouldn't kill me for slighting them. Thanking them would be a mistake, as one must never imply indebtedness to an elemental. However, greeting them was essential, especially as they had addressed me directly. They did not respond to my greeting—not even an ear twitched in my direction, reminding me they were not common hares.

She of the Dark Vale has a message for you.

Hastily, I bowed again, every tendon, muscle, and joint in my body screaming for rest. I wasn't sure which of the hares had spoken, nor exactly to whom they referred. As a failsafe, I bowed lower to show that I would receive the message, without verbal acknowledgement. The less I said, the better. Mountain elementals had a habit of twisting words to fit their aims, and I was wise enough not to give them anything more to work with.

Your mother and sister were killed in the fire.

Maman's ring had led me to the same conclusion—about her, anyway. But Helene? It wasn't possible that Helene… "That cannot be," I gasped, immediately forgetting to stay silent.

We saw the bodies taken. The voice was one and many. The entire drove spoke at once, in my mind. *If they were not deceased, then we do not understand mortality.*

I sucked air into my lungs to stay grounded. Oscarovi lived long lives, but indeed, we were mortal. Or *they* were. I was not truly Oscarovi, nor mortal, I reminded myself. I was not real and too real.

That way lies danger. I looked down. One hare pulled at my chemise again. I could not be certain, but it seemed to be the one that helped me previously. *It is not time to travel in that direction. You must go forward to go back.*

Its eyes swirled with the light of forgotten stars, and I remembered another time I had seen into such depths, but vaguely. "Forward?"

The hare nodded, pulling at my chemise with its claws, so gently it did not so much as snag the fragile, damaged fabric. I bent down to be on eye level with it. I knew not to ask for more information, but perhaps appearing more willing to receive it might speed things along.

The longer I stayed here with them, the more tempted I would be to follow them into the forest and never return. Maman had often mused that elementals snatching children was mere lore, but I knew it to be true. I'd been lured before. Even now, I felt the pull to follow them and never return. Something deep in the forest, far in the mountains, called to me.

The hare placed its paw on my knee, steadying me in my painful crouch. *It is not yet time for you to follow us. You must see your end before you can return to the beginning.*

The message was cryptic, and behind the gentle touch in the creature's paw was a threat. Not to me, specifically, but a menace. I nodded, knowing that if the hare did not say more, there was nothing I could do. Creatures of the limen saw more than we, making their words heavy with meaning, but difficult to parse out. I would not know what the hare meant until it was time.

Deep in the woods, and further down the mountain, a horn sounded, long and mournful. Every hare on the mountain materialized for one brief, terrifying moment, their ears turned in the same direction—toward the horn.

There is no more time, the hare touching my knee warned.

The hunt approaches, the drove said at once, their collective voice a mass of whispers and screams. *You must hide.*

I struggled to rise, but my hands slipped on the damp grass. The hare who'd helped me escape the house pushed its head under my arm as I stumbled. *Run, Mina*, it cried as it helped me to my feet. *Hide!*

There was only one place on the property left for me to go and the hare nosed me in its direction: the carriage house.

We will draw them off, the hare that helped me said. Something in its manner was gentler than the rest of the drove, which faded from sight, their terrible eyes the last thing to dissolve. *Go!*

Sounds of the hunt came closer. Dogs braying, carried by the wind. The hare nosed the back of my legs again as fear gripped me. The only estate close enough to ours to host a hunt that might come so close was House Montclair.

Was Viridian with them? My heart raced at the thought. I pushed myself into motion. The thought of Helene's fiancé catching me again was enough to set my feet running. My legs pumped harder, my arms churning, as though grasping for some hope to hold on to. Frigid wind cut through me as I ran through the overgrown remains of the garden, hoofbeats vibrating through my bare feet.

The hunt neared. Pain laced through me, every step forward agony. The carriage house came into view, just down the hill from the house. It was unfortunately placed near the path the hunt would have to take, but the only cover left on the property. My body slammed into the door, unable as I was to slow down of my own accord. I could hardly clasp onto the iron handle of the door, my hands were shaking so hard.

She of the Still Places watches and waits. The drove's collective voice echoed in my head as the door sprang open under my touch.

I fell into the carriage house. Desperate as I was to hide, I shut the door softly behind me, dropping the heavy wooden bolt lock with as much care as I could. Sound carried strangely in these hills, and if House Montclair was hunting, I could not afford a single mistake. Through the windows at the back of the carriage house, crimson and gold jackets flashed in the woods. The colors of House Montclair. My enemy was upon me.

CHAPTER 3

ASHBOURNE

Dawn crept through Pravhna's undercity, slow and gray. Mist curled around my feet as I trudged home, down one steep cobblestone street after another, from a card game I'd never wanted to attend. I rolled my neck as I walked, stretching my arms out above me after so many seated hours. It had been a long night, but at least it was over.

It was hard to regret helping my partner build our business. There were only a few private investigators in the undercity that weren't completely in the Syndicate's pockets, and we walked a fine line. If we didn't socialize with the Syndicate crews a little, we wouldn't get clients who paid them for protection. And that was almost everyone.

But I wasn't the socializing sort. I'd rather have been in bed with a novel. Fate be damned, I'd have preferred to spend the evening training in the shop basement, rather than playing cards with Syndicate goons. But Skye had asked that I at least try to expand our network a bit, and I hadn't wanted to let her down. Playing cards with some of Karnon Archambeau's crew was the least I could do, and now my head ached from too much ale.

I needed a pot of strongly brewed black tea, a pastry, and a good nap and all would be right with the world. I just had to get home first, and in my drunken haze I'd taken a wrong turn. It was easy to do in this area of the undercity, which was a maze of streets that often dead-ended with no warning, or looped back on one another. The White Lady was the odd pub in a four-block radius of warehouses and small factories that were mostly operational during the day. It made the public house perfect for a quiet, late night card game among criminals.

I should not have had that third ale; my head pounded with a vengeance. I stumbled over a loose cobblestone, bracing myself against the brick wall of a glass factory that I was sure I'd passed at least twice already. I stared at the brick for several moments, appreciating the color of it for some reason unknown to my addled mind. This was why I didn't drink. Still, the glass factory *was* lovely. It was the only brick structure in a sea of clapboard buildings, which made it distinct.

I closed my eyes, breathing through the nausea that threatened to overtake me. What smelled so wretched?

Rubber. Rubber was burning and close by. But there was another smell, something sulphuric and acrid, mixing with the rubber. My head swam, but I pushed myself off the wall. If something was on fire, it wouldn't be long until the entire undercity was ablaze. Drunk or not, I had to help before the trees that canopied the undercity caught flame. The last thing we needed was the elemental spirits in revolt over such destruction.

I groaned as I followed my nose toward the horrific smell. A few blocks away, I found the source of the flames. They shot into the sky at the rubber factory. I was back where I started, across the street from The White Lady. I picked up my pace, my head clearing as my heart beat faster. Urgency took the edge of my stupor off, clearing my mind as I approached.

A dozen or so people had already arrived at the scene and appeared to be fighting the fire. I could take a moment to gather myself. I was sobering up, and quickly, but I'd be no help if I got sick on one of these good folk. Since they already had things well in hand, I braced myself internally, letting the turmoil in my belly calm down.

Assessing the scene brought me back to myself, my nausea receding. Broken glass covered the street, and flames jumped out of the rubber factory, raging and white hot. There was a touch of blue flame that receded by the moment, and was likely the source of the sulphuric scent. Someone had used empyrae here, celestial flame. My gut roiled once more, but this time not from my third ale. This was no ordinary fire, it was another of *those*.

Strange fires had plagued the city of spires for months. They went out so quickly that no one had investigated their origins, but there were rumors they didn't behave naturally. The fires seemed to have no inception point, and no reason for stopping. Nor did they ever spread, according to the rumors. Neither Skye nor Morpheus nor I had ever witnessed one, and the conclusion we'd reached was that they were likely just that: rumors.

Now, I wasn't so sure. Something wasn't right here.

I scanned the people at the scene, identifying the bartenders from The White Lady, and a few overnight guards from some of the surrounding warehouses. They'd opened the block's access to emergency water, something Pravhna was in no shortage of, and were operating the hose. Their movements were odd, stilted somehow.

I recognized Mac, the Oscarovi bartender at The White Lady, by their bright cerise brocade waistcoat. They had a loose hold on the fire hose, but didn't appear to be paying much attention to what was happening. I strode over to them, clapping my hand on their narrow shoulder. "Mac, what happened here?"

The bartender didn't turn to look at me. I moved closer to them, until I caught sight of their face. Their eyes were glazed over and black, the light from the fire reflecting in their glassy depths. It wasn't just their irises having blown out; their *eyes* had gone black entirely.

I stepped away from them, trying not to recoil at the sight. "What's wrong with you?" I asked, though now I did not expect an answer.

Mac didn't respond, but continued to move forward with the hose. I walked around the others, keeping a fair distance from them. Bespelled individuals were worth being wary of. Every single one had the same black eyes. What was worse, they were all completely silent. Only the sounds of their shuffled movements amongst the broken glass and the burning factory filled the street.

They didn't speak to one another, or even move their heads. All were breathing, but there was a stiltedness in their breathing that appeared labored, as though someone else forced air in and out of them. The amount of power it would take to do such a thing wasn't something I could rightly conceive of. Fear slithered under my skin. Only a monster could manage something like this. Controlling others so wholly wasn't just difficult, it was evil. But they weren't doing anything bad—in fact, they were fighting the fire.

Could someone have used their power to make sure the fire went out?

I swallowed hard, watching the dozen or so entranced people operate the hose, their bodies moving like puppets on strings. After a few moments of observation, the truth became clear. They weren't truly fighting the fire. They weren't even pointing the hose anywhere in particular. It was a parody of fire-fighting. And yet, the fire *was* dying. Or perhaps it simply wasn't spreading. Only the rubber factory burned.

A small, animalic part of me knew the best thing to do would be to run, to hide. Anyone who could wield empyrae and keep a dozen people in a trance was more powerful than I should even think of confronting. But I'd never been one to heed my better instincts. I swallowed my fear whole, slowing my pounding heart with a few long, deep breaths.

As unsettling as the entire scene was, I needed to find a way to help these people. The fire was contained, and whoever controlled the trance was nowhere to be seen. I let my eyes fall shut to send my senses of smell and hearing out further.

A soft noise caught my attention, and my eyes flew open, searching for the source. There were very few aetheric street lamps in this area, but the blaze provided some light. Behind a stack of crates, a small Strix child with the visage of a snowy owlet huddled crying. They held a hand to their chest. I rushed to them, crouching down.

"What happened, hatchling?" I asked, keeping my voice as calm as possible. My size was often intimidating for adults. Children had mixed reactions, either delight at how tall I was, or terror. The owlet was happily the former.

"Oh, you're a big'un," they said, their words slurring through their tears.

"Yes," I agreed, smiling as best I could, given the circumstances.

"But you've a kind smile," the owlet reasoned. Something had scared them, that much was obvious. "My mama's over there. She won't talk to me. I tried t'help her, but she didn't even look my way. I tripped and fell, see." They held their little hand out to show me. There was a piece of broken glass stuck in their palm, their taloned fingers quivering.

"That must hurt," I said, after identifying the Strix in the line of silent firefighters that was likely the little tyke's mama. Her eyes were black as the others, though the eyes of the Strix and Corvidae were always dark. But no Strix mama I knew would ignore their hatchling. No wonder the child was afraid.

"Can I help you?" I asked.

"Which House are you from?" the little one asked, suspicious of me. "Not one of those cratties, are you?"

The way the owlet said "crattie" was an obvious accusation, but I could only agree. The aristocrats of Pravhna were a terrible lot. I laughed softly. "No, hatchling. I'm no crattie. Just a common Vilhar, like you."

Many of the fey saw themselves as separate from their brethren, using the word Vilhari to distinguish between the fey that were not indigenous to Sirin. If history were to be believed, we all crashed here on a starcraft thousands of years ago and the elementals and Oscarovi were forced to let us stay. As I could not remember an upbringing where I'd learned that history, or the subtleties of our society, it was all the same to me. Strix, Corvidae, sirens, howlers, and my kind. We were all fey. All Vilhari.

"Will you let me help you, then?" I asked. "Now that you know I haven't a House to answer to?"

The owlet nodded, holding their hand out a bit more. I was no surgeon, but I could tell the glass was wedged in such a place that it might keep the littling from being able to use the hand again. I couldn't help with the fire, nor could I solve the problem of the adults' current bespelled state, but I could solve this.

"Close your eyes," I begged the owlet. It would be better if they didn't watch.

It was a risk to use my power this way. While many could wield celestial power, control over empyrae, its purest form, was rare. It might draw unwanted attention, and I'd worked so hard to keep my abilities a secret, but the child's hand was worth it to me. They squeezed their eyes shut tight, burying their face in their uninjured arm.

"This will hurt for a moment," I warned before pulling the glass out. The littling was brave though, and did no more than wince. I couldn't help but smile as I covered their hand with my own. I used a bit of my celestial power to knit the wound back together, my magic doing the internal work a skilled surgeon might. It was a dangerous thing to do this in public, especially so close to a blaze started with empyrae. I had no doubt that I'd risked making myself a target. If anyone saw what I did, they might think I'd set the fire.

"How did you and your mama end up here?" I asked, wanting to distract the owlet from the extra pain the healing would cause.

"Mama's a night guard for the rubber factory, 'nd I have a cold. So I had to come to work with her tonight."

The little one sniffed a little, their tears obviously compounding the severity of their congestion. My healing work was almost finished, but I would have to cauterize the wound. The owlet winced, but did not so much as cry out.

"Did you see who did this?" I asked as I sent a tendril of cool aether into the closed wound to soothe the cauterization.

The littling nodded, eyes open now and wide, staring behind me. "T'was them," the owlet said through strangled sobs. "How'd they get back here so fast?"

I whirled round, standing quickly, keeping the child behind me. In the street stood four masked people. They wore dark, lightly armored clothes, and their entire faces were covered, but for slits in the masks for eyes. There was nothing showing in their appearance to distinguish whether they were fey or Oscarovi.

The two in front were obviously athletically built, but the pair that stood behind them were in shadow, their physiques difficult to make out in the moving shadows the dying flames from the fire cast —one or more of these people had to be the cause of all this, the owlet was right. The fire and the entranced people made more sense if it were a group controlling the working. I hadn't heard them approach, which was utterly impossible. Where had they come from?

"Run," I growled at the child. "Get to the Merc for help."

Hopefully, the Mercury Room would still be full of Halcyon Gate Syndicate folk at this hour. At the very least, Edith Braithwaite kept rooms in the pleasure house, and if the Syndicate leader was in residence, she'd be able to muster aid quickly. I tried to discern if any of the four figures were using aethereal power, but something dulled my second sight.

The owlet made haste behind me. One of the masked figures attempted to follow. I blocked them, delivering one swift punch to the head as they passed me. I was fast enough that they didn't even have the opportunity to duck. There was no way I'd get so lucky again.

No change in my second sight, nor in the entranced people. That one hadn't been involved in the working here. Another rushed towards me, obviously wise to my speed now.

This one was smaller than me, but more heavily muscled and moving at a preternaturally fast pace. One punch, quick as lightning, landed on my ribs, sending me backward as they pummeled me in the stomach. I leapt away, but I couldn't move fast enough to block as their hits flew at me, keeping me on the defense. Like the entranced, their movements were not quite natural.

Each hit came just a little faster than I could manage, as though my assailant adjusted each hit to meet my mounting defense. I blocked a punch meant for my face with ease, then another on its way to my gut. It was almost like dancing, with them in the lead.

I stepped forward at the same time they stepped back. I blocked as they hit. We were evenly matched, it seemed. I swept a foot out to kick their feet from under them. They slipped just out of reach in the nick of time, then pummeled me in the gut with those preternaturally fast hits again.

They leapt back, their feet dancing, every movement a frustrating taunt. The fight had no momentum. It was as though my assailant had no stake in the contest, no worry that I would harm them, and no intention of actually harming me. In fact, the more I blocked and averted, the more skilled their attack became. And yet, none of the hits were painful. They seemed to be purposely holding back.

Testing me.

The other two masked figures simply watched. Gut instinct told me something about this wasn't right. Had they expected me to be here? Of course, I had no way of knowing that for certain, but the thought persisted as I struggled to stay in the fight.

My opponent had moved faster than me the entire fight, never allowing me to land a hit. But now their movements lagged, as though whatever power allowed them to supercharge their speed was waning. If we fought much longer, I would overpower them. I slowed down, conserving energy, and my opponent matched my speed precisely.

Too precisely. This was wrong. If they wanted to kill me, they'd have done it already. I was a skilled fighter, more skilled than these two, but they had the advantage of speed and whatever force allowed my opponent to read me so easily. If I wanted to end this, I would have to use empyrae.

I ducked my opponent, now focused on staying out of their reach, rather than feeding whatever information they sought in engaging me in a fight. My second sight cleared, and I identified which observer was the source of all the magic being used in the street. I paused to consider the wisdom of lunging for them.

I took my eyes off my assailant for only a moment, but it was enough. All went dark.

When I opened my eyes, the sun had long since risen, and rain pelted my face. I glanced behind me. I was in a seated position, propped up against the door of The White Lady, across the street from the rubber factory. It was morning, but this far into the under-city, the clouds were low and the light was gray.

My entire body felt like a bruise, tender and inflamed.

The owlet sat next to me. "You all right, sir?" they asked.

I nodded, my face smarting from the places I'd been hit, but I was already healing. "I'm all right."

"What was wrong with those people?" the owlet asked. "They moved unnatural-like."

"Yes," I agreed, smiling at the littling's way of reasoning through a problem. I liked the way children thought about things. Straightforward, and so often right to the point. "What did you see after I went down?"

The littling shrugged. "I don't rightly know. T'was like I forgot to keep looking at you all. S'not possible that a person disappears, is it?"

It was an unlikely observation, but I believed the owlet. "Like a greymalkin? Or an elemental?"

The owlet shook their head. "Not at all. It's hard to remember, though."

That was a problem I understood all too well, having been hit too hard quite a few times. My amnesia complicated this situation. Something about the four masked figures felt familiar. But if they were—if I had some knowledge about who they were or why they could fight like that—it was not something I could access. Anything before Skye and Morpheus found me a year ago was simply missing.

Across the street, the fire had died down. The people who'd been fighting it were standing in a row facing the pub, eyes blank, though they'd resumed their normal appearance. Briefly, I wondered why no one else had shown up yet. Why was the undercity so quiet? First shift should have started, and this place should be crawling with people.

The air was heavy with power, as though a blanket had been tossed over this little part of the city. I wondered if that was what kept others from discovering what had happened here.

"Where'd you disappear to?" I asked the owlet. "Did you get to the Merc?"

The little one shook their head. "I was going to go to get help, but I got lost. Don't really know how. I've been coming here all my life, but I kept ending up right back here."

So I wasn't imagining the power that muffled the air. Something kept the littling in, and was probably keeping others out. I shifted position a little, thinking to get up, but the pain in my ribs was nearly unbearable. I would have to sit here for another few minutes and wait for them to heal.

The owlet looked as though they might cry at my wince of pain. "I'm so sorry you got hit so many times. They just kept hitting you after they knocked you out. One of them said it wouldn't slow you down for long. Is that true?"

I smiled, my split lip cracking open, spilling blood into my mouth. I was a fast healer, faster than most Vilhari, but this was more inconvenient than I'd prefer. I spat the blood out, away from the owlet, before answering. "It's true."

A fluffy brown raptor dove down from the low clouds that hung over the undercity. Rue, thank the Lady. Skye must have sent the vicious little howler off to find me when I didn't come back home. His arrival was fortuitous—the little messengers could make it through workings that kept other creatures out. The Syndicate needed to know what had happened here, and fast.

"Hello," I said, wincing at the effort to speak. I was already healing, but it would take time. "I need you to get a message to Skye."

CHAPTER 4

MINA

As the thunder of hooves came closer, I ducked behind the Broussard, a massive presence in the carriage house. I was still visible through the giant windows that let natural light in. We'd never converted the carriage house to aetheric power, so windows still did much of the heavy lifting in terms of lighting. Through the glass, bursts of crimson jackets flashed in the woods.

Hoofbeats were close enough now to make the floor vibrate faintly under my feet, and the sounds of the dogs grew louder. Viridian's family employed a kind of fey dog I very much did not want to encounter. There was only one choice right now, as my joints burned with pain. I wouldn't make it up the stairs to the apartment above the garage.

I would have to get under the Broussard if I didn't want to be seen. The shiny black autocar was high enough off the ground that I could roll under it rather easily. The stone floor was cold on my bare skin and my back ached uncomfortably while I waited. I tried my hardest to lengthen my breath; even a heartbeat might catch the attention of House Montclair's fey hounds.

After my ostentatious rise out of the oubliette, my magic was weak, and I was even more exhausted than I would have been after simply climbing the sea stairs. I didn't have much energy left, but I drew a muffling spell around me with the last bit of magic I had. My fingers moved quickly to weave the working that brought a net of aether over me. It was one of my favorite spells. I'd been a child who benefitted from being as difficult to find as possible.

I tried to get comfortable now, but the floor made that impossible. It was foolish to not at least consider they might be looking for me. I hadn't much in the way of memories about the day I went into the oubliette, but there were two things I knew. Maman had sentenced me to isolation, and Helene and her fiancé Viridian were the last faces I saw before the sea covered the opening to the oubliette. If House Montclair was on the hunt, I had to assume Viridian knew I had escaped.

It took some time, but as the hares had promised, they drew the hunt off—shouts rang out among the riders as they spotted their quarry. The sounds of the hunt faded, but did not completely disappear. My eyes drooped, then fell closed. I neared exhaustion, which was strange to think about. The fetch did everything a body should do. It sent all the usual signals that I needed to do vital things like sleep and rest, but I did not actually need to do any of those things to survive.

The muffled sound of a dog sniffing the carriage house door stole my breath. My body tensed in preparation to fight, but the hellish creature did not so much as bark. The sniffing stopped, and the sound of the creature's footsteps fell away. Perhaps the hunt was for a mundane quarry, after all. Still, I needed to keep my wits about me until I was sure they were gone. I closed my eyes, not to sleep, but to pull up memories of Maman's books on forbidden magics.

Inside my memory, pages spun by until I found the ones I wanted, the words I wanted to remember. *Fetch, doppelganger, automaton*: consciousness attached to a clever bit of technology and magic. Magic that the high echelons outlawed long ago, and for good reason. Whatever I had been *before*, I was not now. Remembering that was at least part of what had gotten me thrown into the oubliette. The rest was just beyond this memory, and I struggled against the slippery block that kept me from knowing more.

Frustrated, my eyes flew open. I turned my attention back to the hunt, listening hard, but there were only the sounds of birds singing in the forest to greet me. A sigh of relief brought fresh air into my lungs—I had been holding my breath.

I rolled out from under the Broussard, staring at it for a few long moments, thinking things through. There had to be clothes somewhere in the carriage house, but if there weren't, I was going to have to get to the village and steal some. A loose plan took shape in my head. If I could not make Maman and Helene pay for their transgressions, I could find out who deprived me of that pleasure and make *them* pay.

But first, I needed clothes, and to get to Pravhna. The season had undoubtedly begun, and I had the best chance of finding out what truly happened here in the city. Somershire was too small to even have an investigative unit. If a case had been opened regarding the fire, the records would be in Pravhna. I opened the driver's side door of the autocar, feeling around for the key Maman usually tucked into the crack of the front seat. I hated the idea of driving, but I did know how.

We hadn't been able to afford a driver in years, so Maman had taught Helene and me both to drive, casting it as another of her eccentricities. People thought Helene and I were practically wild things. The difference was that Helene was so beautiful and charming that they overlooked it. My beauty didn't get me very far, as I lacked Helene's social graces.

The key wasn't in the front seat, and though I doubted I'd find it in the back, I looked anyway. When I came up with nothing, I searched under the seats. The glimmer of a small beaded evening bag underneath the passenger side front seat caught my attention. I stretched to reach it, my exposed skin scraping against the metal underside of the seat, but I managed to fish it out. It was one of Helene's favorites. One from her second season out—the season Viridian proposed.

How did it get here? Helene was meticulously careful about her possessions. A vague memory of Brigitte, who'd played the role of nanny, governess, and lady's maid to Helene, crossed my mind. When Maman had been obsessed with selling off our precious possessions to fund her secret projects, Helene and Brigitte had hidden things from her. Perhaps they'd hidden the purse here.

Not what I'd been hoping for, but helpful all the same. I scrambled into the cold leather backseat, curling into myself as I stared at the purse. My fingers traced the floral pattern of the golden beads, emotion clouding my next move. What had become of my sister? It seemed unthinkable that she could die.

Maman had been so miserable as to have become dull over the years. But Helene was different, as cruel as Maman, but cunning. Vivacious. Alive. But the hares said they saw the body, and it was impossible for them to lie. Deceive, yes, but they had *seen* the bodies. My fingers drifted over the beads of Helene's purse, the smooth texture of them pleasing—soothing, somehow. Without my sister, would Viridian even care what became of me?

That was the real problem. I didn't know why the oubliette had been necessary to begin with, so it was impossible to determine what kind of threat Viridian was. I still needed the answers I'd planned to extract from Maman and Helene. The faster the better. I opened Helene's purse.

A silk scarf, a ring of brass keys, and a small bit of paper money were the only things in the purse, save for a few spare hairpins. The silk scarf was plain, the color of a stormy sea. Helene had used it on long drives to protect her hair when Maman insisted on having the windows of the autocar open to "get the air on us."

I examined the keys carefully. None were for the car. Three were for Somerhaven's many locks, and were now useless. One was for Orchid House in Pravhna, and one was a mystery to me. No matter, the key to Orchid House was all I needed.

Getting to Pravhna was a problem. The Broussard was easily recognizable as Maman's—it would draw too much attention. I would have to take the train. I needed as much time as possible to get to Orchid House with no one knowing I'd returned, so that Viridian couldn't make moves to stop me. Once in Pravhna, society would take notice quickly enough, and that was exactly what I wanted. I wanted them to see me, to be curious, to ask questions. It was the only way to draw out whoever might know more about what Maman and Helene had really been doing.

For a few moments, I debated between driving the Broussard to the station in Somershire and hiking down. Both were risky, but it would be better to make it to the station without Viridian stopping me than to be caught in the woods. Of course, that required finding the car key, and I needed to find clothes.

My chemise was tattered and soot-stained. There was no way I could march into the train station and buy a ticket wearing only this. Now that my body had calmed, my senses returned. The vague sound I'd been trying to block out was my teeth chattering. I needed to find something warmer to wear, now.

Even a coat and a pair of shoes would help. As the house was no longer an option, the apartment upstairs was my only hope for both clothes and the key to the Broussard. Before Maman fired the driver, he'd lived upstairs. It was possible he'd left something behind that I could put on until I got to Orchid House, and I was certain he'd had at least two keys to the autocar. I crept through the garage, carefully watching the windows for signs of stray hunters, or their terrible dogs. The narrow door to the stairs stuck when I pulled it, but wasn't locked.

After a bit more effort, it came open, nearly hitting me in the face. The sight of the dust-covered staircase to the apartment elicited a quiet groan. I took the first step gingerly, my entire body recoiling from the feeling of placing my tender, cut-up feet on the dusty stairs. Despite this, or perhaps because of it, I was more determined than ever to find shoes.

As I dragged my body upwards, I cursed. Part of me missed the oubliette. The only good that had come from being trapped in the hole was that for a time, I'd forgotten about my pain. It hadn't disappeared, but I'd forgotten it, along with everything else. Now that I was lucid, the agony of movement was unrelenting.

It will get better, I promised myself. *I just have to get used to it again.*

Luckily, this was nothing like the sea stairs. Just one short flight and I'd entered the apartment. Every surface was covered in the same thick layer of dust the stairs had been. I gritted my teeth. Touching it would be awful, but it was necessary. It was possible, of course, to weave a spell to clean the dust from this place. However, using magic of any kind might draw attention if Viridian had access to Maman's surveillance nets.

That had been one of her many secret projects, developing spells that monitored magical use and other disturbances. Any information left on that would be in Maman's workroom in Orchid House. Getting into her inner sanctum was another knot in this tangled mess, but that was a problem for another hour. I ripped the hem from my chemise in the cleanest part of the garment, tied it around my face to protect my airways from the dust, and began my search. There was precious little to go through, so it went quickly.

The tall dresser and trunk at the end of the single bed yielded nothing, but in the tiny closet by the stairs, I found a coat. It was long, made from thick brown tweed, and blessedly clean. On the hook beneath it hung a small bag of forgotten laundry, and from the faint smell of lavender that still clung to it, it must have been clean as well. Inside, I found a set of the driver's clean long johns, and several pairs of heavy socks. I took them all, and revealed one last happy surprise, a pair of boots.

They were the wrong size for the big Strix driver, but I hadn't time to wonder who they might have belonged to. I slid one foot in and found they fit me well enough, just a bit tight in the toe box. If this was the best I could do, it would be enough.

I took my armful of treasures downstairs to the tub that had been used for washing hounds, back when the manor was lively enough for such things, long before Maman's time. It had no hot water. I dreaded making myself colder, but my trip into the house had left me sooty and bedraggled, which would catch the attention of curious villagers. It was better that I be as inconspicuous as possible. First, I rinsed the tub, then shed my dirty chemise, rinsing off as quickly as I could.

I used the laundry bag to dry myself, then scrambled into the long johns, socks, and boots. When I finally wrapped the overcoat around me, I'd stopped shivering. As I buttoned the coat, something in the left pocket banged against my thigh. I reached in to find the Broussard's spare key.

A thrill rushed through me as I opened the garage doors. Something had worked out. I climbed into the driver's seat. It only took a moment to put Helene's stray hairpins to use, pulling my hair into a simple chignon; then I tied her scarf around my head, affixing it under my chin. It was a universal style this time of year for women in this area, tweed overcoat and a scarf to keep the wind off the ears. I glanced at my reflection for a moment in the rearview mirror. The face staring back at me was presentable but exhausted, my gray eyes puffy and inflamed, my pale skin dry and dull.

This wouldn't do in Pravhna society, but it was perfect for the Somershire train station. I would be utterly forgettable as I made my way to the station. No one was likely to recognize me if I kept my head down and didn't speak much. Not that any of that would be a problem. I hadn't a single friend in the village. Now that Helene was dead, I supposed I hadn't a friend in the world.

"How sad," I murmured as I started the Broussard. "The only person I truly loved died before I could kill her myself."

Was it true? Would I have killed Helene? As I pulled out of the carriage house, I pushed the thought aside. There was relief in not ever having to find out, and that was a gift.

CHAPTER 5

MINA

The drive down the mountain was harrowing. Even though Maman had taught me to drive, I wasn't any good at it. Still, I made it down in one piece, and unseen as far as I could tell. A thicket of blackberry a few miles outside the village was the perfect hiding spot for the Broussard, key still in the ignition. If some villager wanted the thing, they could have it—it was too distinctive to drive into town without being recognized. Besides, I would never drive again if I could help it.

I trudged into the forest, listening hard for any signs of the hunt. They were unlikely to come this close to the village, but it was best to make certain all the same. The woods were close, overgrown with moss covered brambles, the pervasive mist that covered all of Sirin crawling along the forest floor. Elementals often hid within its depths.

The walk into the station was just long enough to make my joints scream with pain. My mind drifted to strategy, a surefire way to dull the agony of a long walk. There was the obvious: get to Orchid House, and into Maman's workshop, but I had to plan for some unfortunate realities. Getting in would be difficult.

Her inner sanctum at Orchid House was undoubtedly guarded by dangerous spells, and she and Demophon would have planned for them to last long after her death. Most Oscarovi used magic sparingly, unless they were inspirited, as maintaining any working drained their lifeforce. Even the inspirited largely could not maintain spellwork after their deaths, but I knew Maman had found ways around the usual rules.

It was Maman's greatest shame that I had not proven a good enough witch to attract an elemental familiar. Not every Oscarovi was inspirited, but to maintain any kind of power in Pravhna, it was practically a requirement. She had berated me about it every chance she got, perhaps to make up for the unsatisfying fact that to maintain her own power, she had to hide my lack. Though power itself was not my problem. It was only doing as others did, making a show of things.

Maman's perspective was incomprehensible to me. She was a paradox—one of the most naturally talented witches of her generation, creative beyond comprehension. I doubt even Helene comprehended the ingenious aspects of her power. I certainly didn't, and it had caught me by surprise. It had always struck me as odd that she was so concerned with what others thought of us.

There had to be something in that particular inconsistency. It itched in the back of my mind, restless to be understood. If only I could remember what it was I knew. The only way to find out might be to ferret out the people who'd helped her. That much I did remember. There were others, though Helene and I never knew exactly who they were—shadows that lurked behind closed doors all my life.

A bubbling creek startled me out of the daze I'd been walking through the forest in. My heart beat hard in my chest, panic rising in me. I should have been paying more attention, for the hunt, for stray villagers—what had I been thinking, letting my guard down that way? I had only meant to dull the pain a little, not lose track of time and space altogether. I needed to be more aware of my surroundings.

The oubliette had dulled my senses; sharpening things should be a priority for me.

I was just outside the village now, approaching a well-worn path that ran along the bubbling stream. Ahead, I recognized the footbridge, its railings built from bent willow branches. As I approached, water elementals took the form of various flying fish, jumping out of the water in prismatic glory.

Had Helene known who Maman's conspirators were, and what they were up to? Was that why she'd been killed? I paused on the footbridge, mesmerized by the crystalline elementals. I wondered how I might get hold of records regarding the fire once I got to Pravhna, and if it was even worth it.

All citizens were allowed to examine public records regarding events, which was what made it so unlikely that whatever had been written down about the fire was the truth. A twig snapped nearby, and my eyes darted towards the noise. It was only a cat, a sweet-faced little calico, running back towards the village with a small rodent in her mouth as a prize. A swarm of thoughts rushed back at me as my heartbeat slowed. After so long in the oubliette forgetting, it was overwhelming to think so much.

The best thing to do, unfortunately, was to move. My feet were already aching, sharp, biting pain shooting through the tendons in my legs with every step. Long breath after long breath did nothing for the pain itself, but with every step towards the train station, I grew reacquainted with it. Soon, I was able to think again.

The cityguard was corrupt, bought off by the highest echelons. If the fire at Somerhaven had been the result of foul play, which it most certainly had been, nothing of any use would be in those records. A stray thought reminded me that anyone with the ability to use empyrae would be nigh impossible to imprison, or to confront.

That was a problem for later, though. Now, my only avenue for finding out what truly happened, and what was at the heart of all this, was to re-enter Pravhna society. Secrets were currency amongst the upper echelons. I would have to find ways to gather enough to make clever exchanges.

That was going to take careful plotting. Without Helene, I would likely be lost in my overwhelming thoughts. Weak sunlight hit my face as I exited the thick forest. I'd walked slowly through the woods to conserve energy, but I sped up as soon as my feet hit cobblestone. I skirted through back alleys, avoiding the main thoroughfares and quaint shoppes of the village. Unlikely as it might be for someone to recognize me, it was better to be careful now.

Somershire Station was much as it had always been when I arrived. My heart thumped, creating a rhythm in my body that thrummed with anxiety. By contrast, the station was slow and sleepy, which wasn't to my advantage. It would have been easier if it had been a busy morning—I would have been just another face in the crowd. As I stood in front of the ticket window, reading the placard that named all the stops on the line out of this station, I noticed prices had gone up.

Before I could think too hard, it was my turn. The clerk was a kind-eyed Corvidae, with their beak stuck in a book. They asked me for my destination without looking up from their reading. I counted the little wad of money from Helene's purse carefully. There was just enough for a third-class ticket to Orobov. My heart sank. I couldn't get all the way to Pravhna.

"Next train to Orobov," I said quickly, not wanting the attention that waiting much longer to answer might draw from the line forming behind me.

The clerk didn't so much as look up at me, but printed the ticket and handed it over. I moved quickly out of line, doing some quick calculations in my head. Orobov was an outer ring suburb of Pravhna, and at the rate I walked, it would be mid-morning by the time I got to Orchid House, if not later. This was worrisome, and frankly dangerous.

I sat down on one of the hard benches in the station, keeping my head down while I tried to sort everything out. Exhaustion clouded my thinking, as I went round and round with myself. I'd used too much magic trying to free Demophon from Maman's ring. Sadness hit me. Cruel as Maman could be, Demophon had always calmed her. I would have liked to have seen the wolverine elemental one last time.

A little family of Oscarovi I didn't recognize entered the station, catching my attention, though I didn't know why. They were nobody remarkable, just parents, a baby, and a toddler. Their clothes were well made, but they'd been mended many times. They bought tickets to one of the northern aeries, and one of the adults spoke to the toddler about seeing the sirens as they sat down. The little girl, who had lush dark curls and glowing umber skin, tapped her cheeks. "They've got people-faces?"

"Yes, darling," one of the mothers answered, distracted by the cries of the colicky infant in her partner's arms. "Though we're *all* people. You know that."

The little one pulled on her other mother's pant leg, ignoring the correction in a babyish way that held no malice. "And birb bodies?"

Neither answered the child, who frowned. She turned to me. "Birb bodies?" she asked, toddling forward a few steps.

I nodded once, as it seemed no one else would answer her. She smiled at me. I did not smile back, wanting the child to look elsewhere. I was upset by the thought of walking from Oborov to Pravhna, worried that I might push myself too hard, when the toddler spoke again.

She was right in front of me now, her chubby little hands reaching for my knees. "Shiny eyes," she cooed. I recoiled from her touch, squeezing my eyes shut.

"Yes, Zell, the lady has shiny eyes," said one of the mothers. My eyes flew open, but neither of the parents was looking my way.

The little one stumbled into me, and the mother who was not holding onto the infant jumped forward, scooping the toddler into her arms. "Apologies," she said to me, while soothing the little girl, who looked as though she might cry.

I nodded once and looked down. The woman stared at me for a long moment. "Have we met? You look so familiar to me."

"No," I replied, shaking my head. "I don't think so."

"Mel, doesn't she look like someone we know?" the mother replied, bouncing the toddler on her knee.

Mel looked up at me, frowned a bit, then shook her head. Her curls were the same as the toddler's. "A bit familiar, I'd say."

My heart beat wildly. They weren't people I'd met before. My memory for faces was excellent. Names, not so much, but faces I always remembered. How was it possible they recognized me? Then it struck me. I hadn't even considered how Maman might have explained my disappearance. If they'd pretended I'd gone missing, had my picture been in the papers?

I almost spoke again, but they'd gone back to their children, fussing over them with the kind of loving frustration that parents with small children are easily forgiven for. Something deep inside me stirred with longing for something I would never have. The fetch was sterile. I'd read it in every one of Maman's forbidden texts about the topic. I'd never even gotten my moon.

Maman took all that from me. The thought was so clear, so poignant I knew it was memory, not suspicion. Everything wrong with me was Maman's fault, or at least I'd believed that the day I'd confronted her. Rage rose in me, and I knew that if I spent another moment here, my eyes would glow in a way the women across from me wouldn't be able to ignore.

I got up. "Have a lovely trip to the aerie," I said softly, the sound of my voice speaking to others strange, after so long with only myself to talk to. "Please excuse me." There was no chance that they'd even remember me in a few moments, so engrossed by their little family as they were.

As I moved away from them, out of the station proper, my anger with Maman expanded. I shut my eyes tight, leaning against the whitewashed brick wall of the station. The mere buzz of the aetheric lights was overwhelming, my shoes suddenly too tight, the collar of the coat itchy on my skin. My jaw clenched, as I attempted to force some of the stimuli to retreat, but it didn't work.

It was as though I could hear everything, and then for a moment I *did*. I could hear the mothers inside the station talking to their children, the clerk turning the pages of her book, and from around the corner, an argument.

I've told you time and time again to leave me be, Hippolyta.

That's fine. Then I guess I'll go to the rags about your little affairs when I get back to the city.

Have you any idea how easy it would be to rid myself of you?

I do. That's why I made certain to let Karnon know where I was off to.

You wouldn't dare put that brute Archambeau on my tail.

I'd like to keep him out of this, if you'd just give me the information I asked for. Where—

My feet moved, as though drawn to the voices. Quickly, I opened my eyes, stopping myself from going forward another step. The overwhelming rush of noise retreated. I could no longer hear everything happening around me. I was out on the platform now. It was empty, but the sound of low voices came from around the corner of the station. I couldn't make them out so clearly now, but one of the voices was familiar.

Viridian Montclair. What was he doing here? Hadn't he been with the hunting party? I froze as the sound of his voice drew closer. "Stop showing up at these events, *Hippolyta*," he warned. The emphasis he put on the other person's name was pregnant with disdain. Whoever she was, Viridian hated her. "You may think you have the upper hand, but I am very willing to prove you wrong."

A part of me wanted to round the corner and confront Viridian, but my fear of the oubliette was too great. It would be wise to run, but I couldn't do that either. I was as stuck as I'd been at the bottom of the oubliette, and if he came round the corner, I'd be caught. The woman was speaking again, but I could no longer make out the words. My fear had manifested into a roaring flood that suffused every particle of my being.

I stood stock-still, not hearing, seeing, or tracking time until a woman a head shorter than me bumped directly into me. She was dressed beautifully, and her face—well, her face put Helene's to shame, and that was saying something.

"Get into the station. *Now*," the woman hissed, pushing me forward. Somewhere in the distance, wings flapped. I had forgotten Viridian had the ability to transform into an eagle. In a daze, my body moved without much of my help. The tiny, stunningly beautiful brunette pushed me, maneuvering me around the corner and into the lavatory, which was a single, private toilet at this station.

She locked the door behind us, then turned to face me, whispering, "Wilhelmina Wildfang?"

I hadn't the wherewithal to lie. It felt as though I was back underwater, moving in slow motion. "Yes."

The brunette, who Viridian had called Hippolyta, glared hard at me, her hazel eyes narrowing. She was a vision, like a vengeful goddess out of an ancient tale. "You foolish girl. What are you *doing* here? Do you *know* who I was just speaking to?"

I came back around a bit more, a glare of my own forming. "Viridian Montclair. What of it?"

Hippolyta sighed. "I know you probably think he is wonderful, since he was engaged to your sister, but that man is dangerous."

My eyebrow arched with interest. I dismissed the condescension in the other woman's voice. Maman had frequently made light of my tendency to forget social niceties as a kind of quirk. People often thought me rather naive, and the way this woman was dressed told me she was likely familiar with my reputation in society. "Why do you think that?"

Hippolyta leaned against the heavy wooden door of the lavatory. "If you knew what I do about Viridian Montclair, you'd suspect him, too."

I laughed, the sound dry and unfamiliar to my ears. So, this woman knew the *real* Viridian Montclair. Unfortunate for her, but fortunate for me.

Hippolyta misunderstood my laughter as dismissal. "Fine," she said as she unlocked the lavatory door. "Take your chances then, if you don't believe me."

I slammed the door shut, reaching over Hippolyta to lock it again, murmuring, "I didn't laugh because I don't believe you, but because I *do*."

The small brunette turned, her eyes flaring with curiosity. "You know something about him."

I nodded once, then pointed silently to the train station around us, then cupped my ears to suggest that anyone could be listening. Hippolyta nodded, her eyes widening. I shrugged, pointing to the door. I could only hope she understood I meant that we should try to leave together. It would be easier to talk openly on the train. I showed Hippolyta my ticket to make my point.

The brunette rolled her eyes as she read my ticket, snatching the ticket away from me before unlocking the lavatory door. "I can do better than that, Wilhelmina Wildfang."

CHAPTER 6

ASHBOURNE

Wicked storms stole into the city on the heels of the usual morning fog, and now rain pelted the cobbled street outside the office. A cello suite played softly in the background as I flipped another page in my book without reading it. I glanced at the clock, my mouth twisting as I calculated how long Skye had been gone.

"*Shit.*" I swore in pain. My lip was still healing, even a few hours after my return home from the fire.

Morpheus growled from the office window, but stretched out, his great paws flexing, silver spotted fur shining in the firelight. The feline was only dreaming, not responding to my foul language. Not that the greymalkin would care much about my swearing, curmudgeonly as he was. Still, Skye rarely swore, so I tried to watch my language.

I glanced at the clock again, refocusing my attention. My partner had been gone for over an hour. As far as trips to the Merc went, that wasn't long, and it was better that she reported the devilry at the rubber factory than me. The Aestra in the *Aestra & Claymore* sign on the front window came first for a reason. Skye's name had weight in Pravhna, even in the undercity, where cratties like her old world family's House were despised. Unlike the rest of them, the name Aestra was respected, in no small part because of Skye herself.

Skye's clever tongue would weave a better tale for the Syndicate leaders than I could hope to. She'd been saving me in one way or another for nearly a year, and this morning was no different. I'd been lucky that she and Morpheus found me out cold by the river last winter, with no coat, no money, only an enormous claymore strapped to my back. When I woke, I had no memory of my past, or what I was doing in Pravhna, only my given name.

I turned the pages of the book back to the beginning of the chapter I hadn't been reading. The book was a new gothic romance, bought from my favorite bookstore down the lane. It was full of haunted manor houses and a sinister love interest, typically my favorite genre, but I was distracted. Likely, I'd stay so until Skye returned with news on what was to be done about the fires. Halcyon Gate got lucky last night; no one had died. Other districts hadn't been as lucky.

Perhaps another cup of tea would help. As I got up from my desk, stretching my long legs, movement outside the door kept me from heading back to the little kitchen behind the front office. My shoulders tensed, the bulk of my muscles still sore from the fight. A delicately boned Strix woman stood outside, reading the sign on the window before pushing the door open.

The woman had a scarred screech owl visage, and was dressed smartly in a vibrant ochre tweed suit, covered with a lush fur over-coat, a bowler hat pulled low over her brow. The gloves that covered the taloned fingers of her hands had a rich sheen to them. Everything about the Strix woman was an ostentatious show of wealth. I paused, feeling wary as she shook her umbrella out the door, depositing it in the stand. I hoped this wasn't about last night, or the child I'd helped.

The Strix tended to stick together and if the littling had told about my power… Well, I didn't want to think about that. I hadn't asked the tyke to keep it a secret. They hadn't even seen exactly what I'd done. They'd been so upset I'd chosen not to draw attention to it, figuring they'd likely forget most of what had happened. But if this woman was here to interrogate me, I might be in trouble. It wouldn't do to let the truth of my abilities out.

"You're the private investigators, yes?" she asked, skipping niceties altogether.

I straightened up, breathing an inward sigh of relief. She was a potential client, not the child's relative. In that case, I needed to think quickly. Skye typically handled new clients.

"I'm the Claymore," I said, stumbling over my words a bit, then realizing I'd been unclear. "I'm Ashbourne Claymore," I clarified. "Typically, Skye does the intake, but she's out right now. Apologies."

This wasn't starting off well. The Strix narrowed her eyes. "Because she is the female?"

I frowned, not understanding. My amnesia worked strangely, according to Skye, whose mother was a renowned physician in the upper city. According to my partner, amnesiacs usually remembered most things about society and the greater world, but forgot their personal details. I was different. It seemed I'd forgotten many things about our world and society at large, as well as my personal history.

"Does Mlle Aestra do the intake because she is the female? Do you view your partner as your secretary?"

I frowned deeply. "We can't afford a secretary, I'm afraid. I do most of the clerical work though. I hope that won't keep you from contracting with us."

The Strix sighed, already exasperated with me. "That's not what I meant."

I saw my mistake instantly. In some aeries, there were strict divisions of labor, based solely on sex, rather than gender. When I'd learned that fact, it had surprised me, and confused Skye and Morpheus.

They were unsure how I could have gone without such basic knowledge for all my life. Skye had wanted to take me to see her mother, but when I'd seen how uncomfortable the idea made her, I'd refused. Relearning stray facts about the world and how society worked had been part of my recovery.

It was as though I was learning most things anew. Memories of my past were elusive, and I did not chase them. My life here was good, and a feeling in my gut told me that whatever lay in the past should stay there. Still, moments like these were always awkward, and I needed to do better. Business had been a bit sparse lately.

My eyes glanced off the stack of bills on Skye's desk, as I gestured to the seating area up front. "Typically, I'm just the muscle. Skye's really best with people. That's why she does the intake." I put another log on the hearth as I spoke. "Please, sit," I urged the Strix woman. "Can I get you some tea?"

"No," she said, sitting gingerly, as though she thought the leather sofa might be dirty.

It was not, of course. We're meticulously clean, and I think the office is rather cozy. It was obvious in the way the Strix woman turned her beak up at the office that she did not agree. I took a seat across from her, a wingback covered in dark green velvet.

"How can I be of service, Madame…" I waited for her to fill in her name.

The Strix woman sat on the very edge of the couch, perched as though she would fly away if she could. "My name is of no importance. I was told you take cases no one else will… Ones of a more unsavory nature."

The woman's clothes had obviously been made at one of the haughty ateliers up top. She likely saw our usual clientele as unsavory, but the reality was that most of our cases were rather mundane. We specialized in finding lost people, and most of our business was reconnecting families. The fact that this woman found our rather wholesome clientele unsavory elicited revulsion in me, souring my stomach enough that I hoped it didn't show on my face.

Pull it together, man. I wracked my brain for what to do next. Skye's method for handling situations like these was to feign confusion. She claimed it often urged the subject to reveal more than they otherwise would. "I'm afraid I don't know what you mean."

"Apologies, Mr. Claymore," the Strix said, her tone gentling into pure condescension. "I meant no offense. I come as a go-between for my long-time employer. Someone of good standing, who has an enemy trying to destroy everything we've worked for."

There was genuine emotion in the woman's voice now. I believed that she believed what she said to be true. "All right. What would you like us to do to help? Gather information? Assess the threat?" All were our first steps in building up to more actionable commissions.

"No," the Strix replied, her dark eyes shining. "We'd like you to eliminate her."

What had this woman heard about me? Was it possible that word had gotten around about this morning already? I didn't see how, but I had no idea how the trance those people had been in worked. Maybe they remembered how easily I'd fought off the unnaturally skilled opponents. They'd gotten the better of me in the end, but everyone in the under-city was a fairly good judge of a fighter's prowess. I had no need to be the best, but there was no doubt in my mind that anyone who'd seen that fight would know that I was more than I appeared to be.

Morpheus stretched in the window, growling in his sleep. The Strix startled at the noise coming from behind her, and turned to look at the greymalkin. "I don't believe your cat likes me," she murmured, her eyes widening at Morpheus' considerable bulk.

"That's no cat, Mistress," I replied, my outward expression grim, though inside I had a laugh at the Strix's expense. Morpheus was deep into his midday nap; there was no waking him. Still, if the Strix was unnerved by him, that was fine. "Have you ever met one of the greymalkin before?"

"Oh," the Strix woman said, thoughtful now. "My apologies."

She didn't answer my question. I shrugged, as it didn't matter to me if she couldn't identify a fey cat. It was time for this woman to go. I hated to lose business, but I knew Skye would have done the same if she were here. "We don't do that kind of work, I'm afraid. You'll have to go elsewhere."

"That's not exactly true though, is it?" Her words sent a chill through me. *Did* she know about this morning? But how could she? Her head tilted to one side, a shrewd expression on her avian face. "You have certain unusual talents, do you not?"

My skin prickled in warning at her words. This woman knew more about me than she was letting on, and with how little I remembered about my own past, that was dangerous. She had to go, and now.

I crossed my arms over my chest, puffing it out a bit, hoping that my sheer size might be enough to convince the Strix that I meant what I said. "We're not the right agency for the job. You might try Wingate and Stravinski down the road a bit. They won't do merc work either, but they'll serve you well for an investigation, which I'm afraid we cannot provide."

The Strix tilted her head in the other direction, her intense expression unnerving. "We want you."

I said nothing, keeping my expression blank, but stony. Morpheus breathed deeply in his sleep, and I matched the rhythm of my breath with his—calm and even. Inside I roiled with alarm, but outwardly, I was cold serenity defined. I hoped she understood the chill in my stare to mean, *if you put the little world I've built for myself in any kind of danger, I will end you.*

"Fine then." The Strix sighed, apparently accepting, for the time being anyway, that I would not budge. "But keep an eye out for a woman named Wilhelmina Wildfang. She's trouble, and we'll pay for whatever you can dig up on her."

The Strix's eyes went to the stack of bills on Skye's desk, lingering on the telltale blue envelope from the Bureau of Taxation for a long moment. She appeared to think hard about something, then rose and moved towards the door. "We can have your tax fee cleared in an instant, and so much more. Consider our offer, Msr Claymore. Wildfang is a menace to all we hold dear."

Her gloved hand was on the door, but she paused, waiting, I imagine, for what she implied to sink in. That this Wilhelmina Wildfang was a threat to the very thing I protected by rejecting her employer as a client. She thought she was good at the game, leading me to believe she had information on my past, and that the woman she wanted murdered could hurt my future. I wonder what made her think I was such an easy mark, but it wasn't worth following up on.

Whoever Wildfang was, I'd bet good coin the Strix woman was the real danger. I narrowed my eyes, but slightly. "Good day to you, Mistress."

Her little hoot of laughter as she stormed out of the office was derisive, and though the sound did no such thing, it *felt* as though it echoed. Long after she'd left, I stood with my arms tightly crossed, fuming. The Strix had stirred up worries I didn't know I had and still couldn't name. Not that I wanted to.

I was so fixated on calming myself that I missed Morpheus

waking. *Is Skye still at the Merc?* he asked as he jumped down from his cushion in the window. *I'd like lunch at a reasonable hour.*

The beast rubbed against my legs affectionately, purring. "Still gone," I replied.

Morpheus glanced at the clock that sat on the mantel. *She should have returned by now.*

He was right. Skye had been gone too long. "Let me get my coat and we'll go."

Morpheus dissolved slowly into nothing, his voice the last to leave. *I shall not walk in the rain.*

Of course he wouldn't, damn feline. I, however, would have to go on foot. Nothing about this day felt right, and if Skye was in trouble, she could handle herself. I knew that well enough, but a dark mood took me, and part of me relished a bit of a tussle. As I pulled my overcoat from the rack at the back door, a crooked smile curved my lips.

All this energy had to go somewhere, didn't it?

CHAPTER 7

ASHBOURNE

A few blocks away from the office, the rain cleared off, though the air was damp from the storm. The undercity bled into a dense forest at the base of the mountain Pravhna was built upon, and mist from below curled around my feet as I walked. It hung in the air, clinging to pant legs and clay flower pots bursting with chrysanthemums.

Lower down, deep in what was known as the dark districts, a canopy of trees blocked even the dim sunlight we sometimes got here. That was where the mist came from. The mist and the elementals. A gust of wind caused the clouds around my feet to billow up towards me off the cobbled walkway. I shoved my hands in the pockets of my overcoat as the mist reached waist level, not wanting it to touch me. It was irrational—the midnight blue stuff was harmless, but it gave me an unsettled feeling. There were echoes, deep in the recesses of my mind, of billowing mist that I daren't examine too hard.

I cleared my throat, as though doing so would banish thoughts of life existing before all this—before Pravhna and the undercity. My stomach growled as the scent of street food drifted past me. A street vendor, just a block away from the Merc, sold roasted chestnuts and candied apples at the center of a roundabout. They'd set up their stand at the foot of an enormous marble statue depicting a wide variety of Vilhari and Oscarovi. I'd been told it was a tribute to the brave soldiers of the undercity who'd fought in some long ago war against an extraterrestrial threat.

Vaguely, I understood the war had been the reason that the Vilhari and the Oscarovi had finally come together as a blended society—that the foe they fought against had alchemized the two groups. I struggled to recall the name of the invaders, but could not. It was all basic stuff, things school children knew by heart, and yet it was all still a mystery to me, as were the intricacies of Pravhna society.

It was easier here in the undercity, where people didn't pry about a person's past. But it was more than that. People in the undercity were nothing like the fussy upper crust cratties, whose neighborhoods of ornately carved limestone buildings were decorated with sedate gardens, put to bed the moment they dried up in the autumn. I passed a cluster of Oscarovi flower vendors, all calling out prices for their bright wares as I went. A few of them were familiar to me, and I waved as I crossed the street.

Here in the undercity, the avian fey gathered festive flora in their travels into the dark districts below. The Oscarovi used their elemental magic to spell them to last longer than they naturally would and sold them in beautifully arranged bundles. This time of year, our district had the feeling of a perpetual carnival.

The Mercury Room, or the Merc as most of Halcyon Gate called it, was up ahead. I slowed as I approached, honing my focus. Doing business at the Merc meant having my wits sharpened to a knife's edge. I always took a moment to clear my mind before entering the Syndicate's inner sanctum.

The pleasure house was a tall, four story building, whose imposing limestone exterior bore carvings of Strix knights and siren queens and oracles over the enormous arched doors. Flowers spilled out of boxes affixed to the sills of leaded glass windows. Huge aetheric lamps were lit even in daytime, their green glow and the curls of wrought iron flowers and bats luring customers in.

After one last steadying breath, infusing my still-aching muscles with a bit of cool relief, I entered the pleasure house through a side door. The back hallways were crowded. I nodded at various people from the neighborhood as I made my way to the atrium at the center of the building. There was a bar set up there, and at night musicians played and the tables were cleared off the floor for dancing. A paper bag labeled "S. Aestra" sat on the bar, near the till. Skye had ordered lunch.

The Strix bartender nodded at the bag as I read the label. "She paid, but she's talking to the boss."

I followed the golden-eyed Strix's gaze up to the mezzanine. Skye was easy to spot. Her shining white hair was cropped short, from where she'd cut off her Chevalier's braid when she left the upper city for good, a tradition among the Syndicate organizations, apparently. Today, she was dressed in her usual attire of slim-fitting trousers, tall leather boots and close fitting shirtsleeves that clung to the athletic muscles of her arms and shoulders. She'd tossed her gray wool overcoat over the back of her chair.

Her expression was serious as Karnon Archambeau leaned towards her, talking animatedly in a low tone. Archambeau was the Halcyon Gate Syndicate's unofficial leader, mostly because of his infectious charisma. He was a short man, but sturdily built, with tawny skin and a sharply intelligent face. The Oscarovi's dark eyes were serious as he fiddled with the pendant that channeled his elemental familiar. There was no hint of amusement in the motion of his hands—he was troubled by whatever he was telling Skye.

So, what I'd encountered this morning wasn't a fluke. We were right to report in. The undercity thrived, in many ways, because of organized crime, but Skye could never shake the feeling that the consequences of their rule were too steep. Privately, I disagreed. The cratties' hold on the upper city was just as cruel. It just looked nicer on the outside, while the Syndicate was open in their brutality. I didn't need to explain that to Skye. She understood it perfectly and wanted better from everyone. That was where we differed. I expected the worst from people and was glad when they surprised me with better.

On the mezzanine, Skye nodded while Archambeau spoke, her face grave. There was nothing of her usual serenity in her posture. Her shoulders hunched around her ears, and every so often she covered her mouth in what I knew was deep horror. Inwardly, I swore.

Signs had been cropping up for months that something rotten was happening in the undercity. First, there'd been more missing people than ever, more odd murders and unexplained crime. And now, these strange, unquenchable fires that did not spread. Our closest guess was that a new player might be attempting to take control of the Syndicate as a whole.

The Syndicate was a loose organization that operated throughout the undercity. Each of the large lower districts had multiple Syndicate leaders that ran things, taking bribes, offering protection, and keeping our communities prosperous. In the Halcyon Gate, we had four: Karnon Archambeau led the Oscarovi, Vionette Celestine the Vilhari, and Edith Braithwaite the Strix and Corvidae.

The fourth leader, who went by the pseudonym Chopard, operated in secret, ostensibly acting as liaison with the dark districts. It was brutal work, but it kept the more dangerous Syndicate elements out of everyday life. No one had ever seen him. In my mind, he was a likely candidate to be the cause of all this trouble. Perhaps he'd been bought out by one of the darker elements in the Syndicate. This morning had proven that if that were true, all of Pravhna needed to be concerned, not just the undercity.

Anyone who could wield that kind of power was beyond dangerous. From the looks of things, Archambeau already knew what was going on, and the news was bad. Karnon Archambeau wasn't a selfish man; in fact, quite the opposite. He cared deeply about the undercity being run in the ways he saw fit. Though Archambeau and Skye disagreed on many of those points, they shared a belief that the only way denizens here would be taken care of was by their own.

I could take the bag of food and go, now that I'd confirmed nothing had gone wrong with the Syndicate, but something in my gut told me to stay. I slid onto a stool, glancing at the bartender. "Ale, please."

The Strix nodded. He was new, and I didn't know his name. They always had the new ones work the day shift for a few months before taking on the riotous nighttime crowd. "Dark or pale?"

"Pale," I said, keeping my eyes on Skye. The Vilhar could hold her own, but I'd never assume we were safe at the Merc just because we had good standing in the neighborhood.

While I didn't *think* we were in trouble from the way Archambeau was talking, there was no predicting the Syndicate. The bartender slid a glass of pale ale across the luxurious wood bar. I waited to take a drink. Something about the way Skye sat back on the ornately carved settee worried me.

Skye glanced down from the mezzanine at just that moment, her silver eyes locking onto mine. The same chill that went through me on the walk over seeped deep into my bones. Skye held my gaze for a long moment, then turned back to Archambeau. I settled into my stool. There was no way I was leaving now. I turned my attention to the bag of food, opening it to peek inside. It was cold.

"Want me to send it back to the kitchen for a warmup?" the bartender asked, a knowing look in his eyes. "The new sous chef is Oscarovi. They don't mind a bit."

I nodded. "That would be great. Could you have them add an extra helping of the plain poulet as well?" That would appease Morpheus' temper for having been made to wait. There was no telling where the greymalkin had got off to, but as he wasn't here, it was my duty to make sure there was enough lunch to keep him happy. Or at least *less* grumpy than usual.

The Strix took the bag away. "Of course." As he walked away, it looked like he let out a sigh of relief. I couldn't say as I blamed him. There was an atmosphere of tension in the pleasure house that was odd for a weekday afternoon. The usual games of cards were nowhere to be found, and there wasn't a courtesan in sight. The chill spread through me, aching as it went.

Archambeau's voice raised a measure, making him just loud enough to be heard down in the atrium. "...one remembers anything afterward. How is he *doing* it?"

Magic that alters memory is old and complex. The Oscarovi usually can't manage it, even those inspirited with the most powerful elementals. As far as I knew, the most powerful among the Vilhari couldn't do spells like that either, not without a fair amount of inconvenience, anyway. Minds are complicated things, hard to manipulate for even short amounts of time. It's why love and memory spells are unreliable and short-lived, if they ever work at all.

I scanned the atrium bar to see who else was interested in what was going on here today. The pink velvet chairs were empty but for a large man, with long dark brown locs pulled into a neat ponytail, wearing a wine-colored suit. His thick legs were crossed in a casual way that suggested he was at ease—well at ease, as anyone who saw the future might be.

I raised a hand slowly in greeting when Muse felt me watching. My emotional range was frustratingly limited, at times. I felt things outside my fairly even keel, but I didn't stray very often from a rather defined set of emotional parameters. Today, things were different. A feeling of an aperture widening came over me as Muse's dark eyes turned my way.

"Ashbourne." Muse's sonorous voice boomed across the atrium, a bright smile flashing white. As always, his umber skin was the epitome of vibrant health. The man always looked infuriatingly well-rested. "Good to see you."

Muse didn't get up though, or motion for me to join him, which was typical of the seer. Muse and Skye were acquaintances on good terms, and little else. The seer had made it clear he wasn't interested in being friends with "anyone who gets themselves into as much trouble as the two of you regularly do." Muse's table had a full glass of *le fey vert* resting on it, and he appeared to be reading a book. From the state of his full glass, I doubted he'd come to the Merc for a hallucinogenic drink and a relaxing afternoon.

Motion in my peripheral vision caught my attention. I looked up to find Skye, with the bag of food in hand. Her face was smooth and serene, but there was a steeliness in her eyes that concerned me. Skye nodded to me. "Let's get lunch to Morpheus, before he destroys something in retribution."

I started to slide off my stool, making ready to follow Skye home. Time seemed to slow, as instincts I didn't quite understand came awake within me. From secret corners, eyes were upon us. Muse looked up from his book at the same time I reacted to the odd feeling. Deep sadness lingered in the seer's eyes, clarifying further when his gaze rested on me. I wondered what he saw, but also—I had the strong sense I didn't want to know.

Skye paused. She looked around, but then seemed to sense the truth of the matter: by day's end everyone would know what she was about to tell me. "We've been hired to investigate Chopard. We're to uncover his real identity."

I had been right. This would mean war in Halcyon Gate. The peace of our district was dependent on the Syndicate leaders getting along. This was unheard of. I glanced back at the mezzanine. Karnon was gone. "What about Edith and Vionette?" The other two Syndicate leaders had to agree to something of this magnitude.

Skye's countenance was outwardly cool, but I saw the worry in her eyes. "They are in consensus. Chopard is the source of the arsons. His people have been spotted at two different scenes, as well as the masked combatants you fought this morning. He brought the fight to us, Ash. There's no other way."

She was right, of course. There were strict rules around how the Syndicate operated, and Chopard had been flouting them for too long—he'd gone too far this time. I thought of the little owlet, and the blank look in those people's eyes. The way that after the working that had turned them into mindless automatons fell away, they'd still be hollowed out, empty shells. I hadn't even asked if they were all right.

"The people from this morning…" I said, trailing off.

"Two are dead," Skye said, her eyes gentling. "The littling you helped and the mother."

"What?" the room spun out beneath me. The owlet was only a little sick, just a cold, and I'd fixed their hand. How could this be possible? "But the child wasn't even affected by the spell."

Skye shook her head. "We don't know how it happened, Ash. But when Vionette's doctor arrived an hour ago, they were both gone."

A stab of fear ran through me, laced with righteous fury at the hatchling's death. The feeling was old, familiar to me, though I refused to examine it further. I drew myself up, my spine lengthening as my feet hit the rough wooden floors. Skye looked back at me over her shoulder, her expression shifting as mine did. The mixture of fear and anger were a warrior's constant companions, and my partner wore them as comfortably as I did when the need arose. Skye's face was a mirror of mine, her eyes hardening into those of the Chevalier she'd once been.

Each step we took towards the Merc's back doors was a transformation. The mild-mannered private investigators we'd been two days ago melted away, and warriors of a different grade altogether walked out into the bustling streets of the undercity.

"I'm so sorry, Ash," Skye murmured as her pace picked up. "This isn't what I wanted for us."

I paused for a moment, knowing she wouldn't say more out here in the open. That apology was the end of the peaceful life we'd built together over the past year. I could run from this, build the feeling of safety I so cherished again—albeit somewhere else, without her or Morpheus, neither of whom would ever leave Pravhna.

The thought was fleeting. Skye looked back, sorrow and resolution embattled in her silver eyes. My feet moved forward until I was at her back—where I belonged—the menacing shadow to her beacon of light.

CHAPTER 8

MINA

A bit reluctantly, I followed Hippolyta back into the lobby of the train station. It was nearing the time for the next trains to arrive. The station was filling up with people. A few villagers I recognized appeared to be dropping visiting friends or relatives off, but none stayed. Anyone going into Pravhna for work would have left early this morning.

No one gave me a first, let alone a second, glance. My makeshift disguise had not worked on Hippolyta because she was uncommonly perceptive. Everyone else here went about their own business, with no mind for others. What had been such a hardship in my lonely childhood was now a boon. No one knew me, or cared to know me. All was the same as it had ever been. There was a cold comfort in that.

One of the mothers from before was talking with a clerk, a worried look on her face. "But we were told the baby would ride free."

"So sorry, ma'am," the clerk said. "They do ride free, 'til the northern stations, but…"

Hippolyta shooed me away. "Go find us a seat. The station's filling up and we've a bit to wait."

She was right, of course, but worry set into my stomach as I sat.

She'd been talking with Viridian. Arguing, yes, but still in his company. Was it possible he knew I was out, and they'd plotted this together? Some part of me rejected that notion immediately. Their argument had been quite genuine, as was her hatred for him and his for her. Still, he might be blackmailing her into helping him.

But again, that didn't fit well with the conversation I had overheard. I watched Hippolyta buy two tickets to Pravhna. As the clerk gathered them for her, she glanced at the woman I'd talked to before. I searched the station for her wife, and the two children, but the station was crowded now. Winged Vilhari and Oscarovi in giant hats mingled together with Strix and Corvidae alike, the soft roar of a bustling day filling my ears. The station was a colorful riot of feathers and fabrics.

It took me a moment to find the little family amongst the crowd. I had to crane my neck a little, over the newspaper of the Oscarovi sitting next to me, to find them. They had changed seats and were crowded between a Vilhar with the brown wings of a sparrow and a Strix couple who were fighting over who had eaten the last cheese streusel from the bakery in town. The baby was crying, and the toddler clung to her mother. All their eyes were wide with distress.

It had sounded like they might not have accounted for the cost of taking a fourth member of their family north to the aeries. Not a crisis, certainly, but a disappointment. When I looked back up at Hippolyta, her eyes had found the wife and children. There was a mixture of sadness and desperation in her eyes I recognized acutely: loneliness. The kind of loneliness that ached in your gut, making your bones brittle and cold. The kind that gnawed on you at the edges, unrelenting and cruel in its persistence.

The clerk talking to the other mother said something to Hippolyta, who nodded. I'd missed some exchange between them. The woman looked confused for a moment, then smiled gratefully, clasping Hippolyta's hand in hers. I watched as the clerk came back at the same time, handing four tickets to the woman, and two to Hippolyta. They spoke for a moment before parting ways. Hippolyta paused, watching as the little family reunited, their trip to the northern aeries back on schedule as planned.

The loneliness in her eyes lessened a measure, though the sadness behind it stayed. I had no idea if I could trust Hippolyta, but there was no doubt in my mind that we could help one another.

~

HIPPOLYTA PURCHASED us two first-class tickets to Pravhna. We would have to share a sleeping car, but that was not a problem. First-class cars contained two small beds, piled high with jewel-hued silk linens, in the bedroom, in addition to a beautifully appointed sitting room and lavatory. Neither of us spoke further about Viridian until the train was well underway to Pravhna.

Hippolyta had been "freshening up" in the lavatory for long enough that my thoughts had wandered. It was as though a ticker tape ran rampant in my mind, a carousel of fragments driving me into what felt like a trance. Pieces of the day Viridian and Helene put me in the oubliette accosted me, unbidden and out of order. The mechanics of what had happened were there, but the specifics eluded me. I'd woken that day plagued with troubling dreams.

And something else, though at first it stayed just out of sight. That morning, I *remembered* Papa. As the memory emerged, I nearly laughed at the impossibility of it. Alastair Wildfang died before Maman gave birth to me. And yet, I remembered his face, handsome, if rather plain—and the sound of his voice, gravelly and time-ravaged, much like my own. I could have dismissed remembering his face as mere fancy. There were portraits of him at Orchid House. But I had remembered the sound of his voice. I'd remembered it and told Maman.

That morning, I'd struggled to grasp onto the memory, but it disappeared before I could catch it. Whatever came next was a blur, an opaque film drawn over the memory. I saw myself, as though I floated above my body, talking to Maman, pleading with her for the truth. Feeling returned to my body, I was coming out of the trance, but I latched onto one last image. I'd woken at the bottom of the oubliette, Viridian and Helene completing the spell that locked me in, their faces disappearing as the sea rushed in to cover the hole.

"Wilhelmina!" Hippolyta's voice cut through the sound of my screams, echoing in my mind.

My vision cleared as I looked up at the woman's beautiful face, confused as to where I was. Her mahogany hair was tucked behind a pointed ear. *I was on a train, with a perfect stranger, hurtling toward Pravhna. Right.*

My eyes narrowed. "You're Vilhari?"

Hippolyta brushed the hair forward again, her cheeks flushing. "Yes, Wilhelmina, I am."

"Mina."

"What?"

Mother and Helene had always called me Wilhelmina. It had never seemed to fit me correctly, but it was an old family name, one I didn't particularly like or want. "Please call me Mina."

Hippolyta blinked once, frowned deeply as she searched my face. For what, I wasn't certain. Understanding people had never been my strong suit. The woman's large hazel eyes softened ever-so-slightly, her heartbeat slowing to a strong, regular beat.

A smile spread across her face, lighting it with overwhelming beauty. "Call me Poe." She lowered her voice to a whisper. "Not Hippolyta. *Ever.*"

"Why?" I asked, forgetting to soften my words into the more palatable tone Helene had begged me to use, claiming that my bluntness offended others.

Poe seemed to like it, though. The name fit her better than Hippolyta, which matched her regal beauty, but not the wickedly sharp intellect the woman obviously possessed. "Poe" fit the danger I sensed the woman before me might pose to any who got in her way. There was a kind of ruthless determination in Poe that was like a mirror of what lived inside my heart.

"The surname Endymion is common enough, but Hippolyta isn't," she said.

That was true. It *was* a unique name. "Viridian knows it, though."

Poe gritted her teeth. "Unfortunately, yes." She sank into the plush, seafoam green chair next to mine before going to work pouring herself some tea. The train's first-class china was exquisite, painted with snakes and a dark floral motif. For a brief moment, I considered stealing it. It would fetch a good sum on the black market

—having been made especially for the railroad. It's what Maman would have done—it's the kind of thing she *had* done, or forced Helene and I to do, dozens of times.

Poe interrupted my thoughts. "In attempting to get what I need from him, he got something from me first. I'm certain he doesn't know what it means, though."

"Why?" I asked, hoping she would reveal more.

The smile on Poe's face was a sharp, cruel thing. "Because if he did, one of us would already be dead."

How interesting. Their conversation at the train station had sounded dangerous, a push and pull of secrets and threats. That clarified the state of things between them, if not the exact nature of their conflict. Neither seemed to have the advantage over the other, but as Poe hated Viridian, it warmed me to her, though perhaps irrationally so.

A cool calm settled over me. "You'll have to make him pay for whatever he's done to you."

Poe set the teapot down so gently it didn't make a sound, her eyes raising to mine. "I intend to."

We stared at one another for a long moment, neither of us offering more. The calm stillness within my chest spread throughout my body. A desperate, lonely feeling chased the stillness, one I was all too familiar with—one that had gotten me into trouble when I was younger. Giving into it always broke my heart, but something deep within me reasoned that all people couldn't be bad. That somewhere, there must be someone I could trust.

Trust was dangerous, too fickle a beast for my taste. "How did you get into a House Montclair country party if Viridian didn't want you there?"

Poe smiled, her grin a wicked thing. "I had three invites to the party. Not even Viridian could keep me away. It was just the opportunity I needed to put pressure on him." Her face fell. "I worked hard to make those contacts. Viridian kicking me out doesn't serve my purposes."

"What do your companions think happened to you?" I asked, wondering if her social standing had been harmed at all.

Poe sighed. "When Viridian had enough of me, I claimed I'd

come down with the vapors and needed to go home and rest. But we were seen having words."

"I see," I said, thinking over what that might mean for her social status.

Now Poe's eyes narrowed sharply. "What do you see?"

I shrugged, trying to appear casual, though I don't think I fooled Poe. "I've never heard of you, and yet..."

"And yet I'm invited to weekends in the country with some of the highest echelons," Poe finished for me. Her tone was void of inflection, her face and body still, but not rigid. There was no way for me to read her, to tell what she might be thinking.

"Yes," I agreed, making sure to sound as neutral as she had. I was trying harder with Poe than I had in a long time. I didn't want her to immediately dislike me. But the fact remained that I had no time for friends. What I needed was an *ally*.

I stared at the teapot for a long time, not certain what to say next. In times like these, I worried my emotions were broadcast outside my body, that everyone could tell how I felt, even when I was uncertain. The train's low rumble as it hurtled towards the city soothed me somewhat, making it easier to think.

Reasoning through a problem always helped at a time like this. I took a sip of my tea—which was utter perfection—mulling over my next move. It was obvious Poe knew at least the basics of what had happened at Somerhaven. Her explanation would tell me more about her as well.

I took a cleansing breath, smoothed my face, and asked, "What can you tell me about the fire that killed my mother?"

For a long moment, confusion clouded Poe's eyes, then that deep sadness from before welled in them. It was as though whatever she felt was less about what she was about to say, and more about something deep within herself. "Your mother and Helene."

The elementals had said it, but with no evidence, I hadn't really believed it was possible. "So it was confirmed? Helene really is dead?"

Again, Poe looked confused, but she nodded. "Yes, Viridian identified the body. He was quite shaken."

That struck me as an odd thing to say. "Were you with him when he found out?"

Poe's cheeks flushed. "Not like that!"

Now it was my turn for confusion, but I caught on quickly. "I didn't mean to imply that you were…"

A shaky laugh spilled from Poe's pretty lips. "Of course you didn't. I'm sorry to have implied that you *would*. Sometimes our peers can be unkind."

I nodded once, though not sure if I understood completely. There was no question that our class could be cruel. I knew that to be true from painful experience. But it was difficult to understand why or how anyone could dislike Poe. I observed her for a long moment—her sharply defined features, her perfectly styled clothing. Everything about her was subtly better than what most of our peers could manage, even with the help of the modiste and a lady's maid.

"They are unkind to you because you are so beautiful."

Poe let out a little laugh, the sound less of delight than relief. "I suppose they might be. How I look has opened doors, but…" Poe's hands fluttered in a way that seemed uncharacteristic for her, given what I'd seen so far.

"But it makes things very hard, doesn't it?"

Poe nodded. "It does. People underestimate me."

"My sister experienced something similar when she was very young." Memory slipped down my throat, cold and slick. I swallowed hard. "My mother taught her to use it as a weapon."

Poe's eyes narrowed. "A lesson I've learned as well, though I had no mother to teach it to me."

The way Poe's voice cracked, ever so slightly, around the information moved me. Determined as I was not to make friends, every moment in her presence made me question my resolve. *Remember what happened with Rebecca and Caralee*, I reminded myself. *Remember how badly this can all turn out.* Childhood wounds did not heal easily, and I did myself no favors by forgetting.

The tension in the train car had thickened to a nearly gelatinous state. "So, my sister and mother are both dead," I said. "What does everyone think happened to me?"

Poe's eyebrows raised. "You don't know?" She shook her head.

"Of course you don't…Your family said you were kidnapped—about six months before the fire—there was an investigation, but no leads were ever found."

"Who led the investigation? Which investigative unit, I mean?"

Poe shook her head. "The IU was dismissed. The Baldwin Agency was brought in—*oh*." I sipped my tea, regulating the rapid increase in my heartbeat as Poe put the pieces together. She was *very* smart, which was incredibly satisfying. "They're on House Montclair's payroll."

Yes, they certainly were. The knowledge was disappointing, but I couldn't afford to let my emotions get the better of me. My eyes deadened, emotionlessness spreading over my features. "You don't need to convince me that Viridian Montclair is up to something bad. I know quite well what the man is capable of."

"So you weren't kidnapped then?" Poe asked.

I stood, suddenly feeling very tired, though of course the fetch did not actually need sleep. "It all depends on how you look at it. I was imprisoned against my will, by the very people who claimed to be looking for me."

I'm not sure why I told her—it was an instinct more than anything. A test, yes, but one part of me was sure she would pass.

Poe's long lashes brushed against her cheeks as she stared down at her hands. "I'm so sorry, Mina. I don't know what that would feel like… but I imagine it's terrible." The kind of sincerity that cannot be faked laced her words, drawing me in, tightening around me like a snare.

If this was a ruse, part of her incredible social skills, I needed her with me. If she could deploy sincerity this way, whether real or a performance, she was an asset I couldn't afford to lose. There was, of course, the possibility that her actions and emotions all stemmed from genuine interest in my wellbeing. I stared at her for what felt like a very long time. So long, in fact, that she looked up at me.

I found the answer I was looking for in her eyes. There was real concern and sadness there, paired with shrewd calculation. She'd hurt her reputation by getting kicked out of the Montclair party. Poe needed me as much as I needed her.

Whatever this woman was looking for, she wondered if I could help. The idea was staggering. No one had ever so much as wondered if I were an asset to their success before. I had only ever been a burden.

The idea of someone needing me terrified me, more than I could accurately understand. I backed away from Poe. "I think it best if I get some sleep now."

"Of course," Poe said softly. "I noticed that you might need something to wear to sleep in. I put something of mine out in the lavatory. It will be too short for you, of course—"

"Thank you," I said, cutting Poe short. "That is very kind of you."

Inside the lavatory, the aetheric light's greenish glow was tempered by a glass sconce, casting a pool of light into the little room. A beautiful loose dressing gown, made of the finest silk, lay over the warming towel rack. I was tempted to wash, but the shower in the lavatory was like a coffin, small and enclosed. Too much like the oubliette. I settled for keeping the door open, and washing quickly. Not much water got onto the floor, but I soothed myself with thoughts of the giant bathtub at Orchid House.

When I'd dried, I slipped into the dressing gown, which probably dragged the floor on Poe, but only skimmed my calves. Still, it was lovely to wear something so fine—and clean. I stared at my face in the lavatory mirror for a long time. My face didn't appear to have aged a day since I reached maturity. This was typical for Oscarovi, who were not technically immortal, but were so long lived that they might as well be, especially with the use of their jewels. But I wore no jewel, partnered with no elemental familiar for use of magic.

It was my greatest shame. An Oscarovi of my status without an elemental pair was considered incomplete, a failure. There were ways to hide my incompetence, but Viridian likely knew the truth about me and could use it to his advantage. That was something I'd have to be careful about. Yet another thing to be wary of.

In the mirror, as my emotions rose to the surface, my eyes glowed golden as the empyraen magic I wielded as easily as aether. Shadows flickered around my fingers, little clouds of aether, friendly as spirits for me. Yet another of my shameful eccentricities. This was not natural.

I was not natural.

I met my eyes in the mirror, as though looking at a stranger. Maman told people I took after Papa, an explanation for my dark hair, umber in color. But Papa's hair hadn't been this color. Brown, yes, unlike Maman and Helene's nearly platinum hair. But Papa had much fairer hair than mine, barely brown, and his features were nothing like mine, upon closer examination of my face.

The most common use for a fetch, before the Oscarovi High Council had outlawed them, was bringing back a lost child. It was nearly impossible to knit an adult's consciousness to a new body, but children were easier. Though the practice did work sometimes, it had also resulted in terrible monstrosities. Some people's essences never attached properly to the fetch, and they grew to be tortured individuals.

It had been considered unethical, and the practice was outlawed. As early as my twelfth year, I had suspected that Maman might have broken the rules, wanting to bring something of Papa back into her life. That perhaps she'd lost the baby she was pregnant with when Papa died and built herself a fetch to carry the child's soul. *My soul.* That maybe that was why I was so strange, never being able to fulfill Maman's desires for my potential, why I was always in so much pain.

But as I aged, I'd dismissed that as the fancy of an unhappy child. Unhappy families were not so uncommon, after all. In the oubliette, the memory of my childhood fear returned, confirmed by my lack of actual need for sleep or sustenance. Still, the entire time I was in the hole, I'd never once considered there might be another reason for Maman to put whoever I *actually* was in the fetch. I forced myself to do so now. I still could not remember why she'd done it or who I was, but staring at myself in the mirror, I understood.

The fetch looked nothing like my family because they were not *my* family. They never had been.

CHAPTER 9

MINA

The train entered Pravhna well past midnight. Though there was a station closer to Orchid House in the upper city, Poe needed to get off at Halcyon Gate Station and thought it better to hire a cab to take me to Orchid House. She explained that some of the tittle-tattle rags had been sending novice reporters to haunt upper city stations at night, catching sight of anyone sneaking into or out of the city in clandestine hours and printing the information the next day in features some of the rags called "comings and goings."

I'd never been of much interest to the rags. My time in society had always been brief. Maman allowed me to come only to events that would be odd if I'd not been present. She portrayed me as a naive, quirky child—a disappointing late bloomer and an introvert. After a few social blunders in my teenage years, it was an easy thing for most to believe. She'd never spent money on outfitting me properly for society, preferring to dress me in unflattering garments that disguised anything attractive about me.

As I followed Poe off the train, admiring the beautiful job her modiste had done to tailor her overcoat to every curve of her petite form, I wondered what might have been different if I'd been allowed to dress as I pleased. I had an eye for beautiful things, but no clue how to go about picking them out for myself. I envied Poe that ability as we prepared to part ways.

Halcyon Gate Station was run down, its grandeur faded, all peeling acid green paint and dusty chandeliers. Only the cracked painted floor tiles remained vibrant, depicting a forest scene, rife with elemental spirits in flat line drawings. I stared at the drove of indigo hares, peeking out from behind the trees and in the mist. Odd that they were depicted here.

Poe took a long breath in, holding it as she frowned, then handed me some money. "This should be enough to get you to the upper city safely." Her words came out in a tumble and the frown deepened into her pretty face. "I hope everything works out for you, Mina."

The way she looked at me was hesitant, as though she did not want to leave me any more than I wanted her to go. But I couldn't find the words to say that. We'd only just met. I wasn't sure how to tell Poe Endymion that while I most definitely needed her help to navigate the upper echelons, I probably needed her friendship more.

Instead of finding those words, I took the money, returning the sentiment, as was polite. "I hope things work out for you too."

We stared at one another, a kind of longing I wasn't used to building between us. I'd experienced romantic crushes before, the desperate rushes of yearning building to a fever-pitch, lust mixed with infatuation. This was nothing like that. Instead, Poe felt like a missing piece of me. Something about her was kindred—her keen intelligence, her sadness, the sense I had that like me, somewhere in the thick of things, Poe had been deeply betrayed.

Poe's long brown fingers stretched towards mine. I looked down at our hands as Poe placed her card in my palm. "Call on me if you need anything."

I nodded, not knowing what to make of the offer, or the desire I had to offer something in return. Poe smiled at me, then finally nodded. "All right then."

She turned to go, picking her bag up. Without thinking, I caught the sleeve of her coat. It was as if my hands had acted on their own. "Wait."

Poe turned, her brows knitting together as she looked up at me. I wasn't sure what I was about to say, but I didn't want Poe to go.

Our stories intertwined, creating a connection that had not yet clarified, but the part of my mind that always worked ahead, that always puzzled together the unseen pieces—it *knew*. Poe was important.

Before I could try to explain any of that, my skin prickled with the feeling of being watched. Covertly, I glanced around. The station was empty, but for the clouds of mist that crept in, curling this way and that across the mosaic tiled floor.

"Someone's here," Poe said, keeping her voice barely above a whisper.

"Yes," I agreed.

Poe and I stood completely still, though both of us clearly braced ourselves for whatever might come next. The feeling of eyes on us receded slightly, as though whoever observed us knew we knew. When it disappeared completely, she let out a tensely held breath. My shoulders sagged a bit.

"The rags?" I asked, thinking of what she'd told me about the tittle-tattles.

Poe shrugged, her dark brows furrowing. "Maybe."

We stared at one another for a long moment while I gathered my courage. "Do you think there's a way we might help one another?" I prepared myself for her to question my statement in a dozen different ways, rapidly calculating as many good answers as I could come up with. "I'm sure you have a life to get back to here, but—"

"Yes," Poe agreed. "I've been trying to sort out how I could broach the subject all night, but I didn't want to scare you off."

Now it was my turn to breathe a sigh of relief. "So, will you come stay at Orchid House?"

Poe grinned. "And play out the season together?"

I nodded. She understood my line of thinking then. We seemed to complement one another well. If we worked together, perhaps we would both find what we sought.

"Then let's get a cab and get out of here," Poe said, picking up her bag and marching towards the street.

I followed her into the night. On the misty sidewalk, several children, none older than twelve, stood smoking something that smelled of clove and vanilla. They were a mix of Vilhari, Oscarovi, and

Strix. Poe hailed them, handing the little Strix girl that approached her a copper. "Grab us a cab going uptown, yeah?"

"Yeah," the little one with the visage of a tawny owl responded.

Poe tugged on the littling's sleeve. "Someone with a clean conscience, or Herself shall hear about it."

Poe said "Herself" like it was a name, and not just any name, a significant one. The little Strix' eyes widened. "Yes'm. I understand."

She ran off into the night. Interesting. It was as though Poe was speaking another language, though I understood her words perfectly. I cast a long gaze back at the undercity. In the distance, intense string music played, accompanied by the sounds of reveling in the streets. One of the undercity's infamous street balls was taking place, just a few blocks away. My body reacted nearly immediately to the music. A forbidden part of me longed to disappear into that music, to turn my back on whatever waited for me at Orchid House and never look back.

"So then," Poe said, stepping between me and the tantalizing din of the undercity.

It was all she needed to say to bring me back to myself—and my need for the truth. There was no room for such fancies as disappearing into the night. I was not built to let things go. "We'll help each other. You need access to society—and I need help navigating it."

Poe moved closer to me, our shoulders touching, her voice low. "Aren't you going to ask me what I'm looking for?"

I looked down at the beautiful woman. "I suppose we'll have plenty of time when we're alone to spin our sad tales, won't we?"

Poe's eyes narrowed slightly. "You don't seem like the type to trust so easily."

I smiled then, a rare thing for me, given how wicked Maman had always said it made me appear. In the undercity, the buskers' music swelled into an appropriately tense tango. "I said nothing of *trust*, Hippolyta."

Poe's smile matched mine. "Won't we make an interesting pair?"

"I doubt that's the word our enemies will use," I mused, keeping my eyes moving for any other unexpected appearances.

A child ran by us, leaving the station, headed towards the street ball. Poe reached out, snatching the littling by the back of their collar. Their visage was that of a snowy owl, and Poe's eyes narrowed shrewdly. "What color is the peony in winter?"

A secret code. Poe was becoming more interesting by the moment. She was obviously well connected, which could only serve both our purposes.

"Black as the day is long, Miss," the little one answered.

"You know who I am?" Poe asked, keeping her voice soft as a cab rounded the corner, the first Strix child riding in the front passenger seat.

The second hatchling nodded.

"Tell her I'm back from the country."

The hatchling nodded again, and Poe let them go. They disappeared into the night. Her eyes narrowed slightly. "Something's afoot," Poe murmured. "The children are afraid tonight."

I hadn't noticed that, but now my mind raced, trying to pick up the pattern in what was happening around us. A picture formed in my mind, but was too vague to make out. It was frustrating to have to wait, but just a little more time and it would clear. It was unfortunate that I was particularly bad at waiting.

The cab pulled up to the curb, the first Strix child jumping out to join her companions. As they rushed off into the night, the driver got out of the car. Like the hatchling, he was Strix, with a barn owl visage. He wore a bowler hat and a tidy suit.

"Fulston, Mlle," he said with a tip of his hat. "Fulston Braithwaite."

Braithwaite? Not one of the famed Syndicate leader's family?

Poe nodded back, smiling. "One of Herself's, then."

This got more interesting by the moment. "Herself" must be none other than the famous Edith Braithwaite, Strix leader of the Halcyon Gate Syndicate.

"Indeed, Mlle Endymion." The cabbie nodded at me, but did not ask for my name. It was discretion, I realized, not rudeness. "Where can I take you this evening?"

"Uptown," Poe said. "And make it quick."

Fulston nodded, taking Poe's bag from her. "Indeed. Best not linger here for long."

~

THE STREETS WERE dark in the upper city, the gas running low in the wee hours for conservation. When the denizens of our neighborhood had voted down aetheric lighting, they'd been told this was a risk, as had the higher echelons who'd done the same. No one had even a shred of fear that poorer lighting might make our streets more dangerous.

We had the cityguard for that, and not one person voting had cared for their safety or convenience in patrolling the streets at night. No matter, I didn't need to see to know what Orchid Boulevard looked like as we rounded the corner onto the two hundred block. My mind's eye envisioned the tall limestone townhomes lining the street, neatly kept and statuesque.

Looming. Intimidating with their elaborate stone ornamentation, various faces and looping, curved lines making each house unique, even as they were made from the same pale stone. I kept my breath even, forcing it in and out of my lungs.

"Are you getting out?" Poe asked.

I hadn't noticed the car had stopped. I *had* to start paying better attention to what was going on around me, but everything was moving so quickly. Too quickly, perhaps.

"Yes," I answered, following Poe out of the car, while Fulston gathered Poe's bag.

"Shall I carry this inside for you?" the young Strix asked.

"Just up the steps please," Poe replied.

He did so with alacrity and was back in his car and down the street before they could even say goodbye. "Edith will pay him," Poe explained in a soft voice, but I hadn't been worried about that. Perhaps I should have been.

Still, it confirmed that the name Braithwaite wasn't a coincidence. Fulston was a Syndicate man, and somehow Poe was connected to the Halcyon Gate organization. For now, I pushed that aside, starting up the steps, toward the front door. Not a curtain on the street had shifted. It was the dead of night, but I had no doubt that by morning the entire street would know someone had returned to Orchid House. My mind raced, reevaluating the situation as I retrieved my key from my pocket. Poe stood behind me as I unlocked the door.

"Welcome to Orchid House," I said as I pushed the heavy door open. "Lux."

Lights flickered on in the front hallway at my words, sparkling crystal chandeliers reflecting on the marble floors and the grand staircase. There was not a speck of dust, and a hint of Maman's jasmine perfume still lingered, as though she had just stepped out.

"Oh my," Poe said, mouth agape as she entered. "I knew your family was wealthy, but…"

"We are not," I corrected her. "*Were* not."

Poe raised her eyebrows, dragging her suitcase and carpet bag inside. She gestured at the space. "I beg to differ."

I understood how she might make this mistake. It was one Maman had anticipated. She knew people saw Orchid House, well kept and looking like *this*, and then didn't question why they were never invited to Somerhaven for long weekends, or why the Wildfangs rarely spent an entire season in Pravhna. Our peers chalked it up to Maman's reputation for "academic" sensibilities, meaning that she was strange, and not much else.

"It's the last of it. There's nothing else. No money, and of course the country house is gone."

Poe nodded as she closed the front door, wandered through the two story entry hall, and grimaced at the staircase, carved from a creamy marble in a shape meant to resemble an artistically rendered spine. It was beautiful, but absolutely grotesque. "But this house. It's worth a lot."

I scowled, only seeing the monstrosity of the place. Elegant yet disturbing art dotted the long hall that ran through the center of the house. "The entire house is like this—from the fireplace with a gaping maw, to the spinal atrocity that is that staircase. It's gorgeous and horrible. My father had a macabre sense of design."

Poe gazed up at the oblong spiral of six flights of stairs. "We can work with this, though. Is there a telephone?"

I nodded. "In the study. Come."

Poe followed me through the house. It was a rather simple layout on this floor. The formal parlor, with its horrific fireplace, to the left of the entryway, the private sitting room to the right. We passed Maman's study and the dining room, as I made my way back to the housekeeper's office.

Poe's mouth hung open, as she examined every impressive but gruesome piece of art. Some paintings depicted horrific scenes of violence, others creatures not of this world. There were a few family portraits scattered in amongst the gallery of macabre images, but not many. I avoided looking at the statues at all. Since I was a child, they'd scared me.

My heart beat faster the further into the house we went. I wished Orchid House had been the one to burn down. Somerhaven had been oddly constructed and ancient, freezing in both the summer and winter, but it hadn't been *this*. All my worst memories lived here, where there had been no escape from how deeply I disappointed Maman.

The sound of footsteps behind me stopped as I entered the housekeeper's office. Poe wasn't following me anymore. I turned, backtracking through the hall until I found the Vilhar in the library. She smiled prettily at me, clearly meaning to comfort me. "*This* place isn't so bad."

I coaxed a few more lamps into lighting. Poe had obviously used the command, but the house responded most reliably to one of its own—and apparently it still recognized me as such. I wondered why it recognized the fetch as a genuine Wildfang, when I was certain I was not one. That wasn't how domicile magic worked.

Spaces were like people in some ways; they had remnants of magical history that made them nearly independent entities, and as such, there were only two ways they recognized someone as part of a family—blood or marriage. The fetch literally could not be either, so Maman must have found some way around the rules. Which, come to think of it, was just like Maman. Describing her as academic was more accurate than the social slight was meant to indicate.

"It's one of the nicer rooms in the house," I said, feeling almost wistful for the afternoons I'd spent hiding here. This had been my refuge as a girl, the only place in the house besides my attic bedroom that did not feel menacing.

There wasn't room for art here, just books, and most of them were novels. Papa had loved to read, or so I was told. Helene and Maman rarely spent time in pleasurable pursuits, so whenever they read, their taste tended towards spellcrafting and treatises on working with elemental spirits.

Maman's study was just next door, where all of her books were located, as well as the locked door to her workshop. But this had been Papa's domain. As a child, I'd imagined we would have been the best of friends. That my life would have been different, if only he'd lived, because he loved these magnificent books. Now, I wasn't so sure.

Poe walked around the room. "Would it be all right if I took some reading material?"

"Of course," I replied. Poe suddenly looked very young, her eyes wide and hungry. It reminded me that though Poe Endymion had access to what seemed like quite a large sum of money, she might not have grown up with the same resources I had.

"What do you intend to do while you're in Pravhna?" I asked. We were safe here, in the strictest sense of the word. The house's wards would recognize Poe as a guest, since she was invited in along with me. None could enter without my permission. It was time to discuss some of what we'd avoided, thus far.

Poe set down a small mountain of books on one of the heavy library tables at the center of the room. She leaned against the table, her beautiful face glowing in the lamplight. "I am looking for my family—and I have reason to believe the Montclairs know where they are."

She stopped there, but her expression was so serious, so dark, I wondered if the family Poe searched for was alive, or if she simply wanted to know what had become of them. The anguish written on her face—in the wet luminosity of her eyes, the drag of grief on her mouth—evoked a kind of envy I'd never known. I could not remember caring for *anyone* that way.

And no one has ever cared for me that way either, a voice in my head snapped back. The envy gave way to an ache in my chest so profound I was rendered speechless.

When I finally found my voice, venomous irritation came spilling out. "And why do you believe *I* can help you get access to that information?"

Poe's smile was shaky, as though she'd instantly forgiven me for being so rude. "I know you didn't have the best luck in society. I do actually know a bit about you, though not much." She came around the library table and reached for one of my hands.

I stepped back, drawing my hands quickly behind my back. I blinked several times, as though it might slow the panic racing through me. "Don't touch me." My tone was too sharp, my ears ringing with the sound of my blood rushing through my veins. The dull whine of the aetheric lights.

Poe's voice broke through. "I'm sorry. I should have asked."

My entire body froze. Forming words was a struggle, but I pushed some out, trying to remedy the damage I was sure I'd done. "You meant to be kind."

Poe nodded. "I did. But if you don't like to be touched, it wouldn't be a kindness to touch you."

Her words shocked me. So few people thought that way. "It's not that... Not exactly." I dragged my eyes back towards Poe's face. I expected to find pity in Poe's eyes, but instead found something else. *Understanding.* "It takes me some time to get used to people. To want them to touch me."

Poe stepped back, and again, her eyes were full of the kind of understanding that came from experience, not pity. That only deepened the ache in my chest. I looked out the window, watching moonlight hit the golden leaves of the black oak in the neighbors' garden. Knowing what to tell Poe and what not to was tricky.

No one needed to know about my body, about the fact that I might not be *real*. But Poe should know about the oubliette, about Viridian's role in putting me there. "Have you ever heard of an oubliette?"

Slowly, Poe shook her head.

I walked towards the library window, painfully conscious of the fact that the locked workroom was just on the other side of the wall. It called to me, begging me to unlock its secrets. Now was not the time. I focused on the scene outside. Looking at the moonlight on the oak tree soothed me. "It's a kind of hole—a deep, magical hole, used to induce a confusing mental state that causes its victim to forget."

"Like amnesia?" Poe asked, drifting towards the window herself.

"Something like that," I replied. "It's a kind of torture."

"Ah, I see why you are so angry with Viridian and your family then," Poe replied, after I had not spoken for a while.

I gazed into Poe's face. It was clear she had seen some of the worst of the world, but still, she was a person searching for her family—because she loved them. I presumed they loved her in return. "Yes. I only just made my way out this morning. I was headed back to Somerhaven to question them—to find out why they did it. But of course…"

Poe's mouth fell open, then abruptly closed. She was catching on to the fact that I didn't much like pity, or being comforted. That would make things easier.

I needed to redirect the conversation to something more useful for us both. "I don't know what the papers said about the fire…"

Poe looked as though she were trying to remember the specifics. "The investigators said it was a kitchen fire. They found your sister's lady's maid's body near the oven, where they said the fire originated. An accident."

I shook my head. That wasn't possible, given the traces of empyrae I'd detected. A lie then. But who'd concocted it? Viridian was the most likely culprit, but *why* had he lied? He had to have known someone used empyrae to start the fire, and how rare the talent was. But I couldn't explain that to Poe without opening up a line of questioning about myself that I wasn't ready to explain. We were revealing ourselves, but only bit by bit. Poe had certainly not told me as much as I was telling now.

Still, I added the necessary information: "The fire was not an accident."

Poe didn't ask me how I knew, as I had not asked Poe why she believed the Montclairs knew what had happened to her family. Secrets were power, and neither of us wanted to give over all of what we knew to the other. But Poe had spent time with Viridian—it was possible she could tell me more about what had happened to me than she even knew. I needed to take risks if I were to get to the truth.

I took a sharp breath in, considering my next words carefully. "I was placed in the oubliette for remembering some secret my family kept, though the oubliette did its work. Now I can't remember what I knew."

To my surprise, Poe's reaction was completely absent of pity. In fact, her eyes hardened. "So you aren't *just* looking for the truth about the fire."

"No," I replied, relieved that Poe reacted as I would have preferred. She hadn't revealed if she knew more than what she'd already said. That was fine. I wouldn't press her. This was only the first night, I reminded myself, and this was a long game. Much as I wanted to solve this quickly, I was going to have to settle in.

Poe leaned against the deep windowsill, looking up at me. "What would you have done to them, if you'd found them this morning?"

I focused on the tree for a long moment, thinking of how to answer. "Gotten to the truth." I looked down at Poe. "By any means necessary."

Poe was not disturbed in the least by my admission. "And when you had it?"

"I suppose I would have gotten revenge."

Poe nodded. "I like that."

"What about you? When you find out what's happened to your family, what will you do?"

Poe smiled. "The same, I suppose. Someone has to pay for what's been done."

That was most satisfactory to hear. I took a deep breath. "Viridian Montclair helped Helene seal me into the oubliette. It would seem we have a common enemy."

Poe's shoulders shook with laughter. "I thought as much—not about the oubliette, of course—but I *knew* he was involved with you going missing."

I didn't have to ask *how* Poe knew that. It was obvious we'd both been piecing things together since the moment we met. Poe plopped onto the window seat. I sat next to her, each of us leaning against the opposite edge of the windowsill, staring at each other.

"We're going to need a very good plan," Poe reasoned. "And probably some extra help."

I nodded. "You should know, I don't have any money. And I haven't a single friend in the world."

The smile on Poe's face didn't falter. "But you have all this." She gestured at the house. "It's the perfect backdrop for a ruse. Your grand reentry into society as Lady Somerhaven."

I frowned. "That will be a costly venture to do correctly and I am terrible with society functions."

"But I am not," Poe said, one delicate foot kicking out from under her skirts. "And I happen to have nearly unlimited funds."

"How?" I asked.

Poe leaned forward. "You keep your secrets, love, and I'll keep mine."

It had to be Syndicate money, but I wasn't going to press the issue further. Poe would tell me when she saw fit. "That will be just fine."

"Now, I must get a call in to Jeanne Laquoix, if we'd like to be outfitted for the season," Poe said, trailing a finger along the hem of the dressing gown that peeked out from my coat. "You're going to need something better to wear."

CHAPTER 10

ASHBOURNE

My tea had gone cold for the third time. I was rather annoyed, but I wasn't going to make another pot or reheat the old one. It would only go cold again. Skye and I had been up all night discussing our next move, and though she'd made several excellent arguments, I wasn't convinced we needed Syndicate backing to do what was being asked of us. I added another log to the fire in the office hearth, hoping that if the room warmed up a bit more, the cold tea wouldn't bother me as much.

"Explain this to me one more time, Aestra." We only called one another by our surnames in a disagreement. "Why is it worth getting in bed with the Syndicate? We can investigate this on our own."

Skye rolled her eyes. "We've talked this over a dozen times now, Ash." She wasn't angry with me, which was good, but it didn't stop me from being mad at her. "We need the money."

"We can find another way." I was wrong, and I knew it, but I was worried. Spun out of control by the thought of the owlet I'd helped and their mother dying. Worried sick that we were getting ourselves into something we'd never dig our way out of. People who helped the Syndicate this way were in for life. It was one thing to be on good terms with them, and another to work a complex job like this.

I needed Skye to understand what she was asking of us both—

what we were tying ourselves to. I wasn't actually arguing against what she wanted us to do at this point; we both knew she'd already won on that count. I'd follow Skye into a burning building, knowing I wouldn't walk out.

But she needed to see what we'd give up by taking on Syndicate backing. Our freedom, our reputation for impartiality in the district, would all be in jeopardy once people knew we were working under Syndicate pay.

"Chopard is buying up abandoned warehouses, near the Achera," Skye said, repeating the information that Vionette Celestine's spies had picked up. She was the richest of the Syndicate leaders, and had a whisper network that extended across oceans.

"Who cares?" I growled. "Why should anyone care that some rogue Syndicate leader buys up some empty buildings?"

Skye didn't answer because I knew the answers all too well. *Everyone* should care. Chopard was buying up buildings openly, and was suspected of burning others down. There were more murders and unexplained disappearances in the undercity and medial districts in the upper city than there had ever been. Something was brewing and Chopard was at the center of it.

Some in the undercity defended the mysterious Syndicate leader. The businesses he protected brought in more revenue than any others, and from the outside, no one could tell exactly *why* that was. Many of the business leaders in the Halcyon Gate were now more likely to work with Chopard than any of the other leaders. Going against Chopard was dangerous, and we were a miniscule operation. Even with Syndicate backing, it was functionally just me and Skye. Morpheus helped with cases, of course, but the cat was only so much help in a real fight.

We had to take the job—Skye's sense of honor demanded it—but this was the end of life as we'd known it for the past year. A desperate part of me screamed for me to keep fighting, to preserve what we had. But Skye wouldn't be the friend I loved so dearly if she didn't want to do this. I moved to sit at my desk. Morpheus was nowhere to be found this morning, tired of our arguing, I assumed.

Skye's countenance was steady; she was committed to this, committed to helping the undercity she loved, and she wanted my help. Needed it—needed the skill we both knew I could provide if things went sideways. *And they* would *go sideways; shit like this always did.* The thought appeared out of nowhere, haunting me, sure as any ghost.

I growled, flinging my head onto my arms. I wanted a different scenario to argue against. One where the Syndicate was blackmailing Skye, or manipulating her into helping with this horrid plan. What I absolutely did not want was for Skye to be doing this because she was a good person. Because she cared about the people of the undercity, and her honor was worth more than their safety. I couldn't argue with that kind of logic. And I certainly couldn't say no to her.

You're throwing a fit, Morpheus reasoned from the corner of his desk, materializing out of nowhere.

I raised my head to look at both the cat and Skye, in turn. "Fine."

Skye raised a snow-white eyebrow.

"Fine," I repeated. There really was no use in arguing any further. I would follow them anywhere and they knew it. All I was doing now was wasting our precious time. "We'll help the Syndicate figure out who Chopard is."

As I said the words, the eerie widening feeling came upon me again, just as it had in the Merc. Instead of an aperture opening, this felt like oblivion gaping at the edges of the life I'd carefully built with Skye and Morpheus. And we were all about to slip right over the edge into it, though neither Skye nor the cat seemed to care.

If only I could be more like them…but I was selfish, wanting only the peace we'd cultivated here. Undercity be damned, for all I cared; but I'd already agreed, and Skye was moving forward. "Braithwaite has an informant, someone who thinks she knows Chopard's identity," Skye said, turning her attention back to her journal. "She'll give us a name and location later today, but we're to liaise between her and the Syndicate."

"Why?" I asked, curious despite my reluctance to do the job at hand.

"We're a legitimate operation," Skye explained. "We've never been in trouble with the upper city authorities."

That was true enough. We'd even worked with them a few times, when our clients needed the help. Skye had severed her social connections when she gave up her life as a Chevalier for House Aestra, but most people in the upper city still liked her, and were willing to talk to her if need be. Her name was still good wherever she went.

She was lucky her mother hadn't put up a fuss. Privately, I thought Elspeth Aestra was still hoping Skye would come home. That whatever row they'd had could be mended and that all this business in the undercity was nothing more than a phase. If that's what she thought, then she didn't know her daughter very well. Skye might someday find peace with her crattie family, but she was never going back to the life she'd lived before. If there was anything I knew, it was what turning your back on the past looked like, and Skye was a classic case.

"So the Syndicate is willing to use your affiliation with House Aestra as an asset," I remarked, needing to be sure Skye saw the full picture. Sometimes she could be a bit of an idealist. "When this is over, your name might not have the same cache up top that it does now."

Every line of Skye's angular face seemed to liquify with emotion. She stood, clapping a hand to my shoulder. I nearly groaned. My argument had the exact opposite effect I'd hoped for. "I know, Ash. It's worth it. We can't let Chopard get away with this. We have to know what he's up to before more people get seriously hurt."

Again, I couldn't argue with her honor, and she knew what she was getting into. There wasn't anything else for us to discuss. Much as I feared I would come to regret this, it was time for me to stop protesting.

"I'm in. Let's liaise for the Syndicate."

Skye patted my shoulder, then glanced at Morpheus. "Do you want to go tell her we agree?"

The greymalkin blinked once and then disappeared into thin air. Off to tell Herself then. Edith Braithwaite would be pleased. She'd been dying to get Skye on her payroll for years, from what I gathered.

"Disconcerting as fuck, every single time," I complained as the last of the greymalkin's tail dissolved.

Skye snorted as she settled back into her chair and opened her journal. She was in good humor now that I agreed, but I felt I needed to offer some kind of apology, or explanation. "You know why I hesitated…"

She looked up from her journal, leaning back in her desk chair, running fingers through her cropped white hair. "I know. And I promised you back then that I'll never tell a soul what you can do. You've got things under control now, right?"

I nodded, but it was time to tell her. "Someone already knows, though."

Skye, always sharp, put down her pen. "What do you mean, someone knows?"

"Yesterday, while you were at the Merc, a Strix woman came in, asking for us to do a mercenary job. I think she knew about me."

Skye didn't ask how I knew that she'd known, or try to poke holes in my statement. She never questioned my instincts. She stood up from her desk, her mind already working on the problem. "Did she give her name?"

I shook my head, watching Skye pace the floor between our facing desks. She did this when she needed to think. "Did she work for someone, or was she doing the hiring?"

"Said she worked for a crattie who'd been wronged somehow. By someone named Wilhelmina Wildfang."

Skye frowned, then went to the wooden file cabinets that made up the wall behind her desk. She walked past our case files, into the territory where we kept track of bigger issues throughout the city. Murders, organized crime stings, Syndicate operations, and settled in missing persons. Why hadn't I thought to look the name up? I was tempted to smack myself in the face, but instead I got up. Skye would likely be a few, tracking the woman's name through the files. Now that we were done with the hardest part of things, there was no use in drinking cold tea.

I busied myself with the kettle and teapot while Skye flipped through file after file. She'd seemed to find something, setting a file aside, but then kept searching. Finally, as the timer for the tea was about to go off, she raised a newspaper clipping in the air. "Found it."

I poured us both huge mugs of a grassy green concoction, stirring in a lump of honey for her, and taking mine plain. Skye drifted over, taking the mug I'd prepared for her, reading the clipping quickly.

"Wildfang's an Oscarovi socialite, though it sounds like she wasn't all that popular. Her sister though, Helene, she was a real beauty, extremely popular with the upper set. I remember her."

"Was?" I asked, sipping my tea. It tasted of spring fields, and just a hint of citrus.

Skye held up the first file she found. "She died in a terrible fire at their country home in Somershire a while back. Remember that?"

I made a noncommittal noise. I didn't keep up with the news the same way Skye did.

"Anyway, the mother, sister and lady's maid all died in the fire, but the younger sister, Wilhelmina, she'd been kidnapped shortly before that." Her voice rose just slightly in volume, off its even keel. "Viridian Montclair was engaged to her sister, the one who died. He offered a reward for anyone who knew anything about where Wilhelmina had been taken after the rest of the family died, but the case went cold."

"He's one of your set?" I asked, keeping my voice as uninterested as possible. Skye didn't like to talk about her family.

Skye nodded. "He's a real piece of work. If he hadn't had a rock solid alibi for the fire, I'd honestly think he had something to do with the whole thing."

I took another sip of tea. "He's that bad?"

Skye nodded, her jaw clenching tight at some memory of the Vilhar, perhaps, but she didn't say anything else.

"So, if the Wildfangs were associated so closely with Montclair, do you think Wilhelmina is trouble? One of the upper crust might have an axe to grind with her family?"

Skye shrugged. "Hard to say."

"Didn't the article say she wasn't liked very well?"

My partner glanced back down at it. "Not exactly. It's there between the lines, though." She looked up at me over her mug. "You know, nobody liked me much up there either."

She was wrong about that, applying how her family felt about her to them all. I'd seen it time and again. People loved Skye Aestra, in both the upper crust and the undercity. She was nothing short of a legend. But I never argued with her when I knew she was worried about her family. That wasn't my place.

I set my mug down and crossed my arms, giving Skye a rare grin. "Maybe this Wilhelmina's our kind of girl."

Skye grinned back. "Let's not rush to murder her then."

Her timing was so snappy, and her smile so unexpected, that I threw my head back and laughed. "Fine by me."

Skye looked back at the newspaper clipping. "She was probably just awkward. I wish I remembered her. She's about my age, a little younger maybe. Twenty eight, I think." She handed me the clipping. "She's pretty."

I took it from her, gazing at the grainy photo. It showed a pale young woman with large, serious eyes framed by neat but heavy brows and long lashes. Her nose was small and sculpted, cheekbones high and sharp, her mouth a generous downturned curve. She wasn't pretty—she was beautiful. I stared at the photo for a long time.

"Oh," Skye said, stretching the short word into many syllables. "You think Murder Girl is *gorgeous*."

My cheeks burned as I handed the clipping back. "She's fine enough, I suppose." I wanted to change the subject, and quickly. "The mother and sister died in a fire? Think it has anything to do with this Chopard stuff?"

Skye frowned, scanning the article again. "Nothing here would indicate that it does, but it *is* an odd coincidence."

Silence spread between us, chilling the air in the room despite the roaring fire in the hearth. "You don't believe in coincidences," I mused, swirling the liquid in my cup a little.

"No," Skye replied, obviously lost in thought. "But now that I think about it, it's a little odd, isn't it, that on the day someone comes to ask us to *kill* Wilhelmina Wildfang, that the Syndicate hires us to help them identify Chopard?"

There was that aperture-widening feeling again. "Do you think *she's* Chopard?"

Skye grimaced. "That doesn't really make sense. From the little I remember about her, she's rather talentless."

I stared at the ceiling for a moment, noting a place that needed to be repainted. "She could be hiding her true power."

"I suppose," Skye mused. "But I think someone who has the kind of power to do what you witnessed the other night would be hard to disguise, don't you?"

She had a point. The kind of power that both Oscarovi and Vilhari wielded had a signature to it, an aura that was obvious. There wasn't a way Wilhelmina Wildfang could be as dangerous as Chopard and no one had noticed. Before I could give it another thought, Morpheus reappeared. The greymalkin immediately began licking his back foot. We knew better than to rush the cat in the middle of an emergency bath, so we stayed silent.

We're to go to 213 Orchid Boulevard in the upper city today at three to talk to the informant. The two of you should clean up if we're headed out of the undercity.

"Did Edith give you her name?" Skye asked. "The informant?"

No, the cat replied. *We were interrupted. Chopard burned another abandoned building last night, this one in Kyovka.*

Skye shook her head. "That's not good."

It is not. There is one more thing—the Strix child Ashbourne helped—

"The one that was killed?" Skye interrupted.

Yes. Their body went missing from the morgue this morning.

I swallowed the lump growing in my throat. It had the same bitter taste the visit from the Strix woman had left in my mouth. I glanced at Skye, who avoided my eyes. So she felt it too. This was going to get ugly.

CHAPTER 11

MINA

Jeanne Laquoix and her small army of Oscarovi sewists waltzed in at seven o'clock on the hour and did not take so much as a break until they were done at lunchtime. I had no idea it could be so grueling to have a visit from the city's most important modiste. When they left, I collapsed into a chair in the front sitting room we'd used for a makeshift studio.

Two racks of finished garments stood in the entryway, ready to be taken upstairs, which was a marvel in itself. "Oscarovi sewists are…" I trailed off, unable to accurately describe what I'd seen.

The talent and skill involved with using aether to complete an artisanal task, especially with the aid of a spirit, had been dizzying to witness. Demophon and Maman had a tenuous relationship, having made a tense alliance when Maman was young, but the spirits that worked with the sewists had been *happy*.

That was how it was supposed to work—the joining between elemental and Oscarovi was meant to be joyful. Helene's had been with Ariston, an elemental that took the form of a tiny firedrake when it manifested, channeled through her ruby. The spirit would curl around Helene's shoulder, purring like a cat when she was a child, hissing at anyone who bothered her. I'd always been jealous.

My sister had attracted Ariston long before she came of age, and they'd grown together.

Today I felt that same envy, watching the jewel-like spider and bird elementals that aided the sewists. The silent, serene communication between Oscarovi and familiar. The seamless coordination of movement—it was beautiful, and yet utterly devastating to watch.

Poe, who was changing back into the dressing gown she'd worn between fittings, nodded. "It's amazing, isn't it? There are Vilhari sewists of course, but the elementals add a certain something to the process." Poe fastened the dressing gown and sat across from me. "I notice you don't wear a jewel."

"No," I replied, wishing she would not have noticed so easily. I was going to have to do something about this, and quickly. I wondered if the sewists had noticed.

Poe seemed to sense my reluctance to say more. She leaned towards me, under the guise of making herself more comfortable in her chair. I wanted to tell her that it was a sheer impossibility—comfort had been the least of Maman's priorities when selecting furniture for Orchid House.

We were still seated in the parlor, where the walnut armchairs were carved in an ornate floral depiction of oleander and foxglove, and the upholstered backs and seats covered in a rich silk fabric that depicted a garden of poisonous plants in a pale aqua shade that somehow made the subject material more ominous, rather than less. The entire room was decorated in what Maman had termed "a poison motif." Frescoes painted on the walls depicted Oscarovi dancing in a poison garden, expired Vilhari victims at their feet, looking as though they were simply sleeping, but for their bruised lips and stained fingers.

When Poe resigned herself to the fact that the chair itself was the problem, not the way she was seated in it, she spoke. "It's fine that you haven't managed to inspirit yet."

I tilted my head to the side, curious to know what Poe was getting at. Surely she knew I should have done so already, but she was being rather delicate about the whole thing, which I could appreciate. "However, I think it would be better if people thought you had."

I gestured pointedly around the room. "There were almost a

dozen people here today. They have seen me without a jewel. I don't think an obvious lie is the way to start things off."

A slow smile spread over Poe's face. "But *have* they seen you without a jewel?" She stared at my chest, where a long pendant Poe had casually draped over my head right before the modiste had arrived was tucked between my breasts, resting against my skin, blocked from view by my corset. I'd thought nothing of it, as Poe had also slipped a large ring onto one of my fingers and dressed my hair in the low profile chignon popularized by the Ballets Vermeil.

"I thought you were just making me presentable for the Maison Laquoix," I murmured, drawing the necklace out of my gown to look at it. It was nothing remarkable, but I was impressed by Poe's ability to anticipate the kinds of details that would help us later on. "Why didn't you tell me?"

Poe smiled. "I didn't want you to be nervous about it. And it was necessary that you be totally natural about the jewel, or it would appear as an object of interest."

"Ah," I breathed. "But if I'd fidgeted with it, I might have given myself away."

Poe nodded. "And you kept it tucked in the entire time, so no one has seen what it looks like. You can choose anything you'd like now. Oscarovi move their jewels into new pieces frequently, do they not?"

I wanted to laugh. "The rich ones do."

"Besides," Poe said. "It isn't as though you don't have power. You radiate with it."

I glanced at her, worried about what she might have surmised, but Poe's face was neutral, as though it were perfectly normal that I "radiated with power" while not actually possessing a jewel.

Poe stood as a soft chime sounded in the front hall. We'd received a calling card. "You can tell me all about it when you're ready, Mina. I won't ever pressure you to explain things to me. We all have secrets."

Poe left the room, presumably to fetch the correspondence, and something tight in my chest released as I got up to follow her into the hall. The way she said "we all have secrets" struck a chord in me. Whatever Poe was hiding had depth. This wasn't only a case of a missing mother; there was more to it than that.

As we walked together to Maman's private sitting room, Poe's fingers flew through a small pile of calling cards. She sorted through them with speed. Though I couldn't see them from my vantage point, she appeared to have a very definite criteria. "It would seem that Pravhna society knows you've returned."

She handed a select few to me. They were from people I would rather not see, friends of Maman's who'd always given me a distinctly bad feeling. It was overwhelming to read the invitations and requests to call. I wasn't sure how to sort them out. At the secretary desk, Poe separated the remainder of the cards into different piles.

"Those are the ones we both need to see first," she said, as I added a log to the dying embers of the fire. "The ones we need to accept right away."

She was right, of course; the people who I liked least amongst Maman's acquaintances were the most likely to know what she'd been up to. I wondered how Poe had known. "How do you know which to choose?" I kept my voice soft, in case Poe needed to concentrate, curling into the velvet covered sofa. This room was only marginally more comfortable than the parlor, but even a little more comfort was welcome.

Poe looked up, her brown skin glowing with the pleasure of having been successful in our first morning back in Pravhna. "I follow society very carefully... I see... patterns in how it moves."

I smiled at the way she phrased her ability. It was so similar to how I thought about things, but about a subject I knew so little about.

My expression caught Poe's attention. "What did I say?"

I blushed, feeling embarrassed. "Patterns—I like them."

"Mmm," Poe hummed. "But you see them differently than me, don't you?"

No one had ever asked me a question like that before. I was stunned. "Yes, I suppose I do. Not with people, exactly. People and why they do things... That's hard for me to read, in the moment anyway. It's hard to describe."

Poe nodded, looking as though she were putting something fascinating together. "Maybe it's more like you see the patterns in what people do, events and results, while I see patterns in the *why*."

My eyes widened as I considered the implications of what Poe had said. "We could be unstoppable."

Poe grinned, her smile making her even more dazzlingly beautiful than she already was. "I'm afraid you're right." She looked down at the last card she held, and the smile faded. "Edith Braithwaite is sending a liaison for us. The Syndicate wants to use our eyes and ears."

Now Poe's Syndicate connections emerged. I was pleased, feeling the blurred edges of the greater picture that formed in my mind clarify slightly. "Why would *we* agree to something like that?"

Poe gestured to the racks of clothing still sitting in front of us. "Because they paid for all of that."

This was excellent. "Oh," I said softly, allowing it to appear that I'd just now understood the depth of Poe's connection to the Halcyon Syndicate. It was always better if I didn't seem too far ahead, especially with new people. "They are interested in finding out what happened to your family?"

Poe shook her head. "No, they're trying to find out more about a person they call Chopard."

"The fourth Syndicate leader of the Halcyon Gate?" I said, wanting to show Poe that I knew something about how the undercity operated. I had a strange desire for her to think I was better informed than I probably was. It was something I'd have to be careful about. I changed tactics slightly. "Is it true that no one knows their identity?"

Poe nodded. "Yes, but Edith's had suspicions for a long while that it might be someone from the upper city."

"And you think it's Viridian," I said, my mind racing ahead of me. That would explain what she might be holding over him. The upper echelons would reject him entirely if they knew he was involved in organized crime. Not that many of their businesses were any better, but it would be the principle of the thing.

Poe shrugged. "It might be. At the very least, he's dealing in something he shouldn't in the undercity. I've caught him there far too many times. He's visiting pleasure houses, and I've confirmed the types of places he's visiting are not," she paused, swallowing a look of pure disgust. "To his taste… the places he visits in the upper city are *vile*."

I did not want to know more, but a chill slipped down my spine. The upper city made quite a show of being set against flesh work, all while having some of the most terribly regulated brothels in the city. If *that* was Viridian's taste, then it was no wonder he couldn't find what he was looking for in the undercity. The pleasure houses there were places to find actual pleasure, where both sides of the coin had a good time.

My eyes fell shut; it was the only way to stop the onslaught of sensory input rushing toward me. Often, the frustration of sorting out the irrationality of cruelty and injustice brought me to tears, but nothing like this. Perhaps the morning's flurry of activity had taken a greater toll on me than I'd assumed. I'd been so interested in the sewists' work that I'd failed to account for the fact that it had been a very long time since I was around so many people.

"Mina, I'm sorry. Have I upset you?"

My face twisted. "People think I am insensitive." It was hard to get the words out. My very short time in society had exposed me to cruel truths about how I was perceived. "But I feel *everything*. I'm afraid this morning may have worn me out a bit."

Poe was quiet for a long time. She didn't speak until I opened my eyes. "That must be very difficult."

I nodded once, unable to form words.

Poe set her pen down. "What we're going to do may be hard for you at times. I want you to promise me that if it's too much that you'll tell me, that you'll let me help take care of you."

No one had ever understood me so easily, quickly, or fully. It almost felt like a trick. Something to manipulate me into trusting Poe. I let my mind free, let it examine the issue from all sides. Poe wasn't rushing me to speak; in fact, she seemed extremely patient. I considered what Poe had said before about patterns and people. "You're like me, aren't you? You see it all, and feel even more."

Poe's smile was sad. "Yes, I suppose that's true."

"How do you keep it from overwhelming you?" I asked, desperate to know what Poe did to remain so obviously at ease.

"I don't," Poe answered. "It just *looks* like it doesn't."

My heart thumped in my chest, as I let that idea sink in. I looked Poe over. Her casual, elegant posture, the way her face was schooled into a perfectly pleasant expression. If this was an act, no, not an act… A mask. Beautifully crafted, elaborate in construction, and practically flawless, but a mask all the same. *How could anyone who felt what we did keep that up?* "That must be exhausting."

"Yes," Poe said, adjusting the piles of cards into neat piles, her voice perfectly collected and almost cheerful. "It is."

I looked for the tell that this was not Poe's real countenance, and found nothing at first… except… Around her eyes, there was the slightest tightness. Something most would read as "smiling eyes," but I read the exhaustion in that tiny bit of tension. Emotion broke apart inside me, my breath quickening at the idea that Poe was bearing all this alone. "Who takes care of *you*, then? When it's all too much?"

Poe's silence was all the answer I needed. We were a pair, and if I believed in Fate, I might have believed the Lady brought us together for a reason. As it was, I was simply grateful to know someone like myself, someone who would not find me embarrassing, or awkward.

"Well," I said, breaking the silence. "Perhaps I can try."

When Poe looked up, there was no trace of her smile. Her hazel eyes were wide with surprise. "That would mean so much to me. Thank you."

Neither of us seemed able to find more words on the matter, so I asked the next logical question. "When do the liaisons arrive?"

CHAPTER 12

MINA

We only had an hour to get ready. I changed quickly into one of the dresses the sewists left. I would have preferred pants, but apparently the high-waisted style I preferred took longer to make than the dresses that had been constructed so quickly. Poe buttoned the back of the creamy lace dress up for me.

I had taken back my old room, at the top of the house. Though it was in the attic, it was quite nice. I'd always loved it here, far away from the rest of the house. It was quiet. My walls and ceiling were painted indigo, dotted with six and eight pointed golden stars that made strange constellations, like none in Sirin's sky. I'd painted them one winter, after being left here alone night after night while Maman and Helene enjoyed the season's many parties. I could have had a room downstairs; it wasn't as though Maman had exiled me here. This was just more my taste.

The view from the round window under the slanted ceiling looked both down the steep mountainside, into the misty forest below, and upwards to the upper echelons of Pravhna, rising above the clouds, where the richest in Pravhna lived. There were Oscarovi up there, as well as Strix and Corvidae who'd made good. But mostly the highest echelons were occupied by the high Houses of the humanoid fey. They wielded the generative power of aether so easily that most had made their fortunes long ago—their families so obscenely rich that many needn't ever work again.

High above Orchid Boulevard, an airship drifted out of the cloud cover. Air elementals took the form of serpentine dracons and rode the warm wake of the ship before fading back into the clouds. In the distance, a group of Vilhari, taking brunch on a high terrace, stopped to watch the elementals before returning to the lavish party they were having. When power was all that mattered, the Vilhari would always rise to the top.

I turned away from the window to look at Poe, who wore a beautiful lavender directoire gown. The dress draped around her curvaceous figure, setting her rich brown skin aglow, and bringing out the amethyst sheen in her dark hair. I sighed, almost wistful.

"What?" Poe asked, glancing in the mirror. "Is something wrong with my hair? Sometimes I don't get the back right."

I shook my head, sitting down on the bed to watch her put the finishing touches on herself. "No, you're literally perfect."

Poe nodded once, the corner of her mouth tugging downward, her mask falling only momentarily, but enough that I caught my mistake. Inwardly, I chided myself, remembering this was a point of sensitivity for Poe. I needed to try to fix things. "Helene struggled with something similar. People expected less of her intelligence, because of how she looked."

The other woman said nothing, but seemed to wait for me to say more. "Like you, my sister was far more than her looks." I stepped closer to Poe, but did not attempt to touch her. "*And* like you, my sister was all the more dangerous because people underestimated her."

Now Poe smiled, a genuine thing, the miniscule tell of tension around her eyes disappearing into an abundant crinkle that set her entire expression sparkling. "Thank you, Mina," she said, her voice rough with an emotion I couldn't identify. Poe clarified almost immediately. "It feels good to be seen."

My head bobbed once. I was pleased to have said the right thing. There was a clenching in my chest that was not altogether unpleasant, a delicious ache I almost didn't recognize.

Friendship.

Downstairs, the bell at the front door rang. The liaison was here, and I still had to finish lacing the tall boots I wore under my dress. The floor-length directoire style wasn't one I favored, and I was relieved that shorter dresses were as popular for daywear as longer gowns now. However, they were a bit chilly in the colder weather. Tall boots were *en vogue* this season for both fashion and practicality, as they kept the wearer a more comfortable temperature.

"Don't forget your pendant," Poe called as she hurried downstairs.

I laced the dove gray boots as quickly as I could, slipping the pendant Poe had given me over my head and under the high collar of my dress, so that only glints of the gold chain showed through the lace. The creamy shade of the dress was nearly the same color as my skin. Because the dress was sheer lace, it made me appear practically nude. As I hurried past the tall mirror in the attic hallway, I thought Maman would have found the garment scandalous. She would have made me change immediately. Helene would have liked it.

I paused to look at myself, turning a bit to look at the way the dress flowed perfectly over my curves, drifting to and fro as though it had a magic of its own. It was remarkable how the right clothes made me feel like myself, though I wasn't certain what that meant yet.

From my vantage point on the stairs, I heard Poe talking to the liaison, who she had not yet let into the house. "Skye Aestra, what are you doing *here?*"

As soon as I heard the name, I hurried downstairs faster, then crept silently toward the front hall, wanting to eavesdrop. A familiar voice was speaking. "Edith sent us to talk—are *you* her informant?"

"Come inside, both of you," Poe hissed.

"You mean the three of us," a deep voice replied. The voice was so resonant it had to belong to someone quite large. My skin prickled with goosebumps, as though the sound of that voice had crept under my skin.

As though compelled by the sound of the stranger's voice, I entered the receiving hall to see Poe glance down at something. "Fate spare us, is that a greymalkin?"

An enormous cat strode into the house. I'd never seen anything like it; its silver ticked fur gleamed, covering its considerable bulk. Instead of the tall pointed ears that many common felines possessed, it had short, rounded ears, placed further down on its head. When it turned to face me, it wore a look of incredible displeasure.

I am Morpheus, the cat said.

Of course, I knew what a greymalkin was, but they were rare enough to be considered extinct in some circles. I wasn't sure I had ever seen anything that was simultaneously so distinguished, adorable, and absolutely grumpy at the same time. The howlers, Pravhna's vicious messenger birds, were a close second, but the feline could top any ranking, should someone make one.

"I'm Mina," I replied to the fey cat, making a little bow to it, as I'd been taught. Growing up in Somershire had meant a certain amount of education about customs regarding the wild fey, who were to be treated with the same amount of respect as the elementals.

You know the old ways, the cat said, obviously pleased.

"I grew up in the north," I answered, as though that explained it all. And for the greymalkin, it seemed to. I turned to face the two people that now stood inside the entry hall to Orchid House.

They were similar and the inverse of one another at the same time. Both were Vilhari, with pointed ears, sharply planed features, and the bulky muscular bodies of trained fighters. The woman had short snow white hair and silver eyes, while the man was dark-haired, with the golden eyes of a hawk. Instantly, I wondered if he turned into one. He was head and shoulders taller than the woman.

Both were dressed impeccably in tailored frock coats, waistcoats, slim pants, and tall boots. Their clothes looked freshly purchased, rather than handmade. This did not matter to me in the slightest, but I filed the information away nonetheless.

Of course, I recognized Skye Aestra. I was sure I'd never seen the man before, though something about him was familiar. Perhaps, on second thought, it wasn't familiarity, but that he was so outrageously beautiful that it was difficult to tear my gaze from his golden eyes.

As when he'd spoken, it felt as though invisible fingers trailed over my flesh, leaving a wake of shivering goosebumps. A flame that regularly burned low in me flared to life, a coiled beast at the core of me, suddenly ravenous for something to eat after too long asleep. My cheeks heated.

Don't embarrass yourself, said that pesky voice inside my head. Quickly, I bowed my head first toward the woman, eyeing her rapier. "Chevalier, it is my pleasure to meet you again."

The man snorted, as though he might laugh, but his serious face didn't change. A stab of shame fluttered through me for a mere moment, as though I might have said something wrong. However, Skye rolled her eyes to the ceiling, as though her companion was perpetually frustrating her this way. She held a hand out to me in greeting, clasping my forearm when I offered mine in return, and kneeling before me.

"Thank you, mistress, for the honor you bestow me in recognizing my station. But I am Chevalier no longer. House Aestra no more."

She spoke in the cadence of the high fey houses. I sensed that while Skye was no longer a Chevalier for her House, that she was still bound by her honor. It was clear she didn't remember that we'd met before.

My attention slid back to the man, drawn to him as though by some wicked force, heat pooling in my belly as I looked him over. He was almost too tall, both long-limbed and heavily-muscled at the same time. And he stared right back, his beautiful features sharpening by the moment in observation of *me.*

His expression confused me, something between a glare and interest radiating off of him. It was difficult to tell if he was simply an intense person, or if he immediately disliked me. My cheeks flushed deeper in response to the perplexing attention, while my spine straightened. Whether he hated me or admired me was none of my concern.

Skye glanced from the man, then back to me several times, then down to the greymalkin, who seemed to speak only to her. I noticed how carefully she avoided looking at Poe as she spoke. "This is my business partner, Ashbourne Claymore. We're here on behalf of Edith Braithwaite to talk to Mistress Endymion."

Poe rolled her eyes. "Stop it with the Chevalier routine, Skye. Mina knows I've been working with the Halcyon Gate." Poe was obviously flustered. "This is Wilhelmina Wildfang, but the way. The new Lady Somerhaven."

Both Skye and Ashbourne paled slightly, glancing at one another as though sharing some private thought. It passed quickly enough, but it was another thing to file away for later. They'd both reacted specifically to my full name.

Did they know something about me? Something about Maman and Helene, or the fire? Immediately, my nerves set on edge, but I shoved down the hypotheses, which felt as though they reproduced in triplicate. Still, I was left with the question: why were the Syndicate's people so interested in me when they were here to see Poe?

This morning Poe had explained that her association with the Syndicate leaders began with a simple friendship and had grown into something more mutually beneficial. She and Vionette Celestine had met in a popular atelier several years ago, and formed a slow but close friendship over their love for couture.

It developed further when Poe revealed that she was looking for her family, and her belief that House Montclair held the key to finding them. She'd begun helping Vionette by posing as a socialite, a wealthy country heiress from Brektos, across the Pontus Axeinos. Vionette paid her handsomely, funded her wardrobe each season, and Poe passed along any information she gathered that was useful to the Syndicate. In doing so, she'd become quite popular with the three known Halcyon Gate Syndicate leaders.

Something in me tingled, a familiar feeling, as though a piece of the blurry picture in my mind had shifted, though I couldn't yet say how. It seemed we'd arrived back in Pravhna just in time for something, and while others might chalk this up to Lady Fate or coincidence, I preferred another explanation.

One or more of these people, whether they knew it or not, drew us together. That was the way of things. Our desires and fears moved us, not something as amorphous as Fate. I motioned towards the dining room. "Would you care to join us for lunch?"

The greymalkin was the first to go, leading the way as if he owned the house. Skye shrugged, then nodded, and the rest followed.

Ashbourne Claymore's eyes followed me the entire way into the dining room, practically branding me with his narrow focus. I glanced behind me, keeping my eyes cast down, my lashes brushing my cheeks. Through them, I caught the heat of his stare. Desire and fear both mixed plainly on his face. If Ashbourne Claymore hated me, and he very well might, his craving for me was just as strong.

CHAPTER 13

ASHBOURNE

In person, Wilhelmina Wildfang was even more infuriatingly beautiful than in the photograph of her in the newspaper. As we followed her through the long hallway, to the dining room at the back of the house, I understood why I hadn't recognized her at first. In the newspaper she'd been dressed plainly, her hair hanging around her face in an unfashionable way. Here in her home, in real life, she was nothing short of breathtaking.

The lace gown she wore revealed pale skin that was nearly lucent, and her cloud of dark hair had been curled and twisted into a knot of waves that defied gravity in its simplicity, framing her lovely face to such perfection I felt as though I might write poetry about it. When Poe Endymion said her name, the weight of the Strix woman's visit slammed into me. Someone wanted this beautiful creature, luminous as the moon, snuffed out.

That could not stand. It wasn't just that she was beautiful—beyond compare, really. But her eyes held a keen intelligence that made me suspect there was more to her than doll-like perfection. Then came the guilt of having even been in a room with someone who wanted her dead, and letting them escape with their life.

If someone had expressed a desire to have Skye or Morpheus killed, I would have ended them, without guilt, sorrow, or second thought. But I let a woman who wanted Wilhelmina Wildfang dead walk free, and now a war waged inside me. Stay on this job and protect her by staying at her side, or abandon Skye and the Syndicate to hunt down the Strix woman and end her?

You are spiraling, Morpheus chided, without so much as looking back at me, as I found my seat. *Get a hold of your good sense, man.*

The greymalkin's words snapped me back into focus. The cat was right. I *was* spiraling. I only just met this woman, and no matter how deeply my instincts told me to protect her, she had not asked for that. She had not welcomed that kind of attention. And I had my friends to think about. My *family.*

Wilhelmina Wildfang was part of the job. That was the way it must stay, unless she asked me for more. Still, as I watched her move about the dining room, setting plates of food out, heat flushed through me. Skye shot a pointed look at me, as though to say, "What is *wrong* with you?"

I had no answer for that. Temporary loss of perspective? Attraction so intense I nearly went feral over a woman I just met? I almost chuckled at the thought of myself racing through the city, rage-fueled and blazing with celestial fire for this woman. I pinched the bridge of my nose. What *had* come over me?

As we took seats around the table, Poe and Skye began talking, though my focus had splintered apart. I could do little more than watch Wilhelmina move about the room, which was beautiful, in a macabre kind of way. As dining rooms went, it was quite small, just big enough for a heavy round table with a marble top, surrounded by six upholstered chairs. The only other piece of furniture in the room was a buffet, but it really didn't need other decor. The walls were plaster reliefs depicting intricate scenes of various violent acts. I couldn't help staring at them. They were beautifully rendered, but horrific.

Wilhelmina must have noticed my attention. "Awful, isn't it? Not my taste." Her words carried the cadence of sarcasm, but none of the tone. Instead, there wasn't a hint of inflection in her raspy voice, and her face was a smooth mask of serenity. Her utter lack of reaction to my rudeness stirred something primal within me.

She left the room before I could answer her, presumably to get more food from somewhere in the back of the house, Morpheus at her heels. Apparently the greymalkin was going to micromanage the serving of lunch—so very like him. With her gone, I could think a bit more clearly, and a wave of relief rushed over me.

While it was obvious I was attracted to her, what I felt for Wilhelmina Wildfang was different, instinctual. Base in a way that both relieved me and made me uncomfortable. Something in the back of my mind stirred, a remnant of life before the coma: a memory that I'd felt this way before for someone. I pushed that thought away, hard and fast. That was all well and good, but I would not open any door that obviously led to my past.

I turned my attention back to the conversation between Poe and Skye. "…on the beach. She doesn't remember anything about being kidnapped—but it's all been a lot for her." Poe dropped her voice. "She doesn't have many friends, and I can't leave her—so I'm staying here for a while to help her get settled."

Poe leaned towards Skye as she spoke. Skye cleared her throat, canting her body away from the other woman. Poe caught the movement and drew back, her movements sharp, hurt flashing across her face. She opened her mouth to say something, but Skye spoke, also keeping her voice low. "You're staying here because her sister was engaged to Viridian Montclair. Does she know you're using her?"

Poe's expression shifted quickly from hurt to cold fury. "Mina and I are honest with one another. A privilege I don't actually owe *you*, Skye Aestra. How did you get the job as my liaison?"

They exchanged barbs, verbally dancing in a fashion I found dizzying. *Mina.* Poe had called her that several times. *Perhaps she preferred not to be called Wilhelmina.* But why should I care about that? This was just a job, one I wanted done quickly so we could return to our former uneventful lives. I hardly convinced myself. Since the moment the Strix woman asked me to kill Wilhelmina Wildfang, I was invested, though I hadn't known it at the time.

The woman in question returned, carrying a plate of unseasoned canard, chatting amiably to the greymalkin. I watched the way Wilhelmina pulled a chair out for Morpheus, offering him the entire plate of meat. The cat began to eat, his purrs eclipsing the sound of Poe and Skye arguing.

Mina's eyes were serious as she watched the Vilhari volley polite insults back and forth. One lush eyebrow quirked slightly, as though she found what went on between them mildly interesting, but not at all disruptive or disturbing, despite the fact that their volume increased by the moment. My focus had narrowed to the point that I could only see and hear Mina, who fetched a plate of escargot from the buffet for Morpheus.

The dress she wore looked to have been made especially for her, its high collar accentuating the length of her neck. And that face. I had to work not to stare at her face, but also to keep my eyes from sliding down every delicious curve of her body. Yes, a war waged in me. Rationality versus the roar of carnal desire that mounted with each passing moment. I didn't even know this woman and yet I wanted to pull that soft body close to mine, protect her with every instinct I had.

What foolishness.

Poe and Skye were practically yelling at one another now, but it was as though I was trapped underwater, my gaze fixed firmly to Wilhelmina Wildfang, as my body came embarrassingly alive for the first time in what felt like eons. My eyes dropped to the ground, desperately trying to avoid lingering on her full breasts, or the perfect swell of her hips, but her boots, tall and closely fitted, didn't inspire any less lust.

The way they clung to her ankles, caressing the curve of her calves—I could not recall another time that leather had me quite so bothered. Her dress was a popular length that fell halfway between her knee and ankle, and each swish of the creamy fabric entranced me further.

"It's not as though you called on me," Poe spat at Skye, breaking my fevered reverie. "You knew where I was."

"You made it clear I couldn't *do* anything for you. But you've got *her* now, I suppose." I'd never seen Skye jealous before, and now she oozed with the emotion. Across the table, Mina's eyebrow quirked up again.

"It is not like *that* between us," Mina said, her voice low and calm as she glanced at Poe. "I need help, and Poe can help me."

Morpheus looked up from his meal, his paws sweeping elegantly over his whiskers a few times as he swallowed. *We have gotten off track. Might we return to the reason we came?*

Both Poe and Skye immediately sat back in their chairs, staring at the table like guilty hatchlings. "My apologies," Poe said to Skye, after a long pause. "I wasn't expecting to see you today."

"Obviously," Skye snapped, but her expression softened almost immediately when Poe flinched. "My apologies as well. We'll discuss our… personal situation… another time."

Poe's lips pressed together, as though she were suppressing another comment, but her cheeks flushed bright pink, and a little smile flickered at the corner of her mouth. She'd read Skye perfectly. I knew my partner was fired up because she liked Poe, probably more than she was comfortable with. I could relate. No one seemed poised to speak to get us back on track. Morpheus had gone back to his canard, whilst Skye was obviously putting her demeanor back together.

I would have to speak up then. "The Syndicate believes a series of fires in the undercity are Chopard's doing. We've been asked to liaise between you," I nodded at Poe, "and Edith—"

Mina interrupted me. "Does Edith Braithwaite believe the arson at Somerhaven has something to do with Chopard?"

Skye answered for me. "She didn't say so, but I'm inclined to believe she thinks there's a connection. I don't think we'd be here otherwise."

I nodded. It all made sense now, why we were asked to liaise. Herself always had the pulse of things, and she had eyes everywhere. She probably knew the moment these two got on the train together. What had felt like Fate or coincidence fifteen minutes ago now felt like Edith's machinations.

"So," Poe mused. "Whatever Chopard is up to, it started long before what's happening in the undercity."

"Which is what?" Mina asked.

"Someone's setting certain buildings on fire," I explained. "People have died."

Mina's brow wrinkled slightly. "I am sorry, that's tragic…"

Skye jumped in. "And at the scene, anyone who might have

witnessed the event is found in some kind of collective trance. They remember nothing when they come out of it."

Poe and Mina glanced meaningfully at one another. They knew something. Skye and I both waited, but neither spoke up. Something to push on later, when they felt more comfortable with us. For now, there were other questions I could ask. "Mlle Endymion…"

"Poe, please," she interrupted.

"All right then, Poe. We were told you might have information for us after your trip to the country."

Poe frowned. "I'm sure I do, but I'll need you to be a bit more specific if you don't want to hear every detail of the last week of my life. What's she looking for?"

Chopard has burned several abandoned buildings on the Achera. His activities are ramping up, becoming more frequent, Morpheus explained. *One in Kyovka last night, in fact.*

"Kyovka?" Wilhelmina asked. "Please, eat, all of you. I'll be right back."

She left the dining room, walking at a brisk pace, her heels clicking against the marble floors. One of Poe's eyebrows arched. "And Edith thinks I have information about this?"

Skye shrugged. "You must, or she wouldn't have sent us."

Wilhelmina returned with a map as Skye spoke. "This may be why." She pushed a few of the plates aside, spreading the map on the table. "This is Kyovka here," she said, pointing to a tiny village, high in the mountains.

Poe's eyes widened. "Oh—oh. I mean, I suspected him of it last summer, but it came to nothing… In fact…" She glanced at Skye. "The night we met…"

Skye's eyes narrowed, then she shook her head. "I can't believe it. He's just not…that smart." My partner leaned back in her chair, crossing her arms tightly across her chest. "Though I'm afraid it *is* possible that he has the power to be Chopard, and he certainly has the resources."

I sighed. All eyes turned towards me. "Apologies," I said. "Might someone explain?"

"This is Kyovka," Wilhelmina repeated, a long finger tapping the map, "And this is Viridian Montclair's country estate—where Poe just spent the week."

Her finger traced a huge plot of land, and right on the border of that land, far to the west, was Kyovka. "So you believe that Viridian Montclair *is* Chopard?"

Skye covered her mouth with a hand. "It would explain a lot." She touched Poe's hand lightly to get her attention, then snatched her own back, as though she'd made a terrible mistake. "The night we met—he had you cornered in that alley. Had you accused him of being Chopard? Is that why he was so angry with you?"

Poe stared at her hand for a long moment, as though Skye had burned it. "Not in so many words, but I hinted that I knew something. I wanted information in return for keeping what I believed was his secret."

Her last words were accompanied by a deep blush and a pleading look at Skye that my partner ignored. "It wasn't enough? What you had on him—it wasn't enough to get the information you were looking for?"

Poe shook her head, still blushing. I got the feeling Poe's emotions were rarely so on display. She appeared to be struggling to compose herself, shifting uncomfortably in her chair.

Skye threw up her hands. "Maybe because it isn't him. I've known Viridian Montclair my entire life. He's unpleasant, but he's just not *capable* of the things Chopard has done."

I felt the moment Wilhelmina's mind changed on the situation. Her chest expanded as she drew a long breath in. My body betrayed me, my pants uncomfortably tight as I watched her breasts push against the fabric of her dress. This was not the time for such observations, but again I was made all too aware of my embattled interior state.

When she spoke, I fell headfirst into the rich tenor of her voice, the low, breathy unevenness of it, as though her vocal cords had been damaged in some way. "If there is *any* possibility that Viridian Montclair is Chopard, then we will need to work together."

Her words surprised me out of my body's hunger for her. Skye also returned to herself, her attention turning to Wilhelmina, as she formed coherent thoughts more quickly than I could. "Why is that?"

My heart beat faster by the moment, as Wilhelmina considered her words. Morpheus was busy cleaning his face, but it was obvious he paid close attention to the woman who'd fed him. His feline eyes raised to mine, as though he cared to emphasize Wilhelmina's words.

"Montclair imprisoned me."

CHAPTER 14

MINA

Poe was angry with *me* now, but not by much, if I read her correctly. It was getting easier to do, and for some reason she was more open around Skye Aestra. Still, Poe was obviously annoyed with me. "You can't just *tell* people that, Mina. It's not strategic."

On some level, I knew that. But we'd already talked this over. To get to whatever Montclair knew about both our families, we were going to need help. And there was no one in the upper city to trust. But these two—I had known who Skye Aestra was my whole life. She was Helene's age, and my sister had *hated* the Chevalier. She'd made fun of her adherence to old Vilhari codes of honor, and sneered at her kindness, calling it "misplaced idealism."

The fey cat, Morpheus, told me on our trip to the kitchen that all these qualities had earned Skye Aestra an irreversible trip to the undercity. Apparently, the Vilhar didn't talk about it much, but she'd parted ways with her House. Her title was void, she was expelled from the Chevaliers, and ever since she'd been making her living in the undercity, solving mysteries, righting small wrongs. Helping others in ways no one would dream of in the upper city.

One of those people was the enigma of a man she'd brought with her. Ashbourne Claymore was in a strangely similar situation to my own. She and Morpheus had found him a year ago, beaten and unconscious. He'd been in a coma for three days, and when he woke, he'd simply integrated into their lives, having no memory of who he'd been before. Now they were a little family. According to the cat, both would rather not be working with the Syndicate, but whatever Chopard was up to, it was heinous.

They were the kind of people who wanted the world to be a better place. I had no such illusions. The world was exactly as terrible as it was because people were terrible. But it would make them easier to mold to my purposes. If Poe was invested in hero types, that was her prerogative, but I saw only opportunity.

So I held up a hand to stave off any further chiding. "We need *help*, Poe. We can't go up against Montclair on our own." Poe quieted, apparently willing to listen. "The two of you want to find this Chopard because he's doing terrible things, yes? You wish to stop him?"

Skye and Ashbourne both nodded.

"And you," I pointed to Skye, "believe Viridian Montclair isn't capable of doing these terrible things?"

Skye threw her hands in front of her, as though warding off an accusation. Perhaps I'd been too forceful with my words. Or perhaps it was the pointed finger. I forced my hand back to my side. I'd always used big hand movements when I talked. It had embarrassed Maman and Helene to no end.

I glanced at Poe, afraid to see the cringe of secondhand embarrassment that often accompanied my inappropriate social behavior. Poe looked like she might laugh, but not at me, at the look of deep worry on Skye Aestra's face. *Poe wanted to laugh at Skye, not me.* It was a distracting moment.

Skye sounded calm enough when she answered, but it was obvious she was attempting to regain her equilibrium. "If you say he kidnapped you, then I can admit I may have been wrong about what Viridian is capable of."

I had not said he'd kidnapped me. I said he imprisoned me, and I liked to be precise when I spoke. When others weren't it bothered me, and while I knew correcting others was considered rude, I couldn't seem to stop myself. "He didn't exactly *kidnap* me." Though I was not about to tell them all I knew, it was important they be fully aware of what Viridian could do. "He helped my family to imprison me in an oubliette."

Skye clapped a hand over her mouth, her silver eyes wide. Ashbourne went a slightly gray shade paler than he'd been moments before. So they were familiar with the mechanics of the oubliette and the way the spells to maintain it worked. I hadn't thought about it this way yet, but someone had to maintain spells on a long term basis. While Viridian might not have been old enough to have crafted the first spell for the oubliette, someone would have had to maintain or revive it, and that was no small feat.

There were too many similarities between the cases in the under-city and the fire at Somerhaven. The memory loss, the fires them-selves. And still, I couldn't bring myself to say that Somerhaven had been burned with empyrae. I wanted to hold that information back until I was sure of something—I didn't know what right now, only that it wasn't time to reveal it.

"That is *torture*," Skye breathed, her brows knitting together. "Did you just escape… *yesterday*?" I nodded as Skye stood, wondering why she wasn't more concerned about the similarities between the cases. "Then we will go. You should be resting."

Ashbourne shook his head, reaching for Skye's arm to stop her from leaving. "If Montclair is capable of such magic, he'll come for her. We can't leave them to fend for themselves."

Skye's jaw twitched. "This isn't the job, Ash. *They're* not the job."

"But maybe they should be." The look that passed between the two of them was rich with some personal meaning.

Skye took her seat again, shaking Ashbourne's long arm off her. "How would we manage something like that? We'd have to—"

"Move in," I interrupted. "Yes. I think that may be necessary. Though the house is safe enough—Maman was an expert with wards —I think we need the extra eyes and ears. I'm not opposed to helping the Syndicate take Chopard down, as long as Poe and I get what we're after."

"Which is what, exactly?" Skye asked, her gaze pure steel.

I glanced at Poe, looking for her consent. She nodded once, resigned apparently to the fact that we could, in fact, use the private investigators. "Information about what's happened to both our families. We have very different motives, but Poe and I both believe House Montclair is at the center of our troubles. If Viridian Montclair is your problem as well, working together benefits us all."

"We can't just—move in here," Skye said, obviously flustered. "We have other work."

It was Ashbourne's turn to roll his eyes. "Not that you could tell from our ledger."

Next to me, Morpheus grumbled. *Here, lunch might be on time.*

Skye's mouth dropped open. "I am late *one* time—"

Ashbourne rose. He hadn't even touched his food. "We will discuss this in private and return to you with an answer this evening."

Poe nodded, standing up as Skye did. "I'll walk them to the door."

I was tempted to reach out to touch the greymalkin's head to say goodbye, but decided against it. The cat jumped down from his chair, and seemed as though he would stalk away without farewells, but instead, he bumped his head against my boot.

Skye looked back over her shoulder, shaking her head. I stepped forward, my hand reaching towards the Vilhar, then dropped. Poe and Ashbourne were already in the receiving hall, but Skye paused at my obvious attempt to stop her.

"Do you—" I hesitated. "Do you remember me at all?"

Skye frowned. "I'm afraid not. Have we met?"

That was truly embarrassing. I stared at the herringbone pattern in the wood floor of the dining room. "We danced at my debutante ball. It was a long time ago."

The tips of Skye's pointed ears flushed. "I'm so sorry, Wilhelmina. I don't remember that." She paused, then added, "I do remember your sister, though."

"Of course," I said, with a small bob of my head. Everyone always remembered Helene.

CHAPTER 15

MINA

When they'd gone, I stood for a long time at the arched windows in the drawing room, watching them disappear down the street. When an enormous maple finally obscured them from view, I let out a tensely held breath. I hadn't thought about the dance at my debutante ball in a long time. It had been the one nice moment in my entire season. Skye Aestra had seen that no one else asked me to dance, and plucked me from the sidelines—so debonair in her dress blues—a true Chevalier.

Of course, Skye didn't remember one dance; she'd had dozens that night. But it had been my only dance the entire season. Pravhna society ran on appearances, and Maman had allowed me only the basest of coming outs. But I was allowed no new clothes at the modiste, and hadn't even a ball gown. She then proceeded to tell people what a strange child I was, and that I had no interest in clothes.

It had made me an object of ridicule for a short time. Helene's friends Caralee Ellis-Whitely and Rebecca Smytheson pretended to befriend me, and then proceeded to tear me down in a way I didn't understand at the time. When Helene revealed that the people I thought were my friends were actually poking fun at me, I was devastated. She, of course, was smug. After that, I was simply ignored. It was like I wasn't even there. But Skye Aestra was different. She had *seen* me, if only for a brief moment. I couldn't hold it against Skye for not remembering, but it stung all the same.

Poe came to stand next to me, leaning against the deep windowsill. "What was all that about?"

I glanced at her sidelong. "You heard?"

Poe made a grand flourish towards her ears. "They're rather good at picking things up."

The embarrassment of Poe having heard was almost too much to live through. "She didn't remember me."

"No," Poe said, sounding thoughtful.

"She'd have remembered *you*."

Poe turned, her arms crossing protectively over her body. "Is that what this is about? Do you like her?"

My eyebrows flew up in surprise. "*No!* I mean, I suppose I did when I was sixteen, but I'm not carrying a torch for Skye Aestra, if that's what you're worried about."

A little laugh escaped Poe, like a burst of wind. "Thank goodness. I thought our first fight was going to be over a girl, and I was so nervous."

"No need to be," I said, surprised to find myself as relieved as Poe was that there was no animosity between us. "I only meant that it is disappointing to always be so forgettable."

Poe didn't have an answer for that. She seemed to be the kind of person who thought before she spoke, if given the opportunity. I had no desire to rush her, nor to fill space with my own words. I walked over to the heavy brass racks of finished clothing in the hall. The racks were conveniently on wheels, and I pushed one down the hallway. Without asking what we were doing, Poe took the other and joined me. We made our way through the receiving hall and toward the back of the house, to the housekeeper's office.

The room was a cozy nook furnished with a sturdy wooden desk, pushed up against a bank of leaded glass windows that looked out onto the overgrown garden. The blackthorn and woody nightshade appeared to be in a battle for dominance, heavy mist creeping through their branches. Meanwhile foxglove, hellebore, and datura proliferated, still blooming long after their season. Maman's magic lingered in the garden, a haunting reminder that despite her irrationality and erratic behavior, her spells were strong. Stronger than her, apparently.

I turned away from the window to open what looked like an enormous closet door and pushed my rack inside. "To my room, please," I said, pressing my palm against the rectangular crystal plate just above the doorknob.

Poe stood behind me, quizzical, until I opened the door back up and the closet was empty. I pushed Poe's rack inside and shut the door, pointing to the plate. "Press your palm against that, and say 'to the Rose Room.'"

"Should I say please?" Poe asked. "You did."

I shrugged. "I like to be polite."

Poe tried it, then opened the door cautiously, as though she were afraid something might pop out at her. The closet was empty. "*How?*"

It was rather unique. All Oscarovi houses were somewhat magical, a byproduct of generations of magic running through them. But Orchid House had a few mysteries in its closets. "Maman's great-grandfather had an idea that they might eliminate servants entirely. The spell has never worked in another house, unfortunately, but it's become a part of the makeup of this one. Honestly, I think the house just doesn't like anyone unnecessary to be here, so it cooperated."

Poe shook her head. "The Oscarovi are rather ingenious, aren't they?"

I motioned for Poe to follow me. The grocery order I'd made before the Laquoix sewists descended upon us would arrive at any moment. We'd had breakfast and lunch brought in, but that wasn't economical in the slightest, and while Poe had access to quite a bit of money, I abhorred the idea of waste.

We walked down the stone steps behind the housekeeper's office to the ground level. The kitchen was a cozy haven, dark and perpetually spotless. The cabinets were painted a beautiful emerald shade, a sharp contrast to the rest of the house, where lighter colors ruled. When I entered, the kettle all but shivered in greeting.

Poe peeked out from behind me, wide-eyed. "Did the kettle just *move?*"

I nodded, then spoke to the kettle itself. "Water for tea would be lovely, thank you."

Flame flickered underneath the copper kettle. Poe took a few steps forward, leaning on the enormous wood worktable to watch as the water inside the kettle began to heat. "How is it doing that?"

I didn't have an answer for her. Orchid House had simply always *been* this way. Poe glanced up at me, through thick long lashes. "Really, Mina—I don't think this is normal—even for an Oscarovi house. Magic is science, not some nonsensical force."

So the Vilhari always insisted. Again, I shrugged. "I've never thought about it too much, to be honest. And I've been to very few other homes, so I wouldn't know."

Poe was silent after that remark, her mind obviously turning that information over carefully. It wasn't as though she didn't already know that I hadn't any friends. Anyone who'd followed the social seasons over the last decade with any vigilance would know that, and I knew Poe had. Perhaps she'd thought I'd accompanied Helene to her social engagements, and thus had friends by association. If she thought that, she hadn't known a thing about Helene—my skin flushed with anger at the thought.

Even now, the anger faded quickly, chased by my usual guilt for thinking bad things about Helene. It wasn't that I didn't know exactly who my sister was. It was just that she had been the closest thing I'd ever had to someone who loved me. Yes, she'd hurt me, more times and in more ways than I could count. But she was the only one who'd ever cared to see that I was all right after. To make sure I wasn't so damaged I couldn't recover. It was embarrassing to be so attached to someone who treated me so poorly, but I missed her all the same.

To avoid Poe's watchful gaze, I moved to the kitchen door, opening it to the autumnal air. I leaned against the doorframe, gazing upwards as a breeze floated down the alley, rustling some dry leaves that had gathered in a corner. The air was cool, but Orchid House was far enough up in the echelons to get a bit of sun every now and again. I closed my eyes, letting the the sun's rays warm my face.

A shadow falling over me broke my repose. Above me, enormous feathered wings blocked the sunlight. I stepped back inside the doorway as a siren landed with a small wooden crate in their talons. The fey creature set it down gently in front of the door. Her feathers were bronze, tipped with iridescent amethyst, and her face ethereal, that of a beautiful woman, with pale moonlight skin. "Order for Wildfang."

I made a little bow to the siren. They were revered beings after all —their terraced farms by the sea some of the only places food could grow in this region, high above Sirin's near-constant cloud cover. "Yes, thank you."

"Payment is due within the week. Will this be a regular delivery?"

I nodded in the affirmative as the siren held out a talon. A receipt and a contract for future deliveries were tied securely to her leg. Careful not to touch the siren too much, I removed the tightly scrolled bundle. "I'll have this filled out shortly."

"Sooner is preferable to later," the siren responded. They always sounded like that, speaking in the formal way of the old Vilhari.

As she prepared to launch, another avian fey dove into the alley —its trajectory shaky at best. The thing looked as though a cat and a raptor had collided rather hard, yielding a creature that was both adorable and incredibly vicious at the same time. Pravhna's little messengers, the howlers, were a distant relative of the gryphon.

"Oh dear," the siren crooned, her terrible voice full of concern. She stretched a wing out, rotating it slightly to catch the smaller fey. The little one bounced slightly, then perked up. Its eyes were large and dark as its head darted around.

Poe rushed past me into the alley, scooping the little howler into her arms. "Rue, you goose, what have I said about diving?"

The little fey chirruped loudly, in clear indignation. It trilled once at the siren though, blinking sweetly in clear gratitude.

The siren smiled, an uncharacteristic expression for one of her kind. "Be cautious, little one," she intoned as she took to the air. "The skies are not what they once were."

Something about the statement sent a shiver spider-walking down my spine. The sirens were known to traverse the spirit paths, to broker portents as mundanely as they did produce. I glanced at Poe, who cuddled the little howler to her breast, but watched the siren as she rose above the rooftops. When she met my gaze, the same fear that gripped me was reflected in the other woman's eyes. She felt it too, then.

"This is Rue," Poe said, by way of introduction.

I nodded to the little bird, bobbing my head in a little bow. They didn't speak the way the greymalkin or the elementals did, but it was known that they understood speech perfectly. "I am pleased to make your acquaintance."

The howler trilled at me, then hopped onto Poe's forearm, holding out his leg. A tiny piece of paper was attached, in much the same way the grocery receipt had been attached to the siren's leg. Poe removed it, slipped it into her pocket and kissed Rue's head, who made a series of pleased chirps, then took off again.

"No payment?" I asked, knowing messenger birds required something for their services, often shiny rocks or small snacks.

Poe blushed, making her look prettier than ever. "We are friends."

That was odd. The howlers were adorable, of course, almost to the point of being tempting to squeeze. But they were notoriously bad tempered, disliking humanoids, even their Vilhari kin. It was yet another piece of information to tuck away about Poe until a bigger picture formed.

I picked up one of the rope handles attached to the crate of groceries, and Poe the other. We dragged the crate into the kitchen and then went about the work of unloading it, Poe watching carefully where I put items away.

"You got them to bring more than just produce," she breathed.

A faint smile curled my lips. "The sirens may be the only people in Pravhna who like me."

Poe glared at me. "*I* like you."

I nodded once, but didn't prod further. That feeling could always change. It did with others—Poe might not be any different. "What was the message that Rue brought you?"

"Oh, I'd forgotten it…" Poe fished the little piece of paper out of her pocket. There were actually two pieces of paper, rolled up together. Poe read the one on top first, then discarded it. "Rent's due at my flat in the undercity. Edith will take care of it. Someone's already billed her." Her voice trailed off, already reading the other message.

"They've agreed to be our liaisons—Skye and the others."

My eyebrows raised. "That was fast."

Poe shrugged, taking an apple from the ironstone bowl on the island and staring at it, as though it might hold the secrets of the cosmos. "Skye was always going to say yes. She's just angry with me."

As I finished loading the dairy and meat into the ice box, the kettle whistled. I took down a teapot from one of the shelves. "How did you meet?"

Poe drew a stool out of the pantry, and up against the worktable. "We met last summer at the Merc—well, outside it anyway. I was threatening Viridian, and she thought she'd rescue me." Her voice had slipped into a dreamy tone, as though whatever she was remembering was lovely.

I took a tin of Maman's favorite tea blend down from a shelf, scooping it into the teapot. It smelled of vanilla and bourbon, with just a hint of brown sugar. "But you didn't need rescuing, did you?" I asked as I poured steaming water over the leaves.

"No," Poe said softly. "I didn't need her to walk me home, or to kiss me either."

The pain in the other woman's voice struck a string in my heart that I wasn't aware actually *worked*. I identified the feeling quickly as envy, which was surprising in itself. I was envious of the other woman's ability to love so easily. Something inside me tightened. *Love? Surely that wasn't what Poe felt for Skye Aestra.*

Confusion gripped me, my muscles clenching to the point of pain. Releasing them with a deep breath did nothing for the pain, but just a little for my comfort. The feelings that had nearly overwhelmed me dissipated to a manageable level. Left behind was a wistfulness for someone lost that was both foreign to me, and all too familiar at once.

I blinked several times, as tears threatened to surface. "What nonsense," I muttered, not thinking.

Poe looked as though I struck her, but did not speak. I wasn't sure what to do, but realized my mistake almost immediately. "Not you.

My mind drifted. I apologize. I'm not yet used to being in others' company."

The hurt drained from Poe's face. "What were you thinking of?"

Something about the question struck me as odd, but that was surely because no one had ever been interested enough to ask me such questions. "I was envious of your attraction to Skye—that you two might have a relationship—not because of *her*, but because…" I trailed off, not having words for the strange mix of nostalgia and longing I felt.

"Did you lose someone?" Poe asked, setting down a bag of flour, her dark head tilting to the side slightly.

I stared up at the uneven plaster of the ceiling. "I honestly don't know. There seems to be quite a lot I don't remember."

Poe stepped forward, her fingers stretching forward instinctively, as though she'd like to take my hands. She clasped them in front of her instead, to my relief. "You've only just returned. Give it time."

Footsteps in the alley kept me from answering. We both turned toward the kitchen door to find a tall Vilhari, dressed in the oxblood uniform of the cityguard, leaning against the doorway. The guard bore a strong resemblance to Skye Aestra, with her strong nose, and silver hair and eyes. Unlike Skye, his expression held no kindness, only cruel superiority.

"Well, Mlle Wildfang," the smug Vilhari drawled. "It appears you've returned."

CHAPTER 16

ASHBOURNE

As I expected, Skye's apparent hesitance to work with Mina and Poe was nothing more than a show. I got the feeling she did not want Poe Endymion thinking she was too eager—but I saw the signs of her interest in the pretty, tiny woman. Skye agreed to stay at Orchid House before we'd even gotten out of earshot of the house.

"Of course, we're going to stay with them," she said, her movements agitated, as she pushed a strand of fair hair back from her face. The wind raked cold fingers through it, tousling it again. Skye's mouth pressed into a grim line.

I could hardly keep pace with her as she wound down crowded streets in the upper echelon, and apparently neither could Morpheus, who disappeared to tell Edith that the deal was struck. The little bugger was likely napping in his favorite window at the office already, while I was stuck chasing after Skye.

She rounded corner after corner. I had to double my pace to keep up with her. It didn't help that our route home was a network of back alley staircases that lead back to the undercity and Skye was taking the steep stairs two at a time. Even with my longer legs, the steps gave me vertigo, something about the descent putting me ill at ease.

"Skye," I pleaded, coming to a stop. The dark alley swam in my vision, and bile rose in the back of my throat. Skye had been rattling off our packing list, discussing what items we needed from our compact but well-curated armory. But she stopped, nearly half a flight of stairs below me, turning swiftly to gaze back up at me. There were four of her in my vision.

"Sit!" she exclaimed, rushing back up to me as I swayed. Her hands gripped my arms as she guided me into a seated position. *What was happening?* A spell like this had never come over me before. I took a few deep breaths at her guidance, swallowing the bile in my throat. It felt as though the alley was caving in on me, and I muttered as much under my breath.

Of course, Skye heard me. "You're panicking, friend. Just breathe."

Panicking? But why? I'd squeezed my eyes shut while I took deep breaths, but now I opened them a sliver, my vision bleary behind my long eyelashes. The depths of the stairs disturbed me on a level I couldn't quite understand. As far as I knew, I wasn't afraid of heights or enclosed spaces, having experienced plenty of both in the past year in my work with Skye. We'd taken these routes before. They were dangerous, of course, primarily used by the Syndicate and less savory characters. But they were quicker than the main roads and cheaper than public transport. Besides, we could handle ourselves.

So why was today like this?

The weight of my head grew heavier by the second. Sky guided it into my hands, her fingers cool on my face. "Keep breathing, Ash," she murmured. "Everything's all right."

The dizziness dissipated some, and then cleared. When I raised his head again, the sight of the stairs no longer bothered me. Skye sat next to me on the stairs, her hand on my back.

"Are you all right?" she asked, her silver eyes narrowed.

I tried for a light tone as I stood. "That was odd, wasn't it?"

Skye nodded, but her face stayed serious. "I haven't seen you so unwell since right after the coma. Are you sure you're recovered?"

I nodded, taking a few experimental steps down. I was steady enough on my feet. "Yes, I think so." I reached a long arm back to pull Skye up.

She smiled up at me, but the concern in her eyes let me know she was still worried. "I wish I could take you to see my mother. She'd know what to make of this."

Skye rarely talked about her family, and typically I didn't want to pry. But if we were going to live in the upper city—possibly indefinitely—it seemed prudent to ask a question or two. Also, it would take the focus off me, at least for the time being. "Will you see her when we return to Orchid House?"

A long silence passed, the soft sound of our feet on stone the only noise as we descended the alley stairs. This time of day, when everyone was at work and the stairs were lit well enough with daylight, not many were about.

Finally, Skye let out a frustrated noise. "I don't want to, but it may come to that, eventually."

I hated to hear her distressed. I'd stayed away from the subject the entire time we'd known each other, but now I had to ask. "What happened with your family, Skye? Why did you leave your House and the Chevaliers?"

Her pale head shook a few times as we descended further. It smelled like the undercity now, like roasting chestnuts and woodsmoke. "My brother, Niall, and I could not get along any longer. One of us had to leave, and I knew he would not. So I left, and he stayed. My family disowned me for it."

She'd told me versions of this before, and I didn't like that she was still evading the question. I put an arm out in front of Skye, stopping her from moving forward. I kept my voice deliberately gentle, but firm. "That's not an answer. What was the problem between you?"

Skye threw up her hands. "What *wasn't* the problem between us?" She pushed past me. "But the end for us was when I made the Chevalier class, while he could barely rank in the cityguard."

I suppressed a groan. The cityguard were one of the most corrupt organizations in Pravhna. Outside the city, it was often better, but here they were some of the worst criminals of any echelon. They sought out bribes, dealt unreasonable amounts of violence, let cases in the undercity slip into oblivion… I paused.

"What we do, the investigative work—is it because of him?"

Skye nodded, her eyes filling with tears. "Because of *them*. I begged Niall not to join the cityguard, to take up *any* other profession. But my family didn't agree. I was asked time and again to let it go. When I caught wind that he'd been involved in a brutal raid on one of the medial district pubs, I asked one last time."

Each word she spoke was punctuated by a step downward and a tear sliding down her cheeks. "I love my family, Ashbourne. There was no one more loyal to House Aestra than myself. But the injustice of it, the hypocrisy. My parents especially... I couldn't take it."

"So you left?"

She nodded. "The night I met Poe. There was a terrible dinner, Niall and I screaming at one another. My mother said that if we could not find civil ground, one of us would need to leave. As though Strix being beaten for doing nothing more than operating a licensed pub in the upper city was excusable."

It was a story all too common in the medial districts—those that were just at the edge of the line between the upper city and the lower were often subjected to such unjust treatment. Money talked louder than anything else in Pravhna. The Strix that had owned the bar likely couldn't pay the exorbitant rents levied at businesses there.

I wanted to hug Skye, but she hated for anyone to acknowledge her sorrow. We'd come to the door that led into the undercity, anyway. Skye spoke a few arcane words—ones I had difficulty understanding or remembering, even after a year in the city—and the door opened. When we were on the other side, she shut it firmly behind us. We were in an alley in our own district.

The walk home was unusually quiet, as was our packing. I had been mistaken; Morpheus still had not returned from updating Edith on our progress with the Orchid House inhabitants. In the silent sorting of weapons and various clothes, I had too much time to think. My mind drifted to Mina.

The way her dark hair shone in the aetheric lights of Orchid House, the contrast of her long, bony fingers with her voluptuous body. The hint of skin under the creamy lace of her dress. My own skin heated at the thought, my trousers feeling tighter by the moment. It was as if something woke inside me, blooming even, and I couldn't stop myself from wondering what it would be like to—

"I've asked if you could pass me that dagger at least three times now." Skye smacked me with a tall leather boot.

Playfully, I snatched it from across the table at the center of our little armory. Some of the nicest memories of my life took place in this cozy little cellar, surrounded by weapons and gear. A lump formed at the back of my throat, just thinking about leaving.

"Apologies," I said, passing the dagger in question to her. "My mind was elsewhere."

Skye smirked slightly as I adjusted my pants. "Indeed."

Morpheus appeared on the table between us, stepping deftly around the array of blades Skye had discarded. *Your brother is at Orchid House, Skyeling. We must go.*

Firstly, I was shocked to hear the feline use a diminutive for Skye, but only for a moment. Our friend had gone utterly gray, as the fey cat must have known she would. He'd done his best to cushion the blow, but we were in the thick of it now.

Morpheus hopped down from the table, his usually dour face downright grave. *There is a cab waiting outside. I do not think we should leave them alone with Niall, do you?*

It only took a beat for the information to sink in, and then Skye was on the move. I wasn't entirely sure what the two of them worried Niall Aestra might do to Poe and Mina, but I didn't ask questions. I just moved, racing up the cellar stairs behind them.

MINA

"Niall Aestra—what are you doing here? Missing persons isn't your beat." Poe's voice was calm, smooth as silk. Still, I saw the hint of tension in the set of her jaw, the skin around her eyes.

Niall Aestra—was this Skye's brother? Vaguely, I remembered that House Aestra had two primary progeny, but I'd never heard anything about Niall. Skye, when she was still living in the upper city, had been an object of attention. She was popular for her calm demeanor and unusual kindness, rather than the many other vile reasons that made people stand out in the upper echelons.

Niall moved to step inside the kitchen doorway, but Poe made a gentle tutting noise before he could hit the wards. "Now, now, Niall. You haven't been invited in. We haven't even seen official documentation regarding your visit. Besides, you are addressing *Lady Somerhaven.*"

The Vilhar blinked once as his gaze slid to me—looking me over as if he couldn't believe such a thing were true. I took the opportunity to step forward. All day, I'd been watching Poe. Her manners were impeccable, and though I knew I wasn't capable of replicating her warmth, I had other material to draw on to find a public persona that suited me.

After all, I'd watched Helene—with her cold, imperious grace—

navigate society my entire life. A mask of serenity gilded my face, as a sense of eerie calm came over me. I spoke slowly as I held out my hand. I was breaking through the ward, but I was certain that I could more than handle Niall Aestra, if needed. "I am pleased to make your acquaintance, Officer Aestra."

The command was implied, rather than openly given. I had effectively pulled rank on him. House Aestra was of higher standing than Somerhaven, but by the rules of echelon, I was titled and he was not. He had to submit to me.

As he took my hand, bowing uncomfortably, it became clear: he was here on his own agenda, not that of the cityguard. Corrupt as the entire organization was, they were beholden to the upper echelons in nearly every way. No district official would have sent Niall Aestra here without a partner, nor would they ever have sent an officer, rather than a detective. These thoughts spun in my head, piling atop one another.

Niall rose, letting my fingers go as though they'd burned him. He spun to face Morpheus, who materialized behind him. Wards meant nothing to the wild fey, but as Morpheus and the others were returning to stay with us, on my invitation, the house would now recognize them as it did Poe.

Niall openly sneered at the sight of the feline, who hissed right back at him. *Explain your presence.*

"I don't have to explain myself to the likes of *you*," the Vilhar growled.

The cat sat, casually bathing a paw, though his tail swished violently on the stone floor. *Speak quickly, before your sister arrives. These women are under her protection, and I doubt she will offer you grace for this unwarranted harassment.*

"I am here on cityguard business," Niall insisted, the timbre of his voice shifting erratically.

I glanced at Poe. A vein in her neck trembled slightly, though the rest of her countenance remained calm. "Of course, Officer Aestra. What can we do for you?"

She shot a lightning quick look at Morpheus, and I wondered if she was communicating silently with him. Morpheus nearly faded from sight, losing some of his corporeality. Immediately, I detected a shift in the atmosphere, as though the fey cat were no longer in the room, though I could still clearly see him.

Niall did not appear sensitive to this change. "I am here to inquire after Lady Somerhaven's wellbeing and to find out how she escaped her kidnappers."

Poe stayed quiet, but she nodded at me, almost imperceptibly. We'd discussed how I should answer this over our early morning tea. "I am unable to answer you, Officer Aestra, for I myself do not know."

His eyes narrowed in suspicion. "Are you claiming not to remember?"

I didn't react to his obvious disbelief. "I *claim* nothing, Officer. I am *telling* you, I do not remember." When he visibly winced at my haughty tone, I pushed harder, pleased this persona was working so well. "I hope you're not implying that I'm being deceptive."

"Of course not," he replied as a shadow swallowed him.

The kitchen doorway filled with Ashbourne Claymore, who was so large he eclipsed the light from the alley. "I should think not." The Vilhar's voice was low, carrying the icy chill of darkest winter in its undercurrent.

The ice in his voice had the opposite effect on me. Warmth spread through me at the sound of it. As Niall turned to identify the speaker, Ashbourne stepped into the kitchen. He was a head taller than Niall, dressed in only his shirtsleeves, which were rolled up, revealing his muscular forearms. His long hair was pulled into a messy knot at the nape of his neck. He wore no waistcoat or jacket, as though he'd stepped out of his closet, midway through undressing. I nearly blushed at the thought, but tamped the feeling down as hard as I could.

"Whose behalf are you here on?" Ashbourne asked, his head tilting to one side. He moved with the demeanor of the pantheroi of Brektos, all darkness and sleek cunning.

Niall took a step away from him, almost by instinct. "I'm here on behalf of the cityguard, of course. We had reports that there were lights on in Orchid House."

Some might call the expression that crept over Ashbourne's face a smile, but I saw it for what it was—a predator narrowing in on prey. "You took those reports, did you not?"

Niall swallowed. "I did."

Ashbourne leaned against the kitchen island, the picture of calm. "And does your superior officer know you're here?"

Skye's brother gritted his teeth, a noise so grating I had to suppress the urge to wince. "No."

The thing that was not a smile widened on Ashbourne's face. The man was pure apex predator. Something stirred in me, fluttering wildly in my belly. His gaze caught mine and my breath escaped me.

He didn't take his eyes from mine as he pushed off the worktable. "I think you should go, Niall. Scurry back to your superior officer. Let them know that Lady Somerhaven has returned, and is being kept *very* safe."

Niall's eyebrows raised. "I know who you are, Claymore."

Ashbourne didn't break my gaze, his tawny eyes smoldering. "Do you?" I heard the silent ending to his statement as though he'd spoken it aloud: *because I hardly know myself.* We were an odd pair, two people with broken memories.

No, I thought, in an almost breathless correction. *We are not a* pair.

"I will leave you to whatever this is." Niall backed out the kitchen door. "Tell my sister that I was here."

In my peripheral vision, I saw the way Poe's fists clenched at the vicious tone in Niall's voice. Any questions I had about how Poe felt about Skye were put to rest. Relief flooded me as Niall disappeared, the kitchen door blowing shut behind him.

CHAPTER 18

MINA

"Where is Skye?" Poe hissed as Morpheus materialized fully. Her eyes blazed with something I couldn't comprehend. She seemed almost desperate to know where the Vilhar was.

`"Doing a perimeter sweep," Ashbourne replied. "She spotted someone else on your neighbor's roof when we arrived." He glanced at me, his heavy brow furrowing as the fingers on his right hand flexed and then clenched into a fist.

Poe's face changed. "I forgot to lock the front door this morning... There was a herd of elemental ponies in the street this morning… I went to watch them pass..."

"They're very rare," I murmured to Poe, whose smile was watery in return. "But the house won't let anyone we don't approve inside."

Poe frowned. "We?"

I nodded. "I reset the wards to allow you approval."

Ashbourne raised an eyebrow. "Didn't the two of you just meet?"

I glared at him, which elicited a crooked grin. My treacherous stomach flipped. "That's none of your concern."

Ashbourne laughed softly, shaking his head. It was obvious he liked something about my words, but I couldn't tell what. "How do the wards work?"

My stomach wasn't done with its unconscionable fluttering, but I ignored it. "When we are home, any resident of the house may allow someone inside by inviting them in. Otherwise, no one may enter, except creatures for whom wards do not apply."

"Like the wild fey," Poe murmured, glancing at Morpheus, who simply licked a paw in response.

Ashbourne stepped in front of me, pausing, his molten amber eyes boring into me. Once more, I had the impression that he was either extremely interested in me, or hated me outright—his intensity was difficult for me to read.

"Are you all right?" he asked, speaking to me as though I were a gentle lady, disturbed by Niall's obviously nefarious intentions. His expression softened some as he spoke. He really was uncommonly handsome.

"I am," I answered, suddenly wanting to laugh.

No one, in my memory, had ever looked at me like that. It was so wholesomely unwarranted, so deeply misguided. He thought me a delicate flower, when I was crafted from poison. Living in such close proximity to me, he would learn his mistake quickly. My eyes fell on Poe, who was already headed up the kitchen stairs, with the greymalkin in tow.

Ashbourne nodded once, and then turned to the kitchen stairs, taking them two at a time. I followed, though at a much slower pace. The pain was not so bad today, but there was no need to aggravate it into appearing and ruining my day.

No matter how much I liked any of them, they would learn the truth about me eventually. Whether it was the blunt honesty I often could not hold back, or the way my mind rotated every piece of information until it fell into place—people always got to the core of who I was and recoiled. Every friend I'd tried to make in childhood. Helene, despite her own oddities. Maman, before I'd even had the chance to become a whole person.

At the top of the stairs, Ashbourne had waited for me. "It sounds like the perimeter is clear. Niall was alone."

"That is good," I murmured, almost lost in thought. "Did you bring your things?"

For a moment, Ashbourne looked confused. "No, we came as soon as we heard Niall was here."

I nodded, then frowned. "How did you know?"

Ashbourne sighed. "I haven't heard all the details yet, but the short answer is Edith Braithwaite."

I realized Ashbourne likely had no idea where to go next, so I motioned for him to follow me through the back hall, past the housekeeper's office. "The library is that way. Please feel free to take any reading material you like. My father was a great collector of fiction."

Ashbourne peeked in through the double doors that opened into the library. "Any romances?"

I stopped, raising my eyebrows as I turned back to the library. "Yes, there is an entire section, though I'm not sure anyone's ever read any of it. My understanding was that he appreciated the covers."

Ashbourne nodded, stepping into the library. "Romances often have lovely covers. I prefer a gothic romance, myself. Something about the windswept moors and ghost-filled houses satisfies me."

That made a certain kind of sense. He *looked* like the hero of a gothic romance, with his dark hair and impressive bulk. I wondered if he knew it—if that was why he enjoyed them, or if he was unaware of how closely he resembled the heroes he enjoyed.

Or maybe it was the heroines he liked to read about. My mind swam with possibilities. *What were heroines like in gothic romances?* For the life of me, I could not remember, but suddenly had the burning urge to find out.

"What about you?" he asked.

I frowned, my stream of thoughts regarding gothic heroines disturbed. "What about me?"

His brows knitted together, as though he wasn't sure what I didn't understand. "What kinds of books do you like?"

"Oh," I replied softly. No one had ever asked me before. *So many firsts, lately.* It was an odd feeling to be surrounded by people who seemed genuinely curious about me. "I enjoy adventure stories. Far-off lands and all that."

He looked fascinated, his stern expression opening further. "Not stories of dashing heroes and gallant grand gestures of love?"

Something in me quivered at the thought. "Love stories are not for me."

In one fluid step, he'd moved closer to me, his long legs taking him further than I imagined they might. It was a casual movement, but the heat of his body mingled with mine, in the chill library air. Rare golden afternoon light broke through the clouds, streaming in through the windows, hitting the sharp planes of his face. For the briefest moment, I was certain his amber eyes glowed. My breath caught in surprise, but as his head tipped downward to look at me, I saw it was only a trick of the light.

"And why are love stories not for you, Lady Somerhaven?"

The moment was far too intimate. We'd known one another for a matter of minutes, not even hours. *And still.* My chin raised, as though drawn upward by a force not its own. "Because love is a curse, Msr Claymore."

One dark eyebrow arched in response, one side of his mouth quirking into a crooked smirk. He looked altogether too pleased with himself. "Is that so?"

Now he resembled the rogue princes in the adventure stories I enjoyed, wicked and sure of himself. He did not read gothics because he resembled their brooding heroes then.

How had our heads gotten so close? For that matter, how had our bodies gotten so close? I'd only have to raise my palms to press them against the hard muscle of his chest. Something I was not about to do, but still… Flustered, I swallowed hard, embarrassed at how difficult it was to take a step backwards. Being in his orbit felt like grace.

In my second sight, a beautiful face flashed before me—not Ashbourne's. Pale, porcelain skin, hair like flame, eyes wild with fear. Fingers gripped my shoulders, shaking me as the face shouted, screaming words I could not hear, though I knew I wanted to. The face was so familiar, so precious to me. I reached out to touch it, but found myself falling through darkness instead.

I hit the ground hard, surprised to find the checkerboard pattern of the library's parquet floor underneath me. Hands still gripped my shoulders, but they were not the long fingers of the redhead from my vision. Or had it been a memory? I looked up into Ashbourne's dark, honeyed eyes. Like the memory, he was shouting at me, but I couldn't hear.

Not at first, anyway. When my hearing rushed back in, I realized he wasn't shouting, but *was* obviously quite upset. Poe and Skye rushed into the room.

"What happened?" Poe asked, skidding to her knees to snatch me from Ashbourne's grip. For such a tiny person, she was remarkably strong. She wrestled me into her arms, all fierce defense and blazing fury. "Did he hurt you, love?"

Ashbourne rose, his eyes alight with anger. "Of course I didn't hurt her. She collapsed." Skye clapped a hand to his shoulder, reassuring him, apparently.

I shook my head to corroborate. "No, he didn't hurt me. I remembered something."

Poe turned to Ashbourne quickly, the rage dying in her eyes. "I apologize."

He nodded once, then bent down, scooping me out of Poe's grip and into his arms with a degree of ease that surprised me. "Put me down. I can walk."

Ashbourne paused. "Can you?" His words were careful, and he looked as though he regretted touching me.

To my surprise, his touch was comforting. I was angry that he'd manhandled me, but I had no desire to pull away from him. There was something oddly right about his proximity, as though my body belonged in his arms.

Which was, of course, utterly ridiculous. A short huff of a sigh proved my frustration. "No."

"May I carry you then?"

It was as though the rest of the world melted away. There was nothing left but the two of us, staring into one another's eyes. The feeling that I had been in just such a place before echoed through me, a disconcerting sense of time looping to keep me both right here and somewhere else.

Ashbourne broke eye contact first, directing his attention to Poe. "Could you show me to the parlor? She should rest."

"I am right here," I insisted, my voice too loud and too sharp. "Speak to me."

He looked down at me as he followed Poe out of the library. His voice was a low rumble against me, sending waves of vibrations through my body. "I know exactly where you are, Wilhelmina."

This close to him, the desire in his eyes was plain. The pulse of resonance his voice sent through me was too thrilling, too stimulating —*it felt too good*. I was not allowed such pleasure, not in this body. Not that I could remember. My breath caught at the same time his did, and once more, the world disappeared. I felt my grip on reality slipping.

And then he set me down on a settee in the parlor, his strong arms and sturdy chest receding from me at an unforgivable pace. It was as though I were one end of a magnet, and he the opposite. I had to stop myself from lurching forward, which was momentarily humiliating, until I saw the way every muscle in him tensed. Not in revulsion, but as though he too was holding himself back.

His breath came too quick for the little effort it had taken to carry me, the pace matching my own, as though each of us had traversed long distances to end up in such close proximity. Skye and Poe glanced between us, and then at one another. Skye shrugged and sat down on one of Maman's uncomfortable chairs, her face crinkling with displeasure as she did.

"Should I get us tea?" Poe asked.

I shook my head immediately. I didn't want Poe to go, but I did want tea. That might help steady me. Ashbourne stared at me, then moved. "I will get the tea."

"Thank you." My voice was soft as he strode out of the room.

I realized I'd needed him to leave; I wasn't sure I could concentrate with him there. It wasn't as though I'd never been attracted to someone before. I had. But I could not recall ever having such a strong reaction to someone else. I would need to develop a way to combat this, and to understand why feeling that way for him had triggered the memory; for now, I was sure that was what had occurred.

That wasn't something I was willing to discuss, but the memory itself was. I sat up, feeling focused now that Ashbourne was gone. My body ached more than ever after my vision into the past. My muscles had tensed too tightly during the episode, and now everything hurt.

Poe watched the effort it took for me to drag myself into a fully upright position. Though I'd done it as fluidly as possible, I was sure Poe had gauged my level of pain accurately. I was coming to learn that was typical of Hippolyta Endymion, who saw as much as I did, but interpreted it all differently.

"Can you tell us what you remembered?" Skye asked.

I swallowed hard, a lump forming in my throat at the thought of the woman. "I can tell you what I saw, but not what it meant."

Poe's expression fluttered between compassion and frustration as she squeezed her own hand in her lap. Gingerly, I reached out and took one of Poe's hands. Nothing about it was frightening; in fact, as Poe's fingers laced through mine, I found the touch comforting. I allowed my lips to raise slightly, the tiniest smile for Poe.

Poe grinned back, pure joy on her face. To my surprise, tears welled in her eyes. "Whatever you can tell us is fine, Mina."

A warm feeling oozed through my chest as her hands gripped mine. It was entirely different from what I felt pressed against Ashbourne, but it was a kind of attraction all the same. The feeling was pleasant, comforting even. No one had touched me much in my whole life. Not with tenderness anyway. It was a strange sensation to have so many people interested in me, affectionate with me.

Disconcerted by the flood of confusing feelings I had, I focused on the memory. "I saw a beautiful woman with flaming red hair. She was shaking me by the shoulders, shouting at me, but I couldn't hear her words. I don't know who she is, but I have the sense I *know* her."

Poe glanced at Skye, who shook her head. "There are almost no gingers here. Are you sure it was a woman? I know a few folk with red hair, but they're not women."

I frowned. "Why would you expect to know who it is?"

Again, Poe and Skye exchanged confused looks. Skye answered. "Because of the way we grew up, Mina. We know most of the same people, and there are very few people with red hair in the upper echelons."

I frowned again, wanting to argue her logic of assuming that the person I'd seen was someone of our social class. But Poe spoke. "The way your mother raised you was quite sheltered, wasn't it?"

I nodded. That much I couldn't argue with.

"All right," Poe reasoned. "Were there any redheads you can remember in Somerhaven? It tends to be a familial trait."

Slowly, I shook my head. It wasn't that I didn't follow Poe's logic.

The most likely scenario was typically the right one. But neither of them knew what I did: that there had been a time *before* this life, a before that I could not yet conceive of fully. Perhaps I should tell them… But the thought of telling them what I really was, seeing their faces contort with revulsion after all this kindness—I *couldn't*.

CHAPTER 19

ASHBOURNE

I made tea in silence, even though Morpheus had reappeared next to me almost as soon as I'd made my way back to the kitchen. Emotions swirled through me, confusing my mind and body. I breathed deeply, narrating each familiar movement to keep my focus sharp.

Fill the kettle with water. Long inhale.

Light the stove and put the kettle on. Exhale.

Spoon tea into the teapot. Inhale.

Take the teacups down. Exhale.

Slice a lemon. Inhale.

Fill the sugar bowl. Exhale.

As I waited for the water to heat, I leaned over the long worktable at the center of the cozy kitchen, cradling my head in my hands. Morpheus sat next to me, diligently bathing, leaning his heavy body against my shoulder. If I didn't know better, I'd think the beast was trying to comfort me. I tried to let my mind go blank, rather than remembering what it felt like to hold Mina's body against mine.

It is strange, isn't it? the cat asked—finally done with his bath—*How both you and Wilhelmina have damaged memories.*

The feline's words were phrased as a question, but were spoken as a statement. Fact. It *was* strange. I stood, the knot in my brow deepening, as I considered what Morpheus had presented to me. It was an odd coincidence. Too odd to even be a coincidence, really. It smacked of omens, portents, and other uncomfortable topics. I hated all that nonsense with an intensity that suggested it was a long-held feeling. You couldn't do anything about a prophecy, and I preferred to do something about my problems.

The kettle whistled, and I turned to take it off the stove. I poured water into the teapot, then searched for a tray to carry everything upstairs. By the time I turned back to the worktable, I found Morpheus staring at me. His oblong head was tilted to the side, and his eyes had narrowed to an appraising glare.

Had I offended him somehow? The damn feline was too sensitive. "I'm sorry, old man," I apologized, hoping an advance on my remorse might help smooth things over between us. "What were we talking about?"

The cat's eyes narrowed further, and then he twitched, furiously licking his paw. The movement seemed a touch contrived, as though he would prefer not to return to whatever it was we'd been discussing.

Nothing of import, he finally replied, when the paw met some unknowable standard for cleanliness. He jumped down from the worktable, rubbing his head against the thick barley twist legs before trotting upstairs.

I found a tray and arranged the cups, sugar, lemon slices, and teapot, before following him, balancing the tray full of china easily. What *had* we been talking about? I shook my head. I was going to have to pay better attention—my burgeoning attraction for Wilhelmina Wildfang couldn't get in the way of doing my duty.

We were here for two reasons: to protect Edith's assets and find out who Chopard was. Nothing more, nothing less. But my resolve broke almost as soon as I'd fixed it in place. As I approached the parlor, I smiled to see Morpheus already curled up on Mina's lap. It didn't help that she was so beautiful, but it wasn't just that. There was something so at odds about her, ruthless and soft at the same time. Her blunt utterances and obvious vulnerability mixed an irresistible cocktail of desire and protectiveness within me.

The women were already strategizing, so I laid the table with tea, pouring for each of them in turn as they continued without pause for my entrance.

"Mina's memory *could* be connected to Viridian somehow though, couldn't it?" Poe asked, her question directed towards Skye. My partner sat at a mahogany secretary desk situated near the front windows, a stack of paper in front of her.

Skye nodded as she scribbled notes, pausing to take her cup of tea with a grateful smile. "I suppose it could. Perhaps Mina met the woman from the memory at a country party?"

Mina shrugged lightly, her face a mask of impassive calm. But her fingers trembled slightly as she stroked Morpheus' back. He must have told her it was all right to pet him, because that was not something he typically allowed.

Poe, who sat on the same settee as Mina and Morpheus, took the cup I offered her. "House Montclair has connections to Brektos, so I don't think we can discount the idea that Mina might have met her in the country. That is, if your family attended Montclair parties."

Mina looked as though she were struggling to recall. "So much of the season before the oubliette is missing. But I was never asked to go to parties there before that. Maman and Helene always went without me."

I poured Mina's tea, dropping a slice of lemon and a spoonful of sugar in without thinking. Her eyes narrowed when I handed it to her. "How do you know I take my tea that way?"

Morpheus stared at me, his silvery-green eyes wide, his gaze unsettling in its pointedness.

"I didn't," I admitted. "Just a good guess, I suppose."

The greymalkin sighed as he laid his head back on Mina's lap. Again, I wondered what I'd done to offend him so. All cats were like this, secretive about their many grievances, but Morpheus had to be the most curmudgeonly of them all. There was no telling what I'd done to displease him. He would either tell me or forget he was ever unhappy with me. There was no use in obsessing over it.

Mina's eyes relaxed as she took a sip of tea. She set the cup down on the table as I poured a cup for myself, sitting in the chair across from them. As I did, the bell rang at the front door. Everyone looked to me.

I chuckled; clearly I was to be the domestic help today. I stood, leaving my cup on the low marble table that sat in front of the settee. "Let me get that."

They returned to their conversation as I left the room. In truth, it felt nice to be needed for things so pleasant as making tea and getting the door. Too often, my primary usefulness with Skye was intimidation and fighting. Neither of which I minded much, but it didn't help to feel that was all I was good for.

I strode quickly through the entrance hall, trying not to let the impressively grotesque carved stone bother me. The house itself was a terror—beautiful, but horrific at the same time. I'd never seen another like it in Pravhna, but something about it was vaguely familiar. Likely, the artists the Wildfangs had hired had done other, similar work, only on smaller scales. Last winter, when business had slowed, I'd spent a dizzying month in the galleries of the upper echelons, drinking in all the art I could see, with Skye by my side talking over all the artists' influences.

I paused in front of a statue of a Vilhar soldier, my eyes catching on the odd wings the artist had chosen to give their subject. Utterly fantastical: six wings, more like dracons than birds. *Someone had a good imagination.* The bell rang again, more insistently this time, as though the visitor held the button down for longer than necessary. I swore under my breath.

"Coming," I called aloud.

I opened the door to find three Strix youths waiting for me, two of which were dragging huge trunks up the steps. The other had a trunk at his feet. "Herself sent us with your order from the Laquoix woman and the things from your office."

I'd never gotten used to people calling Edith Braithwaite "Herself," as though she were some kind of royalty. It was warranted, I suppose. To her people, she was better than any of the cratties. She cared about the people who were loyal to her, more than anyone in the upper echelons did. That much was certain.

I frowned at the luggage, not sure what could be inside, but the Strix just shook his head, handing me a clipboard. "Not for us to question the boss."

I stared at the clipboard until the Strix dragged a pencil from his pocket. "Sorry about the pencil. It's all I have. Sign for me, so Herself knows you received the packages."

I did as asked, then fumbled in my pocket for a few coins to tip the hatchlings. The one who'd had me sign shook his head. "None of that please, Msr Claymore. We've been handsomely paid." He lowered his voice, looking around. No one on the street was near enough to hear us, but several curtains shifted slightly. We were most definitely being watched. "The old girl says to report in a week's time."

I nodded, thinking Edith wouldn't appreciate these younglings calling her "the old girl," but that was an issue for another time. "Thank you for the delivery."

"Cityguard's been taken care of as well. The Aestra bastard won't come around again," the youth murmured. "Can't keep the press off you though—not for more than a few more days."

"Tell Herself we appreciate it," I murmured back, careful to look down as I spoke. Lip reading was more difficult than average people assumed, but it was still possible.

The three youths strutted off, chatting to one another in a lively, carefree way. They were headed back to the undercity, back to the Syndicate. I envied them deeply as I pulled the trunks inside. There was nothing about this house, or this part of the city, I wanted anything to do with.

Nothing except Mina. The thought ricocheted through me, wild as a stray bullet in a barrel, and just as dangerous.

I opened each of the trunks, trying to determine which should go where when we chose rooms. One was a combination of both my and Skye's things. None of the clothing we'd packed was there, only weapons and a box of files Skye had pulled from our collection. The other two trunks were full of finely made clothing, fit for dukes, not the likes of us.

"Did Edith send those things?" Skye asked, appearing out of nowhere. I'd heard her coming, of course, but was still impressed with her ability to sneak up on me.

"Yes—what do we need all this for? I thought we were meant to be their guards."

Mina and Poe both arrived in the entrance hall. Poe was immediately distracted by the host of calling cards in the bowl near the front door. She moved quick as a forest pyx as she sorted them.

Mina came to stand next to me, looking at the clothes in the trunk I determined was for me. "It looks as though the two of you will be acting as our escorts."

I glanced at Skye. "Would that be… inappropriate? Escorting them and staying in the house together?"

Skye laughed, though she also had that worried look she got when I didn't remember something essential about how society worked. "No—no one cares about that kind of thing in the upper echelons. They bed whoever they want, whenever they want."

Poe looked up from her calling cards. When Skye's eyes met hers, they both flushed deeply.

Mina leaned over with intention, her eyes locked on the neat pile of shirts. I liked that she had noticed our friends' obvious attraction to one another, but was letting them have a private moment. She was uncommonly considerate for someone raised in the upper echelons. I'd never met a crattie I liked so well so quickly, other than Skye.

"These are lovely," she murmured. Her voice still sounded as though her vocal cords were damaged.

"Have you been screaming?" I asked, before I could think better of it.

She looked up at me, her eyes wide. "Yes. I believe I screamed for months on end in the oubliette."

Her voice did not so much as waver. She'd trembled in my arms, her heart fluttering like a panicked, wild thing after her vision, but had no reaction whatsoever to that. As she stood, she seemed unsteady on her feet. "I think I may have done too much today. I need to lie down for a bit." She began to walk away, headed towards the terrible staircase at the end of the hall. "Poe, can you show them how to send their things up the elevator? They can stay in the Oleander and Hellebore rooms."

Poe nodded. "Of course."

Mina turned, took a few steps, then paused. "Nothing in the house is off limits to you, but a word of caution—my mother was very fond of poison and traps. Stay out of the rest of the bedrooms on the second and third floors."

There was a deadly chill in her voice. The fact that she didn't turn disturbed me more than I would have imagined it could. I wanted to see what her face looked like, if there was a mark of some horrific childhood lesson there, or pure fear. As it was, the ice in her voice was enough to send a lick of apprehension through me. What had we gotten ourselves into with this place, this family?

"Of course," Skye replied. "We wouldn't dream of prying."

Mina nodded, glancing sidelong behind her at Poe, her arm stretching out behind her ever so slightly, as though she reached for the other woman. "Would you come chat with me about those cards before you show our guests where to go? We need to decide which to accept."

Poe rushed forward, taking her arm as they walked towards the stairs. I noted the way Mina leaned against Poe, just a little, but enough for me to see things clearly. She was in more pain than she let on. Probably all the time from the practiced, careful way she moved. I watched as they made their way upstairs. Morpheus appeared behind them, following.

When the sound of their footsteps died, I turned to Skye. "She's in a great deal of pain."

Skye nodded, as though she'd noticed the signs I had. "I'm remembering a bit more about her now. I don't remember dancing with her during her season, but when she was a child there were rumors she'd been ill—and that's why she and Helene were kept from society."

Something about that struck me as a lie. The dead woman had obviously fixated on poisonous plants. Had Vaness Wildfang experimented on her youngest child? But why would she? I stared at a family portrait, tucked into a nook near a coat closet. It only portrayed Vaness, her husband, and a small tow-headed creature I assumed was Helene. The littling bore a strong resemblance to both her parents.

None of them looked a thing like Mina, and I wondered if perhaps she wasn't Vaness' child at all. If that was why she'd permanently damage a littling—revenge for an affair. It was the kind of thing we saw all the time in our line of work, sadly. I wasn't sure how that held relevance now, but I'd worked as a detective for nearly a year, and something about all this didn't make sense.

By contrast, the fires were too much of a coincidence to be ignored. What in the Wildfangs' past had drawn them into Chopard's web? I chewed it over in my mind, scowling at our weapons. I wasn't sure how to sort them just yet, so I worked to put the trunks back to rights and close them, while Skye watched. She was just as lost in thought as I was.

When I got the trunks closed, I asked, "What was the sister like?"

"Imperious. Beautiful beyond measure for an Oscarovi. Quite a prize for Viridian. He must be furious that he lost her."

"Why?" I sat down on the trunk that held my clothes. This was as good a place to talk as any. As far as I could tell, there were no comfortable seats in the parlor. I hoped the bedrooms were a different story.

Skye sat across from me, atop her own trunk, silently agreeing with me to not return to the parlor. "Viridian Montclair is rich, connected, and intelligent. But he grates on people's nerves. He struggled to maintain a match, though many were interested in the Montclair fortune. And in the past few years, there have been rumors about the kinds of pleasure houses he frequents."

I grimaced. "Not the ones in the undercity, I take it."

Skye shook her head. "No." She paused for a moment, listening hard for movement upstairs. I did the same, faintly sensing soft footsteps and voices, but not hearing anything distinctly. Poe and Mina were obviously talking still. Skye continued, "Muse could help her remember. She has to know something that would help us. The fire at Somerhaven, her imprisonment... I'm sure it's all connected to Chopard somehow. I can feel it."

I nodded, glad our guts still spoke the same language, that we still thought along the same lines. This mission was cloudy territory, and I had the feeling we were going to have to work on instinct more than either of us liked. Being aligned in our thinking would help ensure we didn't make mistakes.

I kept my voice low. "He could, but getting her to the undercity will be a problem. We're being watched, both openly, and I assume otherwise."

Skye nodded, looking up again, leaning forward. "Edith has eyes everywhere, but I'm fairly certain Montclair has people out as well."

"And your brother?" I asked. "Who's he working for?"

Skye shook her head. "I can't tell, but I doubt he'd have come on his own—someone tipped him off about Mina. I don't like that he's involved in this."

The sound of a door opening and closing upstairs urged me to lower my voice further. "The Strix woman that came to the shop—you think she's involved in this somehow?"

Skye stood, hearing Poe's footsteps as clearly as I did. "I think we should assume that this is *all* connected."

So she was sure then. It both comforted me and set my teeth on edge. Our instincts were built differently. It's what made us such a good team. Skye felt into the subtler side of things, people's feelings, patterns of behavior, when folk lied. But I had a warrior's sense of a fight: when things shifted or turned. When my opponents were closing in on me—and I had that feeling now. Things were building in a way I didn't like one bit. The battle had shifted, but to whose advantage, I was unsure.

CHAPTER 20

MINA

For days after our arrival at Orchid House, we fended visitors off, claiming that I was still quite "done in" from my ordeal. In reality, we spent our time combing the garden for any kind of surveillance spells and reworking the house's wards to our specifications. Niall Aestra's unusual visit put us all on edge, and Skye and Ashbourne insisted we go slow. There was only so much I could do while Maman's workroom was still locked.

Poe and I also spent a good deal of time sorting the calling cards into strategic piles: ones we would never answer, ones we should answer for social reasons, and ones to answer to gather information on both Maman and Viridian's known associates. The trick was mixing the last two groups enough that it would be difficult for anyone observing us closely to determine what we were up to.

Every morning, I rose long before the sun to try the door on Maman's work room. I wasn't keeping it a secret from the others. It was just easier to think in the wee hours, partly because I was having no luck. My frustration was getting the better of me. One morning, on my third day of having no success, Ashbourne appeared beside me in the study, a tray of steaming tea in his hands.

He said nothing to me, just nodded, fixed my tea, and settled into a chair with his own cup, apparently engrossed in a book. He wasn't pretending to read while surreptitiously keeping an eye on me, either. I'd been suspicious when he sat down, but as I sipped my tea, the special calm that came over a room when someone was lost in a story seeped into me.

The man really had just come to keep me company. He seemed to intuit that I didn't want to talk, and just read while I tried every spell, sigil, and secret password I could think of. Nothing worked, but with Ash's calming presence, my frustration lessened. By the fourth day that he joined me, I noticed he had a little notebook he wrote in occasionally.

With sweat beading on my brow from my last attempt at the door, I slumped into the desk chair. The sound of Ashbourne's pen on paper caught my attention.

"What are you writing?" I asked, trying not to sound as grumpy as I felt. I wasn't annoyed with him. Quite the opposite, in fact.

He looked up from his notebook. "I'm keeping a list of all you've tried so far."

"Oh." That was rather thoughtful of him. "There's no need. I'll remember."

His expression was one of thoughtful repose as he continued writing. "The list is not for you, it's for me. I think things through by writing them down."

I wiped the lingering sweat from my forehead with a handkerchief. "Does that work?"

Ashbourne nodded once, then looked up. "It does. For me, anyway."

His golden eyes met mine and a feeling of ease crept through the atmosphere in the room, smoothing all the rough edges that threatened our peace. We didn't talk more. He went back to reading as I pulled down some books from Maman's shelves to read about astral travel, if only to clear my head.

Companionable silence filled the room like a balloon gently inflating. It hugged me, my heartbeat even and my breaths deep and cleansing. It was true that Ashbourne's mere presence had the ability to send me into paroxysms of lust, but there was also this—whatever *this* was. He, Poe, Skye, and Morpheus all drove the loneliness of the oubliette away.

Morpheus. "Could Morpheus get in? To the workroom, I mean."

Ashbourne looked up. "Call to him."

I'd learned the cat could hear a summons from great distance, so I said his name under my breath, adding, "Could you please come to Maman's study?"

The greymalkin appeared at my feet. *Yes?*

"Can you get into locked spaces?"

Most, he answered, staring at the door. *But not that one. That one only opens with a key.*

"A real key?" Ashbourne asked. "Or a magical one?"

The greymalkin seemed to shrug, then rapidly licked some patch of offensive fur on his back leg. *It is difficult to say. The spell is quite complex. A ward around the inner room connects to the lock itself.*

Ashbourne set his book aside to come stand next to me. We both stared at the door. There was no lock. Morpheus curled up by the fire and closed his eyes, having nothing else useful to say, I assumed.

"Have you come across any evidence there's a lock?" Ashbourne asked. "You did several spells to reveal what's hidden."

I shook my head. "No, nothing."

"You don't use a jewel," he said simply. There was not a hint of judgment in his voice. "And yet you are adept with magic."

I nodded, sighing. He was more observant than I'd thought. I might fool people I was around for short periods of time, but I couldn't fool anyone I lived with—a fault Maman had reminded me of constantly. "Correct."

He stepped backwards, sinking back into his chair. "Was your mother resentful of that ability?"

I leaned against the bookshelves, not knowing how to answer that. It was all so complex. "Perhaps. It's not unheard of among us— the Oscarovi have always had access to magic. Some simply have more natural talent than others. But it's rare to have power as strong as mine without the help of a familiar." There was more I could say, but delving too deep would dredge up things I wasn't sure how to explain. Things I wasn't ready for him to know about, first among them that this was not even my real body. That *I* was not real.

He nodded, but said nothing in response. I could not tell him the rest, but I found myself giving voice to one of my most vulnerable realizations—offering it to him like a pearl. "If it had been Helene, I think she'd have been proud. Since it was me—she was ashamed."

I don't know if he understood that I'd pulled something from the horrible dark place at the core of me, that this was a gift. His face was calm, but anger flashed in his eyes, fierce and protective. *Of me.*

"Why?" he asked. "What reason could she have had to be ashamed of *you?*"

The way he said "you" sent shivers through me—as though he could not imagine finding fault with me. The shivers expanded into vibrating waves of heady pleasure. Something was changing inside me, shifting to make room for these people and their apparent care for me. The path I walked now was dangerous for someone like me. I had too many secrets, and it took me far too long to sort out what people's intentions were.

I shrugged, shaking my head. It was time to put my emotions back on more solid ground. "If I knew that, I'd probably remember why I'd been put in the oubliette. I have a strong suspicion the two issues relate to one another."

"So do I," he said, his expression dark. He didn't elaborate, and I didn't push the conversation further.

By the end of our first week together, we'd come up with a solid plan for how to deal with the inevitable questions about where I'd been and what Ashbourne and Poe were doing with us. Since many of the upper echelons had seen Poe at Viridian's country party, we agreed it would be better to hinge my "rescue" on Poe and Ashbourne. As Ashbourne had made a trip out of town the month prior, we concocted a story that he'd found me wandering the beach, soaked to the bone, with no memory. He'd been to one of the aeries just north of Somershire around that time, so it wasn't out of the realm of possibility.

Skye had an isolated little cabin near the Achera River and he'd stayed there for a few days, before traveling north, right past Somershire. In our story, he'd taken me there to recover, until I remembered things like my name and where I was from. We rehearsed telling the story exactly the same repeatedly, then Poe made us tell it more "colorfully," including shared details, from our own perspectives. She even gave us points to argue over, such as whether or not he'd given me his coat right away.

And then we began taking turns about the neighborhood, both in pairs and as a foursome. We let the story slip out, bit by bit, as we naturally ran into many of the people we planned to call on, on the promenade. By our second week together in Pravhna, we began taking callers. There were nearly a dozen each day, Oscarovi and Vilhari alike. None were any of Maman's closest confidants or Helene's friends. Poe wanted to wait for us to meet some of them in public.

She also surmised that this would put anyone who might be anxious about what I might know about Maman's plans on edge. As a result, I was exhausted by endless small talk and the sheer pressure of being around other people. Even alone in my room at night, I felt Poe, Skye, and Ashbourne acutely. It was as though I could hear their very breath and heartbeats, setting me to tossing and turning. Only Morpheus, who melted silently between the limen and the waking world, was gentle on my sensitive perception. Sometimes I didn't know he'd been sitting next to me until he purred, soothing my frayed nerves.

The days inched by slowly, as I did little more than sit quietly and speak in measured tones. But Poe insisted this was the way to meet all our aims. According to her, trying to eke information out of the highest echelons of society was something of a long game. Maman had often expressed similar opinions, though of course, her goals were different from ours.

Calling cards came in daily, the bowl in the hallway filled with more requests to meet with Maman's closest known associates, as well as a few names I did not recognize, but who Poe assured me were people we wanted to be interested in my return. I grew more restless with each passing day.

There was no word from Viridian, nor from any of Helene's set, and instead of relieving me, this made me even more anxious. Poe assured me that we were right on track—that all was unfolding exactly as we'd planned. Though, of course, this part was *her* plan.

Even Skye had to admit that Poe's insight into the upper echelons was far more nuanced than her own.

Ashbourne had little to say about it all, though we'd begun an ongoing game of Squires Spades, leaving our spread out on the table in Maman's study to return to in quiet moments. He told me about the books he read, even trying some of my recommendations and giving me his thoughts.

"Needs more romance," was his usual comment.

I found one of his favorites, *The Gentleman Rogue,* tucked in the basket I used to carry things with me between downstairs and the attic. Though I hadn't started it yet, a brief perusal proved that some passages were quite explicit. I wondered if this was an attempt at seduction, then dismissed the thought. We were simply sharing books with one another, and he enjoyed romances.

One morning at the beginning of the third week I'd been home, we took the morning off from callers at my request. We had been invited to one of the Institute for Research on Interstellar Life's exclusive luncheons—my first public event—and I needed peace to gather myself.

I was headed downstairs after dressing for the lecture when Ashbourne strode in the front door. He'd taken up the habit of a morning constitutional and had been gone an unusually long while. From what I could observe from the front windows, it had made him quite popular in a short time.

I couldn't blame the neighborhood for their interest. Dressed in Mme Laquoix's best, he was a sight to behold: every bit the polished gentleman, though nothing could alter the rugged beauty of his face or the sheer size of him. He was at least a head taller than most Vilhari, who were frequently taller than Oscarovi to begin with.

I couldn't help but think of the description of *The Gentleman Rogue*'s hero ravishing the heroine as I stared at him. I only realized I'd stopped on the stairs when he spoke. "The neighbors say Viridian has arrived at his town residence."

My chest tightened. So the game had changed. "We knew he'd return eventually."

Ashbourne nodded tersely. "And so he has."

He seemed to avoid my eyes entirely. *The Gentleman Rogue* was most definitely not a method of seduction then. Disappointment seeped around the edges of the thought, frustrating me. I took the last few steps of the staircase, moving through the entry hall into Maman's private sitting room, just off her study.

It was the coziest room in the house, decorated in plush cream velvet brocade curtains, with four matching chairs that sat in a circle in the middle of the room. I sank into a chair, waiting for Ashbourne to follow me, which he did. With a few whispered words, the hearth sprang to life. Ashbourne gave it a withering look, and likely for good reason. It was ostentatious, the marble carved with poisonous flora.

"What was your mother's obsession with poison?" Ashbourne asked, breaking the silence between us. His voice was warmer than before, and he leaned towards me, interest in his eyes.

It was so difficult to read him. Was it possible that like me, he was fighting the feelings he had? While I had a few sexual encounters in my past, there had never been romance. I had no idea how to discern what someone felt for me in a romantic sense.

It seemed better to leave all that alone, for now. I wasn't sure how to answer his question. There was the truth, and there was the story I told myself. I never had to tell anyone else, for no one ever dared ask, but I had comforted myself with lies as a child. For some reason, I decided on the truth. "She enjoyed murdering her enemies."

His reaction was unexpected. Ashbourne merely nodded, one eyebrow quirking upward. "A woman with ambition."

"Indeed," I agreed, glad that he did not appear overly sanctimonious about the admission. It wasn't that I defended Maman's predilection for murderous behavior, but I also saw no need to become hysterical over it. There was nothing I could have done to stop Vaness when she lived, and now there was no need to. "The decor, I presume, was to remind people of the fact that not only could she kill them, she was proud of it."

"Excellent," Ashbourne replied, his voice too dry to be anything other than earnest.

What an odd reaction, I thought. *It is almost as if he admires her.* There were plenty of points on which Maman deserved admiration, but combining her ambition and tendency towards murder as positive attributes was somewhat unusual.

Something out the window caught Ashbourne's eye and he stood. "Whatever *is* your neighbor doing?"

I rose to join him at the window, sighing deeply. The door leading to the garden was locked. I fished the house keys out of my pocket, unlocked the door and stepped out onto the terrace. Ashbourne followed me, a warm presence at my back.

"*Miranda.*" I kept my voice low and calm. "What's all this?"

The question wasn't necessary; it was quite obvious what Miranda Willsworth was doing. The pale Oscarovi was yanking on vines of the bittersweet that crept up the wall toward her own garden.

She startled when I spoke, then paled to a grayer shade of white. "*Wilhelmina.* I didn't think it was true."

Everything about Miranda was wan. Her face, her hair, her expression—even her clothes. There was not a single interesting thing about her—unless you counted her sanctimonious attitude as interesting, which I did not.

"Didn't think what was true?"

I tried to keep my temper. One thing Maman and I had always agreed upon was that Miranda was a pain in the arse to live next door to. Honestly, I was surprised Maman hadn't poisoned *her* for all the times she'd meddled with her standing in the Royal Oscarovi Gardening Club over the years.

"Your bittersweet is out of control. It's getting into my garden," Miranda snapped, not answering me.

No matter; I knew what she meant. She didn't think I'd really returned, and she would have preferred it if I hadn't. This was her passive aggressive way of letting me know that she did not approve of me anymore than she had Maman.

Insufferable woman. I glared at her as she shoved her gardening shears into her apron and marched through the open gate between our gardens. "Get it taken care of, or I shall report you to the ROGC."

Before I could answer, she'd slammed the gate behind her.

"Did she just threaten to report you to a *gardening* club?" Ashbourne asked.

"Yes." I sighed again, turning to go back inside. It was the kind of thing Miranda was known for, and the ROGC did have an irritating amount of power amongst the Oscarovi high echelons, so it was something to be conscientious of. Before I knew what was happening, Ashbourne had me in his arms, flat against the deep doorframe.

"Stay quiet," he warned, turning my body so I faced the same direction he did, though his grip on my waist did not loosen. "Do you see them?"

Our view was of the street, as we were on the northside terrace of the house. A block down the street, two cityguard detectives made their way toward Orchid House. Though they were dressed in civilian clothing, as all detectives were, they wore brass eagles pinned to their lapels.

"They're coming here," he warned. "Go inside and warn Poe."

I nodded as he pushed me into the house and disappeared around the terrace, towards the back of the house. "Poe?" I called as quietly as I could.

Poe's dark head popped out from the parlor. "Are you nearly ready to go? The cab will be here shortly."

"Detectives," I breathed, my heart pounding too fast. "A block away."

Poe moved quickly, back into the parlor. I followed, feeling queasy. Something soft brushed the exposed ankles of my boots.

I looked down to find Morpheus at my feet, rubbing his face against my leg. *Fear not, Mina, we will not allow them to harm you.*

Poe looked up from the secretary desk, where she was gathering up her papers, and locked them inside the part of the desk that folded down. "Of course we won't let them harm her, why would you say something like that? Mina knows that."

The cat simply blinked at her, expression solemn as usual.

"Oh," Poe breathed. "*Oh.*"

I wasn't sure what Poe was realizing, but we didn't have time to discuss it. There were footsteps on the front steps. "What do I do?"

"Stay calm," Poe said. "Like you did with Niall. We knew they'd come—you're ready." She guided me towards a chair by the fire, placing one of Ashbourne's romances—not *The Gentleman Rogue*—in my lap, open to a page in the middle. "Read," she commanded. "Do not look up until after I announce them."

I did as I was asked, as well as I could anyway. My mind swirled with worry; knowing Viridian had paid off the detectives in Somershire, what might he do here? My eyes glided over the words on the page of Ash's book. It helped to think of him as Ash, like Skye and Morpheus did. Even Poe called him by the diminutive of his name now. My breath evened out, giving me the appearance of serenity. Morpheus flopped down at my feet, reclining on one massive side, so that his enormous bulk was on display.

He was bigger than most domestic canines, though he would not consent to being weighed, no matter how many times I'd pleaded. He appeared to be sleeping until Poe led the detective into the room.

"She's just in here, Detective Brenton."

Outside in the entry hall, I heard the sound of Skye chatting amiably with the other detective. They'd split them up somehow.

The detective made a small bow in my peripheral vision, but I still did not look up. Poe had not announced them yet. "Mina, this is Detective Brenton. She'd like to ask you a few questions."

Now I looked up, placing my right index finger inside the book as I closed it. I was grateful for it, as my hands had begun to shake, and clasping the book kept that from being visible. Poe really was three steps ahead in situations like these.

I inclined my head slightly towards the chair across from me. "Please, sit, Detective."

The Oscarovi woman sat, looking incredibly uncomfortable. She was a wiry thing, with dull blonde hair pulled into a severe bun at the top of her head, and a sour expression. "We've come to close your case, Mlle Wildfang."

"*Lady* Somerhaven," Poe corrected, her tone somehow sweet and sharp at the same time.

"Of course," Detective Brenton replied. "My apologies, Lady Somerhaven."

"It's quite all right," I said, keeping my voice low and soft, as Poe had instructed. "It is a change for me as well."

The detective, who had been staring nervously at her hands, looked up, a slight expression of surprise crossing her face. *Perhaps no one in the upper echelons has ever spoken to her with kindness,* I reasoned.

"Can we get you some tea?" I offered.

This too seemed to surprise the detective, flustering her a bit. "No, thank you. That is not necessary. I have a few questions for you before we can close your case."

Poe sat on the settee, pretending to take up a book of her own. Anyone who looked at her would think she was relaxed, and perhaps she was. After all, the Syndicate had said they'd taken care of the cityguard. But there was no telling who was working with whom in the corrupt organization, so being too sure of anything would be a mistake.

I made every effort not to look at Poe, but I couldn't help but see Morpheus, who opened his eyes now, stretching his paws out in front of him. His razor sharp claws shone in the firelight, and then he yawned, showing all of his teeth. The fey cat stretched as the detective watched him, horror growing on her face as she realized he was no mere housecat.

When he rubbed his face against my legs before turning twice to curl up at my feet, Detective Brenton's mouth fell open. The greymalkin were legendary for their vicious tricks, bargains that often ended in gruesome violence. Not many people had met one, but everyone had heard terrifying tales of deals gone wrong with the fey felines.

"Perhaps I can make things a little easier for you," I said when Morpheus had settled, glaring at the detective, even as he fell asleep. "As I'm sure you've heard, I remember very little about my time away. In fact, from what I understand, I don't remember the months leading up to my disappearance either."

Detective Brenton nodded, taking a notebook out of her jacket pocket. She jotted down a quick sentence or two, then looked up. "An oubliette could do something of the sort."

I had answered questions about where I'd been in myriad ways over the past few days, but no one had asked follow-up questions when I said I couldn't remember anything. In fact, most had reacted with nothing more than sympathy, seeming to like me more for what I'd been through. People often liked those they perceived as outsiders better when they thought they suffered.

I didn't allow my surprise to show. "I suppose you're right." My head tilted to the side, as I rested my chin on my hand, staring into the fire. "But so could any number of memory-altering rituals and spells, if someone were talented enough to complete them. We've spent the time since I was found searching my mother's library." I paused to turn my head slowly toward the Detective, making firm eye contact. "I am sure you already know about my mother's library."

Vaness' famed library contained records of some of the worst spells and rituals that the Oscarovi had ever successfully performed, many of which were now outlawed. Detective Brenton swallowed hard.

I raised my eyebrows, attempting an innocent expression. "I have none of my mother's interest in such things, of course. But you must understand that I've tried quite hard to find out what happened to me, and come to no conclusions."

The detective looked as though she wanted to ask a follow up question. She had the look of someone who needed the last word. I spoke before she did. "A good conk on the head might have done me in as well. I was covered in small wounds when I regained my senses, but of course, they all healed so quickly it is difficult to know what lasting damage there might be. I am afraid I have no answers for you."

The detective nodded once, looking disappointed. "We understand you have not yet met with Viridian Montclair."

This was not an unusual line of questioning, but it was beginning to seem a bit vigorous for detectives in Herself's pay. The truth was, we had no idea if the detectives were loyal to the Syndicate. Many took bribes with no loyalty in return. It was a dangerous game, but plenty played.

Best to be on guard. I let a small smile creep onto my face. Skye had noticed how unsettling it was the previous evening at dinner, and I was interested to try it out. Detective Brenton was clearly unnerved. Behind her, Poe hid a smile of her own.

"No," I answered. "I have not yet had the pleasure of seeing my brother-in-law." My hand flew to my mouth, my eyes gone wide. "I —I mean… He would have been, you know… If Helene had not…" I let myself trail off. I couldn't quite bring tears to my eyes through false emotion, but I hadn't had a second cup of tea yet. I suppressed the incoming yawn, the necessary tears welling in my eyes creating the convincing effect that this whole line of questioning upset me.

It had the desired effect. Detective Brenton appeared more uncomfortable than ever, and I got the distinct impression she wished she were anywhere but here. It was time for this conversation to end. Any member of the upper echelons would consider this all the information the cityguard would need.

I rose to indicate that I was finished with the encounter. "Is that all? We really must make ready to go. Our autocar will be here any moment, and I do hate to keep the driver waiting. You know they are on such tight schedules."

Detective Brenton nodded. "Of course, my lady. Thank you for your candor."

"Shall you close the case then? Since I have arrived home without harm, and am now in such good care?"

The detective hesitated. "Would you like us to close the case? If you feel yourself in danger…"

Was the detective actually concerned for me? I hesitated for the briefest of moments, but saw a hint of alarm in the way Poe's finger tapped against her thigh. Not concerned then, something else. Best to send her on her way then.

I smiled again, hoping it would have the same unnerving effect it had before. "I am in no danger now that I am back at Orchid House, and amongst those who care for me."

The detective glanced at Poe. "Have the two of you known each other long?"

This was most definitely a more aggressive line of questioning than most of the upper echelons would consider appropriate. Poe looked as though she would answer, but I wondered if it might be better if I did instead.

I kept smiling, my face aching with the effort, as I lightly touched the detective's elbow to guide her to the door. "No, though I wish we had. She is so good to me."

The detective looked a bit flummoxed, as though she wasn't sure how the tables had turned on her. The sickly sweet tone in my voice was nausea-inducing. But the character I had developed, the one I was forced to play to get the information we needed, would say such things. Over the past few days I'd seen the benefit of being perceived as wide-eyed and innocent. Tongues loosened, the usual wariness I was used to dissipating with every effortless-seeming kind word.

Though the detective seemed less dramatically affected by my feigned innocence, her shoulders relaxed a measure, as though something was confirmed for her that she'd suspected all along.

"Of course," Detective Brenton replied. "Unfortunately, because of Msr Montclair's claim that you'd been kidnapped, we are unable to close the case officially. But we will do our utmost to ensure that your privacy is respected."

I paused, widening my eyes a bit further. "Whatever do you mean?"

We stood in the doorway of the parlor now, and I saw that Skye had already ushered Detective Brenton's partner back out the front door. Though Poe stood behind me, my muscles tensed at the detective's statement.

"A member of the upper echelons was kidnapped, Lady Somerhaven. We can hardly appear not to take that seriously, glad as we all are that you have returned safely."

There wasn't time to think of how best to react. I let my face relax, hoping that dropping the smile would help me appear to take the cityguard's efforts at face value. "I appreciate that. Please keep us abreast of whatever you uncover."

The detective's pale eyebrows raised slightly as she stepped towards the door, which Skye held open for her now. "Of course, my lady. We would be happy to. Good day."

I inclined my head, but only slightly. "Good day, and thank you for coming." I turned before the detective could say another word. "Poe," I called out, injecting as much frivolous cheer into my voice as possible. "Is this what I'm wearing to the lecture?"

Poe matched my tone perfectly, warmth suffusing her answer. "I should think you'll need a coat, love."

I disappeared into the parlor as Poe shut the door behind her, my heart beating wildly. When the detectives had cleared off the front steps and retreated down the street, I spoke. "They weren't Edith's people, then?"

Poe shook her head, her mouth twisting thoughtfully as she made her way out of the parlor and down the back hallway towards the housekeeper's office, where we'd been keeping our coats. "Apparently not."

Skye met us there. "They weren't Edith's and they're not Viridian's either, though they're almost certainly on *someone's* payroll. We have another player in the game."

CHAPTER 21

MINA

The car pulled up, its driver a Strix woman dressed in the Braithwaite crew's signature tweeds. I'd begun to recognize the subtle patterns and textures of tweed that only Herself's people wore. Though I wasn't sure what they signified, it was a useful way to tell them apart from civilians.

Ashbourne was nowhere to be found. I hesitated as Skye handed Poe into the car, then held out her hand for me.

"He'll meet us there," Skye murmured to me when I took her gloved hand. As she said nothing else, I thought it better not to ask further questions.

The sunny autumn morning had clouded over, mist billowing up through the streets, out of the undercity, or rather the forest below the undercity. I glanced up at the skyway, watching the airships peek out of the clouds as they passed by. Seeing the sky at all still felt a bit overwhelming after the oubliette.

As Skye helped me into the car, my joints protested. The stress of the detectives' visit had aggravated me, apparently, and the rest of the day would be difficult as a result. I'd have to be careful not to speak too much at the lecture. The pain always brought my defenses up, and I would be liable to say something unpleasant if provoked.

Skye sat in front with the Strix driver, chatting amiably as they pulled away from the curb. Poe joined in from time to time, saving me from having to speak. The autocar wound up the narrow Pravhna streets, passing into posher neighborhoods than my own, where residences took up whole blocks, garden walls spilling over with explosions of autumn flowers.

When we passed into the university district, the buildings grew larger and more impressive. The mist had not yet reached this echelon, and up so far, the near-perpetual cloud cover was less intense. Up here, everything was brighter, but I was not so foolish as to let the atmosphere take me off guard.

Here, where the most powerful ruled, was where I must be the most careful. Everyone was a suspect now, and it would be foolish to assume anything but that the myriad ulterior motives of Pravhna's ruling classes would be on display. I barely registered the conversation happening around me, wondering instead where Ashbourne had gotten off to.

He was still a mystery to me, his mere presence a distraction. I had never been prone to flights of fancy when it came to romance, though I felt attraction for many. Early years of crushing social rejection had stopped me from believing I had a romantic future. Maman certainly had not made plans for me, focusing all her attention on Helene.

My sister hadn't cared for Viridian Montclair even one tiny whit. She'd been betrothed to him as nothing more than a power move, as most people of our class were. That was something Maman had no experience with. To have heard her tell it, Papa had been the love of her life, his death at sea a tragedy she never fully got over.

Maman and Helene still felt real. Present. Every day at Orchid House, I expected one of them to stalk through the front door or around a familiar corner and scold me. It was difficult to believe either were truly gone—that I'd never see them again. Hard as I'd tried to keep track in the oubliette, time had blurred, even when I'd had an accurate count of days. Being trapped in an unchanging hole, affected by the memory-altering magic, made it feel like I'd seen my family only days ago.

Next to me, Poe laughed at whatever the Strix driver had just said. I shifted uncomfortably as the autocar bounced over an uneven section of cobblestones. The streets were narrower here in the university district, making it harder to avoid rough spots in the road.

"Ack," the driver muttered. "Looks like there's a fair bit of congestion ahead. You'll be late for the lecture, I'm afraid."

Poe craned her neck to see, then pulled her watch from the pocket of her emerald gown. She'd unbuttoned her close-fitting frock coat. "We have a half hour until we need to take our seats."

"We're just two blocks away," I said.

Skye looked over her shoulder, into the back seat. "We ought to be dropped off at the front door, though, for propriety's sake."

I stifled a sigh. Propriety was a damn pain most of the time. Poe grinned though, pointing to the little shop out the window. "Problem solved. We'll get out here."

I leaned forward, trying to see what Poe pointed at. I wasn't familiar with this area of town, but the shop was new. Its sign was freshly painted and read "Armande's" in gold lettering. The driver pulled out of traffic and parked. Skye got out first, then helped Poe and me out. As I stepped out of the car, I saw what had attracted Poe's attention.

The most fashionable set of Oscarovi and Vilhari were crowded inside the shop, all of them sipping frothy concoctions. Behind a massive marble bar, a dozen attendants scooped ice cream into fluted pink glasses, topping it with various sodas, syrups, and whipped creams. Some of the liquid sparkled in glittering swirls, while others changed colors as the glasses were passed to patrons. Stands of over-sized cupcakes towered on shelves behind the bar, and chandeliers dripping with jewels hung from the ceilings. It was no wonder so many were crowded inside. The place was a sugary fantasy come to life.

I scanned the crowd for familiar faces, only to find that I knew most of the people inside.

Many of Viridian and Helene's friends were among the crowd. My heart's pace picked up as we moved towards the door.

"Brace yourself," Poe warned as she took Skye's outstretched arm. "It'll be a viper's nest in there."

That was precisely what I was hoping for. Finally, it was time to confront them. As I trailed behind Skye and Poe, I composed myself.

The ice cream parlor was packed tightly with Oscarovi in ostentatious hats and Vilhari who smelled of hothouses and imported perfume. I bumped into a winged Vilhar, dropping my bag. When I retrieved it, I was separated from Skye and Poe. I took a few steps forward as the crowd shifted. My entire body was abuzz with anticipation as the people who'd made me miserable my entire childhood came into view.

Caralee Ellis-Whitely and Rebecca Smytheson sat around a tall marble-topped wrought iron table, surrounded by sycophants. While this was not the group I suspected of knowing why I ended up in the oubliette, there was no love lost between any of us. I was about to walk over to them, several cutting remarks already playing in my head, when Viridian Montclair appeared in the crowd.

He wore an expertly tailored cerulean jacket, the color of a clear morning in the upper echelons. It stood out amongst the darker jewel tones of the season, a discordant note clanging against a symphony of well-practiced melody. The crowd seemed to contract with my severed breath, my lungs straining to take air in. My joints burned with pain, but I did not close my eyes against my mounting terror. There was nowhere to run, even if I wanted to, which decidedly, I did not.

He saw me at the same moment I saw him, and as we made eye contact a smirk haunted the corners of his lips. His arm slipped around Caralee's slender waist. Her dark brown hair was curled into ringlets, tied back with a saccharine looking pink bow. She gazed up at him adoringly, then followed his line of sight straight to me. Something darkened in Caralee's pale green eyes—an intelligence I would not have expected before the oubliette.

I had underestimated my sister's sometimes-friend, perhaps gravely. The two of them had vacillated between rivals and friends for years, the line between the two almost indistinguishable. Though I felt no protective loyalty towards Helene, something about Viridian's arm snaking around Caralee's waist troubled me.

The move was so obviously calculated. Viridian Montclair did nothing by happenstance, but what did this mean? I was nearly immobilized by the swarm of theories crowding my mind. It was as though my body refused to move until it had a plausible explanation for all of this. I was panicking.

Viridian whispered something to Caralee, then began to move through the crowded ice cream parlor. I took the opportunity to search out Skye and Poe, but they'd disappeared in the crowd. My heart thumped hard, but I steeled myself, refusing to move for Viridian Montclair.

It wasn't as though he could drag me out of here by force. Not even the high Vilhari houses had that kind of power, and House Montclair was a middling echelon at best. Higher than the Wildfangs, but not above reproach, certainly. I spotted a sliver of his ostentatious cerulean coat the moment before he emerged from the crowd in front of me.

"A bit close in here, isn't it?" Viridian said with apparent ease. There wasn't a hint of worry in him. He knew that I knew what he'd done. There was no mistaking it in the smug smile that crept from his mouth alone, straight into his eyes. He leaned into me, his mouth grazing my ear as he kissed both my cheeks, and took my hands in his. "I'm sorry I wasn't able to get to you sooner."

It was an obvious threat, but a cleverly disguised one. I refused to allow myself to give into the fever pitch of fear that blossomed in me like Maman's deadliest flowerbed.

Viridian squeezed my hands so tightly I nearly gasped, caught completely off guard. Why hadn't I expected him to behave exactly this way? Perhaps it was that he'd always seemed a bit off-kilter, like he could never quite find his footing in social situations. As difficult as he was, I'd always felt empathy for his situation.

I had been wrong. Wrong about Caralee. Wrong about Viridian. Wrong about so many things. My hands were clammy in his, but I couldn't yank them away. People were watching. My voice abandoned me, along with all the things I'd planned to say to him. I'd rehearsed dozens of biting remarks, clever things I yearned to say to put him in his place, to force him to understand that I would have vengeance for what he'd done.

And now, the moment had come, and he had the upper hand. His grip on me tightened as he straightened up, looking down on me, his cold eyes imperious. "You should have waited for me in the country, Wilhelmina. There was no need for you to travel alone."

A warm hand spread across the small of my back, and a familiar voice rumbled through me. "There you are, love."

Someone pressed a kiss to the top of my head. I tensed for a brief moment, and then my body came unfrozen. Viridian let go of my hands as Ashbourne pulled me into his side. The feeling of his body against mine was comforting and distressing all at once. "So sorry I'm late. Who's this?"

"Viridian Montclair," I replied, using every effort to keep my voice steady as I leaned into Ashbourne. "Helene's betrothed."

Viridian flushed, and behind him, in the distance, Caralee fumed. So they *were* together now. "We have much to discuss, Wilhelmina. We should go somewhere private."

It was a slight not to introduce himself to Ashbourne, but Viridian wasn't known for his manners. Ashbourne's fingers pressed into my flesh, soothing in their unexpected familiarity. The touch radiated through the base of my spine and deep within the recesses of my body. My confidence returned.

"Do we?" I asked, keeping my voice light and sweet. "I understand you handled things with Somerhaven after the fire. I haven't seen Maman's lawyer yet. Do we have affairs of some sort to settle?"

It was a polite way of implying that I suspected him of asking for money. Around us, the crowd tensed. Among this set, there was nothing more vulgar than to discuss finances.

Viridian flushed again. "Of course not."

My eyes landed on Caralee's right hand ring finger. The smile everyone found so unsettling found its way to my lips without effort. I lowered my voice, but not by much as I locked onto the enormous sapphire ring Caralee wore. The entire crowd followed my gaze. Caralee's face flushed beet red, and her hand disappeared under the table.

"What an interesting choice of engagement rings," I murmured softly, putting the subtlest bit of quivering sadness into my voice. There were a few sympathetic murmurs. Ashbourne's hands pressed gently into my back, encouraging me.

"It is a family ring, Wilhelmina. You know that," Viridian spat. I had him off-kilter now.

"Was she wearing it? When you—when she—" I made a show of burying my face in Ashbourne's chest, his arms going around me immediately.

"Oh, Mina," he murmured, as though he spoke just to me. As though the entire shop wasn't hanging on our every word. "Love, don't cry."

I pressed my face against the hard muscles of his chest, my shoulders shaking with hidden laughter. Around us, people whispered, clearly swallowing my supposed grief whole.

I caught only one comment, but it soared through my thoughts. "Do you think he washed it before he gave it to Caralee?"

That brought another round of laughter on, so much that tears streamed down my face. I composed myself and drew my head away from Ashbourne, looking up into his golden eyes.

There was a glimmer of amusement behind his stony mask. The corner of his mouth twitched slightly. He was enjoying this as much as I was. He drew a handkerchief from his jacket pocket and dabbed at my face.

"Beautiful as ever," he whispered.

There were nearly audible swoons, and one "Who is *he*?" in the crowd. We had to stop. It was tempting to twist the knife further, do more damage to both Caralee and Viridian, but Poe had cautioned me against too many public theatrics. The upper echelons had no trouble turning shows of emotion against the unwitting.

I took a big deep breath, making it obvious I was calming myself before turning to Viridian, though I made eye contact with Caralee. "My apologies. I only miss Helene. All my warmest congratulations to you both."

It was the right thing to do, and I hoped wherever she was in the crowd, Poe was proud. I daren't look for her, though. The rage in Viridian's eyes was like nothing I'd ever seen. Ashbourne's every muscle sprang to life, tensed with readiness. I half expected him to throw me behind him. Viridian's fury was obvious.

"You will regret this," he hissed in a voice so low no one could hear him but Ash and me.

Now, suddenly, he was Ash, not Ashbourne. Something had shifted between us, the alteration both imperceptible and monumental at the same time. As if he read my mind, Ash pulled me tighter into his body, his arm snaking around my waist in such an intimate way the world nearly fell away. My breath stopped in my lungs, fluttering like a wet, newborn thing.

"Use caution, friend," Ashbourne warned, using the same low tone. "People are watching."

The ice cream parlor was silent now, everyone openly hanging on the drama of every breath that passed between us.

"Just who do you think you are?" Viridian sneered. "Have you even a House, Vilhar?"

It was an insult amongst the Vilhari to suggest they had no lineage, but Ash did not so much as react. He only smiled. I enjoyed the way my diabolical smile made others uncomfortable, but this—this was something else. The finely planed angles of Ash's rugged face smoothed into something stately, cold, and deadly all at once.

A marble hallway lined with statues, the smell of cypress trees and bergamot carried on a hot breeze, flashed in my mind. It was only a moment, but I was transported to somewhere else. I tried to grasp onto the memory, emblazon it onto my conscious mind so I wouldn't forget—and then I was thrown back into the present moment, as though I never left.

Movement in the crowd stopped Ash from answering as Elspeth Aestra strode forward. Viridian's face smoothed into something more pleasant almost instantly as Skye's mother, revered surgeon and pillar of Vilhari society, placed a hand on Ashbourne's arm.

"Darling," she crooned, in a vibrant, musical voice. "Wherever is my daughter?"

Near the till, the sound of someone clearing their throat caused everyone to turn their heads. "Right here, Mother."

"Perfection," Elspeth remarked as she took my arm. "We must be on our way, I'm afraid, Viridian. Tell your mother I said hello when next you write to her."

Viridian bowed, retreating in a huff. Conversations started again. Elspeth's grip on my arm was too tight as she guided me towards the door. In the crowd, I saw Skye and Poe making their way in the same direction.

"It is good to see you, Wilhelmina," Elspeth said as she dragged me through the crowd. "We will be late for luncheon if you do not hurry, though."

I opened my mouth to explain that we were going to the lecture, but Elspeth Aestra's face was so stern I dared not speak. Outside the ice cream parlor, a grand white Studevale stood idling. It was the most beautiful autocar I had ever seen. A tall Vilhari with the wings of a red-tailed hawk stood waiting next to it.

Skye and Poe hurried out of Armande's after us. "What are you doing here?" Skye whispered.

"Get in the car, dearest," Elspeth said again, speaking at a normal volume. She laughed as though wrangling an unruly child, as she kissed her daughter's cheeks. "It seems you've forgotten our luncheon engagement today."

Skye raised an eyebrow. "My apologies, Mother."

Elspeth's eyes slid to Poe. "Mlle Endymion, how lovely to see you. Please, do join us."

Poe made the tiniest little bow, a show of reverence for Mme Aestra's high rank. "Thank you, your grace."

There was a twinkle in the surgeon's eye that I liked, but Skye practically glowered as we got into the back of the autocar. It was a crowded fit, with me squeezed between Ashbourne and Poe, Skye and her mother sitting opposite us.

When the driver pulled away from the curb, Elspeth's smile faded. "Niall is missing."

CHAPTER 22

ASHBOURNE

Skye flounced back on the bright white leather upholstery of the Studevale, rolling her eyes. She was the picture of teenage angst, and it struck a protective note in me. My partner so rarely appeared young or vulnerable, but she had reverted to some childlike state in her parent's presence, and it brought worry upon me. There was much left unresolved between them, and being drawn suddenly back into family business would not help the situation. Skye was bound to be upset, even if her mother's arrival had rescued us from what was about to be an uncomfortable standoff in the ice cream parlor.

"Mother, *please*," Skye whined. "Niall's off somewhere with his cronies, like always."

"He is not," Elspeth said with crisp surety. "He went missing shortly after he visited Orchid House. I've had him tailed for some time, but my man lost him." She glared at the driver, who glanced apologetically in the rearview mirror.

Skye sat back, her expression melting from incredulous to professional. I'd seen that look hundreds of times—it always meant there was a development in a case, that the knots Skye was unraveling were making sense to her at long last. "Why did you have Niall followed?"

Elspeth Aestra's silvery-blue eyes filled with tears. Tears that, I was certain, were at least partially manufactured. From everything

Skye had ever told me, Elspeth was too controlled to cry in front of strangers unless she wanted to—and she thought it was to her advantage. "I made a mistake, my darling. You were right, I should have stopped Niall from joining the cityguard."

Apparently, Skye agreed with me about Elspeth's demeanor. "Oh, cut the tears, Mother. It's not necessary. I agree that Niall being missing is important." She locked eyes with me, a question there.

I knew instantly what she needed. We'd developed an unspoken shorthand in the past year. "We'll look into your son's disappearance, Madame."

Next to me, Mina shifted a tiny bit to look at Poe, who cleverly had no reaction at all. Even the slightest movement of Mina's body set mine alight. I was far too attuned to her, but Viridian's confrontation had awakened something within me I couldn't deny much longer. The closer we got, the more danger she was in.

To stay clear, I'd need to untangle what made her so alluring, but Mina was difficult for me to understand. It was a mistake to think she was innocent. Mina was as mercurial as Poe, changing as needed to fit the scene she was cast in. However, unlike Poe, whose resilience appeared to spring from an endless well, Mina tired of any ruse quickly, her base nature overriding whatever part she was playing.

I had to wonder if that was part of the attraction. Where I'd tamped every bit of me I didn't want to confront down, she was still free, still wild in a way I couldn't quite identify. Privately, I thought our strategy should be to play into that. Whatever lay beneath the veneer of sweet society ingénue ought to be let out. Every time her lips curled into that terrifying little smile, heat lashed through me. I wanted to see more of that, more of her strength—whether for my own selfish reasons, or that of the mission, I couldn't yet say.

I was so lost in thinking about Mina, I'd failed to track the conversation Skye and her mother were having. Things had grown heated in my inattentive moments. "I don't know what you want me to do, Mother," Skye sighed. "I'm working on an important case, and I can't just drop everything to look for Niall."

"I know what you're working on," Elspeth said, her voice barely louder than a whisper.

Next to me, Mina shivered slightly, her eyes drifting to mine sidelong. *Do not become so distracted you fail to protect her*, a voice inside me cautioned.

"A small group of us has been tracking the movements of this 'Chopard' for some time," Elspeth said, smoothing an invisible wrinkle from the skirt of her directoire-style gown.

Skye sat forward as the car slowed to a halt. We'd stopped in front of a rather nice hotel, The Palais. Nice for people like me and Skye, but for people like Elspeth, practically invisible in the scheme of things. It was neither fashionable, nor run down. It was indistinct, the perfect place for a clandestine meeting. Despite how people often behaved in the mysteries I'd read, places like this were far better for secret goings-on than seedy back alleyways and places of ill repute.

"We've connected Chopard's movements to Wilhelmina's return," Elspeth said. Mina sat forward, Poe went on high alert, and Skye gritted her teeth with obvious frustration.

"How?" Skye demanded.

"Yes," Mina added, her voice deadly soft as Elspeth's. "I'd like to know the same thing."

Elspeth shook her head. "We do not have time for this now. The four of you have an appointment with Muse."

That explained how they'd connected Chopard to Mina. Whoever Elspeth was working with, they must be doing something the seer agreed with. Muse didn't work with cratties, unless he had a very good reason. Skye had always trusted Muse, which was good enough for me.

Fury brought color to Skye's cheeks, though I saw a flicker of relief in her eyes at the mention of Muse's name. Like me, she'd already reasoned that if Muse was willing to help then her mother likely wasn't up to something evil. Though perhaps Skye already assumed that. I hadn't even the barest hint of memory or feelings about my own parents and thus had trouble empathizing. I tensed in her defense, but she didn't need my aid. "If you think I'm going to simply go along with whatever you say without question—"

Elspeth leaned toward her daughter, taking her hands. "Skyeling, I would never assume something so foolish. You've had a mind of your own since the moment you drew breath. Don't you see, my darling? You can move in places I cannot. House Aestra needs you more than ever." It surprised me to hear the sincerity in Elspeth's voice, and I was not so jaded as to immediately suspect her of manipulation.

Perhaps that would be a mistake in any other circumstance, but I knew the kind of loyalty Skye inspired. That had to come from somewhere, and I suspected it came from the kernel of decency I detected in Elspeth Aestra. "I know you think I've been irresponsible with your brother, my politics, and probably hundreds of other things. But if you've ever trusted my heart, please know I want the things you want. I want to see things get better, rather than worse."

Everyone in the car hung on Elspeth's words, waiting to hear how Skye would react, myself included. I would go any direction she chose, follow her down any path she picked out. After what felt like millennia, she nodded once. "Our methods will never be the same, but I believe that much. Shall I ask for Grandmother at the front desk then?"

"No need," Elspeth said with an expression that bore lines of relief. "We chose The Palais because it has private tea rooms."

That phrase seemed to mean something to Skye, who nodded, resigned somehow. What was that about?

Poe too seemed to pick up on what I had, though I couldn't discern from her vague expression what reaction she was having, and then her face changed. The nick of understanding morphed into an earnest smile. "I see where you get your confidence from," she said, looking first at Elspeth, then to my partner. Pleasure shone in Poe's eyes as she gazed at Skye. For a short moment, I wondered if the world would stop turning, just for them.

A little smile crept onto Elspeth Aestra's face as she looked between her daughter and the tiny fey woman opposite her. She suspected what the rest of us did then: the two of them were in love. My chest tightened with emotion at the prospect of Skye's happiness. There was nothing I wanted more than for her to be loved and cared for in every way she could have it.

"Muse and your grandmother both are in the Opal Tearoom. Tell the concierge," Elspeth commanded.

"You're not coming?" Mina asked.

Elspeth shook her head. "No, I have another engagement I must get to. I will call on you, though, later this week. As my daughter is residing with you, it would be strange if I did not."

Rubbish, I thought to myself. She's been shunning Skye for months. This was apparently our signal to leave the autocar though. Skye nodded and got out, helping Poe as she went. I followed suit and helped Mina onto the brick sidewalk in front of the Palais' front gates.

"She's giving us a gift," Poe murmured to Mina as they linked arms. "Her calling on you will open the upper echelons to us."

Mina nodded, obviously understanding what this would mean. Her family name certainly had status, but not like that of House Aestra, which rubbed elbows with the old aristocracy, the last of the Vilhari high courts. Rumor had it in the undercity that House Aestra had been consul to the Court of Aether's queen. Elspeth Aestra was granddaughter to the second-in-command on the Avalonne, the ship that brought the Vilhari to Sirin. Turning the information over in my mind brought up the uncomfortable feeling that always arose when I had cause to think of the Vilhari's history. It should feel like *my* history, the proud history of my people, but more than ever, it did not.

As I followed the women into The Palais, my gut twisted into knots. I had never allowed Muse to read me. I didn't want to know who I was before, or what I was looking for. My steps faltered, my body hesitating. Skye cast a look over her shoulder, immediately knowing I'd fallen behind. Her mouth opened to speak, but soft fur brushed my pant leg.

Morpheus materialized fully, finally deciding to join us. He said nothing, as was his way, but his bulk against my leg was a comfort. There was a plea in Skye's eyes I could not ignore. She needed me, not just to come with her now, but to stay the course and keep my promises to both her and Morpheus. Those promises spoken and unspoken were a comforting weight on my heart, the core of what kept me grounded. My feet moved quickly once more, as long strides caught me up to my friends.

I will not turn away now, I promised myself. *This is my family.*

CHAPTER 23

MINA

Behind us, I felt it deep in my sense of spatial awareness when Ashbourne paused. I nearly turned, but Poe's pace did not slow. She didn't have the same sense for her surroundings that I did, nor the odd connection I'd formed with Ashbourne. *Why was he hesitating? What worried him?*

I longed to turn and ask him, but I kept stride with Poe. Skye fell a half step behind us as Poe greeted the Oscarovi who manned the doors. When Ashbourne's footsteps renewed, relief fluttered in my chest. I shook my head to clear it, focusing instead on the lobby of the hotel. It was modestly but tastefully decorated. Dark wood paneling on the walls echoed the coffered ceilings, which dripped with crystal chandeliers.

An enormous marble podium served as a front desk, and the concierge looked up as we approached. The chestnut-haired Vilhari was dressed in a serviceable gray wool pantsuit, tailored to the generous curves of her body. Her brown skin shone with either well-applied cosmetics or good humor. Perhaps she was simply talented with glamour. Whatever it was, it had a nice effect that I wouldn't mind learning.

"Mlle Aestra," she said in greeting. "Your grandmother awaits you in the Opal Room. Do you know the way?"

Skye nodded. "I do, thank you."

This was a place of discretion then, no unnecessary pomp and circumstance. Of course, I knew there were a handful of places like this all over the city, bland enough to never catch anyone's attention, but clean and discreet. Maman had used such establishments frequently in the last years of her life, but I never knew what she was up to.

Poe squeezed my arm, as though to confirm my previous thoughts. Elspeth Aestra was intimidating, but very good at whatever she was playing at. *No, not playing*, I thought. Whatever the head of House Aestra was up to, it was nothing so inexpert as playing.

Skye led us down a narrow hallway behind the front desk. Tall, heavy doors were staggered on both sides of the hall, each with a gold placard next to the door naming the room. No sound emanated from any of the doors, but vaguely, I sensed occupants in many of the rooms we passed. There was a heaviness in the air I could not identify, as though gravity were different here. I had the heady sense for a moment that I could feel the earth beneath the hotel, pregnant with some massive power, vibrating beneath the surface.

Tempted as I was to dismiss this as foolishness, I was learning to trust my gut more. These impressions rarely led me astray, so long as I kept an open mind about what they might mean. I glanced back at Ashbourne, who appeared to note something in the atmosphere, as I did. His eyes lingered at the door of a room labeled, "The Emerald Room."

"The sound-proofing spells are excellent," he murmured as I fell back to walk alongside him. It was almost a reflex now, and not just because it was obvious that Poe and Skye wanted a moment alone.

Our performance in the ice cream parlor had shifted things between us. While I knew he was playing a part we'd agreed to, there was no ruse to it. We hadn't agreed to act as though there were a romantic relationship between us. The way he'd acted, not to mention the way I'd responded—the way my body had responded— there was no doubt in my mind that was real. I wanted him, and there seemed very few reasons not to indulge if he wanted me as well.

Would it be a distraction? Possibly, but also, I was wise enough to know that if I did not inject a bit of pleasure into my life, my senses might deaden from stress. Yes, to keep sharp, it might be just the thing to let Ashbourne in a bit more. It was more than that, and I knew it, but it helped to tell myself that a bit of physical release was all I sought.

Poe and Skye murmured to one another as they fell in step. The hallway felt endless, and my legs ached with the effort of walking, even on a flat surface. I'd slowed down considerably, but Ashbourne matched my pace. The way he moved when I did, as though in perfect choreography, brought heat to my belly, gathering in my core. What would it be like to be alone together? To move this way, in perfect call and response to one another, in bed? The possibilities were tantalizing, cutting through the pain I was in.

The toe of my boot caught on the carpeted floor. I barely stumbled, righting myself easily, but the jolt sent pain lashing through my joints. He didn't offer his arm, or even look askance at me, but his body oriented towards mine, ready to catch me.

"I will not fall," I said, my tone curt. It felt as though he'd read my mind, the images of all the ways we might please one another dancing in my head as I considered allowing myself respite from all this pain. "There is no need to prepare yourself for a swoon."

A smirk lifted a corner of his lips. "I shouldn't think so. *You* would never swoon."

The tone of his remark was familiar, as though he knew me well. *Had our short time together been enough for such familiarity?* To my surprise, my lips quirked in reflection. "I would not."

"But you are in pain," he added, his voice even and deep, without a hint of condescension.

"Yes," I admitted. There was no use in denying it.

Ahead of us, Skye and Poe rounded a corner at a divide in the hallway. Try as I might, I could not hurry my steps. I'd done too much the past few days, and the increased activity was catching up with me.

"They will wait for us," Ashbourne reassured me.

There was a glimmer in his eyes, an expression that seemed reserved for me. His eyes didn't light in the same way for Skye or Poe. His actions and countenance let me know he cared for Skye and

Morpheus, rather deeply, in fact. But between us there was something else—something deeper than the heat that gathered between my legs—something that keened and growled just beyond the surface of my conscious mind.

Ash has a talent for making people feel safe, Morpheus said as he materialized near my feet. *But he rarely uses it.*

I couldn't respond, the greymalkin's observation nearly stopping me in place. *Was that what this was?* We rounded the corner to find Skye and Poe waiting for us, just like Ashbourne had said they would. They stood in front of a plaque that read "The Opal Room." Skye nodded as we caught up to them and then knocked.

The door swung open under her touch, revealing a staircase cut from opal, its pale fire revealed by the aetheric glow from ornate gold wall sconces. The walls were gilded as well, a sharp contrast to the more sedate appearance of the hotel.

Ashbourne shared a meaningful glance with Skye who nodded once. "This is part of things here. Each 'tea room' is set up this way. You'll see why."

Not even a hint of surprise crossed Poe's face. She was cool as ever. Had she been here before? I wouldn't put that past her. There was so much about her I still didn't know, and she held information close. At the very least, if she knew what to expect, then we were unlikely to be walking into an ambush or other trouble.

There is nothing to worry about, I told myself. Until I looked down at the staircase. My jaw clenched, frustration mounting. *Why must things always be so difficult?*

The stairs were polished to a high sheen. They would be slippery. The soles of my pretty boots were not built for my stability, and sharp pain already shot through my feet. I had no doubt that someone would catch me, should I fall, but the embarrassment of such an occurrence was more than I could comprehend at the moment.

Poe had already followed Skye downward, their soft conversation drifting up to me, though it was muffled as they descended the staircase. Morpheus, as usual, had already disappeared. Ashbourne waited for me though, watching me hesitate with brows furrowed. He glanced down at the slick staircase, then at my shoes. His arms stretched out towards me, an offer of help.

I opened my mouth to protest, but he shook his head, his eyes soft as his fingers stretched towards mine. I took one step down and my knees wobbled. The steps were too much for my terrible balance. Ash took another step back up the stairs. He was as steady as could be. There wasn't a hint of pity in him, only the silent promise that I would get down the stairs without injury or embarrassment.

He lifted me, turning without even so much as a quiver in his muscles. I expected another of those wicked smirks of his, as though he'd won something. But I was surprised. Ash's face was calm, concentrated even. This was not a seduction, or a game to determine which of us had the most power. It was a simple offer of help. He was strong and steady enough to carry me, and I was unable to descend the slick stairs without trouble.

This was kindness, I realized. A kind of protectiveness I wasn't used to. The kind that sought to shield from harm, rather than control. I was glad then that I did not have to walk on my own because the thought of such generosity of spirit was dizzying.

He'd carried me before. This time, I was fully present, and able to feel the increased pace of his heart, thumping against my hand, which was pressed to his chest. My cheeks burned with the sensation of being so closely perceived. In response, I tucked my chin to my chest and closed my eyes, grateful for the assistance, but fighting shame for needing it.

Near the bottom of the stairs, Ashbourne turned, setting me down slowly so that I wouldn't slip. Immediately, I was sure I would have fallen had I attempted to go it alone. My feet ached too much as I stepped down, taking his outstretched hand for stability, the joints in my knees and hips burning.

When my boots touched the rough stone at the bottom of the staircase, my knees buckled, catapulting me into Ashbourne's hard chest. He righted me without so much as a word, his breath hitching as his fingers closed around my waist. So he wasn't so unaffected by my presence. I looked up as he pulled me against him, heat pooling first in my chest, then sinking lower and lower still as his eyes dilated.

"Are you steady?" he asked.

"No," I answered honestly, but it had nothing to do with the pain rushing through me, swirling amongst the blaze of desire lit within my core.

Ashbourne swallowed hard. "Nor am I."

His head dipped slightly, and my lips parted as though by instinct, my back arching into him as one of his arms snaked around my waist, pinning me to him. My breath came in sharp gasps as his hand rose toward my cheek, his thumb grazing my jawline. His face was so ruggedly handsome it was almost painful to look at, as though carved from the finest marble. Even now, he didn't smile, though his lips curved, sensuous in a way that did nothing to cool the flames of desire licking at every sensitive nerve in my body.

Steps brought us both back to the moment, and Ash's grip on me slowly loosened. "You are a beautiful distraction," he murmured as Skye came into view behind him.

"Everything all right?" she asked, her voice a little too bright, eyes sparkling with the light of someone who knows a delicious secret.

"Quite," I answered, my voice high and shrill.

Skye hid a smile as she turned. "This way."

As we followed, my eyes adjusted to the dim light. The sound of water falling filled my ears. It was not a trickle, nor a burbling stream, but the sound of a rushing waterfall. The stone beneath my feet was rough, and though the walls surrounding us were smooth, I could see they'd been carved into rock.

"Are we underground?" I murmured, half to myself. The path was lit by lavender bioluminescent lichen and fungi from below, and some kind of glowworm from above.

"Yes," Skye whispered back, her voice reverent in the dark. "This place is special."

It was indeed. The path widened into a garden that opened up onto a terrace made from a pale white stone. On each side of the terrace, intricately carved arched doorways flanked the common space. Beyond the terrace, graceful skyways crossed the cavern, carved in similar patterns. Lush plant life sprung from window boxes and common spaces alike, scenting the humid cavern with petrichor and perfume.

From somewhere deep inside the cavern came a dim glow of some artificial light, though aetheric power did not fuel it. There was no telltale hum of the aether, only the quiet sounds of water and faraway music. On some terrace I couldn't make out, someone played a harp quite expertly.

We were not alone.

There was an entire city here, underneath the hotel. The architecture was familiar to me, similar to what the high echelons of Vilhari society preferred, but much more intricate. Witchlight lanterns glowed with soft golden light from within the buildings—and in the distance, I could make out a few dark figures, here and there. This place was far from abandoned.

"What is this?" Ashbourne breathed.

Skye smiled. "The wreck of the Avalonne."

I frowned. "How is that possible? This is a city."

"*Part* of a city. The rest of the ship was destroyed in the crash." Skye's eyes widened with sadness as she gestured towards what was left. "This is how my people traveled the stars."

I had seen models of the Avalonne, renderings of what the great ship the Vilhari arrived in four thousand years ago might have looked like. They were nothing like this. Nothing even close to this scale, magnitude, or beauty.

A sliver of unnerving realization skittered up my spine. If this city was only part of the ship the Vilhari had traveled in, the Oscarovi were lucky that they had not wanted to crush us, but only live together in relative peace. When the Ventyr came to conquer Sirin, all that changed. We saw the power the Vilhari had, and we had to adapt.

A shadow of memory danced at the edges of my mind, teasing me. I walked to the edge of the terrace, resting against a stone balustrade so I could crane my neck downward. Waterfalls spilled through arched stone ducts that looked to be made specifically for such use. The memory eluded me, refusing to emerge, but something about this place made whatever came before the fetch feel closer—more tangible.

I chased my thoughts backward, as Ashbourne spoke about the ship with Poe and Skye—back to the Ventyr—another race of winged people, though very different from the Vilhari in many ways. Papa had been a scholar of their ways, studying the stories they left behind after their invasion, until his death. I'd learned much about them as a child, from his books in Orchid House, and now my mind wandered, wondering what that had to do with me.

But it was no use—the memory slipped out of my grip, leaving only the spectacular view of the Avalonne. The impression that I'd almost touched an answer to all that was missing lingered, bitter in my mouth.

"Come," Skye said, touching my arm lightly. "My family's quarters are this way."

CHAPTER 24

MINA

House Aestra's "quarters" were nothing short of a small mansion. Inside, the structure was made of the same white stone as the rest of the city. Furnishings were sparse, but spare in nature, a contrast to the intricately carved stone.

Skye led us to a curved room that looked to be positioned directly under the spillway of an enormous waterfall. The water roared softly behind an invisible barrier. No stray droplets marred the floors under the arched windows that looked out onto the waterfall and the Avalonne. The walls on the opposite end of the room were covered in various mosses and lichens, some glowing softly in the dim light of the room.

Golden orbs danced just below the domed ceiling, which was painted to look like the night sky. The constellations surprised me— they were none I was familiar with. An enormous round table, cut from the same stone as the city itself, sat centered beneath the dome. Two tall figures sat across from one another amongst the many chairs. Skye pulled out a chair for Poe and she sat. Ashbourne held another out for me, and I sunk into it, grateful to finally be off my feet.

On one side of the table sat Mirabelle Aestra, the head of House Aestra and Skye's grandmother. Though we'd never been formally introduced, she was familiar to me. As the head of one of the high houses of Pravhna's elite Vilhari, everyone knew her. Mirabelle's shining white hair hung long down the back of her midnight blue gown. Her skin was the same moonstone-pale as Skye and Elspeth's, and she was rail-thin, like Elspeth.

There were fine lines around her eyes, the only sign that she was aging. And yet, I knew she was nearly four thousand years old. She was born here on Sirin, shortly after the Avalonne's demise. The sheer length of her life was astounding. Oscarovi could live to be a thousand, but it was rare, and we were mere husks of people by that age. I swallowed hard, wondering what the longevity of the fetch would be like.

"Welcome to Avalonne," Mirabelle said as we settled into our seats. "Are you all acquainted with Muse?"

The others nodded, but I had never met the man sitting across from Mirabelle Aestra. He was tall, dressed in crisp white shirtsleeves and a dove gray waistcoat that matched his well-tailored pants and the frock coat that hung on the back of his chair. A sparkle of cosmetics on his rich brown skin caught the witchlight, his tawny eyes shining mischievously at the sight of us. He was a head taller than me, even seated. His arms and shoulders were heavily muscled, and his waistcoat fit his soft middle perfectly. Muse's ebony locs were braided in a thick multi-strand plait that hung down his back, showing his arched ears.

"Hello," he greeted us, then nodded once to Mirabelle as he rose from his chair, walking towards the arched end of the room, near the windows that looked out on the waterfall. As he went, his footsteps grew softer; the closer he went to the waterfall, the less I heard.

"Skye, would you go first?" Mirabelle asked. "While I explain things to your friends."

Skye bowed her head, then got up from her chair and joined Muse by the windows. When she joined him, I could see their mouths moving, but no sound reached me. Something at that end of the room silenced all conversation.

Mirabelle smiled, a serene expression, but severe as well. When she spoke, her words seemed directed at Poe. "What do you know of the Court of Winds?"

Poe's face did not move a muscle. "Only that the Courts were a part of the old world, but not this one."

Mirabelle's smile was practically feral now. *What was this about?* "Come now, Hippolyta."

A snarl so vicious it startled me came out of Poe. She stood, tiny and imperious. "What is the meaning of this?"

At the other end of the room, Muse held Skye's hands in his, their faces calm, eyes closed in concentration. The contrast between the two scenes at play simultaneously was jarring. Something about this was wrong—my heart beat faster, empyrae flaring to life within me, in defense of my friend. Under the table, a hand curled around my knee, warm and firm. I glanced at Ashbourne, whose face was stone, but his eyes burned. The message was clear: *stay put.*

"Don't worry, little Strider," Mirabelle said. "Your secret is safe with me. Not even my daughter knows."

I didn't have to know what Mirabelle was talking about to know she was threatening Poe. Fury rose in my heart, gripping me like a vise. My fists clenched as Ashbourne's grip on my knee tightened, sending a pulse of warmth straight into the apex of my thighs.

This was no time to imagine that hand creeping higher—and yet… *What would it be like to have Ashbourne's fingers on my bare skin?* My mind wandered, merciless in its imagination. In the very real present, his palm moved, inching upwards by only a fraction of an inch, but my breath hitched slightly.

Heat pulsed in my core, all my focus on where I wanted his hand. My eyes slid to his face, where the faintest curve of a smirk played on his wicked lips. It did me no good to see it, for then my imagination went wild with what it might feel like to have his mouth on me. He was distracting me—he'd felt my power flare to life—*but how?*

In my second sight, a vision flashed—*a dark head, buried between my thighs. Cries of pure ecstasy tumbling from my lips as my fingers gripped the hair of that head, pressing fangs deeper into my flesh.* The vision broke, my eyes swiveling to Ashbourne's face. Though his expression had not changed, something in his eyes shifted, desire replaced with fear.

I flinched away from his touch, his hand retreating. His fear at whatever had passed between us infected me. So much so that I didn't notice when he left, and that Skye was back in her seat. Time moved strangely, and the vision played over in my head, getting blurrier each time I tried to remember it, as though a barrier had been erected in my mind. It was like I'd gotten too close to something, and now it retreated from me with unsettling speed.

Muse approached the table, leaving Ashbourne by the windows. "Poe," he said, nodding. "Has anything changed since last we met?"

Poe shook her head. "It has not." She offered her hand to him, and he took it, closing his eyes for a moment. When he opened them, his mouth turned down slightly. "I am sorry, love."

Her chin wavered only slightly, then clenched. "I expected as much." She turned to Mirabelle. "What do you hope to accomplish with all of this?"

Ashbourne stepped towards the table, but did not sit down again, avoiding my eyes, locking his gaze firmly upon Mirabelle. This told me that while he trusted Muse, he did *not* trust Mirabelle Aestra. Skye's ears pinked at the tips, as though she were embarrassed not to have been the one to ask such an important question.

Mirabelle sat straight in her seat, her serenity unwavering. "We merely want more information about the connection between Wilhelmina's sudden reappearance, Chopard's actions, and Niall's disappearance."

"For what purpose?" I asked.

Mirabelle's silver gaze turned on me. "That is not your purview."

Poe stood. "But it is *mine*, Mirabelle Aestra. You have no right to deny my claim to the information Mina asked for."

The sharp breath from Skye's direction had both my and Ash's attention. The former Chevalier stared at Poe in awe, though I could not immediately discern what had elicited such a reaction. It was clear that she'd violated some kind of hierarchical nonsense the Vilhari cared about, but I couldn't immediately determine what it had been.

Mirabelle scowled in response, at first. The sour expression turned, though, shifting into a smile that sent chills through me. "You only have to command me."

Poe stretched to her full height, which was not tall in inches, but imposing in other ways. Her eyes fell half-shut in a regal glare, the set of her shoulders squaring as her spine lengthened. Aether swirled around her fingers, staining them a dark, midnight blue, her nails curving into wicked talons. "House Aestra, you are held to account by your superior. The Court of Winds shall report now to the Court of Aether."

"The lost court?" Skye whispered, her eyes widening further.

Though the Oscarovi didn't care much about the Vilhari's unnecessarily detailed ancient lore, the lost court was the stuff of legends. We grew up with "lost heir" imposters running rampant in Pravhna—Vilhari claiming to be the long lost ancestor of the missing Aethereal princess were a constant source of news. They were all charlatans, of course, trying to seize power in the highest echelons. Their downfall was as much a source of interest as their arrival.

Mirabelle's voice lowered with obvious pleasure at the hush that had fallen over the room. "Name your rank, child, and I shall comply."

Skye's eyes had gone so wide and her skin so gray that Ashbourne came to stand behind her. Morpheus appeared, lounging at the center of the table. While I did not quite follow what was happening, it was obvious this was an important moment. Poe was utterly magnificent, raptorial and fierce.

"You know that as heir to the Court of Aether, which no longer has a representative on Sirin, that my rank is meaningless, Mirabelle," Poe pleaded, glancing at Skye, then myself.

"Say it," Mirabelle hissed. "If you want the information, declare yourself."

The command ignited the indignance I'd seen in Poe before. "It is not yours to command me, Mirabelle Aestra. Henceforth, you shall refer to me only as YRH, Lady Endymion, or simply by Poe." Poe paused for effect, before unleashing one last command. "Call me *child* again, and you'll find out why my rank surpasses your own."

YRH? I asked Morpheus. The greymalkin obviously understood what was happening.

The cat's long fluffy tail swished twice in agitation, but he answered me. *Your Royal Highness. Hippolyta is the lost heir to the Court of Aether, the Strider Princess. Her great, great grandmother was on the Avalonne as an ambassador when it crashed.*

Poe was the *real* lost heir. Immediately, my mind began to twist and turn, pulling various threads, connecting and reconnecting them as the new information changed the pattern. I spun through the little I knew of the old fey courts of Vilhar, what had been on the worlds they left behind when exploring the cosmos in their great ships. I only knew the basics: Vilhar had six elemental courts, four terrestrial, and two celestial. Aether was one of the ruling courts, the Court of Starfire its only equal. The Avalonne had been populated mostly with representatives of the Court of Winds, but an Aethereal princess had been aboard as well, with a portion of her retinue. If Poe was the lost heir, that changed so much.

A pit formed in my stomach. *What was she doing helping me?* Poe didn't need access to society at all. If she'd wanted it, she could be a member of the highest echelons. She would *be* the highest echelon. The look she bestowed on me was one of remorse, and a promise to tell me everything later. I tried to take it at face value, but a seed of doubt once sown cannot be easily dislodged.

Mirabelle had laughter in her voice when she answered. "Certainly, YRH." Poe glared at her, and the laughter died, but slowly. "We believe there to be a connection between these events. They all bear a similar weight, according to the sybil at Orrery."

Some thread in the pattern I was trying to form thrummed as Mirabelle spoke, its vibration discordant. Quickly, I tried to locate it inside my mind, but it quieted, fading from notice almost as soon as my attention turned to it.

"And my people?" Poe asked. "Does their location bear weight as well?"

"We don't know yet," Muse said, placing a hand on Poe's arm. "Though there was no change when I read you, that means nothing until I read Wilhelmina."

Unlike when Mirabelle had spoken, the pattern was silent as Muse spoke. That much made sense, at least. I had wondered if he was one of the sirens' children, and now I was sure. Sirens existed almost completely in harmony with Fate and rarely disturbed events —unless they were meant to—and they could not lie or deceive. Something in the nature of that thought pulled at my memory, but like the discordant thread of a few moments ago, it disappeared.

It was obvious now that Muse was one of the siren's children, though he was a rare genetic anomaly that appeared as a bipedal humanoid. They often acted as inconspicuous ambassadors for the High Aerie, and if the sybil at Orrery was involved, then Muse was likely one of her progeny. The threads connecting everything tightened further. Soon, a bigger picture would form.

"How do you know that?" Ash asked.

Muse stared at him for a long moment, his eyebrows raising slightly. "Because I've read the rest of you, and I *know*."

Ash looked away quickly, his eyes falling to the floor. "I see."

I pushed my chair back, standing. "You may read me next."

Poe was looking for her people, her family, folk she obviously loved, and who loved her back. If *that* was what she was seeking, I understood her secrecy. Though our motivations for learning more about our families were very different, if I could change the course of things for her, it would be worth the risk.

Muse nodded, and beckoned me towards the windows. I followed him, the feeling that someone had wrapped a blanket around my head increasing as we neared the windows. I still could not hear the waterfall outside, but neither could I hear the conversation going on at the table.

"You see things as well, don't you?" Muse asked as he stared out the windows at the falling water. He did not move to take my hands, as he had the others.

"I have been having visions," I explained. "But only for a little while."

"Even so," he said softly, "I cannot read another seer."

"I'm no seer," I scoffed, moving to stand next to him, our shoulders nearly touching.

"Anyone with visions is a seer."

I sighed. There was no need to hide the truth from Muse. He would be able to tell what I was as soon as I took his hands. "They're less visions, and more memories. Suppressed memories. I was in an oubliette for nearly a year, and this body is not my own. I remember nothing about my life before."

Muse turned to face me. "A fetch? That makes more sense. I will not be able to read you at all then. But I *can* help." He opened his hands in offering.

I moved slowly, placing my hands in his. "What do I have to do?"

"Just close your eyes," Muse said. "If there is anything on the surface of your mind that might help you understand what's happened to you, I should be able to retrieve it."

I stared at him for a long moment.

"I will not be able to see what you do. Whatever your secrets are, they will be safe from the others, and I will not tell them about the fetch, so you need not worry about that."

My eyes fell closed as Muse's fingers closed around my hands. Warmth flowed through me, comforting and calm. Time slipped out of forward motion, loosening its grip on me as I shifted between, into the limen's dark heart, and through to elsewhere. Out of time, out of this reality, I found myself at the edge of a rocky cliff, a slate blue sea stretching out before me.

The redhead from my previous vision walked ahead of me, obviously older now, and dressed strangely. She spoke to a similarly dressed, tall woman with short dark hair and golden brown skin. I looked down at my hands, which were incorporeal. Their conversation was faraway, but I could just make out the sound of their voices.

"...after Okairos, you must find my sister. She will need your help as well."

I couldn't hear the other woman's answer, but the red-haired woman locked eyes with me, as though she could see me.

"Open the door, Lumina. Free Sirin and I will come to your aid."

The voice echoed in my mind as the vision blurred. Now, I was immobile on a table, trapped in my body, my corporeal eyes frozen open as two dark, winged figures I could not make out moved above me.

"Work quickly, Penthe—we haven't much time."

"The curse is complete, but the loophole... It won't work. She doesn't love him."

"It will work precisely because she does not. It is what makes it the right *loophole."*

"That makes no sense."

"She is still young, Penthe, and under her father's influence. Away from it, her capacity will be greater than you know. She's the one we've waited for."

"The first of Alcyone's three?"

"Yes. Tighten the loophole, and she will open it with time."

My eyes opened. I was back in my body, back in the fetch. The space between my shoulders ached, a phantom pain that would not relent. I was tempted to try to reach the spot with one of my hands, to try and touch the space that hurt, but did not. None of my pain manifested quite this way.

Muse smiled at me. "Did you find out what you wanted to know?"

None of what I'd seen made any sense to me whatsoever, but a hunch struck me. "I don't know yet. Have you ever heard the name Alcyone?"

Muse's eyes widened. "Yes. She's quite famous amongst my people. On the old world, eons ago, she delivered a prophecy. One that spoke of a great disturbance in the cosmos, an imbalance of power, and the three who would make it right."

My heart beat faster. The three who would make it right. What did that mean? "Can you tell me the prophecy? Or is it written down somewhere?"

Solemnly, Muse shook his head. "I don't believe it is, and I am sorry, I don't know more than what I've told you. My mother would be the one to ask."

"The sybil at Orrery?" I asked, heart sinking. The Orrery Aerie was across the Pontus Axeinos in Brektos. Traveling there was an impossibility right now.

Muse's expression was open and gentle. Under other circumstances, he might be someone I could like. "I am sorry I cannot tell you more. For what it's worth, something is blocking you. I can't read you, but I sense whatever it is."

"Could it be the after-effects of the oubliette?" I asked.

"No." Muse's head shook thoughtfully. "The magic of the oubliette would have worn off moments after you escaped. You did escape it on your own, didn't you?"

"You saw that?" I breathed, wondering how that was possible, given what Muse had said.

He laughed, loud and hearty. "No, I assumed it. There's bits and pieces of you in all the others' surface memories, and from what they think of you, it seems like something you'd be capable of." His eyes sparked with interest. "That's a story I'd like to hear someday."

"But not now?"

"No, now I'm going to tell Mirabelle that my reading was inconclusive. That you haven't been out long enough to tell how you connect."

"Can you do that?" I asked. "I thought you had to tell the truth."

Muse chuckled. "It *is* the truth. *You've* been telling everyone the truth."

I frowned. "About what?"

Muse took my hand again, squeezing hard. "That you don't remember what happened before the oubliette."

"Oh yes," I murmured. "That is true."

I felt no need to pull my hand out of his grip. There was something about Muse that was inherently right, inherently safe for me to be close to. "Will you tell them about the fetch?" I asked, turning my head toward the windows. He'd already promised, but I had to be sure.

"No," he replied. "That is your business, just as Poe's secret was hers. Despite what Mirabelle Aestra thinks, I don't serve her. That's not how the Courts worked, not originally. Her kind has forgotten, but they will be brought to account."

His words had the tenor of portent, and I had no desire to press further. Somewhere in the recesses of my mind, a part of me that existed long before this body whispered that no good had ever come from prophecy. It might be a blessing that I could not reach the sybil easily. Whatever was at work here might be bigger than my concerns, but I was happy to help these people as long as my needs were being met. Right now, however, they were not.

"Do you know anything about my mother and sister that might help me remember the things I've forgotten?" I asked.

Muse shook his head. "I've never had occasion to learn anything about them. I am sorry, Mina. You're the one person here I'd really like to help, and I cannot."

"You don't like Poe?" I asked, feeling shocked.

"I like her just fine," Muse replied. "But her path was set long ago. There's nothing I've ever been able to do to help her. You, I'd like to help. I have a feeling you're the kind of person it pays to be owed a favor from."

At that, I had to smile. "Then you would be a rare one. I don't allow myself to be in positions like that."

Another of Muse's hearty laughs filled me to the brim with comfort. He drew a card from the inner pocket of his waistcoat. "Come visit sometime. For drinks, for fun, for whatever."

I took his calling card, with the distinct feeling that Muse didn't give it out to just anyone. "Thank you."

He bowed slightly to me, then walked back towards the table. I stayed in the quiet for a moment, watching Muse tell them I was no help. I exited the muffled solace of the windowed nook to hear him saying, "It is my conclusion that the four of you are connected. Both to one another, to Chopard, and likely to Niall's disappearance, but not enough has transpired to find out why that is."

Mirabelle Aestra sighed sharply, shoving her chair back from the table. "Then this was a waste of time." She flung a hand at Skye as she stalked out of the room. "Show yourselves out."

Skye nodded, stoic and unreactive. Muse followed Mirabelle, mouthing a silent apology as he went. When Mirabelle and Muse's footsteps disappeared into the upper regions of the Aestra's quarters, Skye spoke. "Shall we find someplace to talk?"

Morpheus was nowhere to be seen, and I envied his ability to blink in and out. Teleportation was a rare and desirable gift that I very much wished I possessed. I considered asking to stay right here —my body ached and fatigue wasn't far behind—but I saw clearly that Poe and Skye wanted to be away. They were both out of their seats and inching towards the door. An old fear of inconveniencing others with my pain fluttered through me.

Slowly, I sucked air in through my nostrils and brought the mask of calm down over the screaming agony that rose in me like an unholy chorus as I stood. Something about unleashing the vision had aggravated my corporeal form. But this was nothing I couldn't manage. I stood without so much as a grimace, proud of myself for hiding the intensity of my body's protest.

My legs crumpled underneath me, and all went dark.

CHAPTER 25

ASHBOURNE

Muse's words echoed in my head, spinning around like a top, torturing me. *Whatever you do, you cannot tell Mina about the offer from the Strix woman. If you do, things go wrong for her. Very wrong,* he'd said, right after he read me. It was a warning, one I took seriously, but it pained me to keep it from her. Especially after the way she'd reacted to my touch, the heat her arousal ignited in me.

Before I could do *anything* about that, I needed to tell Mina everything about the Strix woman and her claims, especially if it was connected to all of this. But neither could I risk her safety, and telling her would do just that. Muse was trustworthy, not just because sirens cannot lie, but because he was a good man, one who stood behind his word no matter what. His reputation in the undercity was unassailable.

Lost in my thoughts, I didn't notice the shake in Mina's muscles as she stood. When she fell, the part of me that was attuned to her recognized something was amiss and I moved without thinking. I only caught her in time to keep her head from hitting the stone table. Poe clapped a hand over her mouth, presumably to keep herself from screaming.

"We need somewhere to go," I whispered. "No one can see her like this."

Poe nodded. "Come with me."

Surprise lit Skye's eyes as Poe moved with purpose, out the front door of House Aestra's massive quarters, into the wreck of the Avalonne. As wrecks went, this one was in fairly good shape. I tried to focus on our surroundings, rather than Mina's scent of iris and white musk. Had my sense of propriety not been firmly in place, I might have nuzzled the space between her shoulder and neck as I adjusted her body to be carried a longer distance.

No one would have seen me do it, but I couldn't trust myself not to linger there, breathing her in. Already, my head spun with her nearness, desire for her racing through my veins. Now that I understood the depth of my need for her, I wouldn't touch her again 'til she begged for it. Something sweet and thick filled my mouth, the taste familiar and strange at the same time. I swallowed the liquid seeping from the roots of my elongated canines.

Faint memory tickled at the back of my mind. This had happened before, with another I'd wanted… I shook my head. There was nothing there for me. Here and now, I wanted her, and only her. She was the only one I'd desired with this kind of intensity since I awoke from the coma. I wanted to keep that for myself, so I diverted my thoughts with purpose.

The Avalonne was a feat of engineering I could not comprehend. The ship itself must have been beyond my puny imagination, for this was a true city, as large as Pravhna, if not larger. We followed Poe through the narrow stone walkways and steep stairs. In the dim light of the phosphorescent plants, the stone sparkled a bit with a faint luminosity of its own.

We took a spiral staircase that looked over a waterfall that fell hundreds of feet, into the misty darkness below. The view stirred something within me, memories of a labyrinth in the mist conjured in my mind. So long as they were not memories of another lover, I let them drift in and out. The less I paid attention to them, the more likely they were to disappear, without effect.

Poe had stopped in front of an enormous arched doorway, drawing a ring of keys from an interior pocket of her heavy coat. Next to her, Skye's mouth fell open. "I've walked past this door so many times, wondering what House it belonged to."

Poe glanced sidelong at Skye. "I don't come here often."

Something about the statement elicited a smile from Skye, a private joke between them, perhaps. The thought of them having jokes to share pleased me as Poe pushed the door open.

"Welcome to House Feriant," Poe said, her voice quiet. "Please never mention this place to anyone."

I pushed past Skye, who'd stopped dead in her tracks. "Hippolyta Feriant. You *are* Hippolyta Feriant."

The name meant nothing to me, but clearly it did to Skye. This seemed like a private conversation though, and Mina stirred in my arms. "Where should I take her?"

Poe's brows immediately furrowed. "Upstairs, second floor, to your left. Any room will do."

Another spiral staircase sat at the end of the entryway, and as I carried Mina up, Skye and Poe's voices carried—they were arguing again. Mina woke to the sound, her face thoughtful against my chest.

"Do you know why they're fighting?" she asked.

"No," I murmured as I stopped at the top of the stairs. The hall stretched out in two different directions. I went left, choosing the first door I came to.

Mina's hand dropped to open the door for me when she saw I'd paused, worrying I'd have to put her down to open the tall, heavy thing. She turned the doorknob, and I pushed the door with my shoulder. The room was pristine, lit by soft witchlights that glowed brighter as we entered. A scent of jasmine and rose hung in the air, as though the room had just been cleaned. There was a canopied bed on one wall, made from heavy, spare wood, hung with diaphanous white curtains. It looked a little like a giant cube. There was no other furniture in the room, save a simple wood bench at the end of the bed.

"Where would you like to be?" I asked.

She looked around. "In a bathtub."

I set her down, watching her sink onto the bench at the end of the bed before I strode across the room. Tall, arched doors took up nearly the entire wall opposite the bed. When opened, they revealed another, bigger room. It was the biggest bathing chamber I'd ever seen. In a nook at the front of the room sat an oversized bathtub.

"There's one in here," I called to her. From downstairs came the sounds of a muffled fight.

"Please run the water as hot as possible," Mina said from the other room. "If there is salt, I'd take some."

There was a shelf carved into the stone wall next to the tub that held various bath accoutrements. I could identify the salt easily enough, but the rest was a mystery to me. Once I had the tub plugged and hot water flowing, I dumped a generous heap of salt in, and went to fetch Mina.

She sat where I left her, obviously listening to the fight downstairs with interest. "So, she's a princess."

I nodded. "It would seem so. Would you like some help getting into the bathroom?"

Mina looked as though she might say no, but when she tried to get up on her own, she winced. I rushed in to help, gripping her forearms before I could think twice. She flinched, grimacing as she recoiled from me.

"I apologize," I murmured. "I should have asked."

She nodded, but said, "Please don't let go. I do need the help."

Together we moved towards the bathtub, her body leaning heavily on me as we went, but she was tense, pulling herself upward with each painful step. Her hands shook in mine.

"Please let me carry you," I pleaded. "There's no need for this. I can see how much pain you're in."

She glanced up at me, her mouth set in a determined, grim line. "You cannot possibly know how much pain I am in."

I stopped, refusing to move another inch. If this was her successfully hiding the true measure of her discomfort, that concerned me. "Show me then."

She stared at me for a long moment, and I thought she'd brush my pleas off, but she closed her eyes. The shift was subtle as she loosened her grip on the mask she wore to keep herself secret. Her shoulders drooped, her spine sagging, her head heavy on what now seemed like a too-weak stalk of a neck. When her eyes opened, I could all but hear the screaming inside her. There was no haggardness in it, only pure suffering, endured over a lifetime. Silent tears slipped down her cheeks, her breath ragged in her chest.

"Let me carry you," I repeated.

"Fine." Her whisper of a voice was barely audible.

Picking her up in this state was different from before. She was both heavier and lighter at the same time. The weight of her pain was unimaginable, but besides that, she felt empty in a way I could not understand. She lay her head on my shoulder, her tears staining my jacket.

In the bathing chamber, I found a bench, a smaller version of the one in the bedroom, and sat Mina down. The room had warmed with the hot water and she was steady enough for the moment, so I returned to the bedroom. I stripped out of my overcoat, frock coat and waistcoat, and rolled my shirtsleeves past my elbows. When I returned to the bathing chamber, she was pouring more salt into the tub, along with various oils and dropperfuls of liquid from different bottles.

Her own coat lay in a heap on the floor, and her hands shook as she found and replaced bottle after bottle. When she could not open the last stopper, I stepped in to help.

"Just one drop of that one," she said. "It has an analgesic effect, but is very potent."

I did as she asked. The tub was full now, and the water shut off automatically. Both of us startled at the realization that it had done so of its own accord. A tiny smile of wonder played at her lips.

She practically vibrated with exhaustion, and though I wanted to give her privacy, it was clear she could not do this alone. "I can help you. I can even close my eyes, if you like. But you need help."

When her eyes met mine, they burned with life. "I don't want you to close your eyes."

My breath caught. Even in this state, with her pain so evident, she was more alluring than any lover I could remember. She turned toward me, her arms hanging at her sides as she leaned against the marble wall. Her eyes did not leave mine as I stepped towards her, my hands going to the buttons on her blouse first. Every button brought her creamy skin further into view, my breath catching at the beauty my fingers revealed.

She leaned forward when I finished, so I could slip it off her shoulders. Her face burrowed into my chest. "There's buttons on the back of the trousers."

I found them, undid them, then pushed them away as she stepped out of them. Under her clothes, she wore a silky ivory camisole and a pair of matching bottoms. My hands hesitated slightly as she pushed away from my chest and turned from me.

"It will be easier for me if I can face away from you," she explained. For a moment, I thought she spoke of modesty, but she braced herself against the wall, allowing me to push the silk bottoms down over the generous curve of her hips. When they lay on the floor, she leaned back against me, her knees buckling.

My arm went around her in an instant, pinning her to my chest, my hand splayed across the bare skin of her abdomen, pushing her camisole aside. Her breath came quicker now as she pulled it off, over her head. I closed my eyes for a moment, trying to still my blood, but she turned in my arms, every delicious curve of her pressing into me as she did so. When I opened my eyes her face was lifted, watching me.

"What is this between us?" she breathed. "Or am I mistaken?"

It was as though she spoke to herself, but I could not help answering. "You are not mistaken."

Her arms went around my neck, and my heart nearly thumped out of my chest. She waited, watching me carefully. "You cannot hurt me more than I'm already hurt."

It was as though she'd read my mind. "What would help you, Mina?" I whispered.

"To feel pleasure amidst all this pain," she answered.

CHAPTER 26

MINA

The words came out of me unbidden and without thought for consequence. It was wholly unlike me, but the pain had caught me, its claws gouging holes in my good sense. Ash's reaction was unexpected. Many men, given the right opportunity, would have ravaged me then and there.

And if he'd have done so, I would have welcomed it. What came next was worse. His mouth met mine, in an infuriating combination of restraint and strength, as he lifted me aloft. His lips were firm and slow, but his tongue tangled in mine with wild abandon.

Hot bath water hit my skin and he paused. "Is it too much? The water, I mean."

"No," I murmured against his mouth. He lowered me into the water, looking only at my face. It wasn't the gaze of false modesty, but one bordering on obsession. As though he wanted to memorize every line of my expression as his fingers grazed the sensitive skin of my jaw then ran down the line of my neck to trace my collarbone.

I'd always hated the way my collarbones disappeared beneath my flesh, when Helene's protruded in such a delicate way. But Ashbourne's reverence made me rethink my stance, the touch reverberating through my entire body as his lips met mine again.

Now that I was settled safely in the tub, the tenor and rhythm of his kisses changed. I was too exhausted to touch him more than to cling to the collar of his shirt, but his hands moved enough for the two of us, pulling out the dozens of pins that held my hair in place.

One grazed my scalp as he did so and I cried out. He broke the kiss, but I pulled him to me, crushing my lips against his. He seemed to understand. There was no way to be gentle with me. Everything caused me some measure of pain now. The only thing to do was to mix pleasure with it so fully that I might find relief.

My hair undone, his fingers moved through it as he kissed me, massaging my scalp to a degree of sheer bliss. Every strand of my hair felt too heavy for my head to carry, and his touch sent shivers of pleasure through me. The heat of the water and the combination of his touch made my eyes heavy.

"You're exhausted," he murmured as he left a trail of kisses from my jaw to my earlobe.

I nodded once, unable to speak now. Ash drew away from me, watching me for a long moment, as though making some determination about what would happen next. His fingers continued to stroke my scalp, pulling gently through my hair to keep it out of the water as I sunk deeper into the hot suds.

"Close your eyes, love," he said.

I shook my head. "Can't fall asleep in the tub." The words came out awkwardly, slowly, and I couldn't be sure they'd exited me in the same order I'd thought them in, but he understood me.

"You're safe," he whispered, sending a shudder of pleasure through me. "I won't let you drown."

There was no way to be sure of that, but the littlest bit of relief had brought all my defenses down and I lost all sense.

I woke in my attic room at Orchid House, my dressing gown tied securely around me. Pillows supported every aching part of my body in an expert placement that surprised me. I raised my head slightly to find Ashbourne sleeping in the chair by the window. The curtains hung barely askance, letting in a sliver of the night. Outside, rain fell in steady sheets.

Slowly, I sat up, listening to the sounds of the house. Rain on the roof, Ashbourne's soft breathing. My pain had receded while I slept, the medicinal bath in the Avalonne helping immeasurably. Careful not to push myself too hard, I swung my legs over the edge of the bed. My muscles were stiff, but nothing was so painful that I couldn't go downstairs for a cup of tea.

I pulled the knitted throw from the end of my bed and covered Ashbourne with it. He hardly stirred at my touch. It was hard not to stay and ponder the sharp lines of his face, the curve of his lip. However, I needed to brew a cup of herbal tisane if I was to feel at all myself when the sun rose. I stole out of the room, closing the door softly behind me as I went.

The back stairs in the attic went straight to the kitchen, but I stopped on the first floor to check the lock on the front door. Viridian knew I was back, and a part of me feared he might come here. I couldn't be sure that my adjustments to the wards would keep him out. When I was satisfied the front door was locked, I checked the terrace doors. Skye had fallen asleep on the divan in Maman's study, a book open on her chest, Morpheus stretched out next to her on his back, snoring lightly. There was no blanket to tuck them in with, so I made my way downstairs to the kitchen.

Though it was dark, I saw Poe without trouble. She stood in the kitchen doorway, a crystal rocks glass hanging from her fingertips as she watched the rain. I know she heard me enter, but she didn't turn to face me. "Are you feeling better?"

Her voice carried a chill I hadn't heard before. "Yes," I answered, turning the dial on the aetheric lamps over the oven so they provided just enough light to make tea by. The green glow was eerie in the midnight hour.

The silence between us was uncomfortable, but I decided to let Poe direct the conversation. When the kettle was on to boil, I turned, and she sat on a stool at the worktable across from me.

"Ashbourne said you prepared your own bath." Poe's words were obviously an accusation, though I could not make out exactly what wrong I'd done.

"I did," I said slowly, spooning tea into a brass basket.

"How did you know what to put in it?"

Another accusation. Still, I didn't understand. I sighed, resenting the fact that she did not simply say what she meant to and tell me whatever I'd done wrong. "I read the labels."

She frowned, as though confused by my reaction. "But *how?*"

"With my eyes, how else?" I hissed, beyond frustrated with her ridiculous line of questioning.

Poe shook her head, her molars grinding audibly. "How did you read the Old Vilhar, Wilhelmina? Who taught you?"

The question was simple. *Who taught you?* Three simple words unmoored me. Three simple words cut the strings that bound me to this plane. Memories slammed into me, out of order and nonsensical, faces and bodies blurry, but emotions all too clear. As I rose out of the emptiest place of my very long existence, the day I'd remembered it all to begin with became all too clear.

The day I'd caught Maman and Helene, playing with forces neither of them should have trifled with. *Maman.* No. Vaness Wild-fang was no more my mother than the teapot I held in my hands, but somehow—somehow, Helene still felt like my sister. That horrifying sentiment shook me out of the stream of memory.

Poe watched me carefully, her hazel eyes sharp. "You've remembered something."

A slow, wicked smile draped over my face as I poured my tea, more relaxed than I'd been since I rose out of the oubliette. "Enough to destroy those that harmed us."

Poe's laugh was soft and dangerous. She pushed her teacup towards me. "Tell me everything."

CHAPTER 27

MINA

We talked long into the night, taking our tea to the study. While the majority of my memories were like watercolor paintings, I understood them well enough to glean that I'd lived a long life before the fetch. I worried at first about telling Poe, given the stigma against unnaturally created life.

Her response surprised me. "After all that happened, perhaps it was a boon."

That was certainly true. Though many things still escaped me, I knew now that the redhead from my visions was my true sister. A half-sister, anyway. When my own mother had died, my father was forever resentful that I resembled her so closely, but could not be *her*. For as a youngling, I showed no sign of having her immense powers, only the most mundane spark of what she'd been, and my father was nothing if not ambitious.

But my father remarried, a woman I loved, and who became like a second mother to me, even after she had children of her own. Twins, a boy and a girl, both far more talented magically than I had any hope of becoming. I could not remember any of their names, and only impressions of their faces. I remembered the wars that lasted lifetimes, the pain of being loved by my stepmother and half-siblings, but never pleasing my father. And then all went dark for a time, though my impression of pain, fear, and an intense longing hunted me still. It had always been there, deep in the pit of my stomach.

"And this was all somewhere else?" Poe asked, setting aside her tea, now gone cold. "Another world?"

I nodded, glancing at the clock. The sun wouldn't be up for another few hours, but night had turned to the wee hours of morning. "Yes, but there was time between when I arrived here and when the fetch was made that I still don't remember. Only that I grew up as Wilhelmina Wildfang."

"So the fetch has grown, just as a real child would?" I nodded as Poe bit her bottom lip. "I don't know much about how a fetch is supposed to work, but…"

Again, I nodded. "That's not how it's usually done. The Oscarovi's fetches were static, everlasting and strong, but they did not age."

"So Vaness had access to some technology or magical knowledge the other Oscarovi didn't."

"Yes," I answered. "I believe that's the only conclusion we can come to. She captured me, and what's more, I think Papa—her husband was involved. I remember him, from before the fetch. Whatever they were doing, he was helping her."

"Why though?"

I had no answer for her. Memories still floated through me, quietly organizing themselves in my mind, but none made much sense yet.

Poe drew a sharp breath in. "But how did you get here? Was it a ship?"

My answer had been theorized about thousands of times over Sirin's long academic history, but never proven. "I believe I came through a portal. Through the limen."

"Like the Ventyr?" Poe asked, naming the only extraterrestrial force to have come to Sirin since the Vilhari.

I paused then. She'd taken the news about the fetch so well, but this was different. From the time we were small children, we learned about the Elemental War. We had named it so because it was the first time the elementals of Sirin agreed to pair as familiars with the Oscarovi, making our kind nearly as powerful as the Vilhari. We had needed that power when the Ventyr came to conquer us.

They were much like the Vilhari in some ways. Stronger than the Oscarovi, with more technical prowess. They had come with the intention of conquering Sirin, and by the elementals' grace and the strength of our alliance with the Vilhari, we had beaten them back. We had become unconquerable.

I still thought of the Oscarovi as my people. It was easier than the truth. The Ventyr were despised on Sirin. It was one of the few things we could all agree on. Telling Poe wouldn't be like it was with the fetch. She might hate me.

I took a deep breath before answering her, knowing I had to be honest. "Not *like* them."

Poe leaned back in her chair, her eyes wide. "*With* them? You're one of them."

I stared at the ceiling for a long moment, tracing the clouds painted there with my eyes. "Yes, and no. I believe I am a high ranking Ventyr, though I cannot remember my name, or the names of my family. I have the strong sense I was left here to be punished. Isolated."

The silence between us made me anxious. I longed to fill it with words, but I stayed silent. There was nothing I could do now. If she hated me, if she feared me, I would have to endure it.

"What was the reason for the punishment you endured?" Poe asked. "Why were you left here?"

I sighed. "That I still don't know. I first remembered all of this—it's why I was imprisoned in the oubliette—on my twenty-eighth birthday."

"Your celestial anniversary," Poe added. "That is a special birthday for the Oscarovi, is it not?"

I nodded, wistful sadness gripping my chest. "But not for me. Maman and Helene had nothing planned for me, other than the barest acknowledgment." It wasn't that I wanted the kind of lavish party that people like Caralee Ellis-Whitely had. We didn't have money for such things.

"Maman refused me the ritual. She told me no elementals were interested in pairing with me, that the forest had denied my soul a pair."

This elicited another sharp breath from Poe, her eyes widening. "Your family's familiars were mountain elementals?"

Rain struck the study windows in violent torrents, obscuring my view of the garden. "Yes, that is the Wildfang tradition."

"That is rather cruel," Poe said, sadness caressing the hard edges of her response. "Mountain elementals are the most powerful, but pairing with them is a vicious process from all I've heard."

I stood, pulling my arms around me for warmth. What she said was true. Mountain elementals required a trial before agreeing to pair as an Oscarovi's familiar. The ritual could be brutal, but I had longed for it just the same. All I had wanted in my childhood was a familiar, but I had been denied over and over. My celestial anniversary had been my last chance; after that, I would have been too old. I had been desperate that night. There was one log left in the basket by the hearth, and I bent to put it on the dying fire. "I went into the forest at Somerhaven to plead with the old ones."

Behind me, Poe was silent. I didn't have to turn to know she wore a shocked expression. No one in their right mind would do such a thing. The Oscarovi were indigenous to Sirin, but the elemental spirits, they *were* Sirin. The old ones were their eldritch gods, the nameless elders that spawned the spirits. They were elementals, and *more*. Creatures best left to forgotten places and legend.

One did not treat with them and live to tell the tale. I had been foolish to do what I did, going to the standing stones to demand reconsideration—or at the very least—an explanation for why I'd been rejected. I got my answer, the forbidden knowledge I'd sought. I was given the reason for my pain, my neglect, my isolation. In the standing stones, the old ones showed me the truth of my body, the carved out reality of my existence.

But all I said to Poe was, "They showed me what I was, and I confronted Maman."

Poe made a little noise. I turned and saw tears streaming down her face. "I am so sorry you were treated that way, Mina."

There was no doubt in my mind that Poe understood more than I'd said, that she had some ability to see beyond a person's words and into their souls. I'd suspected she might have auric abilities for some time—that she could read emotions and possibly even surface memories. It was a rare gift among the Vilhari, one that presented only sporadically. It was treasured, though without proper cultivation, it could be maddening for some. Clearly, she'd mastered her ability to read others. There was no other way she could read between the lines of what I'd told her and the swirl of emotions and memories that flooded me now.

"There's no reason for you to be sorry, but I appreciate the sentiment."

Poe wiped her eyes with the back of her robe's sleeve. "When I met you in the train station, I knew there was something special about you, about us."

I turned my back to the fire, letting my backside warm for a bit. The feeling was delicious on my still-sore muscles. "Oh?" I wasn't following her train of thought.

Poe nodded. "Yes, I read auric energy."

Well, there it was. I'd known, but there was something gratifying about hearing her tell the truth.

"And there was something familiar about yours." She flexed her hands out in front of her, staring at them for a long moment. "I can't see my own aura, but I feel it. And there was something familiar in yours. Something that made me think immediately that we might be connected."

The excitement in her voice was contagious. "And what do you think now that we've spent time together?"

She stood, coming to stand next to me, her backside to the fire as well. "Oh," she said, with a tiny smile. "That does feel lovely. This place is freezing."

A little chuckle bubbled up from my chest, breaking up the tension that had gathered there since she confronted me in the kitchen. It was going to be all right with us.

"What do you know about House Feriant, about the Court of Aether?" she asked.

I shrugged. "That the Court of Aether ruled Vilhar alongside the Court of Starfire, and the heir was on the Avalonne, as some sort of ambassador. And of course, that the representatives of the Court of

Aether disappeared after the Ventyr were beat back, leaving the Vilhari without a ruler."

Poe nodded. "That's the basics. But like the vast variation in the Court of Winds, there are also variations in the ways the Court of Aether presents."

My rear began to feel as though it might catch fire, and I moved to sit on the plush rug in front of the fire. It was the softest textile in the room. Why Maman could not have invested in more comfortable furniture was beyond my comprehension.

It would be painful to get up from the floor, but at least I'd stay warm. "Like the differences between the Strix and Corvidae?"

Poe sat next to me, crossing her legs under her billowing robe. "Yes. The Courts of Aether and Starfire have fewer variations in that way, though there are many fey creatures that made their homes with us. The draconae, for one..." Poe trailed off, deep sadness in her eyes. "I'm sorry. I don't know how I can miss a place I've never seen, a life I've never had."

Gingerly, I took her hand. It felt good to do so as her fingers closed around mine. "Thank you," she whispered. "It's kind of you to comfort me, considering that you actually remember the home you left behind. I only have stories."

The memories I had were sparse, but she was right. I did have them, and more would return. What she felt was a different kind of pain, missing a life she never had a chance to live. "We don't have to have the same experience for me to feel empathy for what's happened to you," I explained.

She smiled. "The point I was trying to make was that a good portion of the Court of Aether were winged, much like the Court of Winds... But different."

"Different how?" A yawning hole opened in my gut.

Poe pulled her hand from mine, but gently, then pushed herself into a standing position. She closed her eyes, and the atoms in the room shifted. The change was nearly imperceptible, but for the six feathered wings that flexed behind Poe. They were midnight blue, the color of aether, glimmering in the firelight with a faint iridescence that shifted green and purple.

Their formation was as familiar to me as my own face. Now I

remembered what else I had lost, long before anyone put me in the fetch. A great howl of grief welled within me, but I only said, "Your wings are like the Ventyr's. Avian, rather than draconic, but the same otherwise."

Poe nodded. "This is not common knowledge amongst the Vilhari on Sirin, Mina. But I think it explains something… On the Court of Aether's home world, on Neamor, House Feriant had feathered wings. House Larae, draconic."

My heart beat faster at the name. "House Larae?" The way she pronounced it, laa-ray, was not the word I was familiar with. "Not, Larai?"

"Lah-rhye, laa-ray," she sounded the words out as one of her wings stroked my back. "Do you miss the sky, my sister?"

Tears fell unbidden, streaming hot down my cheeks. While I could not make the faces of my family clear in my mind, I saw their wings. I *felt* my own. Three sets of draconic wings, just like what Poe had described. The ache between my shoulders was nearly unbearable now that she'd said it. It did not matter how many baths I took, nor how many massages. That particular pain never went away. Even in the fetch, *I missed my wings*.

Loose memories gathered, spinning through me, clustering into stories that made sense. The first time I'd flown, my mother tossing me to the wind, off the top of a tower with a joyful whoop, diving after me as my wings found purchase in the air. My father's angry scowl as he watched my mother sicken and die. The day he married my true mother's second-in-command, and the way Orynthia treated me as her own. The day the twins were born. And the war, the never-ending war.

My mother was Larai. It was why my father wanted her so badly. Her people were unconquerable, and his only choice had been to ally with them, taking their queen for his wife. Was it possible that the Larai were somehow related to House Larae? I swallowed hard, understanding what must be an ancient truth. "The Ventyr are Vilhari. We're all the same people."

"Yes, they are ancient relations. Lost but never forgotten," Poe breathed. "I don't know much, but from the records I found in the Avalonne it is why the ambassador traveled with the Court of Winds.

She hoped to find some hint that the Ventyr, our lost people, still lived."

Had the Ventyr known all this when they came to conquer Sirin? Had my parents known we were one people? If they had known, would it have mattered? I wished I remembered more. In time, perhaps I would, and I could give Poe some of the answers her ancestors had sought. It wasn't enough to make up for what the Ventyr had tried to do here, but if my mother's people had been loyal to House Feriant, perhaps that would be enough for her.

Poe let her glamour cover her wings, and sank back down on the rug next to me. Her frown deepened as she chewed something over in her head. "I would like to find my mother, and the last of House Feriant."

"The lost court," I murmured, thinking of the truth about Poe's heritage. We hadn't had a chance to talk about her revelation in the Avalonne yet. "How were you separated from them?"

Poe shook her head. "Much of what I remember is a blur. I was only five when it happened. All I remember is that there was a disturbance in the middle of the night. Fighting. My mother's lover, Euryale, was the one to bring me to the Avalonne. She was injured though, and died before she could do more than tell me how to access our family's quarters, and the wreck itself. I wasn't left with much."

It was all too much sorrow. We had not deserved such terrible childhoods. I had not deserved two terrible childhoods, but I would not say that. I didn't want Poe to think I was trying to compare.

Instead, I asked, "Why were you in hiding to begin with? Why did they disappear?"

Poe's sorrow was palpable now. "I'm not certain. From the little I remember being taught, they were afraid of something. I was never to talk about House Feriant, never supposed to say my full name."

"But you think they're alive somewhere?" I asked.

Poe's smile was watery. "No," she replied, her voice breaking over the word. "All I want now is to know who killed them, and to find their bodies. I want to do the rituals, to grieve for them."

"And after that?" I asked.

Her eyes hardened. "I want what you want."

"Revenge." I offered Poe my arm. My memory might be fractured, but I remembered what it was to make an oath amongst my mother's people. The Larai were kin to House Feriant, and that was enough for me.

Poe clasped my forearm, her fingers curling around my skin as mine gripped hers. When she called me sister, she meant it. We were more than friends. We were family, and I would not let her down.

CHAPTER 28

ASHBOURNE

I woke to the walls shaking, a lightning strike hitting someplace too close for comfort. Mina was gone from her bed, but I sensed her and the others downstairs. My heart slowed as I assessed the situation. Everyone was safe. Morpheus and Skye slept, while Poe and Mina talked in her mother's study. I couldn't make their words out, but they were calm enough in tenor.

All was well. There was nothing to worry over. I pinched the bridge of my nose, a soft blanket falling off me. Mina had covered me before getting up. Memories of her touch, of her mouth, of her naked skin, came flooding back. I took cool air into my lungs, hoping for relief.

None came. I wanted her too badly. There was only one way to resolve these feelings: I needed to move. Technically, there were two ways, but the one I'd prefer wasn't an option right now. Someone needed to do a perimeter check anyway. I adjusted the massive erection in my pants, then slipped my frock coat back over my shoulders as I stood. I'd been sitting on it, and it retained the heat of my body.

I took the stairs two at a time, not bothering to be quiet. Mina stepped out of the study, her robe dragging on the floor behind her, dark hair spilling around her face and shoulders. "You're awake."

The rasp of her voice was too much. The thin fabric of her robe clung to her, revealing the way the chill in the air had peaked her nipples. My head swam with ideas—so many ideas about the ways I'd like to touch her. I could not stay and listen to her without dropping to my knees and begging her for release. I swallowed my baser urges, clearing my throat in an attempt to gather my wits. "Someone needs to do a perimeter check."

"Is something wrong?" Poe asked, poking her head out the door.

"No," Skye said from the doorway of the drawing room, Morpheus just behind her. Wonderful, everyone was awake. "But with Viridian back, and our trip to the Avalonne, it's probably best that we set up a watch." She stepped forward. "I am sorry, Ash. I should have thought of it myself."

I nodded, feeling bad about her obvious guilt. I only wanted to get out of the house, to find something useful to do with myself. There was never a moment I wanted Skye to feel as though she'd made a misstep, especially not when she had been resting.

"Go back to sleep," I pleaded. "I'm sure all is well."

Skye yawned. The enormous grandfather clock in the back hallway made a soft noise, its cogs and gears turning as the stars on its face shifted slightly. It was a quarter past five. Technically a decent hour to rise, but we'd had an extraordinary day.

"Please," I said as Poe and Mina both yawned in chorus with Morpheus and Skye. "All of you to bed. I will do a perimeter check and then make mushroom tarts for breakfast."

"With cheese?" Skye asked, heading for the stairs. "Something sharp?"

"Yes," I reassured her. "Plenty of sharp cheese. We have a lovely cheddar."

Mina looked back at Poe, reaching a hand toward the other woman. "We should sleep. There will be much to talk about later."

Poe nodded, taking Mina's hand. I noticed the way Skye purposely did not look back. She was still angry then. They'd done nothing but bicker since Mina lost consciousness. I'd hoped they'd have resolved things between them by now, but Skye felt betrayed by Poe's secrets, and I couldn't blame her for that.

Honesty, I'd found, was the most important thing in healthy relationships. It was the foundation of everything Skye and I had built together in our friendship, and it was the reason I needed to get out of the house. Muse had been clear that it was imperative that I keep the visit from the Strix woman a secret from Mina, but I still had doubts.

How could lying to Mina about someone who meant her harm be helpful? But Muse had made an important point. It wasn't that *not* knowing would cause her to be off her guard; it was the knowing that would prod her into making decisions that might ruin everything.

Something about that idea resonated deeply with me. While I could not be sure why that was, I knew the feeling of memory returning when it drew near. There was nothing I wanted less right now than to bring on visions of the past, especially when the people in the here and now meant so much to me. My coat hung in the front closet, in the vestibule. I brought it out, flipping the collar upwards against the storm as I opened the front door and made my way down the steps and onto the street.

The early morning was marked by the storm that raged on outside. Rain fell in sheets, clouds rolling in the sky. Pravhna's storms were serious this time of year, and would remain so until the snow began. Water rushed down the steep streets, into the sewers that ran below the city. I had to wonder if the waterfalls in the Avalonne were overflowing right now, if the ship had ever been flooded out by storms.

I turned the corner on Orchid Street, and made my way up several blocks before doubling back when I was certain I hadn't been followed. It was hard to imagine who would be out in such weather, especially so early. But there was something about Viridian Montclair that reminded me not to get complacent.

He had a quality I recognized, though I could not pinpoint its origin. I knew in my bones' marrow I'd met others like him in the past, bullies who thrived on people believing their motivations were simple cruelty. Viridian Montclair was no fool, and I would not make the mistake of underestimating him.

As I slipped into the alley behind Orchid House, I was rewarded for my efforts. On the roof of the horrendous neighbor's house, the one who'd scolded Mina about the garden—what was her name? I could not remember, but there was an anomalous shadow on her roof.

Whatever my previous training was, I'd learned to pay attention to even the smallest details. The shadow was nothing short of suspicious. As I neared the neighbor's garden wall, my path to the roof became clear. The shadow moved, having spotted me as well.

"Shit," I swore, regretting that I'd told Skye I didn't need her.

There was no time to fetch her. If I wanted to know more, I'd have to follow alone. I raced back to the alley to follow the shadow. Nor was there time to scale the houses on Orchid Street. I would have to pursue them from below, hoping my efforts would fade from sight in the dark alleyways.

After two blocks, I nearly lost them, but gained a tail. So much for being lost in the darkness. There were two of them. But were they separate entities, or were they working together? I had to make a choice. Follow one or catch the other. Some trace of strategy or instinct told me it would be better to chase and let the tail follow.

I increased my speed and the length of my strides. No longer did I try to disappear. Speed was all that mattered at this point—if I could get ahead of my quarry, I could cut them off. As I pulled almost two city blocks ahead of the figure on the roof, I hit the high street. Rather than having back gardens, shop buildings extended all the way into the alley.

One had a ladder that went up the side of the building near the trash bins. I scaled the ladder as fast as I could. Near the roof, I looked back. My tail was on the same block, and had spotted me. *Good.*

The figure from the roof was catching up to me. I moved towards them, meaning to cut them off and confront them, but they paused, spotting me. They were a block away and hesitated for what felt like an age. And they then shifted shape, turning into a starling and flying away. As they rose higher, I noted that one wing appeared injured, though it did not seem to impede their progress any. Swearing softly, I stole to the edge of the roof to find my tail.

They hadn't followed me up the ladder, but had stopped in the alley, watching the starling disappear into the clouds. I caught sight of their scarred owl's visage as they slipped into the shadows, disappearing so quickly it was startling. What they'd done wasn't possible. They were simply *gone*. I scrambled back down the ladder, searching the alley for signs of them, but there were none.

It was as if they'd never been in the alley at all. I'd lost them both, but gained at least a little knowledge. My tail had been none other than the Strix woman, which was complicated, given Muse's pronouncement. At the very least, now I knew that she was far more talented at subterfuge than I might have expected. I wouldn't underestimate her again. The sinking understanding that she would return threatened to send me into a focused rage, but I hadn't time for that. Besides, if the Strix woman was headed anywhere immediately dangerous, it would be back towards Mina.

My best bet was to head back to Orchid House and keep watch. I made haste, pondering the starling, going over all I'd observed as I jogged. I had a feeling that both Skye and Poe would be good resources for which of the high families shifted into starlings. Sunrise threatened in the east. There wasn't anything else I could do now. I turned back towards Orchid House.

I'D JUST PUT the mushroom tarts into the oven and was filling the kettle with water when Skye appeared in the kitchen, along with Morpheus.

"Poe and Mina are still asleep."

I nodded, putting a bit more water into the kettle. Skye often needed an extra cup of tea on mornings when she hadn't slept well. From the shadows under her eyes, I had to assume she was still upset from the previous day's events.

She sank onto the stool across from me. I filled the kettle, then put it on the stove. The house would not fill it for me, the way it did for Mina or Poe, but as I set it down, the stove flared to life on its own, just as the oven had done when I began making the tarts. The house was getting used to me. I opened the kitchen door a crack. It was hot down here.

"We were being watched," I said, keeping my voice low.

Skye nodded, resting her elbows on the island and her head in her hands. "Did you catch up with them?"

I shook my head. "No, the first flew off before I could catch up. The other was the Strix woman from before." Muse had said nothing about keeping news of the Strix woman from Skye, and it was best that she knew what we were dealing with.

Skye raised her head from her hands, her silver eyes narrowing. "That isn't good."

"No," I said, taking a teapot down from the shelves. "It isn't. What's more, Muse warned me against telling Mina about her."

"What?" Skye gasped. "Why?"

I lifted my shoulders to indicate I wasn't sure. "He said knowing would set her on a disastrous path."

Skye leaned back slightly. I knew my friend well enough to see the wheels turning in her head. She was trying to put this all together, just as I was. "She's more than she seems, don't you think?"

My jaw clenched as my body reacted to the mere thought of her in the bathtub, her arms around my neck, her soft mouth on mine, pliable and warm.

"I meant from a tactical standpoint," Skye hissed, though there was laughter in her voice. "You've really got it bad for her."

Morpheus leapt onto the island, flopping down in front of Skye, the tip of his tail moving only slightly. *She is more than any of us bargained for, that is for certain.*

"Do you think she's a danger to us, or herself?" Skye asked, the question directed toward the cat. Her focus was sharp now, as though something about the feline's words or tone was concerning to her. She was better at reading him than I was. His moods seemed rather monotonous to me, but Skye sensed the subtleties in Morpheus.

I believe Wilhelmina is dangerous to the entire world, in the wrong situation. He stared at me as he spoke, as though waiting for me to react.

I had very little to argue with. Mina was most definitely dangerous, quite dangerous, in fact. I sensed a power in her she likely was not even aware of yet.

"Do you know something more specific?" Skye asked. "Or is this another of your vague premonitions?"

She said it with love, but apparently, Morpheus did not appreciate Skye's tone. He disappeared in parts, dematerializing from the tips of his ears down to the end of his tail in a slow, deliberate manner that expressed his displeasure.

She is dangerous and powerful, the cat said as he faded from sight. *We will need those qualities before this ends. It would be better that she were dangerous and powerful* for *us, rather than* against *us.*

When he was gone, Skye swore. "That's rather ominous."

I nodded, glancing at the clock above the stove. The scent of mushroom tart had increased a measure. Skye smiled contentedly as she breathed in the bouquet of rosemary, mushroom, and melted cheddar. "When will the tarts be finished?"

"Not for another half hour," I replied. "And then they must cool."

The kettle sang, and I moved quickly to bring it off the stove, then spooned tea into the pot to steep. Behind me, Skye spoke. "When I found you, you were such a fearsome sight, even passed out. Bloody and so damn *dirty.*"

I chuckled as I brought the teapot and teacups to the island. "And now?"

Skye smiled at me. "Now you're my best friend." Her hand stretched towards mine, and I reached out to take it. Her fingers closed around mine, her large hand looking small and graceful against my rugged bulk. "Be careful, Ash. With Mina, I mean."

I nodded. "She's been through a lot."

Skye sighed. "That's not what I mean. Be careful with yourself. She's dangerous in more ways than what Morpheus meant." I frowned. "She's complicated, and she's not telling us a lot. You sense that, right? That she's holding a lot back?"

I nodded. "Everyone has their secrets, though."

Skye shrugged. "We don't."

I laughed, gesturing to myself. "We *do.*"

"That's different," she said. "You don't have any memory of who you are, or what's happened to you."

"But I remember what happened at the rubber factory," I murmured. "And so do you."

Her expression went dark, thinking of the empyrean fire I'd used to heal the owlet the night this all began. We hadn't had time to discuss that further, with all that had happened since. Everything had moved too quickly. But in any other investigation, I'd be a suspect.

"Do we need to talk about it?" I asked. "It's an odd coincidence, given everything." Something about my words, and the kitchen itself, gave me the sense that I'd had this conversation before.

"There is no way that you're Chopard. I know where you were for every other fire," Skye murmured. "Besides, you used your empyrae to heal. We don't even know if you have the ability to use enough to burn buildings to the ground."

I nodded, appreciative of her trust, but she was hedging and we both knew it. There wasn't any need for more conversation. Skye was always straightforward with her words. I poured the tea, spooning honey into hers, with a little milk. Just a splash. She smiled up at me.

"The one that got away from me before," I said as I poured tea for myself. "They turned into a starling and flew off."

Skye's cup nearly slipped from her fingers. "Was there anything wrong with one of its wings?"

I knew she would know who it was. "Yes, it appeared injured."

She shook her head. "Not injured. Well, not actively so, anyway. Niall broke his left arm rather badly as a child, on a voyage to Brektos with my father. It wasn't set properly, and it healed wrong. He's never been willing to have it broken again and reset."

"So, your brother isn't missing at all."

"It would appear not," Skye said. "But that still leaves us with questions."

"Yes," I mused. "Such as, who is he working for?"

CHAPTER 29

MINA

I picked at my mushroom tart while Poe combed through both the gossip rags and an enormous pile of calling cards. Ashbourne and Skye were off to the undercity to report to Edith Braithwaite's operation. Ash hadn't made eye contact with me all morning, nor spoken even a single word. One nod in greeting was all I got.

I wondered if I'd made that much of a fool of myself in the Avalonne, or if he was simply shy about physical encounters. It bothered me a little, but there would be time to address it later. Outside the front windows, a stream of umbrellas passed by on the street. The rain had continued into the morning. It was a typical Pravhna autumn, cold, rainy, and blustery.

Water elementals played in the rain, turning into beautiful goldfish with fancy tails and swimming through the air. They grew larger as droplets added to their mass, then splattered apart, only to reconstitute moments later. Watching them, it was difficult not to wonder what might have happened if the old ones had answered me in the way I'd hoped for—if I'd been given a partner in this life, rather than knowledge that had shattered any hope of happiness I might ever have.

Without speaking, Poe handed me the pile of tittle-tattles. *The*

Ladies of Chanticleer publication was at the top of the pile, and the most popular of the rags. Poe tapped a long oval nail on its first piece, "Oscarovi Heiress Ostracized at Armande's."

"That's an abhorrent use of alliteration," I muttered. Poe made a non-committal sound, the nib of her pen scratching the paper she was making lists upon. A glance told me she was sorting invitations. It was time to move to the next phase of our plan, evening events in wider society.

It looked like we'd been invited *everywhere* from the piles Poe had sorted. I turned my attention back to the article in the Chanticleer rag. Through the author's lens, Ashbourne had valiantly come to my rescue, and I'd done little more than stand there looking pretty and "surprisingly vulnerable for the heir to the Somerhaven title."

I sat the rag down with an eye roll. "Surprisingly vulnerable."

Poe looked up from her list. "That's a good thing. They're under-estimating you still."

I grimaced, but of course she was right. The longer society thought me a brainless socialite, guileless and without ambition, the better. People's lips loosened around those they underestimated. They forgot to be on guard, and that was exactly what we needed to untangle the knot of our multiple interests and how they wove together.

It was good that they didn't think I was like Helene or Maman. While Helene had been admired, she was feared. Apparently, no one remembered much about me other than my youthful awkwardness, which the Chanticleer author noted that I'd "blossomed out of." It was insulting to think people perceived me this way, but I reminded myself it was all for a purpose. A vain part of me was pleased that they noticed how beautifully I was dressed.

It didn't take long to scan through the other rags. Some mentioned the previous day's outing, but they were mere echoes of the Chanticleer's thoughts. Nothing original. That was the way it always was. The Chanticleer set the tone of things and most everyone else simply followed along.

"Where are we off to this evening?" I asked, setting the pile of gossips aside.

Poe pushed a hand-lettered invitation towards me. "This was delivered by one of the House's footmen this morning."

I opened the envelope, the heavy paper luxurious to the touch. Inside was an invitation to an intimate evening soiree at House Aestra. "This seems a bit last minute for Elspeth," I said as I scanned the invitation.

"It's a viewing for the Orilion Lights." Poe held up a handwritten note. "She says the sky will be unexpectedly clear this evening and the astronomers have deemed them likely to be visible."

I glanced outside, where rain still fell in heavy sheets. "Interesting."

"She also says that she's invited those she believes may have connections to Chopard, and some of your mother's possible connections."

Anticipation thrummed through me. We'd missed our opportunity to sleuth yesterday at the lecture, but gained valuable information from Muse. It was an acceptable trade-off, but it was time to begin our hunt for Chopard in earnest.

"If we are going, I need to respond," Poe said, staring at the front door.

"Have the two of you made up yet?"

Poe shook her head. "And I'd rather not respond without talking it over with her, but..."

I placed my hand on Poe's. "Respond. She'll understand."

Poe sighed. "All right. We'll need to begin getting ready, if we're to make it in time."

I glanced at the clock. It was a little before noon. The soiree did not begin until almost nine, which meant no one of consequence would arrive before ten. The lights wouldn't even be visible until midnight. How could it possibly take us that long to get ready?

SIX HOURS LATER, I understood. Poe had a rigorous routine to ready herself for a high echelon event like this one. This included several small, nutritious meals; treatments for the skin, hair, and nails; and one nap before the real work began. She'd left me to rest, but sleep would not come. Instead, I stared at the slanted ceiling in my bedroom, counting the slats of painted boards, as I'd done when I was little.

I was avoiding the onslaught of memories that flooded me every time I closed my eyes. Everything came back in the wrong order, and though I could discern the basics of my life before the Wildfangs found me, the nuance of it all escaped me. The memories of an extraordinarily long life rushed back, mixing with those of the past twenty-eight years. I was left muddled and confused, unable to find a comfortable position in bed, though my pain was not as intense as it had been the day before.

Downstairs, the front door opened. Skye and Ashbourne spoke to one another, then both came upstairs. I listened as they parted ways. Footsteps grew closer to the door of my room, followed by a soft knock.

"Mina, are you awake?" Ashbourne murmured on the other side of the door, so quiet I could hardly hear him.

So he did not want to incur Poe's wrath. I smiled at the ceiling. "Yes," I whispered, using the same caution. "Come in."

He opened the door, slipping inside on silent feet, then shutting the door behind him without a sound. I glanced at him. Propriety would have said I should rise from bed to greet him, but despite the fact that I resented being told to rest, I did actually need to do so.

"How was it with Edith's people?" I asked as he moved to the chair he'd slept in the night before.

"Fine," he said, removing his frock coat and rolling up his sleeves, as he sank into the chair.

The flex in his forearms was a little too arousing, if I was honest with myself. I'd just had a bath and had only put on my nightgown, since I was still too warm to get under the covers. Ashbourne seemed to notice this fact only after he'd sat down. A pink flush colored his moonstone cheeks.

He swallowed hard. "About yesterday, at the Avalonne…"

"I understand if you were just being kind," I interjected when he seemed lost for words. My voice went flat. "I apologize for my forward behavior. I hope I haven't made you uncomfortable."

"I am not uncomfortable," he said, defense edging his voice. "In fact, I worry I am altogether too comfortable with what happened between us."

Surely he wasn't one of those men that believed women needed to be protected from the wanton desires of men. There were a few of that kind in more conservative pockets of the upper echelons, but most folk didn't subscribe to that kind of nonsense. If he was one of those, I'd made a terrible mistake.

"I only meant that you are a client, Mina," he explained, obviously observing the way my eyes had rolled at my train of thought. "It isn't appropriate for me to bring clients to the heights of pleasure."

"Then you have nothing to worry over."

He scoffed slightly, then frowned.

Perhaps more clarification was necessary. "I only meant that not much happened between us. I hold every confidence that you might please a lover."

He stood slowly, his eyes falling half shut as he rose. "Oh?"

The depth of his voice sent shivers through me, my back arching slightly at the sound. "Yes," I said, planting my body firmly back on the bed. "I am certain you're quite capable."

He crossed his arms, looking down at me. "You don't sound convinced to me."

I raised my eyebrows, and my head, but only slightly from my pillow as I stretched my arms behind my head, arching my back again. "Perhaps I'm not."

The barest hint of a smirk played at his lips. He moved faster than I assumed someone of his size might be capable of. In a flash, he was bent over me, one hand pinning my hands above my head. "What," he growled, "do you anticipate it might take to convince you?"

"I'm not certain," I purred back. "I'd have to be presented with a sampling of your skills to really say."

His free hand gripped my jaw now, bringing my eyes to his. "Please, tell me you are not a virgin, Mina."

My eyes fluttered, rolling again. "Of course not."

He waited. We were still playing, but he was serious. "If you are a virgin, we cannot do this now."

I strained playfully against his hands. "I am not." He frowned, clearly worried I might be lying to him. It was good of him to be concerned, but he need not be. "There have been others. When I was younger—a teenager." I matched his seriousness now. "It has been a very long time, though."

Relief flooded his expression, replaced quickly with simmering desire. "Then we'll need to make this good, won't we?"

My mouth went dry at the promise in his words. I had no doubt that Ashbourne Claymore could make good on the fire burning in his golden eyes. One hand slid down my side, barely grazing the fabric of my thin nightgown, eliciting a shiver of pleasure that quaked through my whole body.

He held his weight above me, only applying enough pressure with his heavy body to give me the feeling of being comfortably caged. He shifted slightly, parting my thighs as he came to rest between them. His eyes didn't leave mine as his wandering hand moved lower, skimming the line of my hip now. The hand holding my wrists above my head flexed, and I opened my palms to allow him to lace his fingers through mine.

"Tell me where you want this hand," he murmured as he lowered his head to my ear. The sound of his low voice sent waves of anticipatory pleasure straight to my core as his fingers dragged lightly across the swell of my belly.

I was no blushing virgin, and I wouldn't pretend to be. "Inside me," I commanded.

His head pulled back from mine so our eyes met again, his fingers leaving my body, though I could not see where they'd gone. "Inside you?" he asked as his thumb grazed my bottom lip.

I glared at his purposeful misunderstanding of my words, but I dipped my chin, capturing his thumb lightly between my teeth. He let out a rumbling growl of pleasure as my tongue flicked over his skin. Two could play these games.

When I released his thumb, I asked, "Where do you want to put that hand, Ashbourne?"

His breath quickened at my words and a muscular thigh slid

between my legs, an answer of its own. My arms broke free of his grip, flying around his neck. I pulled him down atop me, our mouths colliding in a fervent embrace. My hips lifted as I squeezed my thighs around him, desperately seeking friction. My joints ached, but his touch countered the pain in a bittersweet dance.

Some fluttering thing beat its wings inside my chest, my breath racing through me in feverish pants. His hard length pressed into my core, promising me sweet release with each thrust of our hips, then betrayed me as he pulled away. Again and again he moved against me, kissing me as hard as I kissed him.

My fingers coiled in his hair, drawing his head back so I could taste the skin at his neck. Something primal rose within me at the taste of his skin, and I had the insatiable urge to sink my teeth into him, to inhabit him so fully we could not be parted. I wanted him with a desperation I had never known with any other lover. There was no time—I wanted him inside me now.

A knock at the door caused us both to startle, our foreheads crashing into one another. "Mina," Poe chastised from the other side of the door. "That is *not* resting."

Ash buried his head in my neck, silent laughter shaking his shoulders.

"Let her rest, Ashbourne," Poe warned as her footsteps retreated. "Or I shall make you both sorry you defied me."

I stared at the ceiling for a long moment, cheeks flushed hot, Ash's body a comforting weight. My hands ran through his hair as I laughed along with him. He fell onto the bed next to me, pulling my back against his chest. "Poe may be a lost princess," he murmured in my ear. "But she certainly has the giving orders part mastered."

As his arms tightened around me, my backside pressed into him, seeking the proof that he wanted me still. His hand slid down to my belly, pressing firmly into my flesh, pinning me to him, a claim on my body. "Will you not sleep?"

I shook my head, my thighs pressing together. "How could I now?"

The arm that curved up from under me flexed. "I am not risking her royal highness' wrath," he murmured in my ear. "But we will finish this, Mina. You will scream my name before this night is over."

Desire snapped through me like a live aetheric wire, but Ash's arms only tightened around me. "Sleep, you beautiful menace."

Something about those words soothed my soul. Ash saw me for what I was, and he wanted me still. I sighed deeply, smoothing the ragged edges of my breath as my heart sought out the rhythm of his, thumping against my back. My eyes were heavier than I'd thought and before I was finished yawning, I had fallen asleep.

MINA

When I woke, Ash was gone, but there was a note on my pillow that read, *I keep my promises. Dress accordingly, and do not take matters into your own hands.* I swore into my pillow, but couldn't help but laugh. It felt good to do so, and when the sound of my mirth died away, I rolled onto my back, breathing freely, a smile on my lips.

A voice inside me rose up, warning that I must not lose focus. That if I sought pleasure over purpose, I would lose. The voice sounded more like Maman or Helene than me, though, and I whispered aloud, "Lose *what*, exactly?"

There was no force requiring that I hunt down the arsonist who burned Somerhaven down. My survival did not depend on getting revenge against whomever killed my family. And why did I want to kill them, anyway? They'd done me a favor. My anger seemed silly. Childish even.

Nothing in the world could stop me from helping Poe, or Skye and Ash, for that matter. They had offered me aid without conditions, a kind of generosity I'd never known. But I could leave all this anger behind, if I so chose. I could help them find Chopard, and then leave with them. Wherever they went next, I could go too.

I could start over if I wanted. The promises Ashbourne's body made to mine could be fulfilled as many times as we wanted. My skin flushed at the thought, remembering his hands on me, his lips on mine. *Do not take matters into your own hands*, I reminded myself. My rebellious thighs squeezed together, my skin damp with the pleasure he'd wrought from me before my nap.

There didn't have to be more than this. I could have this winding affair, let my feelings get involved in ways that the voice that sounded like Helene railed against. It gave me pleasure to deny it.

I sat up in bed, my eyes meeting my reflection in the mirror on my vanity table. "I don't have to do as you did anymore," I said aloud. To Helene, to Maman. To all those who came before this body, before this life. The ones who'd wanted only to control me, to punish me.

And for what?

I could not remember now.

I only remembered the pain. The pain that had always been with me, in one form or another. Behind it, there was the promise that the well of agony would be endless if I stayed on this path. If I let all these memories in, if I unlocked Maman's workshop door, this would never end. But I had the power to stop. If I wanted to, I could.

I looked at the note again, my fingers moving over the words, thinking of the man who wrote them. Would it be so bad to fall in love with him? To give him my heart? Not tonight, or tomorrow, certainly, but someday.

My throat tightened with every passing thought, a sob clawing its way up my throat. On the sea stairs, I had promised myself that there would be no more tears. Not of this kind. If I let them out, could I let this go?

I nodded to myself, rocking my body back and forth as tears fell, sobs wracking through me as I relinquished all my anger to my tears. None of it mattered anymore. The memories that had crowded my thoughts before Ash knocked at my door receded to somewhere deeper in my mind. They were still there, and someday I could take them out, sort them, and understand why all this had happened.

But for now, I wanted this release. I looked around my room, knowing that when we were done here, I never wanted to see this house again. I would sell it all, and move to the undercity, or wherever my friends were.

My friends. My heart swelled with all the affection I hadn't yet let myself feel for them. For the first time in my life, I had real friends. People who saw me for what I was and did not care. Through the tears that still fell, I laughed. Maman and Helene had been wrong all along. I was worthy of love, and now they were dead. Gone forever.

I was finally free.

A FEW HOURS LATER, Poe put the finishing touches on my hair and declared me perfect. Diamond and sapphire encrusted pins shone in my masses of dark hair. I had no idea how she'd managed it, but the effect was one of undone beauty. The style was less severe than the sleek chignons that were popular now, but still unquestionably fashionable.

Poe was a genius, pure and simple. When she left me to put the final touches on her own ensemble, I turned in front of the mirror in the hallway. I marveled as the light caught the jewels in my hair, the subtle sheen of my dress. The gown was simple, made from a nearly sheer midnight blue fabric that billowed around my legs as I walked. The bodice was fitted, a corset built into it, the light boning covered in plush velvet that created an intricate pattern across my abdomen. It looked a little like I was wearing armor. But my favorite part of the dress was the high neck and billowing lantern sleeves.

The effect was heavy, elegant, and sensual. I was completely covered, but when I moved, hints of my pale skin showed through. I wore scant little under the dress, as that was how it was meant to be worn, but also, because of Ashbourne's note. My skin heated with the promise of his words.

He and Skye were out on some errand, though I had not caught what that was. I made my way down to the second floor, where I found Morpheus asleep at the top of the stairs. I sat next to him and he stretched out, his fluffy tail flicking my leg.

His eyes blinked open a few times before he sighed deeply, appearing to go back to sleep. *You are a good likeness for Akatei.*

"Who is that?" I asked, curiosity piqued.

Morpheus growled in irritation, but did not answer me directly. *Of course, you are not really a witch. Not truly.*

That stung a little, even if it was true. Though I thoroughly hated all Maman and Helene stood for, the Oscarovi were admirable. I wished I was one of them. I wore no false jewel this evening. Poe had promised me she was fetching me something from her own cache of treasures.

"I am no one," I mused. "Not really. Whatever I was before, I'm not now. And you're right, I'm not a witch."

That is not what I meant at all, the cat grumbled. *Have you considered you might be* more?

I was about to ask what he meant when the door to the Rose Room opened and Poe emerged. My mouth fell open. The dress she wore was seafoam green, which contrasted beautifully with her bronze skin, but the dress itself wasn't the marvel. The silver corset she wore atop the dress accentuated her every curve, a flexible cage that moved with her, giving her the appearance of a queen going into battle. She wore no other jewelry.

Poe needed no extra adornment; her face was so beautiful it was hard to look at her for very long. Joy crept through me, a grin stretching my cheeks so far it almost hurt.

"I don't think I've ever seen you look so happy," she said.

The tears I'd shed after my nap threatened to return, but I swallowed them. There weren't words for all the emotions I currently felt. Not yet. It was going to take me some time to find the words to tell Poe how much I appreciated her. I settled on, "You look like a queen."

Her smile was faint, as though her thoughts were far away. "Thank you. Tonight, I feel like one."

Downstairs, the front door opened and Skye and Ashbourne entered, both dressed in tuxedos and long, heavy overcoats. Skye stopped in her tracks when she spotted Poe. Ash shut the door behind her as the two of us watched them float toward one another.

Poe took Skye's outstretched hands. Skye fell to one knee, pressing her forehead into Poe's palms. "I'm sorry," she whispered, kissing each palm in turn, a gesture so intimate I blushed. "Forgive me, Your Royal Highness."

"Skye," Poe breathed. "Don't call me that."

Skye looked up, a devilish look in her eyes.

Poe bit her bottom lip, smiling. "Unless I ask you to."

From the top of the stairs, I struggled to stifle a delirious laugh. It was wholly inappropriate, but also, *I was happy*. The feeling left me giddy. Ash's eyes shot to mine, a slow smile spreading over his handsome face. He'd gotten a haircut, his long hair now shorn into a style that flopped into his eyes, but no longer needed to be tied back.

Morpheus, who still sat next to me, began to disappear.

"Where are you going?" I asked, looking down. He hadn't been around much lately.

I have an engagement of my own to get to this evening. He promptly disappeared, as though annoyed by my question.

Downstairs, Ash shook his head, then took the stairs three at a time to reach me. He sat a step below me, reaching for something in his pocket.

"I picked this up for you. Edith paid for it." He handed me a velvet box, his eyes dark with worry. "I wish it were actually *from* me."

I opened the box. Inside was a beautiful ring, an enormous black opal, set between the metal petals of two *orchis mascula*—a mildly poisonous orchid, whose roots were used in love spells, should one be foolish enough to craft one. It was a beautiful ring, stunning in fact. My heartbeat sped up as I ran a finger over the ring, testing it for traces of magic.

There wasn't even a hint. The ring had been made by mundane means, which was an enormous tell. My heart beat even faster now. A piece of paper was folded up inside the box. Ash shrugged when I pulled it out, showing it to him. I opened it. It was a note written in a neat hand that said,

Mina,

This was given to me to pass onto you when the time was right.

EB

I frowned. "Did Edith say where this came from?"

Ash shook his head, pulling the ring out of the box and looking at it closely. "No, and there's no artisan marks on it either." He closed his eyes, his fingers closing over the ring. "There's not a trace of magic on it. It's like it's empty."

I swallowed hard as he dropped it into my hands. It was as I'd suspected upon opening the box. The ring was a vessel—created with the sole purpose of being inspirited with a familiar. A black opal was a powerful stone, meant to channel an even more powerful elemental spirit. Goosebumps pricked my skin as I slid the ring onto my left index finger, the place anyone who knew what they were looking for would check. Inspirited rings were always worn as such.

Unless someone else held the ring itself, as we had just done, no one would know the ring was still empty. "Do you know what this signifies?" I whispered. "What people will think?"

Ash nodded, his mouth tightening. "It will make you an object of conversation… But also a target."

CHAPTER 31

ASHBOURNE

The rooftop terrace of House Aestra was beyond anything I could have anticipated. I thought I understood what the high echelons were like, how they lived, but this proved how wrong I was. The building itself was beyond comparison, a six story marvel of limestone and granite, twice as grand as Orchid House. The patterns in the leaded glass alone must have taken years to create, and an inordinate amount of money.

It shattered my understanding of Skye, in part, but mostly, it helped me understand her convictions better. That her honor was true, because she'd chosen the life we lived over this one, the under-city over this sparkling world. I loved her all the more for it.

The house was beautiful; tastefully decorated, art gilding every hallway. But Mina was the real jewel tonight. The dark fabric of her gown swirled in tantalizing fashion with even the slightest movement. As we made our way to the terrace, Skye, who had hold of Poe's arm, looked back at me, nodding once to confirm our plans. We'd agreed to go our separate ways for the evening. The four of us together was too much, too intimidating. But split up, we could cover more territory, talk to more of Elspeth's carefully curated guest list. Mina slipped her arm under mine, her fingers curling around my bicep as she leaned into me.

The feeling of her body so close to mine was distracting, but a pleasant buzz of pleasure, rather than the intense waves of desire I'd felt before. It was obvious from the way her pupils widened as she gazed up at me that she wanted all the same things I did. There was something comforting in that, a warmth emanating from her that hadn't before.

"Something is different about you," I murmured softly.

We stepped out the arched doors of House Aestra's impressive ballroom to the garden terrace. Mina nodded towards a bower near the balustrade. Further on, fire moths danced in the tall garden flowers, drawn by the ambrosia of night blooms. People gathered in groups, sparkling wine in hand, chatting under the unusually clear night sky.

"Could we take a moment?" she asked.

"Of course," I replied, following her lead.

The bower was covered in night-blooming honeysuckle, which was covered in fire moths sipping at the flowers. Mina's skin glowed like the moon under the dancing light of the flying insects. One lit on her shoulder as she sank onto the bench inside the bower. Its white furry body was larger than the others, and the glow it gave off was blue, rather than the pale silver light of the rest of the moths. She smiled as it rubbed its fuzzy face against her cheek. My breath caught in my throat, and my body froze.

The picture she made with the elemental creature so close to her beautiful face was like nothing I'd ever seen. Somehow, even with my missing memory, I was as sure of that as I was of the emotions brewing in me. This was more than lust, more than duty. I cared for her, wanted to see her satisfied in all things.

In that moment, I was sure of only one thing: I would do anything to give her what she wanted. Nothing would stop me from protecting her, from being at her side if she needed me, away if she asked it. I would journey miles to find anything she needed, extinguish any who harmed her, and someday, if she let me, I would love her.

The thought stunned me. I loved Skye and Morpheus deeply. They were my family, the deepest companions of my heart. We had forged trust between us with time and experience, in thousands of thoughtful actions and conversations. But this was an altogether different feeling. It was as though my heart already knew hers.

This woman *was* my fate. She was as inevitable as moonrise. Her eyes met mine as the moth whispered silently to her. She nodded once, acknowledging it, but her gaze did not waver. I wondered if she felt it too, the way Lady Fate had her talons wrapped around us. Would Mina buckle in submission, as I was about to?

I took one step towards her, my fingers grazing her chin, her soft jawline. I hesitated, not wanting to muss her hair. My thumb swept over her bottom lip, and she let out a gasp that wove between us, the threads of Fate's magic tightening. Mina's fingers closed around my free hand, tugging me towards her.

When my face was just inches from hers, our breath met in a moment so heavy with possibility I thought she might turn from me. But she did not. Instead, she whispered just one devastating sentence. "I want all of you."

I searched her eyes for telltale signs of lust, but found only raw vulnerability. Yes, there was desire there, as there was for me. It was not the base desire of bodies feverish to make quick contact. Instead, in her gaze, I found the longing that haunted me. Longing for some place to belong, just as I did. For some*one* who could love the monster I knew lurked inside me. I pulled her onto my lap in one fluid motion, wrapping my arms around her waist.

"Then I am yours," I replied. But it wasn't enough. I needed to know that she would promise the same. "Will you be mine as well?"

She nodded once, solemn as a priestess, and destiny ricocheted through me, wounding as it gave me hope. When my lips met Mina's, a drumbeat sounded in the recesses of my mind, menacing in its violent threat. Rather than warning me off the path I walked now, it drove me further, my grip tightening on the woman who kissed me with need that echoed my own. I deepened the kiss, my hands drifting now over the curves of her body, the silken fabric of her gown slick against my touch.

"Not here," I said, my mouth still on hers. The warning in my mind was clear. When I entered Mina, I could lose some measure of control of my magic. She would be safe, but no one else would be. I couldn't risk revealing myself. "I know what I said, but not here."

"What is happening to us?" she asked.

I shook my head, unsure, but glad it was not just me. "I don't know, Mina. Is this what falling in love feels like?"

A helpless little laugh let me know just how unmoored she felt. She was at as much of a loss as I was, then. "I don't know. I've never fallen in love before."

I hugged her to me. "This seems like something people are supposed to know, doesn't it?"

Her breath on my neck was distracting, but sweet in its comforting simplicity. "How do you know this isn't just lust?"

I sighed, knowing it was best to be frank. "I am not a monk, Mina."

She nodded. "Neither have I been chaste, as I said before."

"So how do *you* know?" I asked.

She shook her head, watching the fire moths floating around the bower. Music from further away on the terrace floated towards us. Someone was playing the harp. "For me, it is like I've always known you."

Her words pierced me. For the smallest moment, I thought I might panic, but I could not say why. "Yes," I said, the word slowly leaving my mouth. "Yes, that is exactly how I feel. How strange."

"What is strange about that?" she asked. "I've read some of your romances. Is this not how lovers often feel?"

At that, I laughed. "You are right. Perhaps that's what is strange. I don't have many... How to put it?" She waited for me to speak, her eyes infinitely patient, an expression I'd never seen on her face before. *I'd* elicited this from her. Patience from one of the most driven women I'd ever encountered. "Universal experiences," I finished when words found me again. "I don't often seem to feel or react the way most people do to things."

Mina slid off my lap, taking my hand in hers, pressing it to her lips. "Neither do I. Perhaps that is why we're so drawn to one another."

I nodded, feeling like someone had cut me loose. From what, I could not say, but the unmooring was not unwelcome. In fact, it felt as though an adventure lay before me, new and alluring. I stood. "So, we'll do this together?"

"Yes," she replied. "We'll do this together, and when it's done, when we find Chopard..." she trailed off, as though suddenly unsure.

I finished for her. "We will sail those waters together as well."

MINA

His words sent a fissure through me, cracking into the wall that stood between me and the last of my memories. There was a thick mist between me and all I wanted to know, but one memory in particular floated back to me: the vision I'd had of the women standing over me, talking while they thought I was unconscious. *What had they said? Something about a loophole. Something about love.*

When the memory had first returned, it meant nothing to me. It was only evidence that there had been life before the fetch. But now I wondered—was love part of what I needed to end this? Were their words a benediction, rather than a threat?

If, as I was beginning to suspect, I had been cursed, then some essential part of my nature must have been taken into consideration. Vaness Wildfang was a terrible mother, but she had been a thorough teacher, and I knew that curses only worked if you truly understood someone.

If someone had cursed me before I'd ever encountered the Wildfangs, then it had been someone who knew me. Someone who knew that love did not come easily to me, and would not in any life, any iteration of my essence, as I was unlikely to ever trust another enough to love them. Someone who knew that every curse had to have a loophole to bind properly—and that truly loving another would be an appropriate one for me.

As I looked up into Ash's golden eyes, fixed on me like I was the moon he hung all his hopes upon, I knew. I could love him. And not just him, but Poe, Skye, and Morpheus as well. I'd been right this afternoon. This thing that had plagued me through lifetimes could be vanquished. Though I was not even sure yet what it was, what followed me, relentlessly haunting me, I knew I wanted it gone. And now I had hope. If there was a curse upon me, it could be broken, but there would be a price.

My pride, my fear—they would all have to go. Trust was not built on secrets. "This is not my true body," I said, without hesitation. "This is a fetch, a doppelganger. I am not real or natural." I paused, waiting for his face to twist with disgust. But like Poe, he merely appeared curious.

"You feel very real to me," Ashbourne responded, pulling me to him. The hard warmth of his body infused me with hope. I dared not breathe for fear he would change his mind. His head bent low. "And when I am buried deep inside you tonight, you will know just how real you are. Nature means nothing to me. I want all of you."

Tears welled in my eyes as a fresh wave of arousal flooded my core. This was what true desire felt like, emotion tangled with attraction so strong it could unthaw even the coldest of hearts. "Then, you don't care?"

He shook his head. "You could turn into a wraith, a White Lady, a ghoul, and I would still want all of you, Mina. I want *you*, not the vessel that carries you." The words were spoken with such depth of feeling, I wondered for the briefest moment if they were for me.

Wasn't this all too fast? Too soon? Shouldn't I be suspicious? Thoughts flooded me, trying to overwhelm me with doubt. I shoved them aside. For once, I wanted something good for me. Something that had nothing to do with survival or revenge. What I wanted now was a life, and I was willing to fight for it.

"Thank you," I said. Simple gratitude was all I could manage, the lump of emotion in my throat so potent I could not say more.

"Shall we get to work?" he asked.

I nodded. "And later?"

His grin was a promise, followed by a hard swallow, his throat bobbing with the same emotion I felt. "Later, I will show you what devotion means to me."

~

I'D VISITED some of the upper echelon's homes in my childhood, but House Aestra's terrace was like nothing I'd ever seen. The structure itself jutted out above the city, which peeked out from the mist and clouds below, where every so often, lights sparkled in the depth of the dark night. Up here, the air was crisp and dry, all the stars visible in the clear sky. There was no moon; Fate's lady hid her face from us in her monthly retreat inward.

The fire moths lit the fragrant flowers of the garden. Up here, where the sun could actually peek through the clouds, so many more varieties of flowers bloomed. Pravhna's climate was fairly temperate. Despite the fact that the autumn rain could be brutal, it was merely chilly, not truly cold, as it would have been in Somershire. Scattered amongst the overflowing flower beds were nooks meant for intimate encounters, marked by carved stone arches. Various delights graced tables and the trays that floated unaccompanied through the crowds.

Elspeth Aestra had pulled out all the stops for tonight's party, using so much magic I had to wonder who exactly was pulling the strings. Was she powerful enough to light the gardens and keep floating trays on their paths? Or had she a team of Oscarovi somewhere managing it all? That would be expensive, but she certainly had the capital to do something of the sort.

There weren't so many guests as to feel overwhelming, but neither were there so few that the party felt small. I couldn't help but be impressed. As Maman had not entertained much, I had very little idea how one pulled something like this off. From watching Poe, I knew the answer was "carefully." More than that, I might never know.

My fingers tightened around Ash's arm. If he meant what he'd said, and I believed that he did, my life would probably never look like this. There would be no posh parties, no giant townhouse in the upper echelons. No large events to plan or execute. Relief crashed over me. I wanted none of this. I wanted purpose, and most of all, peace.

Ash took a coupe glass from the tray that had paused before us. It was full of a sparkling rose liquid. I took a sip. Crisp apple burst on my tongue, followed by the sweet taste of burnt sugar and something vaguely floral. He sipped from his own glass and smiled. "Tastes like a day at the orchard."

A smile stole through me, reaching my eyes before it did my mouth. "It does, though I can't say I've ever been to an orchard. But this is exactly what I imagine it would taste like."

Happiness rolled off us as we stared at each other. That nasty voice inside me tried to make a remark, but I couldn't hear it. Over Ashbourne's shoulder, I caught sight of Caralee Ellis-Whitley. "Will you hunt down one of those trays of cheese puffs?" I asked.

Ash followed my gaze, his brows knitting slightly, but he nodded. "I will." He brushed a kiss to my cheek, his breath lingering for a moment. Caralee looked up as his cool knuckles brushed over my jaw. "So beautiful," he murmured as he turned away. I watched him stride after one of the floating trays, stifling a laugh as it moved just fast enough that he'd have to jog to keep up.

When I turned back to the crowd, Caralee openly glared at me. I walked towards her, keeping my pace relaxed. There was no need to rush and risk tripping on the rough stone pavers that formed the terrace's many winding paths. Besides, it agitated Caralee, who so obviously waited to have a confrontation.

As I approached her, I noticed she no longer wore the ring Viridian had given my sister. I could practically feel my eyes glimmering with mirth. "Good evening, Caralee. You look beautiful tonight." It wasn't a lie; she was gorgeous in a ruby colored gown that draped alluringly over her tiny waist. Her mass of dark curls was pulled into a tight bun, and to my mind, the pale skin of her forehead appeared a bit strained. "I always appreciate someone who knows just exactly how much jewelry to wear to one of these events."

She fumed. My heart sang with the pleasure of it. The woman had tormented me for years when we were children, pretending to be friends for months on end, then embarrassing me at the most inopportune moments. All of it had been a game to her.

"Do you?" she asked as she regained her composure. "Have you been to many of these kinds of events, then? I don't recall seeing you."

Good. She was going to play rough. I wanted a fight. "Are you invited to many parties with the likes of House Aestra?" I asked, taking a firm guess that she was here because House Montclair had been invited, and not on her own merit, which meant that Viridian was here somewhere.

Caralee's eyes blazed with fury. "At least I'm not here riding the coattails of some undercity hoodlum."

I felt Ash return before I saw him, felt him tense at Caralee's words, and my own fury rose to meet hers. "No, that's true, Caralee. You come riding the coattails of Helene's leftovers." I stepped closer to her, dropping my voice a measure. "How does it feel to know that you only have what you do because someone *murdered* my sister?"

Caralee gasped, sputtering. "How... *dare* you?"

It had been a calculated move, cruel, but it did as I hoped it would. Caralee searched the crowd for Viridian. She had never been the kind to stand up for herself. She moved in crowds of people who were just as small-minded and petty as she was. Helene had been just as vicious as she was, but never so small.

I'd hit her where it hurt the most, revealing an insecurity, and now she wanted Viridian to come put me in my place. I wondered if she knew that he'd put me in the oubliette. It wouldn't surprise me much if she had, nor would it surprise me to know that he'd kept her in the dark. Ash stepped up beside me, handing me a small plate of cheese puffs.

He followed my gaze, which tracked Caralee's. She had taken a few steps away from us, and was preparing to disappear into the crowd. Her eyes lit when she found Viridian. He was at the opposite end of the terrace, leaning against the balustrade. His coat was tailored close to his trim form, and was a deeper shade of crimson than Caralee's dress, but it was obvious he'd dressed to match her, which was unfortunate. The color did not complement his pale hair or skin one bit. Cooler colors suited Viridian better, I decided. He was deep in conversation with a shorter Oscarovi man, who faced away from us.

The man had pale skin and wan brown hair. There was nothing of interest about him whatsoever, except that he wasn't dressed for the party. His suit was nice enough, and had obviously been tailor-made, but the invitation had specified formal dress. When I turned back, Caralee had disappeared, melting into the crowd. No doubt she was off to tattle on me to Viridian.

"What a terrible woman," Ash said as we both watched the man speaking to Viridian. Ash was looking him over carefully as well. I wondered if he noticed the sartorial misstep. Likely he did. He had a careful eye for detail. "Someone should break all her fingers."

I made a non-committal sound as his words fully sunk in. My curiosity piqued. "Why her fingers?"

Ash swiped a cheese puff from my plate and popped it into my mouth. The melted sharp cheddar combined with a hint of tart cranberry jam and buttery pastry. It was divine. He smiled at my apparent reaction to the puff. "Because then she'd require help wiping her own ass."

My nose wrinkled at the picture forming in my head. It was an awful thing to say. Also, it pleased me so much I wished the crowd would simply disappear so I could tear his clothes from his body. "Wicked boy," I purred.

"Beautiful menace," he replied.

For a moment, it seemed we might forget ourselves and give into our passions without care for who watched. Across the terrace, the man talking to Viridian moved, his face briefly visible. It was a plain face, one most would forget the instant they saw it, but I'd seen it many times before.

"I know him," I said, careful to keep my voice low. "He is one of those who used to come to the house to meet with Maman." I looked at the sky. "Often, on nights such as these."

"The dark moon." It was a statement, not a question. He'd scanned through as many of Maman's spell books as I had recently. The dark moon was ripe for many kinds of workings. Many of them neutral, but many dangerous as well. I had no idea if the timing was significant, but it would be lazy not to assume that it was.

The man shook hands with Viridian, and then turned. Ash took my plate from my hands, leaving it on a bench. "Come, we need to talk with him, then."

CHAPTER 33

MINA

Overhead, the Orilion phenomena appeared as Ash pulled me through the terrace garden. The lights must have been manifesting while I argued with Caralee. Now they danced in the sky, green and violet ribbons of light. Somewhere deep inside me, a resonance built in my chest, behind my lungs. It was as though some part of me vibrated in time with the celestial dance.

I took my eyes off the lights in time to see the faint blue glow of a loping gait, close to the ground. My breath stuck in my throat. It couldn't be. They didn't leave the mountain. The flash of a pale tail stopped my feet—I froze in place.

Ash looked back. "We'll lose him."

My heart beat faster. "Go. I'll catch up."

He shook his head, seeming to sense that I'd seen something important. "No, I won't leave you."

"Go," I insisted. Just beyond him, in a giant rosemary bush, a long ear poked out as a chill breeze kicked up. The hare was behind the bush, waiting for me.

"All right," Ash agreed, though he still held onto my hand. "If I don't return, find Skye and Poe. I'll meet you at home."

I liked the way he said home. I nodded, pulling my hand from his grip. He'd lose the man if I stayed with him, and I would lose the hare. He flashed a quick, reassuring grin at me, then disappeared. A moment of envy caught me by surprise. It would be nice to be so mobile, so quick and free of pain. Even now, after a day of rest and preparation, my body ached. I flexed my shoulders slightly. The place between them hurt more tonight than usual.

Ash had the ability to free me from my pain, to make even the worst bouts of it pass, even if just for a short while. The little of his touch I'd already experienced was enough to know that the ways his body was attuned to mine would be more than a balm. In his embrace, I experienced ecstasy, however brief. That would have to be enough for me. As I made my way slowly toward the rosemary bush, I had the distinct feeling that it would be more than enough.

"Hello," I said as I approached the bush. "I see you."

The hare poked its head out. I couldn't be certain, but it looked like the one that had helped me escape the ruin's collapse at Somer-haven. *You have become distracted*, it said.

"I do not recall you giving me a mission," I replied, feeling tart. "You only told me you'd be watching and that all I do matters."

The hare glared at me, its vicious, cunning paws raising towards its chest. I'd seen common hares box one another before. Surely, this one did not intend to punch me. *You are impertinent.*

"Very likely so," I agreed. "But if you have something you need to tell me, I am happy to hear it."

The hare's head tilted slightly, its terrifying eyes reflecting the dying light of the Orilion. *My brethren dance to the songs of the stars. Can you hear the music?*

I glanced behind me. Sure enough, in the fading lights, air elementals, many in the shapes of serpentine dracon, undulated with the Orilion. Though the lights faded, the resonant music inside me had not. I felt the music, rather than hearing it, but I supposed that was good enough. I nodded. "Yes, I feel the music. What does it mean?"

It is Her song. She gathers us to Her. Which side will you choose?

I knew better, but the cryptic knots the hare spoke in were terribly frustrating. I sighed. "Whatever do you mean?"

Impertinent, the hare scolded. I didn't dare roll my eyes. Already, I'd pushed the rules of etiquette too far. *You must choose between this world and the past. She Who Waits does not mean you harm. But should you choose incorrectly, there will be consequences.*

"Is there some kind of rule that you cannot simply tell me what it is you mean?" Speaking so was a risk, but I was ever so tired, and the revelations of my day emboldened me.

I could have sworn the hare sighed. Its paws lowered, and it stared at the Orilion as it faded, the air elementals dispersing. In the crowd, near the balustrade, the hush that had fallen over the party broke. People began chatting again, and the Vilhari on the harp picked out a soothing melody.

We do not intend to cause you distress. But it is required that you choose without interference. This is our way.

A sharp gust of wind cut through the thin fabric of my dress. "And is this not interference?"

It is a reminder, the hare said before fading. *When you have decided, meet us at the standing stones.*

The mere mention of the standing stones struck fear into me. I'd trifled with the nameless elemental gods once and survived. My base instinct warned me not to think of doing so again, not without good cause. I fought against this new information. I had decided on another path. Anger and fear mixed within me, souring my stomach.

Fear won. I'd been too well educated on the lore of the eldritch origins of the spirits, and the dangers they posed to the corporeal beings of Sirin. I could sell Orchid House, start a new life, whatever I wanted, but the elementals could find me anywhere. There was no running from this. Disappointment flooded me, adding urgency to fear's sharp bite.

A single tear leaked from the corner of my eye. "How will I know that I've decided?"

You will know, came the hare's voice, though it was gone.

I stood staring at the spot the hare had been for a long time, though if it were minutes or hours, I had no real idea. I had decided on another path—could I still have the life I'd imagined, if I was drawn deeper into this mess? A hand touched my arm. By instinct, I flinched, but relaxed as soon as I saw Poe. All made better sense with her by my side.

The hare was correct: I knew exactly which side I would choose.

Hers. Poe was the kind of person who could change Sirin for the better. And I was exactly the kind of person who could support her from the shadows.

Oblivious to my monumental revelation, Poe smiled. "Skye went after Ashbourne. She said we should say our goodbyes and head home."

I stood staring at the spot where the hare had been for a long moment.

"Are you all right?" Poe asked.

"Yes," I said. I wasn't ready to tell her about the hare just yet. The encounter had unsettled me, and I needed to sort things out. "Should we find Elspeth, then?"

Poe nodded slowly, obvious concern written all over her face. "If something was wrong, you would tell me, wouldn't you?"

I took a deep breath. "This afternoon I decided that when we find Chopard, I want to sell Orchid House." I wasn't going to lie to Poe about the hare, but I needed time to think over what it had said.

"You want to sell Orchid House? But why?" Poe sounded genuinely shocked. "What about revenge and finding out what happened to your family?"

My chin quivered, but the warm, safe feeling I got when Poe asked me questions reassured me. Before the oubliette, I dismissed feelings like these, not knowing how to interpret them. Now, I learned to trust myself. And Poe.

"I don't want to know who killed them anymore. I want to be done with all of this." Gingerly, I took Poe's hands, waiting to feel the usual tightness in my chest at touching someone. I felt only comfort as her hands closed around mine, her expression open and earnest. "These past weeks have been the nicest of my life. If you'll have me, I'd like to help you find *your* family."

Poe nodded as I spoke. "Of course I'll have you. But..." she trailed off, her brows furrowing.

My voice dropped a level. "Whoever burned the house down did me a favor, Poe. I'm free. I don't need to know more."

"Muse said that all this is connected. You may find out more whether you like it or not."

She was right, of course, and I'd already considered that. "I know. And that's fine, but I only want to follow this as far as taking Chopard down. The only thing I want for myself now is a new life. One free from the upper echelons."

Poe nodded, then sighed. "You'll get quite a lot of money from the house. What will you do?"

Yes, that was exactly the point—we could stop depending on the Syndicate for money—but I didn't want to say that just yet. She needed time to adjust to the idea, and so did I. "I'd like to find out what I'm good at. I don't hardly even know myself. Vaness didn't raise me to have a purpose."

"I think that sounds wonderful, Mina." Poe took my arm, and we turned to find Elspeth in the crowd. "Will you come live with me? I have a little space you could use as a bedroom, and my neighborhood is darling. So many lovely cafes and galleries."

"Yes," I said, a picture of it forming in my head. Poe let out a shuddering breath, relief coloring her smile. She wanted this too. Hope fluttered in my chest, bright as a newborn chick. To keep myself from any earnest proclamations of undying friendship, I pointed across the terrace. "Look, there's Elspeth and Mirabelle."

Poe's smile was slightly smug; knowing, at any rate. She heard the unspoken proclamations, despite the fact that I'd clamped all earnestness down. I bumped her shoulder with mine, rolling my eyes a little. She laughed softly, nodding as though I'd spoken words she agreed with.

I'd watched Skye and Ash communicate wordlessly and wondered what it would be like to have someone like that in my life, and here she was. The oubliette had taken so much from me, but when I looked at Poe, I came to realize it had given me something precious as well. I said a silent prayer of thanks to Lady Fate, my first ever, promising to plant deadly nightshade to honor her name.

We made our way to the House Aestra matriarchs. Now that the light show was over, the party was breaking up. There were only a few guests left on the terrace. As we drew closer, Mirabelle spoke to Elspeth in fervent, hushed tones. When they spotted us approaching, Elspeth beckoned us to her.

She gripped Poe's arm as soon as she came within reach, alarm in her eyes. "Niall was here," she said, after looking around to make certain no one was within earshot.

"He stole something," Mirabelle added. "Though I can't say what yet. But he ransacked my study."

"Someone saw him?" Poe asked.

"Yes," Mirabelle answered, voice sharp. "Me. He nearly knocked me over, rushing out."

"He was hiding something in his coat," Elspeth explained. "Mother thinks he made a mess to hide what was taken. Where is Skye?"

"Following a lead," Poe replied. "We should get home. Will you send word when you know what Niall took?"

"Absolutely," Elspeth promised. A twitch near her jaw gave me pause. Was she nervous about something? "Go now before Msr VanGuerten makes his way over here. He says the longest goodbyes." She kissed Poe generously on each cheek, her hand lingering on the younger woman's face for a moment. "You are so lovely. I can see why my girl holds you in such high regard."

Mirabelle sniffed a little derisively but did not contradict the statement. Poe blushed. "I feel the same about her."

Elspeth beamed with pride, nodding vigorously. "How lovely," she said, emotion thick in her voice. She was impressed by Poe, happy that she was interested in her daughter. "How very lovely."

My gaze flitted between them, my heart swelling with happiness. When this mess was over, we had much to look forward to.

CHAPTER 34

ASHBOURNE

Skye and I nearly ran into one another. We'd been around the block twice, but the man Mina spotted had disappeared. My frustration mounted. Too many were getting away from us these days. It felt like I was always just a touch too slow for my opponents. I wasn't used to the feeling, and it unsettled me more than I cared for.

"Shit," I swore. "We lost him."

My partner paused before she answered me, her molars grinding together in vexation. She too was losing patience. Undoubtedly, this job was more complex than any we'd worked together, but the basics were the basics, and usually we made headway more easily than this. When she spoke, her voice was strained. "Let's widen the search a few blocks. What do you say?"

I narrowed my eyes, raising an eyebrow. It was unlike Skye to sound so unsure. But she was already walking, and I was right behind her. "What are you thinking?"

Skye picked up the pace. "A few blocks down from here, there's a little park with a smattering of crattie conveniences."

I snickered at the term. "Eateries with all the tiny food?"

She nodded, laughing along with me. It broke up some of the tension that frustration had built between us. "Indeed. What a foolish trend. You always go home hungry and it's twice as expensive as anywhere else."

The casual banter was the lifeblood of our relationship. It got us back on more solid ground. I saw her line of thinking, though. "It would be a good place to catch a cab. If he didn't have a driver of his own, perhaps he went there."

"It's a long shot," she replied, some of the agitation from before still lingering in her words. "But worth a look."

Of course, she was right. Skye was always thorough. We fell into companionable silence for a block. As we reached the square, Skye motioned to me that she would go left, and I'd go right. I'd given her a good description of what the man had been wearing and his build, though I hadn't gotten a look at his face. The goal now had to be to find out who he was. We could bring Mina to him, if necessary.

I began my walk around the square, still amazed by how clear the sky was this far up the mountain. The stars were beautiful, but it felt as though I might float away. Some part of me missed the cloud cover. As I walked, I watched the cab line gathering in front of the little cafes grouped together on the opposite side of the square. The man was nowhere to be seen, but I spotted Skye, whose eyes were fixed on a dark alley.

She glanced over one shoulder, found me, and made the smallest motion of one hand. I couldn't believe it—had she found him? Careful not to draw attention to myself, I strode across the little park at the center of the square. I reached Skye's side just in time to see what she was looking at. A car drove into the alley, one that had just been in the cab line. It had one passenger in the back: Niall Aestra.

The man from the party stepped out from behind some trash bins and got into the car. Skye pushed me out of the mouth of the alley, behind an enormous pot of chrysanthemums. Someone had piled various sizes of pumpkins and gourds at the center of the arrangement. It was artistically done, and very convenient, as it hid us perfectly from sight. The cab pulled out of the alley and headed back in the direction of the undercity.

I shook my head. "He was talking to Viridian at the party."

Skye paused, grabbing my arm. "*Ashbourne*. They're headed toward Orchid House."

That was undeniable. Orchid Street was on the way to the under-city from here. Skye rushed towards the cab line, searching each big black autocar until she found a Strix driver wearing Braithwaite tweeds. She knocked on the window. The cabbie rolled it down. "What can I do for you?"

"We need transport back to Orchid Street, on the double. On business for Herself."

The Strix, who had the visage of a screech owl, raised her eyebrows. "Yeah?"

"Yes, yes. All the nonsense about velvet peonies riding at dawn."

The Strix clicked her beak. "Get in. I'll get you there."

THE RIDE WAS HARROWING, the Strix taking turns at a gut-wrenching pace. I was glad I'd only had one glass of sparkling wine, and no more than a dozen cheese puffs. But we got there in time to find Mina and Poe pulling up in a cab of their own, driven by Fulston Braithwaite, still half a block away. Skye patted the Strix's shoulder in relief, passing her the fare, as well as a generous tip. "What's your name?"

"Evelyn Masterson," she said, voice clipped as she glared out the front window at Fulston Braithwaite. Perhaps they were in some kind of competition with one another. "But everyone calls me Evie."

"You're the fastest cabbie I've ever had," Skye said with a grin.

Evie passed her a card. "Faster than him," she said, nodding at Fulston. "You call me whenever you're on business for Herself. I'll get you where you need to go."

Skye glanced at the card, letting out a low whistle. "The boss doesn't give too many of these out."

The Strix nodded. "That's right. I'm the best. Or I will be when Fulston gives up."

So I'd been right. Skye flashed the card at me, showing me what had elicited the whistle. It was one of the most expensively made calling cards on the market, the kind that came in packs of a baker's dozen, rather than a box. It would let Evie know our exact location if we used it to call for her.

The usual calling cards simply appeared in hallways or mailboxes when you wanted to schedule a visit with someone and didn't take much magic at all. But something like this was expensive for a reason. Edith must really trust this slip of a girl. I was doubly impressed now.

"Thank you," I said as I got out. I glanced back at Skye. "Don't let the girls in the house."

Skye nodded, giving the autocar a pat as Evie drove off. I slipped inside. As soon as I entered, I knew we were clear. Morpheus lay reclining on the steps, cleaning his paws.

There is someone in the garden, he said as I was about to go back out front.

I wondered why he hadn't done something about it, but asking the feline to justify anything was a losing battle. I ran through the back of the house to the housekeeper's office, taking the stairs to the garden two at a time. Sure enough, a shadow lurked in the garden. The figure stepped out of the darkness, into the golden square of aetheric light on the stone patio.

She was tall, with rounded ears and golden brown skin. Her hair was short, like Skye's, but the style was different, strangely cut. And though she wore clothing that was regular enough, slim trousers and a long wool overcoat, her shoes were the oddest thing I'd ever seen: white, and made from a material I could not immediately identify.

"Ash," she said, breathing a sigh of relief. "I'm so glad to have found you."

I frowned. "Are we acquainted?"

The woman's brown eyes narrowed. "That's rather cold of you. A week in the limen together wasn't much for you, eh?" The woman laughed easily, as though she expected I would laugh along. She had a lovely smile, but it faded almost immediately. I sensed something about her, some power that did not make sense.

"Are you not Oscarovi?" I asked, more confused than ever. If what I sensed was right…it couldn't be. The stranger had empyrae in her.

"Of course not." She laughed again, but this time she backed away, obviously nervous. "I'm human. You know that."

"Human?" I asked. The word sounded familiar, but I couldn't

place it. It was the root of humanoid, of course, but I knew of no people who claimed the name.

"Seventeen hells," she swore. "Do you not know me, Ashbourne?"

There was no threat in her voice, nor in her posture. It was obvious she knew me. A weight dropped into my stomach like dread. *She knew me.* Now I was the one to back away. "Whoever you are," I cautioned, "I don't want to know you."

Hurt flashed in her brown eyes, then determination. "Did you find her? Lumina?"

My mind caught on the name, a howl building from deep within my soul. "Get away from me," I growled. "Don't come back here again."

Her hands flew up in front of her, as though in defense, the sleeves of her overcoat falling down her arm. A tattoo of a compass glowed with celestial power. So that was how it got into her, this human. I shook my head. "Get. Out. Of. Here."

"I'm going," she agreed. "But I'll be back. Maybe Bayun can talk some sense into you."

My entire body vibrated with fear, empyrae mounting in my hands. I couldn't go in the house this way. When the woman disappeared, my entire body sagged with relief. Her footsteps traveled away from the house. I listened until they faded away, squeezing my eyes shut tight.

When I opened them, the yard was empty, and I felt a lingering sense of confusion. *What had happened? Why did I come out here?*

WHEN I GOT BACK in the house, Morpheus waited for me by the back door. *Did you find what you were looking for?*

I nodded. "All clear."

The cat turned his lamp-like eyes on me. *No one in the garden?*

"Not a soul," I said. He was in a mood then, because he stalked off, huffing in frustration. I went to the front to give the girls the all clear. The three of them sat on the front steps, Poe leaning against Skye's knees as Skye told them all we found out. Mina had made them a sound dampening bubble, but it encompassed the door to the house, so though I could sense the spell working from the way the sound of traffic on Orchid was muffled, I could still hear them.

"The house is clear," I said, reaching out to help Mina up. I was tempted to scoop her into my arms and kiss her, right here on the front steps, but I wasn't sure how she would react to that.

She leaned on me as she stood. "These shoes are too much," she complained as she let her muffling spell go with a flick of her hand. Little tendrils of aether clung to her fingers. She tucked them into her pocket, sparing a moment for a tiny smile.

"Thank you for going on without me," she said as we walked into the house. Skye and Poe stayed out front, murmuring to one another about more mundane topics. We turned to look at them.

"Coming in?" Mina asked, though the quirk of her lips told me she already knew the answer.

Neither of them looked back at us, so engrossed in one another's eyes as they were. "Be in later," Skye said, her voice thick with concentration.

Mina let out an amused breath as I shut the door behind us. "You should have seen Elspeth Aestra saying goodbye to her. The woman has her sights set on Skye wedding the last princess of House Feriant."

I chuckled. "She's going to be rather disappointed then."

Mina looked back at me, her eyes sharp. "Why is that?"

I held up my hands in mock defense. Had I already done this— reacted just this way? *No, that wasn't right.* I grinned at Mina, banishing the odd feeling. "Stand down, little menace. I only meant that I doubt Elspeth will get a society wedding out of the pair of them."

"Oh," Mina said, a blush creeping onto her cheeks. "I apologize. I'm a bit protective of Poe."

I stepped towards her, our hands brushing. "I like it very much. Your protective side, that is." Her eyelashes brushed her cheek, and I didn't think it was modesty, but she was battling some feeling. I bent toward her, bringing my mouth to her ear as my fingers wound through hers. "Did I detect a bit of that protectiveness when Caralee called me a hoodlum?"

"Perhaps," she said, her damaged voice low and sweet.

"Does that mean you care for me as well?" I asked.

"Perhaps," she replied, this time turning her eyes to mine. "You know I do."

"I do," I said, my voice dropping to its lowest register. Heat rushed through me. "And I believe I promised to show you the meaning of devotion tonight, did I not?"

"You did," she said, turning to the stairs. "The night grows short. You'd better get started, if you've any hope of making me understand."

I swept her into my arms, our mouths crashing together as she wound her arms around my neck. I pulled away just long enough to make a promise. "You will. And if you don't understand the first time I show you, then I'll simply have to demonstrate it again."

CHAPTER 35

MINA

I don't know how we made it to my bedroom. All I knew was the tangle of hands and the power of Ashbourne's body, moving mine at incredible speed. Everything slowed as he set me down in front of the bed. No fire was lit in my bedroom, the night air cold at the top of the house.

Slowly, I turned. "Unbutton me?"

The heat of his body warmed my backside, his breath caressing the shell of my ear as he trailed kisses down my newly exposed neck. "So many buttons," he purred.

The dress fell away from my body, leaving only the meager undergarments I'd adorned myself with. He turned me in his arms, his eyes hungry with desire. "What is this?"

"I believe they call it lingerie," I said, my words carrying a challenge and a bite.

He took them easily, swallowing them down as he dragged one finger over the laces of the close-fitting camisole I wore, sending shivers down my back. My fingers went to work as well, pushing his waistcoat off first, then moving on to the buttons of his shirt. He'd removed everything else before we came upstairs, so there was little else for me to do.

The laces loosened, and he pulled the camisole off me, exposing my bare skin to the chill of the room. My body sang as his hands cupped my breasts, warm as they stroked my pebbled skin. He looked me over, as though afraid he might hurt me.

"I am all right," I breathed as his fingers dragged down the curve of my hips, setting my skin afire.

"You are beautiful," he replied, his dark hair falling into his eyes.

In the dim light of the bedroom, the angles of his face were all in shadow. He might be threatening, his body made for winning battles, but I was more interested in the pleasure it would bring me. He turned my body in his arms, bringing the unclothed skin of my back against his bare chest.

"Lean into me," he murmured as one hand cupped my breast again, the other sliding down to the curve of my belly.

I moaned as his fingers pressed into my flesh. His hard length pressed into the silk of my undergarment, the only thing I was left wearing. "Will you let me show you what devotion means to me, Mina?" he whispered in my ear, his fingers sliding under the scrap of silk that covered me.

"Don't go slow," I begged. "I need you."

He let out a primal growl and turned me around, depositing me on the bed, his body covering mine. Our kisses came fast and hard, his body moving against mine in expert ways. Ways that cleared my mind of any thought but how I might get more of this feeling, more of this friction, this pleasure. My thighs squeezed around his, damp heat building between them.

"Please," I begged, knowing he would not relent until I asked him to. "I need you inside me."

His breath was as quick and labored as my own. My back arched with need as his fingers grazed over the curves of my body, then pulled the fabric of my undergarment aside, cool air meeting my hot, moist skin.

Ash's mouth met mine as his fingers found the places I needed him most. This was sheer torture and the height of gratification all at once. His touch was more than I'd hoped for and somehow not enough. My cries were desperate, pleading for him to go further, as I writhed against his touch.

Harder and harder he kissed me, his hand working in time with each thrust of his tongue, each nip of my bottom lip and then my neck, moving lower to my collarbone. Then his mouth covered one exposed breast, his kiss harder and more insistent now. Heat built in me, gathering into a tight knot at my core. My eyes fell shut as my hips moved with each circle he wove with his fingers.

Ash's breath was hot in my ear as his mouth left my breast, commanding me. "Open your eyes."

I did as he asked, finding his beautiful face hovering above mine as I whimpered with need. "More, I need more."

He nodded, his hands leaving me only for the time it took to remove his pants. And then he fitted his slim hips between my thighs, pushing me open for him. "Is this what you need?" he asked, his voice soft and husky.

"Yes," I murmured as his fingers closed around my chin.

"Don't look away," he pleaded. "I want your eyes right here."

I did as he asked, his body moving against mine. He entered me slowly, carefully, his face tender as I moaned his name. "Yes," he breathed as he filled me. I pulled him down atop me. I wanted him covering me.

"Don't stop," I said. "I want you hard and fast."

He had no verbal response, only the increase in speed I begged for. Our bodies moved in perfect concert, my pain fading as every delicious moment of friction and wet heat brought me closer to an edge I wanted more than anything.

When Ashbourne's mouth met mine again, drawn together as if by some cosmic force, white light flashed behind my eyes. My voice went ragged with my cries, my fingers wound tightly in his hair.

Every muscle in me clenched, my toes curling as his voice met mine. The power of his release took me over the edge and into another swell of ecstasy I hadn't known possible. Our bodies rocked against one another as we slowed, but could not quite stop.

He brushed a damp strand of hair from my face. "You are incredible," he murmured. "Better than I could have imagined."

I raised an eyebrow. "I did very little."

He laughed. "You did plenty. And you will do more before the sun rises."

"Will I?" I breathed, my breath quickening already, my body tightening around him once more.

"Yes," he promised, his words backed up by the reigniting passion that sparked between us and inside me. His hips pushed against mine —and I believed him. "You will take all I give you and more."

"I will," I moaned. "Give me all of you."

He did, over and over, until I knew Ashbourne Claymore's definition of devotion by heart.

CHAPTER 36

MINA

I woke up with a start, my legs tangled in Ash's, his fingers twisted in my hair. He mumbled something incoherent as I pulled out of his grip. What had woken me? I'd been dreaming, but could only remember snippets of the dream. Someone had been speaking to me, arguing with me. My thoughts raced as I tried to hold on to what was left. The argument felt important.

What are you doing here?

Saving you.

I sent word. I told you not to come.

Then hands gripped my arms, dragging me away. When the screaming began, I was shaken awake. I touched my face only to find that tears stained it. I'd been crying in my sleep. My heart pounded, its beat all I could hear—the memory of pain seared into me.

A hand pressed into my back, its warmth a reminder of the pain. I closed my eyes, fighting the tears that threatened to overtake me. "What's wrong?" Ash's voice was careful, as though he feared my reaction.

I shook my head. "It was just a dream."

"Was it?" he asked, sounding a bit relieved. "Or was it another memory?"

"I don't know." My words came out in a strangled sob.

Gently, his fingers closed around my arm, pulling me into his chest. "What do you remember?"

"An argument," I said, after a few deep breaths. "I was arguing with someone about saving me."

A thoughtful hum sent vibrations through me. "Would it help to tell me more?"

I shrugged. Truly, I didn't know anymore. The hare had said I would have to choose between the past and this world. Was there any use in thinking about what had already happened? "There was so much pain," I whispered. "And I told him not to come, but he came anyway."

Ash tensed beneath me. "What?"

I shook my head, sitting up. "It's what I said: *I sent word. I told you not to come.*"

All color had drained from his face, and there was a faraway look in his eyes. "Who were you speaking to?" he asked, his voice devoid of any emotion.

"I don't know," I replied, sitting up. "But I screamed it at him before they dragged me away. After that, it was all just pain." My hand crept over my chest and around the base of my neck, grasping for the spot between my shoulders.

Ash blinked a few times, color returning to his face as he focused on me. "That sounds terrible."

There was something oddly stilted about his words. "Is everything all right?" I asked, feeling suddenly tentative. Had I shared too much? Was this not what people did after intimate encounters? Though I'd had sexual liaisons before, I'd never spent the night with anyone.

A slow smile spread over his face, his fingers playing with my hair again. In the early hours of the morning, he'd washed it for me in the bathtub and it was still a little damp. "Everything is perfect, except for your dream. I wish that hadn't happened."

He sat up, brushing kisses onto my face as he did so. In a movement so quick I could hardly track it, he'd pulled me between his legs, my back resting against his chest as his fingers traced lines over my skin. I pulled the blankets up, not wanting the chill in the air to get to us. Beneath the covers, he teased me, skimming all the parts of me he'd learned last night would make me moan.

My body was sore, in the best ways possible, but I did not think I could take much more pleasure without the consequence of real pain. I winced slightly as his fingers brushed my core. "I'm sorry," he murmured, his hands moving away, wrapping around me in a comforting embrace.

"Please don't be sorry," I said. "Last night was wonderful. I'll just need a little recovery time."

"Take all the time you need," he said, his words warming me. "We never have to rush."

Something about the way he said the word caught my attention. "Never?" I leaned my head back on his shoulder, looking up at him.

There was a glimmer of mischief in his amber eyes. "What are you asking me, love?"

I hesitated, not able to find the right words. He saved me from my struggle. "We have all the time in the world, Mina. This is not a bit of casual fun for me. Is it for you?"

I shook my head. "No. I'm selling the house when we've found Chopard." I paused, watching for his reaction. He only waited, steady, countenance open and curious. "I'm moving in with Poe."

"And what if she and Skye wish to live together?" he asked, a smile growing.

I twisted around, straddling him. I'd changed my mind about the pain. A little more wouldn't do me any real damage. His breath caught as our bodies met, and he pulled me to him.

"You beautiful menace," he growled, before kissing me hard.

Every nerve in my body sang for him, some with pleasure, others with pain. The mix was exquisite, dark and rich as he slid inside me, our movements slow and small.

"If they want to live together," I breathed as his fingers traced my spine, "then I will find a place for myself, and you will sleep in my bed."

"I doubt I will sleep much," he whispered, his hands covering my breasts. "If this is how it is to be between us."

My back arched, and he wrung a keening cry of agreement from me. My vision went dark at the edges, all the tension from the nightmare snapping out of me in one clean break. Another memory replaced it: the set of keys I'd found in Helene's purse. There had been one I hadn't been able to identify, hadn't there?

Under me, Ashbourne found release, his grip on me tightening as our mouths crashed into one another. When our bodies finally stilled, he shook his head. "You got the better of me, love. Are you hurt?"

"A little," I breathed as I climbed off him. "But it was well worth the trouble."

He caught my hand in his as I got out of bed. "I don't want you to push yourself too hard, Mina. I meant what I said. We have all the time in the world. Where you go, I go—until you tell me not to."

I had my robe half on, but I paused, listening to him. He sat up, pulling the robe closed, and tying the sash for me. "Perhaps it's too soon to say this..." For the first time since we met, he seemed unsure.

I touched his face, my fingers running over his cheekbones. "Whatever you want to tell me, it's right on time."

"I want to be with you. Only you," he said. "And all else that comes after that."

His words dazzled me, simple as they were. Nervous energy flowed off him in waves as he waited for my response. "I feel the same," I said, after giving it a moment of thought. "There is no one else. I want to see where this goes."

Ash laughed, a sound so joyful it almost hurt to hear. What we were agreeing to was complex. Pain came with forging a connection like this with someone. But also love, and I was no longer afraid of love's weakening effect. Even the little taste of what was growing between us had me well fed. Love might make me weak in some ways, vulnerable, rather. But in so many others, it had the potential to strengthen me, lift me up.

Joy, I was discovering, was the antidote to pain. Living a life that meant something to me, with people I cared for, was far more important than anything else I'd ever wanted. This was no longer about letting Helene and Maman go, or forgetting them. Poe had been right the night before. I might have to confront all that at some point. Now, this was about finding the place I belonged, and I belonged wherever my friends were. Wherever Ash was.

I wrapped my arms around the man that had just offered me

another avenue to that belonging. "Thank you," I whispered as he hugged me back.

"For what?" he asked as he stood, his arms scooping me up. He walked toward the door to my little bathing chamber.

"For setting me free."

Some point of confusion flickered in his eyes, as though his mind stumbled over my words. Then his eyes cleared, and he smiled at me. "If anyone is mistress of her own fate, it is you."

I wasn't so sure about that, but it meant something to me that he thought so. We dressed at a leisurely pace, taking time to help one another in entirely unnecessary ways. Every touch was bliss, every stray kiss a promise for the days to come.

As we walked downstairs together, arm in arm, I leaned on him. Stairs were hard for me, and I didn't care that he knew it. Letting even a little bit of my vulnerability be known felt like a victory.

Downstairs, Poe and Skye chatted amiably in the dining room. When we walked in, they held hands, and did not spring apart or show signs of embarrassment. Instead, they smiled at us, and Ash smiled back. I nodded once, happy that they too had found solace in one another.

Breakfast was quiet. Peaceful even. I could not remember another such time in Orchid House. Quiet was typically a sign that Maman was angry, and her silence had been deployed as a weapon. This silence was different, carrying with it the comfort of ease and a hint of joy that I had not ever felt in my family.

Morpheus consumed an entire plate of poulet, and then stretched out on the table, purring. Ash left for a bit, and returned with a pot of tea, pouring each of us our preferred serving. Once done, he sat, opening our morning's conversation with a return to the previous night's events. "I believe our first order of business must be determining who our mystery man is."

Skye nodded. "I can visit Mother today, see what she knows, and how he's connected to Viridian. If she doesn't know outright, perhaps someone in her circle might find out more."

Poe squeezed Skye's hand. "That is good thinking. As Mina is the only one who saw him, it might help to employ a sketch artist."

"Do any of you know one not employed by the cityguard?" I asked.

Skye smiled then. "Yes. I believe Muse's lover is an artist who does portraits, is he not?" Her question seemed directed at Poe, whose smile brightened as she answered. "Indeed, Arcturus has done work like that in the past. Mina, Muse gave you his card, didn't he?"

"Yes," I replied, getting up to fetch it. It took a short trip to Maman's sitting room to fetch the card from the secretary desk, where Poe had filed it away. When I returned, I cleared my mind, then pressed my finger to the card, making a request to see Muse and Arcturus at their soonest convenience.

The response was nearly immediate, and I imagined the two of them might still be in bed together. As I had just left such a happy state, it was easy to smile. "They will see us in an hour. We are to bring pastries from the Clotted Calf. What does that mean?"

Ash grinned. "It's the best bakery in Halcyon's Gate. Right around the corner from Muse's place. Tell him we'll be there."

I did as asked, then turned to Poe. "Are you coming with us?"

She shook her head, picking up a piece of correspondence sitting next to her plate. "Vionette Celestine wants to see me for lunch. I asked her to do a little digging for me on Viridian's past. He spent some time in Ismit last year right after Mina's disappearance, and Vionette has connections there."

"Good," Ash replied. "The more we know about his movements, the better."

Poe hummed a little in the affirmative. "Yes, I hesitated to ask before. Vionette can be prickly about her Ismiti connections. Her reasons for leaving were unpleasant, I believe. But I couldn't justify leaving potentially valuable information on the table any longer."

"Thank you," I said.

Poe smiled at me. "Of course, darling. We're narrowing in on something, I can feel it."

As we parted ways for the day, I had to agree. There was an air of possibility hanging around us, as though our story was turning, on its way to a new chapter.

CHAPTER 37

ASHBOURNE

Watching Mina pick out pastries and a variety of cheeses at the Clotted Calf was nearly as satisfying as having her to myself in bed. Nearly. But her excitement at deciding on various delicacies was unmatched, and so endearing I had to stop myself from hugging her. When she had nearly three large bags of treats, and the clerks were dizzy with her requests, I hazarded a touch.

As my hand pressed against the small of her back, she turned towards me, her arm slipping around my waist. In the most alarmingly domestic movement, she lifted her face to mine, her eyes closing. She expected to be kissed. The sweetness of the moment, and her trust that I would oblige, moved me.

I dipped my head to meet her mouth, keeping the kiss chaste as I could manage, but my blood sang at her nearness. It had taken all my effort the night before not to allow my magic to run loose. Even now, I felt the song of empyrae in my blood, and some primal instinct told me to take her behind the building and bury myself in her—in every way possible.

Her tongue slipped into my mouth, evidence that she too was thinking of more adventurous encounters. I pulled back, running my thumb over her delectable mouth. "You are a wicked girl," I murmured as the clerks finished bagging our goods. "*My* wicked girl."

She did not smile with her mouth, but the gleam in her eyes was enough for me. "If only I could show you what I'm thinking," she whispered.

"All's ready," the clerk behind the counter said, a brunette Oscarovi with a pleasant smile. She pushed the bags forward.

Mina took one, and I paid, then took the remaining bags. Outside the bakery, the streets of the undercity filled with people. There was a lively bustle and the smell of the bakery mixed with the distinctly green scent of the florist next door. Mina shivered.

"Are you cold?" I asked, concerned for her wellbeing.

"No," she replied. "Well, yes. But it's not unpleasant. This is my favorite time of year. For weather, anyway."

As we walked, she told me about autumn in Somershire, the fall festivals and the Hallowed Moon rituals. A note of sadness followed every word she spoke, chasing down what should be pleasant memories. From that alone, I understood that she had not been intimately involved in any of the happy events she recalled, but only watched them.

She had spent her life as an outsider. When this was over, when we found Chopard, I was determined to take her to every one of the undercity's ridiculous seasonal celebrations. For her, I would happily make friends, socialize, anything to wipe away the sorrow in her voice. Anything to show her how wanted she was now, and—I paused—now, and for a very long time to come.

It surprised me how much I wanted a future with this woman. How I wanted to watch her enjoy her life. I'd become so distracted by the thought, it took me a moment longer than it might have otherwise to notice we were being followed. I did not turn to look behind us. It would do me no good.

Whoever followed knew what they were doing. Whenever I slowed, even a little, they did as well. We were nearly at Muse's. Though I did not want to frighten Mina, I would have to do a perimeter check of the building as soon as I had her safely delivered to the seer and his lover.

"We're being followed," she said, her voice light as she broke through my thoughts.

She surprised a laugh out of me. "Yes." I bumped her shoulder with mine, careful not to unbalance her with my bulk. "How did you know?"

Mina shrugged. "Are we almost to Muse's?"

We were on his block, in fact. "Yes, it's just there."

Her pace picked up slightly, and though I knew it must cause her pain to do so, she climbed the front steps of Muse's building swiftly. A line of brass call buttons was embedded next to the door. Mina seemed to know which to choose already, and she pressed the third one from the bottom. The speaker placed above the buttons crackled to life.

A rough voice spoke. "Muse is in the bath. I'll be right down."

Moments later, a person as tall as myself, but twice as wide, opened the door. His chest was broad, covered in dark hair exposed by his unbuttoned shirt. He had a mass of dark curls haloing his bearded face and sparkling brown eyes. "Hello," he greeted us. "I'm Arcturus."

"Hello," Mina replied, her voice pleasant. "We are being followed."

"Ah," Arcturus said, eyeing the bags in my hands. "Let me take those then, and show Mlle Wildfang upstairs, yes?"

I nodded, handing off the bags. As Mina disappeared inside the building, I narrowed my eyes at Arcturus, a warning.

"She is safe with us," he assured me. "Do what you need to make sure it stays so."

I nodded once, then turned, rushing down the steps. My gut told me to go back the way we'd come. I walked with purpose, knowing whoever followed wouldn't be out in plain sight, and would likely expect my pursuit, especially if they were after Mina, not me. I turned down several quiet streets, making a circle around Muse's building.

When I'd nearly come back to Muse's block, I caught the sound of a muffled struggle. I paused, locating the sound. It came from the garden level entrance to the townhome I'd just passed. I turned, racing back, before whoever followed me could escape. In the lower level entrance to the house, the Strix woman who'd asked me to murder Mina struggled with a tall, dark-haired young woman.

The Strix was overtaking the woman, or so I thought at first. But as I neared, I saw the truth of things: the dark-haired girl had a firm grip on the Strix's wrist, and the avian woman was punching her repeatedly, trying to get her to let go. I wasn't sure what to do, who to help, but before I could decide, a furry golden body rushed past me, streaking down the stairs.

"Don't let her get away," the dark-haired girl yelled to the cat, for that was what the little beast had been, I was sure of it. "She's one of *his*."

The Strix woman growled something I could not understand, some language I didn't know, and the girl snarled in response.

The cat arched his back, ready to fight, just as the dark-haired girl caught sight of me. She paused, distracted just long enough, and the Strix woman slipped her grip and ran, kicking the giant golden cat and shoving me aside as she went.

I made my way towards the stairs, thinking to see if the girl and the huge feline were all right. I lost sight of them for only a moment as I rounded the balustrade that kept folks on the street from inadvertently stepping into the staircase. When I reached the top of the steps, the girl and the cat were both gone. I ran to the bottom of the stairs, trying the door to the townhome.

To my surprise, it came open easily under my hand. The door swung open with an eerie groan. Inside, the garden level flat was empty. There was nothing inside, no furnishings, just layers of dust on the wide planks of the wood floor. And not a single footprint in the dust.

I stepped back outside, looking for another door, another obvious way the two of them could have disappeared. But there was nothing. Nothing at all. My breath shuddered through me. People did not just disappear into thin air. All the magic in the world did not allow for such a thing. I went back into the flat, sure I'd missed something.

I opened the few doors the little place had. There was only a tiny closet and a lavatory. No other door led to outside, and the walls were solid stone. I stood staring at the flat for long moments, wondering if I might be losing my good sense.

What other explanation could there possibly have been?

CHAPTER 38

MINA

Muse's flat was a wonderland. The walls were painted a rich peachy pink, and caught the light from the leaded glass floor-to-ceiling windows in a magnificent glow. Everywhere there were plants and comfortable places to sit. Plush velvet chairs in orchids and lavenders, sparkling chunks of raw crystals scattered about. Oversized pillows, covered in lush patterned fabrics, were strewn around a low stone table at the center of the room.

An entire wall was taken up by bookshelves, stuffed full of only fiction, most of it titles I'd never heard of. I was mesmerized by the books, wondering what it would be like to read as Muse obviously did, or Ash did. While I enjoyed the odd adventure story, I had rarely read for enjoyment. It wasn't that I didn't like to do so, but that Maman had not approved.

She'd called it a waste of time, and warned that too much fiction would rot my brain. Especially the kinds of books these were—mostly romances and fanciful stories about mythical creatures. Arcturus laid out tea just for the two of us on the stone table, as he asked me for my description of the man. Without thinking too hard, I told him, still staring at the books.

When he'd asked me a few questions, he got out a sketchbook.

"Feel free to sit and have some tea. When I have a basic sketch done, we'll see if we're close."

I nodded, reading more of the book's titles. "Have you read any of these?" I asked.

Behind me, the sound of sketching stopped. "Oh, yes, most of them. Though only half are mine."

"Oh," I said, frowning. I'd seen no pattern in the way the books were organized. How odd. "Which half?" I asked, turning.

Arcturus looked up from his sketch, his eyes lit with merriment. "I have no idea, love. I hardly remember anymore."

"Oh," I said again. "I assumed you meant that either the top half was yours... or perhaps the left side. Are they organized in some way?"

The Oscarovi laughed now. "No, we just shove them in wherever."

I took my overcoat off, draping it over a lavender velvet chair. I arranged a few pillows, then sat down on the floor, across from Arcturus. A gold earring with a dangling pink opal hung from one ear.

I sat quietly as he sketched, not wanting to bother him. Behind the door to the bedroom, a radio drama played, and there were faint sounds of splashing. Arcturus winced, setting his pencil down.

"You are in pain," I said, my voice deep with empathy.

He nodded. "Yes, do you mind?"

I wasn't sure what he asked, but there was a large glass device for smoking poppy on the floor next to him. Did he use the stuff to help the pain? If so, I had no desire to stop him. "Of course not," I said.

He did not reach for the pipe, but instead whispered the words, "Venisci Acraea." *Come, Acraea,* he'd said in ancient Oscarovi.

The opal at his ear glowed with blue light for a few moments, before a large moth spirit appeared, an air elemental. "Acraea helps me when my hands hurt," Arcturus explained.

I watched as the moth fluttered around Arcturus' face. They communicated silently, before she landed on the bridge of his nose, flapping her wings several times. When she took to the air, his eyes glowed faintly blue. "She can see my vision for the image now," he explained.

The spirit hovered over the paper for a moment, then landed. At almost the exact same speed as Arcturus had drawn before, lines appeared on the page, while Arcturus massaged his hands.

"I thought you meant to smoke poppy," I breathed, amazed by the way they worked together.

Arcturus smiled. "I might later. It does help with the pain a bit, but I want to get this done for you first. Acraea was happy to help."

"How did you form such a relationship?" I asked, amazed. Maman and Helene had both acted as though their elementals were servants, meant to do their bidding. Even the Laquoix sewists, who worked in beautiful collaboration with their elementals, seemed to have a working relationship. This was something different, more intimate, deeper. It was what I'd always dreamed of. Someone who understood my pain and who *wanted* to help me.

"It has always been this way between us." Arcturus' eyes fell on my ring. He smiled at me, sympathy in his eyes. "You are not inspirited, then?"

I realized my mistake instantly. My eyes widened with the gravity of my error.

"I'll tell no one," Arcturus said. "Especially none of the cratties you've been mixing with."

"Thank you," I breathed, not knowing what else to say. I'd let my guard down too much these past weeks. I was letting my desperation to quell the loneliness inside me win. It had changed me, having friends. I fought silently with myself. None of the voices within me sounded like me anymore.

The door to the bedroom opened. "Wilhelmina," Muse said from the doorway. "You are thinking so loud you drowned *These Ivy Halls* out."

"I'm sorry," I said, apologizing in a completely uncharacteristic way. But I *was* sorry to have disturbed the seer. "To you both. It has been a strange time."

Arcturus nodded. "That is what Morpheus tells us."

"You've seen him?" I asked, surprised. Though the cat did disappear quite often, he never mentioned where he was going or where he'd been.

Arcturus glanced at Muse, who laughed, gesturing to the fountain that bubbled in the bay window of the flat. It was surrounded by soft cushions, all of which were covered in silver fur. An odd question popped up in my mind. "Does Morpheus live here too?"

Arcturus and Muse stared at each other for the longest time, their faces both incredulous. "He really is gone too much to assume we were his only roommates," Muse said finally.

Arcturus shook his head. "I am truly stunned…though," he said laughing, "I'm not sure why. It is so very like him to let all of us think we were his only family."

I found myself giggling along with the seer and his partner. It was the first time I'd ever laughed this way with people who were so new to me. But if Morpheus lived here as well, if these two were also his family, then there was absolutely no way they were unsafe for me. It was a refreshing thought to trust someone that way, and no surprise that I'd put my trust in a cat.

There came the sound of footsteps rushing up the stairs, and the door to the flat flew open. Ash breathed hard. "Thank the Lady," he breathed. "You're safe."

"Yes," I said with a smile. "Arcturus is almost done with the sketch."

Ash closed the door. "Good."

"Was it Niall?" I asked, wondering if that's why he looked so worried.

"No," he said, shaking his head. Muse stared hard at him. Something seemed to pass between them, though what it might be, I couldn't say. Ash opened his mouth, then closed it, before finishing, "I didn't recognize them."

I frowned, but Muse was already putting the kettle on for more tea. The peculiar tension that had transferred between the seer and Ash had gone, disappearing so quickly I thought I must have imagined it.

Ash came into the flat, watching the moth finish the sketch for a brief moment. "There were two of them," he explained. "And it was the oddest thing, they were fighting each other."

"Maybe only one was following us," I reasoned. "And the other was following the person following us."

Ash frowned for a moment, but then he nodded. "You know, I think you might be correct about that. Odd, still. I think we should take a cab home. Shall we call Fulston when you're ready? Or would you prefer Evie?"

So he'd noticed the two Strix were in competition as well. I smiled. "I'll let you choose your contender for fastest getaway driver."

Arcturus held up the image. "Is this him?"

I tilted my head. "I think the eyes were a bit different. Harder somehow? And maybe a little further apart."

Arcturus set the image down and Acraea went back to work. In the kitchen, which was just off the main room in the flat, Muse bustled about making tea.

"Are you all right?" I asked Ash. "You look a little piqued."

"I'm fine," he said, drawing me to him. "I'm just worried about you. When I realized they'd gotten away and you were alone..."

Strange, wistful joy went through me. "And now I'm not."

He followed my gaze around the room and back to himself. "Now you're not."

"Did you know Morpheus lives here too?" I asked, still scandalized by the news.

"He does not!" Ash exclaimed, as shocked as I had been.

"He does," Arcturus replied. "And we're all the fools." The big man's words were free of malice. He grinned, picking up the image as Acraea clung to his shoulder, both of them watching my response.

"That's him," I said, impressed with their skill.

"That is Lord Eccles," Ashbourne said. "Skye and I did a job for him six months ago. He's a professor at the university and a fellow at the Institute for Research on Interstellar Life."

"From the lecture we missed?" I asked.

"Yes," Ash agreed. "The same. He hired us to find out who had been stealing his mail. He seemed sure someone in his department was taking it for some kind of academic retribution. It turned out that the professor with the office across from his had been gone on sabbatical for a month, and the new mail carrier got them confused." Ash shrugged a little, then frowned. "At the time, it all seemed like an honest mistake, but I remember Skye feeling as though there had been more to the case. We'll have to ask her about it when we get home."

"It doesn't seem like a coincidence now, does it?" I asked.

"No," he answered. "It does not."

MINA

When we arrived home, Skye had returned from speaking to Elspeth, but Poe was not yet back from the undercity. Elspeth had confirmed that the mystery man was Lord Eccles, and that he had not been invited to the party.

"Not because he wouldn't be," Skye explained. "He's very well-respected, but he is a known introvert. Aside from teaching and lectures, he rarely socializes."

"What do we know about him?" I asked. "I've never heard his name, but I know that he was both here and at Somerhaven nearly every month when I was a child. He was the most obvious of Maman's special cohort."

Skye sat down. "He didn't grow up in Pravhna, though Mother wasn't sure where he was before. Apparently, he got a job at the university about thirty years ago, and has been the same the whole time. He isn't a recluse, but he isn't very sociable either."

"We're going to need to find out all we can about Vaness' activities," Ash said.

"Yes," I agreed, a thought emerging. The key, I'd forgotten about the key again. "I think I know how to get into Maman's workshop. Wait here."

I rushed as quickly as I could back upstairs to my vanity, my knees alarmingly weak as my joints screamed with pain. There would be time for a bath later, I promised myself. I rummaged through my drawers until I found the key ring, with only the key to Somershire and the mystery key left on it. I'd put the keys to Orchid House on a jeweled key ring in the shape of an ouroboros that Mme Laquoix's people had brought with them, and forgotten these were here.

There was a knock at the door. Ash entered. "Someone spotted Niall in Halcyon Gate. Edith sent a messenger. I have to go."

"Is Skye going with you?" I asked.

"I asked her to stay here with you." He paused. "I don't want her to have to bring him in. It's too much to ask of her."

I was impressed with how considerate he was of Skye. It bode well for any future we might have together. "Go find Niall."

He narrowed his eyes. "I asked Skye to give you a little time to take a bath before you tackle Vaness' workroom."

I wanted to protest, but he put a hand on my arm. "Please, take care of yourself. We have time."

"All right," I agreed.

Ash disappeared into the bathing chamber. I heard the sound of water running. He was drawing me a bath.

When he came out, he appeared to be torn about leaving. "Bath's filling. I'm going now." He brushed a kiss to my lips and shook his head. "I wish I could stay and bathe you."

"I can do it myself," I replied, a little grumpy that he thought I couldn't manage on my own.

"I know you *can*," he said as he strode to the door. "But it's less enjoyable, isn't it?"

Now I understood. Innuendo was occasionally difficult for me to detect. I would have to adjust my expectations now. I couldn't keep the smile off my face, as exactly what he meant sunk in.

"There's my girl," he said, casting a lingering look at me. "Do me a favor and spend a little extra time thinking about everything you enjoyed last night while you're in the tub."

I nodded, my skin flushing.

"I'll expect a detailed account of your audit when I return," he said as he closed the door.

His words stole my breath, and I wondered how I would focus until he came back.

ASHBOURNE

Evie's car sped away, leaving me a block from the alley where a baker's assistant claimed to have seen Niall. I bought a mug of tea at a street cafe and sat down to watch the alley. Buskers, a string quartet, played music on the corner, though I couldn't remember the name of the song. I watched the alley for a while, not expecting to see Niall.

Something about the report was off. The baker was one of Herself's oldest friends, but the assistant was new. The description the young Oscarovi had provided of Niall was a bit too specific. No one remembered such details unless they were rehearsed.

Still, it didn't hurt to sit here for a bit and simply watch the neighborhood goings-on. I was deep in the Halcyon Gate district, closer to the Night's Door district than I liked—the proximity made me uncomfortable. The Night Syndicate was very different from the Halcyon Gate Syndicate. The Halcyon Gate bosses were cultured, deeply interested and invested in the people they protected.

The Night Syndicate was another story altogether. They were still better than the cratties, in my opinion, but they were less principled. Ruthless in ways that Skye did not approve of, and thus neither did I. I finished my tea, watching the movement in Night's Door, a few blocks away. There was no marker indicating the change in management, but I felt the border all the same.

I left a tip for my waiter, and slowly made my way down the street. As I'd expected, there was nothing amiss here. Neither was there any sign of Niall in the alley. This was either an ambush or a setup. My shoulders tensed.

I was about to leave when someone else entered the alley. A familiar tall, slender woman with dark hair and eyes walked in, accompanied by a large orange feline. A greymalkin.

They were the two from before, from the alley, fighting the Strix woman. For a moment, I couldn't believe the luck of it. Then I understood. There was no luck to it. The reason the report about Niall seemed shaky was because it wasn't real. How had they managed this?

Ashbourne, the fey cat said, as it rubbed against my legs. This was not at all what I'd expected. *Have you so easily forgotten me and Morgaine?*

I crouched down to pet the beast. He was soft as silk, and his body was differently built than Morpheus', more like a lynxcat. He was magnificent. His giant head bumped my hand, and I scratched behind his ears. He was certainly more friendly than Morpheus.

"I am sorry, friend," I said. "I wish I remembered you."

"At least he's being nicer than he was last night," the young woman said.

"Last night?" I asked, looking up at her. She was a handsome woman. Surely, I would remember meeting someone as striking as her. I'd certainly never forget what she and the cat had managed earlier. "Was this morning not the first time we've met?"

Last night I had been rather taken with Mina. It would have been easy to overlook anyone. Perhaps I'd been rude to this woman and didn't even know it. "Were you at House Aestra's Orilion party?"

She raised her eyebrows, and the cat looked back at her, alarm in his eyes. "No, Ash. In the garden at the house where you're staying. Remember?"

I stood, taking a step back from them. "You were in the garden at Orchid House last night?" My heart beat faster now, my stomach suddenly roiling. I stumbled a little, as I had on the stairs a few days ago. But that had been vertigo. My feet were on flat, steady ground now. The woman took hold of my arm, steadying me.

She spoke softly to the cat. "Is it like Rakul Kimaris? Has he been bound?"

No, the greymalkin answered. *It's much worse. He is cursed.*

"Cursed?" The word was bitter on my tongue.

Yes, and I'm afraid whoever placed the spell on you was quite talented. There's no undoing it. You will continue to forget your past until you find the loophole.

"Well, shit," the woman swore. "Then he's no good to us. We'll have to find Lumina on our own."

Unless he's found her already, and doesn't even know it.

Their words were confusing, and my head swam. I held up my hands. "Please, slow down. Who are you?"

The young woman stuck her hand out. I shook it and she replied, "Morgaine Yarlo, and this little lyon is Bayun."

She opened her mouth to continue, but the greymalkin growled. *Tell him less. The curse will only tighten if you try to make him remember. In that way, it's exactly like what we saw with Kimaris.*

"Rakul Kimaris," I said, repeating the name. There was no reaction in my body to that. "Do I know them?"

Morgaine shook her head. "No, I don't think the two of you met. Though I suppose you might have known him *before*."

The way she said "before" was significant. As though we'd known one another only a short time, but I'd lived long before that. I assumed as much, but hearing this stranger say it was disconcerting as her claim that we knew one another.

Hush, Bayun warned. *Nothing so far back as that.*

Morgaine nodded. She looked as though she would speak, but I held up a hand. "Did you ask the baker's assistant to report seeing Niall Aestra?"

The young woman's shoulders sagged a bit. "Yes, I'm sorry we lied. But things didn't go well last night."

I nodded, gathering that we had indeed spoken. I was not inclined to trust Morgaine, nice as she seemed. But greymalkin cannot lie, and Bayun seemed to corroborate all she said. I looked at the golden animal. His topaz eyes were fixed on me. "Do the two of you mean me harm?"

No, the cat answered. *We are your friends, Ashbourne. We mean you no harm and wish you no distress. Once, not long ago, we walked the same path you did. We were at the start of our journey then. Now we only wish to go home. But first we need your help.*

I nodded slowly. Beyond the fact that greymalkin could not lie, I believed the cat wholly. Though I could not remember them, I could understand why I would make such friends. There was something of Skye in the girl, and I always had a soft spot for felines. Perhaps they were the reason I'd trusted Skye and Morpheus so easily. Had I been reminded of these two and not even known it?

My head dipped for a moment, my throat tight with emotion. I was cursed. Little bits of the past few weeks came back to me. Morpheus trying to talk with me about something, something I now could not remember. I didn't struggle against the resistance I felt, not wanting the nausea to return.

Was my reluctance to remember even mine? Or was it the curse? The thoughts slammed into me like a runaway train. Once articulated, I could not unthink them. I spoke without thinking. "I'll help you whatever way I can."

Morgaine nodded. "We'll go carefully then. We're looking for a woman. One you came here to look for as well. Her name is Lumina, and from what we understand, she would be heavily glamoured, but her sister believes she would be tall, with dark hair and a serious countenance. Her eyes are gray, and she has a bit of trouble relating to others."

Lumina. Mina. My knees buckled, and I crashed to the ground. All went black.

WHEN I CAME TO, I couldn't open my eyes. This had to stop happening. There were voices speaking.

He's seen her.

"We can't ask him again, not with the curse."

It is weakening, Morgaine. Ashbourne will remember all he's forgotten soon enough. We should find the last door, before it's too late.

A cool hand pressed to my forehead. "I'm so sorry, friend. We'll see each other again soon." The voice attached to the hand quieted for a moment, then whispered. "We have to tell him."

It could cause him to forget again. I wouldn't.

The hand drew back from my face, but the voice added one last thing. "Beware the Strix woman you saw us fighting, Ash. She means both of you harm."

That much I already knew. So the voices were the people I'd seen the day before. Had we been talking before this? About what? I struggled to remember, finding myself unable to move or think clearly. There was a sound of footsteps and then silence. The cat and the dark-haired woman had gone.

When I could open my eyes, I was alone, and more afraid than I could remember being. The cloudiness of waking up wore off. Bits and pieces of the conversation I'd had with Morgaine and Bayun came back to me, though others remained blurred. Something was there that I could not reach, even if I wanted to. I wasn't sure if I did, but the one thing that was crystal clear to me scared me. My lost memories were not a result of amnesia. I was cursed—a danger to all I held dear.

CHAPTER 41

MINA

After my bath, I was tempted to go right to the study to try the key, but Ash's plea to take better care of myself came back to me. I had a tendency when an idea took hold of me to forget all else, focusing only on what had caught my interest. It never yielded the best results. I often ended up completely exhausted, unable to finish a task. Maman had called me lazy and useless because of it.

My chest tightened at the thought of her. Memories of her disdain, which had once felt almost neutral in my mind, now soured as I recognized them as painful. It was remarkable what being treated better, and treating myself better, changed about the way I viewed my past. The world had opened up so much in the short time I'd been out of the oubliette.

I stared out the attic windows, wondering if it could last. Outside, the autumn rain had turned to sleet in this part of town. Though looking down the mountain, into the undercity, it was obvious it was only the midcity that was getting the freezing stuff.

Nevertheless, I needed to dress warmly. I found a pair of sheep-skin slippers in the back of my wardrobe and slipped them on. Next was a pair of high-waisted wool trousers in a gray tweed, and a silk blouse with a sheer lace back. Ashbourne would be back soon, after all, and so long as my feet were warm, and I fed myself, I could afford a lighter top. I slipped the key in my pocket and made my way down the back stairs, heading straight for the kitchen.

Tea was needed for this venture. Morpheus waited for me on the worktable, blinking several times at me as I came down the stairs. My left knee buckled slightly, still sore from my nighttime activities. I winced as I took the last few steps.

The cat sat up, narrowing his eyes as I leaned against the table. *Is it a bad one today?*

I shook my head. "No, just the consequences of my happily chosen actions." The cat grumbled softly, but blinked at me slowly as I moved through the kitchen, the kettle filling with water on its own. The stove lit, also on its own, and I spooned tea into a teapot.

"Do you need a fountain here as well?" I asked, remembering the little corner of Muse's flat for Morpheus.

The greymalkin's eyes dilated in surprise. *That would be nice. Thank you.*

He didn't address the fact that he had another home, another family outside Skye and Ash… And now myself and Poe. It was all very catlike of him, which should be no surprise. He was a cat, after all. A fey cat, but still feline.

Have you ever wondered at the coincidence that you and Ashbourne both have problems with your memories? he asked.

"That's an interesting question," I replied as I waited for the water to boil. "I hadn't."

Now that I thought about it, it was strange that I hadn't. "He was attacked, wasn't he? On his way into Pravhna?"

The greymalkin tucked his paws under his bulk, in a position Skye called "roast chicken." It was adorable, but I was not about to show that I thought so. *Yes, Skye and I found him near the river.*

"The Achera?" I asked, referring to the river that ran through the forest at the bottom of the mountain Pravhna was built upon. The cat made a noise I took to be affirmative. "What were you doing down there?"

Skye does not remember this, but she had a dream that morning. When she woke, she felt compelled to visit her family's cabin. We found him nearby.

The kettle whistled. I frowned as I poured water into the teapot. "That is very odd."

Confusion battered my conscious mind. My frown deepened. I stared at the cat, whose gaze was so intense I thought it might become tangible. "Why do I feel like this?" I asked, as dizziness sent me swaying. I held onto the edge of the worktable.

You remember what we are talking about? Morpheus asked, sitting upright now.

"Yes, but something—" I clutched my forehead with one hand, gritting my teeth. "It's like something is smothering my thoughts. It's hard to pay attention."

What is your greatest weakness, Wilhelmina? Morpheus' words were sharp, cutting through my blurred thoughts.

My breath came in labored gasps, a clammy sheen of sweat on my brow. I understood. This was magic, strong magic, and the cat looked for the loophole to the working. It was a familiar idea, though at this moment I could not remember why. "Love... And trust. The ways they intertwine. I don't do either easily." I ground each word out with effort. The pressure in my head began to relent, but only slightly.

And, have you learned to love and trust?

I nodded, then winced as the pressure increased. "I am learning. It's getting easier." The pressure relented once more. I rested my elbows on the worktable, my head next to Morpheus'.

Name them, the cat insisted. *Name the ones you love.*

"Poe," I said easily. "And I trust Skye." The pressure was bearable now, but the cloudiness would not relent. I closed my eyes against my fear. "And someday soon, I will love Ash." I opened my eyes, clear about what we discussed. "And I like you very much, but I do not know if you want my love."

The greymalkin rubbed his head against mine. *I believe I would enjoy being loved by you. But this is not enough. The curse will not be broken so easily.*

I laughed, resting my head on my arms. "It wasn't exactly easy to get to this point."

I do not doubt that, child. You have been very brave. I am afraid you must be braver before this ends.

"What does Ashbourne's memory loss have to do with this?" I asked.

Think, the cat said.

I tried, but the pressure returned almost immediately. I stopped trying so hard. Instead, I moved quickly, focusing on bringing the metal basket out of the tea pot, finding milk in the ice box, and pouring it all into a big pottery mug. Each small task sent the pressure running. Soon, I could think through the entire conversation we'd had without it returning, but I could not press on the issue of Ashbourne's memory loss.

"Do you know why this is happening?" I asked Morpheus, careful not to think about it too hard, focusing on the heat of my tea as I took a long drink.

It appears to be a curse, the cat answered. *Every time I attempt to talk to any of you about it, you all forget immediately.*

"Oh, how terrible," I said, wanting to wrap my arms around the cat.

Yes, he agreed, staring at the table in such a forlorn way that I set my mug down. I wondered if this was why he'd been disappearing so much lately. He needed time with people who didn't forget the things he tried to tell them. I was suddenly very glad he had Muse and Arcturus.

"May I hug you, Morpheus?" I asked.

He looked up at me, eyes solemn. *I believe I would like that.*

I wrapped my arms around the great cat, and he leaned into me, his cheek rubbing against mine. I closed my eyes, savoring the contact. Maman would never let us have pets, and because I had no elemental pair, I'd been denied such things as furry hugs. I tried to imagine hugging one of the hares, and snickered.

What is humorous? Morpheus asked, as I let him go.

We walked up the stairs together, towards the study. "I was thinking about hugging a mountain hare."

That is not an advisable action, he replied.

"No," I agreed as we entered the study. "It's not."

I took the key out of my pocket. As I held it up, a lock appeared. Without so much as a thought, I stuck the key inside it, my head still swimming. After all that nonsense with the pressure in my head, I was nauseated. The key fit easily, and then turned, something inside the door hissing.

I would wait a few moments, Morpheus cautioned.

I nodded. "Yes, I expected something like this. There's a toxic gas filling the room right now. It will dissipate shortly." The cat's eyes widened at my feet. "Maman liked to be sure about things."

I leaned against the bookshelves, pressing my ear to the wall. There was still the noise of faint hissing inside the workroom. Footsteps in the hall let me know Skye was approaching.

"I found your stash from the Clotted Calf," she called out as though it might draw me to her. I smiled. If my stomach wasn't so unpredictable, it would have been the perfect lure.

"We're in the study," I shouted back.

A few moments later, she appeared in the doorway. I felt the need to apologize. "I'm sorry my bath took so long."

"No apology necessary," she said, taking my cup of tea from me without asking, and replacing it with the bag of pastries. "You must take these. I took a little nap, and when I woke I ate four pastries. I might burst."

I fished a croissant out and stuck it in my mouth before my body had the chance to tell me it wasn't ready for food. The taste of flaky, buttery pastry was more than enough to quiet any protests within me. I chewed slowly, then swallowed. The first bite having gone all right, I took another, handing the bag back to Skye.

She took it, setting it on the desk with my mug. "Did you get the door unlocked then?" I nodded. She was wise enough to stay leaned against the desk. "Another of your mother's tricks then? What is it, toxic gas? A loose pyxie?"

I smiled at the mention of the mythical creature. "Gas. No pyxies, as far as I know."

She winked at me, a crooked smile quirking up one side of her lips. "Thank the Lady. I was terrified of them as a child."

"Me too," I confessed. *"Bloodbeard the Terrible* used to make me cry."

Skye laughed. "Me too. Niall used to read it to me, just to see me weep."

I put my hands near my face, curling my fingers like claws, "I'll gnash your flesh..."

"And boil your bones for broth," Skye recited in unison with me. "Ugh. That one is the worst."

I shook my head, thinking of Helene reading stories from *The Violet Book of Tales*. "It was Helene's favorite. She insisted on doing the voices as well."

"Ghoulish behavior," Skye said, shaking her head. "We should have known they were rotten to the core, shouldn't we?"

I shrugged. "When you don't know any different, I suppose it seems normal." I pressed my ear to the door harder. It sounded as though the hissing had stopped. Only a few more minutes and the gas would clear.

"What do you think is in there?" Skye asked.

"I don't have expectations. Whatever's inside, if I know Maman, none of it will be straightforward."

Skye nodded, and the three of us sat in companionable silence for a few minutes. Skye stoked the fire in the hearth and I swept up my crumbs off the floor, tossing them into the fire. Though I hadn't spent much time alone with Skye, I saw why Ash enjoyed her company so much. She was easy to be comfortable around.

"I care about him," I said, feeling as though I needed to assure her I was serious about her best friend and partner.

"I know," she responded. "And I am in love with Poe."

A pleased smile lit my face. How nice that she felt she had to do the same with me, as I did her. "Does she know?"

Skye grinned. "I told her last night."

"When this is over, I plan to join you all in the undercity. I want to help her find her family." I motioned at the room. "I want no part in all of this."

Skye crossed her arms, but she didn't appear closed off, only more comfortable in that position. "You don't want to be Lady Somerhaven?"

"No," I said. "And not in the way you left the Chevaliers. I *truly* do not want this. There is no conflict in me."

"There's nothing good in this place." She grinned. "Except us."

I turned from her, but I could not muster a laugh. "I'm not so good either, Skye. This body is a fetch."

I felt her hand on my arm. "I know, Mina. Poe told me a few

days ago. I hope you won't be angry with her, but I'd started to suspect and wondered if you knew."

"How did you know?" I asked without turning.

"The intensity of your pain made me wonder, as well as your gait," she said, mentioning something few knew of. I was impressed with her depth of knowledge on the subject. "Though I think it's something you probably experienced in your former body as well. Automatons can exacerbate conditions like yours, making them nearly unbearable."

I opened the door to the study, taking a big step back. It was best to do so, just to make sure. I turned to Skye. "Do you care? About the fetch, I mean."

She shook her head. "Not a bit. My mother worked with many before the ban, trying to help them. Her belief was that they were no more unnatural than the rest of us, but that the Oscarovi's metaphysical mechanics were not good enough to justify their use." Skye paused. "Do you mind?"

No one had asked me that. "There are things I don't like. I'll never have children."

Skye's eyes widened in empathy. "That is hard. Did you want them?"

"I wanted to be able to choose," I said.

Morpheus rubbed his face against my leg. *It is safe to enter now, littlelings.*

The cat often referred to us as children. "How old are you, Morpheus?" I asked as we followed him into the workroom. It was completely dark inside. There were no windows. No way in or out but the door. As a child, this room had terrified me. Maman often worked here, but Helene and I were not permitted to enter and she'd used all manner of threats to keep us away.

I felt for a switch on the wall, trying to banish the mounting anxiety in my chest. My hand hit a metal nub, and I pushed it upwards. Aetheric lights buzzed, then glowed dimly at first, brightening by the second.

One thousand, three hundred and forty-three, the cat replied to my question as the lights came on.

"Middle-aged, then," Skye quipped as the lights became bright enough to allow us to look around.

The walls were lined with bookshelves stuffed with leather-bound tomes, all of their spines in languages I did not recognize. In the center of the room stood a heavy table with a giant silver bowl resting on it. There was a dark, iridescent liquid inside it, viscous, with a life of its own.

The lekanomance. I swallowed hard at the sight of it, trying hard not to physically recoil. Logically, I knew my fear of it was irrational, born of Maman's attempts to scare us away from her study and the workroom. But still, the things she'd said about it haunted me.

"This is going to take a while to get through," Skye said with a sigh. "We're going to need more tea."

CHAPTER 42

MINA

An hour came and went and Skye and I had done little more than drink tea and sort through the books. None were written in any of the languages used on Sirin, which was notable in itself, but completely useless to us. We'd sorted out the few that had copious illustrations to come back to. Morpheus had given up on us entirely and was sleeping on the hearth in the study, his feline snores audible from within the workroom.

There was no secret cache of notes or records that would tell me anything about Maman's projects that I could easily find. Opening the workroom seemed, at first glance, to have been an utter failure. The thought tickled my mind. It was just the kind of thing that would have delighted Maman. It would have pleased her that anyone who was canny enough to break into her workroom would only find the lekanomance and a bunch of books they couldn't read.

"How is this even possible?" Skye asked, draining the last of our tea.

I'd dragged in an ottoman from the Maman's sitting room about fifteen minutes ago, and was now sitting on it, thinking. "It's not," I said, an idea forming. "It's not possible."

I began examining the room itself, looking for even the slightest anomaly. Skye watched me for a moment, then shook her head. "I give up. What are you doing?"

"It's a kind of magical encryption." I kept looking, running my fingers across every surface. Skye did not appear to be convinced. Perhaps she needed proof. "Try to take one of the books out of the workshop."

Skye raised an eyebrow, but did as I asked. I stopped my search and positioned myself, just in case. Sure enough, as she attempted to walk out of the workroom and back into the study, an invisible force propelled her backwards. As she was far more athletic than me, she needed little help, but I caught her anyway.

"Thanks," she said as she righted herself, setting the book she carried down on the table at the center of the room. She did not appear any worse for having the spell's power demonstrated in such a fashion. "So, the books have to stay in the room. Why is that significant?"

I leaned on the table, careful to keep away from the lekanomance. "Because if they have to stay, it means the encryption is a part of the room itself. If the spell was on the books, you'd be able to remove them."

Skye hummed a little, nodding as she looked around the windowless room. "So we're looking for something to do what? Turn the encryption off, like an aetheric light?"

I nodded. "Exactly. Of course, it could be a word or phrase, which might be impossible to discern. Maman liked puzzles."

Skye's eyes widened, then she began doing as I did, running her hands over the inside of the bookshelves. Just as I did, she pulled each book out individually, waiting for a response that never came. "What was your childhood like?" she asked.

I let out a dry laugh. Was this small talk? I hadn't spent much time alone with Skye, and I was never sure how to respond to these kinds of questions in ways that satisfied others. Vague answers, bordering on lies, for questions regarding family were probably best. "It felt uneventful, but I learned a great deal."

When I looked up, Skye stared at me, frowning. I wondered if I'd answered the question she was actually asking. Or had she not been making idle conversation? I tried again. "Maman was most interested in things like this," I gestured around the room. "She had little use for children, though she saw Helene as her protégé. I am not sure what I was made for, or why she wanted me if I was not her child."

Skye's expression shifted, her eyes widening further, her mouth twisting into a knot. "I am so sorry you had to go through that."

"Thank you," I murmured as I resumed my search. I was still uncertain about the purpose of this line of questions, but I wondered if perhaps I should ask about her childhood. "I assume that Elspeth was a better mother?"

"Yes," Skye answered, though her countenance told me the conversation wasn't going quite as she expected it to. There was a slight friction in her voice and movements, barely perceptible, but strong enough to let me know that I was irritating her. "She and my father made it clear they loved us, but they were a bit like Vaness in some ways. Like her, they were always working."

I hadn't heard much about Skye's father. "Is your father alive?"

Skye didn't answer immediately. I looked up from the shelf I examined, a prickle of heat blooming in my chest. She'd raised an eyebrow at me.

I had the distinct feeling of wanting to disappear. "Was that too blunt?"

Skye's brows knitted together, and then smoothed. It was as though she understood something she already had information about, but was just now seeing for herself. "Perhaps a little, especially if he was not… Alive, that is."

Inwardly, I winced, but I did not apologize. I'd learned long ago that showing remorse for my blunders only drew more attention to them, so if I had not caused harm, I tried to let things go without remark.

"My father is alive, incidentally. He is an airship captain. He travels to Brektos on a regular trade route."

"Oh." I was mildly confused. Most of the high Vilhari did not have true careers, but Skye's mother was a renowned physician and her father an airship captain. "Is that odd for you? That your parents have professions?"

Now Skye smiled. "Oh, yes. My family follows many of the old ways." We'd searched all the bookshelves. Now we moved on to the worktable, Skye on one side, and me on the other.

"The old ways?" I asked, keeping as far from the lekanomance as I could.

Skye nodded. "Before the Vilhari came here, there was a nominal aristocracy amongst our people, a hierarchy used only for determining how decisions were made. But everyone had enough. Everyone worked. What we've devolved into here should be our greatest shame."

I paused. "That's why you are so angry with Niall."

Skye nodded. "That's why I left home. My parents wouldn't reprimand him or stop him from becoming this. And look where it's gotten us. He's obviously wrapped up in something terrible."

I felt sorry for Niall Aestra, in some ways. We'd all been drawn into something terrible. He'd simply chosen the wrong side.

The table yielded nothing. I was frustrated, but Skye was calm. She leaned on the table, staring at the lekanomance. "It's been a long time since I saw one of those. They're very rare, and rather finicky if they're not maintained."

I calmed my breath. There was no harm in simply *talking* about the thing. "You know what it's used for, then?"

Skye nodded, though she watched me carefully, as though seeing some clue I could not discern. "In essence, anyway. I've never been that interested in magic. You ask for what you want and it gives it to you, right? Forms something out of nothing?"

"Not nothing," I explained, my skin prickling with the sheer anxiety thinking about the lekanomance brought on. "The liquid is pure aether, straight from the heart of the limen. It's the building blocks of all matter."

"Interesting," Skye remarked with a sigh. I was sure she feigned disinterest, but not why. Perhaps she'd sensed my discomfort in discussing the thing. I had no doubt fear was written all over my face. "Do we think it's a spoken command then?"

"It must be," I had to admit, relieved that she did not press me more about the lekanomance. Disappointment filled me. I'd been so sure when I remembered the key that I'd unlocked the answers to many of our questions.

"I'm going to go make more tea," Skye said. "And find something for Morpheus to eat before he wakes and gets angry with me."

I sank onto the ottoman, nodding. "Of course."

Her footsteps died away, and I turned my thoughts to Maman. Though I knew her well enough to predict when she might smack me, or find fault in my actions, I knew little about her as a person. The place in me that might have been sad about that was only angry.

My explanation to Skye rang back in my thoughts. Why had she made the fetch? What had she wanted with me, and how did it connect to Chopard? There was no way around it; if we couldn't unlock the secrets of Maman's workroom, we would have to do this the hard way.

I would have to remember what I'd forgotten, and we would have to hunt down Maman's friends. As I came to this conclusion, the front door opened. Though I heard Poe murmur a few words to Ashbourne, there was no immediate answer. Only the sound of his feet on the stairs, and then a door opening and closing.

I frowned. He'd gone to his own room. I walked into the study, about to go find Poe, but she met me at the door. "Oh, you got it open. Find anything?"

I shook my head. "Not yet. Excuse me, please," I said. Then I stopped, smiling faintly at Poe. "Skye's making tea."

Poe looked as though she might argue, her mouth opening once, but then she nodded, sinking to the floor to sit next to Morpheus on the hearth.

I hurried upstairs to the Oleander Room. I knocked softly, once, but Ash didn't answer. "It's me," I murmured. "Can I come in?"

Beyond the door, I heard him sigh. "All right."

When I opened the door, I found him sitting in the dark, head in his hands. I rushed to examine him, worried he'd been hurt. "What's wrong?" I asked. "Did something happen?" I kneeled on the rug in front of him, wary of touching him without his permission, but longing to do so.

He looked down at me, frowning. "I'm cursed," he replied, as though it explained everything. The pressure that had built in my head when I discussed my own situation with Morpheus returned, almost instantly. "That's why I can't remember anything."

My head ached, the clouded feeling returning. I attempted to make the connection between the similarities in our situations. I desperately wanted to talk this over with him. To turn the idea over in each of our minds, seeing how the other's perspective could change what we thought about what was happening.

But my mouth would not open. Not even to allow me to breathe. I tried again and again to make a sound, but it was as though I was frozen in place, unable to move or speak. In trying to calm my rising panic, I recalled what Muse had said about the connections between the four of us.

Our mutual loss of memory was connected. That much was clear. Now I could not move any part of me. Stubbornly, I held onto the thought, refusing to let it go, even as the curse's magic tried to strangle me. I took long, even breaths through my nose, steadying myself. If this curse was aggressive, I could be worse.

Curses were not like other spells; they were more like living things that grew and adapted with the cursed. It's what made them unreliable workings. But I refused to give into the pressure. If this spell had followed me all my life, I would become its worst nightmare now. It could not have me. And it could not have this man. I wanted him for myself, and none would take him from me.

My hand moved of its own accord, the pressure in my head relenting. My voice still caught, but I could move. I reached up to brush hair out of Ashbourne's face. His golden eyes met mine, and I inched towards him. Still, I could not speak, but I hoped he saw the question in my eyes. *Can I comfort you?*

He bent towards me, his lips meeting mine. The kiss was tender to begin with, his hands cupping my face. My arms went around his neck and he pulled me to him, my body resting between his legs. As he deepened the kiss, the magic relented, letting go of my voice.

"I don't care about curses," I said, my lips moving against his. "It doesn't matter."

He pulled away from me, eyes searching my face. "You don't, do you?"

I shook my head. "We belong together. I believe that."

"Show me." His words were a plea, dragged up from the depths of him.

Whatever he had been through before he was cursed, he did not want to remember it now. I feared what might happen when he did, when we both knew why we'd been drawn together in this way. I had the feeling there was not much time. That an hourglass had been turned over, and I watched sand slip through it, with no way of stopping what came next.

Every feeling I'd had of being able to control this, of getting my way, dissolved before me. There was no path that belonged to me now. There was only this moment, this man, and Lady Fate's talons closing around us.

"Show me," he pleaded again, pulling me to him.

My mouth met his, my need rising to a fever pitch, one to match Ashbourne's. If all we had was now, then I would spend these precious moments in ecstasy, not pain.

CHAPTER 43

ASHBOURNE

I woke up tangled with Mina, sharing her breath. A glance at the clock told me we'd fallen asleep, missing dinner and the evening hours after our very long encounter. I pushed a strand of hair off her face. In sleep, she was oddly innocent looking. None of her sharp edges showed, and every instinct I had screamed at me to both get away from her and stay by her side.

How was I to protect her if I was a danger to her? If I was cursed, but did not know why, then I had to admit some hard things to myself. Until I knew the exact nature of my past, and why I'd been cursed, I was a danger to all those I loved... Or in her case, all I *could* love, if only it was safe.

It was in her eyes as she made love to me: she was falling hard. I was too, but I had to stop myself. She was giving me all of herself, and taking every bit of me I would give her, but if we continued on, I would disappoint her.

And there was the matter of my celestial power to contend with, and the Strix woman. Mina had been honest with me about so much, and I knew very well how important trust was to her. I was keeping things from her, for reasons I'd deemed good, but she might not. If I didn't go now, I would ruin it all. I needed to hurt her now to help her the most. To try to save the spark of what we had started.

I said a silent prayer to the Lady as I wrote her a note. *Please cushion this blow*, I begged. *Help her understand all she needs to know and show us both the way back to one another.*

As I placed the note by her pillow, my heart ached. I wasn't sure this was right. Walking away from the women in this house would be the hardest thing I'd ever had to do. They were my family. They had all of me that I could give. But until I knew that who I was wouldn't endanger them further, I had to take some space.

I dressed quickly, stealing out of the room with my boots in my hands. Skye sat on the stairs, as though waiting for me. Morpheus sat next to her. I gestured to the door. She nodded, and they followed me outside.

On the steps, she crossed her arms tightly around her body. "Morpheus thinks you're sneaking out on us. Is that true?"

I looked down at the cat, shaking my head. "Were you spying on me?"

I was coming to cuddle her, the fey cat said defensively. *She seemed worried that I might enjoy Arcturus and Muse's company more than hers. I did not want her to fear abandonment.*

I crouched down to stroke the greymalkin's head. "You must continue to do that, friend."

The feline glared at me. *So you* are *leaving.*

I stood, placing my hands on Skye's shoulders. "Only for a few days. A week at most. My memory loss is not amnesia, Skye. I'm cursed."

She clapped a hand over her mouth in horror. I looked down at the greymalkin. "You didn't tell her?" Greymalkin could see spells more clearly than other creatures. Surely, he'd known.

The great beast sat down hard on the step, his eyes round and wide with sadness. *I tried. She could not remember it, nor could you. If you have this knowledge, then you are remembering as well.* The cat looked as though he might say more, but strangely kept silent.

"I'm going to the cabin for a few days, if you don't mind," I said when I was sure the greymalkin did not have more to say. Skye's family had a little hunting cabin deep in the forest, near the Achera that was hers to use when she liked. "I'll isolate for safety... In case remembering brings on my celestial fire."

Skye had known from the beginning what I was capable of, and we'd worked hard to hide it. It was a rare gift amongst the Vilhari, and a dangerous one. Even those who wielded celestial power could not always summon empyrae. Keeping this fact a secret had been vital to my blending into the landscape of the undercity. Now, to keep them all safe, I needed to go.

The deeper my feelings for Mina became, the more likely I was to emit empyrae during our intimate encounters. And remembering my past could surely do the same.

"Of course you can use the cabin," Skye said. "What should I tell Poe and Mina?"

"Tell them I was called away. That the Syndicate got a lead on Chopard, and I've gone to investigate."

Skye nodded. "We will pursue Lord Eccles in the meantime. Poe says that Vionette has eyes on Viridian at all times. He's been quiet for the past few weeks, rarely socializing outside his small circle of Caralee's friends. We'll keep an eye out for him."

I couldn't argue with any of those points. "Watch for the Strix woman," I warned. "She wants to kill Mina, and if Mina finds out, her path will be altered in ways Muse warns against."

Skye nodded. She knew all this, of course, but I could not help reminding her. But I had not been able to tell her about the woman or the other greymalkin yet. "There's a young woman following her, accompanied by a large golden cat." I looked down at Morpheus. "I believe he is one of your kind."

Morpheus' eyes narrowed to dangerous slits now. *Interesting I have not met another of my ilk for centuries.*

"They know about the curse," I said. "And while I don't think they are dangerous, we must be careful all the same." I ran my hands through my hair in frustration. "It's not a good time for this, Skye. If I had any other choice, I'd stay—"

She clasped my forearms, shaking me a little. "Brother, I know this."

It was the first time she'd ever referred to me that way. Tears sprung to my eyes, and I grabbed her, hugging her hard. "I'm so sorry," I said as I blinked back tears. "I've brought you nothing but trouble."

She hugged back just as hard, and Morpheus wound around our ankles. "You are my best friend in the world, and the brother of my heart," Skye murmured, her body shaking with tears. "The day I found you was one of the best of my life. The Lady brought us together once and she shall do so again."

When I released her, we both wiped our eyes. "I'll see you in a week," I promised. "No more than that."

She nodded. "If you don't come back, I will find you. Anywhere you go, Ashbourne Claymore. Whatever you remember about yourself, know this for fact: You are more than a friend to me. We have a covenant deeper than blood, and I will not let you go. Whoever you were in the past, you choose your future."

Skye sounded like the Chevalier she was, formal and grand, all the rules of chivalry fresh in her mind. Standing in the moonlight, she was a vision of the Lady's right arm, the picture of valor and camaraderie the Chevaliers aspired to. I was as proud of her as if she were my own sister.

My heart ached with some forgotten hurt, but I would have those answers soon enough. For now, Skye's words meant more to me than I could ever say. All I could manage was, "I love you too."

I turned away before I could change my mind. Mina would be safe with Morpheus and Skye, safer than she'd be with me. I had to go before I made a horrendous mistake. As I walked down the step to Orchid House and into the street, it felt as though my heart would shatter.

It would, I realized when I looked back. It would shatter because I'd left it in that bedroom. And when she woke, she might not understand the way Skye had. Skye's reassurances about my leaving might work for a week, but if this took longer... She would never forgive me.

As I walked down the street, I felt the pressure of eyes watching me. I looked back. Skye and Morpheus were no longer on the steps, nor were they at the window. As I had been for weeks now, I was followed.

Good, I thought to myself. *Let the Strix woman follow me and leave her behind.*

CHAPTER 44

MINA

The next morning dawned bright, golden sunlight streaming in through the open curtains. Curtains we'd forgotten to draw last night. I rolled over to find Ash's bed empty, but another note on my pillow elicited a smile. His little notes were sweet, and I loved that he could steal away from bed without my waking. There was something comforting in knowing that I could rest. I opened the note and immediately frowned.

I have to go away for a few days. Didn't want to wake you. Skye will explain.

-Ash

I sat up, pulling the covers around my shoulders. It was an unfortunate development, but not entirely unexpected. We weren't courting under normal circumstances, after all. Likely, he had some part of our puzzle to piece together. And, if I was honest, it might be easier to sort out this business with our curses if he were not here.

If I couldn't talk to him about it, then maybe his absence might reveal more than if he'd stayed. Under other circumstances, I would not have minded taking our problems to bed to solve. However, unlocking this part of what was wrong would take a bit more maneuvering—that I was sure of at this point.

I made my way up to my own bedroom to dress. After some

consideration, I threw on a pair of wool pants, the sweater I'd worn the day before, heavy wool socks, and my slippers. With some effort, I yanked my hair into a nest atop my head, stuck a long hairpin in it to secure it, then headed downstairs. I had thoughts about Maman's workshop I wanted to work out.

As I made my way towards the stairs, I heard Poe and Skye talking in the foyer. It was a bad habit to eavesdrop, but one I couldn't help indulging in from time to time.

Poe said, "Vionette says another warehouse in the country was burned. Same as before, everyone was found in a trance, their memories wiped. Things smelled like sulphur."

"He's gone to hunt a lead down, for exactly that reason," Skye responded. "He's staying at my family's cabin."

"I'm afraid she'll be upset. They're getting close. I don't want to see her hurt, Skye."

"He's not going to hurt her, darling. She will understand."

I peeked around the corner. They were hugging, and the way Skye stroked Poe's hair was endearing. My friend was so tiny, and Skye so tall, she was tucked into the crook of the former Chevalier's arm. The scene made me glad they had each other.

Making sure to cause a bit of noise as I went, I made my way downstairs. The two of them looked up. "Ash left a note. Has he gone after Chopard on his own?" I made sure to look appropriately concerned, but not sad. I didn't want them to worry about me.

"Not exactly," Poe answered. "But he has gone to chase down a lead."

Skye smiled a little too brightly. "Shouldn't be gone longer than a week."

I had to stop myself from laughing at their overt concern. It was sweet, after all, and I did appreciate it. But I was fine. He hadn't abandoned *me*, after all. We had goals, things we were trying to achieve. But I understood why they were worried, why he might be worried. It was one of those things another kind of person might be concerned over, but I was not.

This was good for me. I had no interest in a partner who lived only for me, or who would be constantly interfering in my business. It was good that he was gone now, taking care of our mutual interests. We would be together again soon enough.

"Then he'll be back soon," I said. "I have an idea about Maman's workroom. Where is Morpheus?"

"I think he is a little sad about Ashbourne leaving," Poe replied, as she and Skye followed me to the back of the house. "He went to Muse's."

"But he told us he was going!" Skye added, smiling. "So it's an improvement in his behavior."

I laughed softly. "Indeed. We're all learning, aren't we?"

The two of them looked as though they might be bowled over by a wave of relief.

"I am fine," I insisted, as we walked through Maman's study to the workroom. "Ash will be back soon. Will the two of you be all right without him?"

Skye looked as though she was swallowing some big emotion, but as I had no idea what it was and she and Poe both nodded, I moved on. There were times, like this one, that not being able to discern the nuance of what others were thinking or feeling was a blessing. It allowed me to focus on the task at hand.

We had left the door to the workroom unlocked, but closed with the key inside the lock. I opened the door and turned on the aetheric chandelier, the cold brass of the switch frigid on my fingers. The dark bookshelves seemed to loom over us. Why couldn't there have been a window in here?

My fear of the lekanomance returned as soon as I set eyes on it. I didn't bother to resist it. I would do what I had to when the moment came, but for now there was no use in fighting an emotion so native to my being, so perfectly emblazoned on my young mind.

Now I stood behind the table, gesturing at the bowl of dark, viscous liquid. "Maman used to scare me about the lekanomance, warning me that if I so much as looked at it, it might draw ghasts to the house."

Skye and Poe stood across from me. "How awful," Skye said. "That's not what they do, is it?"

I shrugged. "I suppose it's possible that a witch might conjure a ghast from a lekanomance, but they'd have to really want to. The liquid inside the bowl is pure aether. The same stuff at the heart of the limen, where all aethereal power is generated."

"That seems like a rare tool," Poe said, frowning.

"It is," Skye agreed, taking Poe's hand. "I've only seen one other. It's in the wreck of the Avalonne. Do you know where Vaness got this?"

I shook my head. "Not really. She said it was something Papa's family gave to her when he died. But really, anything might be true. I have no doubt she'd have stolen it from the Avalonne itself, if she thought it served her purposes."

Poe's face crumpled. "Mina," she breathed. "I'm so sorry."

"Why?" I asked, curious.

Poe glanced at Skye. I hated it when people did that. A frustrated sigh rattled through me. "I just..." Poe's words sounded jumbled. "You deserved better. You *deserve* better."

I still didn't quite understand. But what I did understand warmed me. It made her sad to know I'd had an unhappy childhood, and that was a kindness I could appreciate.

"I have better now," I said, my voice sounding unimaginably soft and vulnerable. I smiled at them both. "In all of you."

If I had known they were going to cry, I would have chosen my words more carefully. But from what I could tell, these were happy tears, and I knew how healing those could be. I let my friends cry, forcing myself not to apologize to them. When they wiped tears from each other's faces, both giving me watery smiles, I continued.

"I believe the lekanomance may be the key to the workroom." I paused, taking a deep breath. "But I must admit that while my rational mind knows that Maman was trying to scare me away from it for exactly this reason, I am still afraid."

Poe came around the table to stand next to me. "Do you want to hold hands?"

"No," I said with a small smile. "I have to stick both of mine into the lekanomance, I'm afraid. But please stay near me."

She looked up at me, nodding. "I won't move a muscle."

I smiled at her, then at Skye, just to show them I was feeling brave. Both of them grimaced. "So, that was not my most successful smile?"

"No, darling," Poe said. "Please do not ever do that again."

I laughed now, but for real. Poe smiled back at me. "There's our girl."

It was a reminder that they saw me for my true self and liked that best. That I didn't have to falsify my emotions for them. The knowledge made me brave. Without another thought, I stuck my hands into the silver bowl. The liquid inside, pure aether, was cool to the touch.

It whispered to me, voices both familiar and strange inside my head. I thought I heard my name, but could not be certain; it sounded odd. Before I could think on it further, I whispered words I'd heard Maman say many times over the years, *"Per aspera ad astra."*

Through hardships, to the stars. I'd tried saying it in the room a few times, but it had had no effect. Now it did. It was as though a veil fell away from the room itself. Skye and Poe stared at the bookshelves, their backs turned to me.

"I can read them," Skye said. "Most of them, anyway."

But I was transfixed by the image that seemed to be projected from the pool of pure aether. It was a map of the stars and planets, which rotated slowly above my head. Some constellations I recognized. Others I did not. The planets that popped out from time to time as the image rotated were labeled in golden lettering. The first was Sirin, which I recognized immediately.

The next was a planet called Okairos, then another named Elysium, another called Earth, and the last, the one that stole the breath from my lungs, was named Interra. I watched it rotate, its land masses as familiar to me as my own face, with a growing sense of horror. Every piece of memory that lived inside me rearranged, sharpening to a clarity I had not imagined possible.

Lumina and Ashbourne.

The useless princess and the general prince.

Not the Mina and Ashbourne of today, but two winged immortals, like the statues Papa had been obsessed with. Both Ventyr, but from warring houses. Sworn to seduce and kill the other, we had been enemies—until we were not. Then enemies once more when torn asunder.

Ashbourne Thuellos, his true name, was the reason I'd been discarded here. The reason my wings were ripped from me. The reason I would never fly again. He was the reason for every sorrow within that could never be mended. I'd spent hundreds of years walking this cursed planet alone, unknown, in pain. Only to fall *in love* with him. Now.

Before, back then, I hadn't known if I'd been in love or not. It was too hard to separate the animosity between our families from the feelings we developed for one another. I pushed these thoughts away as hard as I could. Remembering the past this way... it was too much. I could not be Lumina and Wilhelmina at once. My jaw clenched with the effort it took not to break apart.

But nothing could stop my mind from its unrelenting churn once it got started. Every muscle in my body tightened, bracing against the overwhelming flow of information. It was both inconceivable and utterly predictable that this could happen. That this could be the end to the curse. That loving *him* would break it.

Cruel as it was, it made a horrible kind of sense. My aunts, my mother's sisters, were the ones who laid the curse. They were the only ones with enough skill to do so, and enough knowledge of me to craft such a cunning loophole, such a bitter blessing.

They thought they did me a favor; that if we could find our way back to one another, I might be mended by his love. But nothing could or ever would heal the ways his betrayal broke me. If only he had trusted me when it counted. If only he'd stayed away. But he'd thought he knew better than me, that he and his seventeen generals, and all their armies, could save me.

All he'd done was damn me to eternal pain and loneliness. And now, I would be expected to forgive all that, to love him and work together to keep this little shred of happiness that had been gifted to me in another lifetime of eternal pain. Fury rose in me at the unfairness of it all, of being expected to be the one who forgave and forgot yet again. It was always me who was expected to grant absolution. I tamped the storm of rage that brewed within me down as hard as I could.

Poe and Skye were still distracted by the books. They had not seen the map of the stars. Only a moment had passed, though to me, it felt like an eon. I pulled my hands from the lekanomance, my heart a hollow plane.

There was no doubt in my mind that I loved Ashbourne Claymore and hated Ashbourne Thuellos. The two horrible truths collided with the knowledge that if love was the loophole, I was doubly betrayed. *My* Ashbourne did not remember who he was, who *I* was. He did not love me. A feral cry overtook my consciousness, spooling out from my empty heart in a symphony of anguish.

I tried to shut it off, to focus only on the notes of warning and rage, and to reject the sorrow. But I could not turn it down or ignore the knowledge that beyond any other betrayal, I had cruelly forsaken myself. The man I loved was the reason I would spend an eternity in pain.

CHAPTER 45

MINA

P oe's voice shook me from whatever dark place I had traveled to. I blinked a few times, my vision clearing. Poe stood in front of me, shaking my shoulders gently, her face twisted with worry.

"I'm all right," I said as soon as I realized she had been asking what was wrong. "Just a bad reaction to the lekanomance."

It was not wholly a lie. And the present moment, the now I'd left before all had been made clear, was strangely comforting. Though I was utterly changed, this world was still here. Poe, who loved me, and Skye, who would not when I did what must be done.

My breath caught on the thought, as Poe led me out of the workroom, through Maman's study and into the sitting room. *What did that mean?*

"Sit here," Poe said. "I'll fetch you a bit of tea and a snack."

Absently, I nodded, already lost in thought. Fury and revenge had been the undercurrent of my thoughts for nearly all my life, though I had not understood that so well as I did now. I'd always believed what Maman had told me about myself, that I was a wretched child, ungrateful and unworthy of more than I got from her. But my anger had been justified. *I'd been betrayed.* The words played over and over in my mind until I shook my head, trying to loosen their grip on me.

Now was not the time to get lost in emotion. Logic must reign. I'd let my feelings carry me away these past weeks. I could not yet say if I was sorry for it, but it could not stand now that I'd remembered myself. The memory of the day I'd confronted Maman was still not accessible to me, and I could not immediately see why.

If the curse had broken, why could I not remember that day?

All I knew now was that it was more important than ever that I understand why this had happened. Why had the fetch been necessary? It would take me days, at minimum, to untangle my thoughts and feelings about Ashbourne. As much as I wanted to hunt him down and dismantle him piece by piece, my feelings for him were real. The man I'd fallen in love with hadn't acted a bit like the spoiled prince I'd seduced in my youth.

I couldn't see how he, or our past, connected to Maman, or what she might have wanted, so I set that aside as collateral. It did not occur to me that I was pacing, having left the chair, until Poe and Skye returned with trays of tea and toasted cheese sandwiches.

As I watched them arrange their trays on the low table at the center of the room, I knew it was not in me to break them apart. If one of us had to leave, it would be me. If I told Poe the truth, she would side with me. I knew that, without a doubt in my heart. She was steadfast and true in a way no lover ever could be. As I was to her.

I watched as Skye touched the small of her back, pressing a kiss to her temple. Poe had lost so much already, was already so brave and strong. I could push all my feelings aside for now and get us to the end of this. I had to uncover why Maman had put me in the fetch.

A plan formed in my mind. I sat down across from the two of them, taking the cup of tea Skye offered me. One deep breath and all my anger faded into the depths of me. I had no illusions that it was gone for good. But I was good at this. I'd spent the last twenty-eight years learning, and I was now an expert at forgetting.

"I've remembered a bit more about my past," I explained. "How much have you told her?" I asked Poe.

"Not much," Poe assured me. "It is your story to tell."

Skye nodded. "I would be honored to carry your tale."

My eyes crinkled with affection, loving the formal way she spoke. Skye was so very special, and I was glad she would take care of Poe, if ever I was unable. "Long before the Ventyr came to conquer Sirin, I was a princess on a planet far, far from here called Interra. Have you ever heard of it?"

Skye shook her head. "I don't believe so."

Poe took her hand, and they shared a look I could not discern meaning from. Perhaps they'd already talked about this part of things? No matter.

"My mother was the leader of a band of Ventyr called the Larae, a matriarchal lineage of warrior queens. On Interra, they were unconquerable. Our people were always at war, Houses forever locked in conflict. My father's House, House Anemos, was the victor for centuries, amassing land and alliances. When only the Larae remained, my mother knew she would have to give in to him.

"There was no other way to protect her people, and with the whole world united against them, she knew they could not hold out against my father much longer. So she married him, leaving her people in the hands of her sisters, Orynthia, Penthe, and Faedra. Soon after my parents' marriage, I was born, and then there was no other child. My mother could not conceive another after me, and I was not a son."

"Was that so important?" Skye asked, frowning.

It warmed me to hear her say such a thing, to be so innocent. Sirin was not a perfect world by any means, but it was so much better than Interra had been. "Yes," I said softly. "In our society, sons were valued above all else. Not within the Larae, you understand, but Interra at large believed this, while my mother's people still followed the old ways."

Poe smiled then, though her eyes were wet with tears. "The Ventyr are fey, as we are. The word Vilhar is not the name of our people, but the place we are from."

Skye's eyes went wide with wonder. "But how?"

Poe shook her head. "I've searched the Avalonne's records for that knowledge, but I cannot find it. If it was known when we came here, it is lost now." She nodded to me, urging me to continue.

"My father spent so many years looking for ways to conceive an heir by my mother. There were... experiments. I watched her grow frail and fade. Strong as she was, she could not withstand his methods, which were dark and dangerous. My father was not only a tyrant, but also a magician of great strength. Eventually, he killed her."

"Oh, Mina," Skye breathed, her face drawn with sorrow. "I am so sorry."

Her sympathy was fresh, but this was a wound I'd carried for so long it hardly stung. "Thank you. She endured his machinations so none of her sisters would have to. It was her greatest regret that she failed. He replaced her with the eldest of her remaining sisters, my aunt, Orynthia."

I paused, wondering exactly how to tell this part without revealing anything about Ashbourne and myself. The easiest way might be to spin the tale without planning, to keep things as close to the truth as I could. "In his efforts to secure an heir, my father lost control over Interra. These experiments he became obsessed with— they took years from my parents, you must understand. So when he married Orynthia, she brought along her generals and her military prowess. Together, they retook the planet, bit by bit, though Orynthia hated every moment of it."

Skye glanced at Poe before she spoke. "Then why did she help him?"

I swallowed hard, not knowing how to explain this to someone who had not lived through it. "You must understand, our people are as long-lived as yours. There had been centuries of wars. Thousands lost, and millions of lives ruined. Orynthia believed as my mother did —that if my father got his way, if he conquered the planet—that there might finally be peace."

"And was there?" Skye asked, her voice choked with emotion.

I shook my head, understanding that she knew how this story ended for her people, with the Ventyr coming here to conquer a whole other planet. But my mother, my aunts, they hadn't known that at the time. They hadn't even known that was possible.

"They were doing the best they could with the knowledge they had, Skye," Poe said.

Skye sighed. "I'm sorry. What happened when they retook the planet?"

I sighed, frustrated that the only story I had to tell would confirm what she already thought of my people: that we were evil. Even now, as much as I hated my father and all that he'd done, I wanted to believe the Ventyr had good in them. "The wars restarted, and in the midst of them arose a new threat. Creatures we called the Ravagers, with the power to feed off of and influence emotions, to render whole cities listless, void of life. They fed mostly on anguish and pain, which they cultivated like grapes for fine wine. My father believed their power could be harnessed for a time, but his Lords begged him to turn his attention to destroying them."

Poe and Skye both looked as though they might be sick. Poe had turned a shade of gray I didn't like, and Skye wrapped her arms around her waist, hugging herself tightly.

I had to finish this story quickly. "They could not be destroyed. We had to make an alliance with our greatest enemies, House Thuellos, to stop them. Eventually, we did. They were imprisoned in the limen, where they sleep, to this day."

It was a struggle not to explain who Ashbourne was, that he was the youngest son of House Thuellos. That my father, looking for a way for me to be useful, had ordered me to seduce him—to gain access to all his secrets, and all those of our rivals. I sucked air through my nose, hoping that if my face showed the distress I felt that they would simply think I was upset by the other memories.

"Mina," Poe breathed. "That is an incredible story. How long ago did this happen?"

It was a logical question to ask, but I had no answer. "I could not tell you. I lost count of my age when I passed a thousand of our years."

"Incredible," Poe said, her eyes wide with wonder. "But—"

"You are wondering why this is important now," I finished for her, wanting to move things along. "Come with me."

I stood, walking as quickly as I could to Papa's library. I pulled several books from the shelf and handed them to Poe. In turn, she handed them to Skye with a smile and a quick kiss on the cheek. I was heartened to see my story had not struck fear into her, or if it had, she was holding up well against it.

We made our way back to the workroom, where Skye set the books down on the table as I pulled more volumes from the shelves.

Now that I knew what to look for, they were easy to find. "All of these are, in one way or another, about harnessing great elemental energies."

I waited for them to catch up, for them to understand what I saw so clearly now. It was hard not to jump in with the answer, but this was not how people learned best.

Poe's eyes lit with understanding first. "Surely Vaness did not believe that..." She shook her head. "No. No one could be so cruel."

Skye looked lost. "I told you, I'm not a scholar of magics. You're going to have to explain it to me."

I nodded, happy to do so—anything not to get lost in my memories of Ashbourne Thuellos and all the ways he'd torn me apart. "My supposed Oscarovi father, Alastair Wildfang, was obsessed with the Ventyr before his death. These are all stories he collected about them," I explained, gesturing to the novels and volumes of poetry I'd pulled from his library. "I believe if we search in these, we will find stories about the Ventyr, my true father in particular, looking for a way to channel enormous amounts of elemental energy.

"Before his Lords talked him out of it, my father wanted to use a magically gifted person to channel the Ravagers. He wanted to use their power for himself, for more war."

Now Skye's eyes widened. She looked to Poe, who shook her head as I continued on. This was a lot for them. For me as well, but I had to get it out. They had to know. "The Oscarovi had independently found the means to channel elemental spirits. I believe Maman and her cohort thought they'd found a way to do the same, but with the Ravagers. Their intent was to set the Ravagers loose, and use me as the conduit for their power."

"Why..." Skye asked, her mouth hanging open in pure horror. "Why would they have believed that would work?"

My face was smooth, wan with exhaustion. This was all so much to tell, and I had not even told the worst of it, the ways I'd been used to manipulate House Thuellos, then betrayed by my own people. I took a deep breath. Then I lit one hand with empyrae and with the other summoned aether.

Both Poe and Skye stood frozen, their eyes wide with shock. I sent the two opposing forces into a spiraling column above our heads, fire and shadow twisting together. "I can use both."

"Did you burn Somerhaven down?" Skye asked, the moment she found words. "Was it you?"

"No," I said, shaking my head. "It wasn't me. I don't remember it yet, but I believe this is why I was imprisoned. I believe I uncovered Maman's plans for me."

"What did Vaness want?" Poe asked. "What did she think she could do if she turned you into a conduit for such a creature?"

They still didn't understand. It was a testament to them having grown up in this place, free from the kinds of power mongering that had been my bread and butter for centuries. "To rule this world," I explained. "To conquer it for herself, with me as her enforcer, inspirited by the Ravager."

CHAPTER 46

ASHBOURNE

The cabbie dropped me off at the end of the long gravel driveway that led to the cabin. They'd asked if I wanted to be taken all the way, but I refused. I wanted to walk—to be alone with my thoughts. I'd been followed all through the undercity, and through some of the outer ring suburbs, but once I'd reached the mountain villages, my tail disappeared. I figured I had a few hours at least, maybe a day, before the Strix woman found me.

No matter how much time I had, I meant to make the most of it. The mountain air was crisp and cold, and clouds hung low in the sky, the dim light intensifying the golden glow of the birch trees that lined the drive. I felt as though I could breathe again, free of responsibility and worry, even if just for a short time.

My boots crunched on the crushed gravel of the driveway as a gust of wind kicked up, sending a shower of birch leaves raining down on me. It was magical to be surrounded by them. Dizzying, but beautiful. As they swirled around me, the movement distracted me, familiar somehow. I tried to focus on the feeling, grasping at it, though it seemed to slip out of my mind's grip.

The moment I relaxed, I slipped into my second sight, memory taking over as though it were a vision. The curse loosened its grip on my mind, even if only a little.

There had been rose petals. Hundreds of thousands of rose petals floating down from the sky. A celebration. Or at least it was for everyone else. But not for me. For some reason, I had been sad as I'd walked through the crowds of winged people. I'd ducked into an alley, hoping to avoid being seen by anyone I knew, and there she found me.

The next few moments were a blur in my mind. A soft body pressed against mine, the pleasure of her kiss, the sting of her knife at my neck. The gasp of betrayal as mine pressed against her ribs. The fury in her eyes as we both realized the truth of the moment, of the lies we'd told one another for months. The clatter of the knives on the stone street. The heat of her kiss, of our renewed passion.

The fervor, brought on by our mutual betrayal and a thousand stolen glances and brushed fingertips. The sting of her fangs piercing me was nothing in comparison to the pleasure I'd felt as mine entered her. To claim her was the height of fulfilled desire, of divine providence. And it was also my undoing.

The vision ended abruptly, my corporeal sight returning in a tumble of senses. The chill air, the smell of winter approaching, and the leaves that carpeted the ground. Despair barreled into me, nearly knocking me over with its force. That woman, whoever she was, she'd meant something to me. Something horribly important. And I didn't know what had happened between us, but I knew I'd betrayed her, hurt her in ways I couldn't be forgiven for.

I gritted my teeth and kept walking. This was why I was here, to figure all of this out. To know the truth of myself so I wouldn't repeat the past with Mina. The only way to keep her safe now and in the future was to know what I'd done to that other woman. I had to be sure I'd changed enough from the man I was in my vision. And if I hadn't, I would work on it harder; I would find whatever help I needed to be the kind of person who deserved someone like Mina Wildfang. Someone worthy of being permitted to love her.

Clouds moved overhead, and I drew a long breath in as I rounded a corner in the driveway. I don't know what made me so sure of myself, but I knew I was capable of figuring this all out. The cabin came into view, and I had to smile. This was where it all began with me, Skye, and Morpheus. Skye had found me by the river, beaten and unconscious, and we'd spent much of the first month of my recovery here, before I'd agreed to come back to Pravhna with her.

There was wood by the door, but not much. I gathered up an armful of what was left and pressed my hand to the door. While this was technically House Aestra's retreat, only Skye used the cabin, and she'd added me to the house wards long ago. The door swung open.

Inside, the cabin still smelled like summer-fresh wildflowers. I unburdened myself of the armful of wood and placed my bag on the bed in the tiny guest room just off the kitchen. All of the bedrooms were small in the cabin, which was luxuriously furnished, but still rather rustic.

I lit the stove first, setting the kettle on to boil, then went to work lighting a fire. It was easy to feel comfortable here. This was the first place I'd known after waking from my coma. Skye and Morpheus had made me feel safe, in a time when it was disorienting not to know myself. As I looked around the cabin, there were only good memories here, which I'd known since I first opened my eyes wasn't the case with my former life.

Despite my amnesia, I'd been left with the unrelenting sense that my life before had been fraught with pain, both others' and my own, and that I was the cause of most of it. Guilt had wracked me for months, but Skye was the one to convince me that if I had sins to repent for, the best way to do that was to live a better life. Be a better man.

The kettle whistled, and I went about making tea in a large pottery mug as quickly as I could, before going to sit by the fire. The quicker I got about this remembering, the better off I would be. I closed my eyes, and tried to return to the memory of the falling rose petals, the woman's body pressed against mine. Some part of me knew things had gone further in that encounter than a passionate kiss, but I didn't want to remember that.

I wasn't the kind of person who could focus on more than one lover at once. At least I wasn't *now*. Thinking of another while my heart was still with Mina felt wrong. Perhaps I should start with a different part of the memory. I tried to take myself back to the walk —the falling rose petals. What had I seen around me?

A city, very different from Pravhna, with tall stone buildings. But in the memory, I'd been on a hill. There were huge evergreen trees in the distance, and a view of a lake—the Nameless Lake. My heart beat faster as I remembered. What was the city called? Kilm. Yes. That was it.

Kilm, the Emperor's city. But I was not from there. No, I was from somewhere further north. A citadel by the sea… Lyonesse. I could see the promontory in my mind's eye, the rocky shore jutting out into angry water. The citadel, rising out of the stony outcropping of land. House Thuellos.

Outside, a gust of wind blew one of the shutters loose from its fastening. It banged loudly against the house, drawing me out of my exploration of the past. I got up, stretched my muscles, and looked at the clock that sat on the heavy stone mantel. I'd been here for over an hour.

I was making excellent progress. At this rate, I might be able to make it back to Pravhna in a week. It would be slow going at times, I was certain, but if I had a bit of luck and the Strix woman didn't find and distract me, I would be fine. Relief flooded me as I walked outside. This had been a good choice.

The wood pile needed replenishing, and moving my body would no doubt trigger more memories if the curse was weakening, as Morgaine and Bayun had suggested. I found the axe and set up my first log. With every subsequent hack into a log, my body warmed and my mind cleared. I let it empty out, removing my shirt, as my skin was clammy with sweat. One log after another, my muscles burned with the pleasurable effort.

In my mind's eye, an image of a great labyrinth emerged, the strange girl, Morgaine, and the cat appearing. *They had been lost, and I walked the labyrinth daily. I was unable to leave my post for long, but the labyrinth offered relief from the creatures imprisoned within Nihil, and was close enough that I could return quickly if something went wrong.*

When Morgaine and Bayun appeared, they came bearing a familiar power, starfire. And they had spoken names I knew. The names of my family, my enemies —my lover. Though that name was one and the same with my enemy. I tried harder to focus on that moment and Morgaine's actual words, but I remained just outside the range of hearing. I knew the broad strokes of what she'd said, but could not hear the specifics.

Lost in the memory, I did not hear my attackers approach until it was almost too late. My sight moved back into my body and I spun with the axe, meeting the masked figures from the day of the fire.

This time, there were only two, and rather than the slow approach they'd used to test me, this time they attacked in earnest.

They were fast, seemingly flying at me at once. My mind was still cloudy from the memory, but I ducked their lightning quick kicks and hits, taking a wide swing with my axe, which they both sprang away from with no trouble. One rose into the air, lifted not by wings, but seemingly by power alone, though I could not read its source.

They kicked at me, their legs moving at preternatural speed. I tossed the axe aside in favor of grabbing onto their leg, swinging them around hard as I could, and tossing them towards the river. The other was on me the moment I turned, moving so quickly I could not see the hits coming to block them. All I could make out was their masked head, so I butted it with mine, as hard as I dared.

They went down, but the other leapt back at me, now holding my discarded axe. Inwardly, I swore. I'd made a novice's mistake—my head still hazy with remembering. They swung and I ducked, once, twice, thrice, before summoning my fire. This was not going to end the way our first fight had. They were no longer testing me, but were here to kill me. My empyrae sliced through the axe, but my opponent leapt backwards before it could strike them.

They came back in concert now, and it was all I could do to fend them off as the hits kept coming. I blocked as many as I could, but one got me in my right flank before I landed a kick in their gut. They struck me more than I managed to get them, moving so quickly I was unable to track them.

They were wearing me out. The first fight had been about assessing my style. This was about killing me. They were Chopard's people, that much was certain, but why were they so invested in me? Had we gotten too close to finding out Chopard's identity?

Skye. Mina. Poe. They must have uncovered something in the city. Had they already killed them? Even Skye would not be able to fight foes this fast, and I was uncertain what Mina's powers might be able to accomplish. They would wear me out long before I could beat them, unless I ended this now. Empyrae boiled within me as I mustered up the strength to let it flow, my celestial fire fueled by my rage at Mina's possible harm.

It flowed out of my hands, so hot it was blue. Using empyrae would end my ability to question them, but it didn't seem I had another choice. When the fire hit them, it was imbued with my will, wrapping around them to prevent escape. The air filled with their screams and the smell of sulphur. It had been so long since I loosed my empyrae from within.

I fell to my knees, unable to stop the flow of celestial flame, though both of Chopard's fighters had fallen. The bodies still burned with the fire that would not stop flowing out of me. This is what I had feared—I couldn't stop. The empyrae was feeding on my life force now. It had been too long since I used it.

The day I was captured came back to me as I swayed. Not the burning fires on the battlefield, though those were clear enough in my mind. Now that I'd remembered them, I would never forget the sight of so many dead, and for what? My folly. No, what I remembered was her face. The woman from the alley, with the rose petals.

Her wide gray eyes peered in at me, through the bars that separated us. "I sent word," she said, her voice full of anger and pain. "I told you not to come."

She had. Nothing she said was wrong. She'd given me good reasons to stay away, but pride and guilt had made me think I knew better. The moment happened over and over, in a seemingly endless loop. *I sent word. I told you not to come. I sent word. I told you not to come. I sent word. I told you not to come.*

My second sight threatened to keep me in this moment forever, but my corporeal body caught wind of another presence. It was enough to startle me, my empyrae dying as I slumped over, onto the ground.

I'd almost burned out, lost in the memory of her. Of Lumina, who I had thought I wanted to save. Who I came here to find. *Lumina.* All I'd wanted when I came to Sirin was to find her, to apologize. To tell her that I knew better now, and that after centuries of imprisonment, I knew that I had been wrong to ignore her warning, that I understood I was the cause of so much trouble, so much pain. And to warn her—I'd known something she needed to know. But what had it been?

A shadow fell over me. I looked up, into the scarred face of the

Strix woman. "He's still alive," she called out. "He just burned himself out."

She disappeared for a moment. I struggled to right myself, but I had no strength and only managed to flip onto my back. Try as I might, I could not get up. I'd killed Chopard's people, only to make myself vulnerable to this Strix that wanted to kill Mina. A quiet cry of frustration fell from my lips.

Cool fingers cupped my chin, and a beautiful face appeared over me. It smiled, the full lips sensual, but the blue eyes that looked down on me were cruel. "Hello, Ashbourne," the face said.

The woman's blonde hair was pulled back into a tight chignon, accentuating the finely boned structure of her face. Like Poe, this woman possessed the kind of beauty that could be used as a weapon. Her face was so familiar, and yet I'd never met this woman before. I was sure of it. Where had I seen her face?

"Do you know me?" she asked.

I frowned, unable to form words.

"They're dead," the Strix called out. "He killed them."

The woman nodded, crouching low over me, her long fingers caressing my face. "Have you been enjoying living in my house, Ashbourne? Fucking my sister?"

Her sister? *Helene Wildfang.* That was where I recognized her face from: the paintings in Orchid House. Mina's sister hadn't died in the fire. She was alive, and could likely answer all our questions. I struggled to speak, as I knew I couldn't rise.

"Hush," Helene soothed, stroking my cheek again and again. "Don't try to speak. You've worn yourself out."

I glanced at the Strix as she came to stand behind Helene. Why were they together? I remembered then what she had said the first time we met, that Mina had wronged her employer. Helene Wildfang was alive, and she wanted her sister dead. Again, I struggled to rise. I had to get away from them. Reach Mina before they could.

"Brigitte," Helene whined. "He's struggling."

The Strix stepped forward, a large dagger in her grip. Before I could so much as cry out, she hit me on the head with it, and all went dark.

CHAPTER 47

MINA

The moments after I finished explaining that Maman had wanted to rule the world were pure chaos. Poe and Skye both talked at the same time, shouting above one another in their attempts to be heard. It was difficult not to clap my hands over my ears to block them out, but I tried to follow what they were saying.

All I could make out was that neither of them could understand what all this had to do with Chopard. When trying to focus on their voices didn't work, I tried counting all the blue leather-bound volumes on the surrounding shelves. The aetheric power in the crystal chandelier flickered a bit, hurting my eyes. If only there was a window in here. Though I wasn't exactly claustrophobic, the workroom suddenly felt too small, too closed in.

The various ephemera on the shelves—skulls, apothecary jars filled with sharp teeth and shed skin from various reptiles—all began to seem macabre, menacing. Overwhelmed, and desperately wanting them to stop raising their voices, I held up a hand, but neither of them noticed. The noise and the pressure of my memory coming back together were all too much. Something had to stop.

"House Montclair is obviously involved," I shouted, unable to listen to the cacophony of their voices for a moment longer.

Both of them stopped, shutting their mouths. Blessed silence filled the air, calming me as my thoughts and the threads of the pattern began to emerge, clearer now than they'd been before. I needed a moment to think this through, and a bit more information.

I held up a finger, signaling that something was coming to me, but my mind was slow and cloudy still. I needed their help. "Tell me, Poe. Where are Viridian Montclair's parents?"

She frowned. "His parents? They've lived in Brektos for years."

I nodded. "But not always…"

She shook her head, obviously trying to follow my train of thought. "No, you're right. When my people were attacked, they lived here, at the estate near Somerhaven."

Again, I nodded. "Do you see a connection? It seems as though there *is* one…"

Both she and Skye shook their heads. They hadn't watched Maman's cohort gather every month, or overheard snippets of conversation over years and years. Fragments of information that never formed into anything truly meaningful, until now.

I paced along the worktable as it all came together, staying clear of the lekanomance. The Montclair choice of country property finally made sense. It was not their ancestral home, as ours was. No, the Montclairs were *from* Brektos; House Montclair was firmly established in Novo Mala, from everything I knew.

They purchased the estate outside Kyovka, short miles from our own, when Helene and I were girls. And they were friendlier with us than any other family in the area, which, in retrospect, should have been suspicious. While many in Pravhna passed Maman's behaviors off as eccentric, with the disguise of Orchid House's obvious wealth to shield her, country families were different. They'd shied away from us, as though by instinct, though it was probably more a feature of the fact that Maman never participated in country life.

Poe caught my hand, trying to slow my movement. I hadn't noticed her moving, I was so lost in thought. "Come back to us," she whispered. "Tell us what you're thinking."

I frowned. She'd interrupted my stream of thoughts and now I was distracted, discombobulated. Poe seemed to understand, and smiled gently at me. "Take your time. I'm sorry I interrupted."

What had I been thinking? That it was odd that the Montclairs had overlooked our social standing in the country. Why hadn't I thought that was odd as a child, when I'd keenly observed so much else? The faintest of memories materialized at the back of my mind: Viridian Montclair, at ten, sword fighting shadows with sticks, alone by a creek. Letting me play with him when he'd caught me watching, then running away when Helene called me for dinner.

There was a time I'd wanted Viridian to like me. To be friends. Before Helene had seen his value to her social status. I pushed that out of my mind, hard. It had no bearing on what happened here now.

I struggled to return to the present moment, but Poe squeezed my hand again. Her patience with me and her understanding that she'd interrupted my thought process, slowing me down, gave me a boost of clarity. "I think the Montclairs were a part of Maman's cohort, the group that planned to use me as a conduit for the Ravager."

Getting the words out was a relief. I clasped Poe's hand in both of mine. "Thank you," I whispered.

She smiled, pulling my shoulder against hers, our hands still wrapped around one another. I felt no need to pull away. The tenderness I felt for Poe was changing me. *Safety, friendship, love.* These were all things I'd never known, and now I was greedy for them.

Skye leaned against a bookshelf, running a hand through her moonlight hair. "That makes sense." She glanced at me, her face shifting slightly into something I'd begun to recognize as concern. "I don't mean to be insulting, Mina, but Viridian's engagement to Helene was a bit odd."

I waved Skye's worry away, my free hand fluttering in dismissal. "It was. Most explained it away with her beauty... but that's not the point. What they were planning for me, it amounts to a coup. The destruction of everything the Oscarovi and Vilhari built after the Ventyr."

Poe let go of my hand, moving to the workroom doorway. "Thought I heard someone at the door," she murmured, frowning. When she turned back, she shrugged. "Must've been the wind."

I glanced at her, hoping my question wouldn't hurt her to answer. "Would your mother have come out of hiding to stop them from making me into an infernal weapon?"

Her eyes widened, then filled with tears. "Yes, she would have united the courts against Vaness, and likely the Oscarovi as a whole."

The thin veneer of society made it seem as though we had moved beyond the days of brawling for prominence. But those battles had only moved to other outlets—social status, capital, *echelon.*

Skye straightened. "It would have meant war, but the Vilhari would have won if they'd gotten to Vaness before she set the Ravager free—which perhaps someone did."

That was an interesting theory. Had someone killed Helene and Maman because they'd found them out? Skye's eyes went to Poe, who bit her bottom lip so hard I was afraid she might draw blood. Skye's thought had hit her quite differently than it had me.

"The Montclairs eliminated the risk of House Feriant trying to stop them," Poe said, her expression hardening again. "They removed the threat before it could hinder their plans to make you the Ravager's puppet."

My heart ached for her. I had never felt such empathy for another person, such concern for their wellbeing. I wanted to hug her, but feared that I might disturb her equilibrium.

Instead, I nodded. "I think Viridian became Chopard to form an army of his own. While his parents hold your family prisoner somewhere, or have killed them already, Viridian was left here to gain as much power as possible so that when Maman managed to inspirit me with the Ravager, they would have a foothold in the undercity."

"Why all the fires then—and why imprison you?" Skye asked.

"I'm not sure yet about the fires," I admitted. "But confronting Maman about the fetch has to be the reason they imprisoned me. They must have been worried I would escape them before they could enact their plan."

Poe's jaw clenched, her fists balled, her arms tight at her sides. "There's still so much of this we're not seeing." I understood her frustration; I was as impatient as she was to know more. Poe's eyes narrowed with determination. "But we can find out more if we confront Lord Eccles."

"That's dangerous," I said. "We don't know what he might be capable of."

"We need the information, though," Skye reasoned. "Before

Chopard… Viridian… makes another move. If he was willing to imprison Mina to keep her safe for the Ravager, we've got to find out what this is all about before he can get to her."

Poe's jaw twitched. "He's likely had eyes on us all along," she breathed. "He knows Ash is gone. Which means he knows we're at our weakest right now."

I nodded. "And that Ash is in danger as well." I looked to Poe, panic rising in me.

"I'll send for Rue," she said, closing her eyes. "He can get a message to Ash quicker than any other howler."

"Thank you," I murmured.

Skye nodded, gratitude in her eyes before she continued speaking, her voice faraway, as though she were speaking to herself. "If whatever Viridian is doing, burning all these places down, if it's all to get the Ravager here, we need to move quickly. We'll have to go to my mother. The high Vilhari can help us."

Poe's facial muscles tensed as she opened her eyes. "Rue is on his way to Ash," she explained. "We can consider whether or not to tell Elspeth when we find out more from Lord Eccles."

Skye frowned. "Why don't you trust my mother?"

Poe looked down at her hands. "It's not just your mother, Skye… Your grandmother and whatever little group they've gathered…"

Poe was so rarely at a loss for words, her hesitation surprised me. Another part of the pattern flickered in my mind.

"Do you suspect them of something?" Skye asked, her tone chill as a winter wind.

"No," Poe said quickly. "Of course not. I just wish we'd learned more about what they're up to."

Poe was lying. I didn't know how I knew, but I was sure. She suspected them of something else entirely. I had to wonder if she thought what I thought—that if by some chance Viridian Montclair was *not* Chopard, perhaps House Aestra was. They could be working together to achieve some other end, one we couldn't fathom yet. But Mirabelle's attitude had bothered me since the Avalonne. Something more was going on there. I was glad Poe had picked up on that as well.

Skye didn't seem to notice Poe's lie; she sighed with relief. "We'll ask Elspeth what's going on as soon as we can, all right?"

Poe nodded, her smile tight and conciliatory. I had no idea how Skye did not see what I did, but I moved my eyes to my ring, letting the flares of fire within the black opal distract me. This was something for them to work out. When the tension dissipated a touch, I looked up.

"It's settled then," I said, glancing at the clock. "We should get to the university. Perhaps we can catch Lord Eccles before he leaves for the day."

CHAPTER 48

MINA

An hour later, the three of us were on campus, dressed in the casual clothing of Aervale students. Ancient trees loomed overhead, mixing with the gloomy dark spires of the university buildings. Here, in the university district, the buildings were older, feeling almost ancient with their intricately carved arched doorways, every tower capped with stone sentinels, the great gryphon of Vilhari lore.

Some said this was the best example of architecture from the fey's original world, which they called Vilhar. It was not dissimilar in some ways from the more organic ornamentation the Oscarovi preferred, but the university had a feel of liminality, as though doors *between* might open at any moment. Likely, it was all the aether being used here. At any given time, there were dozens of magical experiments happening.

Before we left, Skye had tracked down where Lord Eccles' office was located. Poe and I stood outside the round Heathcliffe Camera building while she went inside to confirm. We were to watch each of the separate exits to make sure he didn't somehow leave without us knowing. Poe was seated on a bench under a stand of maples, ostensibly reading a book.

Students stared at her as they passed. They were right to—she made a beautiful picture, red leaves falling around her as a gentle breeze floated through campus. The day was mild up here, the sun's light golden and low in the sky. I was around the curve of the building, but sat far enough away that I could still see her. I tried to catch her eye, but realized quickly that the rose garden I sat in was likely obscuring her view.

Bells rang over the campus, signifying the end of the last class of the day. I glanced up at the astronomical clock that graced the front of the Lady's temple. A shiver ran through me as I noted, for the first time, that there were statues of large mountain hares scattered through the rose garden, peeking out of the foliage. All stared at the clock.

My breath caught. The statues were obviously quite old, and I'd been to campus plenty of times when in Pravhna. The Vercault Library was one of my favorite places. Why had I never noticed the hares?

The last bell rang. Office hours would begin shortly. Moments later, students came streaming out of the building. A flash of silver hair, moving against the flow of the crowd, caught my eye. Viridian Montclair.

I stood, surreptitiously trying to get Poe's attention, but again, she did not look my way. I would have to follow him without her. As quickly as I could, I merged into the crowd that was entering the building. As I walked through the doors, surrounded by students, I wondered what it would have been like to come here, merely for the purpose of learning things. It was a life I could hardly imagine.

I broke away from the group of people moving purposefully. I didn't know where to go from here. The inside of the Heathcliffe building was stunning. A marble staircase swept up the round walls, spiraling upwards. Light streamed in through the windows on the ground floor and near the domed roof, which was painted with a vivid scene of the Elemental War. Various fey, Oscarovi, and elementals were portrayed as victors, while my true people, the Ventyr, were depicted as wounded and weak.

For the first time, I noticed that when Vilhari artists portrayed the Ventyr, they did not do so accurately. None of the Ventyr had wings, nor had any in any other art I'd ever seen of the War. Only the statues at Orchid House portrayed us as we truly were. I wasn't sure what to make of that.

A fresh faced Vilhar with russet curls and round cheeks flushed pink with the cold bumped into me. "So sorry," she said with a smile.

"Oh, please don't worry," I replied, using the soft rasp I'd cultivated all these weeks in my social visits. This was the perfect opportunity. "Could you tell me where Lord Eccles has his office?"

"First semester?" she asked.

I nodded. "I keep getting lost."

"This campus is a bit of a maze. It will get easier in a few weeks, you'll see." She pointed to the grand marble staircase. "Up two flights, then it's just to your right. 317, I think."

I thanked her, then joined the people heading up the stairs. My knees protested, but I had a purpose that kept me going: stopping Viridian from catching Skye unaware. He had to be here to see Lord Eccles. It was too much of a coincidence, especially after seeing them together at the Orilion party. I broke from the stream of students on the third floor. It was quieter here. I found 317 easily, and tried the door. I had no plans to knock, especially if Viridian was already inside.

The office was quite typical of what one might expect from a university professor, but for the blood that spattered the room, pooling on the floor in glossy crimson sheets. My stomach dropped within me and I stumbled, woozy, not at the sight of all that blood, but the scent of it. Memories of a battlefield filled my mind, my sisters hacked to pieces around me. I'd fought with the Larae once, just before the Ravagers came. I'd gone home to my true family.

I was lost in a swirl of memory and sorrow. Trauma kept me still when I should move, my ancient past devouring me whole. I felt the grimace of disgust stretch my face. Heard the screams of the dying in my head.

"Damn it all," Viridian growled from the other side of the door. His hand went around my arm and he yanked me inside, shutting the door firmly behind me.

I controlled myself, keeping my empyrae down while I assessed the scene. I had to calm down, push the memories back. Keeping my wits about me was of utmost importance now. There wasn't a body anywhere, and Skye was nowhere to be found. Neither was Lord Eccles, but I feared this might be his blood.

"What did you do?" I hissed as Viridian shut the door.

"What did I—" Viridian let go of me, pinching the bridge of his nose. "Lady take you. Mina, you are the absolute *worst*."

I frowned. His entire demeanor was off. This was not the Viridian I was used to at all. There was no bravado in him, only a kind of exhaustion I recognized. The kind that came from keeping too much in, too many secrets. Perhaps he saw it in me too because he pulled me away from the pool of blood on the floor that crept slowly towards us.

"Come away from that, *please*," he cautioned. "Someone has murdered Lord Eccles, and we don't need you caught up in such nonsense. We must go before Niall Aestra gets here. He'll have you in prison in the blink of an eye."

"You'd like that, wouldn't you?" I asked, but the question came out more earnestly than I'd expected. Less accusatory, more genuinely searching. Viridian's usually neat and tidy clothes looked rumpled, his cerulean jacket the same he'd worn at Armande's. It looked as though he'd pulled it off the floor, wrinkled and slightly stained. Something was most definitely wrong with him.

"No!" Viridian said, eyes wild with frustration. He looked around the office. On the other side of the pool of blood, there was another door. "We have to get over there. That door goes to a private study."

I glared at Viridian, who was now bolting the door shut. "Touch nothing," he warned, showing me his gloved hands. "You're not wearing gloves."

"I'm not going anywhere with you," I insisted.

"You must," he hissed, pulling on my arm again.

"No," I argued, angry with his overconfidence. Was he such a fool that he thought I would just meekly go along with him? "You're Chopard. You imprisoned me in an oubliette. Why would I go *anywhere* with you?"

Viridian covered his face with one hand, and I thought he might be crying for half a moment. His shoulders shook. But then his hand fell away, and I realized he was laughing, not with villainous mirth, but nearly hysterical. It was as though everything had gone wrong for him, and I was the thing that might break him. I could empathize all too well. I didn't like the feeling.

Again, he pinched the bridge of his nose, clearly exasperated with me. "I am not Chopard, you silly girl. I'm trying to *find* Chopard and stop you from becoming the conduit for an infernal beast."

"The Ravager?" I asked, hardly believing what I heard. "You want to stop that from happening?"

"Of course I do," he insisted, his voice raising an octave. "That is why I'm engaged to Caralee. Her family is in on your mother's horrendous plans. It's why I was engaged to Helene." He grabbed me by the arms, shaking me. "It's why I helped Helene put you in the oubliette, where you'd be safe—monstrous as it was to do that to someone. Even someone as infuriating as you." His voice has raised to a nearly shrill octave. He really was upset with me. "But you had to escape, didn't you?"

My mind swam. If what he said was true... but how could it be? "But your family was a part of Maman's cohort, were they not?"

Viridian sighed, the noise edged with another shriek of frustration. "No, Mina. House Montclair has always protected Sirin."

"Your people attacked the Court of Aether, though." Let him explain that.

"*Attacked* them?" Viridian tore at his hair. "We don't have time for this, Mina. Niall is never far from Eccles. He will be here in moments."

I crossed my arms. "I can deal with him."

Viridian closed his eyes. "Would you kill Skye's brother so easily?" He had a point. I would not. "I know what you're capable of. The empyrae. You can kill me later, if it pleases you. But for now, could we escape before things become even more complicated?"

"If you promise to explain everything," I said, hating that I followed his logic. "Now, show me how to get beyond the blood."

Viridian Montclair sighed again, this time with relief. "Finally, you see reason."

I gritted my teeth. Reason had nothing to do with it. Viridian was correct; I could kill him later. What I needed now was answers.

Nearly as soon as we'd made it out of Lord Eccles' private study and back into the hallway, there were sounds from within his public office. It was good we hadn't gone out the door we went in; we would have run straight into whoever was in there now.

"Niall," Viridian whispered. The hallway was full of students. "Keep your head down and follow me."

He led us around a corner, to a set of back stairs. They were narrower than the grand staircase and completely empty. I started to ask him for information, but he shook his head. Of course, anyone could be hiding in the staircase. He was right again. It was uncomfortable, Viridian being right so much.

The stairs were quiet but for a stray ghast or two. I kept my eyes deliberately averted. Ghasts had the nasty habit of showing you the way they died if you looked directly at them, and I was in enough pain going down the stairs. When we exited the building, we ran right into Poe and Skye.

Poe rushed towards me, grabbing me, throwing her body between me and Viridian. "You won't take her, you fiend."

I was grateful for her support, both in the emotional sense and the physical. For a moment, I leaned on her, catching my breath as the pain from navigating the many stairs slowly receded.

"You again," he growled, stepping forward, a menacing threat in his eyes. "What do you want with her? I won't let you charlatans turn her into a monster." He lunged for Poe, but Skye drew her rapier, lightning fast.

I looked around. There was a hedge of cedar growing around the back door to the building. We were hidden from sight.

"*Me* turn her into a monster? What about *you*?" Poe screeched.

"Poe," I said softly, regaining some of my strength. "Viridian claims *not* to be Chopard, or a part of Maman's cohort."

She sneered. "He can claim whatever he pleases. He is a lying sack of shit." Skye kept the rapier against Viridian's throat, allowing Poe to ask whatever she wanted. "Where is my family, Montclair? What have you done with House Feriant?"

So we were doing this now. I was fine with that. I leaned against the back door to the building, fusing it shut with a tiny bit of empyrae, then moved my fingers quickly, drawing a muffling spell around us. It would give us a bit more privacy, and enough time to figure out what to do next.

"I'll never tell you where they are, you imposter," he growled.

Poe's mouth fell open in shock.

"Oh yes, I know what you planned to do, Hippolyta. You've been trying to use me to build your credibility for over a year now. Did you think I hadn't guessed your plans?"

Skye tilted her head to the side, a dangerous glint in her silver eyes. "Just exactly who do you think Poe is pretending to be, Viridian?"

This was not at all what I'd expected when we escaped Lord Eccles' office. Carefully manicured lies and excuses, yes. Some weak explanation for what Viridian had done, of course. But him accusing Poe of… whatever this was? This had not been on my list of things to expect from Viridian Montclair.

He shook his head, steadfast in some resolve. "Do whatever you want to me. Kill me, if you have to. House Montclair is loyal to House Feriant, and nothing you do to me will change that."

Skye glanced at Poe, as all our breath drew in. What was Viridian *saying*? My eyebrows raised as I pushed away from the door. Poe's mouth still hung open in shock.

"Do you mean to tell us that you're trying to protect House Feriant?" I asked, as Poe was too stunned to speak.

"Obviously," he spat out. "House Montclair came with the princess on the Avalonne. We took holy vows to protect her, and nothing any of you do will change that. Torture me, if you want to. I'll never tell where they are, and *you* will never claim her title, Poe."

A tear slipped down Viridian's cheek. It was the most vulnerable I'd ever seen him, but then I wondered if I'd ever seen the real Viridian Montclair. His chin quivered. "I'm surprised you'd be involved in this, Aestra. Do you know what this woman wants?"

Poe and Skye exchanged another look. Some invisible conversation passed between them. Poe nodded, and Skye lowered her rapier, sheathing it. "She wants to find her family, Viridian."

His eyes widened, as though Skye's words confirmed just how wrong he'd been about Poe. Poe straightened her spine, the glamour on her dark wings falling away. She looked Viridian straight in the eye, her shocked expression turning defiant and regal.

Viridian fell to his knees. "You're the *real* Hippolyta?"

The name fell from his lips in a cry of despair, as though he realized every mistake he'd made in one moment of horrifying clarity. If anyone had told me a week prior that I would understand Viridian Montclair so intimately, I'd have called them a liar.

"Your royal highness," he breathed. " I have made a grave mistake and will accept punishment. I thought you were trying to assume the princess' identity."

In a moment I could not quite comprehend, Poe bent down, placing a hand on Viridian's shoulder. "Do you know where my family is? My mother?"

He looked up, deep sorrow in his eyes. "Your mother was killed in the raid." He glanced towards me. "The people who want Mina. The one you call Chopard—it's his operation, and they killed her on sight. But the rest of your people are safe. The descendants of House Feriant, the princess' retinue, are safe. My parents guard them, even now in Brektos. We thought you and Euryale had been killed."

"We almost were. She died on the Avalonne." Poe drew her glamour around her again, looking at both me and Skye. "I don't think he's lying. But how can this be?"

Skye offered Viridian a hand, pulling him up. He brushed off his pants, then wiped his eyes. Without his usual mask of bad temper and bravado, the lines of his face were sensitive, noble even. If my sister had known this version of him, she would have hated him.

"Chopard, whoever they are, is the one pulling all the strings." Viridian looked at me. "I believe they were the one manipulating your parents, Mina. I've been tracking their movements for years. It's why I offered marriage to Helene. I thought if I got closer to your family, I might be able to discern who Chopard was, and what their aims were. I didn't want to imprison you when Helene asked for my help, but in the oubliette, at least I knew you were safe."

"Did she tell you why I was being imprisoned?" I asked.

Viridian shook his head. "I'm sorry, no. Helping her was some kind of test. I still don't know if I passed it, but she never told me *why* we did it."

I wondered if he knew I was not the Wildfangs' actual child. I was not about to enlighten him, if he didn't. While I leaned towards believing what he said, it was better to keep some things secret and safe. "Did my sister know about this plan to make me the Ravager's conduit?"

Viridian shook his head. "Not that she told me. But I believe Chopard killed your mother and sister. Like you, he wields empyrae, and I fear they'd outlived their usefulness to him."

It was hard not to be frustrated. We'd solved part of the mystery, only to have more questions opened. I wasn't sure what to say to Viridian. His face was so earnest it was hard to comprehend that the other side of him existed. It was as though he was two people.

"Who do you think is Chopard?" Skye asked.

Viridian stared at the building, his eyes traveling around the round outer walls, as he thought. I wondered if he sensed something I didn't; his eyes kept traveling back to the windows in the staircase. "I thought perhaps Lord Eccles might be Chopard, but that seems unlikely now. He came to find me at the Orilion party to tell me to back off..." Viridian frowned, as though he were trying to work some-thing out.

"Back off what?" I asked.

"You," he answered. "He told me to leave you alone."

The door rattled behind me. Someone on the other side was trying to get out.

"We should go," Viridian said. "It wouldn't be good to be caught here. I will call this afternoon though, and we can discuss this further."

Poe nodded. "We can find you, Viridian. If this is some ruse, know that I have eyes everywhere."

CHAPTER 49

ASHBOURNE

My vision blurred, and I was woozy, but my eyes opened. I lay on the floor of the cabin, near the fireplace. I glanced out the window. Not much time had passed, maybe an hour. The clock was too far away on the mantel, my vision still too fuzzy. I didn't want to risk drawing attention to myself before I got my bearings, so I didn't move, but I could tell I was not bound.

It wasn't necessary to move to know that I was still too weak to do anything but lay here like a lump. There was movement near the kitchen. Helene and Brigitte, the Strix woman. I tried to summon a little bit of aether, anything to help me, but I had no energy. I'd burned myself out fighting Chopard's people.

"Brigitte. He's coming around," Helene said, from the other side of the room. "Look."

The Strix woman, Brigitte, nodded. "That he is. Get on with it then."

Her voice was brusque, almost annoyed. It was an odd way for the Strix to talk to Helene, who was supposedly her mistress. Almost as though Helene were an unruly child. Helene nodded as she came into focus, pulling a chair over to where I lay.

"Do you remember me?" Helene asked.

I figured it was better to play along. Of course, I recognized her from the portraits in Orchid House. She was unmistakable. "You are Helene Wildfang."

"Yes," she answered. "You tried and failed to kill me. I don't appreciate that. My sister isn't in Pravhna. Where is she?"

My breath snagged in my lungs, my heart nearly stopping. I couldn't remember ever having met Helene Wildfang before. I certainly did not remember trying to kill her. What was happening here?

Fear gripped me as I realized the gravity of what she'd said. If Mina wasn't in Pravhna, where was she? I had come here to keep her safe, and now it seemed that I'd left her vulnerable. I longed to ask Helene what had happened to Skye and Poe, but that wasn't wise. Even in my weakened state, I knew better.

I would have to buy some time, let my power rejuvenate. It had been a long time since I used so much, but I had to do whatever I could to draw this out. Making Helene angry would likely work for a little while. She seemed like the type who was used to getting her way. Outright refusal was probably my best bet.

I managed to struggle into a seated position, my back against the heavy, flannel-covered settee, with Helene watching me carefully. Brigitte stood in the kitchen, glaring at me. That was all fine; my strength was coming back, little by little. All I had to do was buy myself a bit of time. "I won't tell you where Mina is."

Helene sighed, standing up so she could look down on me. She was a delicate thing, with rail thin limbs and elegant features. I didn't know what kind of magical power she wielded, but physically I'd have no trouble overpowering her in… a half hour or so, I gauged from the feeling in my muscles. I was sore still, but moving again, a sure sign that my body would recover shortly, if not my magic.

"I was sure she'd come here with him, what with all the fucking you reported, Brigitte," Helene said with a vicious sneer.

She was a beautiful woman, no one could deny that—her hair was like spun gold, her eyes sparkling sapphires—but that *look*. It was pure ugliness. Helene Wildfang had let her mother poison her, ruining whatever physical beauty she might possess.

The Strix shrugged. "And apparently, you were wrong. Again. He won't be happy with you. This isn't what we were sent here to do. We came for Wilhelmina."

Helene sighed. "I thought he would happily kill her. He seemed so bent on it when he burned the house down."

When I burned the house down. The house. Mina's ancestral estate had been burned—that was how Helene, and this Brigitte if I remembered correctly—were supposed to have died.

Brigitte rolled her eyes. "If you say so."

"He was," Helene said. "Weren't you? You were so angry when you arrived looking for her."

Had *I* burned Somerhaven? Dizziness gripped me as I tried to recall, but I could barely think. Why had I been allowed to remember Lumina, but not this? Inwardly, I fought the feeling back.

I had to remember this. Something about this was important. Had I burned Somerhaven? Was I the one to kill Mina's mother? My eyes squeezed closed, the room spinning. Now, more than ever, I had the instinct that it was best to play along. I had no idea what the two of them were after and I needed time to think.

Helene waited for an answer. I had to say something to keep the conversation going. I steeled myself, willing my voice to come out cold and calm. What would happen if I agreed with her? Would she let me live long enough to regain some strength? The words tumbled out of me, a jumble of truth and lies, as I opened my eyes. "Yes, I wanted to kill her. That is why I came to Sirin. But you got to her first."

Helene smiled a victor's smile. What had I said that elicited that look? "Yes. And then the curse got you, didn't it? The closer you got to her, the more you forgot. But you remember now, which means you broke it. What was the loophole?"

She knew about the curse. My stomach clenched with worry. Helene seemed a bit unbalanced, but she knew more than she should. She was more than a few steps ahead of me. I needed more from her, so I shrugged. At least this much I could be completely honest about. "I have no idea."

"Well," Helene said, sitting back in her chair. "I'd rather see my sister dead than what *he's* got planned for her. Do you still want to kill her? You always did before, from what I understand."

My heart beat faster. What did she mean? Had I really gone to Somerhaven to kill Mina? Why would I have done such a thing? Something stirred in the back of my mind—the leaves falling in the driveway to the cabin. What had I remembered earlier, before Chopard's men came? I'd made progress.

Helene placed her elbows on her bony knees, resting her chin in her hands as she looked down on me. "That was what made her hate you so much in the end, wasn't it? That you'd always planned to kill her."

Some part of me remembered what she said, but it was unclear. Wrong... But also, I realized with a sickening lurch, some of it was right. What kind of monster was I? My jaw clenched with the pain of this newly realized knowledge.

I knew I'd been right to leave when I did. These two knew more about the man I'd been than I did. I *had* planned to kill Mina. I choked back a sob, realizing the near miss, the way I'd just barely gotten away in time. If I'd remembered all this when we were in the house together, might I have harmed her? I couldn't bear the thought of it.

"Helene," Brigitte cautioned. "I still don't think this is wise. He'll be angry with you when he finds out."

Helene smiled. "For a little while, perhaps, but then he'll see that *I* am the better choice for his plans."

Brigitte shook her head. "You have lost all good sense, girl."

Helene stood, her hand flying out towards the Strix. It made contact with a loud thud and an explosion of feathers. Brigitte hissed and clutched her face. "He will punish you for this, Helene, and I will enjoy it."

"I won't kill her," I said, interrupting them.

I had to stop them. I could not risk what might come next. The more they talked about killing her, the more deeply I cared for Mina. I could not allow myself to remember how I knew her, or the reasons I wanted her dead. She was my chance for happiness, and I was hers. I could never be the one who ended her life.

"I will never kill her," I said again, struggling to rise. "I will kill you both before I let you at her."

I couldn't do it. I knew that. But maybe they didn't. If they killed me first, I knew Mina could handle them. And if she couldn't, Skye could protect her. My only regret was that I wouldn't be able to say goodbye. But this was the only way to keep them all safe from the monster I knew myself to be, deep down. I had just enough strength for this—I pushed myself off the ground, lunging for Helene.

Brigitte was on me in a second, but I flung her off. She hit her head against the heavy dining room table. It was unfortunate. They'd have killed me faster together. I would have to put up enough of a fight to keep Helene going. This ended tonight.

I gathered my strength as she whispered words I could not understand. The pendant around her neck glowed and an elemental firedrake flew from it, its sharp claws aimed directly at me. It ripped at the skin on my chest as Helene called upon aether, a whip forming in her hands. She struck me again and again, as her elemental spirit clawed at me to keep me from getting up.

This is it, I thought as I surrendered to the pain. *Soon she'll be safe.*

Whatever I'd done to Mina before, something in me was sure that I deserved this now. If she'd hated me, then this was earned. I bowed my head and let the lashes come, only struggling for show.

The door to the cabin flew open. I raised my head, distraught to find the woman I fought to protect standing in the doorway, in a blaze of empyrae and aether. No, she couldn't be here now. Not when I couldn't fight to protect her. Not when I was still a danger to her if I lived.

"Get away from him," Mina said, her voice low and calm.

Helene loosed the lash upon me again, but her elemental rose to protect her. I slumped to the floor, defeated. A hot tear slid down my face. This was not how things should end.

"Come and get him, if you want him so much, *sister,*" Helene sneered.

I watched, helpless from the floor as the woman I loved stepped into the cabin. My heart thumped faster at the thought, panic and desire rising in me, twisting together as Lady Fate's talons wound around my heart.

The woman I loved.

I did, I loved her, and I was so glad to know it in these last moments. To see that she loved me too—that much I could see in her eyes, though there was fury there as well. Frustration and confusion mingled on her face, and they were a familiar sight. *I sent word. I told you not to come.* The words were familiar, but I did not know why I thought of them now.

"You are no sister of mine," Mina said, taking another step forward.

Something in me changed as she moved, shifting. The pressure in my head lessened. Memories rushed back to me, overwhelming in their magnitude. *I sent word. I told you not to come.* An enemy princess. The woman I'd claimed, who'd claimed me, for all eternity. A bond so strong it had brought me through a portal to this world that no one else could reach.

Helene laughed, breaking my concentration, the flow of logic that had almost reached its conclusion. Her words tore the memories away, confusing me.

"You have always been so slow, Mina. Even now, you're just blundering through life." She raised her arm as though to send the whip forward again, this time in Mina's direction.

I could not let her harm Mina. I reached out, using my last bit of strength to grab hold of her ankle, and pulled hard, just as she cracked the whip. Helene stumbled, and Mina's arm caught the whip. My girl, my beautiful menace, smiled then, a stunning, feral thing to witness.

I had seen such a smile before, but not on her face. What did it mean?

In a flash, her aether wrapped around Helene, snapping her neck. "You should have died in that fire, Helene," she said as her sister slid to the ground. The elemental firedrake disappeared, dissolving into smoke.

Mina rushed to me, lifting my head into her lap. "Don't you fucking dare die on me," she growled.

There was fury in her voice, a fire I would not escape. The memories inside me, the ones I struggled to understand? She already knew the truth of them, whatever it was I'd done, whoever I'd been before. I'd meant to hurt her, and now I would pay. As it should be. The last thing I wanted now was to harm her, to regain some part of myself that would be capable of such a thing. I looked beyond her, worried Brigitte might regain consciousness.

But the Strix was gone—I'd killed her, though, I was sure of it. How had she disappeared? As my vision went dark, I whispered the only words that mattered. "I love you, Mina."

CHAPTER 50

MINA

SIX HOURS EARLIER - PRAVHNA

Viridian Montclair sat in the parlor at Orchid House, explaining the way he'd narrowed in on Eccles as someone who either reported directly to Chopard, or was Chopard himself. "I followed him to some of the worst brothels in the upper city," Viridian said, revulsion obvious in the twitch near his eye and the way he wrinkled his nose. "And I tried everything I could to bribe the people he met with. But they would not speak about him for anything."

Well, that explained his trips to the brothels, at least. Viridian's story was growing more plausible by the moment. It pained me, in some ways, to believe him. He had, after all, locked me in a hole beneath the sea. But given what he'd suspected, what he feared, it was hard for me to argue with his logic.

"And now someone has killed Lord Eccles," I replied, thinking of the amount of blood on the floor. "Do you still think he's Chopard?"

Viridian shook his head. "Someone killed *someone* in Lord Eccles' office. There was no body. The cityguard will assume it was Eccles, because they are fools and like things to be tidy. But we have no evidence that it was actually Eccles who died there."

I was already tired of this conversation and becoming distracted. Now that we knew at least some of Poe's family was still alive, I needed to talk to Ashbourne. If he did not remember me, I could force him to remember. He need not love me, but we had to resolve things between us. The curse was weakening, and I needed closure on this part of things before I could move on.

Curses were fickle things, and it was impossible to curse more than one person at once. Even my mother's sisters, Penthe and Faedra, talented as they were, could not forge a curse strong enough for two Ventyr adults. More likely, the curse was laid upon me, and me alone.

The memories I had of Penthe and Faedra speaking over me seemed to confirm my suspicions. The curse was on me, but applied to Ashbourne as well, and likely anyone who realized what was happening between us. But the spell radiated from me, triggered by my proximity to him. The amnestic effect, the gagging of anyone who tried to talk about the curse—those were all typical of such workings. Measures to ensure that the cursed would not escape their punishment until they'd found their loophole.

Before Ash met me in this life, I was almost certain he had been able to think of Lumina, of my former self. It was only when he reached Sirin that he forgot me. I had questions about how he'd gotten here, and I had no doubt that Skye had answers I needed. But would she give them to me?

I stared at her for a long moment. No. She would not betray him to me. Nor should she. Nor did I actually want her to. More than anything else, what I wanted was for him to explain himself to me. To tell me why he'd done what he'd done. And, if I was honest, I wanted him to let me punish him. To let out all my rage and make him pay the same way I had for the choices *he'd* made.

There was only one way that was going to happen. I had to go to the cabin and speak with him. The trouble was, I didn't have any idea where it was located. I needed a moment to myself.

I stood. "Please excuse me for a moment."

Skye and Viridian nodded, continuing to discuss the way the city-guard would handle things. Apparently, he suspected Detective Brenton and her partner of being in Chopard's pay. That did not surprise me. Poe watched me carefully, obviously suspicious. She was going to follow me, that much was certain.

It wasn't as though I could sneak out in broad daylight. I had no idea where to go. Instead, I went to the library and stared at Papa's books, remembering that as a child I had been foolish enough to think we would have been friends. That he would have liked me at all was a laughable idea now, given the fact that before he died, the man had helped Maman kidnap me and imprison me in this body.

I ran my fingers over the spines of the books. My memory of arriving on Sirin was still fuzzy, as many things were, and would continue to be. A curse that persisted for so long would take time to wear off, especially as it had been enhanced by the oubliette's magic. I paused when my fingers traced the spine of a romance. It was the story of a siren and her Oscarovi lover.

The sirens. The reason I still felt so comfortable with them was because they had been kind to me. For years, I'd wandered Sirin alone, trying to stay as far from the cities and the Oscarovi as I could. Why, I could not remember, but I had a reason, I knew that much. I lived among the sirens though, in an aerie across the sea. In Brektos. We grew fruit, apricoft and pairns, in enormous, terraced orchards, high above the clouds.

Sadness had followed me, a constant companion in those days, but I had finally been at peace. I had been slow to trust the sirens, but they had been patient with me—they gave me all the space I needed. A tiny cottage to myself, amongst their unwinged, humanoid children. Those like Muse. They were not happy times, exactly, but they had offered me something I had not expected when I came here. Peace.

Papa, Alastair Wildfang, was the one that found me. I remembered the day, though not much of what happened. I remembered him calling me Lumina in a market, on a sun-drenched mountain I can hardly remember now. All was confusion after that. He and Maman must have killed me, the first me anyway, Lumina.

I blinked away tears, happy enough not to remember that. The memories of my wings being butchered from my body were too much. If I had to remember dying as well, I didn't know if I could survive. My earliest memories after that were of Maman and Helene. Being a child. I had been an adult, ancient to the children of this planet. Then reduced to a mere babe again.

Was it even fair to consider Lumina my true self? I had her

memories, but was I actually her? The question was philosophical in a way I had little patience for. A feline head bumped my ankle as Morpheus materialized.

Ashbourne needs you, he said, alarm in his voice. *Muse had a vision. You must go to him. Now.*

"I don't know where the cabin is," I replied. "Tell Skye. We'll all go."

No, the cat insisted. *It must be you and only you.*

I narrowed my eyes at the fey cat, speaking to him from inside my head. *I don't like to be manipulated. Not even by the servants of the Lady.*

It cannot be helped. Will you go?

I nodded. "Show me where."

I saw the trains I would need to take, the roads to travel down, the curve in the road, and the cabin by the river. It was all very clear. I whispered, "Distract them then. I must get my coat."

Morpheus nodded, and left the room. I headed straight back to the housekeeper's office. I threw a coat on, then scribbled a note for Poe, hoping she would understand what it meant.

"Where do you think you're going?" I turned to find her, hands on her hips, glaring at me. "How dare you think to leave without so much as an explanation. Have you any idea—"

I covered her mouth with one hand, pressing my finger to my lips with the other. With a flick of my free hand, I brought a muffling spell down on us, praying Morpheus could keep Viridian and Skye away for enough time to let me leave.

Bringing my lips to her ear, I breathed in her floral scent. It was comforting as a warm blanket. "It has to be me. I have to go alone. I can't ask you to leave what chance you have for happiness…but—" I slipped the note I'd written her into her hand, then kissed her cheek. "Know I would have followed you to the ends of the cosmos, my queen. We will meet again."

Her eyes were wide and serious as she clung to my hand. "We will meet again. I promise it."

I pulled my hand from hers before I could change my mind. Leaving her was the hardest thing I could remember ever choosing to do. In my long, long life there had been so many things I'd done because I had to. Because I was forced, tricked, or backed into a corner. But this, this was by my own choice. That did not stop the ache of knowing that I might not be able to come back.

That if I had to kill him, Poe might not be able to forgive me. That she might choose Skye above me, and that I couldn't ask her not to. "I love you, Poe," I said as I opened the back door. "You are everything I could have hoped for in a queen, a sister, a friend. Please don't forget that."

"I won't," she murmured as she took the door, tears welling in her eyes as she shut it softly behind me.

I paused there, feeling both our hearts breaking as we stood on opposite sides of the door. Then I turned swiftly, rushing through the garden as fast as I could. Only when I reached the street did I realize that Miranda Willsworth was watching me from her back window, an eerie darkness in her eyes. I hadn't the time to stop to think about it. If I slowed down for even a moment I would go back into the house and beg them to come with me. I'd abandon Muse's mandate, and all my plans to stay with the only friends I'd ever had.

On the train, I realized what the darkness in Miranda's eyes was. They had gone completely black, just like the eyes of the people who'd witnessed Chopard's attacks. There was no way to send a message on the train. I hadn't brought even so much as a calling card with me. Though I didn't know what it meant, I knew it could not be good.

THE TRAIN RIDE was a blur of anxiety, fear of what I left behind, and what was left ahead. I repeated my next moves to myself again and again. Send a message to Poe about Miranda Willsworth at the train station. Hire a car to take me to the cabin. Interrogate Ashbourne, by whatever means necessary, until he remembered what he'd done. Until he explained himself to me, once and for all.

If he was in some kind of trouble, as Muse's urgent message had suggested, I supposed I'd deal with that as well. It was easier to focus on my goals than unknowns. When the train stopped, I hurried off. The little country station was tiny. There was only one clerk at the ticket counter, and no customers in the lobby. When the Vilhari clerk turned to face me, their eyes were black, just as Miranda's had been.

I panicked, running from the station, before I could send a message back to Poe. My body ached with the effort, but I could not stop. I hazarded a look behind me, but the clerk did not follow. There were a couple of cabs waiting outside. I checked each driver in turn. All their eyes were normal.

With relief, I chose a Strix driver that reminded me a little of Evie, though the tweeds she wore were regular. She was not one of Edith's. I gave the address of the cabin and sank into the back seat of the cab.

"It's about an hour, Miss," the cabbie said, her accent a lilting one. She was from north of here, then. "You should rest. Forgive me for saying it, but you look awful."

"Yes," I agreed. "Thank you."

I didn't think I could sleep, but before I knew it, the cabbie's delicate voice woke me. "We're here, Miss."

"Shit," I swore, realizing I hadn't any money left to pay her. I'd used the last of what was in my coat pocket at the train station. I pulled a diamond hairpin from my mess of hair. "I'm sorry. Take this. If you don't want to sell it in town, take it to Orchid House in Pravhna. The women there will make sure you get paid. Ask for Poe."

The cabbie took the pin, her dark eyes serious. "All right, Miss. But this is more than your fare. Should I wait for you?"

"That's your choice," I said, thinking hard about what lie to tell, how to hedge against what might happen next. "If I return, it will be with a very sick man. He may not be conscious."

"Oh dear," the cabbie replied. "Is it the poppy or the bottle?"

For a moment, I was confused. Then I understood. "Both," I said. Why not go all out with the lie? If I had to knock Ashbourne out, she might as well believe he was in a bad way. "He needs a great deal of help. I don't know what state I may find him in. He's gotten himself into some trouble, you see."

The cabbie nodded, sympathy in her eyes. Clearly, she had experience with men who'd given over their lives to wantonness. "I'll wait for an hour. If you don't make it back, I never saw you."

"Thank you," I said, getting out of the cab. I felt a little guilty for playing on the obvious harm that had been done to her, but I would more than make up for it with money, if given the opportunity. "I appreciate the discretion."

She nodded, turned the autocar off, and leaned back in her seat, clearly prepared to take a nap.

CHAPTER 51

MINA

I crept down the long driveway to the Aestra's cabin. In truth, I expected a country manor built by the river, but was surprised to find out that it was, indeed, a rustic little cabin. It wasn't tiny, by any means, but nor was it a sprawling estate.

A window was cracked open at the front of the house. Voices inside let me know Ash was not alone. Silently, I made my way closer to the house, keeping well out of sight. A familiar voice was speaking inside the house, one I'd known my whole life. "…were wrong. Again. He won't be happy with you. This isn't what we were here to do."

I did not have to look inside to know who spoke. It was Brigitte, Helene's governess and lady's maid. What was she doing here? My heart shattered when the next person spoke.

"I thought he would happily kill her. He seemed so bent on it when he burned the house down."

Helene? This could not be. And what she said—did she mean that Ash was the one who burned the house down? When Morpheus said he was in trouble, I assumed he meant that Muse had seen him in anguish, that his memories tormented him, or that he'd been attacked in his pursuit of Chopard.

But this? He'd killed Maman? My heart nearly beat out of my

chest, my breath stalling. I could not find air. Somewhere in the haze of my panic, I had the wherewithal to wonder *why* he'd done that. Why had he burned the house?

Inside the cabin, Brigitte said, "If you say so."

"He was," Helene replied. "Weren't you? You were so angry when you arrived looking for her."

And then I understood. Ashbourne Thuellos had come for me. This time he had come for the right reasons—even after all he'd likely endured, being imprisoned with the Ravagers, his heart hadn't hardened against me. He had found his way to Sirin to find me, to set me free from this prison, and when he found that someone had harmed me, he'd lashed out.

I didn't have to know the particulars of what had happened to know that the Ashbourne of my past would have killed anyone who'd harmed me, without thinking twice. Our bond was complicated, but it was nothing if not eternal. For a moment, my heart sang with joy. The Emperor had been wrong. My true father's last words to me had haunted me for so long, and now perhaps I might be free.

No one can love you, Lumina, he had said as he pushed me through the portal. *Not when they know the truth of you. No one is coming. You will be alone here, unknown and unloved, forever.*

His words had been the true curse. They were all I'd feared my entire life, living on the outside of everything. They were the reason I'd done as he asked so many times before Ash. So much harm had been done because I believed no one could ever love someone like me.

But despite his mistakes, despite all we'd been through, Ashbourne had changed. Proven everyone wrong. He had come for me, killed for me. *Did he love me now?*

"Yes," Ashbourne replied, voice calm and collected. He sounded nothing like the Ash I knew now, but exactly like the prince who betrayed me. My hope died, shriveling inside me like rotten fruit. "I wanted to kill her. That is why I came. But you got to her first."

He was the same as the rest of them then. He hadn't changed a bit. I tried to shrug it off, but the knife cut deep. I couldn't let this matter now, not with Helene's return. My sister wasn't dead. And she was meeting with Ashbourne out here in the woods, in secret. Had he been plotting against me this whole time? My heart felt as though it would shatter into a thousand pieces. I curled into myself, staying still as I could. I needed more information.

Helene spoke again. "Yes. And then the curse got you, didn't it? The closer you got to her, the more you forgot. But you remember now, which means you broke it. What was the loophole?"

At least they hadn't been working together. But they might be soon. Perhaps that was what this meeting was about.

"I have no idea," Ash said, casual as could be. But I knew better. Helene might not, but that was a lie. What was happening here?

"Well," Helene said. "I'd rather see my sister dead than what *he's* got planned for her. Do you still want to kill her?"

There was a long pause. I couldn't see what went on inside, but it seemed as though Helene waited for some kind of response. I wished I could peek in and see what was happening. Finally, she spoke again. "You always did before, from what I understand. That was what made her hate you so much in the end, wasn't it? That you'd always planned to kill her."

She wasn't wrong, but how had she known all that? It wasn't possible for Helene to have known these things. Panic had me in its grip, but I wasn't giving in so easily. I had to get the information I needed and then retreat somewhere safe to sort this out.

"Helene," Brigitte cautioned. "I still don't think this is wise. He'll be angry."

Helene answered. "For a little while, perhaps, but then he'll see that I am a better choice."

Who were they talking about? It had to be Chopard. But if that were true, why would Helene want me dead? Did it even matter? Was Ash going to agree to kill me?

I clutched at my head. Memories of the first time I'd discovered that Ashbourne had orders to kill me rushed back, the scent of rose petals in the air lingering in my mind. It had been nothing like whatever this disaster was. I had my orders as well. Once we'd solved the problem with the Ravagers, the Thuellos prince had to die. My father had seen no use for furthering the alliance between our houses. My mission had been to seduce him, gain his secrets, and then, eventually, kill him.

And apparently, he had been mandated to do the same. We'd discovered one another at nearly the same moment. It had devolved into frenzied lovemaking, fuel for a fire that had been building between us for months. But this was something else. He actually sounded as though he might kill me now. Despair filled me. The man I loved yesterday was gone.

Brigitte spoke, breaking the hold memory had on me. "You have lost all good sense, girl."

A loud thud came from inside the cabin, followed by the unmistakable sound of a Strix hissing. "He will punish you for this, Helene, and I will enjoy it."

My sister had hit Brigitte. It wasn't as though it was an uncommon thing. I'd seen her do it dozens of times growing up. But now that I'd lived another way, it was shocking to me. My sister was a *monster*.

She, Maman, Papa. They were all monsters. People didn't live the way we had. Not average people. I'd known no better as a child, but I did now. I'd had an inkling when I grew old enough to understand the world better, but now I was sure of it.

My thoughts were interrupted by Ashbourne's soft voice, deep and clear. "I won't kill her," he said, interrupting them. What was he doing? A moment ago, he'd said he wanted to kill me. Now he wouldn't?

"I will never kill her," he said, the sound of a struggle following his words. Was he hurt? "I will kill you both before I let you at her."

He sounded like the man I knew now, not the prince of before. Sounds of a scuffle ensued. I expected it to be over quickly. Ashbourne was bigger than these two, faster and a warrior. He could easily overpower them. But the sounds of the fight went on. And what did I expect would happen when he'd fought them off?

What part of what he said had been the truth? Did he want to kill me or protect me? There had to be some place else to hide and think over my next move. I could no longer be sure that I could trust him. I moved as quickly as I could, heading towards the river. There had to be somewhere near the riverbank I could tuck myself away in and watch what happened next.

It was odd how little I felt about the possibility that Ash might kill my sister and Brigitte. But I'd never had any trouble remembering who Helene was. It was only that my perspective on her had changed. When I'd been so little loved and respected, even her toxic love had seemed better than Maman's obvious hatred for me.

But now, I wished she had stayed dead. There was no relief in me that she hadn't died in the fire. I had no curiosity whatsoever about how she'd escaped or where she'd been these last months. I would rather not kill her myself, but I would if I had to. When I rose out of the sea I had been willing to kill her, but now it seemed a bit distasteful. I had loved her once, but if she wanted to kill me, I would happily kill her first.

Ahead of me, a tendril of smoke rose from the ground. I scurried to it, finding two bodies, smelling of sulphur, still burning. Someone had used empyrae to kill these people.

I remembered what Helene said. He'd burned Somerhaven. Certainty grew in me. I'd been right the first time. He'd come for me, and my sister had believed it was to kill me. But I *knew* Ashbourne. Both the Ashbourne of before, and the one I'd fallen in love with.

He came to save me, as he had before. It didn't excuse all he'd done. I still wanted him to answer for the ways he'd ruined me. If he had the power to burn all of Somerhaven to the ground, he could certainly kill two people. I looked carefully at the deep gouges in the ground next to the bodies. He'd burned them, and then kept loosing his empyrae on them.

He'd lost control of himself. The threads pulled tight in my mind. The curse had taken him at Somershire. His proximity to me had driven him out of his senses, and there was no doubt in my mind that Maman had tried to fight him. If she thought he might take me from her, take her chance to use me as the Ravager's vessel, she would have tried to kill him. And he would have fought back, with much, much more power than she could ever have expected.

Perhaps he hadn't been attacked, as Skye and Morpheus had assumed. It was possible he'd been caught in the wreckage of the house he burned, collapsing. After that, the curse must have taken him, causing him to forget everything he'd known. I had no idea how he'd made his way here, but the rest made sense. If he'd burned himself out at Somerhaven, the amnestic effect of the curse would have been strengthened.

And he'd used his empyrae again today, burning himself out again, if those marks in the ground were any indication. My heart raced at the realization. My sister was powerful—more powerful than Maman had ever been. If he was weak, burned out, she might kill him.

I turned back to the cabin, my body moving too slow, too tired to run. As I drew nearer, slow as I was, I heard the sound of a lash. Of Ashbourne crying out in pain. She was hurting him, and he was not resisting. Why wasn't he fighting her?

He believes he deserves this fate, a voice said as I struggled forward. Each step was more painful than the last. I hadn't been taking good care of myself. The voice came from everywhere. *Do you?*

"No," I whimpered, limping forward as best I could. My knees burned with more than their usual pain. I was too tired. If I could make it to the cabin, I could stop Helene and Brigitte with empyrae, but I was too slow. I would hear him die as I dragged this body towards him, unable to help him. What was all this power for if I could not do this?

What would you exchange to save him, little one? the voice asked. *Would you choose our side? Would you choose Sirin over all else?*

"Who are you?" I begged, though I knew the answer. The eldritch god I'd called on at the standing stones sounded just like this. She of the Still Places had found me. The warnings the hares had given me were all coming true.

His time runs out.

There was no other choice then. To save Ashbourne, I must agree to be the puppet once again, rather than the mistress of my own life. I had never been allowed sovereignty over myself. My whole life had been one manipulation after another. Saying no to this nameless god wouldn't stop her from coming for me again. It would only prolong the inevitable.

But I wanted one thing for myself. One choice that was mine alone to make. I wanted to decide Ashbourne's fate. "I will agree to whatever you ask. But he must live to answer for what he did to me."

Granted, the voice said, full of wry amusement. *I am sure you're quite capable of making Ashbourne Thuellos pay for his sins.*

Dark blue light, the light of elementals, surrounded me, lifting me. My body floated to the cabin with ease, and some of my strength returned, though the pain did not abate. Apparently, even a god could not, or would not, remove it from this body. I shook my head, a sneer of disgust crossing my face.

I had agreed to this, but I did not have to like it. There was nothing in our agreement that said I had to be grateful. The god's voice laughed in my mind, as though she heard my every treacherous thought. That was just fine with me. Let her know the truth of the bargain we'd made. I was no willing supplicant to her cause.

When you are done with him, I will see you at the standing stones, the voice said. *You belong to me now.*

"Fine," I gritted out as my feet met the ground, pain shooting through my metatarsals. "But I warn you, you'll likely regret this."

The god's laughter filled my mind. *How wonderful you are, Mina.*

I rolled my eyes, flicking my hand at the door to the cabin, my power renewed and strengthened in some way I could not yet understand. The door flew open, revealing a horrific scene. Rage mounted in me.

Brigitte was sprawled on the floor. She wasn't breathing, and I hadn't the time or inclination to check for a heartbeat. Ashbourne lay near her, bloody and battered as my sister lashed at him, her firedrake elemental keeping him pinned to the ground. He raised his head as my power sprang to my hands.

"Get away from him," I commanded my sister.

Helene loosed the lash upon him again, but her elemental rose to protect her. Ash slumped to the floor, defeated.

"Come and get him, if you want him so much, *sister,*" Helene sneered, her cold blue eyes alight with pleasure.

She was enjoying this. Just as she had enjoyed inflicting pain on me her entire life. I had no idea how she'd escaped the fire, or falsified her death. It didn't matter now. She had harmed the man I loved, and I *did* love him, no matter how angry I was with him now. He was mine, and she'd harmed him.

And now she would pay. "You are no sister of mine."

Helene laughed. "You have always been so slow, Mina. Even now, you're just blundering through life."

She raised her arm, as though to send the whip forward again, this time in my direction. Ash reached out, grabbing hold of her ankle. He pulled hard, just as she cracked the whip. Helene stumbled, and I caught the whip round my arm. The aether she wielded melted into the power that I controlled, becoming mine long before Helen could hurt me.

I smiled then, a wicked grin that was wholly my own, born out of every moment Helene had tormented me. Out of every hurt she and Maman had wrought over the longest twenty-eight years of my life. There was no need to draw this out, or to make big speeches. I was done with this part of my life.

A snake of my aether formed a cord of its own, whipping out at Helene and strangling her without a second thought from me. It snapped her neck with no effort at all, and I did not feel even so much as a whit of remorse. "You should have died in that fire, Helene," I said as she slid to the ground.

The elemental firedrake disappeared, dissolving into a puff of aether. This was the price for tying a life to a life for more power. The firedrake could not exist without Helene's lifeforce.

I rushed to Ash, lifting his head into my lap. "Don't you fucking dare die on me," I growled.

His eyes went soft. He wasn't the prince of our youth. He was only Ashbourne Claymore, private investigator. The man that, a day ago, I had thought held my future in his hands. As his eyes fell closed, he spoke the only words I wanted to hear.

"I love you, Mina."

If only it was not far too little, and far, far too late.

CHAPTER 52

ASHBOURNE

I woke at the bottom of a deep hole, something in me fundamentally changed. Dark stone walls curved around me, the sound of water echoing. Memories of who I'd been mixed with who I thought I was. The dim light of the hole did nothing to relieve the looming feeling that everything had gone terribly wrong.

Or had the scene in the cabin been a nightmare? It seemed impossible that everything had changed so much in just a few short days. In search of hope, I raised my head upward, toward the light. The woman I loved had been stuck in a place much like this for a year, and now she sat above me, her pretty legs dangling over the edge.

Somewhere far beyond, waves crashed angrily, and rain fell on us both. "Good," Mina said. "You're awake. Do you remember what happened?"

I nodded, glancing down at my body. My wounds were healed. I frowned. My clothes had been changed as well. I was warm and dry enough, despite the rain. "Did you heal me?"

I didn't bother yelling. Both of us could hear just fine without the volume.

Apparently, Mina had come to the same conclusion. She

shrugged. "You got the medical attention you needed. I wanted you awake and clear-headed for this."

I was mostly dry, but her hair was wet from the rain. She wore a long white gown, but no coat. I worried she might catch cold, with the rain falling on her, revealing every curve of her body. It was a beautiful picture, if melancholy, but I worried for her health.

I was at the bottom of the oubliette, and if she was sitting at the top, then nothing I remembered was a nightmare. That was most unfortunate.

"I am clear-headed," I agreed, then tried for a lighter tone. "I don't suppose you'd let me out so we could talk this over somewhere a bit more comfortable?"

"I think not," she said, matching the light tenor of my voice. "I think what we need now is some time apart."

Hadn't we had enough of that? It seemed that in the thousands of years we'd known one another all we'd done was stay apart. Things were different now; why continue with the same old mistakes? Looking up at her, at the steel in her eyes, at the sheer will written all over her face, I knew she was the same as she'd ever been, stubborn and convinced her way was the only way.

I sighed, feeling eternally exhausted. "What good will that do us, love? All we've ever done is fuck and fight." The words slid out of me before I could consider them. I grimaced as soon as they hit her.

She peered over the edge of the oubliette, unadulterated fury on her face. A terrible thought crossed my mind; *she was somehow even more beautiful sinister and angry than she was calm.* Why would I think such a thing? But then, I had remembered, hadn't I? The man I was before. And now, I was no longer Ashbourne Claymore. Or at least, I was no longer just that man.

Now I was someone else as well. Trying to reconcile the two parts of me was unsettling, and likely dangerous. Perhaps she was right to have stuffed me down here. That other part of me took over, the prince that had bedded the princess the moment he knew she was out to kill him. The man who was aroused by violence and cruelty.

I stopped fighting it for a moment. Stopped fighting the memories that threatened to overtake all I'd done, not only in the past year, but the centuries of imprisonment I'd endured to become a better man. Now though—it was as though that moment on Interra, eons ago, was merely a day ago. The ghost of her knife at my throat sent my heart racing, the memory of her fangs impaled in my skin lit every nerve in me aflame. I leaned against the wall, letting the wicked grin of a young prince spread over my face.

"Oh good," she sneered, looking down on me. "I hoped this side of you would show up. I was afraid you didn't remember yourself. That you were stuck inside the narrow little tunnel you built for yourself as Claymore."

Mina pulled her legs up with some effort, wrapping her arms around her knees. The sight of her struggle brought me back to myself, back to the present. She was cold, and I ached to wrap myself around her, warm her shivering body with mine. It was as though I was being dragged in and out of the past, moment by moment, the two halves of myself unable to exist at once. I couldn't find the words to say that to her though, not after all I'd done, and all that she'd endured.

"All that Thuellos charm is still in you, isn't it?" Her voice was sad now, but her words still held a bite. My girl was a fighter. And I was willing to take my punishment. But I feared what she was up against. What might happen to her while I was paying for my trespasses.

She had to keep fighting, even if it took making her hate me even more. "As I recall, Lumina, my Thuellos charm is in you, too. Has been in you from that first fuck." My words were coarse, meant to inflame her. She needed to be angry at me now. Needed to hone herself into the weapon I knew she could be.

She scoffed. "Have you forgotten the fetch?"

I laughed, low and cocky. "Do you think my claim was on your Ventyr body? I claimed your soul, and you mine. We are bound forever, my girl. Unless you'd like to come down here and kill me."

She stood, her face distorting with pain. When she spoke, her voice was soft. "I know what you're trying to do."

I looked up at her. She was the most beautiful thing in the world. In all worlds. I had searched for her, even in Nihil deep in the limen, even imprisoned, I had looked for her. I found her once, I could find her again. But if she didn't want me—then none of it mattered.

"Did you know they cut my wings off?"

My eyes fell to the ground. I had not known that. Her wings. The space between my shoulders ached just thinking of it. I would need to remove my glamour now that I remembered myself. Now that I remembered my true form. If I did, I could shift now, toss off my glamour and fly out of here. But I would not insult her in such a way.

But her beautiful wings—severed from her body. It was unthinkable, a betrayal that no Ventyr could forgive. And I was the cause of her pain, of that most grievous mutilation. My breath caught in a sob.

"No," I choked out.

"They kept me awake. Forced my eyes open and made me watch in a mirror. Each time I passed out, they revived me."

Every word was a knife to my soul, as it should be. When they cut her, they knew that someday I would learn of it. That she would hate me for it forever. It was the last thing her father, the Emperor, had said to me before he locked me in Nihil. "If you ever see my daughter again, she will hate you more than any person she has ever known."

I had not believed it at the time. Now I knew what he meant. Years had taught me my mistakes. I'd come here to make things right. To find out if the woman I'd known on Interra was still my mate, still my claimed partner, or if we would have to go through the painful ritual of unwinding our bond. I dreaded the moment she would ask for the reversal.

Her voice was quiet when she spoke again, almost drowned out by the howling wind. "I walked this world, abandoned and alone. Spellbound to my glamour for centuries. When I was finally at peace, the Wildfangs found me, killed me, and turned me into this."

Her voice was softer still, so vulnerable and young. "And it is all your fault, Ashbourne. Because you would not listen. You would not believe the prophecy Alcyone gave to me. Why could you not trust me?"

Tears slid down my face. Honesty was the only way now. Truth would not set me free, but it was my only choice. "Because I could not stand for you to be imprisoned when I walked free."

"I told you," she shrieked, her voice ravaged with the pain of over a thousand years of loneliness and betrayal. "I told you what she said. That if you came for me, it would end like this. In eternal war, with the Ravagers free. All lives forfeit—the cost for what *we* have done."

My shoulders shook with the sobs spilling out of me. She *had* told me. Nothing she said was an exaggeration or lie. I had known when I gathered my generals that the siren prophetess had spoken, and I did not believe her.

I did this. I was the reason for all of this.

"And still I love you," she said, her tears falling into the oubliette. "But love is not enough, Ashbourne. This kind of love is nothing but pain. Do not look for me."

Before I could say another word, before I could beg her to listen, the sea came crashing in, flowing over the invisible seal on the oubli-ette. I waited for the forgetting to begin, welcomed it even. It would be a blessing to forget this. As the hours went by, I realized that was exactly why it would never come.

Mina had not left me here to forget. She had left me to remember.

THE RAVAGED DARK

BOOK TWO

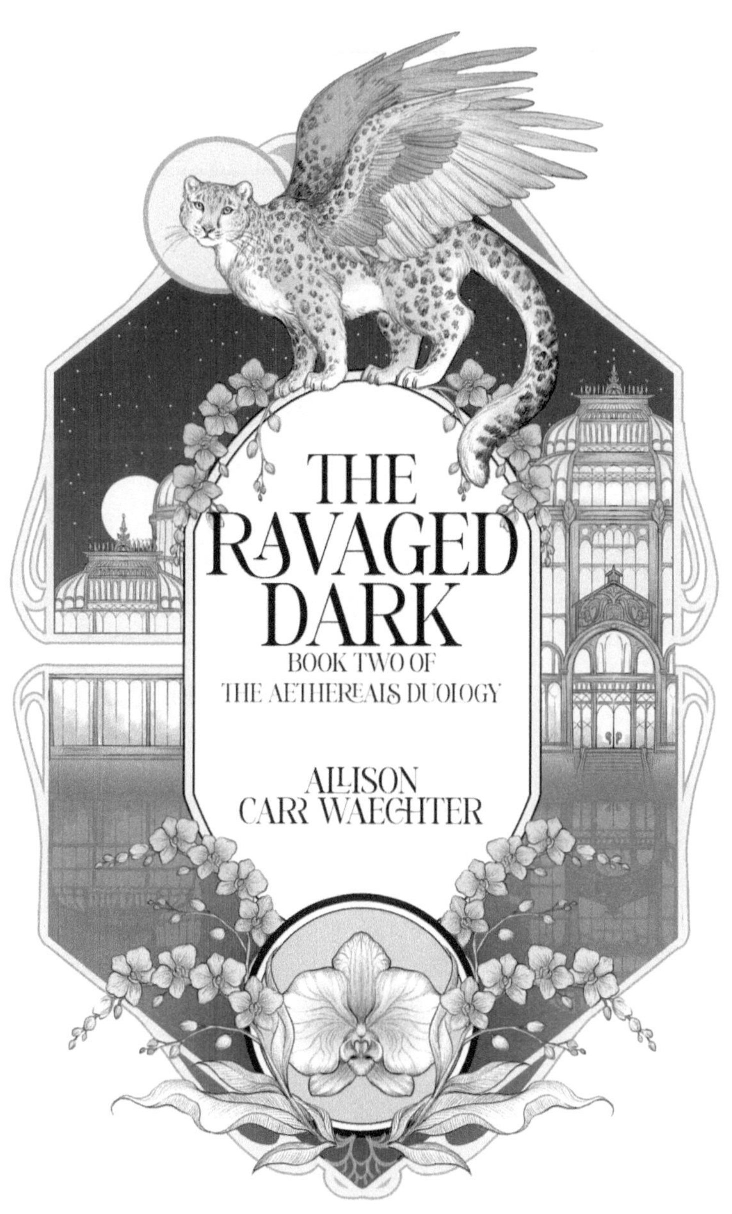

THE RAVAGED DARK

BOOK TWO OF
THE AETHEREALS DUOLOGY

ALLISON
CARR WAECHTER

CHAPTER 1

MINA

Ashbourne Thuellos would haunt me 'til my last breath—no matter what dark hole I locked him in. Icy wind howled through my hair, lashing at the tears I fought to blink back. Late autumn at Somerhaven might as well be winter. While I was impatient to be away—to push all that happened here into the recesses of my mind—I could not. Not yet, and maybe not ever. The memories I'd lost were still coming back to me, still seeping in like a poison that would never stop infecting me.

It was a risk to leave him in the oubliette. Poe and I had not sealed him in, nor had we activated the sigils that would initiate the forgetting. It was imperative that he remember as much as he could —and quickly. It was possible he had information about the Ravagers that was vital to our success. The faster he remembered what he knew, the better.

And... I wanted to punish him. I couldn't deny that. I didn't even want to. He'd made choices that had ruined lives, all while knowing that what he did would cause harm. I loved the man he'd become as Ashbourne Claymore, but the man he'd been as Ashbourne Thuellos must be held to *some* account. And while it was possible that the time he'd spent imprisoned in the world between worlds had changed him, I had no time to watch and wait. We needed answers now.

I wrapped my arms around my body, snuggling into the coat I'd left on the sea stairs. It had been dramatic to wear only this thin white gown to seal Ashbourne into the oubliette, but Poe had argued for it, insisting it would leave him devastated in more ways than one. I had hoped my words would be enough, but I deferred to Poe on costuming.

Down on the beach, my friend stood staring at the angry waves, watching the tide rush in. Poe hadn't come out to the oubliette with me, worried as she was for Ashbourne's safety. More than that, she worried about what Skye would think of *her* when she and Morpheus retrieved him. I pushed away the anxiety that I'd taken Poe from the people who could love her best. She was a grown woman; she chose this. Chose to come with me, instead.

Because if Viridian was not Chopard—and we still had yet to confirm the story he'd told us—we had only two viable suspects: the mysterious, and possibly dead, Lord Eccles... And Skye's mother, Elspeth Aestra. I wouldn't make the same mistake we'd made with Viridian again, though.

Doggedly pursuing just one suspect no longer made sense, but neither did continuing to allow a suspect's daughter full access to all we knew. On the beach, Poe's shoulders hunched. She was crying. We agreed that Skye likely did not know that her mother might be Chopard. We also agreed that she'd be unlikely to help Elspeth willingly, but it was clear how much the former Chevalier wanted to reunite with her family. She might unwittingly help without realizing it.

Between my cursed history with Ashbourne and Skye's potentially compromised position, we couldn't risk staying with the two of them and Morpheus. Not until we knew for sure where the four of us stood. Morpheus understood this, and had agreed to help them both understand things, to be our go-between until things were clearer. The sun sank lower in the sky—something of a metaphor for my emotions, which grew darker by the moment.

This far north, daylight didn't last long. Soon a blanket of sparkling stars would cover the sky, and the bitter cold would set in. Worse, Skye and Morpheus would be here to look for Ashbourne any minute, if my calculations about the train schedule were correct. Poe had asked Morpheus to keep Skye away from the oubliette as long as possible, to give us a little more time, and for everyone's safety. Neither of us thought she would comply. Skye was stubbornly loyal; it was one of her best qualities, but letting Ashbourne out of the oubliette could be dangerous—in more ways than one.

The chill in the air deepened as the sun sank lower. We needed to get going. But Poe's shoulders were still hunched in that terrible way. An uneasy shiver ran through me, but I brushed it off as best I could. The feeling that we should be gone by now stalked me, but Poe had asked for a few moments to herself, and I needed to respect that.

As I watched Poe tremble, an echo of my body's response to the cold, some eldritch prescience used my spine for its ladder. Without turning, I knew eyes bored into me from the forest. We were being watched. Reluctantly, I tore my gaze from the beach to look back at the charred remains of Somerhaven. For half a moment, I expected to see the drove of elemental hares that had helped me the day I rose out of the oubliette. But this feeling wasn't anything I'd ever had around elementals, even mountain spirits.

I searched the area with my eyes, but nothing stood out to me. I slipped into my second sight, but though the feeling of being watched intensified, I saw nothing new. When I turned back toward the sea to check on Poe, Helene stood in front of me, incorporeal, her neck bruised from where I'd snapped it, just days ago.

You finally showed your true self, she said, her voice far away inside my head. *Don't you wonder what else you might be capable of?*

My eyes narrowed as my shoulders tensed. She did not look as ghasts usually did, cast in a silvery diaphanous light. Instead, she was like the elementals, deepest indigo—the color of pure aether—the only difference was that her eyes were gaping, empty holes. I slipped out of my second sight, but only halfway, to see if she appeared in the corporeal world. She did not. So she only existed in the limen, the space between worlds. Aether's true home.

"What do you want from me?" I asked.

Helene's smile widened further, stretching her finely boned face into something grotesque. "Everything," she growled aloud. I slipped back into my corporeal sight, jarred by the noise of her voice in my ears. It was terrible—a thousand malefic notes struck all at once, discordant and confusing. Now she appeared in my corporeal sight as well. "Everything you are and more."

I took a step backwards. It was pure instinct. Whatever the thing before me was, it was not Helene. Not exactly, anyway. There was something of her true essence inside it, though. It solidified gradually, as an elemental spirit might—manifest, but not *real*. The thing that was not quite Helene stepped towards me, smiling again, her teeth lengthening.

In an instant, I saw my mistake. There was not something of Helene inside the thing before me. *It* was inside of *her*. It inhabited her. *But how?* That hardly mattered. I took another step backward and then another, wanting to lead the creature away from the cliff side, away from Poe. And Ashbourne, if I could be honest with myself. Even now, I protected him.

Whatever this thing was that inhabited my sister's body, it was wrong. Unnatural. The difference between it and my fetch, the corporeal form I inhabited, was obvious. The fetch was made of everything I'd been made of before; the shell mimicked my original form. Instead, this thing before me was Helene's form, twisted. It had taken her essential nature, and compounded it into something so grotesque, so evil, its malice ached in the marrow of my bones.

Helene's teeth sharpened into vicious points as the smile pulled towards her ears, unhinging her jaw like a serpent. I was tempted to scream, but down on the beach, Poe still watched the waves, and I did not want to startle her as the tide rushed in, a violent spray of water on the rocky shoreline. It was a dangerous time of day. She should not be down there, but neither did I want her up here.

The thing's mouth snapped open, halving Helene's entire head, turning her inside out in an instant, and into a creature of smoke and teeth. Down on the beach, Poe spun around, looking up towards me, as a creaking groan cracked the cosmos open. Time slowed, the details of each moment coming into sharp focus.

Far out to sea, long past the oubliette in the roiling waves, rose an elemental I'd never seen on Sirin, my memory stirring, but coming up with nothing useful. What good was having my memories back if I could not easily access them in moments such as these?

Every muscle in my body contracted, tensing in preparation as time slowed further. The air around me was thick as molasses, my movements sluggish and heavy as I was forced to watch the creatures rise out of the sea. They were nothing but eel-like skeletons, spiny bones with vacant eyes that bore the gravity of utter emptiness, a ravaged dark that swallowed light whole, rather than existing as its opposite. It was the same gaping nothingness that had been in Helene's eyes only moments before she'd transformed.

Beneath them, there were holes in the sea. Not swirling whirlpools; the water was not being sucked into the yawning wounds. No, there was something else there, but it was too far off, and even with the way time had slowed, I could not quite make it out. I blinked, and the holes disappeared, the angry waves the same as they had been moments before. Time resumed its normal pace in a sickening lurch.

My stomach threatened to empty its contents on the sea stairs, but I swallowed the bile that rose in my throat. The creatures sped upon the waves rushing towards shore. I screamed, "Fly, Poe! Fly!"

Calm as could be, Hippolyta Feriant looked back over her shoulder, glared at the vile beasts, then shifted shape. It was not an unglamouring of wings, but a transformation, whole and true. The humanoid form of my friend was gone, and left in her place was an enormous dark bird, raptorial and fierce. She sprang into the air, her wings beating powerfully, talons outstretched as the creature of smoke and teeth lunged towards me.

I ducked, keeping well away from the stairs, joints aching as I moved. As a Ventyr princess, in the life I'd lived long, long before this one, I had been well-trained in fighting maneuvers. Not that I'd ever been any good. I'd been in pain back then as well. The memory came back to me as my body moved in ways I thought I'd forgotten.

Because I had never been good at fighting, my body aching even then, the General had focused on teaching me to evade. An auburn-haired beauty flashed in my second sight as I tucked into a painful roll on the ground. That was not the General—she had skin black as midnight, the pointed ears of the fey, and half a dozen draconic wings. My memory played tricks on me, but for a moment, the curse was still fighting me. I knew this woman. Had always known her.

Get up, the redhead barked.

Ouriel. My half-sister. Relief flooded through me. The curse had not returned; its remnants simply clouded my thoughts. I stared at Ouriel, grateful to see her face once more. She was as tall as I was, and built similarly, but where I was soft, she was muscular. It took me a moment to realize I was not hallucinating: Ouriel was no longer a phantom, but neither was she actually here. Her bright green eyes, flecked with the same gray as my own, were fierce. *Move!*

The creature's attention snapped towards her, leaving me for the briefest of moments. She'd bought me some time. I scrambled to my feet, every joint in my body aflame with searing pain. I would pay for this later.

The creature's attention was back on me in an instant. It barreled towards me. There was no way I could outrun it. I drew upon the spark of celestial flame within me, determined to give it a blast of empyraen power it would not soon forget.

No! Ouriel screamed. She was standing right next to me now, her pale skin the same shade as mine as she wrapped her long fingers around my arm. Her hands were just like mine. The remnants of the curse within me fought against my memory for one last moment, then cleared as Ouriel spoke. *You'll harm the Strider.*

I followed her gaze, straight up to the sky, just in time. Poe's talons wrapped around my arms, lifting me easily off the ground. We rose upwards quickly, as the creatures became a single mass of bones, teeth, and smoke. The sound of eerie, whispered screams filled my ears. As we hit a bank of clouds, I searched the ground for Ouriel. But she was nowhere to be seen.

CHAPTER 2

MINA

The creature was going to follow us. I nearly panicked as we cleared the clouds, blinking against the soft hues of starlight, my eyes burning as my joints protested the way Poe carried me. *What could we do against a thing like that?*

I'd been foolish to think of using empyrae against it. It went against all the rules of dealing with elemental creatures, of which the thing had certainly been one. Elementals were pure energy. Using magic of any kind might give them more power, rather than destroy them.

Maman had taught me that, of course, but so had someone else. Had Ouriel been there? Somehow, she was connected to this idea. I nearly drowned in the stream of memories that coursed through me like a raging river. There was no sorting through that now. There were too many—I'd lived too long of a life. It was going to take time to get used to remembering it all again.

I was damp from flying through the clouds and the frigid air plastered my wet clothes to my skin. There was nothing to do about it, and I certainly could not complain to Poe, so I closed my eyes against the night, but there was no respite in my mind. The curse had lifted, but I was no better off than I had been before. My molars ground against one another in frustration. There had to be a way for me to remember more, in a way that had some semblance of usefulness.

We must get to higher ground, to sanctuary, Poe said in my head, her enormous talons tightening around me. The way she held me was not comfortable, but it was secure. I was safe with her. *Viridian has the best wards in the region.*

Agreed, I answered in my head. It had been a long time since I made a psychic connection with any creature, but Morpheus and I had practiced a few times, and it was not much of a struggle. *It will give us a chance to evaluate his claims to loyalty as well.*

I felt Poe's hesitation in the way her talons shifted around my arms, and the cadence of her words. *Do you have a reason to mistrust him?*

My immediate reaction was yes. Viridian Montclair had done thousands of things to make me not trust him over the years. Aligning himself so closely with Maman and Helene. Helping to trap me in the oubliette. But I did believe him that he'd done it all in service of House Feriant, of his commitment to the lost Court of Aether and, ultimately, Poe. That he was trying to protect Sirin and Poe's mother's legacy the best way he and his family knew how.

Not any reason that matters now, I finally answered. *I believe what he told us. The more important question is, do you?*

Yes, Poe answered as she swept higher into the cold night sky. *I do.*

Then that is enough for me, I said.

My body quivered, almost uncontrollably, from the cold. I took long, slow breaths, trying to use the tiny spark of empyrae within me to warm myself without burning anything, an old warriors' trick. A small gift from my returned memory.

Though I could deliberately access very little in the messy swirl of aeons within me, apparently some of my more useful memories could show up given the right trigger. That was something to work with, at least. The shivering didn't quite stop, but it slowed.

I closed my eyes, sending my second sight out around us. I found no sign of the creature of smoke and teeth, which somehow made me more uneasy, rather than less. *That thing isn't following us anymore.*

I know. Poe sounded as concerned as I was. *It seemed like it would follow, and then it just stopped, as though it hit a barrier.*

You can see the thing?

Not now, Poe said. *As I said, it has gone. Disappeared.*

My muscles fatigued from shivering, and the after-effects of fear. I struggled to stay conscious by keeping my conversation with Poe going. *But how could you keep track of it without going* between?

My sight in this form is split between corporeal sight and a view between.

That was fascinating. Poe could see into the world between worlds, the limen, at the same time she saw everything around us. I'd never heard of such a talent. The redhead had called her a Strider, as had Mirabelle Aestra, which suggested a medial nature. A way to exist between one plane and another at the same time. *You can use your corporeal sight and your second sight at the same time?*

My body was having no more of my nonsense. Sleep loomed at the edges of my consciousness, threatening. I fought it, attempting to focus harder on Poe's voice inside my head. *Yes, in my Feriant form, my eyes are different.*

My own eyes were too heavy, my eyelids drooping. I could not nod off while flying. I tried tightening my grip around Poe's talons, but I shook too hard from the cold. Pain lanced through my fingers, every tendon in my wrists and forearms alive with the rage of having been used too much, too roughly.

Mina. Poe's voice cut through the haze of exhaustion and pain. *Don't fall asleep! Mina!*

It was the last thing I heard.

I came to wrapped in a warm cloud of soft blankets, snuggled into a simply made canopy bed. An elegant iron candelabra that hung from the ceiling lit the small room with a glow of aetheric light. The walls were covered in various oil paintings, and from the slope of the ceiling, I could tell we were in an attic. Three doors graced the walls opposite the one the bed stood against. The one directly across from me was closed. The one on the right led to a small washroom and the one on the left to what appeared to be a studio.

A rather good seascape sat on the easel at the center of the studio. We were not in a guest room then. I frowned. Next to the bed, Poe slept soundly, curled up in an overstuffed chair covered in a fussy floral fabric. Her dark hair glowed with an amethyst hue beneath the candelabra. Her face was peaceful, and I didn't dream of waking her. The past few days had been more than either of us should have had to deal with.

Out the window, snow fell in big clumping flakes. From what I could see, we were deep in the forest, and the first snow of the season fell around us. I recognized the gatehouse I spotted in the distance, out the window. We had made it to House Montclair. I tried to sit up, but found I was too weak to move. The door to the room we were in opened slowly.

Viridian Montclair's handsome head poked through the door. "You're awake," he whispered.

I nodded, pressing a finger to my lips, gesturing to Poe. Viridian nodded, showing me he understood. I struggled to raise myself up in bed, but the pain was too great. Viridian rushed into the room.

He pulled a heavy sweater from the back of a desk chair, tucked into a dormer window. The way he moved about the room told me all I needed to know. This was Viridian's refuge. It wasn't the bedroom on the second floor that I'd passed on one of the few weekend parties I'd been allowed to attend here. This was his real bedroom. His real space.

Now that I understood that, I felt the wards on the house, the room, more acutely, seeing them with my second sight, but also feeling them on a more instinctual level. This room might be one of the most heavily warded places on Sirin. With a bit of trepidation, Viridian handed me the sweater.

I took it, but struggled to get it on. He watched for a moment, then whispered, "Can I help? I have tea in the next room."

Grateful for his consideration, I nodded. He moved me with the utmost care, then held out his hands. I took hold, and pulled myself towards him, while what felt like every muscle in my body cried out in protest. When my feet rested on the floor, Viridian waited.

Using his hold on me for leverage, I dragged myself upwards. It was strange to hold Viridian Montclair's hand as he led me from the room, but I wasn't stable enough to move safely on my own. Stranger still was how gentle he was with me. The room beyond the outer door to his bedroom was cozy. The steep pitch to the ceiling gave it a feeling of being contained and safe. A fire crackled merrily in the hearth, and the overstuffed couch that matched Poe's floral chair had clearly been slept on.

Viridian left me for a moment and closed the door to the bedroom. I took several small steps towards the leather chair by the fire. He rushed towards me, and as he helped me into the chair, I marveled at how undone he appeared. He wore a pair of shearling boots and soft wool pants, with an emerald green sweater thrown on. There was paint on the sleeve of the sweater, and his long silver hair still appeared sleep-tousled, though in every other way he appeared fresh.

The kindness in his eyes as he helped me lower myself into the chair made me think again that he really was quite handsome. "Better?" he asked, after covering me with an impossibly soft knit blanket.

"Yes," I said, keeping my voice low. "Thank you."

His smile was wan. "Poe told me what happened on the beach. I will have my contacts look into the creature you saw."

They could look, but I felt certain they would find nothing. Whatever that thing was, it was a part of something new to Sirin. I felt it deep in my gut, though my memory still would not give up what secrets it held. "Does anyone else know we are here?"

Viridian shook his head. "No. I send the staff home when I don't need them."

I frowned, fighting the surprise I felt. The idea was so against what I thought I knew about House Montclair, which was one of the wealthiest Houses on Sirin. "What?"

Viridian sat down across from me, pushing the blanket on his sofa back while he poured tea. "I have no need of servants. If there's a party, they come in to help, and then leave after. Those who run the estate live in the cottages."

The "cottages" were a series of small but extremely well-kept homes at the back of the estate, near the stables. I'd always known Viridian's people had good lives, but not that he did not keep the staff on when he wasn't entertaining.

"And are they free to work elsewhere the rest of the time?"

Viridian frowned. "No, I ask that they don't."

Now I frowned, my eyes narrowed with suspicion.

One of Viridian's eyebrows raised in confusion. Then he smiled. "I pay my people very generous full-time salaries, Mina. I just like for them to do what they please when I don't need them. Most are artists like me. A few writers, and a composer."

"Oh," I breathed, understanding. "How did you hide this from Caralee?" She wouldn't have liked him being kind to his servants.

Viridian sat back on the sofa, one leg crossed elegantly over the other. He smirked. "I spent most of our time together at her home."

I wrinkled my nose. The thought of merely kissing Caralee was repulsive to me, despite her beauty. The rest of her was so ugly I couldn't see how it mattered.

Viridian laughed again. "Not like *that*. We haven't consummated anything."

"Oh," I said again, unable to think of other words. I stared at my tea, feeling too tired to speak.

Viridian set his teacup down. From the nearly-invisible shake in his long fingers, and the tension in his jaw, it was obvious he had something difficult to tell me. "I've been making some inquiries." He stared at the fire for a moment, swallowed hard, and continued. "About what it might take to get you back into your real body."

My breath caught in my chest, but I knew from the look on Viridian's face that it was not good news. "It can't be done, can it?"

He shook his head. "My sources say that we would need your bones." He stared down at his hands. "Mina, I'm sorry. But someone destroyed them. With empyrae."

My throat went dry and tight. I bit my bottom lip to keep it from quivering. "I understand."

Someone made sure that I would never return to my true body. Someone anticipated that eventually I might remember everything. Somewhere deep inside, I'd always known. But to be trapped like this forever was still a deep cut, one that followed myriad others, compiling into a history of pain I could not seem to escape. *My wings. My true body. All I had been and could not be now. There was no hope then to return to what I'd been before.*

"I am so sorry," Viridian said.

He sounded sorry. I fought back panic. I could think of too many possibilities for who to blame, and I wanted someone to pay for what was done to me. It simply was not fair that I be allowed to endure so much and all who'd harmed me went unpunished.

I dragged my eyes up to his, determined to move on from this. "Thank you for trying to find out more. We need to get to the standing stones in the forest as quickly as possible."

The memory of the creature on the beach haunted me. If the elementals could tell me what it was, I might have a chance at figuring out what to do next about Helene.

Viridian's mouth formed a grim line. "About that..." He took a deep breath. "The creature that chased you and Poe destroyed a good portion of the forest—the standing stones are gone."

CHAPTER 3

ASHBOURNE

W ater dripped somewhere in the oubliette, but despite the wintry weather above, down here it was warm enough. For now, at least. There was a bite in the air, threatening my skin with the cold that was to come. The space was too small, too tight for comfort, but it wasn't altogether terrible.

Nothing was actively harming me. In all the ways that counted for most people, I was safe. The problem, for me, was that at the bottom of the oubliette, there wasn't much to do but think. If Mina had not disabled the spells that caused one to forget, I would be blissfully unaware. Instead, I was locked at the bottom of a damp hole, the ocean raging overhead, alone with my thoughts.

It was the worst possible thing Mina could have done, and likely also the best. My memories rushed back to me in fits and starts. *My father's palace. The day I met Lumina. The day he told me I would woo her, gain her trust, and then kill her. My sister's death on the White Plains.* All these mixed with snippets of memory from the past year. *Morpheus and Skye mixed with the ancient world of the Ventyr. Of my true people.*

The memory that lingered was that of the White Plains, soaked in blood. Tears wet my cheeks. Thalia's death was too much to think of. Too raw, even after all these centuries. There would never be enough time to mourn her. In a household full of pompous men, my sister had been the bright light, the fierce grace. My best friend and my rock, lost in an instant to the greed of the powerful.

I pushed the memories away, but they shoved back harder, clawing back into my conscious mind with a chaotic vengeance. Views of my mother's skirts, the sound of her laughter. Fighting the endless wars, year after year, never knowing who was winning, until Boreas came to power. And then the creep of empire, the uncountable fallen.

Then came the Ravagers.

We drew them right to us, with our wars, our violence. Ancient foes, things of legend. None in power had believed the stories could be true, at first. The ways entire cities were brought down in weeks, or mere days, by their power was unfathomable to us. And that was how they caught hold of Interra. Our unwillingness to believe in our own fallibility had been our undoing.

Pain shot through me. I had fallen to my knees without realizing it. I gagged on saliva, my tongue too dry in my mouth as I screamed. Did Mina know this would happen to me? Was this how it happened to her? Was this how her memories had returned, violent and unrelenting?

Was this why her voice was so rough? Was this how her vocal cords were damaged? Did she scream for days on end, remembering and forgetting all of this bloody history at once, only to start over again?

If so, she had shown me mercy by leaving me to myself to remember. But no, that had not been what happened to her. She had been lost within herself, unable to remember all she was, who she had been. That was a torture all its own for one so self-possessed as Lumina. Mina. *Which was she?*

The scent of sulphur filled my nostrils. I was loosing empyrae around me, a seemingly endless stream of celestial flame flowing from my fingertips. But it would stop. I would burn out. And then the memories would come for me. They would drive me out of reason, out of time, until there was nothing left of either Ashbourne—Thuellos or Claymore.

Flame spun white hot around me, though it did not burn any part of *me*, or the oubliette for that matter. The flame was blue at the base of my hands, near my palms, which I raised to my face. The empyrae was hot enough to melt ore, to forge the finest weapons. To fuse things together. A train of thought emerged from the chaos in my mind.

This is why she locked me in the oubliette. Her words had been cruel, and I deserved them, but this was why she'd done it. To keep everyone safe from me while I suffered this transformation, this trial by my own fire. It was imperative that I find a way to fuse Ashbourne Thuellos, a spoiled, arrogant prince used to getting his way, with the man I'd been in Nihil. The Warden.

There, through thousands of years of watching over the imprisoned Ravagers, I had learned patience. Control. Grace, both for myself and others. But I had not learned to be a man until I had a family. Until I'd been Ashbourne Claymore, a humble private investigator. Until I'd learned to love—both others and myself.

I struggled to see a way forward. How could I merge the vicious prince, the lonely sentinel, and the good friend I had learned to be in one being? Every iteration of myself competed with the others within me, leaving me in the fight of my life for control. I used my second sight to scan the oubliette's opening. The seal was intact, but not locked. I could leave if I wished.

She had not locked me in. Mina had trusted me to make the right choice—no, it was not trust: she *tested* me. This was a test to prove myself better than the prince I'd been, the one who'd ignored her warnings and brought ruin upon us all. Better than the Warden, who watched the safeguards I was sworn to uphold crumble around me. Better than I'd been as Ashbourne Claymore, a man who'd loved her, but had not been willing to face the truth of myself. I had failed before, but I would not fail now.

Not with Mina on the line. Not with her love just within reach.

Sobs wracked my chest. Not one word Mina had said to me was untrue. I was the cause of all her pain, the cause of all this, really. If I had only listened when Alcyone came to me. If I had only left well enough alone, the Ravagers would not be loose upon the cosmos now.

I had to face my mistakes; all I'd done in arrogance. I would do it for her, yes, but also for myself. To claim honor that I'd never possessed. For the first time in my long, long life, I might be free to live as I chose. To be as *I* chose.

Empyrae burned the last bit of my clothing away, not even leaving a dusting of ash. But the flames did not burn my skin, only burned away all that was untrue about me. The glamour of my Vilhar form fell away as I stretched to my full height, my wings too large for the tight oubliette. I needed to do this in my true form, even with the heartbreaking knowledge that Mina would never again take hers. It felt as though I betrayed her when I shifted.

Lumina loved to fly. *Mina* was trapped inside the fetch, inside a body that could never be true to her spirit. I had done that to her, and I still had this body, this strength. Surely, there must be a reason for that, if only I could find it. My wings folded behind me as I sat on the now-hot stone beneath my feet. The celestial fire had stopped hemorrhaging from my fingertips, but left the inside of the oubliette almost uncomfortably warm.

I crossed my legs as I closed my eyes. If it meant going back to the beginning, I would. I would start at the beginning and remember it all. As long as it took, I would remember every one of my sins in fine detail. I would mark them down, and then I would atone. If there was a way to make up for all I'd done, I could not stop until I found it.

Or you could let me help you, a voice said.

My eyes snapped open. I looked around. I was still alone at the bottom of the oubliette. Was I hearing things?

I am everywhere, Ashbourne Thuellos. And nowhere.

"That is... disconcerting," I answered. There didn't seem to be a reason not to. I was stuck at the bottom of this hole. The least I could do was answer disembodied voices that offered assistance. "What kind of help would you provide?"

I can give the memories back to you. All at once. It will be painful, but it will be as though you had never forgotten.

It was, of course, unwise to make bargains with unknown entities. Wracking the memories I had access to, I found no evidence of having ever been particularly wise. In fact, in most of my various iterations, I had been a bit reckless. But for what purpose—that was the key to doing better. If I were to be reckless, it must be for a higher purpose than simply avoiding thinking things through.

Better to get more information before agreeing to anything. I adjusted my weight so my tailbone did not dig into the rock below my seat. The oubliette was too tight a fit. It was necessary to shift my attention if this were to work.

"How painful would this be?" I asked.

Very, the voice answered.

We would get nowhere by dancing around the point. To get answers, I would have to ask a direct question. "Who are you?"

The Oscarovi call us the Old Ones.

The direct tactic, at least, was successful. The creature I spoke to was one of the mysterious eldritch gods of Sirin. Elementals, if I understood things correctly. "And what will you expect from me in return?"

Nothing you do not already want to give.

My skin prickled into gooseflesh, a clammy chill spreading over me. *A warning.* I would not be tricked so. I had heard rumors about these creatures. Directness had worked well before. It was worth another try. "Be specific."

You will help Mina with the task I've set her to.

Anger flickered within me. How had Mina been drawn into a deal with this god? She was too shrewd for such a thing. "What have you done to her?"

Nothing, the voice answered, sounding a bit annoyed. *She made a covenant with me, just as I expect you to.*

"And what did she get in return?" I asked, unable to believe the elemental creature.

The power to save your life. She was too weak to drag her damaged body to save you from her sister, but I gave her all she needed to do so.

Surprise froze my breath, and then I felt lighter than I had in days. I hated myself for it, but it lifted my spirits to hear that. I suspected she had done all this, at least partially, out of love for me. She might hate me, but Mina... Mina truly loved me, as I did her.

"Yes," I agreed. "I will help her do whatever you have asked of her. But on one condition."

There was a brief rumble of amusement from the voice, and if I thought a god could laugh, I might assume that's what it was. *You are as smart as she is, Thuellos. I like it. What is your condition?*

I spoke quickly, being as precise as possible. "When she has completed the task you ask of her, and it *will* be just one task... You will let her go. You will let her be free."

And yourself?

I could not believe my luck. It appeared that I might have won this round. That alone should make me suspicious, but with Mina involved, it was necessary to take the risk off her and bring it onto myself. "Take me in her place if you need to, but she will be free."

I agree to your terms. She will be free when she has completed my task.

I wasn't sure if the god meant that it agreed to take me instead of her, or if they were simply dismissing that part of my offer. It didn't seem prudent to ask. I could let it be a terrible surprise when the time came.

Now brace yourself.

I did not have time to brace myself, but I scarcely think it would have helped. When the memories came back, they burned. Every fiber of my being caught flame, and I knew pain like none I'd ever felt. The sound of my screams filled my ears and fire was all I knew as I descended into the depths of my mind.

CHAPTER 4

MINA

Poe and I stood next to Viridian in his conservatory workroom. The day was still fresh, and he'd cleared the glamour off what appeared, at first glance, to be an elaborate fountain. Now it was an enormous bowl of viscous silver liquid, which moved on its own.

"I have never seen one so large," I commented, staring at the pool of liquid as it shifted of its own accord. One moment it appeared to be silver and the next, the darkest indigo. I swayed back and forth a little as I watched it move, mesmerized by it.

Viridian smirked. "I am fairly certain I have the largest one on Sirin."

Poe smacked his arm. "Don't be such an ass."

Now he grinned. "You love it, princess."

She smirked as well. "I certainly like it better when you're on our side."

Deep sadness returned to his eyes, as I was learning it did whenever she mentioned the appearance of his betrayal, or having hurt me. He hated himself for what he'd done. *What he'd had to do*, I reminded myself. To find and protect the Court of Aether's lost heir, Viridian had done many things he regretted.

The way his honor returned to him, straightening his spine and broad shoulders bit by bit, was gratifying. I'd always noted a bit of a slouch to Viridian, which I'd assumed was arrogant nonchalance. Now I recognized it for what it was. His years of playing the cad had worn him down. He'd been a part of this charade since he was a child. In some ways, we were all our parents' pawns.

"What can it do?" I asked. "Anything special? Or is it just big?"

Viridian looked as though he longed to make another joke, but he pressed a finger to his lips, tapping once and shaking his head, as though he recognized this was not the time for such things. "The liquid inside a lekanomance is a distillation of aether and iridium which has gone through a complex process of—"

"Viridian," Poe interrupted. "Get to the point."

He rolled his eyes. "It's bigger, so it's stronger and can show you a wider perspective than the smaller versions."

"Thank you." Poe smiled, prim for a mere moment. Her eyes lit up as she stepped towards the oversized lekanomance. "What are we looking at?"

Viridian shoved his hands into the thick liquid, whispered a few words as I had in Maman's study, and closed his eyes. A view of the forest beyond Somerhaven and the House Montclair estate projected into the air above the basin. An entire area was flattened, the ancient trees destroyed, ripped to splinters. Amongst the rubble were fragments of what I assumed had been the standing stones.

"Did the creature we met on the beach do that?" I asked.

Viridian opened his eyes, as his mouth turned down. "I can't seem to get it to show more. Sometimes the lekanomance can see into the past. Muse might be able to help…" He frowned, taking his hands out of the liquid. Though they were dry, he still wiped them on his pants. "I can't show you what happened, but yes, I think it's safe to say that Helene did this."

"It couldn't have been Helene," I murmured, almost afraid to speak her name aloud. Every time I thought of her, I thought of the way I'd killed her. While I didn't have an ounce of guilt over it, the fact that she'd returned mere days after death—inhabited by that thing—was too hard to believe, even for me.

Or perhaps I simply didn't want to believe it.

"I think it is," Viridian said. "I tried to locate the creature you both saw while you slept. There's no sign of it that the lekanomance can show me."

Poe's arms crossed tightly across her chest. "But you found Helene, didn't you?"

He nodded, thrusting his hands back into the liquid. My sister's face appeared, but it was almost blurry. Everything around her was blurry as well. She appeared to be reading something, or perhaps writing. Her face was tilted down and slightly away from us, the edges of the projection amorphous.

"Why can't we see her clearly?" Poe asked.

Viridian gritted his teeth. "Wait."

I got the distinct impression he was afraid. He closed his eyes, jaw still clenched tight. Helene looked up, as though someone had called her name. Her face turned towards us, and the eyes were depthless black holes, and for a moment I saw the face of the creature that had unhinged Helene's head on the beach.

Poe's gasp was quiet but shocked as my heart thumped wildly.

Viridian yanked his hands from the basin, as though he'd been burned. "It's her... but not." He staggered back from the lekanomance.

"That is very troubling," Poe remarked as she placed a hand on Viridian's back. "Do you need a moment?"

He shook his head, his breath as labored as if he'd just raced up a flight of stairs. "No, it takes too much energy to try to find her, though. Something is wrong, and not just because she's supposed to be dead twice over now."

Poe's fingers spread over Viridian's back, comforting him. He nodded gratefully. "Might we talk of something else for a moment, to help clear my mind?"

Poe nodded. "Any word of Lord Eccles? We should probably question him."

Viridian straightened now, shaking his head as he crossed his arms over his chest. "No word yet, but I used the lekanomance to try to find him, and I believe he is still alive, but using some sort of masking spell to hinder those, like me, who might try to find him."

"Does that seem odd for a scholar?" Poe asked.

I shrugged. "I suppose it depends on his field of study."

Viridian moved away from the lekanomance, a bit of color returning to his cheeks. "We'll need to learn what he's published then."

"Something to do when we return to Pravhna," I murmured. "As well as finding other standing stones. Are there others?"

Viridian nodded, pushing his sleeves up. "Let me show you." He shoved his hands back into the water.

A bird's-eye view of Pravhna and the surrounding area showed above the basin. Several lights glowed, pulsing throughout the city and beyond—my breath caught. A chime startled the three of us. The picture dissolved as Viridian yanked his arms from the lekanomance. He laughed, but the sound was anxious, not joyful. "One moment, please. That is the telephone. Still surprises me every now and again."

"So, we're headed back to the city," Poe said, a faraway look in her eyes. I wondered if she was thinking of Skye.

I nodded as Viridian walked away. He left our immediate vicinity, but we could still hear him. His voice was tense. "Thank you for telling me." He slammed the receiver back onto its cradle and strode back towards us. "Caralee is headed towards the gatehouse. You have ten minutes to leave. I'm so sorry. My people will try to stall her at the gate…"

"Viridian," Poe said. "It's fine. We can walk. I have a car stashed nearby."

I grinned at Poe. She always had something up her sleeve. When she smiled back at me, my heart warmed. We would be all right.

"We'll see you back in Pravhna?" she asked.

Viridian nodded. "As soon as I can get there. Head back and I'll meet you there. There are coats by the back door, and boots that should fit you."

"Thank you," I said, taking Viridian's hand. It was a difficult thing to touch him, but I wanted to do it. "For all you've done for us."

He nodded once, face calm, but I saw the tears welling in his eyes. "Of course. I will see you soon."

Poe moved towards the back hallway that connected to the

conservatory. "Did you notice how many of those locations were places where Chopard set fires?"

"Yes," I answered. "It can't be a coincidence."

MINA

The walk through the forest wasn't hard; everything was downhill, back towards Somerhaven. But I was still tired and in so much pain, we had to move slowly. Poe and I spoke little at first, trying to get far enough from House Montclair that we wouldn't be spotted by Caralee, or any of her people.

Viridian would have to maintain his charade of an engagement for a while longer; we'd agreed on that much over breakfast. For now, if there was any sort of information to be gleaned from Maman's former cohort, we had to know. Viridian was our best spy, but he was of the mind that if there was something to find, he would have uncovered it by now.

His supposition was that Maman had never really made the full range of her aims clear to her makeshift coven. That she'd used them somehow, but that they knew very little of her actual plans. Unfortunately, that did sound like Maman to me. She was certainly never complimentary about any of her associates.

"I have an old Broussard stashed just over that hill," Poe said, pointing to the next lump of earth in front of us.

I nodded, but didn't speak. My mind raced. I wasn't happy to be returning to Pravhna so soon after leaving, but this needed to be done. I had a debt to the old one to fulfill, and after what we saw at

House Montclair, it was clear now that finding Chopard was more important than ever. "What is Chopard doing with those fires?"

Ahead of me, Poe shook her head. "Nothing good, that's for certain."

"He's trying to open portals," a voice said next to me.

I nearly jumped out of my skin. A slender girl with the rounded ears of an Oscarovi stood next to me, but she was no witch, of that I was certain. Her hair was cut short, like Skye's, and she had a beautiful face, with dark brown eyes and lucent brown skin. When she grinned, there was something undeniably familiar about her.

Where had she come from? It was as though she'd materialized out of thin air, with not even a trace of magic, aethereal or celestial, to be found.

Shadowy aether wove around Poe's fingers in defense. "Who are you?"

A greymalkin peeked out from behind the girl's legs. Unlike Morpheus' bulky form and silver fur, this cat was a beautiful shade of autumnal auburn, its ears tall and tufted, with giant eyes that glowed like topaz. *A lynxcat.* The memory of the word came back to me slowly, emerging out of a long-forgotten past on another planet.

More evidence that some memories would come back as-needed. It wasn't a comforting thought. I wanted to rifle through my thoughts and memories like a well-organized archive of my experiences. Still, this memory at least was a good one. The big cats were some of my favorite Interran creatures.

I dropped to my knees. The form the enormous feline took was not what I remembered, but I would know his eyes anywhere. "Bayun. What are you doing here?"

The girl frowned. "You recognize him?"

The greymalkin crawled into my lap, purring loudly. I nodded, a lump in my throat. "You have changed, little lyon. But I would know my sister's gryphon anywhere."

Memories of Ouriel, flying through a rosy sunrise with Bayun, myself and her mother, Orynthia, close behind, came rushing back. Laughter rang in my memories. Much of my life on Interra had been terrible, but there were also good times—most of them with Ouriel. It felt as though a vise tightened around my chest.

The girl smiled, stretching out her arm. Poe tensed, looking between us, almost frantic with worry. "It's all right," I reassured her, stroking Bayun's ears as I let the memories of the only family I'd ever truly loved fade away. Those times were over, as evidenced by Bayun's presence here on Sirin, with this strange girl. But the little one would not travel with anyone who could be a danger to me. There wasn't much I trusted from my former life, but Bayun was among the few creatures I knew were good. "These are friends."

The girl pushed the sleeve on her wool frock coat up, revealing a compass that glowed with golden light. Poe took a sharp breath in. "That is pure starfire."

I nodded, recognizing my sister's mark, as well as the particular vibration of her magic. It was an ability I'd forgotten I possessed until this moment. "So, you are Ouriel's lightbearer?"

It was an old term; one I hadn't used in centuries. But my mother's people, the Larae and their descendants, could gift aspects of their power to another. Only temporarily, of course, but the bearer could use the full range of their power in that time. This girl had been gifted with Ouriel's starfire, which, along with Bayun's companionship, made her one of the most trustworthy people on Sirin at the moment. I did not have to know her better to know that.

"I am," the girl said. "I am Morgaine, and we have been looking everywhere for you, Lumina."

"Please," I said, nuzzling Bayun one more time before standing. It was difficult to let the greymalkin go, but I had to. The feeling that time was running out chased me now, spurring me on. "Please call me Mina."

Morgaine nodded. "Ouriel sent me. I have much to tell you and not much time."

So she felt it too, the aperture narrowing. Whatever was happening with my memory, with Ashbourne's, with Chopard, it was all the same problem, and the time to solve it was now. We could not wait longer; we couldn't take time for love or friendship to develop or solve itself. Even my drive for vengeance, which had renewed since putting Ashbourne in the oubliette to sort himself out, must be put aside.

Morgaine held out her hand. "Will you accept the message?"

I nodded, clasping hands with the girl. Poe stepped forward, her hands in the air. "Stop. Stop. What is happening here?"

I couldn't blame her for being worried. If someone approached her with the same aim, I would be standing between them right now, refusing to let them touch her. But we hadn't much time, of that I was certain.

"It's all right," I said, hoping to reassure her. "Ouriel is my sister. This little one was once her closest companion and confidant."

A cold breeze sent a flurry of snowflakes towards us through the spindly branches of the trees. The year was turning darker. Poe's arms fell helplessly to her side. "What is the rush?"

Morgaine glanced behind her, as though looking for something, then back to us, smiling. It was a pretty smile; some might even call it dazzling. "I am being pursued. By Chopard's people. I'm fairly certain they know what I'm here to do and they don't like it."

So that was why she'd turned. If she was being pursued, I could not sense anyone else in the woods with us. I glanced at Poe, who shook her head once, almost imperceptibly. We were alone in the woods—for now, anyway.

The fur on Bayun's back bristled. *They have not pinpointed our location just yet. They will, though.*

Again, I glanced at Poe, who nodded almost imperceptibly. Morgaine had confirmed two vital suspicions for us. Chopard was working with a team, and they were talented enough to manage complex tracking spells.

Morgaine nodded to the greymalkin. "They always do. We should get moving."

Poe nodded, gesturing towards the path she'd been tracing through the woods. As we walked, Morgaine kept stride with me. "Since we haven't much time, I will get right to the point. Chopard's people are looking for you."

Ahead of us, Poe sucked in a sharp breath, her feet crunching on the dry, dead leaves on the ground. Her shoulders crept up around her ears and her pace quickened. *Could the two of us not have a single moment of peace?* I desperately wanted the time to talk to her about the creature on the beach and what we'd learned at Viridian's, but here was yet another problem to deal with.

Still, it was information about Chopard, and we couldn't very well dismiss it—no matter how depleted I felt. "Do you know who he is?" I asked. There was an edge to my voice, a tell I would have to work on before we got back to Pravhna. I sounded tired—weak. I worked to banish it, to even out my tone with my next words. "His real identity?"

Poe paused, seeming to realize she'd gotten too far ahead. Though she didn't turn back, her shoulders relaxed, her head pulling her spine upwards. It was like watching a dancer compose themselves on stage.

Morgaine shook her head as she stepped around a rock in her path. "I only know he's trying to open a portal into the limen, which is making my job harder."

We caught up with Poe. Thoughts swirled in my mind, almost too quick for me to follow. A warm hand slipped into mine and squeezed. Poe's body pressed close, a comforting weight.

"Keep moving," Morgaine whispered, glancing back.

They've narrowed in on our location, Bayun agreed, rubbing his face against my calf. *But I do not believe they've found us yet.*

I GLANCED AT POE, but she looked straight ahead at Morgaine, her face the serene picture of calm. I saw Poe's expression for exactly what it was: a mask. Poe was just as tired as I was, grieving just as deeply, needing rest just as desperately. She pulled me along with her, our pace increasing as she stepped in front of Morgaine to lead the way once more. We were practically jogging at this point, though I felt the effort Poe made to keep her strides as long and smooth as possible. She was taking my pain into account, tempering her fear with my needs.

For her, I had to think harder, faster, better. *The fires.* Chopard was covering them up, obscuring the cuts. It was a solid method, as empyrae would erase all evidence that he was trying to open portals between realms. If he hadn't done it, both the Vilhari and Oscarovi would have ferreted out what he was up to before now. Travel between realms was dangerous and difficult. It wasn't something our people took lightly. In fact, on Sirin, even attempting to do such a thing could generate a great deal of trouble. The practice was not outlawed, but it was certainly socially unacceptable.

Poe's steadying grip on my arm continued as the pieces moved rapidly in my mind, ancient memory mixing with present-day knowledge, connections forming more quickly that I could consciously follow. Suddenly, I understood exactly why Morgaine was here, and why she bore Ouriel's unique power. I stopped short. Poe stumbled against me. "You're closing portals, aren't you?"

Morgaine nodded, stopping as well. "Your sister said you'd understand."

I looked to Poe, who waited patiently for someone to explain all of this to her. I squeezed her hand. Morgaine glanced down at our grip on one another and an expression of deep emotion crossed her pretty face. She understood what we were doing, steadying one another from the onslaught of the terrible things that continued to batter us both. And though I could not decipher her exact emotion, I recognized the understanding in her eyes. What had this girl been through?

I had no time for such thoughts—somewhere at the edge of the forest, there was a disturbance in the atmosphere that was all too familiar to me. The locator spell was honing in on our area. Every muscle in my body tensed. Memories clouded my mind before floating away. I could not reach more information. Bayun and Morgaine looked in the same direction I did.

"Keep moving," Morgaine urged again. "It will make the search harder for them."

Poe moved first, and though she might not have sensed the threads of magic being pulled the same way that Morgaine or I did, she obviously knew something was amiss. "The car is a short distance from here. We can take the two of you with us."

We followed her at a brisk pace, winding a path deeper into the forest. The trees were almost impassable here, they grew so close together. As we moved, I talked, trying to keep calm. "When the Ventyr first came up with the plan to imprison the Ravagers, our scholars posited that if they ever got out, they would open dozens of portals between worlds, searching for realms with more direct access to aether."

Poe's eyes went wide as she worked through my words, the pace of her footsteps increasing with her understanding. "They consume aether?"

I nodded, my breath catching in my lungs. She was moving a bit faster than my exhausted body could handle, but I knew we needed to hurry. "Yes. It was how they nearly destroyed us. Nearly destroyed Interra." I glanced at Morgaine, who was keeping up quite a bit more easily. "Have they returned there as well?"

Tears filled the corners of her eyes, but did not fall. She sidestepped a tree root with the grace of a dancer. More likely, a fighter. Morgaine was a warrior. She reminded me of my Larae family. She was young, too young for this, but then that was how these things so often happened. Ashbourne's sister. Me. Ouriel. Some of us still had our lives, but we had been destroyed by the Ravagers all the same.

"Yes," Morgaine answered, her countenance shifting, becoming heavier. "We tried to stop the one on Interra, but we were far, far too late."

It was as I feared then—the Ravagers had escaped. This was a conversation I'd hoped to have with Ashbourne. He knew so much more about all this than I did, after spending aeons keeping watch over them. That too was among the memories I'd regained. The knowledge that while I'd been punished here on Sirin, he had been given much, much less freedom. He had been trapped in the limen, with the Ravagers.

And now one was loose on Interra. "Are the others still imprisoned?" I didn't hold out much hope for this, given our circumstances, but it seemed worth it to ask.

Morgaine shook her head. "No, the second has been dealt with, though. A third…"

"Is here," Poe finished as she pushed back a thick layer of brush to reveal a navy blue Broussard in a smaller model than the one Maman had maintained. It took me a moment to understand that she did not mean that the Ravager was inside the car. The stress of all this was altering me as well.

"Get in the car," Poe said, her voice much more brusque than I was used to.

Morgaine shook her head. "We can't go with you."

A sense of pressure deepened in my sinuses, and my head felt thick and full. The search in the woods was growing more intense, the threads of reality pulling so taut they might break. There was a kind of pressure in the air that was all too familiar to me. It brought back memories of a time of endless war. A time when I would have done *anything* to have stopped the wheel of suffering.

Rose petals falling from the sky. The bite of a knife at my ribs. Hot breath in my ear. A light in the darkness—an unusual ray of hope. I gritted my teeth, willing the memory to retreat. Not this, not now. The last thing I needed was memories of Ashbourne right now.

Bayun rubbed against Poe's legs, purring loudly to comfort her. *We will help you if we can, but we have our own work to do.*

"Closing the portals Chopard is opening?" Poe asked, her words rushed and breathless.

Morgaine slumped against the trunk of a tree. Her eyes held the kind of exhaustion I thought only immortals felt, and I knew now what she was. She was *human.* I hadn't seen or heard of her kind in a very long time. It made her embodiment of my sister's power that much more unique. Morgaine must be very special indeed.

"That wasn't my mission," the human girl replied, "but yes, I've remediated a few of his. I'm here to deal with the Ravager's damage."

Poe frowned as she looked around, sensing what we all did, that our time together grew shorter by the second. She wrapped her arms around herself. "I hate feeling so behind." Poe bit her lip hard, seeming to realize we didn't have time for detailed explanations. Through her coat, I could see her balled fists. Her hazel eyes had widened with fear. "Do you know what Chopard wants?"

Morgaine pushed off the tree, her shoulders barely lifting. I could only hope she was strong enough to finish her task on her own. "I don't know. But every attempt I find in time suggests he is looking for something in the limen." She turned swiftly, sensing something that apparently Poe and I could not. "Do you accept Ouriel's message?"

"Yes," I answered, holding my hands out to her.

Morgaine held onto my hands. Both our hands slid upward, onto each other's forearms. Immediately, Ouriel's face filled my second sight. We stood in darkness, atop an endless expanse of dark blue sand that rose and crested in enormous dunes, shifting in waves, as though they were water. This place was not familiar to me, and yet something in my soul recognized it.

Behind Ouriel loomed an ancient structure I could not quite make out. We stood quite a distance from it, and still, I could sense its enormity. My second sight focused on my sister. She was different from when we were young, with the rounded ears of an Oscarovi, a face sprinkled with constellations of freckles, and beautiful auburn hair, just the shade of Bayun's fur. Her wings were nowhere to be seen.

"Sister," she breathed. "I have missed you."

I knew I couldn't speak back to her, that this was merely a recording, but I answered her anyway. "I missed you too."

"Morgaine will have told you what she is to do, and by now you have likely parsed out that Ashbourne's failure to listen to you brought about the release of the Ravagers. He was never meant to be the Warden forever, Lumina. He is destined to be the shrike and you the thorn. You were meant for one another in all patterns, all times. Forgive him if you can. There is no solving this without him, my love. He is the only one who can bring about the end."

Ouriel's green eyes narrowed, as though she were blinking back tears. She looked over her shoulder and nodded to someone I cannot see. "I know. I'm coming." When she turned to face me again, she smiled. "I wish I could see you again, Mina. Even just once. I will try to help you however I can. I am working on something big, but I am not sure I can manage things in time. Whatever you do, don't break the ward on Sirin. It's the only thing keeping them out."

I opened my mouth to ask her what she meant, before remembering she couldn't hear me. She faded from sight and I was left on the shifting indigo sands that moved faster, a great wind howling as the structure in the background was swallowed by the sea of dust. What I witnessed was not part of the vision Ouriel sent to me. It was something else, something harder to understand. As the vision faded, I tried to remember all I'd seen while Ouriel spoke.

I let go of Morgaine's arms. "Thank you," I whispered, wiping tears from my cheeks.

She nodded. "You understand, then?"

"Yes," I said, though there were things I decidedly did not understand. There was nothing Morgaine could do about that, and she needed to go. We all did. "I understand. You should go, as should we."

Bayun rubbed against my legs. *We will meet again before we leave.*

"I'd like that," I whispered as Morgaine's arm glowed with starfire.

A knife appeared in her hands, glowing with celestial light. She cut an elegant slit in the fabric of reality, and she and the greymalkin slipped through. She waved once, and the wound closed, sealing at her touch.

"What *was* that?" Poe gasped.

"Let's get in the autocar and I'll explain," I said.

CHAPTER 6

ASHBOURNE

When I opened my eyes, there was no more pain. The bright light of the sun caused me to squint. The air around me was cold and crisp, snow on the evergreen trees in a hidden bay outside Lyonesse. *I was home.* Why did it feel as though I hadn't seen this place in ages? There was an ache in my chest for something I'd lost, but I could not determine its source.

"Where'd you go?" Connoch asked.

I glanced at my older brother, grinning. "Nowhere."

"Ach," he scoffed, punching my arm. "You were thinking of *her* again."

"I wasn't," I said. But he was right, much as I hated to admit it. "Have you noticed the way Rosalind's hair has a bit of a sapphire sheen to it?"

Connoch groaned. "Please, Thalia will have your head. They are best friends."

He was right, of course. Our little sister was very protective of her friends. Rosalind was likely not the woman for me. But she was beautiful, with all that indigo hair and alabaster skin. Besides, with her talent with aura, she would make an excellent partner. Still, if I broke her heart, Thalia might eviscerate me. Likely, it was not worth the trouble of romancing her, but it was better than pining over women I could never hope to court. I banished thoughts of the silver-eyed princess who'd plagued my mind for years. She was not for me.

Connoch cast his line into the quiet waters of the bay. "If you're not going to fish, then why did you come?"

"To talk you out of this thing with Aislin," I replied.

Connoch groaned. "Not this again. It's a political marriage. Besides, it will be years 'til we actually marry."

"She's Boreas's plaything," I said, trying to keep my tone even.

"We all do what we have to," Connoch said, settling down on a rock, just a few feet away from me.

It felt as though we'd had this conversation before. And we had. We'd been talking about Aislin for years now. But that wasn't it. It was as though we'd had this *exact* conversation before. I remembered the angle of the light as it hit my brother's face. In exactly three seconds, the line would jerk out of his hands and be pulled underwater. Sure enough, the line tugged. Connoch stood, and it was just as I remembered it—the line jerked out of his hands. A giant silver body writhed just underneath the surface of the water as the fish got away.

I remembered this day.

"Damn argenti," my brother said with a laugh. "The giant bastards ruin all my fun."

Yes, he'd said that before. Next, we would get into a screaming argument about the wisdom of Connoch Claiming Boreas' former mistress. Movement in the corner of my eye caught my attention. I turned, swearing I saw a figure moving in the bushes behind me, a huge spotted feline body disappearing into the forest, its iridescent wings glimmering under the bright light of the sun.

That wasn't possible. The animal I'd just seen did not live in this part of the world.

"I am going to take a piss," I said. I'd said it before as well, but not because I'd seen something. Because I'd finished a whole bottle of ale in under an hour. The bottle sat empty next to me on the rocks. But I was not drunk. Not even close.

Something was wrong.

Connoch nodded as I followed the shadowy movement into the thicket of bushes behind me. Instead of the dark wooded glen behind the lake, I found myself on a burning battlefield, Thalia's name on my lips as I frantically searched the bodies for any sign of my little sister. She was not supposed to come, not supposed to be here today, but her giant heart had betrayed us all.

She'd come to protect the people of this little northern village, and now no one could find her. Connoch's voice had echoed mine just moments ago. Now it fell silent. Feral keening startled me into turning. Seventy paces from me, Connoch kneeled on the ground. Blood smeared his face where he'd buried it in her shoulder, our little sister's body cradled in his arms as he screamed for her to wake.

Her body was broken and battered, covered with livid red lesions that told the story of this battlefield all too clearly. She'd given all to save the people here. She'd given all, so they wouldn't have to. Villagers stood at the edge of the forest, weeping for their princess. Weeping for the woman who gave her life to protect them.

Connoch's eyes locked with mine. "Boreas will pay for this."

The words were a promise, a threat, a premonition, all in one. He would rebel or retaliate. I knew not which, but I knew my brother—my sister's death would push him over a very specific edge. One he would not come back from, I feared.

As I stepped towards them, meaning to calm Connoch before he said something he could not take back, I found myself clean, inside the palace at Lyonesse. Soft fur brushed my fingers, but when I looked down, I only saw the roughhewn wood floors. I looked up, feeling ill at ease. Across from me, my father sat at his desk. Notus' heavy brow was creased, his pale blue skin the same shade as mine and Connoch's. I felt as though I hadn't seen him in years.

The temptation to lurch across the desk to hug him overwhelmed me. But I was smashed in a chair that was far too small for my enormous frame. It was only now that I noticed the oddness of having wings again.

Again? I'd had wings my entire life.

My father was talking, and I'd stopped paying attention. Why had my attention drifted? "...think that the best way to keep them in for good is to imprison them in Nihil."

"The heart of the limen?" I asked.

He was talking about the Ravagers, of course. It was all we talked about these days. How to stop them. What the implications of their arrival were. How soon the world might end. How soon after that the others would fall, if we did not do *something*. Now the scholars had a plan, and it hardly seemed real. Nihil was dangerous to begin with, unstable with the sheer volume of pure aether—otham, a substance as dangerous as it was vital to all life existing.

My voice went on without me, as though it did not need me to think or speak. "Near the remnants of the labyrinth? Do you think it wise to keep them so close to the nexus of life?"

Had I asked this question before?

My father shook his head. "No, I don't. I don't think any of this is *wise*, Ashbourne. I think it is a foolish gamble. But Boreas is up to something bigger."

"Then why go along with it?" I asked.

"Because he's calling himself *Emperor* now," Father said, his voice cool and filled with fury. He ran a big hand through his freshly shorn hair, sending it flying in all directions. My stomach lurched.

Empire was evil. Our people had resisted empire for centuries, preferring to fight with one another over territory and resources than to collaborate, all in the name of refusing anything that resembled what elders like Notus and Boreas left behind. We were no longer servants of Empire. We ruled ourselves.

My father continued, sounding tired. "I have no way of stopping him from claiming the title. No way of shaking his hold on the planet. He's already taking credit for saving us from them."

I growled with frustration, my nails digging into the soft wood of my chair. House Thuellos had captured the Ravagers, and built the mechanisms that kept them imprisoned. It had taken nearly a decade. Interra was a shadow of its former self, but at least the drain on our power, on our people, had stopped. "It was *our* mages that constructed the vivarius devices."

"And his resources that made it possible." Father pounded a large fist on the surface of his desk. "He's too powerful." My father leaned back in his heavy desk chair. He stared out the window at the angry winter sea. "Coming here was a mistake. Boreas is no better than House Vecarius."

I swallowed hard. This wasn't the first time I'd heard my father express regret over leaving the Vilhari Empire, but it was a rare thing. The elders didn't talk much about why they'd left our home on Neamor. Only that the high courts had failed us all, and that we were better off on our own. The promise the elders had made when they came to Interra was to start anew, with a culture all our own.

"The people know who saved them," I said, trying to bring my father some peace. He was not perfect, by any means. Neither he nor my mother were, but they were different than the other elders, more like the Larai. They often seemed to regret not aligning with the warrior queens more closely, but that too was something we did not discuss. So many secrets.

"The people know who has the most power," my father replied, always the pragmatist, turning from regret to what action we might take. "Boreas looks to other worlds."

My eyes widened as horror shuddered through me. Other worlds meant expansion, and I understood too well why Boreas called himself Emperor now. My mind wheeled with the implications. "The elders would never allow it."

Notus shook his head. "Which elders are not under his thumb, my son? Even your brother bows to his every whim now, forcing me to stay my hand."

It was true, but I did not want to believe it. Didn't want to think of what Boreas might bring to worlds beside our own. Our situation was bad enough here, and we had only a slim chance of resolving things.

My father continued speaking. "He has one weakness left. His children."

I shook my head. "We can't get near them. Orynthia's Larae General is with them at all times." My father smiled. I shook my head, realizing what he had. It was devious. Devious, but brilliant. I would finally have my chance with her. "But not the eldest."

Father shrugged. "It's not ideal. Boreas values the twins more, for their power, and the fact that the boy will inherit. But Lumina was the child of his heart. He loved her mother. Orynthia is simply a means to an end."

I nodded, thinking it over. I hated the thought of destroying the princess, but when I weighed the options, it was an easier death than the one she would have if House Thuellos conquered House Anemos. "If I kill her, he will just come after us."

"I don't want you to kill her," my father replied. Relief flooded me. Ever since the night I first saw her at a party, I'd wanted Lumina Anemos. "Not if we can turn her to our side. I want you to seduce her. Claim her. Make her yours in every way possible. Find out as much as you can."

It would ruin her chances for a political marriage. My father didn't say it, but then, he didn't have to. It was a good plan, a savvy one that would both weaken Boreas and give me a sliver of the revenge Connoch and I sought. The Emperor, as he would have us call him, had stolen my little sister from me with his lack of action. Thalia was the purest good in this world. And now I would take something he loved, and corrupt it. It was a satisfying thought.

I nodded, getting up to make the arrangements. "It will work."

"Yes," Notus said, his eyes going back to his papers. "You are perfect for this job. It will all work out, perfectly."

Something about his tone struck me wrong, as deceitful somehow. My stomach lurched. Did he know my secret? Mother's secret? I paused, but my father did not look up. I read too much into things, worried too much.

As I turned to the door, I remembered the lake and fishing with Connoch. It had happened months ago, but now it felt as though it had only been moments. When I pushed the door open and stepped through, I found myself in an alley. Rose petals fell from the sky. Everywhere, there were sounds of cheering. This. This had all happened before.

CHAPTER 7

ASHBOURNE

I looked about, my eyes searching for some sign of the winged cat I'd seen before, but there was no such creature here. Or anywhere in Kilm, I reasoned. I was having a difficult day. It would be better to go home and sleep. This celebration was poised to go on into the wee hours. I couldn't blame my people for their joy. The "ravaged years," as people called them, had been long and exhausting, and they were finally coming to a close.

Soft footsteps echoed in the alleyway behind me, her scent of clean musk and a fresh spring day filling my nose. I spun as she drew close, dragging her into my arms. Our bodies crashed into one another.

This couldn't wait another day. Notus had ordered me to kill Lumina Anemos a month ago, and yet I hadn't. The Ravagers were imprisoned. We had all the information we were going to get—and it still wasn't enough. The past year had driven my father to desperate measures.

It was time, but her body was so sweet, so soft and pliable. Her luscious thighs spread at the merest hint of my hand moving between them. She was as desperate for me as I was for her. Fervor had us in its grip. I didn't want to kill her. Knowing her had changed me, broken apart my every desire for vengeance through her destruction.

We were alike in so many ways. We both saw the possibilities for a world without endless war.

I didn't love her. I didn't love anyone. Not really. But I wanted her more than I'd ever wanted another. And from the moisture on my fingers as I entered her, I knew she wanted me too. She moaned in my mouth as I pushed my fingers deeper into her silken depths. I was so hard it hurt, but as her wet desire coated my fingers, her soft body undulating against mine, all I wanted was her release. My name on her lips as she came apart around my fingers.

I kissed her harder, knowing full well this couldn't go on. I had to kill her, before my ideals and all hope for Lyonesse died here in my poor choices. This woman could not be the end of me, of my family's desire for a better world, my father's vision for a brighter future. The path there was brutal. It was time to hone in on my prey.

I pulled my fingers out of her, feigning as though I was unbuttoning my trousers. Instead, I went for my knife. As I pressed it beneath her ribs, a sharp sting cut into my neck.

Delight filled me, as well as fear. She had intended to kill me, and she was more than capable of doing so. We were the same. We had always been the same inside, different as we were. "Was this always the plan?"

She nodded, her mercurial eyes wide with delight. "Was it for you?"

Heat flushed my skin. With her knife digging into me, I wanted her even more. I tossed mine aside, my fingers moving to my pants. She watched my progress as I freed the hard length of me that would not behave with her around. I fisted my cock, watching her watch me fit myself against her.

She did not take the knife away from my neck, but her leg curled around my waist, her eyes blazing with fury as she pulled me inside her, just a fraction of an inch, positioning herself above me. She teased me, rolling her hips just a little as she moved me inside of her and out, never letting me fully inside. Her knife finally dropped to the ground as she sank down on me, taking me to the hilt.

There was no gentleness between us. I took her hard and fast, sweet venom dripping from my fangs. The fervor took over. It was a sign. When her canines sank into my neck, I howled with pleasure.

Mine sank into her as we writhed against one another. Again and again, we fed from one another's power, exchanging our lifeforce in every way possible.

"You are mine," she hissed.

"From now until the stars go out," I growled. She screamed with pleasure as I impaled her in every way possible, again and again. I was hers. She was mine. It would be so forevermore.

There was no feline made of shadow this time, only the fading light from the alley. Now I stood on a terrace at Lyonesse, my bedchambers behind me, my bed still neatly made. It had been another night of sleepless pacing, trying to figure out just exactly how to keep Lumina from being punished for being my Claimed. They had taken her from me, imprisoned her, and I could not rest until she was free once more.

A siren sat in front of me, an annoyed look on her humanoid face. "My prince, it is as I have explained. If you leave Lumina be, they will keep her safe."

"Imprisoned," I snarled, furious. My Claimed. She was mine, and they dared keep her from me. I would punish House Anemos, burn Boreas' city to the ground to get her back.

"Yes," the siren agreed. "Imprisoned, but *safe*. If you attempt to take her, the Tapestry shows no other options but utter destruction."

I glared at the creature before me. Prophecy was something of the old worlds. Of the Empire. I had failed Lumina, and now this old woman wanted me to simply let her fester in prison because she had a *vision*. Impossible.

Gods, true immortality, foreseeing the future. Those were things of the past. They had no place in our modern society. These old birds only wanted power, and I was tired of sharing. "She is my Claimed. I have rights to her."

"They will not harm her, my prince," Alcyone said again, a plea filling her voice. "Boreas is baiting you, don't you see?"

"Do not think to tell me my business," I snarled. "You know nothing of what you speak. Go."

Alcyone turned, sighing deeply. "Your decision will be the end of Lumina, and the world as you know it. You will loose chaos on the cosmos for your foolishness, Prince."

I laughed, the sound harsh, even to my own ears. "Peddle your superstition elsewhere, old woman."

Some part of me knew I was acting irrationally—that I was giving into my baser instincts, and pure pride. And I did not care. I had lost too much at Boreas' hands and I wanted Lumina back.

"She asked me to come here, you know," Alcyone said softly, her voice even, but restrained. "I told her the same as I told you. She asked me to help you understand. You must leave her be."

"You lie." I laughed again. This time, the sound was weaker. I knew I was wrong, and yet I also knew I would not stop. My generals wanted vengeance for how House Anemos had treated House Thuellos. Taking Lumina back was an act of retribution, a powerful move that would bring Lyonesse back to its rightful seat of power. We would not fail again. Boreas' hold on Interra would end now.

There was too much talk of other worlds. Too many dangerous plans being maneuvered into place. We'd lost Connoch to Boreas, though I could not understand how. The only way to get my brother back was for House Thuellos to rule. For Lumina to be mine, and for Boreas' reign to end. I could see no other way, and would hear no further objections to my plans.

The shadows filled my eyes, a heavy animal body leaning against my legs, a great wing wrapped around my body as I slumped over. When my vision cleared, I was at my sentencing. The memories came back faster and harder now, each transition making me more aware that somewhere, in my corporeal form, I was in an incredible amount of pain.

A voice echoed through the vaulted ceiling, raised a hundred feet or more over the heads of the gathered crowd. "For the crime of violating the Nihil Treaty Accords, Ashbourne Thuellos is sentenced to eternity as Warden of Nihil, Guardian of the Ravagers, Sentinel of the Ten Kingdoms."

I gazed up at the frescoes painted far above me as the gathered crowd gasped. The paintings were freshly finished, though they had taken years to complete. The scene depicted there was House Anemos, defeating the Ravagers, once and for all. It was not remotely how it had happened, but it was how it would be remembered.

There was no true history. Only accounts colored by those who conquered. Those under their heel would be forgotten to time, their stories twisted and misshapen for the next bad ruler's ulterior motives. What would history recount about me, I wondered.

Would I be remembered as the foolish prince who betrayed his lover? Or the Warden of the limenal prison that kept the Ravagers in? I remembered all too well what Alcyone had warned. My only redemption would be in keeping the Ravagers well in hand. The rest of my long life would have to be dedicated to that purpose. I could not let what Alcyone had warned come to pass.

The future of all worlds now rested with me. It was enough to change a man.

The shadows filled my eyes again. A tiny, brown-haired witch visited me, over and over. A little one that reminded me of Thalia, in both her earnest sweetness and her sharp humor. We walked the maze of the labyrinth together for years as she grew into a woman, until one day everything changed all at once. The memories spun past me, faster and faster.

The Ravagers broke loose, one by one. The consequences of my actions came to bear upon me. All abandoned me, and I set out to find Lumina. To pay penance for what I had done. To put myself at her mercy before the end. To beg forgiveness for my arrogance and the consequences of my actions.

And when I found her, Vaness Wildfang had imprisoned her once more, and thought to attack me. I lost my temper and all reason. I lashed out with empyrae, losing control and consciousness. The same temper, the same arrogance that started this all, brought me low once more.

The stream of all that had been now made sense. I woke alone, sitting at the bottom of the oubliette, my throat raw from screaming, the truth of my mistakes weighing me so far down I could not think. The old one had been right to call the process painful.

This has all happened before, the eldritch god said, still lurking close, it seemed. *It is time for this era to end, and another to begin. You are no longer the Warden, Ashbourne Thuellos. You must become the Shrike.*

CHAPTER 8

MINA

Blessedly, Poe was a much better driver than me. After a half hour of watching to make sure we weren't being followed, my heartbeat slowed, coming down out of my ears and settling back into my chest where it belonged. The leather of the Broussard's seats was cracked and worn, but it was clean and smelled of cigar smoke and Ismiti vanilla. I traced the cracks in the seat with my finger, waiting for Poe to speak.

Meeting Morgaine in the forest had done more for us than deliver Ouriel's message. It gave us vital information about the kind of power that Chopard's team possessed. The kind of magic they were capable of using was suspicious. It took a good deal of skill and power both to track someone with the ability to cut the threads of reality. My sister's power, even on loan to a human, was rare. I glanced at Poe, wondering if she was wondering the same thing I was —that it looked more and more like Elspeth and Mirabelle Aestra might be our next best suspects.

Poe still said nothing, focusing on the road. Her mouth twisted slightly, and her eyes narrowed enough that her long lashes brushed her cheeks every time she blinked. From the tense posture in her shoulders and the way her knuckles whitened around the steering

426

wheel of the Broussard, I felt comfortable assuming she might be angry with me. I dared not ask, though.

Fear wormed its way into my heart, as a nasty little voice in my head calculated how long it would be until she was sick of me, until she realized I was a burden on her, a dead weight around her neck. It occurred to me that I feared little else in the world more than finding out that I did not mean as much to Poe as she did to me. Even the sting of learning the truth about Ashbourne did not elicit the same terror in me that this did. Lovers were not to be trusted, him most of all. But a true friend? To lose Poe might be the end of me.

I chewed on the inside of my cheek as I attempted to calm the raging sea of emotions within me. We drove in silence for a time, the tension between us thickening into a veritable stew of frustration on both our parts. Finally, she sighed, her long oval nails tapping the steering wheel as we drove through a series of country villages with narrow cobbled streets and stone buildings. Nobody much looked our way, but the streets were quite crowded.

Despite everything, I was nervous about returning to Pravhna without Skye, Ash, and Morpheus. Orchid House would feel lonely without them. I snuck a look at Poe. "Are you ever going to tell me what Skye said when you told her you were leaving?"

Poe glanced over at me, taking her eyes off the crowded street as she slowed the car to let a herd of sheep cross. Each was dyed a different pastel color, and wore a matching satin ribbon around its neck, which was quite odd, but neither of us commented on it.

Poe only asked, "Are *you* going to tell me what all that in the woods was about?"

I nodded. "Of course. It's just that I'm still thinking it all through."

The candy-colored sheep were slow, but obedient to the Strix youth that led them, ringing a small brass bell to keep them in line. What *were* they doing? The tension in Poe's shoulders relaxed. Her hand drifted over to mine. I turned my palm over on the bench seat of the old Broussard. She slipped her hand into mine and we both squeezed. Relief suffused my entire body. Things were all right then. She understood.

"Can you think and listen at the same time?" she asked, her voice soft, as though she didn't want to disturb me.

"Yes," I said. "It's all just running in the back of my mind."

Finally, the sheep were past us, down another alley, and traffic resumed, though now we joined a host of lorries and painted wagons, moving at a glacial pace. I leaned forward to look up at the colorful pennants and late fall blooms that were strung between the buildings. Had we hit some kind of local festival?

Slowly, we passed an adorable little inn, right at the edge of the village. I craned my neck to look back at it, frowning. The Broussard slowed as Poe took her foot off the gas pedal. Poe let out a little huff of frustration. "You want to stop, don't you?"

It wasn't just that I wanted to stop. It was that I was desperate to slow all this down so I could think. "I know we have to get back to Pravhna. But I need a day or two, I think."

"I don't think we'll be able to get a room," Poe said, as traffic slowed again. "The preparations have begun."

"Preparations?" I asked, feeling as though I'd missed something quite vital.

Poe's smile was wan. "Yes, for the Grand Exhibition, have you forgotten?"

My eyebrows raised. The Grand Exhibition took place over the winter every decade in a different city, with scholars and artisans from all over coming to showcase their work. I hadn't realized it was this year. The last had been in Ismit, and I had not been allowed to go with Maman and Helene. The expense was considered too great.

"I had forgotten it was this year," I whispered, my throat tight at the thought of Helene. The memory of her on the beach at Somerhaven was almost too much to bear. Had that only been yesterday? It felt like months. "We'll have to return to Pravhna then, I suppose."

Poe hummed a little in response. "I would like to have rested a bit as well," she said softly as the traffic cleared. Our velocity increased as we passed vehicles and carriages headed into the village. "What was your sister like?"

"Helene?" I asked, my heart pounding, thinking of the creature on the beach.

"No," Poe answered. "Ouriel."

"Oh," I breathed out, then sucked in air that I imagined tasted like the cold, brisk winds of Interra. "Ouriel was my half-sister. She was fierce from birth." I stared out the window at the trees that canopied the road. We had entered the forest that would soon become the undercity. "A warrior, with the kind of power that made grown men jealous... and devastated her twin brother."

"Why?" Poe asked.

"Because in our line, power was meant for men. The right of primogeniture passed over both myself and Ouriel, though both of us were more magically talented than Luciel." I gritted my teeth, thinking of my brother. "She trusted him too much. Too deeply. Ciel was our father's creature."

Poe frowned, then, keeping her voice even, asked, "How does all this connect to the Ravagers?"

I shrugged, letting memories wash over me. There was still a lot I couldn't quite make out, pieces I didn't understand. "I don't know if it does, but it might. When I was banished to Sirin, my father had shut me out, obviously. In the time I was imprisoned, he'd begun working on something big, something he thought would give him power over more than just Interra."

"What?" Poe asked.

"He found a way to get to other worlds, without spacecraft."

Poe frowned, tapping the steering wheel again. "Through the limen?"

I nodded. "I think so. From the little I could discern, he planned to send his people to at least three different worlds. He worried the Ravagers had done too much damage to Interra."

"Oh," she huffed out. "He thought he could just *have* another planet?"

I didn't have a chance to answer her. Ahead of us, a stag darted into the road, a giant beast crowned with antlers so large they looked as though they might pull his elegant head down. Poe slammed on the brakes of the Broussard, turning the wheel with a violent twist of her arms. The stag leapt out of the way just as we came to a screeching halt.

"I'm so sorry," Poe blurted out. Her hazel eyes were wide with panic. "Are you all right?"

She was breathing too quickly. I honed in on her, listening to the sound of her heart, which beat far too erratically. Mine did as well, but my breath came in long, even strokes. Tears welled in Poe's eyes, her head falling into her hands. Great sobs wracked through her as she gasped for air.

I slid over on the bench seat of the Broussard, taking her into my arms. I looked behind us and ahead. The stag was gone without a trace. Had it really been there? Or was it a vision? It couldn't have been; Poe saw it too. There didn't seem to be any traffic coming in either direction, but with preparations for the Grand Exhibition, I knew we weren't truly safe here in the middle of the road.

I hugged Poe tightly. "I am going to get out, all right?"

She looked up at me, confused.

"You are panicking. I will drive."

She could not stop crying, even now. I should have anticipated this. Should have seen it coming. For as different as we appeared outwardly, Poe and I were so similar inside. She had been through too much, too fast, and could no longer process her feelings quickly enough to wear that mask of perpetual calm.

I kissed her forehead, then slid away from her, getting out of the car in calm order. She slid over to the passenger side as my feet crunched on freshly fallen snow. Winter was upon us, and I shivered a bit as I climbed into the driver's seat. I closed the door behind me, taking a deep breath as I moved the car as far onto the shoulder as I could. We both needed a moment to reset before I could drive us the rest of the way to Pravhna.

"He left me here after the War, but whatever Boreas wanted from Ciel and Ouriel, he had not managed to get it right." Poe nodded. Her sobs had slowed, and listening to me seemed to help a bit. "All I know is that Interra was not enough for him. When he left me here, he told me I was a seed he'd planted. That someday I would be part of this planet's subjugation."

Poe sucked in a gasp. "Why would anyone want that?"

I shook my head as I gripped the wheel. "I have lived thousands of years, Hippolyta, and I still cannot fathom why anyone wants that kind of power. It is a sickness."

She nodded as I gripped the wheel. "You can do this."

I wasn't sure if she meant facing my memories, or driving the rest of the way to Pravhna. I didn't ask. Whether I wanted to or not, I was bound to do both.

CHAPTER 9

MINA

The rest of the drive to Pravhna was slow, but uneventful. By the time I drove the Broussard into Orchid House's carriage house garage, Poe was asleep and the sky had gone dark. As I sat listening to Poe breathe, I peered into the night through the carriage house windows. No lights lit Orchid House, and my stomach tightened. There was no Skye, no Ash waiting inside. No sweet Morpheus for me to beg for a hug.

It was just me and Poe now. I closed my eyes, trying to fight back my own tears. How had I let myself grow so attached to these people in such a short time? I gazed at Poe's sleeping face. A little drool seeped out of her mouth and I could not help but smile. For as beautiful as she was, she was still a person.

One that I loved with my whole heart. And one that I did not want to drag back into the poison of Orchid House, or the trouble brewing between myself and Ashbourne Thuellos. Not to mention Helene, as the creature she'd become. But Poe was linked to all this, inextricably, in her position as crown princess of House Feriant, the lost heir. She was not yet queen, but someday she could be. I had no idea what that meant for Sirin, but if Poe could influence the way this world worked for the better, I knew she would.

Sirin had never had royalty. It was not really our way. What would we do with a Vilhari queen? What would that mean for this world? Would it even matter if the Ravager took hold of the planet? The thoughts swam together, struggling to keep their heads above the roiling waters of my mind.

But Poe's heartbeat, slow and steady, brought me back to myself, back into my body, which ached from sitting for so long. As quietly as I could, I opened the Broussard's door and stretched my long legs, feeling the pull of my muscles soothing the deep ache that seemed to seep directly into my bones. I arched my back, stretching the space between my shoulders.

I felt eyes on me and turned, assuming it must be Poe. But she was still fast asleep. I searched the dark carriage house, slipping into my second sight, just to be sure. There was no one here. I moved to the carriage house windows, arched and leaded, mirroring those of Orchid House. There was no one in the house, as far as I could see. But the lights were on next door.

My breath hitched as I caught sight of the figure at the window. It was our neighbor, Miranda Willsworth. She was backlit by the lights in her parlor, so I could not see her face, but she was staring right at the carriage house. There was no way she didn't see me. The day I left to find Ashbourne, she'd watched me in just the same way, her eyes gone black.

Instinctively, I longed to shrink back from the window. My skin crawled in reaction to the malevolence in the slump of her shoulders, the intensity of her attention. Instead, I forced myself to straighten my spine, increasing the power of my own countenance. Though I couldn't be sure how much of me she saw, I narrowed my eyes into a steely glare.

On Interra, as princess of House Anemos, I had been known for my cold, intimidating nature. I was not the one people loved. That was Ouriel. I was the one they feared, the one who unsettled them with her uncanny movements. I pulled all of that energy out of my memories and into my body, willing it to infuse every particle of my being, every thread of my power.

"I am not afraid of you," I whispered.

"Who are you talking to?" Poe asked from the car.

"No one," I said, tearing my eyes from the window. Poe was too tired for this truth tonight. The last few days had been too much, and we could go over everything tomorrow, or even the next day. Taking care of her was my primary goal right now. "Let's get you into the house."

From inside the car, she nodded. A soft knock came at the carriage house door. Both of us startled. I spun back to the window —Miranda was gone. "Stay there," I commanded Poe, aether and empyrae both sparking within me. Whatever inhabited Miranda, I was not going to give it a chance to harm Poe, or myself.

My heart beat faster as I moved toward the carriage house door. It opened into the alley behind Orchid House. My muscles tensed painfully as I moved. I was in no shape for a fight, but I trusted my power—the power the Old One had unlocked for me. I took a deep breath as I put my hand on the doorknob.

"Who is it?" I asked, working hard to keep the shake out of my voice.

"Viridian," a masculine voice whispered.

Poe, who did not stay in the car as I'd asked, let out a sigh of relief behind me. I shot a glare over my shoulder at her, to which she simply shrugged. "I wasn't going to let you fight some unknown foe alone, you goose."

I chuckled as I opened the door. Viridian Montclair stood outside. He looked more disheveled than I'd ever seen him, his long silvery hair a mess around his shoulders. He wore a beautiful cerulean frock coat, but had no waistcoat or jacket underneath it, and his shirt was unbuttoned to his waist, revealing his muscled chest.

I raised an eyebrow. It looked as though Viridian had left his bedroom mid-tryst. Given the way we'd left him, I wondered if he and Caralee had consummated things. He rolled his eyes at me, his finely boned face twisting into a sarcastic sneer. "Yes, yes, I am a mess." He pushed past me, into the carriage house. "But I am here." He made a small bow to Poe. "Your Royal Highness."

She sighed. "I would rather we dispense with all the YRH nonsense, if possible."

Viridian straightened, frowned, then nodded, smirking a little. "Of course, my queen."

Poe groaned. "Lady damn you, Viridian."

Now he grinned. He was fooling with her. Joking. Poking fun. Viridian Montclair was... comfortable. It was still an odd sensation to recognize this, because I too was comfortable with his presence.

"Did you deal with Caralee?" Poe asked.

He rolled his eyes. "Yes. She wanted to measure the garden, of all things."

"For what?" I asked.

"The wedding," he said, his shoulders slumping. "It was all I could do to get away from her before she wanted to…"

"I thought she was a bit of a prude?" Poe framed the statement as a question.

Viridian wrinkled his nose. "Apparently, wedding planning makes her amorous. I told her I had a meeting in the city and left her with my butler."

"And she believed you?" I asked.

Viridian shrugged. "She's not the most intelligent woman, Mina."

That was not exactly true. Caralee Ellis-Whitely was a fool, in many ways, but she was socially savvy. It didn't seem like the moment to scold him for misjudging her, though. Viridian had enough problems with Caralee, and of course, I had a bit of trouble telling if he was being humorous. Perhaps he was only joking about her intelligence. There were times when dry humor escaped me entirely.

Viridian shivered. "It's rather cold. What about a spot of tea?"

We made our way through the carriage house and into the garden. I kept my eye on Miranda's house. Viridian followed my gaze, narrowing his eyes. He nodded once to me as Poe walked ahead of us. Either he knew what I looked for, or at the very least, he understood that there was a possible threat next door.

The thought was mildly comforting. Viridian Montclair was no littling or youngster. He was a full-blooded Vilhari mage, a powerful enemy, and for the first time in my life, I had the comfort of knowing that was all working to my advantage.

I could let him help me tonight, and tomorrow we'd get back to the realities of the situation. Tonight, we needed rest. Rest was integral to making a good plan. Anything I said now would only hinder that rest, and the kind of strength we would need in the coming days.

Moving slowly rather than rushing ahead was not my strong suit, but to do all this right, it was the way.

Poe waited for me at the kitchen door. She could open it, of course, the house would respond to her, but I understood her impulse. I pressed my hand to the door. We had only been gone a few days; there was no need for a key. The door clicked open under the pressure of my hand and I entered the kitchen.

"Lux," I murmured. The lamps that dotted the corners of the cozy room lit, casting pools of warm light into the darkness. "Water for tea, please," I said softly. The copper kettle on the stove shivered with delight, filling itself with water. As the water began to boil, I let the sound of the bubbling kettle soothe me.

The kitchen had always been a world apart in Orchid House. The smell of tea and spices filled my nose. I could practically taste Ash's mushroom tarts. I missed him. The only time this house had ever felt like home was the short time the four of us had lived here together.

Would life ever feel like that again?

Poe settled onto a stool at the ancient worktable at the center of the room. She melted onto the battered surface of the table, her head resting on her arms. She should really go straight to bed, but I wasn't about to start ordering her around.

"What kind of tea would you like?" I asked. While she thought it over, I glanced at Viridian. "Check the alley?"

Viridian nodded, moving to the door at the back of the kitchen that led to the alleyway. He opened it slowly, then stepped out, looking first right and left, and then up. "All clear."

I let out the tense breath I'd been holding. We were safe then. The house's wards would not allow anyone inside that I did not approve of. If no one was lurking, then we only need worry about Miranda, for now. And even that could wait until tomorrow. Poe moved off her stool and began getting down things for tea. There was a nice blend we had delivered right before everything had gone to shit, one with lavender and lemon zest that sounded delightful right now.

As I searched through the various tins and crocks for it, Viridian made eye contact with me. "I think I should do a quick perimeter sweep."

Poe nodded, and I added my assent to hers. "Thank you."

Viridian slipped out the door, into the alley. "Will I be able to let myself back in?"

I whispered a few words to the house, which vibrated a little in my second sight. "Yes," I assured him.

Only moments after he left, the kettle whistled. Poe dragged herself off the worktable and joined me by the stove, choosing a fragrant floral tisane, rich with rose, valerian, and some kind of citrus. It wasn't the one I'd searched for, but it was one of my favorites all the same. I heaped spoonfuls of summer honey into the heavy stoneware mugs she chose instead of teacups. One for her, one for me, and one for Viridian.

Upstairs, the sound of soft footsteps caught both our attention. Poe grinned. "Morpheus!"

Her joy at the sound of the greymalkin's footsteps was infectious. I hadn't known she cared for him so deeply. "You go," I said, feeling a bit of cheer at the thought of seeing the grumpy feline. "I'm sure he's looking for us."

She smiled, reaching up to touch my face. "It's all going to be all right. You know that, don't you? We are going to figure all this out, and before you know it, we'll be back with them. He'll make amends, and we will live happily ever after, just like in Ash's stories."

Tears pricked at the corner of my eyes. It was difficult for me to share her view of things, but I liked the vision she saw. Since we were not confronting reality tonight, what harm would it do to agree with her? I nodded. "Won't that be lovely?"

She brushed a kiss onto my cheek, then turned to rush up the stairs. I stirred each of the mugs a bit to incorporate the honey and then picked up the tray. Upstairs, I heard Poe calling out for Morpheus. Trickly little feline, he was likely running away from her —that adorable act he did where he looked back over his shoulder, just daring you to catch him.

The greymalkin was a dangerous beast, to be sure, but he was also too like a sweet house cat not to be completely adored. With him here to update us on what went on with Ash and Skye, it was easy to imagine that Poe's vision for the future was possible. I let that feeling carry me up the kitchen stairs and through the dark hallway on my way to the sitting room, where a lamp was already on.

As I walked through the doorway, all my hopes shattered. Poe lay on the ground, a wound seeping blood at her temple. I screamed for Viridian as the tray fell from my hands, aether and empyrae sparking within me. Whoever had done this, however this had happened, I would fight.

But before I could do a thing, even turn, something sharp pierced my neck, stinging as poison coursed through me. All went dark, as my last, helpless scream echoed in my ears.

CHAPTER 10

ASHBOURNE

"The Shrike?" I whispered into the dark abyss of the oubliette. "What does that mean?"

But the god was gone; it did not answer me. Now I was alone, but for the rush of memories that plagued me. Somewhere in the oubliette, water dripped onto stone, echoing just enough to be disorienting. I took a deep breath, attempting to refocus on what to do next. Thinking too hard about my regained memory now would do nothing but haunt me. Instead, I assessed the situation at hand.

It appeared my empyrae was under control, but I wasn't sure if I could trust myself around those I loved just yet. Perhaps I should stay here, in the oubliette, at least until I was sure. The frigid sea roiled in aquamarine eddies above me. The tide was going out. There was no lock on the oubliette. I was free to leave whenever I wanted, whenever I thought it best.

Mina had trusted me that much. It was a scrap of hope, but I knew it was purposely left for me. My Mina did nothing by chance, nothing by instinct. She worked things through and had a plan. If I was not trapped in the oubliette, she thought I could be trusted to choose when to leave.

I knew full well this was a test, but it was one I was willing to take. I stood, searching the oubliette once more for the god, but it was well and truly gone. The memories I'd gained were still taking shape in my mind, but I understood what the elemental wanted from me. It wanted me to protect Mina, to help her in her task, to sacrifice myself for her, if necessary.

Understanding who I was and how I'd reached this point was the start to helping her. And as that was exactly what I wanted to do, there was nothing in the world stopping me from beginning now. I flexed my wings as much as I could manage in the tight squeeze of the oubliette, dropping into a crouch. It was unfortunate that I'd burned my clothing away, but that was a problem for later. I tucked my wings in tight and closed my eyes.

I sprang off the rocky ground, using a power I'd forgotten this past year or so on Sirin. My body shot upward, as it was meant to, hurtling through the tunnel of the oubliette, breaking through the water and straight into the sky. I had a view of the ruins of Somerhaven as I rose into the sky, which did not surprise me, but further up the mountain and deeper into the forest, a fresh path of destruction caught my eye.

My wings beat steady and true, holding me aloft so I could survey the damage to the mountainside. The enormous evergreens had been flattened in a path that led from the sea to what had once been a grove in the forest. I felt the same pressure I'd felt in the oubliette—the otherworldly presence of the god. *The Ravager is here and already interfering,* came the god's voice in my head. *Your friends are on their way to you, but you are needed at Orchid House.*

I flexed my wings and changed course for the road. If Skye and Morpheus were on their way to me, I would meet them. "Why don't you just go to her directly?" I asked, curious about the god's choice to speak to me, rather than to Mina.

We made a covenant, the god explained. *She must come to me through standing stones. I did not anticipate the quick rise of the Ravager. I believed we had more time.*

There was a hesitation in the god's voice that worried me. This ancient being had been tripped up by a technicality? I chuckled to myself.

There is nothing humorous in this, Ashbourne Thuellos. Why do you laugh?

"Not to you," I laughed, then sobered, thinking over the god's words again. "What is going on in Pravhna?"

The god's voice was distant when it answered, and I could not quite catch all it said. *...maintain the connection... you must hurry.*

The Old One was right. There was nothing funny about this. If Mina was in trouble, I had to go to her. I searched the ground as I flew, watching for Skye and Morpheus. Strong as I was in my Ventyr form, I would have to shift back into my Vilhari alternae; I couldn't be seen in Pravhna like this. The sight of a Ventyr male would strike fear into those who remembered the war, and I had no desire to create chaos.

Below me, I spotted movement on the road. A shining white Studevale sped up the mountain towards Somerhaven. It was Elspeth Aestra's autocar. I dove, tucking my wings into my body. Wind whipped past me as I hurtled toward the autocar, grinning. I had missed this without even knowing it. Flight was a pleasure I never wanted to give up.

Guilt wracked me as soon as the thought came to completion in my head. My Lumina, Mina, would never fly again because of my choices. I swallowed hard, all the joy of the moment gone. My feet slammed down on the rough dirt road, rock and debris cutting into my bare skin. I shifted as quickly as I could, but I could not stop Skye from seeing my true form as the Studevale slowed.

Her mouth opened slightly, a frown knitting between her pale brows. When she stepped out of the autocar, there were tears in her eyes as she flung herself at me. "You're all right," she gasped, words bubbling out of her in a torrent of concern. "I was so worried. Poe said they wouldn't harm you, but still... they've come undone, Ash. Lost it. The things Poe said... That she accused you of. She and Mina..."

"Were all true," I replied as my arms went around her. "Everything they said is true. You saw me. You saw what I truly am. And anything Hippolyta and Mina have accused me of—it's true."

She shook her head. "It can't be. I know you. You are good."

I pushed her away from me, and for the first time, Skye seemed to notice I was unclothed. She frowned. "They said you're the reason the Ravagers are loose. That you're a Ventyr prince... That you are the reason Mina was punished… terribly."

I nodded. "Yes. All that is true. I am so sorry, Skye. If I could take it all back, I would." She looked up at me, her silver eyes wide, emotions battling behind them. "If you no longer trust me, I understand, but I must get to Pravhna to help Mina. Something is wrong."

Morpheus appeared at our feet. *You should dress first, then. We brought dry things for you in the car. Poe suggested you might be wet when we found you.*

"Only naked," I said, attempting a smile.

Skye's expression was helpless for a moment, as though she wasn't sure exactly what to do. I took a deep breath, wondering if I could do all this without her. I'd move faster that way, but it wasn't what I wanted. It would be better for us to be in this together, as we always were.

"Was anything about the past year real?" she asked.

"It was all real," I said. "Every moment. I've only just remembered who I was, and what I've done. The man you knew and trusted existed because of you."

Skye swallowed hard. "And where is he now?"

Still here, Morpheus answered, narrowing his eyes at me from the ground. *Still much the same, but different somehow as well.*

"Yes," I agreed. "I am both Claymore and Thuellos now... but who I was as your partner, Skye, that man wasn't a wholly new creation—" I paused, the realization growing in me as I spoke. A lump formed in my throat. "That is the man I could have been, if I'd never been a Thuellos. If I'd never known the cruelty of the Ventyr, or the endless wars."

Skye's jaw tightened, tears welling in her eyes. "Can I trust you?"

"Yes," I choked out, hoping to all the nameless gods that it was true.

She nodded once, wiping her eyes with the back of her shirtsleeve. "Then get in the car and get dressed. I'll get us to Pravhna."

I placed a hand upon her shoulder. She was shivering in just her close-fitting trousers and shirtsleeves. "Are you sure?"

She smiled at me, watery but steady. "I am always sure of you, my brother. That has not changed."

~

Skye drove swiftly as I dressed and recounted all I'd experienced since we parted ways. My voice cracked around the story of how I failed Mina, how she'd had to kill Helene to save me, but somehow I got through it. She didn't say much. I asked once what had happened to her, but she only shook her head.

Not now, Morpheus said, caution lacing his words. *Later, when we are all safe.*

So, whatever had transpired between Poe and Skye, it had been bad. I had no doubt that Poe was with Mina now, that she'd been with her when I was put in the oubliette. The two of them were closer than lovers ever could be. Their bond was stronger than any I'd ever seen; it rivaled the Claim.

My blood stirred to think of it. The Claim. What would it be like to see her again now that I knew what drove the passion between us? I had to control myself. If she wanted to reverse our bond, I would accept that. The spells were powerful, and the ritual would be painful, but I would do it for her.

I wasn't a brute, like my father, or the Emperor. Both had used the Claim like a weapon against women who could not have loved them otherwise. If Mina did not want me, no longer wanted to honor our bond, I would let her go, hard as that would be. But until then, I knew how powerful the link between us could be. I'd seen its power before, felt its intensity.

As we drove, Skye caught me up on some of what I had missed, though she carefully avoided the topic of what had transpired between herself and Poe. Her most surprising bit of news was that Viridian Montclair was not our enemy, Chopard, or any other vile sort, but rather had been on the same search we were on. He'd been looking for Chopard, in service of the lost Court of Aether. When Skye explained it, the pieces fell into place for me, as I was sure they had for Mina.

I wondered how she took the news that she'd been so wrong about Viridian. It had been hard for Lumina to admit she had been wrong about something, and I could not help but be curious if the same was true for Mina Wildfang.

The undercity whipped by us at dizzying speeds. The narrow streets were shadowed by the canopy of trees, witchlights glimmering in the foliage above us. Clouds of aether billowed out of alleyways, blanketing the street with a thick fog.

I hadn't been gone long, but it felt as though I was coming home, nonetheless. I'd never considered how much I loved the undercity. But coming back to the city with my memory intact felt like coming home in a way that surprised me.

"Don't tell Herself you can drive like this," I said from the backseat. "She'll hire you to drive for her."

Skye chuckled a little, but I heard the nerves rattling her. "How are we going to play this?"

"I doubt it will help if I knock on the door," I reasoned. "What do you two think?"

Morpheus huffed slightly, as though agreeing with me whole-heartedly. *I will go, see what is happening at Orchid House, and return with a plan. If they are in danger, it would be prudent for us to know what we are walking into.*

"Yes," Skye agreed. "That would be best. We will wait for your return." We'd crossed through the Halcyon Gate and were headed to the upper city. The aethereal mist cleared somewhat as the treed canopy cleared.

If I do not come back before you arrive at Orchid House, do not come in after me. Use caution, Morpheus warned before dematerializing.

In the backseat, I slipped into the charcoal-colored frock coat Skye had brought for me. We didn't speak as she sped through Pravhna's crowded streets. Traffic was worse than usual, the preparations for the Grand Exhibition having begun in earnest. In all the bustle of the past months, I'd forgotten about it completely.

The silence between us was awkward. I wasn't sure what to say, and it appeared Skye was at a loss as well. I had to try, though. "Thank you for coming to get me," I said, leaning forward as Skye parked the car a half a block away from Orchid Street. I knew all the views from Orchid House; we were just barely out of sight from the front windows.

"You're welcome," Skye whispered.

I placed a hand on her shoulder, squeezing. "Put your coat on, please. It's cold."

She nodded and pulled her frock coat off the passenger seat, shrugging into it as best she could. The frown on her face let me know how much she worried. The moments ticked by in mind-numbingly uncomfortable silence.

I ran my fingers through my hair, pulling at the shorn ends. I missed my longer hair a bit. "He should be back by now."

Skye nodded, worrying at her bottom lip with her teeth.

"Are we going to do as he asked?"

Skye looked back over her shoulder at me, rolling her eyes. "Of course not." She pushed her car door open, and I followed.

As we walked, she spoke in a low tone. "Circle back around the house. Be ready for my signal."

I nodded, attuning my hearing as well as I could to her. I wanted to hear every moment of what she said. Her heartbeat increased as we parted ways. I looked back over my shoulder at her, but she did not look back at me. I focused hard on her heartbeat. This was a skill we'd worked on many times in our partnership. Vilhari hearing was exceptional, but it took effort to focus it.

As I sped through the alley, I heard Skye knock on the front door. There was a long pause. I tensed as I waited. Finally, she knocked again. It took a few moments, but this time, the door opened.

"Skye Aestra," a voice answered. It was Poe, but her voice was stilted, formal, with none of the warmth she usually had. Things had gone badly between them somehow, but I had no idea they'd gone this badly. "Now is not a good time."

Skye gasped. "Your head, what happ—"

"Now is not a good time, Skye Aestra," Poe repeated in that same forced tone.

The chill in her voice sent a shiver through me that had nothing to do with the cold city air. Poe wouldn't speak to anyone that way, let alone Skye. It didn't matter how angry she was. My stomach clenched tight.

"All right." Skye's voice was even, but I knew she had to be as suspicious as I was about Poe's responses. "My apologies for the intrusion."

My muscles tensed, ready to spring into action as the front door shut with a definitive bang. There was a long pause, as though my friend stood staring at the door before Skye ostensibly headed back towards where the Studevale was parked. Instead, she circled back around, into the alley behind the houses on Orchid Street. As I caught on to her change in direction, I moved to meet her. She met me near the kitchen door.

"Her eyes," Skye gasped, her voice barely a whisper. "They'd gone completely black."

It wasn't as though I was surprised, but the pit of dread that opened in my gut was loathsome. Whatever went on inside Orchid House had to be stopped.

"Like the people at the fires," I breathed.

Skye's brow furrowed. "We should get to Muse, see if we can find out more before we make our next move."

My molars ground against one another, my fangs protruding, dripping with venom. Mina was inside. I sensed her. A Claim forged thousands of years ago was strong, not like it was when we first drove into one another, rutting in an alleyway much like this one. The bond was hungry to taste her again—a wet, live thing, as ravenous for her body as I was.

I could hear Skye's words as she spoke. Something about caution, about not acting in haste. I heard her, and there was a part of me that longed to do as she said, to behave as Claymore would have. But I could not.

My spine lengthened as my glamour fell away.

"Ash!" Skye cried. "Stay here."

"No," I answered, my voice steady with rage as my eyes locked on hers. Someone had trapped Mina. Someone hurt her. This ended now. "*No.*"

CHAPTER 11

MINA

1 *0 minutes earlier.*
My face was an oozing mess, my left eye swollen shut. I was bound to a chair in Maman's sitting room, one of the horrifically uncomfortable ones, which made the past twelve hours that much more unbearable. Poe sat across from me, weeping. Her knuckles were bloody, and every time she looked at them, she wept harder.

I tried to comfort her through the gag in my mouth, but I couldn't manage anything discernible. I hope she understood the look in my eyes to mean, "I don't blame you." Hot, angry tears slipped down my face as Viridian's black eyes bored into mine. He was fighting the control better than Poe had; he was holding back his punches.

My darling Poe hadn't been able to, hitting me again and again. I'd heard her right hand break an hour ago, but she only kept pummeling me. Every time I thought I was out of tears, fresh ones spilled out of me. I don't think I'd ever cried this hard, for this long.

In the chair next to me sat Helene, dressed in a snow white directoire-style gown that clung to her curves. Its neck rose high enough to hide the wound I'd created just days before when I killed her. Her form was completely corporeal now, but every so often, she faded around the edges, as though she could not quite hold onto this plane of existence. She smiled sweetly at me, her blue eyes compassionate.

"You see, my darling. It's as I always told you. No one loves you. No one cares for you but me." She locked eyes on Viridian. "Hit her again."

His fist met my cheekbone, and I cried out, but it hardly hurt. His jaw clenched hard. He was still fighting it. I tried not to look too hard at him, lest I tip Helene off, but I was tired.

Helene tracked my gaze, fury building in her posture. Her delicate fingers clenched into fists. "Useless," she snarled, moving with an unnatural gait, the creature within her exposing its gaping maw as she stood and lurched towards Viridian, backhanding him across the face. His eyes returned to their usual pale blue as he stumbled backwards.

"You again." Helene motioned to Poe, regaining her composure. "Stop mewling and get up."

"No," Viridian gasped. "Use me." He hung his head, shame flushing his pale cheeks. "I won't fight it anymore."

His eyes met mine, and I nodded once, giving him permission to let go, to stop fighting to protect Poe. At first, I thought Helene only meant to intimidate us. When we'd woken, bound with some metal that kept us from using magic, I'd thought that eventually my sister, inhabited by the Ravager, would see reason. That she'd reveal whatever it was she wanted. But now I had my doubts. This had gone on for too long. Now I wondered if she only meant to kill me slowly, to use the people who loved me to break me.

From the back of the house came footsteps. Brigitte entered the room, her taloned fingers clutching a huge grain sack that growled piteously. Whatever was inside it was furious, but injured. My heart ached to hear it.

Please don't let it be Morpheus, I prayed to whatever gods might still listen.

"The greymalkin." Brigitte crushed all my hopes as she sat the bag down by the fire. "I caught it trying to sneak in. Should I destroy it?"

"No," Helene crooned, her voice saccharine. "It will have its time."

I couldn't understand how they were both so strong, so fast. The three of us had tried to fight back at first, but there was nothing for it. I had been foolish not to consider that if the Ravager had Helene's body, if it was using it as a vessel, that it could enter the house. That we weren't safe here. Orchid House had never been safe, but my carelessness had cost us dearly.

"Get up," Helene commanded Poe.

Rage boiled in my gut. No one should speak to Poe that way. Poe's eyes went dark, but I knew from all the times before that whatever vile power my sister wielded, it allowed Poe to see what she was forced to do. That she was present for every sickening punch, every cut of the knives on the table next to me. I healed, and then she hurt me again and again.

"Do you understand yet?" Helene asked me as Poe stumbled awkwardly towards me. "Are you ready to let go?"

My words were muffled against my gag.

"What's that?" Helene asked, as Brigitte sat down on the couch next to Viridian. He glared at the Strix, but could not move a muscle. "Oh, you're gagged, that's right," Helene said with a girlish giggle. My sister had never acted like this. Like me, Helene was a serious creature who rarely laughed. No one who grew up with Maman had much room in their countenance for joy.

Sometimes she seemed like the person I grew up with, and sometimes she did not. This giggling monster was both Helene and *not* at the same time. It was as though the creature had burrowed inside Helene and twisted, and twisted, until this hideous thing had appeared. It looked like Helene, and sounded like her, but it certainly was not *wholly* Helene Wildfang.

For one thing, I knew without a doubt that my sister had died. I killed her myself, and I would carry the weight of that forever. Whatever this creature was, it was not Helene, but also not a fetch, like the body my spirit inhabited. It was Helene's body, and at least part of her soul, but it was also the Ravager within her.

I made a noise against the gag again. This time, Helene sighed and moved towards me, gently prying the cloth away from my mouth. "There," she soothed, running her ice-cold thumb over my cheek. "Is that better?"

I nodded, working my jaw a little, trying to get saliva to activate in my mouth again. "What do you want?" I managed to rasp out.

Helene smiled. "You're not ready to know yet. You pretend that you are, but you're protecting them. When you hate them for what they're doing to you, *then* we will talk."

She pushed the gag back into my mouth. Her touch was sweet, gentle, and she kissed my cheek when she was done. Only Viridian and Poe hurt me. Helene touched me with kindness. I knew what she was doing. She'd made it clear that she meant to make me hate Poe and Viridian, but not why. I watched closely as she moved towards the bag that held Morpheus.

"I wonder what this one might do to her under my control," she mused to Brigitte.

The Strix sighed, picking at the damask on Maman's uncomfortable sofa. "This is boring. Besides, you're not following the rules. You were supposed to bring her to our side, make her see our way of thinking, not beat her half to death."

Helene rolled her eyes. "You haven't been paying attention, Brigitte. I have been doing exactly that. She won't see *our* side until she hates *this* one." She gestured towards Poe, Viridian, and Morpheus.

This was as much as they'd spoken to one another. Thus far, they'd been careful not to let too much be known. Now I wondered if they'd gotten careless.

"Hit her again, Poe," Helene commanded.

Just as Poe drew her arm back to do so, there was a knock at the door. Helene startled, but composed herself quickly. "Muzzle him," she commanded Brigitte, who tore a strip from Viridian's fine shirt. He groaned. "Have you any idea how much that cost?"

Beneath my gag, I laughed, hysterical tears springing to my eyes. The warmth in his cool eyes gave me strength as Brigitte shoved the fabric into his mouth. I had never loved Viridian Montclair as much as I did at that moment. The pure strength of will it took to keep that kind of attitude was something I admired deeply. And he used it to lift my spirits, and Poe's, buried deep as she was under Helene's will.

Poe's fist came down on my face. A bone protruded from her

knuckles as she hit me, the fracture breaking her skin and mine at almost the same time. She didn't make a sound.

I locked eyes with Viridian, tears spilling freely from my eyes now. Helene's efforts would fail time and time again. She only made me love Poe more. The more she hurt me, the more I knew that my Poe would never do anything so cruel to me. I trusted Poe more deeply than I ever had.

I locked eyes with her, gazing into those obsidian depths. *I love you*, I said to her, trying to reach the part of her that could hear me. It worked in her Feriant form, it had to work now. *I trust you.*

"Again," Helene commanded.

There was another knock at the front door. Brigitte stood, narrowing her eyes at me and Poe, who had not yet hit me again. "She's trying to mindspeak with her. It's getting through."

"Damnit," Helene swore. "Answer the door, Poe. Tell whoever it is to go away. Tell them this is not a good time."

Poe nodded once, then started to walk towards the front door. Brigitte ran after her with a pair of gloves, and shoved them onto her hands before pushing her towards the door. They were a pair of black lace day gloves that had been Maman's. They weren't much, but they would hide the wounds on her hands for anyone who wasn't looking too carefully.

"The rest of you will be perfectly quiet," Helene said, picking up the sharp poker from amongst the fireplace tools. She nudged the bag that held Morpheus. "Or I will stab the greymalkin, many, many times." Her eyes lit merrily at her words, as though she relished the thought.

The slow sound of the heavy front door opening was torture. I longed to scream, but I believed Helene when she said she would kill Morpheus. I closed my eyes.

"Skye Aestra," Poe said, her voice strained. "Now is not a good time."

Skye. Skye was here. As was Morpheus. Was Ashbourne here as well? I tried to do the calculations in my head. Could they have gotten to him already? I had not locked him in the oubliette, trusting that he would make his way out when he was ready—when he understood my perspective.

Out on the front step, Skye gasped. "Your head, what happ—"

"Now is not a good time, Skye Aestra," Poe repeated.

Surely that flat tone had to make Skye suspicious. And her eyes were black. Would Skye notice? Much as I wished for calm rationality, we could not take much more. Panic infected every breath I took, every thought that crossed my mind.

"All right," Skye responded. "My apologies for the intrusion."

My heart sank as the front door shut. She was going, and there had been no sign of Ash. Perhaps Skye was too angry to notice Poe's eyes. The scene between them before Poe joined me had been difficult, from the little I'd gathered. Love was occlusive. It hid what was right in front of us. Skye was an experienced private investigator, an expert when it came to details, but her love might keep her oblivious to what she'd seen. Poe came back to the sitting room, her eyes still dark with Helene's strange power.

"Sit," Helene hissed, pacing back and forth now. She glared at Brigitte. "I thought you said Skye Aestra was out of the city. Gone."

"She was," Brigitte insisted. "I can't be blamed for her coming back. I don't control them, Helene. *I* don't have that power."

Helene smiled. "Of course you don't, my love. Only I have that gift."

Brigitte rolled her eyes, but Helene stroked her face. "Go after her. Follow her. Find where she's off to." Helene sat on my lap, plopping down like a bony sack of flour. "We will be just fine here on our own." She kissed my face, her lips cold on my hot skin.

The dynamic between them was more strained than it had ever been. When we were children, Helene and Brigitte had seemed so aligned. As Helene aged, they'd disagreed more, been more at odds. Now, it was almost as though Helene had taken something vital from Brigitte. Through the haze of pain and confusion that clouded my mind, I wondered what it could be.

Brigitte left the sitting room, and then the house, out the front door. When we were alone, Helene stroked my face. "What kinds of games should we play while Brigitte is gone? What would you like to do together now that we are alone?"

I narrowed my eyes—even that hurt, due to the damage to my face. Helene's words were edged with a kind of sickness I wanted nothing to do with. Her expression turned dark, interpreting my confusion as hostility. I needed to buy some time. A tiny bit of confidence built within me, rationality taking the reins once more.

Skye would work out that something was wrong with Poe. Their parting might have been difficult, but not so difficult that she would believe Poe would treat her that way. Besides, if Morpheus was here, Skye was most definitely waiting for him. When he didn't return with news of us, any suspicions she had about that strange encounter would solidify. Yes. Skye would help us. My job was to give her time to work out a plan.

I shook my head and nodded toward Viridian and Poe. Helene smiled. "Oh, you don't want them here? I understand. There are things sisters can only say to one another in private." She hopped off my lap. "Come," she ordered. Their black eyes blinked in unison and she led them out of the room.

Their footsteps echoed through the main hall and to the back of the house. There was a long pause, and then came the snick of a lock. She'd locked them in the housekeeper's office then. My heart raced. Whatever Helene wanted to do with me was likely nothing good, but we weren't truly alone.

In fact, the tie on the bag Brigitte had trapped Morpheus in was very loose now. I wasn't sure how it was keeping him in to begin with, but I figured it had something to do with the substance that had bound the rest of us. Now the bag was open and one of Morpheus' paws snuck out.

Promptly, it disappeared, though the bag still looked as though he was trapped inside. If Helene looked at it too carefully, she would see that he was not, but that just meant that I had to distract her. The heels of her pretty leather boots clicked on the marble floors as she walked back to me. I prayed hard that Morpheus could help Poe and Viridian get loose, at least. If only they could escape, they could find Skye, and the four of them could get Ashbourne together.

I feared the thing inside my sister was too strong to be fought by normal means alone. We needed empyrae, and if I was bound, then only Ashbourne could fight her. They would bring him. He would help me. This much I knew. My head was so heavy. Everything was *so* heavy.

"Don't sleep," Helene sang as she plopped back down in my lap.

I must have nodded off for a moment. I didn't see or hear her coming. She stroked my face again.

"Poor little Lumina," Helene said, but this time it was not my sister's voice that came out of Helene's mouth, but the sound of myriad whispers, mixed with screams. It was the sound of power and braying hellshounds. "So much damage to one weak little body, but still you fight." Helene's palm slammed against my aching chest, pressing against my heart as though she would reach through my flesh and tear it out. "It is why I want you so much."

Her face was close to mine now, her breath hot on my skin. "You will want me too before the end." Her fingers dug at the tatters of my dress. "You will want me so badly you'll beg for me to take you."

I recoiled from the hideous words, from their heinous undertones. Somewhere in the back of the house, the tiniest of noises caught my interest. The thing inside Helene was too focused on me to have heard, but it would not be distracted for long.

I nodded, speaking one word against the gag. *Yes.*

Helene's eyes narrowed, glittering like sapphires. She pulled down the gag. "What was that, little mouse?"

Her voice was her own again. I feigned exhaustion, which was not hard at the moment, nodding. "Anything..." I rasped out. "Anything to make it stop."

Helene smiled. "Do you expect me to believe you are that weak?"

I caught the movement behind her before she had a chance to react. "No," I said, before ducking as much as I could while bound.

Morpheus had materialized on the mantel, and now launched himself at Helene, throwing her to the floor. She snarled with anger, trying to grasp onto him. But he simply dematerialized, only to reappear the next moment, hooking his claws into her and tearing at her dead flesh, then disappearing again as she screamed.

And then Ashbourne Thuellos was in front of me, naked, glorious, and vibrating with power. It took me a moment to realize he had shed his glamour, that he was in his Ventyr form. Helene roared from the floor, still fighting Morpheus, who tormented her so fiercely it won new depths of respect from within me. A feral scream boiled out of me: "Release me."

CHAPTER 12

MINA

Ashbourne knelt behind me, fussing with my bonds as the scream died in my throat. His fingers were gentle, and he didn't say a word, but I felt the intensity of his gaze. The man I knew, in all lifetimes and iterations, would be marking every cut and bruise on my body.

I was angry with him still, but more than that, I needed his rage to bring me back to life. The impact of the past hours came rushing down on me and I feared I might be too tired to provide much aid.

"Empyrae," I managed to squeak out.

I smelled sulfur, and just as I got free, Helene caught Morpheus in her hands. Her nails dug into him, eliciting a hideous yowl.

"Go," I begged, slumping against the side of my chair. Morpheus did as I asked, disappearing as I stared up at Ashbourne's beautiful face and wings. Three sets of powerful draconic wings. They were strong enough to carry me away.

"You came." I swayed as unconsciousness threatened to take me.

"Of course I did," he said, as he gathered me into his powerful arms, pressing me against his bare chest. "I will always come for you." As he drew my head closer to his, he whispered, "I always have, haven't I? No matter how ill advised."

I managed a laugh. It was inappropriate, of course, but the joke was good, all the same. Helene lunged for me, grasping my hair. She was strong. Stronger than Ash, I feared. My body, now broken and exhausted, recoiled from her as Ash sprang back. She would have me in her grip in moments.

Ash's eyes locked on mine, a question in them. We had no time for words. I nodded, sensing what I knew he did. The Claim's bond had snapped back into place, active once more. It had merely been dormant when we had forgotten one another, a mere shadow of what it truly was.

Now that we remembered one another, it was hungry. This was part of why I'd locked him beneath the sea, merely to have some time away from this feeling. Now, the magic that bound our souls wanted blood, wanted fuel to feed its unquenchable raging fire. Whether it would work as it should in this body was anyone's guess, but this was our best shot at escaping Helene.

We'd both fought Ravagers before, and the look in Ashbourne's eyes told me he knew we weren't getting out of here alive if we fought. We had to escape. That was our only chance. My Claimed opened his mouth and latched onto my wrist. My neck would have been better, but this would do. As soon as his venom hit my blood-stream, I knew it would work. Fangs this body had never possessed protracted from my gums, venom miraculously appearing in my mouth.

It shouldn't be possible, but it happened all the same. My body knew the Claim no matter what form it took. Ancient, unknowable magic, irrational and unguarded, flowed through me.

He shoved his wrist in my mouth before Helene could do another thing. As we both drew blood from one another, my body strength-ened. Helene grabbed my hair and dragged me away, my skin tearing as Ashbourne's fangs were ripped from my body. She had me in her grip, but the little I'd tasted of my Claimed had been enough.

"Now," I whispered, knowing that Ash could hear me.

I loosed pure otham, the most concentrated form of aether I could muster, at Helene. It knocked her backwards, as I threw myself at Ashbourne's feet. I had to trust that Poe and Viridian were already taken care of. Empyrae flew from Ashbourne's hands, blasting towards Helene. We would burn with her, if he was not careful, but Ashbourne Thuellos had not been High Commander of his father's armies for nothing. One arm scooped me from the floor, pinning me to his chest as though I were light as a child. From his free hand flowed white-hot celestial fire that engulfed Helene.

"We must go," he said to me, his voice gentle and deep. "Hold tight."

I nodded, wrapping myself around him in every way I could. And though I knew it was a terrible mistake to do so, I kissed him. I kissed him so hard I didn't even notice when Orchid House slipped away. I only knew that he had gotten me out of there.

As we stole through the house, and leapt into the air, he kissed me back. I recognized the feeling of flight, though it had been centuries since I had been able to do so myself. Speed, power, and then a certain sense of weightless joy. I had no desire to look down, to see the city below. The only thing I wanted to do was cling to Ashbourne. I squeezed my eyes shut against everything.

It was shameful to want him this way. To feel so safe in his arms when I was still so angry with him. When we landed, I held tightly to him, afraid of what would happen when I opened my eyes.

"It's all right," he said, stroking my hair. "Mina, please."

I slipped out of his arms, feeling grass beneath my feet. The smell of night air hit my nostrils, petrichor signaling that rain would begin soon. We had to be on one of the high echelons for so much to still be growing. Still, I could not open my eyes. I was afraid to see anything, know anything but Ashbourne's hands on my back.

I fell to my knees on soft grass, retching. Ashbourne gathered my hair in his hands, holding it for me as I heaved. As I had nothing in my stomach, this was little more than exhausting, but my body would not calm.

"Mina," his deep voice vibrated in my ear. "You are safe."

"Poe?" I managed to choke out, but couldn't manage more words.

"Safe, with Skye. I promise. Viridian and Morpheus too. They'll be here soon."

Relief filled me as I opened my eyes. "Promise?"

"Yes," he breathed, his golden eyes locking on mine. "I would never lie to you about something so important. They are safe. Morpheus let me know."

I nodded, my chest still heaving with sobs, though it seemed I was out of tears. He sat down on the ground beside me, still holding my hair back, watching me with so much care, he might have been looking at treasure. "Where are we?" I managed to choke out.

"House Aestra," he said.

Finally, my body seemed content that there was nothing left to retch out. The heaving slowed, and I was left shivering. "You're bigger than I remember," I said as I fell over onto the grass.

He looked down at me with amusement, then gestured to his Ventyr form. He *was* at least a foot taller, his skin a light, opalescent blue, his dark hair falling into his face. The beautiful lines of his Vilhari alternae were harsher now, more rugged, and if possible, more handsome. My body suddenly felt less ill, heat pooling in my belly as my eyes traveled downward, past the wings that flexed behind him, to the erection that stood proudly between his legs.

It wasn't really the time for such things, but the Claim worked in mysterious ways. Rather than blushing, or covering up, as the Ash Claymore of just days ago might have, Ashbourne grinned at me. "Do you like what you see, princess?" he murmured, so much cheek in his words I nearly slapped him.

There was no hiding that I liked it, that I wanted him inside me, that I would climb atop him right now and ride him into oblivion. It was something I was deeply considering, in fact, having remembered at just this moment that the healing properties between Claimed were more intense if the bond was renewed during intercourse. My body was still battered to pieces, and I needed help.

But my pride ran too deep. I wished I had not kissed him—had not stirred this violent need for him. I wished I had never seen his beautiful face again, or needed his help. My mind raced with all my wishes, all my thoughts, until he reached out one long arm, his knuckle dragging softly over my bruised cheekbone.

He leaned towards me, his lips brushing my ear, as his fingers trailed lightly over my wounds. "Why don't you let me fix this?"

"No," I growled, scooting away from him.

For a moment, he looked hurt, but my movement sent my scent

into the air. Ashbourne Thuellos smirked at me. *Smirked.* My hatred for him was thousands of years old, and it boiled to the surface now. That smirk did it to me every time—reminded me of who he really was.

"Just because my body thinks it wants you, doesn't mean *I* do," I snarled. *Lies, lies, all lies.* "There is a difference between the bond and *me.*"

There really was not. Perhaps there had been, once. But now? Now, despite my most fervent wishes to the contrary, I feared I was wholly aligned with the Claim. It was not a thing I could give into, though, however much I wanted him.

Ashbourne drew back from me. Sorrow filled his eyes. His mouth opened, and I thought for a moment he might apologize. He looked like the man I fell in love with until his lips closed and the mask slammed down. He was pure Prince Ashbourne now.

"Then gather the supplies we need for the bond reversal," he said with a casual smile. "If you want to be rid of me, you only have to say the word."

His words slammed into me, hitting right where he knew they would hurt. My fear of being unlovable—I had confessed it to him in the little time we had together in that life before. I had told him that I thought I could trust him. I had told him how easy it always seemed for others to use me, discard me, *abandon* me.

Something flickered behind his eyes as the hurt sank in, something like regret, but I would never know because I forced myself to my feet. "I am too injured for the bond reversal," I said, trying to keep my voice steady. "You know I wouldn't survive it."

He shrugged, but I saw the concern in the tense set of his shoulders as I said what we both knew to be true. The bond reversal ritual was brutal. Survivable, if both parties were healthy, but the tearing of two intertwined souls was no easy feat. In the best of times, I would be damaged from it for months, if not years. Now, in this body, with all this pain… It might be worse.

That was a risk I couldn't take right now. Wind cut down from the top of the mountain, tearing into me until I shivered uncontrollably. I stumbled towards the door to the house. I remembered the way from the party we'd attended here not long ago.

Ashbourne scooped me into his arms. "No need to walk, princess."

"Don't call me that," I grumbled.

He yanked me closer to him, pulling my face close to his. His fingers knotted in my hair, at the base of my neck, forcing my eyes to meet his. Every nerve in my body sang with pleasure at his touch. My back arched as my breath quickened, plush heat gathering in my belly, swirling as it moved lower.

"What do you want me to call you then? Lumina? Mina? My beautiful menace?" His last word was a snarl: "Lover?" My breath came in fast, wet, pants now as the arms that held me tightened. "The only thing I want to call you is *mine*," he snarled.

A flood of heat rushed between my legs. *His.* I was already his. I had been for centuries, and my body had just been waiting, biding its time, hungering for him. My arms twined around his neck as a whimpering mewl came out of me, needy and wild as I felt inside.

"Yes," was the only word I could manage.

"Yes, *what?*" he demanded. His tone was harsh, but there was a plea beneath it, a desperation.

There was no denying it; we would have to fulfill the Claim, or it would drive us both to distraction. This was the fervor. It usually affected those who had coupled, but not Claimed one another, those who were ripe for the bond. But it could affect Claimed pairs that had been separated for long periods of time as well. If it was not fulfilled, or the bond broken magically, then it could cause us significant problems perceiving reality.

Neither of us could afford that right now. I wanted this on so many levels, but more than that, I needed it. Needed him. Needed the healing he could provide, and if I was honest with myself for even a moment, I needed any scrap of love I could get right now. Something to ground me after the hours I spent in Helene's company. He could make all that go away for a little while. He could make me forget with just his touch.

"Make me yours. Now."

His mouth met mine in a fury of lips and tongues.

"Is there anyone here?" I asked, breathless from the kiss.

"We have a few minutes," he answered as he crossed the terrace in four short steps to a tiny gazebo. He was just as breathless as I was.

The terrace was lit with witchlights, but the gazebo was enclosed in glass for the cold season. Ashbourne sat down on one of the benches, pulling me atop his lap. He ripped my undergarments from me like they were wet paper, pulling me down atop him. My body was more than ready as I sank down on him, letting him fill me.

The feeling was pure bliss. Venom filled my mouth as I moved on him, undulating my hips to chase the waves of pleasure coursing through me. Ashbourne's hands slid up my body, his eyes burning with reverent desire.

"Is this what you wanted?" he asked. "Is this enough?"

"No," I snarled, moving faster as his hands gripped my hips, driving me down on him harder. "Is it enough for you?"

"No," he growled, yanking me closer. "It won't be enough 'til I fill you completely. 'Til you are mine completely."

"Do it," I commanded, arching my back.

His hands cupped my breasts, and he smiled, wholly the wicked prince in this moment, his thumbs grazing over the peaks of my breasts until they stiffened under his touch. "Next time, I will bite you here."

"There will be no next time," I replied, though my reply sounded weak.

He smiled again, pulling me closer to him, slowing my movements. Without thinking, I whimpered.

"Such a soft and needy thing," he murmured, one hand skimming down my belly, lower and lower, dipping under the hem of my dress that pooled between us.

When his thumb met the spot I needed him most, his words set me aflame. "There will never be enough of this, my beautiful girl. Not for you, and certainly not for me."

His mouth claimed mine, our venom mixing with each slide of our tongues, the taste intoxicating as he deepened the kiss further, his thumb's ministrations intensifying between my legs as he allowed me to increase the pace of our lovemaking once more.

Heat built in me as each movement brought me higher. Ashbourne kissed me harder, until I could take no more. I broke the kiss as my back arched, my entire body tightening around him as white light filled my eyes, shadows of aether flowing from me, twining with the light that escaped him. His fangs closed around my neck as I screamed his name, power flowing between us as he emptied his release into me.

The pain in my entire body receded for a few brief seconds of blissful relief. Nothing hurt, all was pleasure as he filled me with everything I needed to survive. As the high wore off, and my vision cleared, my shadows receding back into me, we stared into one another's eyes.

His mouth opened, as though he would say something, but I shook my head. "Say nothing." I climbed off him. "We only did this to stave off the fervor. We can't do it again."

The evidence of our encounter slid between my thighs, which I pressed tightly together. "Do you understand?"

"No," he said, a smug smile on his lips. "I hear what you're saying, but I think you'll climb into my lap again." He took my hand, his lips grazing my fingers.

"We solved our problem," I said, snatching my hand back. "The fervor. It will be sated now. And when I'm better—"

Ashbourne stood, his cock still at attention. He drew his hand across my face and cupped my chin in his fingers. Fingers that smelled of me. He tipped my chin upwards and pressed a gentle kiss to my lips. "When you are better, *nothing*," he said as he straightened. "The fervor is the least of your problems, beautiful girl. You love me."

CHAPTER 13

ASHBOURNE

Mina glared up at me, her beautiful gray eyes glossy with lust. She was magnificent, glowing with the power of our bond. It was all I could do not to pull her down on me again. The fervor had gone—she was right—but to think that I was sated was foolish. I only wanted more of her.

"Love is not enough," she snarled, gorgeous in her ferocity. Nameless gods be damned. Everything she did was sensual.

"Nothing is *enough* when it comes to you and me," I growled back, matching her ferocity, beat by beat. "That is what makes us, *us*. That we cannot get enough of each other."

Her breath shuddered through her. I kneeled before her, my hand sliding up her bare leg, between her thighs. "You see?" I whispered as her legs opened for me. "There is never enough. You want more already."

Her lips parted. "Ash," she begged as I stroked my fingers over her slick skin, teasing her, strumming her pleasure like a lyre.

She shook beneath my touch as I pulled her towards me, and brought my mouth between her legs, closing my lips around her. Her fingers wound into my hair, pressing me harder into her. From deep within the house, I heard Skye arrive with Poe and Morpheus. Beneath us, the house was waking up.

No matter, Skye could explain it all to them. We needed to be right here, right now. I filled my mouth with Mina, feasting on her with a hunger I hadn't felt in years. I'd let myself forget the way she felt, the way she tasted, but even in the fetch, she was the same as she'd been the months after we Claimed one another. The sounds she made as I touched her spurred me on.

"Yes," I urged her. "Take what you need from me."

She tensed, then pulled away. "What I *need* is time."

Her voice was clear. We were done playing then. She was safe, she was mostly healed, though I could tell her pain was already creeping back in. I stood, then made a show of sucking the evidence of her off my wet fingers.

"You are terrible," she said.

"Am I?" I countered.

She turned towards the door. "I don't want to do this, Ashbourne. This thing we did back then. The banter, the angry love-making—I want none of it." She looked back over her shoulder for a moment, her eyes full of sadness. "I fell in love with a man who loved me wholly, without all that. Ashbourne Claymore is the man I loved, but he does not exist anymore."

She pushed the door to the terrace open and disappeared inside the house. I could not move. It was as though I could feel every inch of the bond crack. A tiny fissure, to be sure, but I felt the pain of losing her acutely. She loved the man I'd been before I remembered my true self. Before *she* remembered Ashbourne Thuellos.

And now that she remembered who I was, this was all I was good for: quelling the fervor. Indignation, arrogant and cold, rose within me. I loved Wilhelmina Wildfang, loved her more deeply than I had ever loved another person. It made her abject rejection of who I was, who I'd been, sting that much more. And a part of me wanted to lash out with cruel words. To hurt her and twist her back toward me, as I would have done long, long ago.

As quickly as it came, my arrogance faded. I stared up at the night sky, the cosmic dance that crossed universes above, and whispered an ancient prayer, one I had not spoken in centuries. It was a prayer for battle, but was not a war prayer. Those inflated things had never meant much to me, even as High Commander of House

Thuellos' armies. This prayer was for a restitution of spirit, for a measure of peace I no longer knew how to find.

If I made the same angry mistakes now that I made when we were young, all would end up as it once had—in ruin. I could not afford this, and not just because I liked Sirin, loved it even, and wanted to see it remain whole. But I also wanted more for myself. All these centuries of life, and I had never truly lived.

I'd had a taste of life as Ashbourne Claymore, but while that was not a false self, it was not the truest of my inner lives. It was, as I had told Skye, the self I could have been if everything had been perfect for me. I had to find a way to reconcile all of my myriad, ancient parts with the person I'd been with Skye and Morpheus, the man Mina fell in love with.

The door to the terrace opened. I waited, still staring up at the night sky, as Skye made her way to me. "I brought you clothes," she said, as she came to stand next to me.

I took the garments she offered. There was a way, of course, to shift without destroying my clothing, and I would have to practice that skill if I did not want to continue to spend so much time unclothed. I shifted back into my Vilhari alternae and dressed quickly. "Is Poe all right?"

Skye's entire body tensed. "No. Mina is with her now."

I nodded. "That is best. How did she sustain those injuries?"

My friend's chin quivered, and she shook her head, as though she couldn't bear to speak the words. She grimaced as she spoke. "Viridian says that Helene forced them to beat Mina. Took them over by magic—like the people found at the fires."

My stomach tightened with fear and rage. "How is this possible? What was that thing I saw? You cannot tell me it was Helene. People don't come back from the dead."

But that was not true, and I knew it. There were ways to bring a soul back. Old ways. Dangerous ways. Ways that should never have existed. If someone had brought Helene back from the dead, we were in terrible danger.

The knuckles on Skye's hands went white as she clenched her fists. "I don't know, Ash. We're so far out of our depth."

"Is that why we're here?" I asked quietly. "Are you hoping your mother and grandmother might illuminate all this for us? Or do you have something to prove?"

There was something Skye wasn't telling me. Something that happened between her and Poe while I was away that she didn't want to tell me. Skye walked to the heavy stone balustrade and bent over it, resting her forearms on its wide surface.

She craned her neck to look up at the stars, as I had only minutes before. "She and Mina are worried. They think my family might collectively be Chopard."

I took a long breath in, turning the idea over in my mind. As a princess, Lumina had been one of the most strategic Ventyr I'd ever known. When she made a mistake, she adjusted quickly and in harsh measure. Once she'd discovered how wrong she'd been about Viridian and House Montclair, she would have gone over all the evidence again. I could see why she'd landed on House Aestra.

I didn't believe that she truly suspected them of being Chopard, but if she thought as I did now, she suspected them of *something*. In the past, I had been reluctant to confront uncomfortable truths with Skye, preferring to let her come to her own conclusions. After all, who was I to tell her how to think about things?

Now, with the weight of vast experience in my memory, I spoke with as much gentle kindness as I could muster. "You can see why they might be suspicious, can't you?"

Skye's jaw twitched as she glanced sidelong up at me. "Yes."

Her terse answer told me all I needed to know. This is what she and Poe had fought over. Skye saw reason—the investigator in her understood exactly why her family was in question—but it had damaged her pride. She was allowed to be angry with them, criticize them, even hate them, but no one else was.

"Show her she was wrong, and then admit you were as well," I said.

Skye let out a wry laugh. "And will you be doing the same with Mina?"

I chuckled. That was a fair assessment. "Eventually," I said, mimicking Skye's position against the balustrade. "You are right. We are out of our depth here, and we must learn to swim quickly."

Skye nodded. "Indeed, we must. Let's go inside then, and begin to practice."

CHAPTER 14

MINA

By the time I got downstairs, Viridian had allowed Elspeth Aestra to administer a healing tonic to Poe, and she was resting in an upstairs bedroom that I was fairly certain had been Skye's when she lived here. The room was sparsely decorated, in muted tones of sage and cream. Someone had bathed Poe's face and dressed her in soft, comfortable clothing. She was tucked into Skye's bed, and was near sleep when I entered.

She winced as soon as she saw me, looking away from me. My heart pounded so hard I thought my chest might crack open. Helene had not broken me, but perhaps she'd never actually meant to. Perhaps she'd meant to break Poe, to make her hate me—that would be a much easier task.

My hand went to my chest, as though I could quell the fear that pulsed through me like a living thing. A horrible noise came out of me, a sound of uncontrolled panic at the thought of Poe hating me. Her head turned slowly, but she took altogether too long to drag her eyes up my body, and see that I'd healed. When her gaze finally met mine, her bottom lip trembled. "I can never apologize for what I've done."

I rushed to the bed, kneeling on the floor next to it and taking her hand in mine, careful not to squeeze too hard. "If you apologize, I will scream," I said, kissing her hand as gently as I could. "I don't blame you for one bit of what happened."

Never had I seen Poe so lifeless; she was nothing if not vibrant, but Helene had taken something from her. Her voice was flat, emotionless. "I don't know how you could forgive me."

I looked up at her. She looked nothing like my Poe, open and loving. It was as though she had shut down entirely, everything that made her emptied out, lost. I knew that feeling all too well. What could I do to help her? What would help me?

"There is nothing to forgive," I said, even knowing she would not believe me.

Indeed, she looked away from me, pulling her hand from mine. "Go away, Mina," she whispered. "Leave me be."

I stood, looking around the room. There was a sturdy wood chair at the desk in the corner under the tall window that looked out on the city. I dragged it to the bed and sat down in it. "No."

A sob broke over her, shaking her small body. Usually, it was easy to forget that Poe was a rather tiny person. She took up space with her spirit. But now she looked small and fragile, not the dynamic woman who'd led me out of so much darkness. It was time for me to be her light. She taught me how to do this. The least I could do was return all the love she'd given me.

I let her cry for a bit before speaking, gathering as much wisdom as I could as I waited. If it were me in the bed, I knew she would only have one chance to change my mind. But Poe was better at all this than I was. I collected every scrap of empathy she'd taught me in the time I'd known her, stitching the pieces together like a quilt.

When I spoke, my voice shook, but I knew the words were ones she might have used. "I know what you are telling yourself. You're reciting all the ways you've faltered, all the mistakes you have made, all the wrong moves and bad ideas you've ever had."

Her sobs quieted, as though she considered what I said. I was on the right track, then. "You are calling yourself terrible names, names you would never call me, or anyone you love. The voice inside you is busy berating you, ranting about your own unworthiness."

She was silent now, breathing evenly, but still not making eye contact with me. That was fine. It was more comfortable to talk without it, at least for now. I needed Poe to hear me. "I know you, Poe. All of the social graces in the world cannot hide your true self from me. It's all a mask. You do it so that you can stave off the voices you hear now. The voices that sound right because you just spent the last day viciously beating me."

She took a sharp gasp in, a shrill sound of pure agony seeping out of her. These words were the right ones. They hurt, but did not injure. This was the pain of clearing the wounds of infection.

"Cry, my darling," I said as tears sprang to my eyes along with hers. "Let it out. Let it all wash away. You were forced to be vicious and cruel, but we survived. We survived because you did not fight her. You saw what happened when Viridian fought back. You read her right. Letting Helene use you for her cruelty was cunning. It bought us the time Morpheus and the others needed to get to us."

We sat in silence for a long time. I felt her thinking, fighting all I'd said, but I did my best not to say more. She had to work this out for herself. Finally, Poe's hand stretched towards mine. I took it, clasping it tightly. It was not the broken hand. That one she held close to her chest.

I breathed a sigh of relief. "We survived because you saw things clearly. You have nothing to apologize for."

"How did you know?" she whispered.

I smiled. "Because it is exactly what I would have done. I would have hated every moment of it, as you did, but I would have beat you to a pulp to keep her going, if it had been the other way around."

She nodded. "So long as she didn't ask me to kill you, I couldn't fight her. She was getting something out of it."

I nodded. "Yes. You are right. We learned something from it, didn't we?"

Now Poe nodded. "We learned many things." Her eyes looked too heavy to keep open.

I bent over, kissing her forehead. "We did. And now you have to sleep."

"What if it's not safe here?" she murmured sleepily.

"Nowhere is safe, my darling," I whispered back as she drifted off. I turned off the lamp and sat with her in the dark for a long time, listening to the even noise of her breath.

I strongly suspected that I'd arrived just in time. If she'd been allowed to sit with her thoughts much longer, they might have taken root. Poe needed someone to tell her that all the ways she was calculating did not make her bad. Usually, her skills went unnoticed, and though I had not seen it at the time, it came to me almost immediately after that what she had done had been genius.

In the dark, I whispered to Poe, "Now we know that the thing inside Helene revels in the more twisted versions of pain. Not all Ravagers like the same flavors. This one is a true sadist." All Ravagers fed on strong emotions, outrage, violent conflict, even illness. But this one liked something else, something much more personal. Its choice of Helene was purposeful.

I stood and went to the window to look out. "Did you know when you made this body for me?" I whispered to the darkness. Maman could not answer, of course, but I wondered all the same. "Did you know its tastes, even then? Did you hope it would break me?"

It bothered me how much the Ravager reminded me of her. It was confusing at first, because Helene had taken after Maman in many ways, but not this. She was cruel, but she never reveled in cruelty the way Maman had. She used it as a means to an end, while Maman *enjoyed* hurting others. Hurting me. And Helene.

When we were girls, she had frequently set us against one another, creating arbitrary reasons for us to hate one another. I learned early how to be a less interesting target. How to respond enough that escalation became unnecessary, but not so much that Maman became amused by my reactions. It was a delicate balance—one I did not always succeed at.

If the Ravager shared Maman's nature, perhaps she had thought they would make good partners. That she could control it more easily than one of the others. I tried to remember what I could of the original Ravagers. I hadn't been privy to as much information as Ashbourne had, but I scarcely wanted to discuss this with him.

I long suspected that the first of the Ravagers was with us from the very start. That from the Ventyr's exodus from Vilhar, from our home world of Neamor, it had followed us across the stars and burrowed into Interra, poisoning us from the beginning. That one loved war and violent conflict. It had seemed to me to be the most tortured of the three.

It had wanted something it could not have, and as such, spent its existence railing against it. I had argued with the mages' insistence that we imprison the creatures. It had seemed a recipe for what we dealt with now, but they had assured me the Ravagers would stay imprisoned forever. That there was no way for them to escape.

"There is always a way," I said aloud, shaking off these dark thoughts, at least for the moment. I returned to my chair. I needed to close my eyes, if just for a few moments. Viridian would keep watch, of that I was assured, but I would not leave Poe's side tonight for anything.

CHAPTER 15

MINA

I woke to find that someone had moved me from Poe's bedroom to one of my own. Like the room she was in, the furnishings were spare, with cream and light blue dominating the room's decor. The sheer curtains were open a crack, letting in weak autumnal light. I rose and splashed water on my face in the small washroom that adjoined the bedchamber. After a quick bath, I slipped into the soft cotton robe I found draped over a chair.

Everything I'd worn yesterday was covered in my blood. A glance in the mirror showed me that my face was nearly healed. Another day or two and it would be like nothing happened, outwardly at least. Inwardly, I wondered if what I told Poe last night was true, if I really held nothing against her. I didn't think I did. I'd meant what I said. But the heartbreaking reality of her hurting me had done damage.

It hadn't affected my trust in her, or my belief in our relationship, but it had altered something in me. It showed me the truth of our bond, of all close bonds. They could be a strength, but they could also be used against me. I'd never had relationships like these. There had never been people who saw the whole of who and what I was and who not only accepted it, but loved it. Loved me. Helene had twisted that love and tried to use it against me.

Suddenly, I was freezing cold. I riffled through the tall wardrobe next to the window. Many clothes that would fit me were already here. No doubt, that was Viridian's doing. I dressed quickly, selecting a pair of beautifully tailored wool trousers and a deep green sweater with a sweet rounded collar. Dressing kept me busy, but once I'd slipped my ring back on, thoughts began to creep in again.

If Helene managed to trap Ashbourne so, and use him against me, it might break me. And not because my love for him was stronger than what I had for Poe, but for the sheer fact that I did not trust that love. The love between us was erratic and unpredictable, while Poe and I were a sure bet. There was no doubt in my mind about Poe. And there was nothing *but* doubt in my mind about Ashbourne. My muscles tensed painfully. I let a few tears drop before shutting them away. Downstairs, voices filled the house. The day had truly begun, and I couldn't hide up here forever.

Outletting my emotion was necessary, but I could not let fear take hold. Fear would deaden my senses, cause me to make rash and foolish decisions. Fear was nothing but a hindrance. It was as insidious as love in some ways.

I took several deep breaths, smoothing my face into comfortable neutrality before leaving the bedchamber. Downstairs, just a level down from where I was, everyone had gathered, and it seemed Elspeth and Mirabelle were being held to account from what I could tell. I sat down on the top step, feeling wary.

More conflict wasn't what I needed right now. I needed space to think things through, to try to see all the pieces of this puzzle at once, so I could begin to form the bigger picture that loomed in my mind. But the arguing downstairs was nearly too much. I twisted the opal ring Ashbourne gave me as I listened to the din of everyone speaking at once.

From what I could parse out, Skye was defending her mother against Poe, who demanded an explanation for the secrecy Elspeth and Mirabelle were shrouded in, the interrogation they'd put us through with Muse, and what they were doing in their "little group." Though on the surface they were arguing over particulars, what I heard was a battle between them about trust.

Skye was angry that Poe did not trust her judgment of her family. Poe was angry that Skye did not trust her objectivity. And at the heart of it all was Poe's YRH status, I thought. Something about it scared Skye, though I could not tell what it was. Soft, silver fur brushed against me.

"Why is Skye scared of Poe's title?" I asked, keeping my voice soft.

The greymalkin saw more than I ever could, though whether he would answer was another story altogether. He set his two front paws and chest on my lap, raising his head for ear rubs. I obliged, and he purred as he explained things to me.

She is scared of the ways the title will affect their future. Historically, it has been difficult for Vilhari queens to maintain strong romantic relationships. Their duty to their people must always come first.

"Oh," I breathed. "Does she not believe that her duty to her queen holds weight?"

Morpheus narrowed his eyes slightly. *Explain.*

"As the queen's consort... if that is what they chose, of course..."

Of course, Morpheus agreed.

"Skye's duty would be to devote herself fully to Poe, to making her happy. It seems as though she has a strong enough heart to do that unselfishly."

Inside my head, Morpheus chuckled a bit. *You are right in that. Perhaps her true fear is not being chosen. Of Poe's duty being so grand that she would not choose Skye.*

I got the feeling we weren't just talking about Poe and Skye. "You think that is what Ashbourne fears as well."

Yes, Morpheus agreed. *It is different between the two of you. But he has chosen you unconditionally—*

"He has a strange way of showing it," I interrupted, my voice raising to a level louder than I'd intended.

Wilhelmina, Morpheus chided. *You cannot see his devotion to you?*

I could. That was part of the problem. I saw it and it scared me. All that raw love that he wanted me to take on trust. When all evidence pointed to the idea that this was a man who had hurt me grievously, had been the cause of all my pain, and that he would do so again.

Was he though? Morpheus asked. I knew the greymalkin could skim surface level thoughts from a person's mind, but it startled me all the same. *Was he truly the cause of your pain?*

That was a hard question to answer. Ashbourne's choices had initiated so much harm. For me, the world, and now all worlds. But I thought back to the mages who would not listen when I'd suggested that imprisonment was not our best defense against the Ravagers, or my father's insatiable need for more resources and power. Ashbourne's actions in an unjust world had been the initiator, the spark that lit the fuse. But he had nothing to do with the fuse itself, or the explosive it was affixed to.

"No," I admitted. "But that doesn't make me trust him. It doesn't fix things."

Of course not, Morpheus replied, rising up to bump my face with his. *Only time can do that work. Time and the two of you together.*

Elspeth Aestra appeared at the bottom of the enormous circular staircase, her long face stern. "Come down."

With a grumble, Morpheus extracted himself from my lap. Elspeth's expression was pinched and worn. Though physically she did not look any different from the last time I saw her, there was an air of weariness in the set of her shoulders. I waited until she turned back to the parlor to pull myself upwards.

Coming down the stairs with everyone waiting was terrible. I was slow and my joints flared with so much pain that by the time I reached the bottom of the stairs a flush had bloomed on my cheeks. In the parlor, everyone sat silently, though I realized immediately that no one but Ashbourne had been paying any attention to me.

Poe sat in a chair by the window, arms crossed tightly across her chest, her spine ramrod straight, her skin a shade of gray that worried me, even though she looked much better otherwise. Across the room, Skye sat in nearly the same position, with the difference that she slouched in her chair, her legs stretched out before her, almost languid. If her face had not been clenched so tightly, I might have thought her relaxed.

"Where is Viridian?" I asked.

"He went home to fetch something," Ashbourne said.

Like Skye, he sat in a relaxed position. Unlike her, his face was also the picture of ease. I tried my hardest not to look at him, not to think about what we'd done in the gazebo last night, but it was impossible.

He was dressed in a pair of well-tailored gray tweed trousers and a matching waistcoat, his shirtsleeves rolled to his elbows, revealing his long muscular forearms. Under my observation, one hand flexed, and I dared not look at his face, but my treacherous eyes moved upward, anyway.

His dark hair was tousled artfully. My eyes slid to his face. A faint shadow of stubble gave his beautiful Vilhari features an air of ruggedness. Just as I expected, his lips quirked into a smug smile.

My stomach flopped. I tried to tear my eyes from him, but found that I could not, so I schooled my face into cold impassiveness. The smirk faded somewhat, to my pleasure. It was as though we were locked in orbit around one another. Nothing else seemed to matter.

"Follow me," Elspeth said. When none of us moved, she glared imperiously. "Now."

My friends got to their feet. I thought I heard Skye grumble, but when I cast my eyes in her direction, her face was pure innocence. Suddenly, I understood her odd casualness, despite the obvious tension between her and Poe. She was comfortable here in her childhood home. Comfortable with her family, who she might disagree with fundamentally, but whose love she was sure of.

The knowledge felt like a punch to the gut, and I nearly doubled over with envy. Elspeth walked towards the staircase that led further into the depths of the house. Poe and Skye followed her, keeping a good distance between them. Morpheus was not far behind, leaving Ash and me to walk together.

He stood just behind me as I moved to follow. "It's hard to watch, isn't it?"

I increased the pace of my steps. Not that I thought there was any chance of outrunning him, but he was too close. My heart threatened to beat harder, and I took a long breath, deliberately slowing the pace of its beating, and my strides. Long and even.

"What?" I asked finally, unable to ignore him.

"How comfortable they all are together. How sure they are of the inevitability of their love—that all will work itself out, eventually."

Ashbourne's voice was low, as though his words were meant only for me. "Neither of us has ever had such a thing."

His words cut deep into what I'd observed since sitting at the top of the stairs. The argument between Poe and Skye wasn't the kind that threatened their relationship. It was the kind that worked things out. They were managing their feelings, and it didn't look perfect, but they were facing their fears head on, and together, despite their anger with one another.

Long fingers brushed mine, if only for a moment, as we reached the top of the stairs. "Take my arm," Ashbourne said.

I couldn't discern if the phrase he uttered was a command or offer, but it hardly mattered. There was no way I would take his arm or his help. He blocked the way, looming over me for only a moment, then his head bent low. For a split second, I thought he meant to kiss me, but he only brought his face close to mine.

"You need the help. There is no shame in it. Use the tools you are given."

As he drew away, his eyes locked on mine. The intensity burning in them shocked me. On his face, and in his countenance, I saw the war within him. The fight between the man he'd been as Ashbourne Claymore—loyal, steady, and true—and the one he'd been as the Prince of House Anemos—cunning, powerful, and arrogant. The qualities mixed within him, creating something altogether new and familiar at the same time.

Without thinking more about it, I stretched an arm towards him. He wasn't wrong. Every part of me hurt. The wounds Poe and Viridian had inflicted on me under Helene's influence might technically be healed, but they left behind an ache that wouldn't soon subside.

He swept me into his arms, picking me up so easily I had no time to protest that I'd only meant to take his arm for support. "Please don't argue," he murmured into my ear. "I would like to catch up with our friends sometime soon." I glared at him. The expression he offered in return was one of wicked humor. "Unless you'd like to sneak back upstairs with me? I could probably ease some of your discomfort."

My thighs tightened in response. He felt the clench of my muscles and smiled as he stepped down. "No, of course not. You want to know what Elspeth Aestra is up to more than you want my face buried between your legs for the next hour."

Heat flushed through me. His words were barely a whisper, meant only for my ears. In fact, now Ashbourne's lips grazed the shell of my ear, his breath caressing every sensitive nerve ending there. "But later, when we've found out what these fey are really up to, you will need a nap. You will need rest after your ordeal, and then you will let me do as I said."

"I won't," I said, keeping my voice terse, but my arms tightened around his neck, my breath quickening in my chest. *I would. I knew I would.*

Ashbourne took another flight of stairs. This house was far too tall, with too many stories, I decided. I craned my neck to look down. The others were three flights below us now, waiting.

"If you are a good girl and ask me to help you, I will give you what you want without teasing," Ashbourne countered, moving far slower than I knew he was capable of, even carrying me. "If you are a bad girl, and my darling, I *do* hope you choose to be difficult, I will make you beg me for every ounce of pleasure."

I squirmed in his arms as we reached the landing. He set me down, but caged my body against the wall. Much to my frustration, I had no inclination whatsoever to get away from him. My back arched off the wall as he stared down at me, my lips parting just enough for me to lick them once.

Ashbourne's eyes glowed, the Claimed beast within him alive with need. I reached up to fist his shirt in my hands, pulling his face close to mine, so I could whisper, "Whatever in the world would make you think that it will be *me* begging for release?"

His body tensed against mine. I arched my back harder, so that my breasts pressed firmly into his chest, drawing his head even closer to my lips. "Isn't that what you're doing right now? Begging me for your pleasure?"

A low growl vibrated in his chest. An arm snaked around me as his thigh parted my legs, pinning me between his hard body and the wall. But he had no teasing words for me now.

That was fine. I had plenty for him. "Isn't this all just you begging for another taste of me? Begging to be let inside?"

"Yes," he gritted out, his hand moving to my throat, his fingers gentle as they wrapped around my neck. I practically hummed with pleasure at the hint of pressure. "The difference between us is that I am not too proud to beg for you."

Like lightning, he was gone, leaving me to walk the rest of the way on my own.

CHAPTER 16

ASHBOURNE

It was wretched of me to leave her on the stairs when I knew she needed help, but if she'd spoken even one more word, I would have lost all reason and dragged her upstairs with me. What were we even doing? What was *I* doing?

"Where is Mina?" Poe asked, her voice shrill.

"Coming," I growled. "She didn't want my help."

Skye patted me on the back. Elspeth Aestra rolled her eyes. Morpheus simply sighed and disappeared. He reappeared a few moments later on the stairs, Mina walking slowly behind him. Her face was composed, though her porcelain skin glowed with what I knew to be fury. Keeping her angry with me had been a tactic I'd used long ago, when we first met.

I'd irritated her, aroused every bit of her, and fucked her into oblivion. Fucked us both into oblivion, to be honest. In retrospect, all I'd ever wanted back then was to possess her so fully that she could not get away from me. From the moment I met her, I wanted to crawl inside her, consume her, keep her for only my own.

She was right when she'd said that wasn't love. It wasn't. It was lust and fear, hopelessness born from a life starved of joy. Torment was the only way I'd ever seen love work. But it wasn't for us anymore.

It was effective still, as I saw plainly from the flush in her cheeks as she passed by me, the faint scent of arousal still clinging to her. But it would burn her out, burn us both out. We would never be happy. A memory crossed my mind, sharp and dangerous: the day I took her to Muse's. All I'd wanted was to make her happy, to end her suffering —to spend the rest of our long lives giving her every tiny scrap of joy I could.

I caught her hand as she passed me. She paused, looking up at me with such a terrible mix of fear and fury that I nearly let go. "I am sorry," I said, keeping my apology simple.

She nodded once, but the tension drained out of her shoulders. And then she surprised me. "As am I."

There was an unusual quiver in my jaw as I smiled. I think it was the first genuine smile I'd given her since reuniting. We still held hands, and I would not be the first to pull away. Instead, I drew her arm through mine, letting her lean on me. It was a less intimate gesture, but it kept her near me.

"Are we ready now?" Elspeth asked, her voice dry.

Mina nodded, leaning harder against me for support. Skye and Poe still did not look at one another, but both nodded as well. Morpheus was nowhere to be seen. I assumed he'd gone ahead, to wherever Elspeth intended to take us. She took a key from the pocket of her gown and unlocked the door we stood in front of.

"This is what we've been working on," Elspeth said as we filed in.

The room was located at the center of the house. A domed glass ceiling allowed soft, ambient light into what would otherwise be a dark, windowless room. The pin-board at the center of the room stood just to the side of a giant brass orrery that depicted the planetary system containing Sirin. Several tall library tables, strewn with papers, circled the orrery. It was clear this was an inner sanctum for Elspeth and Mirabelle, though it was not obvious to me what their aims were.

Elspeth followed us, shutting the door behind her as we fanned out around the room. "This is what we've kept from you. We've been tracking the most powerful players on Sirin for centuries—since the last Aethereal princess."

Mina and Poe both went to examine the material affixed to the pin-board, then began whispering to one another. Skye came to stand by me, frowning as she watched them move from the board to the tables, examining what looked to be maps, and notes. It was not immediately obvious to me, nor to Skye, what we were looking at. But Poe and Mina were a different story. They had moved to stand in front of the orrery and were pointing at different glowing lights, as it slowly rotated.

I walked over to the pin-board, frowning at the timeline at the top of the board. It was difficult for me to tell exactly what was being tracked, but Skye took a sharp breath in. "That is when Mina was born." She tapped a spot on the timeline. I couldn't make out the code it was written in, but clearly Skye could read it. "And that is when Alastair Wildfang died."

She glanced at Elspeth. "You tracked the Wildfangs' movements?"

Elspeth nodded. "Yes. We suspected their group of something nefarious. Alastair Wildfang's travel made no sense for his business."

"What did he do?" I asked.

Mina glanced back at me. "Imports and exports."

I raised an eyebrow. "Was he part of the Syndicate?"

Elspeth shook her head. "No, he worked on his own until he and Vaness met. We knew they meant to cause trouble, but for a while it seemed they were most interested in furthering an agenda that would put the Oscarovi in charge of Sirin. It didn't come to much..." she trailed off, pursing her lips.

Mina's eyes widened. "But you didn't know what they had planned for me, did you?"

Elspeth shook her head. Her hands clasped tightly in front of her, and from the way she wrung her fingers out, I guessed she felt some amount of guilt for this now. "If we'd known..."

Mina waved a hand. Her voice was soft, dismissive. "Who would have guessed that anyone would do such a terrible thing?"

Poe's eyes narrowed dangerously. "*Someone* should have."

Elspeth nodded as she trailed after Poe and Mina. "Yes. We should have."

Morpheus materialized by Mina's feet, reclining and cleaning his paws, as though something momentous were not about to occur. Casual fey feline. I envied his composure.

"You are tracking the portals then," Poe said, pointing at the orrery.

Elspeth nodded. "Yes." She pointed to a few different spots in the orrery that glowed with silver light. "We know Chopard is opening these, and then covering them, quite clumsily, with empyrae."

Mina turned to look at the table behind her again, her fingers gliding over a stack of papers that she fanned out. "It's like Morgaine said."

My attention snagged on one of the papers Mina grazed over, the word "Laniidae" standing out to me. My heart beat faster, but Mina paid no mind to the piece of paper. Something else held her attention as she riffled through the papers, but for the life of me I could not focus on it, only that she had not seemed to care about that one word.

Poe nodded, still staring at the orrery, face thoughtful as she tracked the spots that glowed bright blue. She stepped forward and pointed to them. "Are these natural portals?"

There was something odd about her question, but I could not quite put my finger on it. Still, it was a good distraction from worrying over Mina. I glanced at Skye, but from the deep crease in her brow, she was confused as I was, and Mina was still utterly transfixed by the stack of notes on the table. The notes about the Laniidae had been discarded, and I breathed a sigh of relief.

Elspeth shook her head. "No, there are no natural portals on Sirin. There hasn't been a single one since the War of Elementals."

Mina took a sharp breath in, turning away from the notes. "Standing stones?"

Now Elspeth smiled. "Yes, good."

Mina turned to look at the board of equations again and frowned. "I've seen equations like these before. On Interra."

I stared at them, but they were foreign to me. If our scholars had used equations like these, I would not know the difference.

Elspeth walked to the equations and pointed to one row. "We are trying to decipher why the natural portals stopped opening."

Mina's jaw went taut, and her eyes focused as she moved towards the board. "Do these coordinate? They look similar."

Elspeth smiled. "Yes, if we can figure out how to reverse what happened after the war, we'll be able to use the limen for interstellar travel again."

"No," Poe breathed, her voice shrill. "You must not."

All of us turned towards her. "Why not?" I asked, keeping my voice low and gentle. It was obvious she was afraid.

She shook her head. "I... It's not..."

I elbowed Skye sharply. She looked up at me, clearly annoyed, but her expression softened when Poe covered her face with her hands. Mina moved towards her friend, but I stepped between them. "Let Skye help her," I murmured.

Mina glared at me, to which I responded with a smile. Skye's arms went around Poe, who melted into her body. She cried quietly for a moment, burying her face in Skye's sweater. Skye held her tighter. I looked to Elspeth Aestra, expecting to see irritation on her face. Instead, I found relief.

She had worried about their fighting, then. She wanted her child to be happy. Next to me, Mina tensed, and I heard the choked noise she made. It was so quiet that none but me could hear. Her arms hung stiff at her sides, her fists clenched into tight balls. I covered her fist with my hand, prying her fingernails away from her palms.

To my surprise, she let me. All the muscles in her arms relaxed, her opposite hand unclenching as well. I had promised the god I would help her. My behavior over the past few hours had been abominable. I had to do better.

She pulled her hand from mine, gently, rather than a violent yank, then wrapped her arms about her body, taking a few steps backward. It was as though she couldn't bear to be so close to Skye and Poe. The position was protective, but there was little tension in her now.

She looked up at me, eyes soft rather than defiant. It was all the thanks I needed, but I couldn't help myself. I stepped nearer to her, standing just behind her, wedging myself between her and the library table. She tensed for only a moment, but when I made no move to touch her again, she relaxed into me, her back meeting my chest.

I felt her let out a tensely held breath, her body relaxing against mine. I longed to wrap my arms around her waist, to pull all her weight against me and kiss the top of her head. Someday soon, I promised myself. If I moved slowly, she might trust me enough to let me comfort her more.

Poe took a shuddering breath and pulled away from Skye, looking up at her gratefully. Skye, to her credit, seized the moment, cupping Poe's face in her hands and kissing her gently. It was too much to watch; Mina and I both averted our eyes, but she leaned harder against me, her hand reaching backwards towards mine. Our fingertips brushed lightly, but she did not quite grasp on. It was as though she could not quite bring herself to ask for the help. She rolled her neck, stretching both arms out behind her now, as though she were in pain.

And perhaps she was, but I saw the movement for what it was. She was hiding the fact that she nearly reached for my hand. She had wanted the comfort I could give her as much as I wanted to offer it. We were making progress then. Slow progress for what I'd prefer, but I would take anything she gave.

Mina took a sharp breath in, as though it pained her to do so, and then wrapped her arms about herself once more. The urge to hold her was more than I could bear. She was obviously as torn as I was, but I couldn't force her into anything she didn't want. I couldn't irritate her into my arms, or frustrate her into giving into my will.

None of that was fair to her—or me. I had to know she wanted me for myself. For all of me. The monster I was as Thuellos, and the man I'd become as Claymore. I placed a hand on her shoulder and squeezed, then moved away from her. I hoped she understood that I wanted her too much, that the desire to protect her with all I had when she wasn't ready was too strong.

Instead, as I moved away, her shoulders slumped. She had not understood at all. It wasn't as though I could stop and explain to her right now, but causing her more pain was not my intent. I nearly broke all social protocol to tell her anyway, to confess all I felt for her here in front of all these people.

Elspeth shook her head. "Why do you say we shouldn't?"

Poe took hold of Skye's hand, as though for strength. Skye

brought it to her heart, and Poe looked back at her, gratitude welling in her eyes. "Why do *you* think we should?"

Elspeth huffed in irritation. She wasn't used to being outranked; that much was clear. "The Ventyr locked us in. They closed Sirin to the limen."

"Did they?" Poe's head tilted in that birdlike way she had.

As I did not know the nuances of Sirin's history, only the broadest strokes, I couldn't tell what the perception of this issue was on my own. But from the look on Mina's face, I gathered that this might be new information.

Elspeth Aestra stepped towards her queen. "That is what we have always believed."

"Yes, I know," Poe said, weariness in her voice. "That is what you were meant to think. My grandmother sealed Sirin off when the Ventyr were expelled. Now, only someone with the power to manipulate starfire can get in or out."

"The purest form of empyrae," Skye breathed, wonder in her eyes.

"To do such a thing, your grandmother would have had to pull energy from the heart of the limen, pure otham," Elspeth said, her voice shaking.

"Yes," Poe said, looking at me.

"She weakened the walls at Nihil." I spoke the words as they came into my mind.

"She didn't know, Ashbourne. We didn't know what had happened to the Ventyr after the exodus. The Avalonne was trying to find you."

"We were on a diplomatic mission," Mirabelle Aestra said, appearing as though from nowhere, though it was obvious now that she'd come out of one of the alcoves at the back of the room. Her steel gray eyes locked on me. "The crown princess wanted to make amends between our people, to try to forge the relationship we once had."

"She is the reason the Ravagers were able to escape..." The words came out choked with grief. When the first one fled, I blamed myself. Blamed my lack of vigilance.

Mina stepped between me and Mirabelle, a ferocity in her that thrilled me. She saw I was vulnerable, and like a lioness, she protected me. "She wanted the Larae back. Not the Ventyr who left Neamor—the Larae. Her bodyguards."

Mina pronounced the word La-ray, but we had always called them Larai on Interra. They were her mother's people, the warrior queens. The Unconquerable. A dynasty of Ventyr so strong even the Emperor could not defeat them, but had to marry them to have even a slice of their power. A power that rested in her.

I wondered if Poe understood that power, if she knew all the Larai had been capable of. If she could even fully comprehend the power that Mina held within her, like a seed—the power her sister Ouriel had possessed. I looked down at Morpheus, who had once warned me that Mina was more powerful than Skye and I assumed. Had he always known?

The cat blinked sagely at me. *You are* finally *catching up*.

Poe spoke quickly, clearly trying to placate Mina. "She did want that, but Mirabelle isn't wrong. She was on a diplomatic mission to mend things. Her own ancestors made many mistakes she sought to mend."

Mina's hands clenched into fists again. Poe's confession clearly distressed her. The intricacies of what was wrong between them was personal, but also ancient and political. The problems between the Ventyr and the Court of Aether were myriad, and began aeons before our time. But for creatures such as us, long-lived as the universe itself, if nothing stopped us, grudges were borne over generations.

This was something the two of them would have to work out on their own. Neither Skye nor I could help them. Poe tore her gaze from Mina's, refocusing her attention on Elspeth. "My grandmother sealed Sirin to protect us all from the Ventyr. She used the last of her immortality to complete the spell and sent my mother to watch the seal. To protect it."

Elspeth and Mirabelle wore twin expressions of wide-eyed realization. "But she trapped us in."

Poe shook her head. "No, she kept them out. Don't you understand? The Ventyr, under Boreas, were too strong. Once they found us, they meant to destroy us." She shot a pleading look at Mina, who averted her eyes. "*Boreas* meant to destroy us, and likely to mine Sirin for all the power it possessed." Poe stepped towards Mina, taking her hand. "He would have destroyed the Oscarovi in the process, the elementals—"

Mina nodded. "I know. You should have told me." She turned toward the stairs and walked away.

I moved to follow her, but Poe threw an arm in front of me. "Stay here. This is for us to work out without your *interference*."

Poe spat the word at me, not as queen of the Vilhar, but as Mina's best friend. I held my hands up in defeat, taking a step backwards to allow her to pass me.

Mirabelle Aestra patted me on the shoulder. "That was smart of you."

CHAPTER 17

MINA

"Mina," Poe called behind me. "Please wait."

I didn't stop. Instead, I took step after step, though it hurt my knees and hips to do so, climbing the stairs. She would argue with me all the way up, just as I wanted. I clutched the torn piece of paper I'd taken from the library table, tucked inside my blouse, beneath my sweater. It was safe.

"I know I should have told you about all this sooner," Poe said, as she caught up to me.

"Yes," I agreed. "How long have you known?"

I didn't care one bit how long she'd known that her grandmother was the one to seal Sirin. It was the right thing to do, just as it was the right thing to keep it secret. The fewer people that knew, the fewer that would try to break the spell. Keeping the Ventyr out was wise.

If my father had wanted in so badly, he would have returned with a greater force than he'd come with the first time. And he would have done worse to this world than any Ravager could have. Or at the very least, he would have been just as bad.

"Since the night in the Avalonne," Poe explained. "In my mother's chambers, there has always been a box I could not unlock. But that night... It opened. And it had her diary in it. I read it all. I didn't know when the right time would be to tell you. I worried you'd be angry with me, that I would lose you." She reached out to grab my arm. "Mina, *please.*"

I yanked my arm away from her, continuing on. "Do you think I haven't *always* known the relationship between the Larae and the High Queen?"

Behind me, Poe's voice was quiet. "You didn't remember it at first. And when I understood it, I didn't want to tell you."

"Well," I huffed as we neared the top of the house. We were almost to the terrace. "I knew the moment I remembered my people." I pushed through the doors to the rooftop garden and reached back to grab Poe, pulling her outside with me.

The second the door shut, I pulled the threads of aether around us in a muffling spell and yanked Poe to me, hugging her as tightly as I could. "And I have never cared. The arguments of our ancestors have nothing to do with us."

Poe stood still for a moment as my words and actions sank in. Then she was clinging to me just as hard as I was to her. "Thank the Lady," she sobbed, as we sank to the ground. She grabbed my shoulders, pushing me just far enough from her to look into my eyes. "Why would you *do* that?"

"It seemed better for them all to think we're at odds until we decide what to do next." I pulled the scrap of paper I'd found from inside my shirt sleeve. "Look at this."

Poe opened the paper, examining the diagram I'd found. It was, if I'd read it correctly, a map of the standing stones in Pravhna—half was missing.

"This is what Niall Aestra stole," she breathed.

"Yes," I hissed. "Do you think they know?"

We stared at one another for a long moment. Then she shook her head. "Those tables were covered in dust when we arrived, Mina. I don't think anyone had worked with those notes for a while. I get the impression that Elspeth and Mirabelle felt they'd hit a wall."

I nodded. I'd gotten the same impression. "They're not Chopard."

Poe shook her head, staring at the map. "No, but this confirms that Niall is working for him."

I couldn't disagree. "Can we trust them?"

Poe sighed. "Trust? I have no idea. But I think we have to try to work together. That orrery is well made, and we may be able to recreate these measurements."

I nodded; her assessment was just as mine had been. We were back on the same page. "I'm sorry I let you think I was angry, but conflict between best friends makes a good distraction."

Poe smiled. "You're always thinking."

I returned the smile. "Just like you."

She pulled me back into her arms for a hug. When she let go, she was laughing. "Did you steal this when Ashbourne was trying to comfort you?"

I let out a small, guilty puff of air. "Yes?"

Poe snickered. "You really are a menace."

I shrugged. "He would have done the same if he'd had the chance."

Poe's head tilted slightly to the side, and for a moment I saw the Feriant in her movements. "No, darling. I don't think he would have. But you were smart to use him as a shield."

"So, we'll work with them then?" I asked, dismissing her statement. I wanted her reassurance about what to do next. "Skye, Ashbourne, and the rest of the Aestras?"

Poe nodded. "Yes, I think we should."

I dropped the muffling spell. Somewhere outside, far below us, someone knocked at the front door. Poe and I walked to the stone balustrade to peer over. It was Viridian. He looked up, his mouth pressed into a grim line. Whatever news he had, it wasn't good.

"I suppose we ought to go find out what that's about," Poe said, coming away from the balustrade.

We linked arms and went inside.

We met Viridian in the first floor parlor, where he sat with Elspeth. "Ash and Skye had to visit someone in the undercity," Elspeth explained. "Viridian has some news for you, Wilhelmina."

"Just Mina, please," I said as I sat down on a light blue settee, opposite Elspeth and next to Viridian. An enormous bouquet of hothouse flowers sat on the table between us. I could hardly see over the blooms. I was relieved that we didn't have to deal with Skye and Ash just yet.

Elspeth nodded. "Noted, for the future."

Poe spent an uncharacteristically long moment deciding where to sit, then chose the seat next to Elspeth on the mirroring settee. House Aestra's furniture was much more comfortable than Maman's, but it was still very formal and built on a small scale. We were all sitting too close to one another, the effect made worse somehow by the oppressive bouquet.

Viridian tried to shift his weight so that we wouldn't touch, but it didn't quite work out and resulted in him banging his bony knee into mine. I repressed the urge to sigh.

"The interior of Orchid House is not in the best shape after our escape," Viridian said. "It is salvageable, but will cost a great deal to restore."

"Clear it out and sell it," I said, without even a second thought.

Viridian nodded slowly. There was obviously something else he wanted to say. "Yes, well, that will be a problem."

"Why?" I shot back. Sitting so close together, and so close to the flowers, was agitating.

Viridian tried to lean away from me, sensing my irritation or experiencing some of his own, but the springs in the settee didn't let him get far from me. He sucked his teeth slightly before grimacing as we collided again. "While she was not there when I arrived to retrieve your things, Helene has been seen in society."

That shocked me into silence. I had the vague sense that I was falling through vast, endless darkness. Why had I not anticipated this? It was because she was *dead*. The knowledge confused me, rattled me so deeply that words simply wouldn't come. Suddenly, Viridian's nearness was less aggravating. I slumped against him, feeling as though I needed to catch my breath.

Viridian glanced at Poe first, who shook her head; she had no immediate words either. He turned to Elspeth. "Do you receive the Lady Chanticleer?"

Elspeth grimaced at the sound of the name. "That gossip rag? I should think not."

Poe smiled sweetly. "There's a copy on your hall table, actually."

Elspeth got up, wearing an expression that clearly conveyed that she very much doubted what Poe said. She exited the room with all the haughty grace of an empress. When she returned, she sighed. "Apparently, Mother gets it."

She handed it to Poe, who tore it open and shook her head. "Viridian is right—"

"Did you think I was *lying*?" Viridian interrupted, aghast. Though he had revealed his true self to us, there was much about the original Viridian Montclair about him still. His absolute horror at the slightest implication that he might have been lying about Helene brought me back to myself, back up out of the abyss.

"Of course not," Poe reassured him. "A simple turn of phrase." She paused, a true diplomat, waiting to see if Viridian had more complaints.

He said nothing, but he pursed his lips somewhat as he crossed one leg over the other, away from me. Despite his body language, he leaned against me, his body creating a comforting weight for me to rest against. It was obvious he was a bit put out, but was still being a friend. It felt good to trust him.

Poe scanned the front-page story. "She's peddling some story at any event she can gain entrance to…" She flipped the page, shaking her head. "She says that while the two of you were out of town, reuniting, someone set fire to the house."

"Damnit," I swore. "How are we going to handle this? I can't go back there. None of us can."

The four of us were quiet for a long time. Finally, Elspeth spoke. "I have an idea, but I worry that you will not like it." I guessed her idea before she spoke, but it seemed to genuinely surprise Poe when she said, "What if you and Skye were engaged?"

Poe seemed at a loss for words, but managed to sputter out, "To be married?"

"Yes." Elspeth smiled. "It would give us a reason to have you all here. Especially if you let it be known that you are the lost heir, and that Mother and I have verified your identity."

Poe stared at me, her jaw clenched as her head shook. We had walked right into this particular machination. Elspeth continued, "If you make this announcement and name Wilhelmina as your Lady Chamberlain, no one will expect her to return to Orchid House. And! If you and Skye are engaged, it would be expected that you all stay with us, as your family no longer owns property in the city."

I thought Poe might explode. Viridian wrinkled his nose and closed his eyes. He looked as though he wanted to crawl under the settee and hide. Poe's face shifted into her beautiful mask of equanimity. "I will certainly talk that over with Skye when she returns."

"Of course," Elspeth replied. "Now, if the three of you do not need me, I have a few things to attend to."

We nodded, like the bobbing-head toys sold in droves at Yuletide, as she left. When we heard her shut the door to the conservatory, I turned back to Poe, who sighed as she stared at her nails, fussing with a cuticle. "I hate that it is such a good idea."

"Do you think she's already talked to Skye about it?" I asked.

Poe shrugged, fiddling with the hem of her blouse. She only fidgeted like this when she felt unsure about something. "I don't know."

It was hard to imagine that she worried that Skye might not agree to the plan. It was early in their relationship, but people got engaged for lesser reasons all the time. Perhaps Poe didn't want to talk about this more. I changed the subject quickly. "Could you explain to Viridian what we found downstairs?"

As Poe explained that the Aestras had been trying to unseal Sirin from her grandmother's protection, I pulled the piece of paper I'd swiped from the conservatory from my pocket. "Do you think this is what Niall might have stolen?"

Viridian examined the paper carefully, then stared off into space for a few moments. "This makes sense. The standing stones are conduits to the part of the limen the elementals exist in. It is separate in some ways from the limen proper, but if someone were trying to open a portal out, and didn't have a good grasp on starfire, then the standing stones would be the best place to begin."

"Yes," I agreed, wishing I'd thought of it myself. "But *why* is Chopard doing this?"

Viridian shrugged. "That's the real question, isn't it? I think you're right about Niall stealing half of this chart. I also think taking the calculated risk to tell Elspeth and Mirabelle everything would be prudent at this point."

Poe breathed slowly, staring at her nails again. Her voice was quiet now, resigned, but calm. "I agree. Their methods haven't been up front, but I don't think they mean harm. They only thought of regaining what we had in the past."

"Or they want to go home," Viridian said, his voice wistful.

I frowned at him. "What do you mean? Both of them were born here."

Viridian smiled with his mouth, but his eyes were sad. "Many of the Vilhari miss a planet they've never seen."

"Neamor?" I asked, naming the homeworld of the Court of Aether, and at one time, the Ventyr.

"No," Viridian said. "The Court of Winds had their own world, each of the courts did. And many Vilhari would like to go back. Perhaps the Aestras are the same."

"We would hardly fit in," Poe said. "It has been thousands of years. We don't even speak the right language anymore; all our languages have merged with the Oscarovi. We belong here now."

I shifted uncomfortably in my seat. "I am sure there are Oscarovi who wouldn't mind if the Vilhari left. That's why Elspeth and Mirabelle tracked the Wildfangs to begin with."

Poe nodded. "I'm sure you're right. That is why I'm worried about Elspeth's idea. Even if Skye and I agreed to this, wouldn't it cause problems to announce me as the lost heir? I'm not the queen of anything here."

Viridian smiled authentically then, his eyes and his mouth in harmony. "Your mother felt the same. She expressed that many times to my parents."

Poe reached across the small occasional table that sat between the settee to take Viridian's hand. "Thank you for keeping these memories for me. And for honoring my wishes."

Viridian nodded, flushing slightly at her praise. "So, what should we do?"

"I need to talk this over with Skye first," Poe said. "She will have a better idea of how to navigate things between her family and myself."

The pink in her cheeks told me that there would be more to that conversation than discussing navigation, but I kept my thoughts to myself.

"I think it might be helpful if I went and explained what we suspect about Chopard and Niall," Poe said as she stood. She walked to the window and looked out. "Perhaps the two of you can sort through the things Viridian managed to rescue from Orchid House. If we need to have Madame Laquoix here, I'd like to know as soon as possible."

"That reminds me," Viridian said, joining Poe at the window. He pulled a stack of envelopes from his pocket. "I gathered the correspondence from the front hall. I doubt I'll be able to return once Helene and Brigitte take residence, but I thought these might be useful."

Poe shook her head. "Give them to Mina to evaluate. You sort through the clothes."

"We have our orders then," Viridian said with an elegant bow. "Let us get to work."

Poe tweaked him on the nose before heading towards the conservatory. I picked up the discarded Lady Chanticleer off the occasional table as everyone cleared off. A small headline caught my eye: *University Custodian's Body Located, Lord Eccles Headed Home From Ismit!*

CHAPTER 18

MINA

The piece was short, more of a write-up of the crime blotter than anything else. Apparently, Detective Benton had located Lord Eccles, who was on his way back from Ismit, where he'd been visiting the Universitaire d'Ismit's palatial library system. The blood Viridian and I found in his office was not his, but a custodian's.

I sank back on the settee, frowning. At least that explained why we hadn't been able to find him. But it didn't quell my curiosity about his involvement with Chopard or Maman. He was firmly back on my suspect list.

Someone would need to tail him when he returned, at the very least. It would be better to talk to him ourselves. I read the article again, noting when he was set to return to Pravhna. Not for another week, it seemed. I sat down at a small writing desk near the back of the parlor.

The small pile of correspondence was mostly uninteresting invitations and requests to call from folk I knew Poe would ignore. A heavy linen envelope at the bottom of the pile caught my eye. I plucked it out and carefully pried it open. The paper was almost too pretty to mar with my nails, but I wanted to see what was inside.

It was a beautiful, hand-calligraphed invitation to a series of opening events for the Grand Exhibition. I scanned the list, noting an airship party at the end of the week, and a series of private lectures to follow in the weeks to come. I recognized many of the scholars' names as prominent Oscarovi, and a few Vilhari, but one stood out: Lord Eccles. *That* was why he was on his way back to the city. At least that gave us good cover for questioning him. We would be expected to be at all such events anyway, especially with the jump in status Poe was about to experience.

The front door opened, disrupting my train of thought. Skye and Ashbourne entered, both brushing off a dusting of snowflakes. This far up in the echelons, late autumn's perpetual rain often turned to snow. Ashbourne had snowflakes caught in his eyelashes and he blinked them away as he removed his heavy woolen coat. Skye stopped to hang both their outerwear in the vestibule, but Ashbourne found me immediately.

A cool wall slammed down between us. "Good morning, Mina," he said as he took a seat near the writing desk.

"Good morning," I said, trying to evaluate this greeting, to parse out the particularities of each syllable—to no avail. Ashbourne's countenance was inscrutable, for me at least. Poe might have had some insight, but I flushed at the mere thought of asking her to tell me what she thought he might be thinking. "We have received invitations to the opening events of the Grand Exhibition," I said as Skye joined Ash.

She sat down in the chair next to his, reaching forward to pour them both a cup of tea from the set that had appeared while I was busy reading our correspondence. I frowned at it. "Does your mother employ servants?"

Skye smiled. "No. One of her best friends as a child was a talented Oscarovi. They created a network for Alabaster House that responds to our needs much in the way that Orchid House's does."

I raised an eyebrow. "It seems a good deal more advanced than ours. Orchid House doesn't anticipate our needs."

Skye shrugged, smiling. I had thought our home was unique, but here again, I was reminded that I had not actually had much experience with how others lived, given my relative social isolation. I tried not to let it make me feel ill at ease, but I could not shake the feeling of having misunderstood something. That, at least, was familiar to me.

Ashbourne glanced at me. "Would you like some tea?"

I nodded, and he fixed me a cup. A slice of lemon and a spoonful of sugar, just as I liked it. As he handed it to me, our fingers brushed, sending a vibrant current of energy through me that settled at my core, tingling with anticipation. I met his golden eyes, thinking again of how much they reminded me of a raptor. They were wholly focused on me now, as though he took in every aspect of my being.

Though the feeling was slightly uncomfortable, I couldn't deny that it was also exhilarating. *As it always has been,* some voice in me whispered. I didn't bother to try to hush that voice. There was no helping this. Now that the curse was lifted, it would simply be like this. We would both be perpetually haunted by our shared pasts, both recent and ancient.

This was why I was in no hurry to dissolve the Claim. The process would ultimately be brutal, and I was not yet strong enough to handle the ritual. As well, dissolving the Claim wouldn't—couldn't—stop the effect that memory had on me, or emotion. The Claim, after all, had nothing whatsoever to do with love.

I sipped my tea. It was perfect. Skye had taken up the invitation to the Grand Exhibition's opening events while Ashbourne and I stared at one another. She seemed determined to let this moment pass without notice. Eventually, she nodded. "This lines up with what Edith found out." She picked up the Lady Chanticleer. "You read about Lord Eccles then?"

I nodded. "Yes. What did Edith find out?"

Skye and Ashbourne exchanged a tense look before Skye answered me. "She thinks he killed the custodian. They were Strix. One of hers, so she's got people on it."

That was another black mark against Eccles, in my opinion. Perhaps we'd finally got a hold on things. If Lord Eccles was Chopard, it meant that whatever he wanted aligned with what Maman and Alastair had been plotting to begin with. Somehow, their aims matched. Nothing about that surprised me.

"Lord Eccles looks more suspicious all the time," Poe said from the doorway to the parlor. I wondered how long she'd been there.

She seemed to hesitate to come in the room any further. "Did Edith say anything about the Merc to you?"

Skye's eyebrows knitted together. "Nothing in particular, why?"

Poe held up a fresh piece of paper. From here, I could see a freshly drawn map of the city. They'd found the missing standing stone locations; the ones Niall had stolen. "It's one of the locations Chopard hasn't hit yet."

CHAPTER 19

ASHBOURNE

That too, Edith had found out, though she'd been cagey with us about what she knew, or where the stones might be located. On the way home, Skye posited that she simply wasn't ready to tell us yet. And though I agreed, I wondered if it might be something more. There was more to Edith Braithwaite than anyone knew, I was sure of that much. Not that I thought I had any hope of untangling the myriad strings the Syndicate leader had tied to everything in Pravhna, but still. I was curious all the same.

I glanced over at Mina, who expertly avoided my gaze. So she was still angry with me about this morning. I couldn't really blame her. I'd done all I could to make her mad. We both watched as Poe drifted into the parlor, the skirts of her silk gown making soft swishing noises. When she reached Skye's chair, she pressed one finger to the former Chevalier's arm. It was a light touch, but Skye's lips parted, her pale eyes raking over the curves of Poe's body.

Poe was practically breathless when she finally spoke. "I need to talk with you about something private."

Skye frowned, but rose quickly to follow Poe out of the room. I watched them go, unable to stifle my curiosity, apparently, because Mina answered the question that must have been obviously on my lips.

"Elspeth believes that the best way to deal with our Helene problem is for Poe to reveal herself as the lost heir, and for Skye and Poe to become engaged to be married."

My eyebrows lifted, and what was likely an ill-timed chuckle slipped through my lips. "Elspeth's not even trying to hide her ambitions, is she?"

Mina shook her head, some enigmatic expression in her eyes I could not read. "Will Skye agree to this?"

I shrugged. "I think it's obvious they are in love, but I cannot say."

Mina bristled at my statement. I leaned towards her, as though by instinct. Everything about her drew me in. The way her sweet little sweater clung to her curves, the fire in her eyes as she recoiled from me. "What made you uncomfortable about that?"

She glared at me. I'd promised myself to stop antagonizing her, but bad habits died struggling, and this one was ancient. I tried to keep my tone neutral, but I couldn't stop myself from asking, "Was it my mentioning how clear it is that they are in love?"

Another glare, and my heart raced. Her glares were as alluring as her smiles, her frustration with me as sweet as any pleasure. This was not how I should feel, was it? Wasn't love supposed to be about making someone happy, deliriously happy? I was greedy, desperate for any attention from her, even if it was irritation.

The glare was her only answer, so I got up and went to stand behind her chair, to read over her shoulder. The flex in her shoulder blades as they came together, the small of her back arching in the smallest, most exquisite fashion, took my breath away.

"I would rather you did not stand behind me," she whispered after a moment.

There was a catch in her voice I could not read, but immediately I stepped to the side to kneel in front of her, looking up into her sad, gray eyes. They were wide with fear, and now her shoulders were tight, her teeth grinding audibly against one another. I was glad to have moved so quickly. I never wanted to see that kind of fear in her eyes, especially if I had been the one to cause it.

"I am sorry." Slowly, so she had a chance to say no, I reached for one of her hands. She did not pull it away, but watched as I took it in mine. "What is wrong?"

Her eyes fell closed, as she attempted to relax her jaw, and then her shoulders, forcing even breaths through her lungs. "My wings," she whispered so quietly, even I could barely hear her. Then, "It is... unnerving... for someone to stand behind me." The words came out in horrific little bursts, as though she had to shove them out of herself.

Her memories had returned. All the trauma of what was done to her returned as well. I should have known, should have thought of this myself. It took all I had to control myself. To keep from squeezing her hand too hard. She had been hurt because of me. Damaged beyond repair. But mages were wondrous creatures. With our knowledge combined, I was sure we could find a way for the Oscarovi to help her. "We can fix it. There are ways—"

Mina shook her head hard. "None of them will work. When the fetch was made, my true body was destroyed. I can never return to it. I'm trapped inside this *thing*."

Rage boiled within me. I don't know why I assumed her true body had been preserved, or that at least her bones still rested somewhere, but I had. Without them, she was right. There was no returning to what she was before. But to hear her call herself a thing was abhorrent. I could not bear it. I cupped her chin gently, waiting until her eyes met mine.

"You are not a *thing*, Mina. You are a powerful woman. Perhaps one of the most powerful women who has ever lived..." There was a clear pause at the end of my statement, but fear gripped me. The words were clear in my mind, but if I let them out, she would have all the leverage between us. She would know exactly how I felt.

Mina leaned towards me, coming into focus, her movement cutting through my fear. Her pale skin glowed in the wan autumnal light of the parlor, her pink lips damp where she had just wet them with her tongue. The sight of her sweet mouth sent heat through me, my trousers feeling tighter by the moment. She thought we'd quelled the fervor. Perhaps we had, but nothing slowed the craving I had for her.

Her fingers gripped the arms of the desk chair, the sound of her breath so captivating I could practically feel how soft the inside of her mouth would be if it closed around any part of me. As I watched her chest rise and fall in short, desperate little pants, I realized what she wanted. She *wanted* me to say it. She had me on my knees, and we both knew this was exactly where I wanted to be.

"And?" she asked, her eyes smoldering with desire.

My words ripped out of me in a feral growl. "And you are *mine*."

Her lips parted as my words sank into her. The grief drained from her eyes, her shoulders straightening as my recognition gave her strength. This was the biological function of the Claim, to provide the Claimed a solid foundation of strength. The knowledge that they were wholly accepted, wanted, and cared for. It had nothing to do with love, and everything to do with security.

If she did not want my love just yet, I could at least give her this. I swept my thumb over her bottom lip, watching as her fangs protracted. This *was* what she wanted. Her long fingers swept over my face. "I am yours."

"Yes," I hissed, pulling her down from her chair and into my lap, so she straddled me like a horse. I didn't care who found us here like this. I needed to touch her, to hold her against me. "Who destroyed your true form?"

Her eyes were glossy with desire, her breath coming in shallow pants as she adjusted herself. The center of her rolled against the hard length of my erection, sending a jolt of pleasure through my abdomen.

"I don't know," she replied in a faraway voice as she pressed harder into me. "Why does it matter now?"

"Because," I said, my fingers wrapping gently around her delicate neck. "When I find who did this, I am going to eviscerate them." Her breath caught as she fit her body against mine.

"Why?" she breathed, arching her back so that her breasts pressed against my chest. Her warm core slid over my cock. I needed these clothes gone, now.

I gripped her hips, pulling her hard against me. "Because, Wilhelmina," I explained. "No one harms what is mine without consequence."

Her head tilted slightly. "And what if I want to kill them myself?"

I smiled at my beautiful menace. "Then I will be the shrike to your thorn. We will do it together."

CHAPTER 20

MINA

He was never meant to be the Warden forever, Lumina. He is destined to be the shrike. You were meant for one another in all patterns, all times. Forgive him if you can. There is no solving this without him, my love. He is the only one who can bring about the end.

Ouriel's words echoed in my mind. Was this what fate was? He offered himself to me, that much was clear. But did he *love* me? Did I love him? I had to wonder if it even mattered. Love was one thing, but trust was another. And beyond the Claim, beyond this bond between us that clearly neither of us intended to break, there was something else.

The seed of trust. The knowledge that all he'd done, the mistakes he'd made, they were all for me. Since that day in the alley, when the rose petals fell down upon us, he had only ever meant to protect me. And though I had not been the one who made the grave mistake between us, I *was* capable of forgiveness. If I held out, deprived him of it for much longer, because of fear or pride, then I would be the one at fault.

"Neither of us deserves more pain," I said as my fingers moved over the exquisite lines of his face. His golden eyes sharpened. Every aspect of him was tuned to me. His grip on my hips loosened, and I nearly cried out from the loss of his touch. But then his arms wrapped fully around me, his hands pressing into my back as he brought me closer.

"Can you forgive me?" he asked. "For all that I've done?"

I nodded once. "Yes. But I believe a period of groveling shall be necessary."

Ash's eyes narrowed further and his hard length pressed into me. A small sigh of pleasure escaped my lips as his fingers pressed harder into the flesh of my back. "I agree. I have amends to make."

One of his hands disappeared from my back, then returned to cup one of my breasts. "I wonder," he mused. "Should our period of groveling begin now?"

"I can't think of a better time," I gasped as he pinched me, sending waves of anticipation deep into my core.

In an instant, he had me in his arms. We were on the stairs before I could blink, and in a bedroom before I could take another breath, the door closed and locked. He sat me down in an elegantly curved wood chair and knelt in front of me. "Then I believe I should start here," he whispered. "This is the correct position to grovel from, is it not?"

I nodded, barely able to find words as his hand went around my right ankle and unlaced my boot. "I don't like these," he said. "They are not sturdy enough for you to fight in. We will need to have better ones made."

There was no processing what he was saying, as he removed my boots and then each of my stockings. "What are you wearing under these trousers today?" Ash didn't wait for my answer. His hands slid up my thighs, then moved to unbutton my pants.

"Raise your hips," he murmured.

I did as he bid and he slid my pants off me, discarding them on the floor. The cool air of the room hit me as he parted my legs to find the lacy lingerie I'd donned earlier. "Is this one piece or two?"

"Two," I gasped as his fingers dragged lightly between the fabric and my skin, exposing the most sensitive parts of me to the air of the bedroom. His head dipped between my thighs and his breath warmed that same skin, but did not touch it. His fingers dragged down my inner thighs, and then I felt his mouth caress me, his tongue dragging languidly over the thin fabric of my lingerie.

"Do you know how difficult it is not to rip this off you?" he said when he raised his face to mine.

"No," I breathed. "I can't imagine why."

He smiled at me, a wicked gleam in his eyes. "Then you must let me explain. Will you?"

I nodded my consent, and he slid his hands over my torso, lifting my sweater first, and then the blouse I wore underneath it. When he saw my lingerie, his breath drew in sharply at the sight of my peaked nipples through the lace. His tongue ran over his lips.

"So beautiful," he said, his hands moving to cup my breasts. His thumbs circled lightly over the lace that covered my nipples. My back bowed as I cried out, feeling every point of contact between my thighs.

"You are so perfect, and I do not deserve you," he whispered.

When I started to reply, he shook his head. "No, my love. Let me beg for you. Let me worship you."

His words stole my breath. I felt them everywhere. The only thing I could do was nod. Ash took my hand, pulling me gently on the floor beside him. "Will you sit here, in front of me?" he asked.

His voice was gentle, and I understood why he asked. I had told him how hard it was to have someone stand behind me. To not feel afraid. To give him my back now was a show of trust. He rested against the wall and spread his legs. I turned, then edged slowly into his embrace.

As my back hit Ash's chest, his arms went around me so tight I almost could not breathe. "You are safe," he murmured in my ear. "Close your eyes and let me help you understand how I feel."

I nodded, leaning into him. My body, which had tensed at the exercise of backing up, now relaxed a measure as his knees raised to create a cage around me. "Will you let me touch you?" he asked. "This explanation needs many supporting examples."

"I do like a man who can show his evidence," I murmured as his fingers dragged lightly down my arms.

"Then let us start here," he whispered in my ear. "With these soft, beautiful arms. The first time I saw you, they were bare and I could not stop imagining what it would be like to have them wrapped around my neck."

"When?" I asked, desperate to know to which past he referred to.

"That day by the Lake of the Nameless," he said.

"The twins' twelfth birthday party." That was years before either of us had been forced to seduce and murder the other. "I had forgotten that was the first time we met."

"I haven't," he murmured, his fingers sliding between mine. "I imagined your fingers laced through mine, just like this—all night long."

A small gasp came out of me as he tightened his grip on me, just slightly. "I wondered what it might be like to hold your hand in the moonlight, to walk you around the lake and kiss you. To take you on the grassy hill, your hands above your head, with mine in yours. Just like this—feeling every soft curve of you from the inside."

"Even then?" I panted, heat building in my belly.

"Even then, and every time after. When my father asked me to seduce you, it was hardly a chore. I already wanted you more than any other woman on Interra. You were one of the few I could not have, and that made the ache for you all the sweeter."

His grip on me loosened, and his touch reappeared on my neck, slowly unbuttoning each of the tiny buttons on my lace camisole. "And then it was the skin just here, in the hollow of your neck, or the swell of your breasts in all those gowns."

He pressed a kiss just below my ear. "To say that I am mesmerized by the merest hint of your skin would be the height of understatement. To touch you now is a privilege I scarcely deserve."

"I wouldn't go quite so far," I replied, feeling very generous as his fingers sent chills into every sensitive nerve-ending in my body.

"Then let me go further," he said, as one hand dipped lower, grazing over the curve of my belly, then between my legs. When he had my bare thighs spread between the strong cage of his legs, he began to stroke the spot at the apex of my thighs, slowly, lightly. "My desire for you goes deeper than the Claim."

My back arched against his chest in an attempt to press his fingers harder into me. His free hand went around my neck as he trailed soft kisses across my jaw, groaning into the sensitive shell of my ear.

"Is this for me?" he asked as one finger slipped easily inside me, drawing out the wet evidence of how he affected me.

"Yes," I moaned.

"I can't believe I get to touch you," he whispered, another finger joining the first. "I don't deserve this."

I could not form words as his thumb traced circles around the spot I needed him most.

"Please," he growled in my ear. "Please, let me add another finger."

"Yes." I bucked my hips against him as he stretched me further. He slowly pushed in and out of me, my desire coating his hand.

"Thank you," he snarled, sounding nearly feral. His cock was hard against my backside. I heard him inhale as my legs opened wider so I could take his fourth finger. "You feel so incredible."

I yanked my camisole down to expose my breasts.

"Will you touch yourself?" he whispered as he pushed into me, filling me with all four of his fingers.

I pinched my nipples, playing with them until they stood in stiff peaks.

"It isn't your body, Mina," he whispered in my ear, a desperate edge in his voice now as the hand around my neck moved lower, to cup the curve of my belly. "Though every single curve and angle of you drives me to distraction."

The fingers between my legs pulled out, leaving me empty. I whimpered with need.

"It's the sharp edge of your tongue," he said before he kissed me, our mouths meeting in a tangle as his wet fingers traced deliciously tight circles between my legs. Ash played my body like a lyre on a sultry summer night, slowly strumming every note of pleasure from me. I writhed in his arms, wanting more, deeper, harder, faster.

"It's the way you look at me when you've had some brilliant thought."

"Ash," I pleaded, begging for release. I gazed up into his eyes.

"It's the way you saved my life," he said as his mouth captured mine again. When he broke the kiss, his eyes were as glazed over as mine. "It is not just the Claim, Mina."

I twisted in his arms, not wanting him to say more. I understood what he was trying to say, but I couldn't hear about love just yet. Swiftly, to distract him, I worked to unfasten his pants, freeing his hard length.

His eyes held mine as I climbed on top of him. "I know," I said as I sank down on him, letting the tortuous exhilaration of him filling me wash over us both. A low vibration spread through the places we connected.

I leaned back, pressing myself harder into him as he moved in me. "I'd forgotten you could do that," I murmured as the sensation increased—a hidden benefit to the Ventyr body that lurked under his glamour.

He smiled at me, earnest as Claymore, wicked as Thuellos, wise as the Warden. He was all three, all I needed, all I wanted, all I had ever loved. Heat built in my core as my hips undulated. Shadows of aether wound around my hands, my eyes glowing bright.

"Shift," I commanded. "I want all of you."

Worry filled Ash's eyes. "Are you certain?"

I nodded. "All of you. *Now.*"

"Fuck," he groaned. His glamour slipped away, his clothes going with it. Inside me, he lengthened, the ridges not apparent in his fey form caressing my inner walls, the vibration between us intensifying.

He was taller in his true form, bigger in every way possible. He sat forward to allow his six magnificent draconic wings to spread out behind him. He grinned, his fangs showing, then ripped the bottoms of my undergarments away, like they were nothing more than sopping wet paper. His wings wrapped around us as he pulled on my hips, thrusting deeper still inside me as my aether swirled around us.

"You are all I have ever needed, or wanted," he breathed as my breasts pressed into the hard plane of his chest.

His eyes glowed with celestial light. We held tight to one another as I bared my neck. His fangs slid into me with only the slightest pressure. When he pressed his wrist to my mouth, my own fangs protracted. As soon as they pierced his skin, I felt the difference. In his true form, the Claim was stronger than it had ever been.

Stronger than I remembered it being on Interra, when I was in my own true form. The thought confused me. How could the Claim be more powerful now than it had been when we both possessed a

Ventyr body? The taste of celestial fire, sulphurous and smoky, mixed with his blood. When my mouth broke free from his skin, my eyes burned with his power.

Heat drove through me, curling tight in my belly and then snapping taut in response to Ashbourne's cry of pleasure as he spilled into me. Empyrae wove with aether above us, harmless in my power's embrace. Release was not far behind, my body responding to every last movement of my lover's ministrations. I don't know when my eyes fell closed, but when I opened them, Ashbourne watched me carefully.

"Are you satisfied, love?" he asked.

"Yes," I breathed. "More than I have been in a long time."

CHAPTER 21

MINA

Ash left to find us a cup of tea, and I took the opportunity to bathe. His room looked out over the city. The day had turned cloudy, a mix of rain and snow obscuring most of the view, but in the short glimpses I got of the city as the clouds parted, there was plenty of movement below. Pravhna was bustling with energy, preparing for the Grand Exhibition.

"Our clothes have arrived," Ash said as he entered. "Viridian's people just came from Madame Laquoix."

I frowned. "More clothes?"

Ash nodded. "Poe went ahead and called her with an order. She'd already been at work for us, apparently. I have a feeling Edith had a hand in that."

I frowned, feeling uncomfortable about the prospect of being on display in public. "Poe is preparing for after the announcement."

Ash seemed to share my discomfort, and his jaw clenched so hard a muscle in it twitched. "Where would you like your clothes? I don't believe I know which room is yours."

I glanced around the room he occupied. It was quite large. I knew exactly what I wanted to say, but the words were stuck at the back of my throat. Ash watched me as he set the tea tray down by the marble hearth. I hadn't noticed I'd done it, but I was gripping the edge of the tub.

"Stop that," he whispered, taking my hands in his. "There's plenty of room here, if you'd like to stay with me."

I nodded once, grateful not to have to force the vulnerable words from my mouth. Ash's fingers wrapped around my chin, guiding my eyes to his. "But I must tell you something important first."

My heart beat faster. "All right."

He stepped away from me, my fingertips slipping through his hands like water. I had the sudden sense that I was falling, that whatever he would tell me would change things. For better or worse, I wasn't sure. He had a word with whoever had delivered the trunks, and I saw the pile in the hallway. Poe had gone overboard with the wardrobe. Ash stepped back inside and closed the door.

He smiled at me, but the expression didn't reach his eyes, which were narrow. "In the oubliette, the god came to me."

The air in my lungs froze. That was not at all what I was expecting him to say. I managed to nod to show that I understood Ash's words. Faintly, the sound of flames in the hearth kept me tethered to the room. Kept me from floating away to protect myself.

"The Old One helped me with my memory, showing me our past —my past—in an order that made sense," he said as he came to stand in front of me.

"That was very helpful," I said. No emotion stirred in me. It was as though I'd simply stopped. "What did you give in return for that aid?"

Ash's knuckles brushed against my cheek. "You know all about these deals, don't you?"

I nodded once, my chin shaking. *He knew what I had done for him.* "I do."

He brushed a soft kiss to my temple, then another to my lips. I melted into him, clinging hard to this moment, lest what came next shatter my fragile security. "I am to help you in your quest, and at the end, you'll go free," he said, wrapping his arms around me.

"What about you?" I asked, my face buried in his shirt.

"We will see," he said. "The terms were... ambiguous."

I gasped, pounding my fist against him. "That was foolish of you."

He grinned at me. "But *you* will be free."

The words tumbled out before I could stop them. "As if that would mean anything to me without you."

His grin widened. "Won't it?"

I glared, and he wrapped me in his arms again. His voice rumbled in his chest. "All that matters is that we get you to the right standing stones. Bird by bird, love. That's how we're taking this."

It took effort not to scream at him. My muscles tensed, but that hurt, so I let them relax. Ash lifted me into his arms, bringing me out of the tub. I was quiet as he dried me with a warm towel, then wrapped me in his robe. Lazily, as though we had all the time in the world, I followed him to a pair of chairs next to the hearth. He poured us both tea.

Before I took a sip, I said, "I prefer to look at the bigger picture. None of this bird by bird nonsense."

He smiled at me, the arm that held me gripping just a bit tighter. "I know. So you look at the big picture and I'll knock the birds down, one by one."

I wasn't exactly sure what he was saying, but I got the gist. He wouldn't try to change the way I did things, but I shouldn't interfere with his way, either. It didn't have to be my way or his. We could work together. "All right," I said, finally.

We stared into one another's eyes, and the cosmos shifted. I felt the whole of my emotions for him; the idea of spending our lives together spread out ahead of me. It was much the same as it had been when I'd imagined it just days ago, but more real somehow. I no longer thought we could ignore the problems of our past, or what transpired in the here and now.

There was no choice but to do as he said, to knock the birds down, one by one—whatever that meant. He would focus on what was directly in front of us, and I would put the pieces together so we would understand what was actually happening here. And after that, there would be other challenges. Nothing would ever be easy between us. We were too different for that.

But there would be the ease of knowing that we were a good fit.

That where one of us left off, the other began. And there would be love, too, if we could both let it in. A smile blossomed from deep within me, spreading into the corners of my mouth.

"Are you happy?" he asked.

I nodded, so overcome by emotion that I couldn't speak. He took my cup and set it aside, reaching for me. There was a soft knock at the door. Ash sighed. "Come," he called out.

The door opened, revealing Skye and Poe. Both looked rather anxious. Poe held up her right hand, where a giant sapphire sparkled on her pointer finger. "We are engaged."

Skye grinned, then, taking our position in, frowned. "Are the two of you..."

Ash pushed me gently off his lap and into a standing position. He rose behind me, my body still resting against his as one arm went around my waist in just the right amount of protectiveness. He steadied me, making sure I wouldn't fall. "We have come to an agreement of our own."

Poe raised her eyebrows at me. I shrugged, but I knew there was a sparkle in my eyes. I could feel it, the peace that simply choosing a path had brought me. There was no way to control the future, but fighting my feelings for Ash made no sense. I needed every bit of my acuity for understanding what we were up against with the Ravager and Chopard.

"Congratulations," I said, stepping forward to take Poe's hand and admire the ring. "This is lovely."

She hugged me, whispering, "It's real," in my ear. When she pulled away, there were happy tears in her eyes. "I know it seems fast..."

I shook my head. Behind us, Skye and Ash were having their own soft-spoken version of this conversation. "It's not fast if this is what you want."

She smiled at me. "There would always have been a political marriage, eventually."

I frowned. It sounded as though she was making the best of things.

Poe's hands fluttered in front of her. "That's not what I meant... I mean, I love Skye. I've been falling in love with her since the moment we met last summer. This is fast, but we have time for it to deepen and grow. And I know it will. It's like there's a tether between us, something that ties us together. Do you know what I mean?"

I didn't. Not exactly. But there was a scrap of that idea that made sense. It was the way I knew that Ash and I would bicker over what to eat for dinner and how to spend our leisure time, but that we would finish one another's sentences when it mattered, and know one another inside out within a month. There was an eternity in front of us, and somehow I knew how we'd spend it. It wasn't a perfect-looking fantasy; it was a life. A full, thriving, wild life that I desperately wanted.

I nodded. "I understand."

"I thought you might," Poe answered. "Now, you don't have to do this job forever, but will you take your place as my Lady Chamberlain?"

I frowned slightly. "What exactly does that entail?"

Poe smiled. "On the old world, it made you my second in command. Here, it will be a little like being my lady of honor. It's a social position more than anything else, since I will have no real power as the heir."

"That hardly matters," I said. "If it lets me stay with you for even a little while longer, of course I will accept."

Poe hugged me again. "I will never let Helene get her hands on you again, Mina. I promise."

It was a kind thing for her to say, but both of us knew very well that if Helene wanted something from me, she would get it. Inhabited by the Ravager, her power might be limitless. We were going to have to work fast to find out how to destroy her, and Chopard.

I pulled away from Poe. "So, what are our next steps?"

CHAPTER 22

ASHBOURNE

The next three days flew by in a flurry of action as the five of us worked with House Aestra to try to find each of the potential locations for the standing stones and determine how to get to each of them before Niall and Chopard. Not knowing what they already knew was a deficit, but as we examined each potential location a pattern emerged.

These were not abandoned buildings, or remote locations. Each was heavily guarded, or very public. None would be easy to get to and complete any kind of ritual that expected privacy. Skye pointed out that this was likely why he'd hit the abandoned locations first. Unlike what Mina and Poe described with Morgaine Yarlo's quiet cuts through the fabric of the universe, we had to assume that Chopard's process was more complicated, otherwise, he'd already have found whatever it was he was looking for. This slowed down our progress, but it would also slow Chopard's.

In the meantime, House Aestra released an announcement about both Skye and Poe's engagement and Poe's claim to the seat of the lost heir in every major newspaper. A flurry of high society callers came, many with tests of their own to administer. Poe passed every single one with flying colors. Some were merely questions, intimate questions, but Poe knew all the answers they wanted.

Others tested her blood, her magic, and asked her to shift into the Feriant, which she did so many times that Elspeth had the parlor furniture moved so she would stop knocking over the centuries-old porcelain planters with her wings. The whole thing made Mina anxious, and so my duty was to keep her thoughts elsewhere.

That was no chore. In fact, it seemed as though any spare moment we had was spent relieving ourselves of the need to hold back our desire for one another. The fervor was finally dying down. We had renewed the Claim enough times that the distracting levels of lust had finally lessened. I could wind my fingers in her long, silky hair without feeling as though I needed to bury my fangs in her neck now.

Mina was restless for other reasons, wanting to get to the standing stones being first among them. But we were being so closely watched that we had to be extra careful now—not only by society, but by Helene. She had sent several calling cards, and our last Oscarovi caller had let Mina know that she was voicing frustration quite openly that House Aestra was "keeping Mina from her."

We would have to see her soon, lest society suspect something more was going on. But tonight was not that night. The day had been icy, and it turned off our stream of callers. When cancellations came pouring in, Mina had gone back to bed. Skye and Poe followed her lead. Tonight was their first official social event as an engaged couple, and Poe declared that we all needed rest since the weather was poised to keep us from our usual frenetic pace. We were attending an airship party this evening that would kick off the Grand Exhibition's opening events.

Mina sat in bed next to me, looking over the list one more time, her long hair wrapped in curlers. We should be getting dressed, but instead we were still laying about. There was something luxurious about the act of putting off the hustle and bustle for another few minutes, and I was enjoying our time alone.

But Mina had been quiet for far too long, reading over the guest list for this evening. "Is something wrong?" I asked, wondering if she'd spotted some evidence that Helene might be in attendance.

"No," she said, but her voice was too quiet. "Not exactly. It's just..." She got out of bed. I smiled, watching her walk across the room, her sheer nightgown trailing the floor. It was such a domestic scene. She didn't even reach for a robe to cover herself. She stood at the desk by the window, rifling through papers on the desk she'd claimed for herself.

When she turned back towards me, a few strands of her dark hair had come loose from her curlers and her face had a fresh look to it that reminded me of a summer's day in Lyonesse, the home of my childhood. I could practically see her in my tower bedroom, looking just as she did now. Past and present collided in a thousand ways as she walked towards me, holding a piece of paper.

"Do you ever miss Interra?" I asked as she climbed back into bed.

She turned the aetheric lamp next to the bed on. It emitted a greenish-gold glow and Mina leaned towards it, examining yet another list. "No," she replied. "Never."

I raised an eyebrow as she sat back, leaning into the pile of pillows I'd stacked behind her. She closed her eyes. "There was never a life for me there, Ash."

It took everything in me not to argue with her about the beauty of the world, about missing the *land*. She had no good memories of home. My siblings and I had grown up with harsh Ventyr parents, and the endless wars, but I was never in doubt that my mother and father loved us. Looking back now, I recognized that they were wrong in many of the ways they raised us, but at the very least, I knew they loved us. Mina hadn't had that.

She'd lived most of her life without her mother, and Boreas had only loved her, in his whole life. He was obsessed with his children—or rather how they could serve him—but cared nothing for them as people. And because he'd loved Mina's mother, he'd shown her more affection than he had the twins, but it wasn't clear to me if Boreas was even capable of love. I hadn't known the difference between us was so stark until I'd had nothing but time in Nihil. By then it was too late.

I shook off the memories and picked up the list she'd been reading. "What is this?"

"A list of the lecturers for the opening week." She sighed. "Most of them are coming to the party tonight, but I was hoping Eccles would be there, and he's not."

I pulled her into my lap. "Are you so eager for things to be dangerous and miserable again?"

Mina laughed, and I was relieved to be able to smile with her. Sometimes she didn't catch my humor, but making her laugh was quickly becoming one of life's great joys. She didn't smile or laugh genuinely very often, and it was one of my objectives to give her more to smile about.

"No, I just want this to be over." I could not agree with her more. She passed me the original list. "But he's not coming, or wasn't invited."

I glanced over the list. The guests were primarily Vilhari, with only a few of the richest Oscarovi. Vionette Celestine, one of the Halcyon Gate Syndicate leaders, had wrangled an invitation, and I spotted Muse and his lover Arcturus near the end of the list. "Who is giving this party, anyway?"

"One of Mirabelle's friends," Mina answered. "Which is good, in some ways, as Helene will not be invited."

So her examination of the guest lists really wasn't about Helene. "Do you really think that Lord Eccles might be Chopard? We have so little evidence."

She frowned, setting the lists aside. "That's the problem, isn't it. Even with the work Mirabelle and Elspeth have done for years, and all of the Syndicate's resources, there's just so little to go on. How has Chopard kept his identity such a secret?"

I shrugged, feeling less concerned with the whys and hows of machinations past, and primarily concerned with how we were going to end this, and what the consequences of our actions might be. We too were operating in secret, and the potential for that creating some sort of backlash was increasingly worrisome to me.

I stared at the ceiling, trying to follow Mina's train of thought. If she was worried about this, I had to assume she was onto something important. "Do you think that if Lord Eccles were Chopard, that he would let himself be so obviously associated with Niall?"

She fussed with the blanket, worrying it between her fingers. "That's what's bothering me. After so long being careful and so successful keeping his identity secret, why would he leave so many clues now?"

I took one of her hands in mine and kissed her fingertips. "It seems unlikely, doesn't it?"

She nodded, but the furrow in her brow told me she wasn't convinced. "It does. Logically, it does."

There was a part of me that wanted to dismiss her worry, to tell her she was imagining things. But I had learned my lesson about that, and it was time to prove it. "We can look into Lord Eccles' history further tomorrow."

The way her eyes lit up almost hurt. She was used to being dismissed about things like this. Not by Poe, I reminded myself. It bothered me that I had not been the first to show Mina the respect she deserved, though not in a way that made me resentful of Poe. Quite the opposite.

I was grateful for the opportunity to do better for the woman I loved. Further, I was grateful that she had friends to love her, as well as myself. For the first time in a long, long while, it felt as though time stretched further ahead than the present moment. Like there was a full life ahead of all of us, a future where we continued on, rather than another ending.

Things were not settled with the god, it was true, but it had never seemed cruel to me before. Perhaps I was too trusting, but it didn't make sense to me that it would trick us simply to use us up and punish us needlessly. But I had been wrong about such things before. The consequences would be dire if I was wrong now.

As I sat brooding, Mina got up. She disappeared into the bathing chamber and dressing room. The quiet sounds of her getting ready for the evening were a balm to my soul. I closed my eyes, listening to the soft click of various instruments and jewels. Candles flickered on the bureau across the room. I could almost fall asleep.

Are you doing as I asked, Ashbourne? The voice was soft inside my head, as though it whispered.

Yes, I answered silently. *But if you are here now, why not simply go in there and help her yourself? Give her whatever she needs to do your will and be done with it.*

Alas, the god answered. *There are rules, even for one such as myself. We made a covenant between us, and now both of us are bound to it. She must meet me at the standing stones.*

You could at least tell us where to go, I argued.

If I knew, I would. Even I do not know which are the right ones, or where we shall meet. That is all up to one greater than myself.

Lady Fate? I asked.

Fortune, fate, destiny, she has gone by many names. There was a long pause. Just when I thought the god had gone, it spoke again. *Time runs astray. Beware.*

And then the god was gone. It was hard to say exactly how I knew, but I was sure of it. I got up, dressing quickly, thinking over its words. Behind me, I felt when Mina came out of the dressing room, rather than seeing her. Her arms wrapped around my waist.

"What did it want?" she asked.

"How did you know?"

I felt her sigh go through me. "I don't know. Could it have been the Claim?"

Her words drifted through my mind, as though searching for some lost knowledge. But the truth was that the Claim was little understood, even by our forebears. Its limits and possibilities were unknown because the Ventyr had only seen it as a tool for dominance over one another.

I wondered then about my nephew, about Connoch's son, Finbar, and his little witch, Harlow. It was the first time I let myself think about them. "Connoch and Aislin had a child."

Mina turned me in her arms. It took everything I had not muss her. She was dressed in a pair of plum colored high-waisted trousers with wide legs, and a matching diaphanous silk blouse that was cut low, giving a scandalous view of her decolletage. It was an alluring mix of masculine and feminine style that I deeply appreciated. Pinned at the shoulder of her blouse was a shimmering dark bird, covered in dozens of tiny black diamonds. She wore no other jewelry but the ring Edith Braithwaite had bade me give to her.

"Eyes up here," Mina purred. When I complied, her smile was faint and her eyes serious. "What was that about your brother and his unfortunate wife?"

Memories of Lumina and Aislin verbally sparring fluttered about in my mind. My beautiful menace had been one of the few people

Boreas would not destroy for slighting his former mistress. "They had a child, who is now a full grown man."

Mina raised her eyebrows, twisting the opal ring on her finger. "Is he as terrible as they are?"

I tweaked her nose. "No. He seems very different from Connoch. More like Thalia, actually." It was bittersweet to think of my sister. She would have loved to have known Finbar, and he was so like her, meticulous and a born leader. I wished I wouldn't have let that fact get in the way of me getting to know him better. "He and his partner were trying to fight the Ravager on their own world."

"Okairos?" Mina breathed. "Is she one of the Ventyr as well?"

"No," I replied. "She's a witch, a sorcière. Like you."

Mina's eyes widened, and for a moment I thought she might be putting some incredible thought together, having some kind of a breakthrough. But instead, her gray eyes filled with tears. "They're like us?"

Suddenly, I understood. She was moved by the idea that there was another couple like us out there, torn apart by the Ravagers, just trying to make it through. I brushed a kiss to her cheeks. "There is no one like us. Because there is no one like you."

She smiled up at me; it was more of a grin, really. Laughter and a smile, all within the span of an hour. I was the luckiest man in the cosmos. "I love you."

The words hit me harder than I expected they ever could. Of course, I loved her, and I'd hoped that she loved me too. But in this moment, this was more than I ever could have hoped for. Tears pricked at the corners of my eyes and my throat tightened with emotion. "And I love you."

There were no beautiful speeches, no poetic lines. Just those three little words that meant everything in the world. The words that banished the curse once and for all, but more than that, healed something in both our souls that had been broken long before we met one another.

Her hand slipped into mine. "Come now, or we'll be late."

I pulled her close to my side, pressing one kiss to the top of her head and another to her lips. "Anything you say, love."

CHAPTER 23

MINA

The airship was beautifully appointed. Crystal chandeliers sparkled with aetheric light, shuddering a little as we took off. They cast a warm glow on the floral carvings in the wood-paneled walls. But I was pinned to the window, my attention on the city below as we rose slowly from the platform we'd boarded in House Aestra's Nepheline Echelon.

As we left the ground, I found myself a bit queasy. The ship shook from time to time, and I was unsteady on my feet. I had never been afraid of heights before, but something about leaving the ground in such a vehicle turned my stomach, despite the luxurious accommodations. Ash's fingers closed protectively around mine when my heartbeat's pace quickened.

"Turns my gut a bit too," he murmured, looking down on Pravhna with me.

The evening was a cloudy one, though not rainy, for a change. The spires of the Nepheline rose out of the cloud cover, like a city of their own in the stars. As the airship ascended, my feeling of unease lessened somewhat. Up here, above the clouds, the sailing was much smoother. Perhaps that was all that feeling had been, a bit of turbulence.

I took a deep breath and then turned to the interior of the ship.

The decor was luxurious, all gleaming wood and brass fittings. The ceiling was spelled to resemble the night sky, the light from sparkling stars refracting through the crystal chandeliers in a dazzling array of opulence. It was so rare to see the stars, unencumbered by clouds, that I couldn't help but be impressed.

A string quartet played from somewhere deeper in the ship. A casino night had been set up to keep the party-goers busy, but I disliked gambling, so felt no lure from the tables. When I said so, Poe and Ash shared a smile. I hid my irritation. They meant no harm in whatever their shared feeling about me was.

Poe was resplendent this evening in a sweeping midnight blue gown and a crown of diamond starbursts in her thick hair. She looked every bit the lost heir, her cosmetics subtle, but effective, and no jewelry but the diadem. Her gown was simple, but so beautifully made that no one could deny its quality.

Skye appeared with a tray of drinks in hand, looking debonair in a tuxedo that matched Ash's. She handed the tray to him and sighed. "Could I borrow you and Poe?"

Ash frowned, stepping closer to me. Skye's head tilted to the side. "I'm sorry, my godmother wants to meet the two of you, and she is a bit rude to Oscarovi sometimes, Mina. You can come…"

I shook my head, taking a glass of sparkling wine from the tray Ash held. "No, thank you. I will be fine alone."

Skye breathed a sigh of relief. "I am sorry."

I smiled at her, attempting to show her I was all right, but it only served to make her frown. Poe touched my arm. "What did we talk about regarding false smiles?"

It wasn't unusual for Oscarovi and Vilhari to have issues with one another. So while I didn't hold Skye to account for her godmother's opinions, it didn't exactly feel *good* to be told I wasn't wanted. I narrowed my eyes at Poe and bared my teeth. "Is this better?"

"Yes," she said, completely serious. "That is, actually."

Ash kissed my forehead as they walked away. "I like all your faces, for what it is worth."

I rolled my eyes and turned back to the windows, watching the clouds for air elementals. Anything to avoid having to talk to anyone. So far, I hadn't been able to find Muse and Arcturus, and it was impossible to tell where Morpheus had gotten off to. Better to stay here alone than to venture out into the crowd.

Viridian was here somewhere, but he'd been forced to bring Caralee, and besides, it would be strange to see us socializing in a friendly way at this point. It was well known that we did not like one another, and we'd already risked things with his visits to House Aestra.

Alone it was, then. I sipped my wine slowly, listening to the sounds beneath the music and conversation. Something was making a noise I recognized, but could not yet identify, somewhere deep in the ship. This often happened. When I was stressed or overstimulated, I could hear the aetheric power running through the lines, or a slight mechanical anomaly in an autocar. Likely, it was nothing, but it was something to do to try to parse it out.

"All alone?" a smooth feminine voice asked.

"Go away, Caralee," I said without looking to my left. She stood too close to me, close enough that I could see the little stain on her right-hand glove, where she'd likely gripped an hors d'oeuvre earlier in the evening.

"Why?" she asked. "When you and I have so much to discuss."

I glanced at her. Her cheeks were flushed red, as though she was in a pet about something. I sighed. "Get to whatever point you're coming to, please."

"Why didn't you tell me Helene had returned?" There was an uncharacteristic note of panic in her voice. Interesting.

I turned towards her, frowning. "We are not friends. Why would I have done such a thing?"

She heaved a petulant sigh, causing her small breasts to strain against the too-tight bodice of her crimson gown. It was an ugly choice for her to have made, as it did not fit her well, but I understood why she wore it. She must be hoping to entice Viridian with it. I almost felt sorry for her.

"You and Viridian have been getting along better," she said. "I know he's come to pay homage to the lost heir several times. I just thought maybe you would have—"

I held up a hand. "Caralee, stop. You pretended to be my friend when we were children so you could tell my secrets to…everyone. Do you remember that?"

Her shoulders flounced. "What does that have to do with anything?"

In one horrible instant, I realized there was no way for me to understand her. "What does it… I—"

It took every bit of strength I had not to slap her silly. How could anyone betray another person that way, even as children, and not understand how I felt? It was possible, I supposed, that Caralee had no sense of right and wrong. But if she had no sense of it, then why would she be angry with me now? Enervation snuck in. I would give anything to be anywhere else—for her to simply disappear.

"Mina!" a deep voice rumbled behind me. "I have been looking everywhere for you, dear girl." Muse came to stand beside me. "Hello, Caralee," he said with much less warmth. "Would you mind giving Mina and I a bit of space? Arcturus and I had a terrible fight, and I need to talk."

Caralee's lip curled. "Good luck talking to *her* about it. She hasn't a scrap of emotion for anyone but herself." She stalked off into the crowd.

Muse watched her go. He wore a beautiful three-piece emerald suit, and tonight his locs swung free of his usual bun and were decorated with tiny glowing fire-moths. The effect was enchanting.

"You look beautiful," I breathed, deeply impressed with his sense of style.

"Thank you," he said with a smile. "So do you."

I shrugged, but appreciated the compliment. "I am sorry about Arcturus. What can I do to help?"

Muse bumped my arm, an affectionate warmth in his dark eyes. "Apologies for my deception. Arcturus and I argued over what to have for lunch today, so not technically a lie, but I think we are all right."

"Oh," I said, feeling confused. "You're sure?"

He smiled, looking a bit smug. "Oh yes. A good argument can be quite a lot of fun, don't you think?" He arched a thick eyebrow at me, mischief glimmering in his eyes.

I nodded, color flushing my cheeks. "Yes."

"I just don't like Caralee," he said, keeping his voice soft. "Will you come sit with Arcturus and myself?"

"Thank you," I said, following the seer as he turned away from the window.

We wove through the crowd. Feathers brushed my sleeve from a Vilhari with the most stunning ebony wings. A few Corvidae mixed with the group of winged Vilhari, and they glanced at me with intrigue as Muse and I passed them. The news about Poe had, indeed, made me an object of interest. I lowered my eyes as I followed Muse.

Knowing that people were watching helped nothing. If I didn't look, it was easier to ignore it. The sound of people enjoying themselves dulled in my hearing as my ears strained to hear whatever noise I'd heard before under the music. It was louder now. Muse glanced back at me; concern clear on his face.

"You hear that, don't you?" I asked.

He nodded towards Ash, Poe, and Skye, who headed towards us, weaving through the crowd. "Yes, I hear it," he said. "And I think they do too."

Morpheus materialized at my feet. *Something is amiss.*

I caught sight of Viridian's cerise brocade smoking jacket before anything else. He appeared as though out of nowhere, at my side. "Do you hear it?" he whispered.

"I hear *something*," I whispered back as Muse began to walk again. I let him lead, as Morpheus and I followed. Now I could see where Arcturus sat in a corner of the room, where several plush velvet chairs were arranged in a semi-circle facing a couch. Muse reached him first, touching his forehead, as though he were in pain, whispering something to his partner. Morpheus jumped up on the couch next to them, rubbing his face against Muse's leg.

Poe and I both sat, while Skye and the men stood behind us. Viridian bent to speak to me, a quick flourish of his hand weaving threads. The natural sounds of people talking and laughing faded, the string quartet going next. Now, I heard the sound of the airship's engine, the beating heart of the ship. And something else—whispers that masked screams, and a low creaking that sounded like the universe was breaking open.

"What is that?" I murmured, unable to grasp the memory that danced just out of reach. It was there. I knew it was, but I couldn't latch onto it.

Viridian shook his head. "Nothing good."

I glanced back at Ash, who'd gone a bit gray. "It is the sound of otham."

Now I remembered. It wasn't just one memory, but hundreds. I'd heard the sounds of distressed otham on Interra so many times that it had ceased to be interesting. My stomach roiled at the collection of memories. As uncomfortable as it was, it was information about the return of my memory, another piece in the puzzle to turn over in my mind.

Muse blinked a few times, his face animating. "Not the sound of healthy otham."

Ash shook his head. "No, that is the sound of otham that is being drained too quickly from the heart of the limen."

Skye threw a hand up. "Could someone please explain?"

Poe took her hand, pressing a kiss to her palm. "At the heart of the limen, the world between worlds—"

Skye pressed a kiss to Poe's hand, smiling at her, mirth sparkling in her eyes. "I *do* know what the limen is, my love."

Poe smiled back, her eyes filling with emotion. I felt it as she did, the way Skye leaned into her. The devotion in her eyes. This was all I wanted for my friend: to be loved just exactly like this.

Muse leaned forward before Poe could speak again. "But do you? Do any of us really know what the limen is?" He looked to Ash. "You must know it the best of all of us."

Skye frowned at Muse, watching Arcturus take his partner's hand in a protective gesture. The Oscarovi was worried about something. "We all know what the limen is. It's the first thing you learn about magic." Her face took on an expression that was very like Elspeth's. "All aethereal power comes from the limen, the world between worlds. The place that connects all worlds and lives within everything. It is the basis of power."

Muse nodded. "Of course, that is correct. But it misses the point. Why does the limen exist?"

Dread pooled in my gut. Muse knew something we did not, and

he was struggling with whether or not to tell us. Suddenly, I understood the way his face had gone blank. He'd been trying to determine what the consequences for telling us might be. It was dangerous business to tempt Lady Fate into noticing you. Arcturus' grip tightened around Muse's hand. He was worried as well.

I stood as Morpheus curled at Arcturus' feet. "Don't say anything else."

Muse looked up at me, his dark brown eyes embattled. "I want to help."

I nodded, bending to take his free hand. "I understand. But you've seen a future where telling us goes wrong, haven't you?"

He nodded, his warm hand slipping from mine to cover his mouth. His eyes squeezed shut. "Yes. But…"

"Darling," Arcturus pleaded. "Don't. Please."

Ash crouched down, placing a hand on Muse's shoulder. "My friend, we know you are not withholding knowledge from us to be malicious."

Muse looked at Ash as though he'd seen a ghost. "In so many instances, I tell you, and it saves you all."

Viridian broke in. "And in others, we die horribly." He pushed his long, pale hair away from his handsome face. The irritation in his previous words drained away. "This is the way of Fate. It is not your fault, Muse."

The seer nodded. "I understand. I only wish I could help." He looked at Arcturus. "You were right. We should not have come tonight."

There was pain in Arcturus' eyes. He knew—whatever it was Muse had seen—he knew what it was. He was Muse's secret keeper. The one the seer told all the unimaginably hard things he saw. Arcturus was Muse's steadying force, his lifeline to sanity.

Poe stood, her jaw set tightly. "There are safety vessels. Morpheus, do you know where they are located?"

The cat nodded solemnly. *But there are not enough for everyone on the ship.*

"Take Arcturus and Muse and get back to the city. We will deal with whatever is happening here," Poe ordered. She sounded like a queen. Morpheus rubbed his face against Muse's leg, and it appeared to me that he was saying something comforting to the seer. Both he and Arcturus followed Morpheus out a door that led to a stairwell just behind where we were seated.

"So it begins in earnest, tonight," Ash murmured as he took Muse's seat. Viridian and Skye both sat as well.

"What?" I asked, panic mounting in my chest.

His eyes were sad. "Our fight with the Ravager. That sound—it is the sound the otham made at the heart of the limen. In Nihil. Thousands of years in the limen, and I have only ever heard the otham make that noise when it is in deep distress."

"It is here," I breathed, hazarding a glance at Poe, whose eyes closed. But the look on Ash's face told me everything I needed to know. Something terrible was about to happen on this ship.

CHAPTER 24

MINA

A long moment passed in silence, tension mounting as the seconds passed. Poe's eyes snapped open, and her spine lengthened as her chin lifted. Whatever she'd needed a moment to digest, she had re-centered herself now. Pride welled up in me. It was as though she'd gone from being my friend to being queen in the mere space between heartbeats. This was what royalty looked like, and I understood why the Larae had followed House Feriant for so long.

Poe nodded to Viridian, Skye, and Ash. "What should we do next?"

A queen who could delegate. The vision was an attractive one. Sound had returned to the room, fading slowly back in as Viridian's working wore off, but I could still hear the otham's whispered screams. The Ravager was somewhere on this airship. I twisted the opal ring, trying to keep the tremor in my hands from showing.

"First, we need to find out if anyone has seen Helene," Viridian said. His tone was overly bright, unusual for him. "The last time we encountered the Ravager, it wore her face."

Skye and Ash nodded. Neither seemed to notice that Viridian was as scared as I was. The idea made sense to me, so I nodded as well. Skye took a deep breath, and I wondered if she was trying to steady herself. Were we all frightened? "We also need to keep everyone calm."

"Distracted would be better," Ash added.

Skye let out a wry laugh. It sounded forced. "Yes. Agreed."

Poe reached out to take Skye's hand, her eyes wide and her voice low and gentle. We *were* all afraid. "Then we should announce our wedding date."

Skye's cheeks flushed as she lowered her eyes. "That would be a good distraction, I think."

"I will circulate through the crowd," Viridian said. "Find out if anyone has seen Helene tonight."

Ash made a thoughtful noise, but when our eyes went to him, he nodded. "Yes, that seems prudent."

"What about us?" I asked.

Ash smiled at me. Of all of us, he showed no signs of fear. "You and I are going below decks."

Viridian's gaze sharpened. "You don't think Helene is here, do you?"

Ash shrugged. "I think it best to cover all angles. You find out if anyone has seen her. At the very least, if she isn't here, that will give us a good read on what she's been up to."

Poe took a deep breath. "That would be helpful. People have been reluctant to discuss her while we've been at House Aestra."

Skye blushed again. "It's Mother. She's always cultivated a very... formal... atmosphere."

"Then we have our marching orders," Viridian said, standing. He looked as though he wanted to say something else, but settled on, "Stay safe, everyone."

I understood his choice. The idea of facing the Ravager on an airship was terrifying. Not because we feared for our own lives, though I was certain we all did. But because there was no easy way to keep the rest of the ship safe.

We were responsible for these people now. Poe as their future queen, and the rest of us as her Court. Viridian left our little group first. I pulled on Poe's sleeve. "If this goes sideways, get off the ship any way possible."

She frowned at me. "And what about you?"

I raised an eyebrow. "I will be with Ash. If necessary, he can take his true form." Poe looked as though she might argue. But if I was truly to be her Lady Chamberlain, then she should take my advice. I straightened my spine and did my best to inject more authority into my voice. "There aren't enough safety vessels because most of the Vilhari can transform into birds or have wings to start with. If something goes wrong and the ship might go down, get *off.*"

Poe kissed my cheek, standing on her tiptoes to do so. "You are a wonderful Lady Chamberlain, Mina Wildfang. Like the stories of old."

I didn't know which stories she spoke of. I hadn't had the benefit of growing up in a culture that venerated the old Empire's ways. When the Ventyr left Vilhar behind, they created a new culture on a new world. But I liked the way Poe looked at me, so I bowed my head to her.

Ash and I watched as she and Skye walked back into the crowd to find Elspeth and Mirabelle. I knew they would warn them that something had gone wrong. Whatever we found here, they would get everyone out if need be.

"Can you manage the stairs?" Ash asked. His tone was completely neutral, not a hint of condescension or judgment. It was exactly what I'd come to expect from him.

"Yes," I replied, following him to the same stairs we'd sent Morpheus and the others down moments ago. My feet hit a plush runner as I steadied myself on the brass banister. "What is our plan?"

Ash's voice was softened by the gleaming wood walls and the patterned rug on the tight spiral staircase. "Surveillance first. We need to determine exactly what we're dealing with."

The sound of whispers clarified as we descended, or so I thought at first. When we reached the bottom of the stairs, I realized that I was not hearing the sound with my ears, but inside my head. What clarified was the pandemonium within the otham's noise. As we reached the bottom of the stairs, the sound of screams condensed somehow. A chaotic element remained, but behind it was a clear chant.

"What language is that?" I whispered aloud. It was none I'd ever heard, and though I read many languages I had never heard spoken, there was nothing in the otham's chant that I recognized.

Ash stopped on the tight spiral staircase, his shoulders tensing. "You hear it?"

He turned slowly to look back at me. As he did, he kept his eyes cast down. I knew that particular motion well. I'd used it many times to hide the way my eyes glowed with celestial light. *But why was Ash hiding that from me now?*

"Ash?" I murmured. There was no way to keep the fear that clawed its way through me out of my voice.

When his eyes finally tipped upward, I saw clearly what he had hidden all this time. The Ravager's presence must have activated it within him—a kind of primal opposition to the pure otham that screamed below us. Rather than the golden glow of Ventyr celestial illumination, his eyes burned with a deeper flame.

"What are you?" I asked, taking the steps between us with only a modicum of pain. When I was close enough to touch him, I placed a hand on each of his cheeks, raising his eyes to mine.

"A forbidden thing," he said. "A secret, even to my own family. Only my mother knew." My heart beat faster at his words: "I am one of the Laniidae."

Blood rushed through my veins, almost audible now, as the dizzying truth hit me all at once. "But how?"

The Laniidae were, in some ways, the alternate force to the Feriant. The empyraeic opposition to the giant aetheric bird Poe could transform into.

Ash shrugged. "My mother had an affair. My father was not my true father. She never explained further."

There was a faraway look in his eyes now, and he did not have to explain why. What his mother had done was an offense that would have been punished in unimaginable ways. To cuckold a Ventyr king was dangerous. To birth an illegitimate child was unforgivable. Further, to create a child who could transform into the Laniidae meant that his mother had coupled with a Vilhar from House Serapion, the ruling house of the Court of Starfire.

And *that* should have been impossible. But here was Ashbourne, carrying the Thuellos name, but not a Thuellos. Not truly. He was something, someone, else entirely. Something shifted deep within me. I understood Ouriel's message to me better now. He was never meant for the role of the Warden—to guard sleeping horrors for eternity. Ashbourne was meant to be the shrike, the Laniidae, the fierce warrior.

His mother had not explained her actions to him to keep him safe. If he did not know her sins, he couldn't be held accountable for them with her, should she ever have been found out.

"Well," I said, finally. "That is very good."

His eyes met mine. "You think so?"

I nodded. "The Laniidae are as powerful as the Feriant. Why would this displease me?"

His cheeks flushed red. "Because it is yet another way that I can take flight, and you cannot."

A wry laugh coupled with the chanting in my head, winding through it, turning sinister as it drifted away from me. The noise was twisting my mind. I clung to Ashbourne, closing my eyes tight as he reached out to hold me. "We need all the help we can get."

"There is no *we*, love. Not for me. There is only you." His arms tightened around me. "You are the reason for all I am now."

I smiled against his chest.

"Are you angry with me for keeping this from you?"

I shook my head. "No. I understand why you did."

The miraculous, wonderful thing was that I did. I was not angry or resentful. Only glad that if I could not fly, that there was never any doubt that he would be able to. That even if I never flew again on my own, I would always have wings.

CHAPTER 25

ASHBOURNE

The bowels of the ship were cold and noisy, but not noisy enough to block out the eerie chanting that filled both our heads. We made our way as quietly as we could across a tiny iron catwalk. There wasn't much light in the undercarriage of the airship, in the voluminous space where the engine was housed, making it feel as though we walked into an abyss.

Mina kept her gaze cast down, searching out threats from below, while I scanned the space ahead of us. It was difficult to see or sense much with the noise of the engine, but the internal chant grew louder in my head as we progressed further into the ship. As my eyes adjusted to the light, the various catwalks that crisscrossed the underbelly of the ship came into view. The Ravager might be anywhere.

The catwalk turned about ten feet ahead to run along the outside wall of the airship, but shadows on the wall suggested that we were not alone. I looked back at Mina, who squeezed my hand to let me know she saw what I did. We backed up a few feet.

"Stay behind me," I said. "I don't want you to use your powers unless you absolutely need to."

Her face was solemn as she nodded. Later, I needed to assess her skills in the fetch. I only knew the bare minimum of what Lumina had been capable of, and I was certain now that no one knew the extent of the princess' powers. Maybe not even Boreas.

My mind caught on the thought. *Had he known she could wield both empyrae and aether?*

"Ash!" she cried, pushing past me. I spun to face whatever she'd seen while I was too busy with my head up my own arse.

Ahead of us, Niall Aestra came stalking down the catwalk, his eyes dark as starless oblivion. Indigo smoke curled around his feet and wrists. He wasted no time speaking, but pushed his hands forward, as though reaching for us. Mina frowned, assessing his efforts, but I saw his aim. Whatever force controlled Niall Aestra, there was a momentary lag. Niall didn't possess the ability to wield aether, and his body could not channel the smoky substance that followed him now.

I pushed Mina behind me just in time. The aether that stalked Niall grew louder, the sounding of chanting ringing in my head so that I could hardly think. I'd never seen aether so dark and menacing before. It was as though the sentient aspects of the substance were tortured, screaming souls, hells-bent on destruction.

There was only one way to combat such a substance. Empyrae flared at my hands. Behind me, Mina gasped. "Ash, no. The ship."

I gritted my teeth. "It's the only way. I'll be careful."

The aether came screaming at us then and I felt Mina drop into a crouch, but I could not look back at her. Empyrae glowed in my palms. Instead of loosing it towards the oncoming shadow, I focused on creating a barrier between us and the onslaught of feral, primal magic.

An orb of empyrae encircled both Mina and me. I felt her magic merge with mine. It was the first time she'd used empyrae in my presence in a very, very long time. The way her magic mingled with mine was sweet music in contrast to the screaming aether.

As the cloud rushed over us, I spotted faces in the mist, skeletons and bones, teeth. Everywhere there were teeth. This was not pure aether. No, this was certainly not the pulsing otham I'd spent centuries guarding in Nihil. This was something else entirely. I watched as the skeleton creatures took form within the mist, dread pooling in my belly.

"He's summoned wraiths from Cocytae," I murmured.

Mina hissed as she drew in a sharp breath. "Cocytae is a myth, a story meant to scare children."

The evidence that she was wrong swirled all around us. The skeleton creatures took form now, their hollow eyes glowing with darklight. I didn't have to argue with her. I knew how she thought. It wasn't that she didn't believe what she saw with her own eyes—she was processing it all. Scheming.

I glanced over my shoulder at her. She was crouched down, her dark head struck downward in deep thought as golden empyrae leaked from her hands, feeding the barrier that kept the creatures from a world most thought was pure myth away from us.

"In the Red Book of Lore, Alyosha was only able to defeat the Cocyti with their own power," Mina murmured. I didn't know the folklore she referred to, and assumed it must be a tale indigenous to Sirin. "I will fight the Cocyti. You must stop Niall."

The creatures writhed in the mist around us, their sharp teeth gnashing. They were capable of draining one of our kind of all their power in mere moments. Through the mists in the limen, I'd seen into their world many a time. I'd seen them damage an elemental being, almost beyond repair.

"No," I breathed, my throat clenching. I just got her back. I couldn't lose Mina now.

"Ashbourne," she growled, rising slowly. "You know better than to treat me as though I'm made of glass."

I turned fully to face her, strengthening the ward of empyrae around us as she drew her power back into herself. My beautiful menace glowed with her power. A wicked smile played at the corners of her mouth. And then she did something completely unexpected. She stepped backwards, away from me, grinning, her eyes glowing like infernal embers.

"This will be fun," she said, the voices of a thousand warrior queens in her lineage echoing in every word. She was more than a woman; she was an elemental force. And though I could tell that every step brought her pain, as I watched her step beyond the barrier of my ward, there was a fluidity in her movements that I couldn't deny.

Lumina Anemos had been a formidable fighter, though almost no one knew it. I was one of the few she let see her true face. A warrior in constant physical pain, whose mental acuity was all she needed in a fight.

The Cocyti rushed her, the smoke of poisoned aether swallowing her whole for one horrible moment. Pure blue aether, wreathed in the glowing golden light of empyrae, pierced the shadows. The Cocyti backed off immediately, and through the mist, Mina spoke, but I could not hear her words. Her eyes glowed with a ferocity I had not seen in eons. She was the woman I fell in love with—twice. Magnificent in the face of the ravaged dark.

I let down the barrier of empyrae between myself and the eldritch horrors surrounding us, turning to face the possessed Niall Aestra. He emerged from the mist, smiling. "General Thuellos," he said, in a voice not his own. "It has been some time."

The strange mixture of Niall and whatever possessed him confused me, but I had no time for that. Niall launched tendrils of poisoned aether towards me. I wanted to look back, to make sure that Mina was still all right. But I could not risk it. I drew empyrae out, intercepting the aether with my own fire, emphasizing each short blast of power with force from both my mind and body.

The screams in the aether increased in volume, their shrill cries a death knell. Mina was winning. A slow smile spread over Niall's face. "She is glorious, is she not?" Niall's attention turned back to me, his otherworldly black eyes narrowing. "You have never been worthy of her."

I bowed my head once. "In that, we agree."

He snarled, sending a blast of aether straight at me. I rushed forward, ducking as I went. A flash of empyrae behind me suggested that Mina was blocking the aether from hitting her. I punched out at Niall's power with my own, meeting shadow with fire as I leapt towards him, angling my body carefully as I went. My foot met his chest with full force. It was as though he hadn't even thought to protect his physical form.

As Niall Aestra flew backwards, I understood more fully. Whoever, whatever controlled him, cared very little for his body. But Skye—my Skye. Skye would care if I killed her brother.

The thought pained me, but my head cleared. The aether's screaming had stopped. I hazarded a glance back at Mina. Every curve of her body glowed with empyrae, shadowy blue aether curling around her fingers. At her feet were the skeletons of the Cocyti. They twitched, itching to reanimate.

She bent down, sending a lick of empyrae through them, incinerating the last of their half-lives with the light of a thousand stars. I could not recall seeing another fighter use empyrae so precisely. Every flame was wreathed in aether, keeping it from spreading past the boundaries of her will. I was mesmerized by her skill—she didn't need me to assess her, let alone train her. She was already an expert with her power.

Movement on the catwalk sent vibrations through my feet, telling me Niall would soon rise. Mina stumbled as the last of the skeletons disappeared. She'd used too much energy. Her ability to channel power from the universe was nowhere near burned out, but her body was.

In my peripheral vision, Niall rose, an unnatural movement. Rather than crouching as any person would, he rose stiff as a board, as though someone had pushed his prone form into a standing position. The sight was beyond unsettling, but I made my decision.

In three long strides I had Mina in my arms. "We're getting out of here."

She shook her head. "He's not stopping, Ash."

A burst of aether came rushing at us. I curled my body around Mina's, unable to think clearly with her in danger. But no impact struck my back. I opened my eyes. I was surrounded by a barrier of her shadows. Though she was little more than liquid in my arms, she still fought, a ghost of that menacing smile lingering in her eyes.

"Whoever controls him won't stop," she murmured, looking down. Below us, in the bowels of the ship, a scream of metal made a hollow, wretched sound. It was unmistakably the sound of something dying. "Poe and Skye will get everyone out. You have to fight him. Give them time to save everyone."

I nodded, lowering her gently to the metal grate of the catwalk. "Protect yourself," I commanded her. "Stay as close as you can manage. When this ends, I will carry you home."

She nodded, her face resolute. Though her body sagged with exhaustion, the strength in her eyes gave me pause. There was no one like her in all worlds. That determination was singular. It lived only in her, and I would protect it with everything I had.

Niall's aberration of aether launched at us again. This time, I fought back as I would a physical opponent, sending fiery punches at every burst of shadow he sent my way. Mina's shadows, unique to her, slid over my body, caressing every muscle, every inch of my skin with slippery grace. A roar of pleasure coursed through me as the barrier of her power encompassed my body.

Never had I felt so *good* while fighting. Her heartbeat was as close to me as though I held her in my arms, as though I drove myself into her again and again. We merged, the space where I ended and she began dissolving, just as it did when I fucked her. The power of the Claim dawned on me: it was more than sex, more than love, it made us *one*.

Every move I made became more precise. Niall stumbled as my empyrae-fueled punches shoved the corrupted aether he wielded back towards him. I watched carefully as he attempted to gather more force, more power, but I did not relent, targeting every weak spot I could find in his defense.

I would rather fight him with our bare hands, but whatever sinister power controlled Niall Aestra now would not allow such a thing. Niall's shadows waned under my relentless pressure, but still he channeled more power. Livid red lesions spread across the pale skin of his face and hands.

"He's channeling too much raw aether," Mina gasped. She did as I asked, following close behind me. "It will eat him from the inside out."

I had only seen such a thing one other time, on a battlefield long ago. Thalia had sacrificed herself in just such a way. My sister had done it with purpose, to turn the tide of a never-ending war. Her efforts had been in vain, but nothing erased the honor of her actions. But this was different. The force that held Niall Aestra wanted nothing more than destruction.

"Get back," I snarled. Behind us, around the corner of the

catwalk, was an escape hatch, made for the winged fey who typically operated the airship. "Get to the escape hatch."

"He's going to blow the whole ship up," she cried.

"The escape hatch," I growled, digging deep within myself, finding reserves of power I didn't know I held. I sent out a stream of empyrae, creating a barrier much the same as I had to protect Mina and myself minutes before, surrounding Niall Aestra. It wouldn't hold, but it would give us vital time.

My physical strength was fading, and I knew I had to reserve some for what came next. I couldn't carry her to the door if we were to escape with our lives. She had to make it there first. "Jump."

I didn't look back. It took all my concentration to make sure she would get there, that she'd get off the ship. I couldn't stop until I knew she was out. "Jump and I will catch you," I murmured, as the vibrations in the catwalk told me she did as I asked.

CHAPTER 26

MINA

"Jump and I will catch you," he said, so softly I almost didn't hear him. He was losing strength, and I was so drained from fighting the Cocyti that I barely had the ability to fulfill his wishes.

Ashbourne, who could lift my body with ease, who could fuck and fight for hours without waning in strength even a measure, was drained. And yet he maintained control. He never pulled so much power from the cosmos, from the limen, that he risked what Niall Aestra now did, becoming an incendiary device of such magnitude that it could level cities.

Pravhna. Were we still above Pravhna? I ran, forcing my last bit of physical strength into my limbs. I would not need the strength much longer. Unlike Ashbourne, my ability to channel power was nowhere near gone, but my body threatened to stop cooperating, pain lancing through me with every push towards the escape hatch.

I threw open the door, relief flooding me. We were far beyond Pravhna now, over the Pontus Axeinos heading into the waters off Cerne's coast. I had no idea how we'd made it out so far past the city, but in the distance, I spotted the lights of the escape pods. I focused my mind, trying to find Poe. If she was in Feriant form, I might be able to reach her.

Are you still on the ship? Her voice was frantic inside my head.

Yes, I replied, relieved to have reached her. *Are you?*

No, she said, and fear edged her voice. *We got everyone out. You're alone.*

Good, I replied, looking back at Ash. He had created a barrier around Niall Aestra, a wall of empyrae that grew thinner by the moment. At the center of the orb, Niall was in a wretched state. The power flowing through him ate away at his muscles, revealing his bones. And though I could not hear him, because of the wards Ash erected, I saw clearly that he screamed with pain. He would not survive this, and neither would we if we didn't move quickly. *Get everyone as far from the blast as you can.*

The blast? Mina—

To cut Poe off, I erected a wall in my mind. I needed every bit of concentration I had now. I summoned my power, the last of my connection to the aether, and whispered a prayer to whatever gods might be listening. And then I jumped, sailing deep into the dark night sky, the sea far below me.

We were high enough that I had time to watch the waves below, to see the water elementals that played in the waves coalesce with air elementals. Dozens of draconae, serpents of the air and sea, flew past me towards the airship. I spread my arms, reveling in the feeling of their immense power as they passed me. Tears flowed from my eyes, but fear couldn't touch me.

A cushion of warm air slowed my fall, and then there was a giant bird beneath me, Ash's Laniidae form, glowing with empyraeic light, the light of distant stars; the light of home, of an empire long abandoned by our people. I smelled fresh clear air, tinged with the scent of rain. It was nostalgic, and though I could not identify it precisely, it smelled like home.

A home neither Ash nor I had ever known. As my body fell onto the giant crimson bird, I buried my face in his feathers. He smelled like Ash, and like a distant star, a forgotten world, a future we would never see, and a promise still yet to be fulfilled. I could not explain the rush of emotions that came over me as Ash beat his wings several times, putting distance between us and the ship.

I threw up a hand behind me, pulling the threads of reality as quickly as I could to reinforce the raw power I channeled. A shield of shadow and fire followed us. I hadn't enough strength to send an orb around the entire airship, and I didn't need it, for the draconae performed a wild dance around the falling airship, pushing it back into the sky, higher and higher.

The night was cloudless, the stars spinning above us as Ash flew faster, away from the inevitable blast. The ship disappeared from sight. And then it blew. The initial blast sent reverberations through us both, but the second blast came on a deeper, more essential level as Niall Aestra imploded, his body becoming a device that affected the world around us on a pure atomic level. Everything shook so hard my teeth hurt.

And then a memory, clear as day, played out in my head. *A dark world, full of ancient ruins. Evidence of a civilization long-dead. Boreas pushing me through the overgrown brush in what looked to have been a temple before whatever befell the world's inhabitants, berating me for being so slow.*

Ashbourne let out a feral cry of pain. His senses were obviously heightened in his Laniidae form. I leaned over to wrap my arms around his neck, burying my fingers in his soft feathers, leaving the terrible memory behind.

How will I tell Skye about Niall?

I sucked in a deep breath of night air. My heart ached for him, or maybe for myself and the girl I'd been in that memory, being shoved around by a father who cared nothing for my well-being. Perhaps it ached for both of us; we'd certainly both been through too much. *We will tell her the truth. It's all we can do.*

My head filled with his memory of me falling towards the sea as he dove after me. The feeling of joy and pride he had at realizing that I was not afraid, and that I trusted him to catch me. A smile so big it stretched my cheeks spread across my face. I hugged him tighter and each of his feathers glowed with celestial light for the briefest of moments. Warm starlight caressed my skin, taking the chill of the night air down to a pleasant sensation.

We can't fly in to Pravhna this way, he remarked. *It would bring up too many questions.*

I agreed. Just as I was about to suggest we head to the cabin, Poe's voice appeared in my head. *Did you make it out?*

Yes, I answered, a gust of cold air that felt like winter hitting my face. *We're headed back.*

Don't come to House Aestra, she responded. *It burned to the ground while we were in the air. Orchid House as well.*

I could hardly believe her words. The cold spread through me. I hadn't ever loved Orchid House, but to think of it gone was unimaginable. It was hard to believe the house would even stand for such a thing.

I relayed the information to Ash, who asked, *What about the office, our place in the undercity? Or Poe's flat?*

I relayed the question to Poe, but the answer was a long time coming.

Gone, all gone. Chopard made his move, Poe said.

Indeed, I answered. The truth of it sank in. I had to let Poe know about Niall, if only so she could be prepared for Skye's sake. *Niall is dead.*

I will tell her, Poe said, sadness in her voice. *Chopard got the cabin as well. Muse and Arcturus' flat was vandalized, but not burned. Someone was clearly looking for something there, but it's such a mess they can't determine if anything was taken.*

I wondered at that. What did it mean that the Seer's flat had been ransacked, but not burned? Did Chopard have a conscience? It certainly didn't seem so, if Niall was sent to kill all of us. So why hadn't he burned Muse's building?

Before I could think on it further, Poe continued, *Elspeth and Mirabelle have gone to ground, for the moment. They're staying in the Avalonne, along with Muse and Arcturus. Meet us there?*

Of course, I answered. *We'll be there as quickly as we can.*

I felt it when the connection between us severed. At least we had someplace to go.

I woke in the soft, sparely decorated room Ash and I had stayed in previously in the Avalonne. Our arrival was blurry in my memory. I rolled over in the bed, enjoying the feeling of the impossibly soft sheets against my bare skin. Ash was still asleep.

At rest in his Vilhari form, he was almost too beautiful to look at, his dark hair spilling across his forehead. It had grown a little since he cut it, and it had a carefree tousled look to it that was sweet in contrast to the hard muscles of his body. Nothing about him was for show—he had the body of a warrior, and one that knew how to use his weaponry.

I hesitated to touch him. He needed sleep to recover himself. In our former life, the amount of power he'd expended last night would have been nothing. But we were both out of practice now. The Vilhari and Oscarovi of Sirin both depended on technology far more than we ever had on Interra, using cosmic energy sparingly. And since there was very little conflict in the way of war on this planet, magic had taken on a more creative role, used to enhance the beauty of life, and for business purposes, rather than for raw power.

Like anything, being out of practice at utilizing battle magic had a draining effect. Ash certainly hadn't lost a bit of prowess, but the toll it had taken on him was written all over his face. Though his body was completely relaxed, the muscles around his eyes and mouth still looked tight.

I stroked a hand across his forehead, taking a deep breath of the cool scent of green growing things and subterranean water that filled the room. House Feriant was quiet, for now. I turned over to look at the small crystal clock on the bedside table. It was a little after nine. At House Aestra or Orchid House, we would have all been up, eating, readying ourselves for callers and the day ahead.

The stillness of the house reminded me that everyone had been through too much yesterday. Morpheus materialized at the end of the bed, still curled in a ball, as though he'd teleported in from the exact same position in someone else's bed.

Muse is restless as well, he said before stretching all his paws out towards Ash. He rolled onto his back for a moment, blinked at me, then stood. The feline fey arched his back, yawned, and then curled up by Ash's thigh. Deep rhythmic purrs emanated from his chest.

I will make certain he gets the rest he needs, Morpheus promised.

I slipped out of bed, noticing that someone had removed our pile of dirty clothes from the night before. We'd both ended up coated in detritus from the exploding airship and bathed as quickly as we could when we reached the room, neither of us able to stay awake for longer than it took to rinse off and stumble naked into bed.

An elegant cotton robe hung from a hook next to the washroom door. I walked carefully towards it, favoring my aching joints as I went, stretching and rolling my muscles slowly to help ease morning's initial pain to a dull roar. Once I had the robe tied, I pressed a kiss to Morpheus' head, and then Ash's, before leaving the room.

I didn't remember much about House Feriant, but as soon as I closed the door to our bedchamber, I made out the soft sounds of someone on the terrace on the level below us. I made my way slowly down the stairs at the center of House Feriant's quarters and found the arched double doors to the terrace. The glass was etched with images I didn't understand, of Vilhari and Ventyr, of creatures most thought of as lore, and a great labyrinth at the center of the image the two doors created.

Things long gone, long forgotten. Perhaps unwisely so. There was movement beyond the glass, and though my view was obscured, I recognized Muse, sitting at a table on the terrace. I pushed one of the doors open slowly and slipped through without a sound.

"Hello," I said as I stepped onto the terrace.

The light was dim, as we were technically underground, but witchlights sparkled across the city that was formerly a spacecraft. The sound of waterfalls echoed throughout the cavern, and the fresh smell of growing things mingled with the fragrant scent of the florals in the tea Muse sipped.

"Hello," he said, smiling at me. He was dressed, as I was, in a cream-colored cotton robe, his long locs drawn back in a low bun. The Seer's eyes were tired, but his expression was comforting nonetheless. "There's enough for two, but I made the pot to my taste. If you care for honey, rose, and lavender, you may enjoy it."

I bowed my head gratefully, taking the chair to Muse's left at the heavy table. The terrace was carved from what appeared to be a solid block of stone, and the furniture outside was as spare here as the stuff inside the house.

"Were all the Vilhari of old so enamored of this minimalist style?" I asked as I took the cup of tea Muse offered.

It was companionable to sit next to him, rather than across from him, and look out at the subterranean city beyond. Unlike the last time we were here, most of the other quarters were dark, but witch-lights still bobbed about the interior atrium.

"I don't believe so," he said. "This style was favored by the Court of Air, in my understanding."

"What do you know about the old world?" I asked. It was out of curiosity, but something bothered me that I couldn't put my finger on. The etchings in the glass had stirred it up.

Muse's head turned, and he looked at me for a long moment, thinking deeply, apparently. I felt his eyes on me, but I kept mine straight ahead. "Is this your version of small talk, Lady Somerhaven?"

I took another sip of my tea and avoided the question, as it was obviously meant as a gentle sort of ribbing. The kind of comfortable jokes that friends made. Typically, I struggled with this kind of humor, but in Muse, I understood it. "I am not Lady Somerhaven, apparently."

Muse's low laugh was wry. "That thing masquerading as Helene Wildfang is no more your sister than I am. It simply wears her face, bears her memories. It is not truly her."

I hummed softly in response. "Then what is it?" I asked. "I know it's a Ravager—but what *is* a Ravager?"

The question was more rhetorical than anything else. I knew how difficult it was for Muse, or any Seer, to tell what they knew about the future or the past. There were so many ways to influence what might happen, and those with the Sight often held themselves apart, seeing too many threads of possibility at once.

And indeed, Muse sighed, rather than answering. Long silence passed between us as we sipped our tea. So he would not answer me, not directly anyway.

"At least you are asking the right kind of questions," he finally said. "That will help."

I nodded. "I wish we'd known each other before I was put into the fetch. When I lived with your people." The statement was impulsive.

Muse's reaction was unexpected. A smile spread across his face, as though he was recalling a delightful memory. "There are so many parts of my gift that are difficult. Occasionally, though, seeing so many possibilities is a pleasure for me."

He paused, thoughtful as he sat his cup of tea down. "Ours is just such a case. There are not many threads of possibility that do not include us being friends."

As we were not yet what I would consider friends, but more pleasant acquaintances, this was not exactly a surprise for me. A path to our friendship was easy to spot out, to trace from our previous interactions, straight through the one we were having now and project that into the future. The part that was surprising to me was how pleased Muse seemed by this idea.

"Does that mean that in other 'possibilities' we met earlier and were friends?" I asked, though I knew full well that an answer was unlikely.

Muse simply smiled again. It was enough of an answer for me. When he spoke again, he shifted the conversation. "Perhaps we should turn our attention to our present predicament."

This was an area I found comfortable. I took a deep breath, letting the pieces in my mind shift and shuffle, until a new perspective formed. "We need to get back onto finding the standing stones. I assume the map that Mirabelle and Poe generated is gone."

Muse's grin widened now, his dazzling white smile sparkling in the dim light of the terrace. "Yes. Good."

He took a deep breath, and then took a moment to sort through his own thoughts. I saw it then, the threads of kindred countenance and intelligence that linked the two of us. I might not see the threads of fate, the thousands of possibilities, as clearly as Muse did, but my mind worked in a similar fashion.

It was soothing to talk with someone whose mind worked like my own. Hope sprang in my chest, blooming like spring flowers as I realized that every person in my life now, the people I'd become close with after the oubliette, all had that in common. We all thought a bit differently than many people and found it more comfortable to be with one another than anyone else.

This was new, but I could see a future in these seedlings of relationships. Tender shoots that would grow into a vastly interconnected ecosystem of love, trust, and mutual understanding. Tears welled in my eyes and my throat tightened with emotion. This was what family was supposed to feel like.

When I met Muse's gaze, his expression mirrored my own. "Yes," he whispered. "Yes, this *is* what family is supposed to feel like."

I reached for his hand and he for mine, and when they met, not a shudder of anxiety went through me. These were my people. I finally had a home.

"Now," he said, taking a deep breath. "I *can* help you remake the map. Can you find me some paper?"

CHAPTER 27

MINA

A few hours later, the household was awake and bustling with revived energy. Muse had perfectly recreated the map of the possible locations of the standing stones, and Mirabelle had revealed a piece of good luck for us.

While most were directly located beneath highly trafficked areas, one was accessible from the Avalonne. Ash and I sat in the tiny kitchen of House Aestra's quarters with Mirabelle. Skye and Poe were with Elspeth, who wasn't faring well after the death of her son. Hesperos Aestra, Skye's father, had sent word that he was sailing back from Ismit immediately, but he could not leave his ship's cargo and fly home alone. It would be several days before he arrived, and in the meantime, Skye was devoted to helping her mother.

Ash watched Mirabelle carefully as she brought a cast-iron kettle off the strange stove. "What powers it?"

Mirabelle pushed the sleeve of her embroidered silk robe back, glancing up for only a moment before pouring hot water into the teapot. It was remarkable how much she looked both like Skye and Elspeth; their bloodline was pronounced, obvious. Between her silvery white hair, and the sharp cut of her facial features, both her daughter and granddaughter echoed on her face.

Why had I never noticed how little I looked like Maman and Helene? I shuddered thinking about Helene. But it haunted me that I'd tried so hard as children to see the resemblance between us. I'd always thought we had similar facial structure. Now I know I was projecting my hope onto her. It was difficult to know whether to be relieved or sad. Even now, I wished things had not turned out this way.

Mirabelle put the lid back on the teapot before answering Ash. "Empyraeic power. Much the same in concept as aetheric power, but longer lasting, easier to store, and much more powerful for space travel."

It was my turn to frown. My father had tried to harness the power of empyrae for years. He'd manipulated Luciel and Ouriel in countless ways, trying to get at their power, but he'd never managed to replicate Vilhari engineering. We'd been effectively stuck on Interra until he found a way to master travel through the limen. I bit down on the inside of my cheek, trying to banish the flood of memories and connections my mind wanted to conjure up.

The longer our search for Chopard went on, the harder it was to focus only on what was at hand. There was too much to worry about. "If you can use the stove, why couldn't the Vilhari leave Sirin?"

Mirabelle's smile was wan. "There is enough to power the interior of the ship for another dozen centuries, but not enough to leave the planet. Or at least not enough to get us anywhere meaningful. That was always the problem. Something drained the core, though we've never known exactly what it was. Landing on Sirin was our only option."

She brought the tea tray over to the small rough-hewn stone table we sat around and distributed the tea bowls first, then poured. The tea was a soft green hue and smelled like fresh rain on a spring garden. I sipped it and found it was the perfect temperature, and had a light taste that reminded me of vanilla, despite the floral scent. Creamy somehow.

I was so lost in trying to decipher the notes in the tea that I almost missed Mirabelle speaking. Tearing my attention away from the tea was difficult, but she explained that there were tunnels under the Avalonne—carved centuries before the Vilhari landed here. "They go to the river," she said.

"What river?" Ash asked, a flicker of tension showing in his jaw.

Mirabelle set her tea bowl down. "Why, the Acheron, of course."

Ash drew in a sharp breath, then nodded. "Of course."

There was something to what Mirabelle said that bothered him. But why would the river be of any concern to him? Schoolchildren knew of the subterranean river under the surface of our world. It was a subject of lore, for the most part. All the science was rather boring, in my opinion. Or at least it had never been any interest to me as a young person.

Now, I wondered.

A long silence passed between us, which Mirabelle broke. "I believe the tunnels should take you to this location." She brought a sheer piece of paper out of a parchment folder on the table. It looked to be a map of the tunnels and the river itself. "I generated this to overlay, like so."

My brows knitted together. I wasn't sure what she meant by having "generated" the map, but looking at it, those questions flew right out of my head. All of the tunnels intersected with the possible standing stone locations. I glanced at Ash, who stared at the wall, his golden eyes narrowed, expression fraught with some emotion I couldn't discern.

"This one is closest to us," Mirabelle said, pointing to the map. "This one is under the Mercury in Halcyon Gate, and this one under the clock tower in the university district."

"They are under these locations?" I asked, as it did not appear that Ashbourne was even listening.

Mirabelle nodded. "Yes, Muse and I both believe so, though of course, there may be some variations we cannot account for about how the stones may appear. The tunnels are known to be unpredictable, and if they function as portals to the realm the elementals inhabit, they may manifest in a variety of ways."

She spoke as if I understood the metaphysics of the portals, and though I did not, I didn't ask further questions. Something strange was going on with Ash. Though his expression hadn't changed, the energy coming off him was intense, though hard for me to read. I found it hard to concentrate on anything Mirabelle said.

Mirabelle seemed to notice both our difficulties. "I will leave you to discuss this."

I nodded absently as she rose from the table. The light in the kitchen was soft, giving the warm gray room a kind of blurry glow. There were no windows here, but it was cozy. It took my mind quite a bit of work to imagine this entire place hurtling through the cosmos. I struck that thought aside, as I felt my mind burrowing into a distraction, and touched Ashbourne's bare arm. His shirtsleeves were rolled to his elbows.

"What's going on in there?" I asked, curling my fingers around the hard muscle, turning his forearm until the back of his hand rested on the table, palm up. I slid my fingers lightly down his skin. He shivered, glancing over at me, his notice finally breaking from the wall.

When his eyes locked on mine, I laced my fingers through his. He closed his hand around mine, capturing my hand in his. "The Pyriphle has many names. It takes many forms. Once it was a great sea of sand, on a world long forgotten. Now, it flows through many different worlds."

That made almost no sense. How could a river flow through many worlds? I frowned, trying to puzzle it out, but even on Interra, where our ideas about how the cosmos worked had been more expansive than those on Sirin, this was not lore I was familiar with. A feeling of having missed something vital oozed through me.

The sea of sand. That was familiar. The vision I'd had when Ouriel's message came through. There had been a sea of sand in it, hadn't there? Ash watched me, running a finger over the lip of his tea bowl as he waited for me to finish thinking. He looked almost meditative, his golden eyes soft, as though he could wait for me forever.

I'd never asked him about the limen. About Nihil. It came up in conversation a few times, but Ashbourne slid past it quickly. I told myself I'd been respecting his obvious wish not to talk about the place, but now I wondered if not asking had been more for my comfort than his. My skin went a bit clammy.

If I was going to forgive him, trust him, it was a mistake not to at least ask. "What was it like in Nihil?"

Ashbourne's raptorial eyes went wide for a moment, then closed. "At first, it was just adjusting to the feeling of being so close to the heart. That much power is overwhelming. But the worst thing was the pods. We weren't to move from them for at least a century, to give the heart time to adjust to our presence."

I hadn't been a part of the team that imprisoned the Ravagers to begin with, but it had been an enormous undertaking to first capture all-powerful elemental beings and then lock them away from everything. A honeycomb of stasis pods had been built close to Nihil itself, the heart of the limen and source of the purest form of aethereal power, otham. This was to keep both the guardians and the Ravagers just sustained enough so they would not be uncomfortable. The team suggested that this was a compassionate solution, but really it was the only one we had; no one had been able to figure out how to actually destroy a Ravager.

The guardians were meant to act as Wardens, watchers and minders, of the pods and the Ravagers themselves. I'd never considered what they'd actually go through in Nihil. I don't think anyone thought much about this. It was a necessary sacrifice, and everyone else involved knew they wouldn't be asked to make it.

"Did anyone leave the pods?" I asked, wondering if Ashbourne and his generals had followed the rules they were given.

Ash shook his head. "Not at first. But eventually most everyone left at some point or another. Mostly, we slept. But when we were awake, it was all arguments and blame... by the time things went truly bad, it was clear they hated me."

I grimaced. The thought was painful, but not surprising. Ventyr culture under Boreas' thumb had been vile. No bond was sacred, no loyalty true. Those with true honor had been punished for it in so many ways. I was almost glad, in this moment, that the curse had made me forget all that. I'd lived so much life, strange and distant as it was to think about, after coming here.

This felt like my life now. This version of me felt true in a way that Lumina Anemos no longer did. I wondered if Ash felt that way at all, but I wasn't brave enough to ask. Instead, I asked, "How long did you argue for?"

His eyes met mine, hollow as my heart had once felt. "Centuries."

The shudder that went through me reverberated through our connecting fingers. Ash squeezed my hand. "It was not so bad as all that. We took turns leaving at first, exploring the limen. I have looked into dozens of other worlds, seen things I still cannot believe were real. Time passed in a blur until the first Ravager got loose."

Movement in the doorway caught my attention. It was Poe, dressed in a sumptuous orchid-colored silk dressing gown. She nodded once as Ash glanced over his shoulder at her. "There is plenty of tea, if you'd like some."

I didn't need to ask if he felt more real in this life, more fulfilled. My answer was written in the way he spoke to Poe, so casually trusting. He didn't guard himself in front of her, but simply kept speaking about what others might consider private matters. This life was better than what we started with, complicated as it was. Sirin felt like home in a way Interra never could—not for me, at least.

Poe nodded, but stayed silent as she prepared herself a cup. Ash continued. "One day, I woke to a sudden feeling of dread. One of the chambers was empty, only a tiny crack in the barrier. That was all it took, the tiniest of cracks."

"How did it get there?" I asked.

Ash gritted his teeth. "I believed one of the generals was in the thing's thrall, but maybe it was Poe's grandmother. Time meant very little to me then, so it is difficult for me to place exactly when it happened." He paused to look at Poe. She only nodded calmly, urging him to continue. Something in me hummed with comfort and pleasure to watch them interact so naturally. "I could never determine who had done it, though. That was just the first betrayal."

It was Poe's turn to frown now. "The first?"

He nodded. "Eventually, they all left, but that was later... I was alone." He shook his head. "I'm not telling it well. Truth be told, it's difficult to recall. The stasis chambers warped your sense of time."

That I remembered. "They were a bastardization of an old Vilhari design, weren't they?"

Poe's eyes lit with interest, but Ash just nodded, face solemn. "Yes. Our scholars changed the original design, I believe—the engineers found a way to acclimate them to the limen—supposedly to keep us all safe—isolated. For all the good that did."

My heart warmed as Poe spoke. "That must have been very lonely."

Ash's lips turned up in a sad smile. "I wasn't always alone. There was Larkin—and eventually the others."

"Larkin?" I asked.

"A young Dreamwalker, Harlow's sister," he answered with a faraway smile. How had his nephew's sister-in-marriage found her way to the limen? Dreamwalkers were rare amongst the fey and Oscarovi alike. I wasn't familiar with the range of their power, but I hadn't realized it might include travel to the world between worlds. The expression on Ash's face was so bittersweet, an ache set into my back teeth.

Tears sprang to my eyes. Dreamwalkers were rare, but Ash had known another, as had I. Thalia Thuellos, Ashbourne's beloved sister, was one. My father had destroyed her for possessing the talent. Made sure that House Thuellos would never prosper from her skills.

Memory crashed into my conscious mind, erasing the room before me. Boreas had drawn one of the Ravagers north, to a village close to Lyonesse, one where Thalia often visited, though I did not know why. She tried to defend the villagers. Tried and succeeded, destroying herself in the process. My head hung as the memory faded, as my tears fell onto my cheeks.

Ash squeezed my hand, but didn't address my tears. There were too many hurts between our families to apologize for every single instance of loss, and with Poe at the table, now was not the time to discuss this. My queen's eyes slid to mine, worry settling into them, but she did not interrupt. She was here, as I was, to witness Ashbourne's knowledge of the Ravagers. Of our true enemy.

Chopard was but a man. Destroying the Ravager was another task entirely. One we were ill-equipped for, as it took the scholar-mages of Interra decades to work out just the problem of the stasis pods, and those we'd had models for from the Empire. Destroying the Ravagers was practically impossible. They were pure energy, and energy could never truly be destroyed, only transformed.

"What happened to Larkin?" Poe asked. "How did you meet?"

Ash smiled. "One day, I found her in the Labyrinth. She walked its lonely paths singing and I walked with her. She was barely ten at the time. It wasn't safe for her to be alone there."

Something I did not know was rough inside me smoothed then,

an edge I hadn't realized existed. We had been treated horribly by our parents, but Ashbourne had not turned that same energy on a child when given the chance. His instinct had been only to protect the girl. "What happened to her?"

He shook his head. "I don't know. She and her sister came the day everything fell apart. The rest of the Ravagers got loose. One went to Okairos." He gritted his teeth, a terrible sound emanating from his throat. "I sent them after it. I sent *children* after a Ravager alone."

"Why?" Poe gasped. "Why would you do such a thing?"

He shook his head. "The generals... they had all gone. I had to choose."

Poe's hand went to her mouth. I saw the puzzle pieces moving in her mind, as they were in mine. It would have been an impossible decision. "How?" she breathed.

One tear slipped down his chiseled cheek. He didn't bother to wipe it away, but his fingers closed more tightly around mine. "The one that went to Okairos—the world my brother apparently escaped to after my imprisonment—it changed somehow before the escape. Larkin's sister, Harlow, she was a Strider."

Poe's mouth fell open. "What an extraordinary family."

Ashbourne smiled now, pride filling his face. "My nephew Finbar's Claimed. On *her* first visit to Nihil, she caught its attention. It calmed somehow in her presence."

Poe suddenly pressed a hand to her heart. "Calmed?"

Ash's eyes darkened. "Yes. It became more at peace somehow. Its thoughts of destruction all but stopped. It was quiet for a long time. When they escaped, I knew it followed her, and that the other might come here."

"But how?" I asked. "How could you know something like that?"

The dim light of the kitchen cast shadows across both Ash and Poe's faces. Ash squeezed my hand again. "Because the other thought only of you, and I had a good idea of where you were."

CHAPTER 28

ASHBOURNE

Mina's hand flinched in mine. She didn't yank it back, but I felt the tendons tighten. The tension in her fingers alone was enough to tell me she was shocked by what I'd said. Why hadn't I told her sooner? I wanted the truth to be that we simply hadn't had time. And in some ways, that was true. But there had been plenty of quiet moments, times when I could have shared all this with her.

With Skye even. But the things I'd regained in the oubliette, the lifetimes I'd recalled... They were not ones that I wanted to remember. Not as the man I was now. Those memories reminded me of all my failures, of the life I'd ruined with my arrogance. I wasn't proud of myself. Not as a general in my father's army, nor as the Warden of Nihil. The only life I'd ever had that I was proud of was this one.

The only person I'd ever been that I was proud of was Ashbourne Claymore. That was the man I desperately wanted to be. Relaxed, good in a fight, loyal to my friends. Simple, in so many ways. The other lives I'd lived complicated all that. Knowing who I truly was hadn't set me free; it had burdened me with more responsibility than I knew what to do with.

So I'd avoided talking about all this. Hells, I'd avoided even thinking about it—especially when it came to remembering Nihil. It just made it easier for me to embrace my cowardice that the nature of the stasis pods had turned time into a convoluted mess. Mina's mouth was tight, pressed into a thin line. She practically vibrated with some emotion I couldn't read.

"What do you mean, it was *thinking* of her?" Poe asked.

I kissed Mina's hand, hoping she would hear me, though I understood why she would be angry with me right now. Or perhaps even afraid of what I might say. "So much of my time in Nihil was a blur after the first two Ravagers escaped. It wasn't until Larkin began visiting that I tracked time again. That was when the otham's usual ambient noises turned to something else. When they grew restless, sounding more like voices.

"When the remaining Ravagers awoke, I knew something had shifted somewhere in the cosmos, so I began to search the open portals that I knew of, tracing the spirit paths over and over, attempting to find any trace of you. If I could, I wanted to at least apologize and warn you of the trouble that was coming. But I also wanted to find out if what I'd felt before we were separated was real."

Mina made a choked noise. She closed her eyes, but nodded, urging me on.

"I knew you'd been sent somewhere as punishment. And since Boreas's attempts at building spacecraft after we reached Interra had totally failed, I knew he'd have taken you through the limen. That he might have brought you right past me in those initial years, when I was still locked in my stasis unit."

Poe's eyes widened as she understood. "It saw her."

I drew a long breath in. It was time to tell my last secret. "I believe what it saw was Boreas. Yes, he had Mina with him, but I think what interested the Ravager was Boreas."

Now Mina frowned. "Why is that important?"

"All of the Ravagers hated him. They knew him. Recognized him as their captor. Their enemy," I replied.

Mina let out a soft noise, something between a huff and a laugh. "Then we are aligned in that."

"I think the Ravager saw you with Boreas and became interested in what it could do with you to hurt him. I believe that is why Chopard is using it now. Its interest in you would be to his benefit, if

Chopard truly was aligned with what Vaness and Alistair Wildfang had planned to do with you."

Poe shook her head. "I don't like this."

I smiled at her, hoping to offer some comfort. "Neither do I, but there must be a way to turn this to our advantage."

Mina sat back in her chair. She hadn't taken her hand back, but she had withdrawn completely. She was lost in her thoughts now. I'd give anything to know what that brilliant mind put together with all this information. But I understood I had to wait, that I'd kept too much back from her and now she was calculating whether or not she could still trust me.

Her hand slipped out of mine, like water through open fingers. I watched carefully as she clasped it to her chest, as though she warded off danger. "Is that all you've kept back?"

I nodded. "I am sure that we both know things that we don't yet know the significance of, but yes. That is the last of my secrets."

"Good," a familiar voice said from the doorway. Skye leaned against the frame of the door, Morpheus at her feet. Her eyes were shadowed with grief, and lack of sleep, but her expression was avid. She was devastated by the loss she'd endured, but still she kept going.

It was something the four of us held in common. I couldn't help but wonder if that trait had done us any good. But there was nothing to be done for it now; forging ahead was the only way to the future we all hoped for. Even that was a blank space now, though. Once, I thought the four of us might have a future together in the undercity, happily running our private investigation firm together. Now, that future seemed unlikely.

"So." Mina's eyes drifted to Poe. "What is our next step?"

Morpheus disappeared, then rematerialized in Mina's lap, turning twice, then snuggling in for a nap. His purrs were loud and rhythmic, which let me know she was hiding her distress over my revelations, but that they were present all the same. I was grateful to the cat for helping her when I could not.

Poe looked to Skye, then back at Mina and myself. "We have to head back to the upper city."

Skye said nothing, but when I glanced at her, just to make sure she was all right, she nodded. "It's time for me to rejoin the Chevaliers. We need allies."

We did. The longer this went on, the clearer it became that Chopard had the upper hand. But still—I swallowed hard. Never would I hold Skye back, but if she rejoined them, my vision of our perfect future would end. I had to be sure I didn't influence her unduly—whatever she wanted most was what I wanted too. But she had left the Chevaliers under difficult circumstances. Returning to their ranks, especially as consort to the lost heir, would be a thorny process. "Are you sure about that?"

Poe's smile was wan. "Neither of us is sure about anything. But it seems like the best course of action right now is to split up. At least for a bit."

"Divide and conquer," Mina murmured. There was no doubt in my mind that she was puzzling through all I'd said, only listening to us talk with half her mind, while the other half searched for the bigger picture.

A restless feeling came over me, as though we'd been seated for too long. "And what about us?"

Poe touched the map that Mirabelle had left. "You two must hunt these down. It's time to figure out what the elementals want from Mina. What does Sirin require her to give?"

Skye still didn't know what I'd promised the elemental god. I didn't have the heart to tell her, even if that made me a coward. It was bad enough that Mina knew. I couldn't let Skye worry for me.

Mina nodded. "It's past time."

Poe reached across the table. Mina met her in the middle, grasping onto her hand. The love in both their eyes was astounding. It rivaled what I felt for Mina, what she felt for me. No, "rival" was the wrong word. But the feeling between the two of them was just as powerful, just as nourishing. My eyes went to Skye. It was what I felt for her, for Morpheus.

This was our family. We didn't have to walk the same path for that to be true. No matter what happened next, everything we were to one another would still exist. It always would.

Separating would be difficult, but my hope was that it would make coming back together all the more satisfying. Skye took a few steps into the kitchen and placed her hands on Poe's shoulders. "If you're ready, Mother's found us a house to let in the highest echelon."

I let out a low whistle. "Moving up, then?"

Skye nodded. "Not only for the optical benefits, but the tactical."

She didn't have to explain. The highest echelons in Pravhna were better protected than even the one House Aestra had lived in for centuries. The expense, whatever it might be, was worth it to protect the Aethereal Court's heir and her consort. It would be the perfect seat for us to operate out of, once Mina and I found the standing stones.

"We'll meet back together in a week," Poe said. "Or sooner, if you have success. All the details of the new house have been left for you."

Mina nodded, her eyes sad. Poe rose from the table, skirted past me, and pressed a kiss to the top of Mina's head. "We'll be together again before you know it."

"We will," Mina agreed.

Skye and I simply shared a look. The last time we parted, we said all we needed to. What we had did not require more words now. When they left, Morpheus disappeared, saying, *I will see you both soon.* His words lingered in our minds after he'd completely gone.

Mina said nothing. She simply got up and walked out of the room. I followed her through House Feriant, up to our bedroom. Clothes had been left for us. I sat in a chair, watching as she undressed. She didn't speak, and her face was blank and expressionless, but I did not sense anger in her countenance. Just deep thought.

She faced away from me, surveying the selection of clothing. "Pants would be best for reconnoitering, yes?"

The chill in her voice stung. I held my arm out to her. She was dressed in nothing but her lacy underthings, and arousal stirred within me. "Yes, but we don't need to hurry." Her eyes didn't meet mine right away, but when they finally did, I saw that she was lost to me. So far away I couldn't touch that part of her. My arm dropped. "I'm sorry."

She turned to look at me, irritation flickering in her eyes at the hint of petulance in my tone. I had forgotten this about her, and was learning it again. Lumina had not had much patience for managing my emotional outbursts either. We were relearning one another, moment by moment, finding out what the aeons had changed, and what had been left the same.

I wasn't proud of having shown my disappointment. "No," I said slowly. "That came out wrong. I am sorry for not telling you all of this sooner. The Laniidae, everything about Nihil." I rubbed the back of my neck, frustrated that I could not manage to put exactly how I felt into words. There seemed no way to tell her the depths of my remorse.

For a long moment her body stilled, tense, wound so tight she might burst. I could *feel* her thinking. Her mind was so powerful that in times like these her thoughts were practically tangible.

Mina's forehead smoothed, her body language relaxing in some mercurial shift. Was she pushing whatever those thoughts had been away? Or had she simply come to a conclusion? I didn't have the opportunity to ask, as she spoke, coming to stand in front of me. "I am not upset about any of that. We haven't had time to talk much. And besides..."

Her expression softened as her muscles relaxed. Heat built within me as whatever disturbing thoughts she had the moment before slipped away. Her pale gray eyes went molten as she searched my face for something. I lifted my chin, my lips parting with desire as her eyes locked on mine. "We've been busy reconnecting in other ways."

In a deft motion, she was on my lap, straddling me. The beauty in her movements was unparalleled, especially when I took into consideration the amount of pain she was in. My breath quickened as her hands drifted down my chest, tracing every line of my musculature. Her pupils dilated as the hard length in my pants grew under the warm core of her.

Her chest rose and fell in time with mine, her voice's usual rasp intensified by the pace of her breathing. "We've lived long, long lives, Ashbourne." She leaned forward, her breasts grazing my chest as she brushed her lips to mine. "There is so much to remember, so much to sort through. I can hardly manage it all myself."

That was hard to imagine, but if it were true, then perhaps I could stop berating myself for not being able to put it all together quickly enough. Change had never come particularly easily to me, but with her, with Skye, with this little family we'd formed together, I wanted to change. I wanted to be the man I'd been as Claymore, but with all the skills and wisdom I'd gained as Thuellos and the Warden. With Mina in my arms, I felt as though all that was possible. When she Claimed me, I felt my true potential.

"Touch me," she begged, her lips soft against my mouth.

With gratitude for the permission, I slid my hands over her luscious thighs and onto her backside, fitting her tight against the bulge in my pants. She unfastened the clasps that held together her brassiere, her breasts bouncing out as she freed them, tossing the lingerie aside.

Her creamy skin was soft as silk, the pink tips of her breasts pebbling in the chilled air of the bedroom. Everything about her was soft, curved, and elegant. I had the urge to tear it all apart, to reveal the vicious creature that lurked inside her. The menace she worked so hard to hide from the world.

She worried, I know, that it scared others. But I wanted them to be afraid of her. I wanted the world to fear her so deeply they would never dream of harming her. What she worried was her least attractive feature was, in truth, her greatest beauty. At least in my eyes.

I pulled her harder against me, eliciting a soft cry of pleasure as I pressed the rock hard length of my erection into her soft, warm core. There felt like miles of fabric between us, when I wanted to sink as deep as I could inside her. But this too was pleasurable. The tease of the damp fabric between her legs as she became more and more aroused. The shudder of exquisite pleasure as I dragged her body over mine. My name on her lips as I captured those pink nipples in my mouth.

"Ashbourne," she moaned. "Yes."

I was relentless in my ministrations, moving my mouth over her skin and her body against mine. I wanted to see her come undone.

"More," she begged. "I need more."

"Not until you scream for me."

CHAPTER 29

MINA

Ashbourne's mouth on my breasts, his hips bucking into me, both were sublime. But my mind was too busy for teasing. Release was the only thing that might clear it—and I was getting nowhere on my own. I needed help, the solace the Claim and his body could provide.

I grabbed his face in my hands, dragging his eyes to mine. "I need you."

Venom dripped in my mouth, sweet and enticing. My fangs protruded, and I let my mouth fall open so he could watch them grow. Now he was the one to groan. I rose up onto my knees, ignoring the pain it caused to do so. He watched me carefully as I pulled the wet fabric of my undergarment aside.

"Feel how much I need you," I commanded, taking one of his big hands and bringing it between my legs.

As his fingers sank deep inside me, he let out a growl, his own fangs appearing as he explored me, his movements slow and sure. I took the opportunity to unbutton his pants, freeing his erection as I rode his fingers. I stroked his shaft in long, languid motions, watching his fangs drip venom.

I lifted myself off his fingers, feeling instantly hollow. He let out a low growl as I moved to fit the head of his cock to my entrance. "I need you," I reiterated, hovering above him.

His golden eyes glowed as I sank down on him. We readjusted and as he filled me, my heart felt as though it would break open. All the emotions I hadn't been allowing myself to feel flowed out of me as Ash pulled me closer. Wet heat smoldered between us at the place where our bodies met.

My back bowed as I took him deeper, leaning back so he could watch as I rose and fell on him, watch as he filled me, watch as I ground my body against his, seeking pleasure in the friction of our flesh meeting. His fangs were at full length now, ready to impale me, and I had never wanted the Claim so much. Not even the fervor drove me the way seeing him like this did now.

Our movements were small in scale, but no lovemaking between us had ever been so intense. His eyes locked on mine. "I love you more than anything," he said, voice so soft I could hardly hear him.

"And I you," I whispered back.

Our words triggered the crest of the wave we both rode. As it broke over us, he brought his mouth to my breast, impaling me with his fangs as his lips and tongue caressed my nipple. The bite of pain, mixed with the soft pleasure of his mouth was everything I needed as his venom flowed into my body.

I grabbed his wrist, shoving it into my mouth, letting my fangs sink into his skin, piercing his veins. I tasted myself in his blood. My essence flowed through him. I was inside him, as he was buried inside me, in every way possible. My hips moved faster now, harder as I took him so deep I saw stars.

More, I needed more. There wasn't enough of him for me. He seemed to know exactly what I thought, as I thought it, and he shifted, his Vilhari form melting away. The chair broke with the force of his wings and we crashed to the floor, but I felt no impact, no pain.

Only the pleasure of him filling me to the brim, of him shielding me with the power of his body. My mouth closed harder around the wrist of his true form, taking his strength, his love, his promises for a better future. An intense vibration emanated from the base of his cock, sending waves of pure ecstasy through me.

He groaned against my breast, still seeping venom into me, still sucking at my nipple. Every bit of me was swollen with the driving need for him, for release, every thought I had disappeared as my focus narrowed blessedly on the two of us.

There was no outside world, no Ravagers, no dead sister come back to life, no outpouring of magic, no secrets kept for far too long. There was only Ash and Mina. Only the love we'd trapped in time, released now so that it flowed as freely between us as the tears that fell on both our cheeks.

Light and shadow burst from both of us, twining together, moving in the same desperate time our bodies did. His mouth broke from my breast as he flipped us over, one arm sweeping the wreckage of the broken chair away in one fluid motion.

He was above me now, his wings spreading and flexing as he thrust deeper into me. My legs fell open as my hips rose to meet him, increasing the power of each of his movements until he hit just the right spot within me.

"Yes," I cried out, and he did not alter his angle, or the power of his movements, but repeated them, driving so deep within me, it seemed possible I might burst. I screamed his name, clinging to him as power reverberated through me, bringing me to life. He followed after me, roaring as his release filled me with power.

When our bodies slowed, we still held tight to each other. My arms ached from the effort, but I could not fathom letting go of him. So often, we struggled to find the right words with each other, to talk as easily as I did with Poe. When we hit our stride, Ash and I could talk for hours. But sometimes we floundered in our efforts, even now.

There was nothing wrong with that, I realized as we held each other. We were so different, and yet exactly right for one another. Being the same was not necessarily an asset. We did not have to agree about all things, or see things from the same perspective, to be this deeply in love. And as I pulled back from our embrace to push a lock of dark hair from his forehead, I realized that we were more in love than I'd ever imagined possible.

The past we shared was part of that, but so too was our hope for the future. "I wish you would not have offered yourself to the god," I said. Ash opened his mouth, but I shook my head. "Please let me finish. I wish you would not have, but I need you to know that I will not be set free when you are bound. Whatever the god wants from you, it will take from me as well. Wherever you go, I go too."

He nodded. "No more being separated."

"Never again," I agreed.

His hands cupped my face as he kissed me sweetly. When he broke the kiss, the battle that was so often fought behind his eyes was finally put to rest. He looked at peace. I had no idea if that could last, but I was more than happy to let him have it now. To let us both have this moment of respite before whatever came next.

THE TUNNELS out of the Avalonne were wide, smooth, and well-lit with aetheric lights. Ash and I had dressed warmly in wool trousers, heavy boots, and fishermen's sweaters. At his urging, I tied a silk scarf around my braided hair for extra warmth. We looked ready for a country adventure. Somewhere far above us, our friends were making their way back to the city.

We walked down the tunnel Mirabelle had marked for us for what felt like hours. The rounded walls were perfectly smooth, glazed with some shiny black lacquer that created a similar illusion to walking in a hall of mirrors. It was unsettling to feel the echo of our forms moving around us, warped out of recognition. As hard as I tried, I couldn't banish the feeling of being trapped.

When I asked Ash how long we'd been walking, he checked his pocket watch. "Ten minutes. Bored already?"

I sighed. "Apparently." After a moment, I added, "But I'd rather be bored than have another incident like the airship."

He nodded, taking my hand. "Do you want me to find ways to distract you while we walk down this incredibly mundane tunnel under the city?"

I couldn't help but smile, appreciating the way he modulated his voice so that I understood he was making a joke. "Yes, please distract me."

He bent down in front of me and tapped his shoulder. "Hop on."

I scoffed. "I'm fine. These are good shoes. I'm not even in much pain."

He shook his head, laughing. "Get on so I can entertain you."

That had not occurred to me as an option. I frowned, but climbed onto his back, trusting that he knew what he was doing. He gripped my legs and hoisted me up. "Hold tight."

His words sounded like a warning, so I held on a little tighter, burying my face between his shoulder and the base of his neck. He smelled incredible. Then he began to jog. "I haven't been able to teleport since I got to Sirin. Have you?"

"No," I said. "I don't know if it works here."

He ran faster now, picking up speed. The aetheric lights on the tunnel walls blurred. "It would be a lot more convenient if we could," he said.

As he ran, the light from the aetheric sconces grew dimmer, and the tunnel walls less perfectly smooth, the glazed lacquer fading away. They were still obviously carved by machine, but a different one from whatever made the tunnel closest to the ship. The floor shifted from shiny black tiles, to an older, rougher tile carved from slate.

Ash slowed as the terrain changed, peering ahead of us. "Did you see that?"

I squinted ahead. The tunnel darkened, as though the lights had gone off. I saw movement in the darkness: a flash of feathers, then the hint of a distinctly feline shape. Ash stopped cold, and his hold on me tightened. Neither of us breathed for a long moment.

"I saw something," I whispered into his ear. "But I don't anymore."

He nodded. "Keep your wits about you."

As he walked forward, I saw the reason the tunnel appeared to go dark: we had reached an unexpected dead end. My heart beat faster as we approached and saw that the tunnel ended in an enormous circular room. Whatever this place was, it wasn't supposed to be here. Ash stopped again as we neared the threshold and I slid off his back. By instinct, I reached for his hand, and found it waiting to close around mine.

Dozens of doors sat along the curved walls, and carved into the floor was a parliament of owls, flying outward from the center of the floor in a chaotic pattern. Between the doors, sconces flickered—not with aetheric lights, but empyrae. This was not Oscarovi technology, but old Vilhari. Imperial technology. My blood ran cold at the sight. The room was empty, though. Whatever had moved in here was gone. I couldn't say if that made me feel better or worse.

"You saw something move, didn't you?" Ash asked.

My fingers laced between his, so I could hold his hand tighter. "Yes."

He shook his head, but said nothing else.

The light from the sconces did not reach the ceiling of the room. There was something terrible about this place. Something terrible, and strangely familiar, though I could not yet say why. For a long moment, we said nothing.

Ash broke the silence. "This wasn't on the map."

I shook my head. "No, it wasn't."

"Was it missing because Mirabelle simply didn't know it was here, or are we being tricked somehow?" Ash shook his head, frustrated. "I can't quite bring myself to trust her."

A sigh hissed out of me. "Neither can I, but there's another option."

"What?" he asked, hesitation in his voice.

I could not begrudge him the feeling. What I was about to say was not good news, and he read me well enough to tell. "Perhaps this room is not always here."

Ash growled. "Wonderful. More Vilhari tricks."

"We should try the doors," I suggested, moving to the right. "You go to the left."

"No," he said, firm. "I go where you go."

I nodded, going toward the first door and he to the one just beyond it. Each was arched at the top, and made of some heavy, dark material that I could not identify. It was nearly black in color, and was neither metal nor wood. The door handles seemed to have been carved from the same piece of whatever material the doors were. They were one thing, rather than several parts, which was quite curious. We moved methodically from door to door.

All were locked, and we weren't even halfway around the enormous room. We could spend hours trying to open them all. My stomach clenched, as something about the room deeply unsettled me. The air was too still, as though the room *itself* waited or watched, maybe both. After a few more tries, we both stopped, listening hard. For what, I was not sure, but then I heard it—water. Somewhere deep beneath this room, water ran in an underground river.

Ash pulled the map from his back pocket and unfolded it. He frowned at it. "There really *isn't* anything about this on the map."

We had to talk about something more mundane. The feeling that something had gone terribly wrong crept through me, as I was sure it did him. Before it burrowed too deeply into either of us, we had to shake it off.

I shrugged, trying to keep my movement light and airy. Poe did this often, masking what she truly felt so that others would be more at ease. I had to try it now. "There wouldn't be, would there?" I doubted Mirabelle had ever actually been down here. "The Vilhari have never been that interested in looking beyond what was right in front of them."

Ash smiled. Though both of us had been born on Interra, we had grown up with stories of the selfish fey, and the Vilhari Empire, who thought of nothing but themselves. It was why our people had left them. Why our ancestors had abandoned the Courts for something different, hoping for a better way of life. We'd mucked it up as badly as the fey had, but our parents had been certain they'd done better somehow. The elder generation was stuck in their ways.

It was hard not to wonder what had become of all of them. The Ventyr we'd lost track of. The Vilhari Empire itself. Were they all still out there somewhere, or were we the remnants of the lost and forgotten? I reached out for Ashbourne's hand. "You said you met Connoch's child, and his Claimed?"

Ash nodded, eyes sad. "Yes. For a short while."

"And?" I asked. "Were they well? Have they found happiness? Is Aislin finally happy having a world of her own to rule?"

My last memories of Interra were of my guards talking about Boreas sending the two of them through the limen with a small force meant to conquer another world, to make it ready for the Interran Ventyr. Boreas had been so worried that Interra might not recover from the Ravagers that he'd made every attempt he could to find new worlds for us to plague. But Connoch and Aislin, and the people they'd taken with them, never returned. They simply disappeared into the limen.

Knowing they'd kept Okairos for themselves was not unexpected. In fact, it was almost satisfying. I didn't have to like either of them to admire their determination to leave Boreas and his endless hunger for power behind. Ash looked down at me, stroking my cheek absently for half a moment before answering.

The wistful expression in his eyes tugged at my heart. "No, love. I don't think any of them are happy, though Finbar and Harlow are well matched, it seems. Perhaps they are happy now. I hope they are."

There was a hint of love in his voice when he spoke of his nephew. I swallowed the lump that grew in my throat. I couldn't tell what emotion welled in me, but his words made me feel strange. Uncomfortable, I grasped at the feeling, wanting to know what it was. "Are you envious of Connoch's offspring?"

Ash shook his head. "No. I told you on Interra that I did not want children; that has not changed."

Unexpected relief flooded me. Though the fetch was sterile, there were other ways to have children, other ways to become parents. But there was nothing in me that wanted that. Nothing that made me feel fit to care for a young one when I struggled so to care for just myself.

Ash continued. "Though I wish I had more time with Finn. And with Harlow. They were *better* somehow." He shook his head, the tears that pricked his eyes apparently surprising him. "I don't know if I can explain it."

He didn't have to. "I think I understand... We... we've lived so long. Even Poe and Skye seem like children to me at times, though I see them as our equals."

Ash swallowed hard again. "Yes."

He waited for me to finish my thought. "But the things that have happened to us marked us. The worlds we've moved through. The endless wars, the destruction... the things we had to do. I never liked your brother, and Aislin was my father's creature, through and through. But it sounds as though their son is a better person than either of them."

Ash bent and brushed a grateful kiss to my lips. "Yes, I think he is."

I wrapped my arms around his neck. "The same way that Poe and Skye will do better than we ever could. They won't pass on the same harm to their children that was passed on to us."

"No," he agreed, as his arms went tight around my waist. "They will not. They will make Sirin a better place than those that came before them. What's dead is dead for them, even if it cannot be for us."

His words looped through my mind. I slipped away from him, turning several times. Our mundane conversation had unlocked an old memory. My breath quickened. "Do you remember any stories of the Vilhari labyrinth?"

Ashbourne's face went dark. "I recounted them many times in Nihil. Why?"

I reached out, pointing to the doors. "Could this be the Nekromanteion?"

Blood drained from Ash's face, leaving him gray. "Fate be damned, Mina. I hope you're wrong."

CHAPTER 30

MINA

Ash walked away from me, his stride purposeful and predatory. He examined the doors more closely, looking at the strange material they were made from. The longer I looked at them, the more I saw elements of stone, metal, and even aether within them. It was as though understanding what this room might be triggered something in the room itself. A deeply unnerving thought occurred to me—was the room sentient? My skin prickled with anticipation.

One of the reasons the Ventyr mages had chosen Nihil for the Ravager's prison was its proximity not only to the heart of the limen —the most powerful concentration of pure aether in the world between worlds—but to the labyrinth itself. No one truly knew where the labyrinth had come from, but for aeons it had existed on the first of the Imperial planets, Citadel.

That must have been what Ash had meant about the Pyriphle, or Acheron, whatever it was named. Somehow the river and the labyrinth had made their way off of Citadel and into the limen, and other worlds' more limenal spaces. The metaphysics of how something like that might happen were complicated; best not to get caught up in them now. The sense that the room was waiting grew stronger in my mind, a deep, subtle pressure. I had no time for my myriad stray thoughts.

But the labyrinth itself snagged at my attention, perhaps because I couldn't remember the exact reason the Vilhari had for using it. Something about a covenant with their gods, some arcane ritual that was likely all mythology, anyway. Superstitious nonsense our parents' generation had believed, though most of them had not yet been born when the stories were already ancient. But I remembered the Nekromanteion part of the story well. It had always fascinated me as a child.

The fey warriors entered the Nekromanteion, a hidden room within the labyrinth, and faced "the beloved ascended." That is what the book I'd had on Interra called them, and as a child, I'd assumed they meant the dead—probably because I'd wanted to see my own mother again so badly. Stories of the Vilhari were our stories too. Technically, we were one people, as Poe had explained to me not so long ago.

My heartbeat felt erratic as my level of agitation rose. The pressured feeling in the room had increased, as though it too was impatient for us to make another move. Did it really matter what the room was? There was no way to move forward on our path and try to find the standing stones without going through one of these doors.

Ash's brow furrowed further as he circled back to me.

"Well?" I tried to keep my tone even. It wasn't his fault that this place made me so anxious. "What do you think? Could it be the Nekromanteion from the stories?"

He nodded. "I think so, though I admit I'm not sure if I remembered the stories correctly, or if they were a flight of fancy in Nihil."

I wondered if what he knew matched my own knowledge, and if it might possibly get us somewhere. "What do you remember?"

He shrugged. "To get to the center of the labyrinth the warriors had to complete six trials. Is that what you know?"

I nodded; perhaps we *were* getting somewhere. "Essentially. Though I didn't recall there were six until you said that. I just remembered the Nekromanteion."

He made a humming noise. "Yes, the beloved dead. It was the last trial before they won their prize, was it not?"

"I remember it as the beloved ascended," I mused.

Ash shrugged. "Is there a difference?"

My eyebrows raised. "Perhaps to them there was."

He squinted at something at the foot of one of the doors across the room, and I saw that something lay on the floor that hadn't been there before. "I suppose we'll never know," he said, walking quickly to the flat object in front of the door.

I walked after him, trying hard to remember the story. Not much else was coming back to me. It hadn't been one of my favorite tales. Just the part about seeing those who'd been lost—that much was attractive to a forlorn girl missing her mother. My favorite tales as a child on Interra were those of worlds where the draconae roamed the seas and skies, and mysterious flora and fauna poisoned the world.

Anything to take me far, far away from the hellish environment my father created when my mother died. Anything to forget his cruelty—the way he'd changed when she passed. It wasn't a past I wanted to remember. Maman had been a terrible parent, and Helene wasn't much better, but they were somehow better than Boreas had been when I was small. There was nothing so terrifying as a man used to getting his way who'd lost the woman he loved.

My mother's death made my father a monster, and I had become his creature to save myself. So lost was I in my thoughts that my steps slowed, though my eyes stayed on Ash ahead of me. I wasn't even ten strides behind him, but as he reached the door, time seemed to speed up.

The object on the ground was a feather. As soon as Ash touched it, the door it lay in front of shivered, and before I could launch myself forward, he was sucked through. There was nothing more than a feeling of constriction. I'd simply blinked and he was gone. I rushed forward, desperate to follow, but the door had not even opened. Ash had just disappeared.

A feral scream ripped from my throat, aether and empyrae both flowing from my hands. I stepped back, my rage consuming me as I pummeled the door with my power. Nothing happened. There was not so much as a burn on the door. It was impossible. I'd launched pure starfire at it. There should at least be a *mark*.

My throat hurt from screaming. Hot tears slid down my face in a torrent of rage. Every breath I took was painful as I turned, looking for some answer, some way forward, to wherever Ash had gone. I rotated slowly, horrified to find that the hallway we'd come down, the tunnel back to the Avalonne, was gone, leaving only more doors.

Across the room, directly opposite to where I stood, lay another feather. This could not be happening. It wasn't possible. The kind of magic it would take to create a space like this was unimaginable. When I suggested it might be part of the labyrinth, I hadn't really meant it. It was only a theory.

The longer I stood here, staring at the feather, the more I wondered if I could be right. I went through everything I knew about the labyrinth, both real and fictional: the labyrinth had existed for aeons on the planet Citadel. Though its atmosphere was compatible with our physiology, the place was nearly uninhabitable, as it was primarily covered with what our mages had called "a sea of sand." They'd said the sand was not like the Black Sands deserts of Interra, vast dunes and an arid climate, but a substance more like liquid.

That reminded me of Ash's theory about the river, but the mages' stories told of an actual sea of aether and silken dust, populated by creatures beyond what I found it reasonable to believe might actually exist. The only habitable places on Citadel were outcroppings of rock that jutted up from that sea, mostly tiny islands and small villages. Citadel had only one great city, where the labyrinth had been built, and one smaller port for the Empire's greatest library.

When the labyrinth disappeared from Citadel and its great concentration of aether, it reappeared within the limen, near the heart. In Nihil. The mages had found the heart by locating the labyrinth, through means I had never understood— likely because I hadn't cared, then. We'd found a solution, a place to put the Ravagers. *How* we had found Nihil wasn't my concern.

Now, I wished that I had cared more. What if knowing was the difference between getting Ash back safely or not? I tried to calm my breath, which came in shallow rapid gasps. My heart beat faster. Ouriel's message, and the vision embedded within it, played over in the back of my mind. Were we always going to end up here? Was this Fate stepping in, playing her hand? I fell into a crouch, the details of the labyrinth turning round and round in my mind.

Sea of dust and aether. Citadel. Great library. Fey warriors. Beloved ascended. Feather. Trials. Nekromanteion. Sea of dust and aether. Feather. Citadel. Great library. Fey warriors. Beloved ascended. Trials. Nekromanteion.

Over and over, the ideas swirled in my head, whispering, screaming, clawing at my mind. I was trapped here in this room, as I had been in the oubliette. *Trapped. Sea of dust and aether. Citadel. Feather. Trapped. Great library. Fey warriors. Trapped. Beloved ascended. Feather. Trials. Nekromanteion. Trials. Nekromanteion. Feather. Sea of dust and aether.*

Feather.

Feather.

Feather.

Ash had touched the feather, and the door had opened, sucking him through. But it didn't take me. The feather had not been here when we entered the room, and the second feather hadn't arrived until he was gone. There was only one thing to do if I could find no help in what I knew: I had to act.

If I couldn't think this through, I would have to pick that feather up.

Shaking, I struggled up out of my crouch, pulling my hands from my face. I forced my arms to my sides as my joints screamed in pain. Every step towards the feather hurt more than the last. Every few moments, I glanced back at the door Ash had disappeared through, hoping he would reappear. He did not.

Fear gripped me, tightening around me. This place was affecting me more than I wanted to admit. The feeling of being closed in while the room just *watched* was terrifying. What if I was stuck here forever?

"Why is this happening?" I asked aloud as I reached the feather. It was large, as though it came from an enormous wing, and was the deepest shade of indigo.

You made a bargain, a voice said.

It was the voice from the forest outside the cabin. The elemental god that had given me the strength to kill Helene. "Ash made a bargain, too," I shot back through gritted teeth.

And I uphold my promises, Ventyr princess. Do you?

The most stubborn part of me bristled at the implication that I might not hold up my end of our agreement. "Of course."

Then pick the feather up.

Still, I hesitated. "Will this take me to where Ash is?"

No, the voice answered, resignation in its tone. *But my intention is not to separate you.*

There was a finality in those words that I understood. There would be no further explanations. The elemental god had already stretched the limit of their patience for my corporeal thinking as far as it was willing.

"All right," I said. "Know that I don't trust you, though."

That is wise, child. I have no interest in earning your trust. Pick the feather up.

I took one giant deep breath, as though I might be plunged headlong into a body of water, and picked the feather up.

CHAPTER 31

ASHBOURNE

All was dark. I stood on firm ground, but the feather I'd picked up was gone. Mina was gone. Despite my steady footing, it *looked* as though I floated in deep space, distant starlight pricking holes in the deepest dark of the cosmos. A great stone archway stood about seventy paces ahead of me, if I assumed there was ground beneath my feet.

A guardian stood before it, a giant soldier nearly twice my height, dressed in heavy armor. Instead of a head, it had a galaxy of dust and light, a mix of empyraeic and aetheric power. The strange soldier seemed to observe me, but did not move towards me, nor did I sense any menace in their observation. They were alert, but relaxed.

Hello, Ashbourne Thuellos.

The voice spoke in my head, like Morpheus or one of the elementals. It sounded calm and ancient, like I was speaking to an enormous tree, or a mountain. There was a timeless quality to the soldier that I found instantly soothing. Cautiously, I stepped forward. My movement caused a ripple in the surface of whatever I stepped on. It was liquid, still and clear as a mirror that reflected the sky above us.

Relief went through me, and I took another step forward. The ground beneath my feet was steady, so I walked towards the soldier. "I apologize, great one. I don't know how I arrived here. Is this the Nekromanteion?"

No, the soldier replied. *This is a place that once was and is no longer. A memory, a shard, an idea.*

I frowned, wishing Mina were here. This kind of abstract thinking was her specialty, not mine. I tried my hardest to think of what she would do, were she here rather than me. She would ask questions.

"Do you know why I am here and not where I was supposed to be?" It was a simple question, probably too simple, but perhaps it could act as a start.

The cloud of smoke and light that acted as the soldier's head turned towards me, and I sensed a kind of quizzical interest. *What once was will always be in some form. You came here, instead of the Nekromanteion, because bits of you belong here.*

Bit of me belonged here? I let out a heavy breath, nodding as I puzzled through the soldier's words, trying to think of another question. The Nekromanteion was a part of the labyrinth of old, what it was before it disappeared from Citadel and reappeared in the limen. The soldier seemed familiar with the Nekromanteion… what did it all mean?

I tried another question. "Am I close to the Nekromanteion? Can I get there from here?"

Of course, the soldier answered.

The flicker of interest it had in me was gone now. I sensed I'd made a mistake, not only because it had not told me how to get to the Nekromanteion, but because there was something else I was missing. Mina would know what question to ask. She would see the pattern in all this.

The pattern. Was that it? I doubted I could ask for exact information. The soldier had already proven to think much differently than I did. But perhaps a more roundabout way of asking might help.

"Is this part of the labyrinth, as the Nekromanteion once was?"

The interest the soldier had in me returned. Again, their strange approximation of a head turned my way. *This is the door once used by the victors.*

The trials that the fey warriors went through in the labyrinth, of course. If I remembered correctly, each ended with some kind of prize. If I'd reached that place, might I win what they once had?

"Can I use the door as they did?"

The soldier shifted their feet, their armor making a metallic sound as it moved. *No. The way is closed to the realm of the immortals.*

I frowned. "But I am an immortal. Why can't I access it?"

Now the cloud of aether and empyrae contracted, as though the soldier focused narrowly on me. *Your immortality is figurative. Not literal. Your kind no longer have immortality.*

From a technical standpoint, the soldier was correct. We *could* die. Certainly, we lived longer than what we considered mortal creatures. But the Ventyr, the Vilhari, all fey creatures—we all lived indefinitely if we were not killed. I crossed my arms, assessing the soldier's position.

They guarded the gate. The way was closed to anyone but true immortals. That had to mean that at one point, the fey used this space to communicate with such beings. But why? Though I was curious, that was not what was truly important now. Finding Mina was.

"Does the gate you guard only go to the realm of immortals?"

Of course not, the soldier answered.

"Could I use it to go back to my partner, Mina?"

No… the soldier replied, but seemed to hesitate. I sensed agitation in their voice and in the clouds of elemental power swirling above their shoulders. I needed to tread carefully. The soldier tolerated me now, but might not for much longer if I annoyed them. *But you might use it to put yourself back on the right path.*

"The Nekromanteion," I mused aloud.

Yes, the soldier said, sounding peaceful again. *You could use the gate to reach it. If that was where you were meant to go, then your path might be righted.*

"But why did I end up here?" I asked, my thoughts leaving my mouth before I could consider the wisdom of voicing them aloud.

Are we so different? The soldier asked. *That you do not recognize one such as yourself?*

I spent countless years in Nihil, watching over entities that neither kept me company nor cared for me one way or another. Eventually, after so many years of bitterness, my generals no longer wished to speak to me, and ignored me, even when we were awake. I had been so lonely. So lonely that when Larkin Krane, a witch from a world completely unlike my own, had arrived in the limen, I had simply been grateful to talk to her, to find someone who often thought similarly to myself.

I had found a friend. Someone to care for, to speak to, to wonder after in the bleak eternity of my guardianship. It had been such a relief, and for years, I'd thrown all my efforts into making sure the child was safe when she visited the limen. "Did you bring me here?"

I gazed around me, watching the slow dance of the stars. They moved, but only slightly, and so slowly it was barely perceptible. This was not much to look at. At least in Nihil, the aether was always at work, shifting and changing in its perpetual quest to *become*.

I did not mean to, the soldier answered. *You have my apologies. It has been aeons since I saw another of my kind. You are a guardian, as I am, are you not?*

"I was," I agreed. "But no longer."

It is not a role one can easily shed.

"No," I agreed, thinking of the way I felt about Mina, Skye, Poe, and even Morpheus. "No, it is not."

You would do anything to protect those in your care, would you not?

"I would. I would do anything for them."

Then I brought you here for a reason. For more than my own lonely heart. I am bound not to tell the secrets of this place, Thuellos, but this is where it all began, and this is where it must end. You were meant to come here.

"I wish I knew what you meant," I said with sadness.

You will, the soldier said. *When it is time, you will know the truth.* The soldier raised the staff they held in their left hand, and brought it close to the gate. The atmosphere of the gate shifted as the staff touched the liquid that flowed through it.

I saw worlds within the gate I could never have imagined, peoples I'd never imagined, and then void. It wasn't darkness, not really. My mind could not make sense of what I saw. Cold terror ran through me.

Run, the soldier urged. *I cannot change the destination of the gate for long.*

I ran, hoping I would end up with Mina, wherever she was now.

CHAPTER 32

MINA

Aether clouded around my feet, whispering to itself. I was somewhere in the limen, but this place felt more real, more grounded, than other places in the world between worlds. A silver frame, with a hint of indigo in its sheen, hung suspended in the darkness in front of me, more solid than the shadowy reproductions usually found in the limen.

I walked towards it, the aether curling around my feet, taking the shape of dozens of hares, first—then shifting quickly into a battalion of leopardi kits. I smiled at them. The leopardi were cousins to the gryphon of Interra, both winged demonae—animalic immortals that were both like the fey and unlike them simultaneously. It pleased me to see them.

I crouched down, smiling as the incorporeal baby animals played at my feet, rolling onto their backs to show me their round bellies. Some snapped at my fingers or arched their backs in mock aggression, their little wings spreading out behind them.

"You always loved our winged brethren," a voice said.

I dared not look up. I'd never hoped to hear that voice again. My eyes squeezed shut, tears falling onto my cheeks. "No," I whispered. "Not her. Please. Take any form you like, but not her."

"Lumina," my mother's voice said, soft and sweet. "My darling, this is no trick, but we haven't much time. Please be brave, my girl."

I raised my tearstained face, the leopardi dissipating into clouds of aether as I did. In the frame was my own dear mother's face. Her face was practically a mirror image of mine. Suddenly, I understood why Boreas was both obsessed with me, *and* seemed to have hated me. I must have been a terrible reminder of her, the only person he'd ever really loved. I lunged towards her, thinking to reach into the frame and pull her out. Aether sprang up before me, pushing me back.

"That won't work, love," she said, her eyes sad. "I am on this side, and you on the other. Until you join me, we will be parted."

"Then I will come to you." I fell to my knees in front of the frame, gazing longingly into it, desperate now that I had found her.

My mother—my true mother, not Vaness Wildfang—had been one of the few people who'd ever truly known me. Who'd ever *tried*. She was the only safe place I'd ever known. Even now, much as I grew to love and trust my friends and Ashbourne, I wanted her most.

"No," she said, voice sharp. "It is not time for that."

I took a step back from the frame, trying not to wail like a small child. Since my memories had returned, I'd shied away from thinking of her. After she'd died, the only thing I could do was try to forget her. It had nearly broken me to do it, but surviving Boreas had required that I grow up strong. Missing her had not been an option, as the mere thought of her had made me weak.

I sucked in a familiar, steadying breath, pushing my feelings deep down within me as I stood. "All right."

She smiled. "My darling. You still have so much life to live. You must live now."

I shook my head, stubborn. Now that I saw her, I only wanted to be where she was, where there was a chance for peace. "I would rather be with you, I think," I whispered. "It is too hard here. I don't understand the way this life works. The people… I'm not like them. I cannot understand them. And they cannot understand me, no matter how I try."

"My darling," she soothed, watching me cry. There were tears on her face as well. "Your path is hard, I know."

"Everything hurts," I sobbed. "All the time. It is too loud. Too bright. Too much."

"Yes," she agreed. "I know. But there is love, is there not?"

I nodded. "*Now* there is."

"And you deserve that love. Hippolyta, Ashbourne, Skye, Morpheus, Muse… They are the family you have always deserved, little one. Would you give that love up so easily to join me here at rest? Even knowing that I will always be here, and that I will always welcome you when it is your time?"

I considered what she said, my breath evening out, my desperate sobs quelling, though my body still shook. "You promise you'll wait for me?"

My mother smiled, radiant as the sun, and just as warm. "Always, my darling. You are all I hoped for and more. I will be here when it is time, and not before."

There was comfort in that. A terrible voice inside me flared caution, warning me that what I saw might be some trick, some figment of my imagination, or a joke the aether played. But there was no way to know for sure and I had to go back. It felt better to believe that she was real, that she *was* my mother. To leave with the idea that she was proud of me and that she waited for me at life's end? That was enough.

"I will go back to them."

She looked behind her, at something I could not see. "We haven't much time left. I have watched you for centuries, my love. I've watched all that has happened to you." Her eyes darkened. "You must find Alistair Wildfang."

Suddenly, there was no longer air to breathe. I was drowning, suffocated, trapped. Find Alistair Wildfang? He was dead, wasn't he? "What do you mean?"

She spoke, but I couldn't hear her anymore. I tried to read her lips, but I couldn't. "I love you."

Her head tilted, tears falling on her beautiful face. She pressed a hand to her heart. I didn't have to hear her, or read her lips, to know she said she loved me too. It was as though a shadow had fallen over her. I could hardly see her now.

My mother's face disappeared, and though I knew better now, I nearly launched myself through the frame as she vanished. Another face approached, this one familiar as well. "Thalia?" I breathed as Ashbourne's sister came into view.

"Hello, Lumina," she said. "I was expecting my brother."

I shook my head, about to explain that we'd been separated, when a rush of frigid air hit my back. And then Ash's arms were around me.

"Mina," he cried, hugging me tight.

"Ash," I said, slipping out of his grip. If Thalia had as little time as my mother had, we could not waste any. "Talk to your sister."

His eyes went wide as he took Thalia in.

"She is real," I said. "Or at least my mother was." I took a few steps back. "Don't touch the mirror," I warned. "It's not for the living."

He nodded, then brushed a quick kiss to the top of my head. I stepped away, wrapping my arms around myself, drawing aether to me to create a muffling spell. I'd had my moment with my mother alone. He deserved the same with his sister.

With his beloved dead.

And I needed a moment to myself to cry. To break down over losing my mother all over again. I believed everything Mama had said about love, but that did not make the pain of losing her a second time any easier to bear. Within the cloud of aether that swirled around me, I curled into myself, closing my eyes against the onslaught of emotions that threatened to undo me. Seeing my mother, my real mother, was more than I could easily process. And out beyond the aether, Ash was going through the same thing with Thalia.

My questions about how he got here and where he'd been warred with what my mother had asked me to do. Find Alistair. Papa. The man who had forced me into the fetch, to live a life without hope. How could Mama ask me to find *him?* And what was I supposed to do when I did?

If I'd been thinking more clearly, I would have stayed and asked Thalia myself. But I couldn't imagine barging out there now to interrupt whatever precious time Ash had with his sister, when I'd had uninterrupted time with my mother, however short.

We would figure it all out on our own. Or, rather, together. My mother's words about love stayed with me, lingering bittersweet on my tongue. It made me happy to think she'd seen the connections I forged with my friends, with Ash. That she thought they were good choices.

A hand reached through the clouds of aether, followed by a voice. "Mina?"

I pulled Ash into the cloud with me, burying my face in his chest the moment he was in my orbit. His arms went around me, and I clung tightly to him, relishing the feeling of safety and stability his bulk lent me.

His heart, which beat rapidly at first, slowed, beating in time with mine the longer we held one another. It was a lovely feeling, delicious in its intimacy. One hand stroked over the back of my head, smoothing out the silk of the scarf that covered my hair.

"Is she gone?" I asked, even though I knew full well he would not be here with me if his sister was still out there.

"Yes," he said. The wistfulness of his voice caught my heart, winding the threads that bound us together tighter. "We need to go. This place is only safe for a little while."

I nodded, raising my head to meet his golden eyes. "Do you know how to get back?"

He smiled. "I do, Thalia told me how. Hold tight."

I did as he asked, clinging to him, and the world went dark as we teleported.

CHAPTER 33

MINA

When we emerged from between, we stood on a mezzanine inside a glass domed atrium. From down below, harp music drifted up to us. I peeked over Ash's shoulder to see the harpist, a lovely Vilhari with bobbed black hair and moonstone pale skin. Her eyes were closed as her elegant fingers strummed over the harp.

"Ashbourne Claymore!" a soft wisp of a voice exclaimed. "As I live and breathe, how did you manage that?"

Ash's grip on me loosened, and he turned towards the voice. I followed him, catching sight of a Strix with a barn owl's visage, who wore a pattern of tweed that had become familiar to me. Her suit was perfectly tailored and complemented her feathers beautifully.

"Edith Braithwaite?" I asked.

Though the Strix did not smile, technically speaking, delight sparkled in her dark eyes as she made a little bow. "At your service, Lady Chamberlain."

I almost scoffed at the title, but decided to simply accept it. Now that the word was out, more people would use it. I would have to get used to being seen as more than the useless Wildfang girl.

"It's good to see you, governor," Ash said. "We couldn't have ended up in better company, but I think we need to move quickly."

Edith let out a tiny two-woo noise. "Muse warned me this day would come, and what I should do to save us all." She looked down below at the single figure on the floor of the atrium, at the harp. When the harpist looked up, I saw it was Vionette Celestine, her narrow eyes clear when she saw us. She made eye contact with Edith, who stared back at her.

For a moment, I wondered if they could communicate silently. There was no way to know, of course, but when Edith nodded and Vionette went back to playing the harp, my suspicions grew. The melody Vionette played changed. A slow, sleepy feeling swept through me, as though I could lie down on the carpet and sleep for years.

"I wouldn't listen too carefully to the music," Edith warned. "Try thinking of something else. Vionette has a way with music that will help you now, but it's not meant for you."

I understood immediately what she meant, my chin dropping in an enormous yawn. Ash stuck his fingers into his ears and raised his eyebrows at me. Edith shrugged. "I am immune to it after all these years of listening to her play."

There was something about the way she said it that reminded me of Poe, or how I felt about her, at least. Edith and Vionette were close, like we were. I nodded slowly, and stuck my fingers in my ears. The sleepiness that came over me when Vionette's melody had changed faded somewhat.

Edith motioned for us to follow her, and we headed towards the mezzanine stairs. When we reached the ground floor, Edith unlocked a door just across from the stairwell. We followed her through to a garden, hidden at the center of the Mercury. Roses climbed the stone walls, and though most of the flowers had ceased to bloom, there was an otherworldly lushness to the foliage that was not quite congruent with this time of year.

At the center of the garden was what looked to be a circular patio, perfectly made for chairs, but there were none. In fact, the irregularly blue slate stone was clear of any object but one, a simple black marble plinth. Pravhna's ever-present mist crept through the skeletons of echinacea and milkweed, gravitating towards the plinth.

Edith glanced back at us as she approached the center of the patio. "Stay off the stone, please."

She pressed her gloved hand to the center of the plinth, whispering something that even my keen hearing could not discern. A groaning noise warned me that something was about to happen. Though we had not stepped onto the patio, Ash pulled me back further, closer to him.

The stone shifted, lowering first, then rotating. As each section of the patio disappeared, another shifted into place. Once the entire patio had disappeared, stones rose from the outer edges of the patio. As they loomed above us, the same feeling of being watched I'd had in the Nekromanteion returned, an eldritch sentience in the stones that I could not deny.

Edith stepped away from the plinth and walked towards the door. She patted me on the shoulder as she went. "I will leave the two of you to it."

Ash nodded in response, but Edith looked to me for a verbal answer.

"Thank you," I said, realizing that if this worked, she had given us a gift—one I had a feeling might cost us later. If there was even a small chance that Boreas was somehow a part of all this, I had to take the gift and pay the price after.

As soon as Edith left the garden the mist thickened with aether, turning a deeper indigo and taking on a more sentient shape. Ash moved closer to me as we watched the clouds undulate around us in silence. I glanced at Ash to gauge his concern, but found he wasn't worried in the slightest.

In fact, his face was smooth, his eyes bright and calm. He was practically serene. It made no sense at first, and then it did. We'd made it here. He'd done everything he could to help me get here, and whatever happened next was out of his hands. While that made me wildly anxious, it calmed him. I didn't know whether to find comfort in that or to be frustrated by our opposite reactions to things. As I tore my eyes away from his face, a figure materialized in the center of the stone circle.

Hello, said a voice that was now all too familiar. *You have learned much, and yet still have so much farther to go.*

The elemental god, She Who Watches, She of the Dark Vale, finally took shape. I had no doubt that this was not her true form, instead one of many that pleased her most, but this one was striking. She was an enormous snow leopard the color of aether, with indigo wings that shimmered in the now-dim light of the afternoon—an adult version of the leopardi I had played with in the Nekromanteion.

You are confused, she said, before we could speak. *You wonder why I cannot simply tell you the things I know and you do not.* Ash let out a dry laugh. Solemnly, I nodded. *This is to be expected for those as young as you.*

"Young?" Ash scoffed. "We are older than the majority of the elders on this planet."

Yes, the god answered. *And I am older than you by millennia. Your lifetime, long as it may seem to you, is merely a speck to me.*

"Excellent," Ash said. His shoulders sagged with exhaustion. His energy for all of this was lagging, as was my own. "We understand. You are old and know more than us. We are young and know nothing."

A hare formed out of the mist, then loped towards us. I was sure of its identity as soon as I saw it. It was the hare that had helped me multiple times now, at Somerhaven, at the Orilion viewing party. *You are impertinent.*

Yes, the god said, a laugh in her voice. *They are impertinent. But such is their charm.*

The hare looked away from us, raising its nose in the air. It reminded me so much of Morpheus that I almost smiled. Almost.

Tell me what you have learned of Sirin's problems, the god said, and it sounded like a test.

It felt as though we didn't know nearly enough. I glanced at Ash, but he shook his head, a helplessness in his eyes. He wasn't sure how to deal with the way the god spoke, the way it talked around things. But this was where I might excel.

I bowed my head—wanting to be respectful of the elemental god and her time. Sometimes people did not like the way my mind worked, needing to think many ideas through before I got to a point. The last thing I wanted to do was annoy a god. "Do you have a few moments to listen while I talk this through?"

The hare's terrifying eyes turned to me, as it focused on my face.

Its attention was discomfiting. The snow leopard narrowed her eyes at the hare. *Do not intimidate them. They are doing their best.*

The hare looked away again. The god nodded. *Take the time you need, child. Your way of thinking is no burden.*

I swallowed a lump in my throat, and glanced down at the hare, whose posture had relaxed. They were not annoyed with me, then. Something in me calmed.

"We know Chopard has been setting fires with empyrae. Perhaps trying to open a portal to another world." I paused for a moment. The god nodded once, while the hare stared off into the distance. Briefly, I wondered what it could see. It seemed to be looking at something, not just idly staring into space. The thought tickled, but I put it aside. "Chopard has an alliance of some kind, acolytes helping him. We have assumed so far that because of Maman, Vaness Wild-fang, I mean—because of her goals that they are in some way aligned."

Again, I paused. It was as though I wanted approval, or acknowledgement from the god. Again, she nodded. Though she did not explicitly confirm this, I took this to mean that she agreed, or at least did not disagree, with my assessment thus far. "We know my mother and several other Oscarovi hoped to harness the power of a Ravager to take power for themselves."

The god shifted on her haunches, her eyes narrowing. I sensed she wanted to speak. *My children have been restless for power since the Vilhari arrived here.*

I nodded, a smile playing at my lips. It was comforting to hear her refer to the Oscarovi as her children. Stung as I had been by my own family, Oscarovi culture was beautiful. When this was all over, I hoped to know more about the people of this world and their connection to the elemental world. What I knew was from books, and Maman and Helene's twisted views, but there was more to it than how they thought of power.

The god narrowed her eyes at me, now. It was as though she could read my thoughts. I might have been mistaken, but I thought she seemed pleased.

"We also have the problem of Alistair Wildfang. My mother indicated in the Nekromanteion that he might be a problem for us."

Again, the god inclined her head but once. "So we will have to fight them all," I said. "And I have to stay away from the creature that took Helene—the Ravager. It wants to inhabit me."

No, the god said, proving to me once and for all that she had been agreeing with me before. *It wants to destroy you.*

Ash hissed, and I realized just how still he'd been. Fury burned in his eyes. "Give me the power to protect her," he growled. "I will do anything."

My hand flew out in front of him, as if I could shove his passionate words back in. It was terrible practice to promise such a thing with elemental creatures.

Calm yourself, Wilhelmina, the god said. *Ashbourne says nothing I do not already know. It does not serve Sirin for either of you to be destroyed.*

I could not quite breathe a sigh of relief. "Tell us what to do. Please," I pleaded.

That is not the way this works, the god said. *I can only give you the power to make the right choice and hope that you will make it. Anything more, and I might alter what is to be.*

So the god saw ahead, the way Muse did, and bore the burden of knowing what might happen if they told too much. "How do you bear it?" I asked, feeling impulsive. The god's eyes went sharp for a moment. "The weight of knowing. Is it unbearable?"

The hare turned its fierce face to mine, its terrifying eyes widened in awe. The god's features softened. *No one has ever asked such a question. Why do you want to know?*

Ash looked down at me, obviously surprised as well. I shrugged, slightly. "I am curious, I suppose."

Curious after my wellbeing? the god asked.

I thought about it for a moment. That was not how I would have termed it originally, but it was not in any way inaccurate. "Yes, I suppose that's what it is."

The warmth in the god's eyes was apparent. *You are more than I hoped for. When you leave this place, you will be able to summon any elemental who can help you. We trust you will be judicious with this power.*

The gravity of what the god said hit me with full force. A pairing with a familiar was for life. Would that be what happened? "But... an Oscarovi can only pair with one familiar."

The god looked up at the sky. *But you are not an Oscarovi, Mina. Neither are you a Ventyr princess any longer. You are open, with the capacity to be more.* The god narrowed her feline eyes, a pensiveness in her face that set my heart racing. *Will you be more?*

Will you be more? The question hung in my head. No one had ever asked for me to be more, only ever less. Less of myself. Less troubling. Less disconcerting. Could I be more, now?

My hands balled into fists, my nails digging into my palms as fear of not being enough to be more threatened to crush me.

Ash's warm hand closed around mine, gently prying my nails away from my palms. When he had the knot of my fists undone, he laced his fingers through mine and squeezed tight, a promise that he would always be there. I looked up into his golden eyes, so full of love and pride, and nodded. "I will."

CHAPTER 34

ASHBOURNE

My heart felt as though it might burst with pride. It didn't matter that it was for the good of Sirin—my beautiful menace finally accepted that she was *more*. I wasn't sure if that scared her or not. Despite the Claim, she was still difficult for me to read.

And maybe that was what I liked about her. She was difficult to puzzle out. Too many people were simple to understand. Their motivations became obvious with only a little digging. Especially after my year with Skye, picking up even more tricks of understanding why people made the choices they did, what pressured them, what made them make mistakes when they should take care. But Mina was different; she was a perpetual knot to be unraveled.

That tangle drove others away. For me, it was powerfully attractive. I hadn't a doubt in my mind that if I tried to get to the heart of her, to sort her out so I could understand her, that she would still surprise me. I could spend the rest of my life being surprised and delighted by this woman and her depths.

"Thank you," Mina said, making a bow to the god. "How should I best use this gift?"

The feline stretched her great paws, arching her back, her wings expanding as she yawned. *That is for you decide, Wilhelmina. I see all possibilities. You must be the one to discern what the right choice is.*

Mina bit her bottom lip, then nodded. "I think I understand."

The rabbit hopped forward. It stood by Mina's knee, pawing at her pant leg. *When you need us, call for the element you want. Someone will answer.*

Mina crouched down, so her eyes met the hare's. "Thank you." Her head tilted to the side. "Is it all right to call on you other times? When I am not in danger?"

The hare glanced at the snow leopard, then back to Mina. *Why would you need to do such a thing?*

Mina frowned a little, her delicate features a mix between amusement and confusion. "To talk with you. Understand how we can best help one another. This is a great gift. I would like to honor your skills, work together to maximize our power... And, perhaps, if you would like it, be friends."

Friends? the hare said. *You wish to befriend us?*

The hare's tone was not harsh, but rather a mix of surprise and disbelief.

"Yes," my sweet girl whispered. She had such capacity for violence, such a propensity for exacting her rage. But she was also gentle and considerate of others. The mix was a heady aphrodisiac, in my opinion. "But if your people would be offended by it, or bothered by me..." she trailed off.

My heart clenched to see her anticipate the hare's rejection, but I knew better than to interfere. She had made herself vulnerable to these powerful entities for a reason. Some instinct told her this was the way—the path forward—no matter how difficult, and I had to honor that. It was not my place to protect her so much that she could not be hurt. I understood that now.

Slowly, the terrifying little creature stretched up towards her, its horrific cosmic eyes closing as its ears relaxed down its back. It was more solid than usual as it brushed Mina's face with its own. *You may call upon us whenever you like, princess.*

I could have cried, and in fact, had to grit my teeth to avoid making a spectacle of myself. This was her moment, and I would not take the attention off her. But I had seen the way she'd been treated all her life on Interra. After her mother died, she was always shoved aside, forgotten. Even Ouriel, who loved her best of those people, often forgot her elder sister. It was a natural thing, and the girl could not be blamed, but Mina had spent her life in the shadows.

And for once, I was thrilled to see that it had helped her. These elementals understood her. Like her, they were an ambient presence in this world, forgotten unless they were a curiosity or a tool. They saw her as she saw them. The affinity between them as she closed her eyes to accept the affection the aethereal creature offered was pure grace.

I locked my gaze on the snow leopard, whose head turned slowly to meet me. In my head, I said as clearly as I could, *Thank you.*

The god blinked once. *She always has a home with us, Ashbourne Thuellos. Will you accept the same offer? Will you give yourself to Sirin? Will you let this be your home as well? Can you find purpose in protecting this world forevermore?*

A single tear fell onto my cheek. A home. With the woman I loved, and a purpose I understood. Mina looked up at me, tears shining in her eyes, and I knew that she had heard the god as well.

"Well?" I asked. I would do nothing without her say-so.

"Yes," she whispered, her voice full of emotion.

I nodded, keeping my eyes locked on her. "Yes," I agreed. "We accept the offer you've made. Sirin has our commitment."

Understand this, the god said, her voice taking on a grave tenor. *If you choose this, you will not die. You will not age. You will not ascend. It will be as it was in the beginning, for just the two of you. You will be like us, everlasting.*

There was an old story about the fey and the gods, that when we were made, they made us to live forever, as they did. We lost true immortality. But this god offered it to us now, and I understood it was not exactly a gift.

"We'll be here long after the people we love move on," Mina said as she stood. "But we will have you." She nodded to the hare and the god. Now she looked up at me, her face serious. "And each other."

"Always," I agreed, as I took both her hands in mine. "Always each other." There was no handfasting needed. This was our marriage ceremony. "Forever."

She squeezed my hands. "In imperfect union, you and I."

A mischievous sparkle in her eyes told me she had no plans of making the long years that stretched out in front of us easy. She would always be the exact right amount of difficult—pushing and pulling in all the ways that drove me wild with desire.

I cleared my throat as heat built in me. "Undoubtedly."

In my head, the god chuckled. *You will find that as your Claim on one another deepens, that Mina's power will grow.*

The god was dissolving now, fading back into the aether. The hare was already gone. "Wait," I cried. "What does that mean?"

As the god disappeared from sight, her final words lingered. *You will know when it is time.*

The stones receded back into the earth. I pulled Mina back from the circle before it began to rotate. "Do you feel any different?" I asked her.

She shook her head. "Not now, but I will need to try to communicate with the elementals on my own, I think."

"I agree," I said. "Where would you feel safest doing that?"

Mina's hands went to her face. She rubbed her eyes a little, as though she was tired. It was then that I saw the shake in her muscles, barely perceptible, but there all the same. She was exhausted and in pain. Deciding where she would be safest would be a challenge for her right now, one I could help with. Her mind was so busy, but I could calm it with some simple choices. "We can stay here, at the Merc, if you like."

She frowned, shaking her head slightly. "Edith has her own motivations. There's something she knows that she isn't telling us."

I sighed. "That very well might be. But like Muse, or the god, it might be for our own good."

Mina groaned, obviously frustrated as she turned away from me. "I am tired of secrets that are for my own good. I can make allowances for Muse or the god. There are reasons for that." She crossed her arms, hugging herself tightly. "I want Poe."

"Of course," I agreed. I closed my eyes, wondering if I might still teleport, but the way between was closed to me. Whatever I'd done in the Nekromanteion, I could not replicate it now. "We'll need to find a cab."

Mina smiled. "I'm sure one of Herself's dueling drivers might be able to help us."

I pushed a strand of hair that had come loose from her braid off her face, cherishing the fact that she smiled around me now. For so long, she hadn't. Her smiles were rare, precious gems. She stepped into my orbit. Her arm snaked around my waist as she leaned into me. "Let's go. Today was too much."

I looped my arm around her shoulders, then pressed a kiss to the top of her head. I hadn't taken much time to think about the day, or what might have happened if we hadn't found each other in the Nekromanteion. We'd made it back to Pravhna, and had more good luck than bad in the process. Perhaps that was all I could hope for.

CHAPTER 35

MINA

Elspeth's house in the upper echelon was unlike anything I'd ever imagined. It wasn't just the size, though the thing *was* a behemoth, but the amount of sunlight was astounding. Most of Pravhna saw the sun at some point each month, except in the darkest quarters of the undercity. But here, light flowed in through the enormous floor-to-ceiling windows all the day through. Every wall was painted a crisp, bright white, the furniture all perfectly matching. There was no art to speak of, besides a plethora of marble statues.

I hated it. The entire thing made me long for the lush dark of Somerhaven, or even the macabre grace of Orchid House. But as we were guests, I did not say this—and of course, they were both gone. All our refuges were gone. We only had one another.

Ash, apparently, felt similarly about the house. We had only arrived an hour prior, and it appeared his forehead would be permanently furrowed from the way he squinted in the bright rooms. We had been let in by the winged Vilhari I recognized as Elspeth's driver, though he did not introduce himself to us, and now we waited for Poe and Skye.

Apparently, they, along with the rest of the household, were out. The Grand Exhibition events began two days ago, and they were currently at a conservatory luncheon in the university district, viewing all the exhibits that included delicate flora. Ash and I sat by the fireplace. That at least was merry enough—though I half expected it not to give off a bit of warmth.

"Was this a mistake?" I asked. "This place is..."

"Unnervingly bright," Ash answered. He sat on a hard upholstered chair that was far too small for him, sipping tea. The chair was covered in a yellow and white striped satin fabric, and he kept slipping forward. "I hate it." He sat the fine porcelain cup on his saucer and then set them both back on the tea tray. "Also, this tea is terrible. I hate it as well."

I nodded, staring at the fire. The tea really was terrible. Oversteeped, most likely. "Perhaps the house will be more tolerable when the sun goes down. I fear there is no help for the tea."

Ash stared up at the ceiling and then pointed to the enormous chandelier. "They have these everywhere, but no lamps. My guess is that they turn them on in the evening and light this place up like a bonfire."

I stared up at the aetheric bulbs in the chandelier and imagined what he described. I shuddered, looking around the room. It was true. There wasn't a cozy lamp in sight. If Ash was right, the chandelier would cast a harsh, bright light on the room in the evening. There was nothing pleasant about the idea.

"Was this a mistake?" I asked again. It felt like we didn't belong here. Something about this place was not *us*. The air felt too thin, too hard to breathe. Outside the window, air elementals played in the clouds, shaped like tiny draconae, diving and pouncing playfully. At least that was pleasant.

"No," Ash replied. "It is just uncomfortable. When Skye and Poe return, all will be well."

I wasn't so sure. I'd felt sure at the Merc, with the god, making our promises, but here in the highest echelon, I felt small and powerless. The house itself was unwelcoming, as was every beautiful house on the street. This wasn't my Pravhna. Nor had Orchid House been. Suddenly, I longed for the lush dark of the undercity, the bustling markets, and cozy tea shops. That had never been my home, and yet I was homesick for it.

It wasn't a thought I could voice aloud at the moment. The

cruelty of wishing for a place we could not go, and a peace we could not yet have, was too much in this bright light. Somewhere in the house, a door opened. Voices I didn't recognize rang out, boisterous and cheerful. They went with the house—too happy, too carefree, too loud.

Ash held up a finger, motioning for me to wait, and then stole into the hallway, closing the door behind him. All of the doors in this place were exceedingly heavy, which I assumed was some kind of safety measure, so I couldn't hear exactly what went on, but Ash's tone was calm, so I turned back to the window to watch the air elementals.

That felt better than looking at the stark white room. I reached out with my mind. *Hello.*

The elemental draconae turned their heads toward me. *Hello,* one answered as the three I'd observed came to the window. *Are you the Ventyr princess?*

Once I was, I replied. *Now I am something else.*

The hares say you wish for friends, another of the little reptilian spirits said. Because they were not corporeal, there was no need for them to flap wings to stay aloft. Instead, all three floated just outside the window.

If you would like that, yes, I answered. *Would you like to be friends?*

They looked at one another, seeming to speak without my awareness. Finally, the first replied. *Come to the roof when the stars come out, and we will bring others to meet you.*

It was not exactly the answer I wanted, but I nodded, speaking aloud. "I will. Thank you."

They faded from sight as Ashbourne re-entered the parlor. "Chevaliers," he said, as though that explained everything. My expression must have belied my confusion, because he provided more explanation. "Apparently, they have welcomed Skye back with open arms. They're to have dinner with the family."

The tight set of his shoulders told me he was jealous. I went to him, wrapping my arms around his neck. "Things were bound to change."

He nodded, but did not make eye contact with me. "She won't be coming back with me. To the undercity."

It was as though he'd heard my thoughts, there was so much longing in his voice. "Perhaps not, not permanently, anyway."

Ash looked down at me. "You are rather good at puzzling through things." I nodded, wondering what he was thinking. If he had the same thought I did—if we wanted the same things, here at the end of one thing, and the beginning of another. "What do you think of changing the sign on the office door? Wildfang and Claymore?"

"Ash," I breathed, joy filling me. "Yes."

"Back there, at the Merc... It felt like we crossed a threshold..."

"It felt like a handfasting," I finished for him. "To me, at least."

"It did?" he asked, a grin spreading over his beautiful face. "Then you'll be mine?"

I nodded. "I already am."

"We should have had a party, rings, all that," he said. "You deserve that."

I brushed a kiss to his lips. "We will. When all this is through. But it will not make us any more paired than we are at this moment. It will simply be a celebration."

"You are everything I've ever hoped for," he breathed. "My whole life, Mina, I waited for someone who would make me feel the way you do."

I bowed my head, my cheeks flushed with happiness. "And I have waited for someone to see the whole of me. The true whole... And not run."

"Poe hasn't run, nor Skye nor Morpheus," he reasoned.

My head tilted to the side. "But none of them see all of me, the darkness and the light. Not the way you do."

Ash arched an eyebrow. "I think Morpheus might."

"You're likely right about that," I agreed. "And so he should. He's probably done worse than either of us could imagine."

Ash let out a deep laugh, one I felt in my belly. I frowned. "Was that funny?"

He kissed me. "Yes, love. Your sense of humor is unparalleled."

I hadn't meant to be funny, but I liked that he thought I was. Often, when people laughed at the way I saw things, I felt left out of the joke. Nothing could be further from that with Ash. With him, I felt included. That, at least, he had in common with Skye and Poe.

Outside, movement caught my eye. Skye and Poe came down the front walk, along with Elspeth and Skye's father. They paused to look at the dried hydrangea husks, waving in the breeze, pointing at something in the garden. Suddenly, I was very tired. We'd been shown to a bedroom that had been prepared for us when we first arrived. "I need to lie down," I said softly. "Can you send Poe in?"

Ash nodded, kissing my cheeks, then my mouth. "Of course."

CHAPTER 36

MINA

I tried to rest in the bright bedroom we'd been given, but as there were no shades on the windows, and no way to make the room darker, I was stuck in a place of agitation. I did not want to be with people, but nor did I want to be separated from them. Frustrated and tired, I did something I hadn't done since I was a child. I opened the door to the bedroom and lay down on the floor to eavesdrop for a while. The benefit of this was that on the floor, I was in the shadow of the tall four-poster bed.

Below me, I heard sounds of Ash meeting the Chevaliers and Skye's father, of condolences for Niall's loss. Mirabelle made an appearance, but was, apparently, busy setting up the new workroom. This property had always belonged to House Aestra, I heard Elspeth explain, but until the fires, they'd let it out to vacationers who wanted to experience the life of the upper echelons.

Nothing said was of particular interest, but the sounds of life going on around me, not needing a thing from me, was comforting somehow, despite the brightness of the room. I stared at the pile of clean linens in the chair next to the bleached white wardrobe for a long while. We'd arrived while the house was being opened back up, and I hadn't managed to put the linens on the bed yet.

Like everything else in this place, they were expensive—silk, I thought. Impossibly soft, and bright, bright white. Ash would help me put them on the bed later. For now, the plush rug beneath me was comfortable enough. I traced my fingers over the tone-on-tone white and cream pattern in the tufted wool. My eyes were heavy, and they drifted closed.

Before I knew it, a cool finger stroked the bridge of my nose. I smiled before I opened my eyes, her rich floral perfume giving her away. "Poe."

"What are we doing on the floor?" She whispered, a playful conspiratorial tone in her voice. I opened my eyes to find the bedroom door closed and Poe lying next to me, a mirror image of my position. Before I could answer, she smiled. "Did you enjoy our nap?"

"Our?" I asked.

She yawned, then nodded. I couldn't help but notice that her high-waisted wool pants were winter white, as was the cashmere sweater she wore. She looked as though she matched the house. "Yes. I found you here, laid down to talk to you, that little brat showed up, and then we were both asleep."

I followed Poe's gaze to our knees, where Morpheus curled between us, little snores reverberating through his body, and both of ours now that I was aware of it.

"He thinks we need more rest," Poe remarked. Again, she sounded playful, but her eyes darkened a little as she rolled halfway onto her side. "He's not being fussy, is he?"

I brought my hands up around my face, making a pillow of my arms. They were stiff and aching. "No. I think he knows that what comes next will take power—energy both of us are running danger-ously low on."

Poe nodded, staring at the ceiling. It was still uncomfortably bright in the sparsely decorated room. "This place needs curtains."

I laughed. "And lamps. There are only chandeliers."

She grimaced. "Elspeth and Hesperos plan to give us this residence."

I reached out to touch the sleeve of her cashmere sweater. She turned towards me. "You and Ash won't stay, will you? Up here with us? When this is all over, I mean."

I shook my head. "No, this isn't the right place for us. But we aren't leaving Pravhna."

Her voice shook with the words: "Or Sirin?"

I shook my head, and set about telling her what the god had told us, and what had passed in the Nekromanteion. Between us, Morpheus rolled onto his back, stretching his spine. With his silver fur, he looked as though he too matched the house. He wasn't sleeping, but neither were his eyes open.

"What about you?" I asked, poking him gently in the belly. "What are you going to do when all this is over?"

He opened his eyes. *Enjoy the benefits of multiple homes.*

Poe snickered, which turned into giggling, which infected me. Soon, tears flowed down both Poe and my faces, the laughter turning to a blessed release of tension between us.

When we curled towards each other again, comfortable on the plush rug once more, she took hold of my hand, squeezing hard. "I am so sorry. For what happened at Orchid House."

I frowned. "I am all right. It is unfortunate it burned before we were able to examine Maman's workroom again, but—"

"That's not what I'm talking about." Poe pushed herself into a seated position, crossing her legs and smoothing the white wool of her pants with her palms. "I am sorry for what I did."

It was my turn to sit up. "We already talked about this. Are you still upset by what happened?"

She nodded. "I can't stop thinking about what it felt like to hurt you. How part of me *liked* it."

For a moment, my entire body went cold. I had to stop myself from recoiling from her. Was she no better than Maman? Fear rushed in—fear that I'd chosen wrong—that Poe wasn't who I thought she was. This was Caralee and the others all over again.

Poe was still talking, staring down at her hands. "I've never felt that way before in my life, Mina. I—I am so afraid of hurting people. So afraid to do anything wrong. It was like a nightmare come true. I was hurting you, and I..." A sob wracked through her, so harsh it shook me out of the cloud of fear that coiled around me like a vise. "I enjoyed it."

Her last words were practically a wail, desperate and lonely. She'd been grappling with this all on her own. Worried she was something she wasn't—something she feared. The last piece of the puzzle snapped into place.

My arms darted out, reaching for Poe. I grabbed her by the shoulders and shook her gently, forcing her to look me in the eyes. It was terribly uncomfortable—for us both—but I needed her to see me. "It wasn't you."

"What?" she gasped. "What do you mean?"

"It was the Ravager that liked it. Not you. It can read our worst fears. It's why it chose you and Viridian to hurt me."

Poe frowned. "I don't understand."

She was resistant to hearing this. Perhaps she even thought I was making things up to help her feel better. That wasn't it, though.

"It seems convoluted, I know. But hear me out, please."

Poe nodded. Morpheus crawled into her lap, purring gently. He blinked at me. *I believe Mina is onto something.*

"This Ravager enjoys inflicting pain. It gets pleasure from it. And the best way to hurt all of us, both in the moment and in the days to come, was to exploit all our fears. My fear that I am not loved. Your fear of hurting others."

Poe's eyes widened. "And Viridian's fear of being disloyal."

I nodded. "Yes. To drive us apart both in the moment, but also after. The Ravager knew we'd escape—perhaps it even meant to let us go. This was meant to fester between us and cause problems."

Poe took a sharp breath in. "But it didn't quite work, did it?"

I sighed. "I think it worked on you better than the rest of us."

"I *am* the weakest of the three of us." She looked down at her hands, which rested on Morpheus' back.

He bumped his head against her chin. *That is not true, Hippolyta. You are attached differently to this existence than either Mina or Viridian.*

I saw what Morpheus meant, immediately. "He's right, Poe. You care about others in a deep, fully present way, while Viridian and I both see the wider picture of the past and future. It allows us distance from things like what happened at Orchid House. And I—well, I have lifetimes of such experiences. You, thankfully, do not."

Poe nodded slowly, though her pretty face was twisted in concentration. "I don't like that explanation, but it makes sense."

I made eye contact with Morpheus, who cuddled further into her lap, purring more deeply, more rhythmically. "Poe, I don't think what happened at Orchid House was meant to hurt me. I think it was meant to hurt *you*."

As the words came out of me, they felt true. The Ravager knew how important she was. Both to me, and to Sirin. Poe had some role to play in all this—as the lost heir, as a Strider, as my best friend—that was vitally important. And the Ravager, in all its ancient cunning, discerned that and wormed into her mind, finding a way to eat at her confidence, her trust in herself.

"I don't know what its aims are completely," I said. "But I know that it wants to hurt me—hurt Sirin—and if it wants to hurt Sirin, it will do all it can to hurt you."

Poe frowned at me. "I don't know what that means."

I shook my head. "Neither do I. Not yet. It's just a hunch. But I need you to trust me on this. Whatever the Ravager is up to, Poe, you did not like hurting me. It did. It liked every moment of the pain it could force you to cause me, and it enjoyed knowing that this too would happen."

Understanding oozed through her, first in waves of horror, then anger, and finally relief. When her shoulders finally relaxed, I knew that she had accepted what I said enough to begin the work of internalizing it. I had the instinct that we shouldn't dwell here.

I pushed myself to my feet. The sun had gone down while we talked. I had somewhere to be, and I wanted Poe to come with me. "Will you come with me to the roof? I have something to show you."

CHAPTER 37

ASHBOURNE

U pstairs, Poe and Mina were having a long talk. Skye was worried about Poe, I could easily tell that. But she'd wanted me to meet her father and her Chevalier friends. We'd been sparring in the gymnasium, which was as cursedly bright as the rest of this place, for over an hour, after a tedious late afternoon luncheon. Far, far too much time had elapsed since Mina and Poe had gone upstairs.

I'd been polite as long as I could and needed a break. It was not my intention to be rude, in fact, quite the opposite. I didn't want to hurt Skye's feelings, but I wasn't interested in socializing now, or ever really, with people who'd abandoned Skye so easily.

She watched, a frown furrowing at the bridge of her nose as I excused myself from another round with the Chevalier I'd sparred with. Outside, the sun was setting and the early evening air was crisp this high up on the mountain. A silver-haired figure appeared next to me on the marble steps of the gymnasium.

Hesperos Aestra was tall, with moonstone pale skin, eyes, and hair. He was even paler than the rest of the Aestras and moved with an otherworldly grace that spoke of ancient days. He was a quiet man, from what I could tell, and though Skye had always described him as kind and loving, I sensed a dangerous quality behind his cultured exterior.

"My daughter is young, Ashbourne," he said. "Give her time to come to terms with the responsibility she has taken on as the High Queen's consort."

I arched an eyebrow, gesturing to the city below us. "You think that will matter to them?"

Hesperos smirked. "Power always matters to them, whether real or perceived."

He could not have stated things more plainly or accurately. The powerful ruled Pravhna. It did not matter who a person was, where they came from, what they looked like, or how much they had when they arrived. If they could wield some kind of power, amass enough of it, this city gobbled it up.

Hesperos continued as he walked down the gymnasium steps, obviously expecting me to follow. "It is significant that Hippolyta is truly powerful, as well as being the heir. Skye will have her work cut out for her, keeping her safe."

I kept pace with the man who fathered my best friend in all worlds. "I agree." And I did. When thinking about it plainly, I understood the enormity of the undertaking. The lifelong commitment it would take to make their lives safe and productive. It was only my desire not to lose her that caused me to hesitate.

I'd told Skye what I could in such a short time about the Nekromanteion and our conversation with the god, but I had done so in private. I took a deep breath. "Mina and I will help, of course. But we have our own mission."

Hesperos slowed as we neared the house. We stood on a gravel path in the garden, the smell of newly tilled dirt still in the air. "You have been called by Sirin, have you not?"

I was surprised enough by those words to take a step back.

Hesperos sighed. "I have traveled this world for most of my life, Ashbourne. And while I am nowhere near your age, I do have a bit of experience."

I couldn't help but laugh. "Sometimes I don't feel very old at all. I spent so much of my life locked in Nihil with the Ravagers."

Skye let me know that she'd told her parents everything. It had irked a bit to know she'd revealed my secrets without my leave, but they had suspected worse; she'd needed to allay their fears about the Ventyr returning.

I held out my hand to Hesperos Aestra. "Mina and I want this to be our home. We aren't going anywhere, and we will help Poe and Skye any way we can. But we won't do it from up here."

Skye's father nodded once, then clasped my arm. "Then we are aligned in our goals. Thank you for helping us, Ashbourne. The coming days will need more warriors like yourself. Like them." He nodded towards the Chevaliers inside the well-lit gymnasium. "This won't end when Chopard is dealt with and the Ravager is gone. You understand this? There is work to do to make Pravhna a better place."

I took another deep breath. "Yes, first Pravhna, and then Sirin. We've let too many of our ancestors' mistakes proliferate here."

Hesperos let go of my arm, seemingly satisfied with my answer. "The avian fey and the Oscarovi must be brought in to lead. We Vilhari have pushed too hard for too long. Elspeth and I made mistakes. We thought that Niall and Skye would be part of a change from within."

"You could not have anticipated what happened with Niall," I said, watching Skye trounce yet another of her Chevalier friends inside the gymnasium. They shook hands, laughing with one another. I rarely saw her so relaxed. She was in her element.

Hesperos laughed, and though there was no joy in the sound, there was a certain warmth. "You don't think that."

"No," I agreed. I hadn't wanted to criticize him. No matter how wretched Niall was, he was this man's son, and he was grieving. But as I was called out, I wouldn't lie. "I don't. You should have listened to Skye. She told you how dangerous the cityguard were. How poor of a choice it was to allow Niall to join them."

"We made a mistake," he replied. "One we will not replicate. We will listen better from now on."

Elspeth opened the terrace doors, carrying a tray of mugs that steamed in the cold evening air. There were only three. She gestured to a set of wrought iron chairs that sat facing the gymnasium. The chairs were painted white. Why was everything here painted white?

Elspeth's face was drawn as she frowned at the tray. "I made cocoa."

Hesperos frowned. "*You* made it?"

Elspeth sat the tray down on one of the small tables between the chairs. "Gerard made it after I ruined the first pot."

Hesperos laughed. "At least you tried."

She shrugged imperiously. "One cannot be good at everything."

I took the mug she offered and sat down next to the couple, who argued in good nature about what exactly Elspeth was good at. There was something comforting about listening to them talk, a paired couple that had lasted hundreds upon hundreds of years together. They were still younger than I was, than Mina was, but this felt like being among equals in a different way from what it sometimes felt like being with Skye and Poe.

These two had seen thousands of years pass, and they understood the complexity of a situation such as ours. If we could defeat Chopard and the Ravager, *when* we defeated them, the work didn't end. We might solve this problem, but there would be others that followed.

That was what made our agreement with the god, and the partnerships we cultivated now, so vital. Sirin had to change, had to rise to meet a new way of thinking about ourselves and our relationship to the world, or we would continue to be vulnerable to such attacks.

Our separation, our insistence upon secrets and factions, had harmed us for far too long. This new Sirin could not be the work of warriors. It must be the work of people like Skye and Poe. Of Elspeth and Hesperos Aestra. Of Edith Braithwaite and Karnon Archambeau. Mina and I could do the necessary work to protect this world when it needed powerful heroes, but we would never be well suited to solving the intricate problems of figuring out how its peoples might get along with one another.

That took another sort altogether. I set my mug down, resolved. "I think I'll rejoin Skye and the others."

Hesperos Aestra smiled, and his expression warmed me all the way through. It was a father's smile. One of understanding and pride. Of watching a child work through something on their own and knowing they would be all right. I hadn't felt a parent's love in a long, long time. I bowed my head to Hesperos and Elspeth, then strode across the yard to join their daughter.

Movement in the shadows of the garden caught my attention. It was the tiniest thing and could have been a small animal. A nuthatch perhaps, or a red squirrel headed to bed after a long day. But for the wary prickling of my skin, I might have ignored it. I did not pause, but changed my trajectory a bit, as though I'd meant to walk to the second entrance to the gymnasium, the one further into the garden.

The movement stopped, and then as I turned my back to enter the gymnasium doors, a figure dashed across the yard, making for the house. Hesperos Aestra stood, pushing Elspeth back as he drew a knife from somewhere within the captain's uniform he wore.

His wife summoned aether as the figure ducked past them. I sprinted across the yard, my long legs pumping hard as I could, but the dark figure was already in the house, headed for the stairs. They wore a hood so I could not see their face. I listened hard, extending my Ventyr hearing as far as I could. Mina and Poe were on the roof. Outside, Hesperos called for the Chevaliers.

I paused. The intruder had a head start and was gaining ground fast. I lurched towards the stairs, feeling desperate, then wondered, slowing. The god had said that Mina's power would intensify as time went on, which had left me to wonder about my own, and the privileges the god intended to give us.

It was a risk, but I stopped. My eyes fell closed, and I felt for *between*. It was there, the feeling in my gut that let me jump spaces instantly. I opened my eyes, stepped to the base of the stairs, and looked up, gauging where the intruder was. Third floor.

I slipped between, emerging on the fourth floor at the top of the stairs. Down below, the Chevaliers rushed up. As the intruder rounded the top of the stairs, I caught sight of their eyes. They were familiar to me—the devious eyes of a particularly cruel Strix woman.

"Hello, Brigitte," I said. "What are you doing here?"

She stopped, glancing behind her. "How did you…"

"No matter," I said, turning my head when I heard the sound of a door opening on the floor above me. My heart thumped hard. Brigitte could not be allowed near Mina or Poe, but I endeavored to stay calm. And so I kept my voice calm. "Darling, close the door, please."

MINA

A *half hour earlier*

UNLIKE AT HOUSE AESTRA, there was no garden on the roof here, just a small terrace, with a few chairs and some potted fruit trees that looked as though they should have been brought in weeks ago. Poe and I settled into two of the chairs.

"What are we doing up here?" she asked.

"The elementals asked them to meet me here after the sun went down."

Poe raised an eyebrow. "Really? Do you know why?"

"To become friends," I said.

We sat quietly for a few minutes, watching the moon rise and clouds move across the sky. Thick mist rolled over the rooftop, behaving in a way it absolutely should not. Poe took a sharp breath inward, drawing her feet up underneath her body.

"What is it doing?"

"They're coming," I said.

Figures solidified in the mist. Hares came first, then large weasels and a few wildcats. From the clouds, a pair of eagles broke out and swung down towards us, along with the tiny draconae from before. As the draconae drew closer, I saw that in the droplets of water on their scaled backs, tiny sea creatures took form.

As the draconae lit on the balustrade that guarded the roof's edge, the creatures in the droplets of water shook off in a spray, landing on Poe and my clothes. Poe lifted a tiny crystalline crab on her sleeve to her face, eyes alight with wonder. "Hello," she said.

Hello, your majesty, all the little creatures on her clothes replied in unison. Shadowy aether billowed around her fingers and the crystalline elementals played happily in it.

Poe twirled her fingers, making little castles out of her shadows. It gave me an idea, and I too began to construct shapes from the aether, building a garden around us, made from the stuff that created life itself.

The elementals explored the spaces Poe and I generated and I felt them, rather than hearing their voices in my head. It was as though I could see what they saw, feel what they did. One of the hares stood next to me, a sentinel as it watched its brethren chase the weasels around.

This is not all of them; more will come. Everywhere you go, they will come. Are you sure this is what you want?

I nodded. "I think it is. Will they want to talk to me?"

More than you will enjoy, perhaps, it replied.

"Why do you say that?" I whispered, crouching down beside it so I could look into its fathomless eyes. It was nearly corporeal now that we were so close.

Some of your kind think of us as pests.

My eyes widened. I had never heard such a thing. I'd heard Oscarovi talk about their familiars as frustrating, like children or servants they could not manage. Was that the same thing?

Perhaps it didn't matter if that was not my view. "You are not pests to me."

Poe ran around the roof, being chased by a small band of indigo woodland creatures, laughing so hard I thought she might cry. It was good to see her have fun. She collapsed in a heap, letting them catch her, completely unafraid.

We'd been taught to fear elementals. The lessons we'd learned as children were meant to teach us respect, but instead taught us to be afraid. The way the creatures responded to Poe now made me wonder if we'd been doing things wrong.

"Do you all like to play like this?" I asked.

The hare stared up at me. *Of course.*

Oh, we had made so many mistakes. So many things had to change. "I think people didn't understand that you wanted to connect with us."

Why else would we agree to form bonds with the Oscarovi? We want to be a part of the world you inhabit.

"Oh." The word fell out of me in a long breath.

These creatures had tried to ally with us, and we'd treated them like tools. They had approached us as equals and we'd behaved as though they were beneath us. It hurt to think about it that way. We were lucky they did not want revenge against us. This was their world, as much as it was ours.

One of the eagles on the balustrade let out a harsh noise aloud, then spoke directly to me. *There is an intruder in the house. A Strix. She wants to harm the queen.*

"How can you tell?" I asked.

The hare pawed at my knee. *That is a hard question to answer, Mina. Sometimes we see more than you, eagles especially.*

I nodded, willing to accept that. It was well known that while the elementals were not the same as the animal avatars they chose to represent them, they often chose them because of their essential nature—because of some fundamental thing about the animal that aligned with their own capabilities.

Several snakes slithered out of the mist, along with a pack of wolves. I motioned to the snakes. "Come with me. Weasels, draconae, you too?"

They followed immediately. One of the weasels nipped at my fingertips. She was easily the size of an otter, but when I extended my hand to her she scrambled lightly up my arm, weighing almost nothing until she wound around my neck.

"Stay close," I told the others. "Will the rest of you stay and protect Poe?"

The leader of the wolf pack stepped forward, baring her teeth. *The Queen is safe with us. None shall touch her.*

Poe tilted her head to the side. "I can defend myself."

"I know," I replied. "But I'd rather you flew if it came to it. Shift please, and be ready to do so if need be."

Poe rolled her eyes, but she nodded anyway. I raised my eyebrows at her and she shook her shoulders. Her humanoid form melted away, leaving nothing but an enormous raptor in her place.

Thank you, I said, speaking to her in my mind.

Yes, yes, she said, before preening the feathers on her right shoulder.

The eagles looked pleased at Poe's transformation, and several grew a few sizes to match her. I bit my bottom lip, satisfied with how this was turning out. "All right," I murmured as I opened the door. "Be on alert."

Ash's voice drifted up to me. "Darling, close the door, please."

I waited for the elementals following me to fly, hop, and slither through before doing exactly as he asked. Then I slipped through, closing the door behind me. I crouched down to whisper to the hares. "Let no one who would harm the Queen pass."

They nodded, their serious faces fierce in the brightly lit hallway.

What should we do? one of the snakes asked.

Can you be harmed? I asked, not wanting my new friends to be put in danger.

Not by the usual means, and most definitely not by the Strix, the weasel wound around my shoulders answered. *Tell us what to do.*

Snakes, I said. *Find the intruder and stop them.*

They grew larger, then slithered quietly away from me. I heard Ash let out a string of curses, likely as they passed him, and then begin to laugh. The draconae flew after them.

"That's one way to do it," he said.

I walked to the stairway and bent over the railing. The huge elemental snakes wound around a masked figure, holding them in place. The Strix looked up and a lump formed in my throat as I saw Brigitte's face. Tiny draconae flew between the snakes' coiled bodies, disarming her, bringing each weapon to Ash, who looked up at me.

"Nice work," he said. "What should we do with her?"

Given the way things ended with Niall, I feared keeping her in the house. If I was honest, I feared what she might do if we let her go. There was nowhere safe from Chopard now. The message he sent was clear. Only one option was left to us. "Kill her."

Ash raised an eyebrow, then shrugged. He stared at her, his brow furrowing slightly. "I can't think of a reason not to."

Skye appeared on the steps behind Brigitte, followed by several of the Chevaliers. "Take her to the basement. There is a room for questioning people down there."

"Skye," Ash said, speaking softly. "I don't think that is a good idea. If Chopard has equipped her as he did Niall…"

A flare of desperation shone in Skye's eyes. "We have to know what she knows, Ash. If she came here for Poe…" She trailed off, but Ash and I both heard it—the love she had for Poe, her need to do anything it took to protect her.

He heard the plea of his closest friend, and I the desire to protect mine. We softened at exactly the same time. It was unwise to keep Brigitte, but if there was any possibility we might learn something from her, I had to agree with Skye. I bent over the railing and spoke to the snakes. "Go with them, if you please. Make sure she is secure —and if you need to go—"

We will help the Chevaliers until the Strix tells all she knows, the snakes answered in a single voice.

Brigitte shuddered at their words, and a childhood memory snuck back to me: Brigitte in the garden, running screaming from a tiny garden snake. They sensed her fear and would use it against her.

Skye glanced over her shoulder as she watched the Chevaliers go. Her father waited to assist them at the bottom of the stairs. "That was far too easy," she said.

Ash nodded, glancing back up at me, both our fears for what Brigitte was here to do renewed. "It was."

The weasel around my neck whispered in my ear. *We must find out why she wanted to be caught so badly.*

I nodded, though I felt sure I knew already. If Niall was any sort of barometer for what Chopard wanted from us, we didn't have long to find out what Brigitte might know. I turned back towards the door, as I needed to make sure Poe was secure. "Send whoever can mitigate a blast of empyraeic power," I said to the weasel. "We are going to need help."

You will need elementals from the deep crevasses, from the ocean. It will take time, the weasel said, pressing its soft furry cheek against mine.

"We don't have time," I answered as I opened the door. "Make as much haste as you can."

CHAPTER 39

MINA

By the next morning at breakfast, we knew no more than we had the night before, and the weasel had not returned with elementals to help us guard the house and Brigitte. Mirabelle and Elspeth went to work strengthening the wards around Brigitte's cell. It would not stop a blast of empyraeic power, but it might contain it long enough for us to escape. Brigitte would not talk, no one had slept, and the rest of the elementals I'd sent out to spy for us had returned with no news.

My nerves were frayed, and I'd taken to pacing, watching out the windows as people passed the house, staring. The eagles had stayed, perched on the roof like sentinels. I had a strong feeling they identified closely with Poe and her Feriant form. People stopped on the walk in front of the house to stare up at them, and then were equally terrified when they caught sight of the hares that lurked in the front garden.

The whispers began. When Viridian showed up just after the breakfast plates were cleared, he looked pleased as punch. "Everyone is talking about House Feriant and the blessed heir. That's what they're calling Poe," he added. "The Blessed Heir. For her fortuitous alliance with the elementals."

Poe rolled her eyes. "It's Mina, not me."

I shrugged. Though I thought she was wrong, I wasn't going to say that right now. She seemed in equal parts pleased and agitated by the attention she was getting as the heir. "I'd like for them to think it was you."

She sighed, taking her tea into the parlor. We followed her. Though I didn't want to make her more anxious by telling her the theory swirling in my head about her position as the Aethereal heir and the spirits of Sirin, they seemed so closely related to one another, their affinity natural. "The elementals like you."

Poe smiled, probably thinking of the way she'd played with them the previous night. "I like them too."

Viridian hadn't taken off his coat. "Are *any* of you ready to go? I sent word this morning that Lord Eccles had been confirmed as back in the city and no one responded."

Poe's eyes widened. "Oh goodness. We were invited to the opening lecture of the Grand Exhibition. That's today."

Skye shook her head. "I don't like thinking about you out there. Too many variables."

I didn't much like thinking about her, or any of us, staying here in the house with Brigitte. But Lord Eccles was going to be there, and someone needed to at least try to find out what he was up to.

"One of us has to go," Poe insisted. "It's necessary that someone from our household be there."

Viridian threw up his hands, as if to say "what am I? Chopped liver?"

Poe merely patted him on the arm. "No one knows you're a part of our household, Viridian. But perhaps now would be a good time for them to learn. Did you do what we talked about?"

Viridian nodded. "Yes, I broke things off with Caralee a few days ago. The gossips all have it now. She isn't going out. Helene has not reacted in any way, nor has she called."

"She won't," I said.

He nodded at me, his pale eyes softening a little. He was sharply dressed today in a light blue tweed suit that complemented his skin and hair. A navy frock coat was draped across his shoulders like a cape.

I shared a long, lingering look with Ash. It was difficult to think of separating now. All I wanted to do was stay near him and Poe both, with the threat of Brigitte's true motives at large still. But Poe was right. It would be better to appear as though we weren't worried, and we did need to investigate Lord Eccles. I wasn't sure what might be gleaned from hearing his talk at the Grand Exhibition's opening lectures, but perhaps an opportunity would arise to speak with him.

"Can you protect them alone?" I whispered.

Ash nodded, love shining in his eyes. Like me, he didn't want to do this separately. That was becoming a theme between us. It was healthy to put some distance between us, even for just a few hours.

"I'll go with you," I said to Viridian. "If people see us in public together, it will give them much to talk about."

Skye smiled. "Which will take some of the attention off us."

Poe nodded, taking Skye's hand. "Yes, exactly. We will create a little distraction with Mina and Viridian out together in a social situation, which should keep anyone from talking too much about where you and I are."

Ash stood, his jaw tight. Neither of us was pleased with the plan, but we had made a decision. One way or another, we would see this to the end. He walked across the parlor in two long strides and cupped my face, kissing me deeply. My knees practically buckled before I remembered we were not alone. When I pulled away, I felt the flush in my cheeks.

"Let me just get my sweater," I said, then glanced at Poe for approval. "This will be fine for the lecture, won't it?"

She appraised my monochromatic ensemble, a blackberry colored pair of wool pants with a matching vest and high-necked blouse. "Yes. Please skip the sweater and wear the matching overcoat. The one with the fur collar."

Viridian's eyes lit up. "Perfection." He grabbed my arm, pulling me to the front hall, calling out for my coat, as though it might suddenly appear on its own.

Gerard appeared, though, his hawk's wings tense around his shoulders. "There is no need to shout, Msr Montclair. I will retrieve Mlle Wildfang's coat. One moment."

Viridian watched Gerard go with a bit more interest than I expected. "Do you..."

"Hush," he said with a smile, but he was still holding onto my arm, and his hand shook a little. "He makes me nervous is all."

"Nervous because you *like* him," I whispered.

"Hush!" Viridian insisted again.

I heard a soft laugh and looked over my shoulder. Ash stood in the doorway to the parlor, looking happy, though there was still tension around his eyes that let me know he wasn't altogether pleased with the plan. "Have a good time at the lecture. Be careful."

I nodded, but could not manage to return his smile. It was time to finish the god's task for us. Lord Eccles might have the answers we sought. I hated that we had to split up to find them, but it was necessary.

Ash rushed forward, as though he couldn't bear my leaving. He pressed another kiss to my lips, then sighed. "I should get down to Brigitte. While you're gone, I'll make sure they're safe."

"Be wary of her," I warned.

He nodded. "I promise. Be wary of Eccles. We don't know how dangerous he is."

"Of course," I murmured as he walked away.

As he disappeared, Gerard returned with my coat, handed it to me with an imperious air, glared at Viridian, then stalked off. Viridian sighed, his lips curving into a wistful smile. I shook my head as I put my coat on, then pushed Viridian towards the front door. "Let's go."

THE GRAND EXHIBITION lectures were all scheduled at the university. As we walked through the double doors of the Lady's temple, I got the strange feeling again that the astronomical clock had a significance I hadn't yet realized. There was something anomalous about it, how its mechanical construction utilized aether in a way that wasn't quite congruent to other aetheric power.

These were the kinds of things about me that had frustrated Maman to no end when I was a child. All my curiosity and endless processing of details drove her to fury. I tried to push the feeling that I was missing something aside, as Viridian guided me towards the lecture hall where Lord Eccles was scheduled to speak. The topic of his talk was "Aethereal Matter: Understanding the Dark Force Behind All Life." It had the added benefit of being pertinent to everything we were currently looking into.

The lecture hall was crowded, making it feel as though the paneled wood walls were closer than they actually were. I tried staring at the carvings in the ceiling, identifying the flowers in the pattern to distract myself from the room filling up. Apparently, this was a popular topic.

Staring at the ceiling wasn't helping, so I tried to count all the people I knew in the room. The technique was one I sometimes used to ground myself, to keep my attention from floating away when I got anxious in a crowd. I recognized many of the scholars in the room as ones I'd read in the past. Mostly Oscarovi, a few Corvidae and Strix, and a small handful of Vilhari. Otherwise, there were students and a few people from the high echelons.

I recognized only one other non-scholar face in the crowd: Karnon Archambeau. I'd never met the Halcyon Gate Syndicate leader, but I'd spotted him once as a child, and Helene had told me who he was. Today, he wore a velvet suit the color of pomegranate arils. When he caught my eye, he nodded once, acknowledging me.

I frowned and turned back around in my seat. "Do you think Karnon Archambeau knows who I am?" I whispered to Viridian.

"Yes," he replied. "Why?"

"He's here," I said.

Viridian raised an eyebrow, but didn't look back. He was good at this. He checked his pocket watch. "Ten minutes 'til this show starts."

A few people looked back at us, whispering to one another. Though the audience was mainly scholars, the students and the few society patrons were more than enough to get tongues wagging across the city.

Someone passed a pile of leaflets through the audience. Viridian took one and passed the pile on. I leaned over to examine the one he'd taken. It was a schedule for the events of the Grand Exhibition. The words blurred a little in my eyes. I blinked a few times. I was tired. The kind of tired that went bone deep.

Viridian leaned towards me, his shoulder pressing into mine. "Are you all right?"

His voice was soft, barely audible in the noisy lecture hall. "Not really," I answered honestly. "All of this has been a lot to take in. I am often overwhelmed by the intensity of all that's happened."

Viridian didn't answer for so long that I felt compelled to look at his face. He had leaned back away from me, but not as though he were repulsed.

"Yes," he whispered.

It was just one word, but the tight set of his mouth, and the way his shoulders had hunched up, told me that Viridian Montclair knew what it meant to be tired and overwhelmed by circumstances. I thought about how long his parents had lived overseas with the remaining Court of Aether. How long he'd been on his own, managing a complicated ruse, taking responsibility for so much.

Yes, Viridian knew all too well what I meant.

My thoughts were interrupted as a sudden hush fell over the lecture hall. I glanced up front. My heart skipped a beat, every organ within me shuddering as Helene walked towards the podium. Today, her too-slender body was encased in a ruby-red silk directoire gown, her blonde hair pulled tightly back from her face in a low chignon.

Viridian gripped my hand as she smiled out at the crowd. He was as frightened as I was. Seeing her here, looking so alive, so well—so normal—was disconcerting. There was a healthy glow in her cheeks, and her eyes glimmered with life. This was not the awful creature who had tortured us, nor the dead girl from the beach, nor even the real-life sister I'd killed.

The Ravager's power held onto some piece of Helene and had created something else from her parts. She smiled out at the audience, making eye contact with Viridian. "Welcome to the first lecture series of the Grand Exhibition. It is my pleasure today to welcome Lord Eccles back from his sojourn at the Universitaire d'Ismit."

Viridian's grip on my arm tightened. His eyes stayed locked on hers, though. I gave him credit for that. He did not so much as blink, his face hardening into something vicious. I'd seen that expression many times before. It was one I wouldn't want to be staring back at, if I were Helene.

But she just kept smiling. It was unnerving, that smile—steady, as she described the talk that Lord Eccles was about to give. I could hardly pay attention to her words. The audience was as stunned by her presence as Viridian and I were. No one so much as whispered, but I saw the small movements, the way people nudged their neighbor or glanced around them to see the reactions playing out in the lecture hall.

I hazarded a look over my shoulder. Karnon Archambeau rose from his seat and walked slowly out of the room. "Archambeau left," I said, covering my mouth with my hand.

Helene was uncannily good at lip-reading in life. In whatever state she was in now, I had no doubt that her ability still existed. Viridian squeezed my hand, apparently afraid to answer. I couldn't really blame him.

Helene stepped away from the podium as an Oscarovi walked out of the wings behind the stage. He was tall, pale, with wan hair—and as he approached the podium cold sweat broke out over my body.

"Viridian," I hissed, almost physically unable to keep my voice low. "That is Alastair Wildfang."

Viridian narrowed his eyes. "What do you mean? That is Eccles."

I blinked, looked around, then looked back. It was clearly Alastair Wildfang. How could Viridian not see that? How could anyone not notice? No one else was having the reaction I was. Did they not see what was right in front of their faces? A man, nearly thirty years dead, brought back to life. But everyone was still looking at Helene.

The crowd focused on her, but Helene's focus had shifted. Now she stared at me, a smug smile on her face. It *was* him. I'd seen that expression thousands of times; every time she won something, she'd wear that look of triumph for days. My emotions ran too high for me to discern what it might mean in this context.

Lord Eccles, Alastair Wildfang, whoever he was, thanked the audience for attending, and began speaking. I could not hear the words he said; my blood roared in my ears. Helene moved to sit on a chair at the edge of the stage. Her eyes drifted over the crowd. When she reached the seat Karnon Archambeau had sat in, a tiny wrinkle formed between her brows.

"Keep an eye on her," I whispered to Viridian.

He looked at me as though he might argue, but in the end, he nodded. I was going to find out why Karnon Archambeau left the lecture. I snuck past Viridian and the other people in our row of seats and slipped through the side door to the lecture hall without looking back.

Archambeau had just reached the stairs, but I didn't want to call out to the Syndicate leader, lest the people in the lecture hall hear. I rushed as quickly as I could to reach him. Apparently, my pursuit was noted, as Archambeau stopped on the spiral staircase to wait for me.

When I reached him, he motioned for me to follow, pressing a finger to his lips. I nodded, keeping quiet as he led me to a secluded alcove on the floor above the lecture hall. When we reached the alcove, Archambeau flicked his fingers and a muffling spell encased us.

"You want to know if I know that Lord Eccles is Alastair Wild-fang," Archambeau said, with a smile.

I nodded. "And apparently you do."

Archambeau crossed his arms across his chest. "I do."

It was obvious he was not going to be forthcoming with me. "What are you going to do about it?"

Archambeau narrowed his dark eyes at me. "Nothing, for now. But I do find it curious that your twice-dead sister and your long-dead father showed up together today, don't you?"

Alastair Wildfang was not my father, but I wasn't going to argue that point. Thinking about Boreas right now was the last thing I wanted. I had enough problems.

I sighed, irritated with the man already. "Of course I do. That's why I followed you out here."

Archambeau chuckled. "Edith likes you. I see why."

I had no idea what amused him about any of this. "Are you going to say anything helpful, or is this all I'm getting out of you?"

I heard Archambeau's molars meet in an irritated grind. "I don't have anything particularly useful to say. Isn't it your job to help *us*?"

I took a step back from Archambeau. I didn't know how he knew about Ashbourne and my agreement with the god, but it surprised me. "Yes."

Archambeau nodded, apparently happy with my answer. "Is

there something else? Or can I go? I need to talk with Edith about this development, and I sense you need to do the same with your people. This is something Mirabelle and Elspeth will have a perspective on."

He was right. I should go. But I hadn't ever spent time with Oscarovi other than my family, and given my realizations over the past weeks, I had a question for the Syndicate leader. I was uncomfortable for a moment. It was so hard to know how he might react. "I am… not Oscarovi."

Archambeau checked his pocket watch, frowning down at it, as though he were late, even though he meant to attend the lecture. "You refer to the doppelganger that your mother created for your Ventyr soul."

Again, I wasn't sure how the Syndicate leader knew about that, but it didn't surprise me much. For a moment, I worried that I bothered him. But it was as he said. I was supposed to help the Oscarovi, and to do that, I needed to know the answer to my question.

Karnon Archambeau had a reputation for being one of the most talented Oscarovi of his generation. I took a deep breath and then asked. "I'm worried about the elementals, about how I can best work with them if I'm not a witch. If I'm not truly… real."

Archambeau's eyebrows raised. He looked at me as though seeing me for the first time. He leaned forward, observing something I could not see. Some Oscarovi could see the threads of life, the foundation of all that was, of magic itself. I wondered if he was one such witch.

He reached out, as though he might touch my face, but stopped short, touching the air in front of me instead. His eyes widened. "You *are* one of us…"

My heart beat faster. "What?"

He nodded. "It's strange. You are something else as well. Not Ventyr; a creature built, rather than created. I see the threads of your making, the weaving that created you. Yours is the most sophisticated fetch I have ever encountered. But it *is* Oscarovi. You *are* one of us, Wilhelmina."

I stared at Karnon Archambeau for a long time. His face changed as I searched his countenance for evidence that he might take his pronouncement back. "You are Oscarovi, Mina, despite not having been born. You are one of us. We will accept you as ours, if that is something you would like."

Something in me cracked wide open. In my thousands of years alive, I had never fit anywhere. Never been right. Too weak for my mother's people, who were warriors. Not impressive enough for my father's hunger for power. When I lived with the sirens, I'd been tolerated, but not accepted. And whatever I'd been to Vaness Wildfang, I'd certainly never been made to feel loved for who I was.

With Poe, Ash, Skye, and Morpheus, I'd found a family.

With the god, I'd been given a purpose.

Karnon Archambeau offered me a people, a culture, a thread in the great tapestry to call my own.

I nodded. "I would like that very much. Thank you."

He touched my arm. "I know there is more you'd like to know. More you think I can tell you about Alastair Wildfang."

"Yes," I said slowly, drawing out the word into a long hiss.

He shook his head. "The truth is I don't know much. I only know that where you are most definitely one of us, Alastair Wildfang is not."

Shock reverberated through me. "What does that mean?"

Archambeau frowned. "I don't know. That is what troubles me. It is why I must go."

"Don't go," a voice said, cutting through Archambeau's muffling spell. Helene appeared, as though she stepped out of nowhere. Her smile revealed sharp teeth. I pushed Karnon Archambeau behind me. He'd have been away from here, away from her, if I hadn't stopped him. He sputtered momentarily with frustration, no doubt thinking he could defend himself.

He quieted when he saw the swirl of empyrae and aether I conjured at my fingertips. "Stay back," I warned. The muffling spell was still in place, so I turned my head so Helene could not see. "Get away from here, fast as you can. Find Viridian Montclair and have him help you find out just exactly what Alastair Wildfang is."

I didn't have time to see if Karnon Archambeau would respond. Helene lunged for me. I threw up a shield of empyrae, wreathed in aether. She hissed at it, those sharp teeth showing. The whispering began as Archambeau's muffling spell fell away. I didn't take my eyes

off Helene, but I felt Archambeau slipping away. He made sure of it
—made sure I knew that he was going. It was an amazing piece of
magic, nuanced in every way. I wanted desperately to know how he
did it.

When I got the chance, I would ask him to show me. Now, I
worked to bend my shield around Helene. I hoped I could trap her
somehow, though I didn't know what I would do if I caught her. Her
thin arms pierced my shield, flesh searing as she broke through. It
was horrifying to watch, stunning me for a second too long.

What remained of her fingers latched onto my outstretched
hands, lacing through my fingers. "Time to go," she said, that
horrible voice the last thing I heard as we slipped between.

CHAPTER 40

ASHBOURNE

The house was quiet. Too quiet. Though they had instigated jealousy, I already missed the noisy camaraderie of the Chevaliers. Now they were silent and serious. Mina's elemental creatures were quiet as well, watching Brigitte—waiting for her to say or do anything that would hint at what might happen next.

I sat in the room outside the holding cell in the catacombs beneath the house, watching Brigitte through the barred door. She sat calmly on the floor. She didn't so much as fidget. I'd run perimeter checks all night, helping Elspeth and Mirabelle to check and strengthen their wards, using my empyrae to test them.

Mirabelle's theory was that Chopard might use the Ravager, as he had with Niall, to turn Brigitte into an incendiary device. I wasn't sure how the metaphysics of that might work, and neither were they, but as soon as we'd shored up the wards, the two of them had gone to work trying to eke out an answer from the little we knew.

I'd come down here to take the next shift watching Brigitte. Now that Mina and I had renewed the Claim, I needed much less rest than usual, and I didn't tire or get bored the way the others did. Centuries in Nihil, watching and waiting, had prepared me for this. This was nothing in comparison to that.

Morpheus materialized at my feet. *Nothing?*

I shook my head. Mina told me she'd had success vocalizing telepathically with Morpheus, and though I hadn't had much success in the past, I tried now. *Brigitte seems content to be here.*

Morpheus bumped my leg with his head, his naturally dour face showing signs of being pleased with me. *Have you tried talking to her?*

I nodded. *Yes, she doesn't respond. She just sits there. Waiting.*

Morpheus growled. Brigitte looked up. For a moment, I thought she might speak, but she just shook her head.

"I don't think she likes you much," I said to Morpheus aloud.

The Strix have always hated greymalkin, Morpheus responded. It was an untrue, blanket statement that I knew the cat did not personally believe.

From the way Brigitte's eyes glittered, she definitely heard him. I kept my voice low—conspiratorial, but casual. "Mirabelle thinks Chopard will possess her and blow the place up, like Niall did in the airship." Brigitte made a little snorting sound. I pretended to ignore her, continuing with my purposefully inaccurate statements. "You don't think her head is going to break open like Mina said Helene's did, do you?"

Doubtful, Morpheus replied. *Helene was already dead. But then, he did kill Niall. Maybe he'll do the same to her.*

There was no way Brigitte did not know we were baiting her, but secrecy wasn't the point of this exercise. Anger and frustration stirred people up, loosened their tongues. The fact that we were obvious in our attempt to manipulate her might make her even more angry than a more subtle approach.

I walked a bit away from the cell door. Morpheus followed. "Any progress on how Chopard is possessing them?"

None, Morpheus replied, playing into my little ruse. *Mirabelle can't find any spells powerful enough for him to possess multiple people at once.*

Brigitte snorted now. It was a soft noise, and sounded almost involuntary. She was silent right afterwards.

"I'm going to try questioning her," I murmured—quietly enough now that Brigitte would not hear me. "Go see if Elspeth has found anything else out."

Morpheus nodded once to me. *I'll ask her to come listen.*

I assumed that only I could hear that, but I did want her to come, so I was glad the feline knew me well enough to understand my methods.

I took a chair from a simple table placed in the middle of the hallway of holding cells. It was an odd thing to have a small prison in the basement of your home, and I'd said as much to Skye when we locked Brigitte down here. She'd flushed with embarrassment, and told me Hesperos and Elspeth hadn't constructed it, but a long-term tenant had it built without their permission.

There were so many problems with everything she'd said that I simply couldn't address them, nor did Skye need me to. She knew. All this was why she'd elected to leave the high echelons. The cell Brigitte sat in, the chair I held in my hands, all were part of something rotten.

I sat the chair down on the expensive white tile in front of Brigitte's cell. Even this part of the house was unbearably white and bright. Reasons for that swirled in my mind. The way blood would appear even more livid—terrifying against the stark white. The way the black bars of the doors to each cell were even more imposing against all this bright white everything.

This isn't how things should be, I thought as I sat in the chair. Aloud, I sighed. "No more games, Brigitte. I know you won't tell me anything, but I'm going to ask you, anyway."

Brigitte's beak clicked softly. She didn't look straight at me, but at a spot behind my head. Long seconds ticked by. The air was still down here, the climate perfectly controlled, which led me to believe a spell could make it any temperature the person controlling it desired. The thought sent shivers down my spine.

"This place is unsettling," I said, resting my elbows on my knees and my head in my hands. "A year as Claymore was enough to change me—I assumed I grew up the way most of the undercity did. I can't say I know how you feel about things, but—"

"No," she interrupted. "You do not know how I feel about anything."

Brigitte had been nothing but unkind to me, unkind to Mina growing up. But I couldn't make myself hate her for some reason. I wished I could understand what motivated her so I could try and sway her to see things from another angle.

Perhaps it was foolish, but I wanted to try. "Helene hasn't ever been kind to you, from what Mina has told me. Why do you serve her?"

Brigitte looked me straight in the eye now, her gloved hands clenched into fists. "I don't."

An interesting answer. Not true from an objective standpoint, but the obvious emotion behind Brigitte's words piqued my curiosity. There was something of value here. I leaned forward, a question forming in the back of my mind that I could not quite grasp.

Footsteps on the stairs to the basement distracted me. Viridian Montclair rushed down, looking harried, followed by Karnon Archambeau and Skye. Viridian grabbed my arm. "Helene's taken Mina—"

Karnon interrupted. "And Lord Eccles is actually Alistair Wildfang. Helene introduced him at today's talk."

It felt as though something detonated in my mind. If the Ravager helped Chopard and Helene was with Eccles, who was actually Alastair Wildfang, this all made terrible sense. It had all been right there, all along, but we couldn't see it. I pushed Viridian towards the stairs. All of this was personal for Brigitte. She wasn't like Niall, who likely hadn't known he'd be blown to pieces when he got on that airship.

Brigitte came here on purpose and allowed herself to be caught. She hadn't been with Helene for all those years, she'd been with Wildfang, who so obviously *was* Chopard. He'd faked his death so that he could be Chopard, so that he could take more power for he and Vaness' plans to use the Ravager to take Sirin over.

Brigitte had been part of those plans all along. She was a zealot for their cause, not Helene's faithful servant. I underestimated her involvement, thought it was simply loyalty to Helene, despite having seen them interact. We couldn't stay here another moment.

"Get out," I growled. "Get everyone out. Now!"

I didn't bother to gauge Brigitte's reaction. She was exactly where she wanted to be, as everyone rushed up the stairs shouting to one another. I couldn't help looking back as I reached the stairs.

"Better go," Brigitte said, her voice quiet. "If you want to get out alive."

Empyrae sprang up at my fingers. I let it spread out around me, creating a shield. "I will be fine."

She laughed a little. "I told him you would be. He doesn't want you dead, you know."

"Wildfang?"

Brigitte laughed again. "Mina's father wants her happy, Ashbourne. Make no mistake about that. He wants to give her more power than she could possibly conceive of. He will make her a god."

I backed towards the staircase. "At what price? Your life? Niall's? How many have to die for Alistair Wildfang to get his way?"

Brigitte was still, her eyes closing. "He will have his way, no matter how you fight, Thuellos." Her eyes opened as chasms, black and limitless, sucking in light and destroying it. "How you surrender will determine your fate and hers."

Despite my shield of empyrae, instinct moved me. Whatever was coming out of Brigitte next would be different than what happened with Niall on the airship. I ran. Outside, everyone was shuffling about, trying to take account for who was out of the house and who was in.

The second I spotted Poe and Skye, I no longer cared about anything else. "What are you doing?" I screamed as I reached them. "Run."

But there wasn't time. The ground shook from deep under the house. I let my glamour fall away, falling to my knees as I extended my shield over the small crowd of people in the yard. I ignored their screams as the house erupted, a prayer to the elemental gods of Sirin on my lips.

"Please help me," I begged. "Please help me save them."

CHAPTER 41

MINA

We reappeared in the carriage house at Somerhaven. There was no trace left of the humble garage it had been for my entire childhood. It was now crowded with bookshelves, comfortable chairs, an orrery with a lekanomance, lush rugs and enormous plants. The space had been transformed into something between an Oscarovi workroom and gentlemen's lounge.

Alistair Wildfang stood at the worktable at the center of the room, making notes in soft scratches in a thick, leather-bound notebook. "Hello, my darling," he said. "I am so glad you could come."

My arms crossed over my chest. I glanced sidelong at Helene, who still gripped my arm hard enough that she might bruise me. She looked as she had in life, her fingers perfectly healed. "Are you Helene at all?"

I hadn't meant to ask the question aloud. But it came out all the same. She stared at me, her eyes widening, and in her face, I saw a flicker of what had been my sister. The girl she'd sometimes been when she allowed herself respite from Maman's machinations.

"Were you ever just Helene?" I asked, yet another impulsive question leaving my lips.

"I don't know," she whispered, her grip on my arm loosening a measure. "Maybe I have always been this." The Ravager emerged, smiling with its pointed teeth. "Or maybe I haven't. Who can say?"

The thing had no good sense. I struggled against it. Alistair Wildfang slammed his notebook shut. When I turned slowly to look at him, his demeanor appeared calm, but the fury in his eyes was familiar to me.

I pulled my arm free of Helene's grip. "Whatever you want from me, you won't get it."

Alistair walked out from behind the table, smiling. "It is amusing that you think you have a choice in the matter."

He moved toward me so fast I could hardly track his movements. It wasn't possible for Oscarovi to move so quickly, even with their familiars' help, nor did Vilhari move in short, sharp bursts that way. In all my life, I'd only ever seen Ventyr move like that.

Alistair stood an arm's length away from me now, smiling. "Do you understand yet?"

No. *No.* My mind railed against the idea that presented itself. He'd left me here, hadn't he? Before the original Aethereal princess had locked everyone out, he'd gone. Hadn't he?

A memory cropped up, intrusive and unwanted. *Boreas and I on Cocytae. Rain pelted down from the sky, and our retinue had been reduced to the two of us and two warriors. The Cocyti had picked off the rest of them. I hadn't any idea where he planned to take me, but I knew Cocytae hadn't been the answer.*

Something had gone wrong on Earth. Something terrible had happened to Boreas' plans to conquer the strange planet. I'd been in my cell and he'd rushed down with his soldiers just in time for them to grab me. And then a bright light occluded my vision. Then Cocytae for days, running from the Cocyti, looking for the portal. By the time we reached Sirin, I was barely conscious. And then he was gone.

My mind cleared, and I was no better off than I'd been before. The memory hadn't made it clear what had happened. I thought it had happened differently. I thought he brought me here deliberately. I shook my head, trying to remember more, but I could not.

Tears rolled down my cheeks, my breath escaping me. This could not be true. It just couldn't. I swallowed hard, my chin quivering as I looked back at Helene. I didn't know if the Ravager was letting her have this moment, or if it was simply resting, but she appeared more like herself than she ever had.

There was only one question I could manage. I didn't want to look at him or talk to him. I wanted *her* to answer me. "Are you my real sister?"

She looked away, her pale cheeks flushing red. It was all the answer I needed. Helene Wildfang was my true sister. She was Boreas' child, just as I was. My heart sank like a shipwreck into a dark abyss. When Chopard was merely a man, even a man as diabolical as I believed Alastair Wildfang to have been, I thought we could win. But Chopard, Eccles, Wildfang… They were all the same. They were all Boreas, and I'd been foolish enough to believe it wasn't possible he was here on Sirin.

No one could win against Boreas Anemos. No one ever had. I stared at Helene, wishing I'd known. Wishing I could go back somehow and fix this, the way Ouriel and I had fixed things. Why couldn't we have been friends?

Boreas grabbed my chin, forcing me to look at him instead. He glared at me, so obviously and predictably angry that in the moment of his big reveal, I'd chosen to care most about my sister, rather than him. I pushed him away from me, hard, spinning as fast as I could to take hold of Helene before the moment passed. I heard Alistair hit the ground behind me, crashing into a potted plant.

Pain seared through me, every moment made harder by it, but it cleared the clouds of confusion from my mind. I grabbed my sister, shaking her thin shoulders. She felt so frail in my grip. "Why didn't you tell me?"

Helene's blue eyes were sad. "They never cared about anything but you."

"Was our childhood what you would call *caring*?" I snarled, nearly feral in my fury. "None of that was love. But *I* loved you."

Tears filled her eyes. "And I hated you for it."

"Why?" I cried.

"Because I was a mistake, and everything about you was planned for," she murmured.

Behind me, Alistair—Boreas—scrambled to his feet, yanking on my hair to pull me back, away from Helene. "Daughters will be the end of me."

"Dear gods, I hope so," I growled, elbowing him in the stomach, then stomping hard on the arch of his foot.

He howled with pain and fury, his hold on me releasing. I lunged for Helene. "Get us out of here," I said, as I grabbed her hand, desperate. "Let's go somewhere and talk." The Ravager was back, I could tell, but it didn't matter. "You hate him. Why would you *help* Boreas?"

She touched her necklace, the one she'd worn every day of her life since she had paired with her familiar. "I am as trapped as you are."

I couldn't tell if it was the Ravager that spoke from within Helene, or my sister. "Please," I begged. "I will find a way to help you."

Helene shook her head, but she didn't look at me. It was obvious she watched Boreas. I drew empyrae and aether to me too late. All of it was too late. Something hit me on the back of the head and all went dark.

WHEN I OPENED MY EYES, I was strapped to a chair. Immediately, I tried to summon aether or empyrae. Nothing happened. I attempted to call out to the elementals of the forest—I was blocked.

Helene sat next to me, bound as I was. Unlike me, she wasn't struggling. Our father was at his worktable. Though he still wore Alastair Wildfang's face, I saw Boreas in him now as he moved, and understood why he had pretended to die. Growing up with Boreas in my first childhood, the only way to survive was to know him better than he knew himself. Knowing who he was, how he thought, and even how he moved was imperative to daily survival.

If he had stayed with Vaness after they made my fetch, I would have remembered sooner. I would have recognized him. Watching him work made me sure of it. Though I could not see what he did at the worktable, a dreadful pit grew cold in my stomach as I examined the bonds on Helene's arms and mine. Both were made from iridium, a substance that could dampen connections to elemental powers. There would be no way to summon my power, or the elementals, as long as we were bound.

"Why are you helping him?" I whispered to Helene, hoping the Ravager would answer.

Her eyes opened with those telltale pits. I'd gotten my wish, and now I regretted it. The Ravager repeated what she'd said before I was knocked out: "I am trapped. Always trapped."

I gritted my teeth, knowing Boreas could hear everything I said. It didn't matter; I had to try. "You and I are not so different."

Helene's body smiled, but I knew it was the Ravager. "I will hurt everyone you love. You know that, don't you? When he forces me into your body, I'll kill them all."

It was a terrible thing to hear, and I believed the Ravager capable of such a thing, but nothing in me reacted. In fact, I felt nothing at all. I looked down at the iridium restraints and wondered if it were possible that they dampened my emotions as well. Maybe they did.

I frowned. Boreas' movements slowed. He waited for me to answer the Ravager. I gave the answer of my heart, the one I'd give if I hadn't gone so strangely numb. "Please," I whispered. "Please leave them alone."

There was little I could do to buy myself time. I could hope against hope that someone would figure out where to find me, but it was clear from the state of things that Boreas would have the Ravager into me first.

Helene smiled again, and this time, the Ravager appeared almost peaceful. "Don't worry, Lu, you won't feel a thing when I rip them apart. You can run and hide. I'll do all the work."

The words were so cruel, so punishing, and yet purposeless. In much the way that Helene's actions had been in Orchid House, with Viridian and Poe. I'd tried and tried to make sense of why she or the Ravager acted as they did, but there were still mysteries in what I'd observed.

Things I still couldn't understand.

Lu. It sounded like a nickname. Only one person had ever shortened my name. Ouriel. Ouriel had called me Mina first, as children.

Was there a connection here I was missing? Was there something I didn't understand?

Sweat beaded on my forehead and in the small of my back. Without thinking about it, I'd tried to use magic, tried to summon aether through the threads, or empyrae—anything that might help me. Desperation clouded my thoughts, but still I struggled to put the pieces together.

"Stop trying so hard," Helene said. "Give in to the inevitability of this. I have."

Boreas nodded. "She's not wrong, my darling."

"What will happen to Helene when you put the Ravager into my body?" I asked, though I wasn't sure why. Every part of me was scattered, scrambling, erratic in its futile struggle to make sense of all this.

Boreas picked up a knife now, coating it in the substance he'd been busy preparing. It was a thick, viscous liquid. "You killed Helene, Lumina. She will die a true death. Slowly, because she is half-Ventyr, and quite painfully, I am afraid. Isn't that what you wanted?"

I stared at my sister, hoping that whatever was left of Helene inside could hear me. "No, it isn't what I wanted. I didn't want you to die. I wanted you to be my sister. That's all I ever wanted."

The Ravager blinked Helene's eyes, and for a moment I thought I saw some flicker of her inside it. But neither it, nor she, said a word. Boreas walked over to us carrying the knife. He drew a long cut down the inside of Helene's forearm with the coated blade.

"Please don't do this," I begged. The words tumbled out of me, but were wholly sincere. I hadn't been afraid before, but now, with my father standing in front of me, with no other way out, all I was left with was words. "Please. You loved me once."

Boreas drew the blade down my arm and summoned empyrae. "And I love you now, Lumina. I have always loved you best of all my children. You will be my greatest achievement."

"What about Helene?" I murmured. The world had gone blurry around the edges. Whatever that viscous liquid was, as it seeped into my bloodstream, heaviness overtook me.

"Stop worrying about Helene," my father said in a soothing tone.

"She was always the contingency plan. She's played her role like a good girl, and now you will play yours."

"No," I said. Tears flowed down my cheeks. Why did things always turn out like this? Why, in the end, no matter how hard I tried, did I always end up as someone else's pawn?

Boreas' hands glowed with empyrae. The flame coalesced into what looked like a fine web, which he affixed first to the cut in Helene's arm, and then to mine, effectively creating a tunnel of empyrae. Neither of us burned from the celestial flame touching our skin.

Darkness flowed out of the cut in Helene's arm. The screams of tortured otham rang loud in my ears as the rest of the world fell into blurry nothingness. The only thing left was to watch as the poisoned elemental creature seeped out of my dead sister's body and into mine.

Though I hadn't much concept of what went on outside of the net, I was vaguely aware that my body convulsed. That I vomited. That I screamed. Strange, that in this moment, of all moments, when the fetch would cease to be mine altogether, that I would finally think of it as *me*.

But it was. This body was mine, and I had no intention of sharing it.

CHAPTER 42

MINA

We stood in a dark place, Helene and I. But it wasn't really Helene. I knew that. Of course I knew that.

"Where are we?" I asked.

"Your mind," she answered. "None of this is real, and yet..." She sounded exactly like Helene, and nothing like the Ravager. It occurred to me that perhaps it was odd that I could tell the difference now.

"Helene?" I asked.

She nodded. "The Ravager is coming. I can't stop that. It has its own plans, its own desires, which you will have to tangle with. There is so much I can't tell you." She gestured to the space around us. "But this is where it has to end."

I stared at the arch that appeared behind Helene. There was a guardian standing in front of it, armored, without a corporeal head. It was the creature Ashbourne had described to me. This was the place he'd gone instead of the Nekromanteion.

Helene touched my arm. "Focus, you fool."

Even in death, she was still treating me terribly. "Speak nicely to me," I snapped back. "For once, treat me like I am your equal."

She threw up her hands. "Your equal? I have never been your equal, Mina. Never."

"Fuck you," I said, turning away from her, crossing my arms. "Just let the Ravager come."

She yanked on my sleeve. "Don't you *understand?*"

When I turned to look at her face, every line of her beauty was pulled taut, her eyes too wide. Her jaw clenched far too tight. She was in pain. "No," I said. "I don't think I do."

"I've never thought I was better than you. How could anyone be better than *you*, Mina? You who could do magic without a familiar, who Maman protected at all costs, while I was thrown to the wolves of Pravhna. Do you know how much I hate those people? How much I longed to stay home and safe, like you?"

Rage burned in her eyes. I'd never once heard her say such a thing. Nor had I given much consideration to how she might have felt, or what she wanted. It hadn't occurred to me that she might not have wanted the life Maman gave her. I knew we were both forced to be the people Vaness wanted us to be, but I hadn't thought much about what Helene herself might have wanted.

I frowned. "You never said."

"No," she snarled. "How could I trust you?"

"You hurt me," I said, still trying to make sense of it all. "You put me in the oubliette."

"She forced me to," Helene screamed. Of course, I assumed that. But again, I also assumed that Helene had wanted what Vaness wanted. Tears flowed down her cheeks. "She forced me to. Forced me to put you down there so you wouldn't know."

Was there something I hadn't yet remembered about the day I'd remembered who I was? I went over it in my mind. I'd confronted Maman about the fetch, told her I had memories I couldn't understand, and then all had stopped. I'd woken in the bottom of the oubliette.

Helene shook her head. "You don't know, do you?"

My confusion must have shown on my face.

"I had to carry the Ravager for you. Maman didn't think you were ready. So I had to let it hollow me out, burn me alive from the inside out. So that *you* could be the vessel and wield all its power."

"How long?" I asked. "How long did you carry it?"

She shook her head, her whole body shaking. "It took years to prepare… So many spells…"

"It's all right." I tried soothing her, making shushing noises, but she didn't seem to hear me. She'd borne it in her Oscarovi body. No wonder she'd been so completely deranged when I killed her. The thing must have been driving her out of her mind.

Helene spoke again, almost to herself, rather than me. "Gods… Viridian. Do you know I actually thought he *liked* me? That maybe someday he could love me." She stumbled over the word love, as though it might choke her. As though it already had once, and her throat was still battered and broken from its dreadful grip.

Though this was only my mind, I had the distinct sensation of my stomach dropping. I knew what else she would say. "You found out… That he was spying on us."

She looked away from me. "All I wanted was to get away from Maman. To finally be free. Viridian Montclair was my way out, and even that turned out to be all about you. You and the lost heir. He never wanted me."

"Oh, Helene," I breathed. So much made sense. Why I loved her, when I'd never loved Maman. She had been broken, just like me. A victim that turned into a perpetrator trying to survive. "I am so sorry. I never knew."

"Don't give me your pity," she growled. "I twisted myself in knots my entire life for Maman, and it was all for nothing. Not one person ever loved me, but I'm still here to help you—"

I couldn't help but interrupt her, even though I had the sense that outside us, time likely grew short. "I always loved you. You were the only person in this life that I loved… For so long."

Something in her eyes softened, but her jaw stayed tight. "Wouldn't it be nice if we had time to talk this all out?"

I laughed. It was inappropriate, but it was all I could do. "Yes. It would. But there is never time, is there?"

Helene grabbed my hands, squeezing them tight. "It's coming. That gate. You have to get it to the gate and push it through."

For a moment, I thought her grip on me loosened. But it was only that she was fading. "I did love you," I said as she faded away.

If I ever made it out of this, I knew she would be gone for good.

There would be no other chance to change things or tell her this. "I always loved you. And I forgive you for not being able to love me. I understand now."

Her eyes were dry as a bone as she faded away. "Imagine a life where I loved you. Try to remember me that way, if you can."

I nodded. "I will."

The gate faded from sight, along with Helene. My spirit body got cold. This was only my mind, but I felt the acute change in atmosphere as the Ravager entered me fully.

"Hello, little witch," it said as it took over. "What shall we destroy first?"

I DRIFTED in and out of consciousness. In my brief moments of lucidity, I was aware of the Ravager moving my body. That I walked the beach with Boreas. That I now wore Helene's necklace. There was something in the space where her familiar should have been. Some substance I didn't understand, and could only sense. While the Ravager was perfectly content for me to resist inside my mind, every time I tried to take control of my body back, things went dark.

The day wore on and it got harder to stay present. Time slipped away, but every time I worked my way back to consciousness and tried to take control of my body back, I was thrown once more into senselessness. Eventually, the sun went down.

Boreas flicked his hand at hand at me. It was the first time all day that I could make out what he was actually *saying*. "Go on. I'd like some privacy."

The Ravager moved my body, slipping out of the carriage house. I was vaguely aware that we moved through the garden, towards the sea stairs in the dark. The night was cloudy, and though I couldn't access any of my physical feelings, I knew it must be cold. But the Ravager didn't look for a coat, nor did it seem bothered by what I knew must be incredible pain in my joints as it walked down the stairs.

It had threatened me with suffering; perhaps it enjoyed the pain. I wasn't sure how any of this worked, or why I was even still here, if this was no longer my body. Some distant part of me wondered if it was even possible to rid a body of its original host—after all, Helene had been left inside her body. Perhaps it wasn't possible… I tried to follow the thought, but could not.

When the Ravager moved my body into the water, I felt the cold. The saltwater was like a clarifying agent. I gasped, feeling air, frigid and sharp, fill my lungs. The thought I'd had before the water touched my skin came back to me: perhaps there was a benefit to the host's consciousness being left intact.

The science of possession was strange. And of course, it was essentially illegal in the modern age, so all scholars knew about it was theoretical, but there were some who posited that a host might be left intact so that their talents were retained. The thought shifted, nebulous and soft one moment, and then sharp into focus as I realized what the Ravager now possessed: a body that could channel elemental spirits, that could use empyrae and aether.

"Good," the Ravager said. "You're with me now. You must stay close. Your sister made a bargain for your life."

Why would Helene do such a thing? I asked from within my own mind.

"Not Helene," the Ravager answered. "Ouriel."

What did she promise you? I asked, not understanding how any of this was possible.

"That you would give me the revenge I seek. To destroy all that Boreas loves."

He claims to love me, I reasoned.

"Yes," the Ravager agreed. "It is quite a conundrum, isn't it? Your sister bargained for your life. But I want to see you destroyed."

Had the creature lost all grasp on sense? *We are trapped in this body together.*

"Yes," the Ravager whispered. "And I want to feel your suffering. You will live within me, but we will do so many things together you will hate. I will feed on your suffering, and in time, we will be strong enough to defeat Boreas."

Dread filled me. The friends I'd made. Ashbourne. I knew what the Ravager required. I saw it all play out in my mind: The cruel words to Poe. The ways I would twist the love Ashbourne had for me into something vile. When it showed me what it wanted to do to Morpheus, I stopped it before it could elaborate. *I won't survive that.*

"You will," the Ravager said, looking out at the sea. "You will survive it because you made that fool's bargain with the elemental god. And because your sister made a similarly foolish bargain with me. All your stopgaps, all your trying. It's come to nothing. Do you see that?"

Yes, I replied, darkness pulling me deep within myself.

"Say it, Mina."

It has all come to nothing, I replied, letting hopelessness wash over me. *You've won.*

CHAPTER 43

ASHBOURNE

No elementals rushed to aid me as the house detonated. Without Mina, I couldn't reach them. Couldn't hold the line against the blast at my back. Pain lanced through me, for the briefest of moments, but I had no capacity to pay it any mind. I had to keep my empyraeic shield up. I had to protect them.

Poe stood directly in front of me, where Skye had shoved her. Her dark eyes widened as the blast blew detritus around us. It wasn't just the new House Aestra that was destroyed. Every house around us fell as the blast moved outward. There was no time for a warning, no time to rescue anyone else. There was nothing but my power flowing over us and the incredible blast of Brigitte giving her lifeforce to Chopard's magic.

But I had saved Poe and Skye—and what was left of House Aestra's dynasty. Poe's eyes fell closed and she whispered something I could not hear, the graceful lines of her face set with determination. I watched as her hands went up, aether flowing from them, extending the shield over the little crowd of people huddled outside the remains of the house.

A ripple of understanding went through the group. Skye's hands raised, and though she had little in the way of magical prowess, her gifts came more from her inner strength than creative forces. A trickle of magic joined Poe's efforts, as well as my own. Every hand in the crowd went up. Bits of power shielded us as the blast reverberated behind me, patched together like a quilt.

Poe's eyes flew open, wild with fear. "It's not enough," she screamed. "It can't hold through the aftershocks—we have to move."

I don't know how she anticipated that, but I trusted her. "Tell them," I replied. "Tell them we have to run. Together. If any fall, pick them up."

She closed her eyes again, and projected an inner voice that reminded me of Morpheus through the small group of family and Chevaliers, as well as a few neighbors who had managed to join us in the street. *Run! Head for the lower echelons, but keep the shield up for as long as you can.*

It took a moment, but our small group began to move. Behind us, there was a feeling of constriction, as though the horrific burning might stop. But it wouldn't. The aftershock would be just as bad, if not worse. The pain in my back thrummed through me, but I couldn't pay it any mind. This was more important.

My bare feet pounded into the ground as I took up the tail of the running crowd. There was nothing left of the houses that had lined the streets here. The entire upper echelon was gone. I wasn't sure how to feel. These people weren't my enemies, but nor were they my friends. Pravhna, and Sirin as a whole, were worse because of them.

But I hadn't wanted them to die. Not like this.

Ahead of us, one of the Chevaliers stumbled. The neighbors who had joined us pushed over him. He was too far away from me for me to do anything but scream for someone to help him. Hesperos Aestra let out a sharp, concentrated blast of aether towards his neighbors, stopping them from trampling the Chevalier. He helped Skye's comrade to his feet and we kept running, leaving the fallen neighbors behind.

My emotions were conflicted as we left them sitting alone in the street. They were willing to trample someone who'd done nothing but try to help them, but they would die without us. Skye glanced over her shoulder, and saw my hesitation.

"Leave them," she yelled. "They chose."

I nodded, my head heavy, but my conscience clear. If Skye said to leave them, then it was right. Hard as it was, I kept going, keeping the shield over us as steady as I could. My power would burn out soon. I was already tired, worried that there might not be a way to get these people to safety, when a blast of renewed energy flowed into me. Viridian Montclair appeared next to me.

He grinned, before yelling at me. "That help?"

I nodded, trying to keep the shield of empyrae even at our backs. "It does."

"Healing magic," he yelled. "Learned it in Ismit."

This was certainly not the time to play get-to-know-you, but it occurred to me that Viridian Montclair had no real grasp on what was appropriate. He was odd, but more than that, he simply didn't care. The heat of the blast intensified. The whole of Pravhna's upper echelons was on fire.

It didn't take much reasoning to understand what Chopard—Alastair Wildfang—had done. He'd eliminated the upper echelon of Pravhna society. Not only did it clear the way for him to take power, with few to oppose him, but it would win him allies in the undercity. To kill so many of the cratties… Well, there were plenty who wouldn't see a problem with that.

Even I was conflicted about whether or not this was wholly a bad thing, especially as the people I loved were safe. I had never been so glad to have been separated from Mina. Wherever Helene had taken her, at the very least she was safe from this.

Everywhere there were screams. My shield weakened as the blast of celestial fire finally receded. Poe and Skye were still directly in front of me, and though the Chevaliers kept running, my friends slowed as I did. Viridian's chin quivered as he rushed to catch me. I hadn't realized I was about to fall.

Elemental eagles swept over us, picking up the people in the streets and carrying them to safety. And what was more wondrous, by far, was the pod of great indigo whales that flew through the sky. Sea elementals, I realized as water fell in streams from their mouths, onto the burning buildings. The scene was horrific in so many ways, but in all my long life, I had never seen such a thing and probably never would again.

As foolish as it was, I wished Mina could see it. "They came for you, Poe. Because you are the Blessed Heir," I murmured, feeling groggy and hot. Too hot. "Mina would be so proud."

Poe nodded, tears in her eyes, her hands cool on my face. Aether wove through her fingers. "Be still," she whispered. Her voice shook and her eyes filled with tears as she cradled my head in her hands. "You have been badly burned. You may not feel it now, but you will. I am going to stop the worst of it, all right?"

I didn't know what she meant. Burned? Was that the ache in my back? I tried to look over my shoulder as I rested against Viridian's chest, but couldn't manage to turn. Why couldn't I move?

Poe's magic joined Viridian's, and it felt as though I'd smoked poppy, something I'd only tried once and did not particularly like. My head felt too big for my body, but nothing hurt anymore. My face pressed against the hard planes of Viridian's body. He had quite a nice chest, now that I thought of it.

I smiled up at him, delirium taking me. "If I'd met you before Mina, I'd probably have fucked you."

Viridian smiled at me, but there were tears in his eyes as well. "Of course you would have." He shrugged, as though he hadn't a care in the world. "Anyone would."

Poe rolled her eyes, pushing to her feet. "Help me get him into that alley."

Where was Skye? "Skye?"

Poe bent down. "She can't right now, love. She can't see you this way."

Cool aether flowed over my skin, flowing into my nostrils, my ears, into every part of me and I knew no more.

CHAPTER 44

MINA

We arrived back in Pravhna under the cover of night. My father was altogether too pleased with himself. The Ravager did not sleep, but sat on the bed in the tiny spare room of the flat Boreas brought us to. There was no evidence of the cohort he had helping him, from what I could tell so far, and in the flat we were alone.

When morning came, Boreas left without speaking a word to us, which surprised me. Why was he so sure the Ravager wouldn't just leave? It had something to do with Helene's necklace, which was now around my neck. When Boreas had been gone for nearly twenty minutes, the Ravager moved silently through the hallways, as though it were worried someone might hear. Perhaps Boreas' people were not in the flat itself, but were nearby.

The city smelled like smoke. From the views from the windows, I determined the flat was located on the penthouse floor of a building in the university district. Sure enough, it appeared the smell came from the upper echelons. Something was burning higher on the mountain. The Ravager didn't let us look for long, but paced the flat instead.

Dark mahogany bookshelves lined almost every wall, and the floors creaked and moaned, despite the Ravager's efforts at silence.

Some of the books were meticulously organized, and other shelves were stuffed full, without any rhyme or reason. It was obvious that this place had been lived in for years, and was not one of the clean, well-kept flats for visiting scholars.

Boreas had been here for years. The entire time I'd been on Sirin. The thought of it was more than I could properly process in my current state. I had always thought he'd gone, leaving me stranded, but when Poe's grandmother had locked Sirin, she must have locked him in. With the Ventyr ability to shift shape, he'd hidden among us for all this time.

Most Ventyr were only capable of limited alternae, faces and bodies that *belonged* to them, but were not their true form. They were a kind of camouflage, and most of us were typically limited to one or two alternae. But some Ventyr were true shifters, shifting to a variety of forms. One of Boreas' best kept secrets had always been the true range of his power. Even my mother hadn't known all he was capable of.

The Ravager stopped in front of one of the bookcases in the hallway, apparently looking for something. I scanned the titles. Many were familiar to me. They were the same as the ones I'd identified as Papa's favorites in Orchid House. Boreas had been living here for quite some time, then. I was frustrated by the Ravager's acquiescence, and that it wasn't speaking to me.

Despite all it had said to me, I was determined that we should work together. My only chance was convincing it to help me. Still, I wasn't sure where to begin to forge a connection. Could the creature even feel such a thing? I didn't know what a Ravager really was, or if it even had emotions. But I had to try something, and I certainly wasn't going to give into it.

When the Ravager wandered into the tiny kitchen and lit the stove, I started with something easy, a peaceful opening salvo, of sorts. We didn't need to become best friends. We only needed to speak, to start off with, at least. *Where are we?*

The Ravager filled a black, painted enamel kettle with water. The painting depicted gryphons in a forest. "Lord Eccles' flat."

It wasn't much of an answer, but I felt lucky that it answered me.

It was a small victory. After so much failure, it felt a little like traction. *Why are we here?*

With the water on to boil, the Ravager walked into the dining room, where frames crowded the intricately carved sideboard. Like Orchid House's macabre design, the sideboard was an elegant rendering of a whale's skeleton. My father's obsession with death was evident, even here.

The Ravager sighed, picking up a sepia toned pictograph. It showed Lord Eccles with Vaness Wildfang and several other Oscarovi, including both Rebecca and Caralee's parents, though neither of them were present. Helene was at the back of the group, and looked to be in her mid-twenties. She looked absolutely miserable.

Why did they take this picture? I mused.

"Odd, isn't it?" the Ravager answered. "To think they found comfort in anticipating *me*." My fingers traced Helene's face. "It was unfortunate what they did to her. She hated every moment of it. Did she tell you that?"

She told me some. I purposely did not say more.

"She thought of many ways to try to protect you from your fate, but Boreas and Vaness were always so many steps ahead of her."

And you never tried to help her?

"What would have been the point?" The Ravager turned away from the picture. "I have always been as trapped as you have. Since the moment Boreas found a way to capture and contain us…"

It trailed off. I felt bad for it for a moment, empathizing. But it was difficult to forget the thousands it had killed on Interra alone. *You were destroying our planet.*

"Yes," it agreed. "Has anyone ever asked why?"

I'm sure many have asked you. It's the sort of thing people ask when they are tormented. This probably wasn't the way to the Ravager's heart, but I couldn't seem to help myself.

It chuckled. "That is true."

We weren't getting anywhere with this line of conversation. *So, Boreas is a shifter?*

"Finally," the Ravager said. "You're starting to catch on. I thought you were supposed to be highly intelligent."

That smarted a bit, but at least we were talking now. *I have been through quite a lot recently. I am not at my best.*

"Certainly we can agree upon that," the Ravager said, walking back to the flat's parlor. There was a stack of newspapers on the occasional table from the past day or two. A headline caught my attention.

Pick that one up, I insisted, thinking of the smoke I'd seen at the windows. *The one about the fires.*

The Ravager laughed. "Oh, this is wonderful. Brigitte finally met her terrible end."

The Ravager set the paper back down before I could read much, but I caught the line, "Ashbourne Claymore was gravely injured" before it tucked the paper under a book. When my body didn't respond to my distress, I panicked. I'd spent so long thinking of myself as separate from the fetch, but now that it wasn't connected to me any longer, it felt like mine. I wanted it back—to feel this fear fully, instead of just in my mind.

Please, I begged, desperate now to know what had happened. *Please send them a message. We can call a Howler. I know one that can get a message to Poe.*

"No," the Ravager replied, eliciting yet another wave of despair in me. "Your sorrow is too sweet."

What is the point of all this? I screamed. My keening mingled with a shrill whistle in the kitchen. The water had come to boil.

"I've told you," the Ravager answered as it walked back to the kitchen. "The point is for you to suffer until I've gathered enough strength to destroy Boreas."

It took the kettle off the stove, and as the shrieking died down, so too did my emotions. A highly irrational sense of resolve set in. I would find a way to thwart this thing, and my father too, if it took everything I had to do it.

I hadn't lost this fight, not by a long shot. In fact, the battle had just begun. For whatever reason, Boreas had not banished my consciousness. Perhaps he underestimated me, or maybe he just didn't care enough to. But leaving me awake and able to communicate with the Ravager was a mistake I was determined to see him regret.

I had to stop panicking and make more careful moves, ask better questions. *How did my father trap you to begin with?*

The Ravager took a tin of tea down from a shelf next to the sink and shook its head. I sympathized. Apparently, my father had no taste for good tea. "Do you really think I'm foolish enough to tell you how to trap one of my kind?"

I actually hadn't considered that at all. *No, I suppose you wouldn't. The people I know—*

"The people you *love*," the Ravager corrected. It leaned against the counter. My body was calm. Either it was enjoying this conversation or it didn't have many overt emotions.

Yes, I replied. *The people I love could help us.*

I felt my cheeks stretch into a smile without my say-so. It was a terribly disorienting feeling. "But then I wouldn't get the pleasure of making you miserable."

Desperation tickled the edges of my conscious mind. I wasn't sure how to deal with a creature such as this one. *Is suffering really so pleasurable?*

The Ravager didn't answer. Could anyone really find power in suffering? The thought struck me harder than I imagined it could. My life had been nothing but suffering, and now, were I not trapped inside my own body, I was probably one of the most powerful individuals on Sirin. And the empathy I'd gained in all my suffering was what got me here. Understanding the elementals had brought us closer together, made it easier for them to trust me.

Suffering most certainly could bring someone power. There had to be a way to use that to change the Ravager's mind. If that was possible, perhaps we could find a way together to defeat Boreas. *Why are you doing everything he tells you to?*

The Ravager touched Helene's necklace, bringing it in front of my face so I could examine the stone. It glowed with some otherworldly depth. "He has a bit of me."

A bit of you? The Ravagers were elementals, mostly non-corporeal. *How is that possible?*

When the Ravager used my voice, it didn't sound like me, which was comforting, somehow. "Like the elementals of this world, once my people were curious about corporeal life. And so we made worlds to walk in, friends to converse with, bodies to cavort in. Somehow, your father found part of me. Part of my real body."

How does it work? The necklace, I mean.

"There is a tiny piece of my true form inside the necklace, which I cannot take off. I couldn't take it off when I wore Helene's body either." It paused, as though considering the wisdom of telling me more, then shrugged. "He has a second piece with him at all times. Before you ask, no, I don't know where he keeps it. I've never been able to tell."

Never? How long had Boreas had hold of the Ravager? It had been inside Helene for a year. Had there been others? I sensed I would have to be cautious about how many questions I asked. If it wanted my suffering so badly, it would be better not to give it too much information.

The Ravager poured the tea, then brought the cup to my lips. The liquid was still hot enough that it would burn my mouth when it drank. *No*, I said firmly. There was a time long ago, on Interra, when I had hurt myself to relieve the turmoil I felt inside. I would not go back to that. *Do not do that.*

The cup lowered, and the Ravager's grip on me lessened. I was in control for a moment and I set the cup down on the counter, tears threatening. But still the Ravager stirred inside me. When the cup was safely on the stone countertop, steam rising from it, the Ravager took control back, crossing my arms over my chest.

I had no idea why it had stopped. Had I wrested control from it?

Outside, the sky was overcast. Rain drizzled down, barely forming into drops. Though it was still early in the day, the flat was as shadowy as if it were twilight. The Ravager and I stood, watching the steam rise from the teacup together in billowing clouds. Somewhere in the building, someone played a brass instrument, perhaps a saxophone. The melody was haunting, lonely even, but soothing.

The moment was an odd bit of respite from someone who'd seemed so committed to my suffering before. *What do you want?* I asked. *Really?*

The Ravager walked out of the kitchen to stand before the floor-length windows in the sitting room. This part of the city was on a steeper incline than other echelons and buildings seemed to spring forth from the mountain, scaffolded by elaborately carved stone buttresses and walkways that carried students from place to place.

The Ravager watched them for a long time before speaking. "There was a time when I would like to have seen this world burn, simply for the pleasure of it. To punish my ill-begotten children."

If I were in control of my body, I felt sure my heart would have stopped. The elemental god had called the Oscarovi its children— but there were more people on Sirin than the Oscarovi. Was the Ravager claiming to have *created* the Vilhari?

There were, of course, creation myths where gods created life, but rarely were whole civilizations' existences attributed to gods. Moreso, it seemed they were guardians, entities that were more powerful, more responsible than we were.

Did you come here for the Vilhari, or for Boreas? I asked, thinking of Ash's theory that the Ravager had come for me. Somehow, I didn't think that was true now.

The Ravager pressed my hand to the window. It was freezing cold. Winter would be here soon. "Both, perhaps. I thought I followed Boreas, but I cannot say that I would not relish punishing the Vilhari."

For what?

The Ravager sighed. "We may be trapped in this body together, Mina, but I have not asked you to reveal your secrets. Leave mine alone."

Fine, I agreed. *But you still haven't answered me. What do you want most?*

"To be free," it answered. "To kill Boreas, and to be free."

CHAPTER 45

MINA

The Ravager's words were a relief, but I had no time to bask in my success, nor did the Ravager have a moment to take even a sip of the tea they'd brewed. The door to the flat swung open and Boreas, dressed as Lord Eccles, walked through.

Behind him were three people I did not recognize, but that seemed very familiar to me. All looked to be Oscarovi. Three men, all tall and pale, built like warriors. Their faces were all strangely similar as well, as if they were related, and yet, there was something unnatural about the way they looked, as though their faces didn't quite fit their bodies.

Who are they? I asked.

For the first time, the Ravager answered me silently. *You don't recognize them? They are Ashbourne's generals. His closest friends.*

My mind spun with the information. Of course they were. Ashbourne's generals, the ones imprisoned with him in Nihil, had been some of the most powerful Ventyr on Interra. The most talented. The ones who knew him better than anyone else. Somehow, it didn't surprise me that Boreas had found them.

How did they get here? I asked.

When Vaness and Helene destroyed Nihil, they came back with them, the Ravager answered. Vaness and Helene destroyed Nihil? How had they managed that? I had so many questions. So much I both wanted to know and which my weary mind wanted desperately to hide from.

Boreas waved a hand to the generals. "Search the place. Make sure no magic has been used."

They stared at me for a long moment, and then disappeared. Boreas nodded to the chairs in the sitting room. "Sit, please."

The Ravager did not suppress me so much now. I felt the pain in my joints again, as it sat. I wasn't yet able to move my body on my own, but at least this was something. It had never occurred to me that there might be a time when I was grateful to feel the burn of pain lashing through me.

I felt the Ravager's amusement at my thoughts. I hadn't realized I was projecting them to it, but it was difficult to tell what I could keep to myself and what I could not. *There is much you can keep from me*, the Ravager said as we waited for Boreas to deign to speak. *And much that I can keep from you.*

It had always been difficult to read my father. Not because he was not expressive, but because he was a master at manipulating others. He had no tells. Everything he did was an elaborate act. It made all the sense in the world that he could also shift shapes, be anyone—perhaps any*thing*. There were a few Ventyr with that talent.

The Ravager's breath caught in my lungs.

Can he shift into objects? I asked.

It did not answer, but by the way it held its breath, I knew the answer was yes. So much about how Boreas had conquered Interra made sense now. He had always been dozens of steps ahead, and now I knew why. He must have been spying on his enemies, hiding in plain sight.

"I would like to speak to my daughter," Boreas said. The Ravager nodded once, to show it understood. "Good. How are you feeling, my little dove?"

I'd forgotten that he called me that. It turned my stomach to hear it. "Let me go."

Boreas laughed. "Will that always be the refrain between us, do you think?"

Pain lanced through me. Not physical pain, not exactly. But the memory of my wings being severed from my body was so vivid, so acute, it might as well have been. My screams—my pleas for my captors to let me go—had been endless. And he laughed now?

"You are a monster," I said, but the Ravager spoke with me. It was an eerie noise, its voice combining with mine. The blood curdling screams that lived within the Ravager blended now in perfect harmony with the hatred I felt for my father.

For a split second, I saw fear in Boreas' eyes. It disappeared as quickly as it came, but I had seen it. Something wild woke within me, alive with hatred and purpose. The Ravager's suppression of me lessened further, allowing me more control. All my focus narrowed in on Boreas, my mind putting together everything about him in quick succession.

It was like my puzzle pieces, but faster as I felt the Ravager lend me its ancient acuity. Boreas' hair was slightly mussed. His brown wood suit had not been pressed well. His left pinky had not been filed as evenly as the rest, a tiny notch broken off of it. The blood vessels in his eyes had been treated with either magic or drops of some kind, but earlier in the day, as they were beginning to redden again. There was a tiny piece of paper affixed to one of his sleeves.

He was stressed and covering it up. The amount of power he'd wielded over these last months, controlling the Ravager, so many of his lackeys, and the people who'd witnessed the fires... Even for him, it was all too much. He was both the most powerful he'd ever been, with the Ravager inside me at his beck and call, and the weakest. Boreas narrowed his eyes, sitting forward ever so slightly. We had been quiet for too long.

He is spread too thin, I observed to the Ravager. *He's used too much power.*

It all but purred with delight. *I like this side of you, princess.*

"Stop talking to one another," Boreas snapped.

The Ravager and I smiled together, a feral expression I hoped was unsettling. It had the effect I desired. I felt my consciousness dull, as though the room had gone a little dark. But I saw the way Boreas' ring finger on his left hand touched the ring he wore on his pinky. It was the tiniest of movements.

As things dulled further, I locked my sight on the sharp letter opener on the occasional table between us. *The pinky ring,* were the last words I could manage before things blurred so intensely I no longer saw through my eyes.

But the Ravager was fast. Faster than I could ever hope to be. It leapt over the occasional table, the letter opener in its grip. I felt the way that Boreas had restricted its use of power. We could not have used aether or empyrae if we tried. And though Boreas certainly started to throw up his own defenses, he was too late.

The Ravager sliced his pinky clean off in one brutal swipe. It grasped onto the ring, but let the pinky fall to the floor. All became clear again. Boreas threw up an empyraeic shield, shouting, "You fools, help!"

Run, I screamed. *Don't fight. Run.*

Empyrae loosed from my fingers, as the Ravager did as I asked, creating a wall of fire behind us. I could only pray that none in the building would be harmed. I felt Boreas' ring slide onto one of my fingers for safekeeping.

We were in the hallway, then scrambling to a door. A bit of empyrae shut it behind us as we flew down several flights of stairs. There was so much pain. So much pain, but still I managed to pause when I spotted the metal lever at the bottom of the stairs.

Pull the alarm, please, I begged.

The Ravager did as I asked and the noise was unbearable as we fled onto the streets. *Elementals of air*, I called out. *Help me.*

There was a rush of wind, as though they had been looking for me, waiting for me to escape. An eagle practically as large as Poe in her Feriant form swept down into the alleyway and lifted my body into the air.

"Take us to the god of the Vale," the Ravager said. "We need to see the god."

No, I cried. *I need to see Ash.*

"Child," the Ravager said. "We have larger problems than your Claimed being injured. We need the god."

CHAPTER 46

SKYE AESTRA

Ash lay sleeping on a special table in the Avalonne's medical bay, face down so that his back could heal. His wings had been so severely damaged in the blast that the only choice had been to amputate. I worried that it was too cold in here for him, but Mother had assured me the low temperature would aid in his healing process.

His healing process. My head sank into my hands. It was so hard to look at the damage he'd taken protecting us. My entire life, I'd been taught to hate the Ventyr, to fear their return because of their incredible strength. But seeing his burned flesh made me grateful for it. Grateful that his inherent strength had not only protected the woman I loved, my family, my friends, and myself... but had allowed him to live as well. No Vilhari could have survived that blast.

Ashbourne had only lost his wings. I'd argued for preservation as long as I could, but in the end, he begged for my mother to take them. He'd refused sedation, refused any kind of pain medication. All for penance. It was the bravest, stupidest thing I had ever seen him do. Morpheus lay spread out against him now, purring. The feline claimed it also aided in healing, but I thought the little fey could not stand to be parted from him.

I could not blame the cat. I felt the same.

Everyone had asked me time and again to rest, but I could not budge from his side. When Morpheus and I found him a little over a year ago, he was in bad shape, but this was worse. Seeing him in his true Ventyr form, how strong and vital he'd been, and now this. Even in sleep, he looked broken.

My mother's soft footsteps padded down the hallway, her feet nearly silent on the stone floors. She held a syringe when she entered the room. "I am going to give him something for the pain now," she whispered. "I know he said no, but his body *must* be allowed to rest if he is to make a full recovery."

I nodded, and she slid the needle into his arm and plunged the medicine into him. Immediately, his body relaxed further, the frown lines in his forehead finally smoothing. My mother nodded once to me, and then made to leave. I caught the finely woven sleeve of her medical uniform. It was a jumpsuit I had never seen before, something that belonged with the ship. Apparently, it was made from a special fabric that helped maintain sterile conditions during surgery.

"Will the loss of his wings affect his Laniidae form?" I asked, wishing I knew more about my dearest friend's abilities. He'd kept so much to himself, and though I knew there were reasons for it, it ached to be made acutely aware of the distance between us.

My mother turned, her face so like mine, her pale eyes softening as she stroked my cheek. "No, darling. That form is a spiritual manifestation, completely separate from his true body."

I nodded, swallowing hard, my chin quivering. "Thank you for helping him."

Mother bent down so that her eyes met mine. She brushed a kiss to each of my cheeks, stroking her fingers through my short hair, just as she had done when I was a littling. It felt good to be mothered. I'd missed her so much. "He was incredibly brave, darling. As were you."

I shook my head, leaning against her, feeling more like a child than ever as the moments passed. I needed her to comfort me now. We'd been close my entire life, until I disagreed with her. Now, it felt like we might have a chance at having that closeness back, and all I wanted was to be as open with her as I once was. "We should have known better. We shouldn't have kept her in the house after what Niall did…"

She nodded. "You are right."

To her credit, she didn't say anything else in our defense. I wouldn't have wanted to hear it. It didn't help to admit I was right now, when I'd been wrong then, but it meant something to me that she didn't argue or try to make me feel better.

"He will survive this, Skye," she said, stroking my face again. Though I objectively knew she was right, it didn't feel that way right now. Mother crouched down. "This is not your fault."

"Isn't it?" Tears wouldn't come, but there was a sob in my voice nonetheless. "If I hadn't argued with him…" I shook my head and held up a hand as her mouth opened to speak. This was most certainly my fault. Even Poe thought keeping Brigitte was a bad idea. I made a mistake, and Ash paid for it. Nothing anyone could say now would absolve me from my guilt. "Is Poe back yet?"

"No," Mother said with a sigh. She was so obviously frustrated with me. "Though I had word from her little Howler friend, Rue— they haven't found Mina yet."

My head dropped into my hands. This was all so far out of control. Where had the days gone when our biggest problems were keeping the ledger in the black and getting Morpheus his lunch on time? I loved Poe, had loved her since that first night at the Merc, and I wanted the future we saw together, but I also desperately wanted the peace of those days back. The more time that passed, the more they felt like a fiction—something I'd merely dreamed up. All of this was too real.

"Will you eat something?" Mother asked, standing. She'd obviously given up trying to convince me that this hadn't been my fault.

I shook my head, and she pressed a kiss to the top of my head. "Wearing yourself out won't help anything, darling."

Though I nodded, I had no intention of resting. Mother spoke a low word and the lights dimmed. As her footsteps retreated, my eyes grew heavy. The sound of Morpheus' purrs got louder, longer, slower, and more hypnotic in their rhythm. I scooted my chair closer to Ash's bed. It wouldn't hurt if I rested my head for a few minutes.

WHISPERS in the hallway woke me. Viridian and Poe, from the sound of it. Morpheus' golden eyes opened. *Go on and see what they've found out. I will come if he wakes.*

I hesitated, but the cat glared at me. *You are stopping me from doing my best work. All your tortured thoughts and angst are too much to work around.*

"What are you *talking* about?" I whispered.

Morpheus huffed loudly through his nose. *So ignorant. My purrs have healing qualities. But your psychic energy is getting in the way of me doing my best work. Be off with you and leave this to me.* Then he growled at me.

I couldn't help but let out a little huff of my own. "Fine, then."

Morpheus glared at me as I stood and backed slowly away from the table. We'd known each other for years, and he was still so unpredictable to me. When I left Ash's room and entered the hallway, Viridian had gone.

"He's been called back to Brektos," Poe said, worry etched all over her face. "His mother is ill. I couldn't bear to tell him we needed him here." Every note in her voice was strained, tired, pushed far beyond the brink. Poe, my beautiful Poe, stood leaning against the wall, her face drawn with exhaustion. She raised her big hazel eyes to mine and shook her head. "I cannot find her. It's as though she's disappeared."

She held something in her fist, though. I took her hand in mine, loving how tiny and delicate her fist was in my palm. I prised open her fingers, as though helping a flower to open. Everything about Poe was pure poetry. A small, flat disc sat in her palm, emitting some terrible energy. My nostrils flared as I tried to take a steadying breath. "What is that?"

Poe shook her head. "I hardly know. I flew to Somerhaven, wondering if Helene might have gone back there. The carriage house had been converted into living quarters. Someone has been staying there. They didn't bother to take anything with them…" She paused, smiling faintly. "I'm sure they thought their wards would be sufficient for keeping anyone who might come by out. And they were quite good. I almost didn't even see that there was a lamp still on inside."

I frowned. "The wards were good enough to make the carriage house appear empty?"

She nodded slowly. It was the kind of power that most folk did not possess—but one notable exception existed outside our little circle. Chopard had the kind of power it might take to do such a thing.

And if Alastair Wildfang really was back, as Archambeau had said he was, under disguise as Lord Eccles, then it would make sense that he might return to Somerhaven as his retreat. And if that kind of power guarded the carriage house, then there was no doubt in my mind.

"So Alastair Wildfang is Chopard," I said.

Poe nodded. "Yes, I think he must be—and what's more—look at this." She held up her hand, to give me a closer look at the disc.

She had wreathed it in aether, a subtle containment field, but I still felt a terrible revulsion when I looked at it. "What *is* that thing?"

She shook her head. "I don't exactly know, but it has a terrible amount of power."

I nodded. That much was horrifically clear. A dark shadow fell on us and I looked up to find Muse standing at the end of the hall. He shook his head as he approached us. "I had hoped it wasn't true," he murmured, reaching for the thing in Poe's hand, but stopping short of touching it. "I've seen it in my dreams so many times. But I see so many things, things from different worlds sometimes. And I *knew*, but I did not want to know."

I wasn't sure exactly what Muse meant, and he did seem to be talking to himself more than to us, but I deeply understood the part about knowing and not wanting to know. There were so many things I'd come to understand in the past few years that I wished I could give back to the universe.

Poe's fingers closed around the object. "I don't think it is good to look at it for long." She slipped it into the pocket of the pants she wore.

Muse shook his head, as though he might shake off the feeling of dread I assumed we all shared. Likewise, I blinked several times.

Poe took several deep breaths, then rapidly shook her head. "Don't bother. It's too powerful, whatever it is." She touched Muse's arm. "Can you tell us what it is?"

Muse nodded. "I certainly can. If it's here, you'll find out one way or another soon. Though you won't like the answer."

Poe glanced at me, and I nodded, urging Muse on. "Please, tell us."

"Have you ever heard of the Prophecy of Alcyone?" Muse asked. When neither of us said we had, Muse sighed. "The Prophecy was about Ash, the Ravagers, and the end of all worlds. When all eight of the wards break, something terrible is supposed to happen."

"That doesn't tell us what this is," Poe replied, patting her pocket.

"It is one of the wards," Muse replied. "Though I am sorry to tell you, I cannot tell which one. That object may well bring about an apocalypse of all things."

CHAPTER 47

MINA

The elemental eagle was fast, taking us high into the clouds. It did not speak to me. I sensed the creature's unease; it could feel the Ravager within me, no doubt. But it sensed me as well, which I supposed was a good thing.

"Thank you for helping," I said. "I know what I carry within me feels wrong to you."

Wrong is not quite the word I would use, the eagle replied. *It is only that I have never carried a god.*

Within me, the Ravager made a satisfied sound. Cold spread through me, deeper than the damp from the clouds. If the elemental eagle could tell what rode within me, what would Sirin's god make of this?

We landed on the tower of the university's astronomical clock. The day had darkened significantly as thick mist from the forest penetrated the campus. There were pinpricks of light from the lamp-posts below, but not much more was visible. I squinted, trying to see the damage that had been done in the upper echelons, desperate for some information that might tell me what had happened to Ashbourne.

By now, I'd determined that if Poe or Skye had been lost there would have been headlines, so I was not as worried about them, but not knowing what had happened to him was destroying me. But the mist was too thick. I could hardly make out anything surrounding the tower now. Aether curled around my feet.

The eagle melted back into the air as it called back to us. *She comes.*

The leopardi form of the god appeared, forming from the mist itself, it seemed. Within me, the Ravager vibrated with interest, speaking through me.

It has been so long, it said.

I could have done with longer, the god replied. They knew one another? This was too much. I had questions, but the Ravager had erected a wall, and wasn't letting me through. *I do wish you would have stayed away, or found something productive to do with your time, but you and your brethren never were satisfied, were you?*

Never, the Ravager answered. *Though you've always thought yourself so superior, haven't you?*

The leopardi sighed. *Have you come simply to torment me? Or will you go?*

I'll go when Boreas Anemos is dead. Beyond a shadow of a doubt. Not before. I will need use of your gate key.

Trapped within myself, I stopped fighting to speak and just listened. What was this gate key? Could it refer to the gate the mysterious soldier guarded?

The leopardi god narrowed her eyes. *That will be a problem. It was stolen.*

Boreas, the Ravager hissed. *I knew there was too much power in that carriage house, but I could not discern where he was hiding it.*

If you find it and you can eliminate Boreas Anemos and his generals, the leopardi said, *you are free to make use of it.*

My head bowed. *Thank you. Are you certain?*

The leopardi inclined its head. *I am satisfied with my existence here. My children are all here and all is well—or it will be when this is over.*

The key can only be used once, the Ravager said.

The leopardi turned, flexing her wings as she crouched, preparing to spring. *I have no use of it. When you have helped Mina, if you can find it, it is yours. I only wish to be free of you, once and for all. Do what you need to and let my seneschal go.*

I sensed the first true emotion past rage from the Ravager. Sadness. It echoed within me, resting finally in the spot where I regretted the way things had ended between Helene and I. The leopardi god sprang into the air, disappearing into the mist.

That sadness increased within me, and the barrier the Ravager had erected to keep me quiet fell. *Is that your sibling?* I asked, going on a hunch.

Once, the Ravager replied. *But no longer, I think. I saw to that.*

It felt too pedantic to ask if all the hideous murdering and destruction had been what did it. Even I could give the Ravager a moment to feel that genuine sadness that permeated my body now. This thing had nearly destroyed Interra—it *had* destroyed many other worlds—but I got the distinct impression that something terrible had been done to it…and its brethren, if I inferred correctly from what the leopardi said.

Something terrible had been done to them before Boreas had imprisoned them. Something that made them hate all Vilhari—including the Ventyr. The answer was ancient, and with the resources we had on Sirin, I doubted there was much I could do to find out what it all meant, but my curiosity was piqued to a fever pitch.

Rain fell in big, fat drops from the heavy clouds that gathered around the tower. Though the leopardi god had gone, something still thrummed with power up here.

You feel the passage, the Ravager said. We watched, face raised to the sky as one of the elemental draconae peeled from the air and water in the sky and wound towards us. *This place, and others like it, are soft spots in the universe. Not quite doors, like the ones Boreas has been making.*

Finally, information I could use. *Where do they lead?*

That is the trouble, the Ravager answered. *It is difficult to tell.*

The draconae settled on top of the tower, solidifying from crystalline water and frigid air into an iridescent white form. *Do you wish to use the door?*

Inwardly, I looked to the Ravager for wisdom. It asked, *Where does it take us today?*

The draconae contemplated its answer for a moment before saying, *It will take you where you need to go, so long as your compass points true.*

I stepped back from the door, noticing that I could choose to move my body once more. My body. Not *this body*, or *the fetch*. Mine. I sighed deeply, the strangest feeling of comfort washing over me. "Thank you," I whispered aloud. "You have given me a gift."

The draconae seemed to know I did not speak to it, and politely turned its head away. Inside me, the Ravager did not feel small, but it no longer felt so large. *I did not mean to*, it answered—a note of surprise in its ancient voice. *But I am pleased to have done so all the same.*

I couldn't wait to tell Ash and Poe. Sudden pain lanced through me as I remembered the news of the fire. How had I forgotten?

It was me, the Ravager said. *I pushed your worry for him to the back of your mind. I needed you to stay calm, and you were thinking about him too much.*

I barely heard the Ravager, though now I thought it might sound apologetic, at least a little. Three long steps took me to where the draconae lay waiting. "What do I have to do?"

Fix wherever you wish to be firmly in your mind, and then step past me, just here. It used one of its enormous talons to point at a spot on the tiled roof.

"And this passageway is always just... here?" I asked, worried about the implications for its further use.

It is, the draconae answered. *But I am its guardian and act as the key. None may pass without my permission.*

The ache in my heart would lead me, I was sure of it. *Send me to wherever Ash is.*

CHAPTER 48

MINA

The Ravager was blessedly quiet within me as we stepped through the portal and appeared in a dimly lit room. I recognized the Avalonne from the lighting and fixtures immediately, but I was not prepared for what else I saw. Ash lay face down on a table that appeared to be specially made for the need. From the rhythmic rise and fall of his breath, I determined he was in deep sleep.

He rested in his true form, but the line of gauze on his back where his wings should have been stunned me. There was a simply made chair next to the bed. I stumbled towards it.

I expected some kind of horrific remark from the Ravager, some indication that it was pleased by my sorrow. But it said nothing, though I felt its observation, its hunger for my suffering. My heart beat wildly now, as I tried to determine if he was all right. If he was still in there. The line of energy that ran between us, that was the Claim made manifest, told me that he was drugged but his mind was still intact. He was just resting. My hands shook as I braced myself on the chair. I could not quite look at his back.

"What happened?" I whispered, even knowing he could not answer.

He shielded the rest of them from the blast, the Ravager said. *The article I would not let you read. That is what it said. He saved them, the Aestras, your Poe, and the Chevaliers within the house.*

I slid to the floor, shaking from the stress of all that had happened. Tears slipped down my cheeks, rough, ragged sobs wracking my body. I rocked back and forth, trying as hard as I could to soothe myself. Every time I tried to think of Ash, and his beautiful wings, the choking sobs came faster and harder.

Air didn't reach my lungs; my breaths were too shallow. The word *no* tumbled from my lips, over and over, a chant, a plea, an empty promise. It felt as though my mind would break, as though all I was would shatter apart. This had happened to me before, many times when I was little, and sometimes when I was alone as a teenager and adult. No one could see me like this. I crawled into the corner, trying to stop the rocking of my body. If anyone saw, they would scold me, as Maman had.

Give me your suffering, the Ravager said. *Let me have it, child.*

There was hunger in the Ravager's words, but also kindness. And yet so much had been stolen from me. Even this feeling, which I hated more than anything in the world, I was tempted to keep for my own. Now that I had control of my body and emotions back, I was reluctant to let go of them. Even so, the panic was unbearable, the racing of my mind untenable.

I will not take it from you without your permission, it said, *and I will not take it all. It will not hurt you to allow me to help.*

"Fine," I managed to gasp between choked sobs. I could hardly breathe.

Little by little, the Ravager siphoned off the worst of the feeling, my panic moving from a raging sea to a gentle storm. The thunder of it still rocked through me, but the waves had quieted some.

Is that better?

"Yes," I whispered, my sobs quieting naturally now. "Thank you."

Is it always like this? The pain, I mean. Both in your mind and your body.

"Yes," I said, my voice coming back a little louder now. "Something always hurts."

Close your eyes against the light, the Ravager advised. *You are tired, we are here. Rest and breathe.*

The thing that had murdered thousands, maybe millions, told me to rest and breathe. What was this? Would it help me simply because the leopardi god had told it to?

The tears that fell onto my blouse lifted, turning to living shadow before my eyes. A bit of aether seeped out of the black opal ring I wore, the ring that was meant for my familiar. It twined with the shadow-tears, alchemizing before me. The shadows slipped inside Helene's necklace, and I felt it fill with something new.

"What are you doing?" I asked, my breath finally evening out.

I don't know yet, the Ravager replied. *An experiment. If it works, I will tell you. I am tired now. I think I will rest. Wake me if something happens.*

And just like that, the everlasting being of malevolence and suffering that lived within me curled up like a cat and went to sleep. Ash stirred. I wiped my face and struggled to my feet, pushing myself out of the corner.

"Mina?" he mumbled.

"Yes," I answered, taking the hand that reached out for me. He tried to glamour himself, his usually pale skin creeping over the light blue skin of his true form. "Don't try to shift," I cautioned. "Save your strength."

He lifted his head out of the hole in the table, his golden eyes ablaze with love. "You're here."

I nodded. "I should have been there." He shook his head, his eyes closing. The pain was too much. "You need another sedative."

"No," he said, struggling to push himself off the table. He growled with fury when the pain between his shoulders kept him from being successful.

"You'll tear a stitch," Elspeth Aestra said from the doorway. She held a syringe in her hands. "Mina."

I nodded to her, waving her in. "You have to let Elspeth help you," I whispered, pushing a lock of dark hair back from his eyes. "I'm here now. I'm safe. Now you must heal. We have work to do."

Elspeth had already inserted the syringe into his arm. His eyes fell closed, but with his last bit of consciousness, he murmured, "I love you."

"I love you," I whispered back, pressing a kiss to his forehead.

When he slept once more, Morpheus materialized. *You have returned. Poe and Skye are upstairs. I will stay with Ashbourne.*

I kissed the grumpy feline next. "Thank you, friend."

He grumbled, turned thrice, and then curled in next to Ash.

~

"So," I said, staring at the flat metal disc on the table between us. "That thing can bring about an apocalypse?"

The four of us sat around the small kitchen table in House Aestra's Avalonne quarters. Muse shook his head. "Not exactly. That's just one interpretation of the Prophecy."

Skye rolled her eyes. "Prophecies are the worst."

Poe giggled, brushing Skye's hand with hers. As much as I wanted to, I could not feel relief at being back with them. It wasn't just the condition Ash was in. It was the Ravager within me. No matter if it seemed to have acquiesced, or if we had a plan to get its way, I couldn't rest easy with it still inside me.

My friends had both been surprisingly accepting of the idea of using it to help get rid of Boreas. That troubled me as well. I couldn't blame them for being afraid of Boreas. I'd grown up as they had, believing the Ventyr had almost subjugated us, and that it was a narrow miss that we'd gotten rid of them. I didn't question the narrative, but nor did I share their relief in having the Ravager's help. It might be a sibling to the leopardi god, but I did not trust its motives.

Muse and I had only a few moments alone, but I'd confessed my fears to him. He had only nodded, which some might not find helpful, but I did. It confirmed for me that there was a future where this path led us to victory, but that I was right to be concerned. I still wore Boreas' ring on my index finger, though it was a terrible weight to carry.

The Ravager had not yet woken, even though I'd asked it to join us several times now. It seemed extraordinarily tired, which I could relate to, but it worried me that it was so relaxed now, when it had been so vicious just a few days ago.

I shivered, unable to tell if the kitchen was cold, or if my body was affected somehow by the Ravager's presence. I trusted nothing at this point, knowing that it could manipulate me so easily.

"Can I hold the seal?" I asked.

Muse nodded. "It is safe to touch, though it isn't comfortable to do so."

"Where did you find it?" I asked Poe, hesitating.

As I reached for the disc, she explained. "I didn't find it. Not exactly. The hares at Somerhaven showed me where Boreas buried it."

That further confirmed my theory that the elementals saw her as kindred to them somehow—that and the fact that they had helped her when Brigitte detonated herself. An odd idea wove through my memories, but I could not yet see its shape. It would reveal itself in time, I was sure of it. The tickling feeling was just the tease that came before the payoff. I picked the disc up, and the moment my skin touched it, I was transported.

A sea of indigo sand, moving as water did, rather than dunes in a desert. Above swirled dark, ancient stars, so far from my vantage point. Six tall figures stood in a circle. All was darkness, and then light burst through a newborn star. The myriad paths of a crumbling labyrinth flashed before my eyes, and then I was pulled through a stone archway, away from the scene with the figures. I found myself before the headless soldier Helene had shown me.

The Larae had stories about beings such as these, elemental guardians. I bowed to the soldier, who noticed me slowly, as though they had not seen me coming. *Hello, little princess.*

"Hello, great one." I held out the disc in my hand. "Will you tell me what this is?"

It is a ward, a key. A seal, an opening, a prison. A cursed thing and a miracle, they answered.

I looked down at it in my hand. "Will it end the universe if I use it?"

None can end the universe, the guardian replied. *But an end will come to pass if you use that for what it is meant for.*

"Something always ends before something else can begin," I replied.

The cloud of gas and light that swirled above the soldier's shoulders coalesced. *Yes,* they agreed. *That is also true. You must return home now, but remember that a gift given opens more doors than a selfish act.*

I looked down at my hands, surprised to find that they were solid.

Was I actually here? I looked up at the guardian again, then pulled Boreas' ring off my finger and held it out. The soldier bent down and plucked the ring gently from my hand.

"Can you keep this safe for me?" I asked. "It is not a gift, exactly, but I think it might help if you kept it."

A rumble emanated from the soldier's head. *Yes. I will keep it for you. Come see me again and we will sing the songs of old.*

It felt right to give the ring to the guardian, as though another of my puzzle pieces snapped into place. I had no sense of the Ravager within me here, which helped. Perhaps I could trust this moment and this choice. I made a silent promise to have more faith in myself when I got the Ravager out of me.

I pressed my fingers to my lips in farewell, in the old way of the Larae. The ancient ways that taught me how to converse with creatures such as this one, creatures so great that they could not be fully understood. Orynthia, Ouriel's mother and my aunt, taught us to flow with beings such as these, to let their abstract logic glide over us like water, like aether, like sand.

My eyes opened, and I looked down at my hands. Boreas' ring was gone. I looked around the table. "Did I disappear?"

Poe shook her head. "No, you closed your eyes for a moment, but you stayed here."

The feeling of the puzzle coming together strengthened. Another piece was in place, though I still could not see the full picture. Something was still missing, and I worried it had to do with the Ravager. Still, I held my hand up. "The ring is gone."

Muse smiled. "So it begins."

Poe sighed, her shoulders rounding as she shook her head dramatically. "So it begins... the beginning of the end. The end of the beginning."

Muse narrowed his eyes at her. "Do you mock me, your highness?"

"I do," she said, raising her chin defiantly. "I mock you."

Muse shook his head. "Such a pity. For now I will have to mock you as well."

Poe shrugged. "Such is our life."

Skye laughed, and from the next room, where Arcturus was reading, I heard him laugh softly as well. For just a moment, I let the future spin out before me, long years of conversations like these ahead of us, if only we could stop whatever Boreas had planned. None of us thought that my escape meant he would stop. We had only slowed his progress.

There was no doubt, for any of us, that he was regrouping. And I feared that he already had another plan. I stared down at the disc in my hand, as the Ravager woke. *That is the leopardi's seal.*

Yes, I said, choosing to speak silently to it, as my friends continued their conversation. A spark of inspiration had stayed with me from my strange vision. *What is your name, Ravager?*

Clever girl, it replied, but did not answer.

I touched Helene's necklace and wondered. Aloud, I said, "I know how to kill Boreas, and get the Ravager off Sirin." In a lowered tone, I asked, "You will help still, won't you?"

So long as Boreas dies, yes. I will give you aid.

"Perfect," I said, though I didn't trust a single word it said now. "Here is what we must do."

CHAPTER 49

ASHBOURNE

I sipped a cup of hot broth while Mina told me what she wanted to do. It wasn't a bad plan, but it had one obvious issue: we had no idea where Boreas was, or how to find him. Mina and Skye had already sent both the elementals and Chevaliers to look for him, and for my generals, for that matter. There had been scant few leads to follow, and it was difficult to wait for word back.

Another long draw off my broth and I'd drained the cup. I rolled my neck, trying to work up the courage to stretch the space between my shoulders. It was amazing to me how Mina dealt so easily with the pain she endured. This was like nothing I'd ever experienced in my life. I'd been injured dozens of times, probably hundreds, but no injury compared to this loss. While my back had physically healed, I felt as though something would be fundamentally wrong with it forever.

She stopped talking, watching me. "It will get better in some ways," she said. "And worse in others."

We'd moved back to our bedroom in House Feriant's quarters in the Avalonne. Elspeth had cleared me a day ago, and I was free to move as normal, but Mina was still acting like I had open wounds. "Will you please come here?"

She shook her head, frowning. "I'm afraid I'll hurt you."

I spread my arms out wide, bringing them in front of me and behind me in various stretches. The pain that burned through my muscles was not the kind I was used to, not the pain of hard-won fitness, or even injury from a battle. It was darker, altering me in ways I hadn't imagined possible. I'd lost something central to my identity, and the pain I felt as a result was harrowing.

Mina got up from her chair in the corner. I set the cup my soup was in down on the bedside table, reaching out for her. She climbed slowly into bed, her gray eyes wide. "I am not alone. Doing anything with it inside me still… Feels wrong."

I wasn't pleased that Boreas had managed to get the Ravager into her, and I worried, as she did, that we didn't understand it fully. Skye and Poe weren't suspicious enough, in my opinion. It was a reminder of how young they were still. They had not lived long enough to see empires rise and fall, to be betrayed by those with no reason to do so. They had not seen what we had, Mina and I.

So we would stay watchful for them. It was the promise we'd made to the god and Sirin, but I felt that promise more deeply. It was the promise I'd made to her, to the people we loved. They could live their lives in hope, but she and I would stay suspicious, on guard. Even if they thought it was silly.

Mina had paused, as though listening. She rolled her eyes. "Be that as it may, I am not having an intimate encounter with you watching. I don't care how many times you've…" she stopped, blowing a big huff of air out of her lungs, puffing her cheeks out like balloons.

I grabbed her, pulling her hard against me. She was so tense, so frustrated. I could fix that in normal circumstances, but if she didn't want to be intimate right now, I didn't want it either. The way she melted into me was enough. Like I was safe, and she was free to be as frustrated and prickly as she actually was around me. She curled up against my chest, grumbling something to the Ravager about going back to sleep.

"I will be so happy when we don't live together anymore," she said, her lips turning down in an exaggerated frown.

I raised my eyebrows, and she looked up at me, then burst into hysterical laughter. "We can't stop arguing."

I kissed her forehead, relishing the way her long fingers clutched at my shirt. There was nothing in the world more beautiful than Mina Wildfang, and nowhere I wanted to be more than right here with her, even if she was preoccupied.

A soft knock at the door interrupted. Skye stuck her head in. "We're on for the conservatory event. Lord Eccles is on the guest list."

Boreas was bold, I granted him that. At the very least he wasn't hiding from us. Whatever he wanted, he wanted us to know he was making his move.

I glanced at my pocket watch on the bedside table. "Do we have time to get there?"

Skye shrugged. "Not if the two of you stay in bed."

"All right then," Mina said, sliding off the bed as Skye left. "Let's do this."

THE CONSERVATORY EVENT was the first true event of the Grand Exhibition, and one of the jewels of the entire festival, from what I understood. This year, though the event did not require formal dress, it was held at night to showcase the Royal Oscarovi Garden Club's bioluminescent orchids.

Mina's plan was simple enough: we were to find Boreas, confront him, and then she and I would make the jump to the center of the labyrinth, to the gate the elemental soldier guarded. We would shove Boreas through, and then hopefully the Ravager would leave as well.

Neither of us thought it would be that easy, but we were out of options and ideas. The only way to do this was to jump in and think on our feet. With the Ravager watching Mina constantly, it was an unspoken agreement between us that some element of improvisation was necessary. She couldn't tell me more, but I knew she had some idea she wasn't saying for fear the Ravager would know it.

I trusted her, and I trusted Sirin's god. I believed we could do this.

Mirabelle and Elspeth's little cohort of conspirators were at the ready to clear the area; on our signal, when we'd found Boreas, they would announce fireworks on the terrace. It was a blessedly clear evening and fireworks would get the rest of the patrons out of the conservatory proper.

The Chevaliers were in attendance, ready to fight if Boreas brought the generals. Each was paired with an elemental spirit, an unusual collaboration, but one that all seemed amenable to trying. It chafed at me that my former comrades would align with Boreas, though I found it easy enough to believe. Their resentment of me, and our imprisonment, went deep. My mistakes came back to haunt me at every turn.

Edith and Karnon had sent conspirators as well. The entire staff for the evening were Strix, Corvidae, and Oscarovi who stood at the ready. If Boreas made his move, we had a failsafe—a veritable army of help to keep him from escaping us. And yet, something still bothered me. We'd done all we could, but we didn't know enough about Boreas' plans, what he wanted.

We never found out exactly what Vaness Wildfang had been up to, or who the rest of *her* conspirators were. We were simply out of energy, and running out of time and advantage. The only edge we had was someplace safe to stay—as it seemed that Boreas hadn't yet found the Avalonne— and the fact that the Ravager was cooperating with us, for now anyway.

As we walked into the darkened conservatory, I sent up a warrior's plea for good fortune. I hoped that somewhere the god of Sirin heard me, but tonight there was no answer. Mina's hand was firmly in my grip. She looked lovely in a smart pair of navy trousers and a high-necked blouse in the same shade. She'd taken to dressing this way, all the same color, and I liked it. Her dark hair was pulled back into a low bun, and she wore practical shoes.

Good shoes for running. The thought disturbed me more than I wanted it to.

The conservatory was especially noisy tonight with the opening of the Grand Exhibition. Everyone who wanted to see and be seen was here. There was nowhere to go that wasn't crowded, the press of bodies almost overwhelming. Yes, I saw why Boreas chose tonight to make his move. He thought we wouldn't respond as stringently as we might otherwise, wouldn't take as many risks with all these civilians about.

I scanned the crowd. There was a mix of Vilhari and Oscarovi here tonight, as well as the avian fey. Expensive perfume mixed with high street colognes, feathers and tweeds mixing with country wools and corduroy. All wanted to see the orchids. Nearly all adults, not a child in sight. A satisfied smile curled my lips. If Boreas truly knew what he was doing, he would have picked an event where more children were present.

Boreas didn't know his daughter at all. Didn't know how vicious she truly could be. I, however, had no doubt that Mina would sacrifice every adult here tonight for the greater good if she had to. But had there been children here, I knew she might have hesitated.

Mina's ring pressed into my hand. I held it up as we walked through the flowered archways that led into the bioluminescent exhibit. "When this is over, I will buy you another ring. One that symbolizes our union."

She did not smile, but the look in her eyes was one of pure adoration. "And I will buy you a ring as well. Would you like something with a large stone?"

I shook my head. "Something simpler, I think."

"*I* would like a large stone," she mused.

I chuckled as I kissed her hand. "Ah, I see. That can be managed."

"Perfection," she murmured. "The Ravager says that Boreas is here. It senses him."

I nodded, looking behind us to Poe and Skye, who were our decoys for the evening. Both were dressed in spectacular fashion, Mme Laquoix's best work yet, I thought. Their deep blue ensembles were dotted with tiny silver stars, made from diamonds. They looked like the night sky, and Poe wore a diadem in her long brown hair that sparkled in the glow of the magical plants.

With everyone else in casual dress, they stood out. Poe had grumbled about how inappropriate it was, and was practically beside herself with worry that people would think she thought herself above them. She and Mina had gone off together to discuss it, and when they came back, Poe had worn the ostentatious clothes without another complaint.

They were to stay near the archway into the exhibit once we'd determined if Boreas was here. As we'd done on the airship, they would lead the crowd away. Only this time, we hoped not to have such a dramatic end to our evening.

"He is by the orchids," Mina murmured, keeping her voice low, dodging the wing of a Vilhari who'd stopped to admire the flowers.

I nodded, letting go of her hand to steer her to a bend in the path. People stepped aside for us. "Let me get one for you," I said, as though she'd asked me for a drink. "Wait here."

She nodded, face solemn. Though her shoulders were straight and her face was calm, I knew she was far from relaxed. She was talking to the Ravager. I couldn't wait for the thing to be gone. It had been cooperative enough, but something in me warned that perhaps it had been too cooperative.

A Strix waiter, one of Herself's, squeezed through the crowd with a tray of sparkling wine. I nodded to him, and he to me, as I took two glasses. I turned back towards Mina, who nodded once at me. She'd located Boreas then. I glanced back over my shoulder at Skye, who took one long deep breath, then blinked both eyes very slowly.

Our plan was in place. I had to trust that whatever we did next, however scantily prepared we were, that somehow, we could win this. I brought the glasses to Mina, handing her one and keeping the other for myself.

"Shall we go look at the orchids?" she asked.

"Yes," I agreed, following her deeper into the veritable jungle of the conservatory. There were fewer people here. Though the noise was still nearly overwhelming, the crowds hadn't gotten this far in yet. The distinct smell of hothouse flowers was intoxicating, as was the warm, damp air.

Behind us, I heard Elspeth announce that to celebrate the inaugural event of the Grand Exhibition, there would be fireworks on the terrace. A few people streamed by us, going the opposite direction. We walked slowly, keeping on in the same direction. In just a few moments, the conservatory had quieted considerably.

We found Boreas right where the Ravager told Mina he would be. He stood staring at a cluster of nocturnum orchids that glowed with a soft sea-green light. "Remarkable, aren't they?" he asked, not bothering to turn. "Vaness loved orchids, but she always struggled to grow them. She would be sick with envy were she here."

Mina's jaw clenched, her entire body going tense at her father's words. She set her glass of wine down on the low wall that lined the conservatory pathways. I did the same. I waited for her to respond to Boreas, but she did nothing of the sort. It seemed as though she would wait for him to speak.

He turned to look at us. I don't know how anyone else had missed the resemblance; he looked exactly as he had in the paintings at Orchid House to me. People really were not very observant, I'd realized. They only saw what mattered to them.

"Children," Boreas said with a smile. "How lovely it is to see the two of you together again."

People only saw what mattered to them.

Mina had let go of my hand.

Too late, I saw what was wrong, understood the mistake we'd made.

It all happened at once. Boreas teleported across the small space we stood in, grabbing hold of Mina's arm. I lunged for her, my arm snaking hard around her waist, as I attempted to pull her away from her father.

To no avail. Instead of taking only her, he took us both. We slipped out of the conservatory, between.

CHAPTER 50

MINA

We appeared exactly where I'd meant to take us, but not by my direction. The guardian of the gate turned, observing us in silence. My heart thumped in my chest, loud, but not fast. I panicked, but my body did not. I buried my satisfaction deep. The Ravager could not know that I knew. Not yet.

What have you done? I asked, injecting as much of the panic I felt into my voice as possible. I was truly afraid. There was so much that could still go wrong.

What I was ordered to do, the Ravager explained. *If it brings you any solace, I regret that I was forced to lie to you.*

It brought me no solace whatsoever. The only thing that did was that at least we were away from Poe and Skye, away from all the people this confrontation could hurt. Boreas shoved me hard, meaning, I'm sure, to push me to the ground in a position of subjugation.

But Ash held me tight against him. He had not let Boreas take me alone. I hadn't meant for him to come with us. I'd wanted him to stay behind to protect Poe, and where I knew he would be safe. But somewhere deep within me, I was glad he was here. I arched into him, steadying myself as my father stepped away from us.

"Oh for gods' sake," he sneered, glaring at us both. "Aren't you ashamed of yourself, man, clinging to her?"

When I had my footing, Ash answered. "Ashamed of myself for what, Boreas? For loving your daughter?"

Boreas sneered. "For letting a woman lead you around by the balls. Have some self-respect, man."

The way he said the word woman made me sick. My father had always thought the women of his court below him, despite the fact that they were some of his best warriors, his most prominent politicians and scholars. Still, he thought of us as weak.

Ash shook his head. "My self-respect is intact, Boreas. I honor the woman I love, and her many talents. Your daughter is no bargaining chip, no pawn to be moved for gaining power. She *is* power itself, and I am honored to serve her in whatever way I can."

My father looked as though he might choke on Ash's words. The Ravager was strangely quiet, but I felt it stir within me, though it let me move on my own now. The entire time, it had been doing as my father had asked. I had my suspicions, but I still wasn't certain why.

"What was the point of all this?" I asked. "Why did you let me go?"

Ash looked down at me, sorrow filling his eyes. He held me tighter, as though he might drag me away from all this. But I knew if he could teleport out of this space, he would have done so already. The defeat in his eyes told me all I needed to know.

This was the end; we'd reached the limit of what we could do. We had Boreas here, but he wanted to be here. There were no other options but to see how this played out. I crossed my arms over myself, grabbing onto Ashbourne's arms. My Claimed, my husband, my partner in all things, even this. I wished there was some way to let him know what all this meant, so he did not have to go through it alone.

Boreas smiled. "I let you go so that you would understand there is no escaping me. I don't need a ring or a necklace to control you. You will simply do as I ask, or I will kill everyone you love and make you watch. If you think seeing your lover's wings burned off was bad, just wait until you hear about the things I've thought up for Poe and Skye, and that pretty little greymalkin."

"Stop," I growled. "Just... stop." I let go of Ash's arms and turned to face him. "He will never stop this. I have to do what I can to make it right. You understand?"

As he nodded, my heart broke. "I do."

Inside me, the Ravager reveled in my misery.

"I am so sorry," I said. "I didn't mean for it to end like this."

"I know," he whispered, lowering his forehead to mine.

I could only hope he understood some measure of what I was about to do as I pulled away and walked to my father's side. "Why are we here?"

Boreas smiled now, taking my hand. His touch was repulsive to me. I fought to think of anything but his clammy skin on mine. "Because they are accessible here. We can reach them."

"Who?" I asked.

He sighed, as though I were a foolish child, and I repressed the urge to vomit as his breath touched me. Every sensory aspect of being so near to him was repugnant. "My armies, of course. Aislin summoned them to Okairos, but they never made it there. Connoch's offspring stopped them. But I've found them, and now all will be well. We will finally have Sirin for our own."

Ouriel's warning not to break the ward sang in my memory. I had tried my best not to let the Ravager see it. It was strangely quiet in me now. I tried to ignore the way Boreas clutched at me. He'd been one to talk about Ash clinging to me. His hand touching mine was the worst thing I'd ever felt, and I had been in pain my entire life. "You plan to use the gate for this?"

The guardian turned. *The gate cannot be used in such a fashion.*

I knew that to be a lie. The soldier had sent Ashbourne back to the gate. And yet they lied now. They, at least, were still allied with me.

I am allied with you as well, the Ravager said, finally speaking. *Despite being controlled by Boreas. The things that passed between us were not a lie.*

I did not believe it. I couldn't be so foolish, but a little bit of hope bloomed within me. Perhaps this would work.

Boreas continued talking, but as he did, I slipped out of his grasp and moved backward, inch by inch. For all he said about needing me, he didn't seem to notice that he no longer held onto me as he spoke. "No, the gate goes to the otherworld. It's practically irrelevant, except for the fact that this is the one place that accesses all parts of the limen." He looked back at me. "Where are you going, child? I need you to open the gate. Don't make me hurt Ashbourne."

I shook my head, letting my shoulders slump. "No, you won't have to hurt him. I will do as you say. Please, just… don't touch me."

Boreas grimaced. "I'd forgotten about your odd distaste for being touched. As you wish. Come here."

I shook my head, turning slightly, which caused Boreas to track me. Yes, now he watched me. Slowly, so slowly we moved. I quickened my breath, hoping the Ravager would not give me away. "No," I gasped. "Not until you promise you won't touch me again."

Boreas growled with frustration. "I've already done so. Now come open a passageway to the limen."

"Why can't you do it yourself?" I asked, continuing to stall for time. "You opened all those other doors."

Boreas groaned, as though he might start screaming at me. A small part of me, the part that was still a child, shrank back, remembering what it was to be screamed at. He wasn't so tall anymore, especially as Lord Eccles, or Alastair Wildfang, whoever I was supposed to believe he was. But the child within me remembered what it felt like to be intimidated by him.

How I'd had to learn every move he ever made, so that I could anticipate how he would react. And act accordingly, adjusting moment by moment to survive. If he'd known he was training me for this very moment, he might have behaved better.

I very much doubt that, the Ravager said.

Will you fight this? I asked the Ravager. Perhaps it was unwise to ask. I'd done so much work to keep this secret from it, suspecting as I was of its betrayal. But now, I found I wanted it to know and agree with me. *Or will you stay still?*

As an answer, it said nothing, but went incredibly quiet within me.

At the same time, Ashbourne moved. He couldn't teleport, but he was preternaturally fast in his Vilhari form, and as he moved, he shifted. Now he moved in a blue blur of naked glory. One moment he was yards and yards from Boreas. Now he held onto him, pinning his arms to his side.

Thank all gods above and below. My Claimed had guessed what I was about. He knew his role. He knew what it meant to be the shrike. Ashbourne Claymore knew *me*, all of me. He knew the way I plotted and planned, the way my brain pieced things together and he'd known exactly what to do in precisely the right moment.

I had chosen my mate well. Pride in both of us sang within me.

"Now," I shouted, summoning as much aether and empyrae as I could.

Ash shoved Boreas as hard as he could towards the gate, while I loosed a spear of empyrae straight towards his heart. It pierced his chest, sending him flying towards the gate at an alarming rate, but he dug his heels in. I walked forward as quickly as I could manage, loosing spear after spear. Through his chest, his eyes, and as he screamed, his mouth.

There was no time to ask him questions. No time to find out why he'd done what he'd done, or what he planned to do next. There was no time left at all. I shoved Boreas through the archway meant only for true immortals, holding him steady in it as his body burned. My hands went unharmed.

Boreas was always so many steps ahead, but he had trained me to be better with his cruelty. He'd been the mastermind behind the downfall of dozens of Ventyr civilizations. He'd ruined worlds. But he made me this.

He and Vaness both. And now he burned for it. I watched as my father turned to ashes, then pushed those ashes through the gateway as well, watching as they disintegrated to nothing. It was over. He was dead.

I looked back over my shoulder at Ash, who grinned. He was naked as the day he was born, but he'd performed beautifully all the same. The shrike to my vicious thorn.

I looked up at the guardian. "Thank you," I said. "Could I have the ring I gave you back?" They dropped the ring into my hand. "It is time," I said. "I have the seal, but I don't think we need it, do we?"

The guardian's gaseous constellation seemed to pulse with interest as it looked within me. *No*, it answered. *If you destroy the ring, as you did your father, the entity within you will no longer be imprisoned.*

Ash came to stand next to me, his fingers lacing through mine. I tossed the ring in the air, sending a blast of empyrae straight to it. An eldritch scream released from it as it turned to dust.

"You're free now," I said to the creature within me. "I believe that if you go through the archway, you might find peace."

The Ravager listened, but did not stir. I felt fear, though it was not my own.

I looked up at the guardian. "Will it be welcomed there, on the other side? Or will it be punished?"

The guardian contemplated my question. *There is no punishment in the divine realm. A god can do no wrong there.* The soldier bent down a little. *The two of you will be welcome there someday, I believe.*

Ash's responding grin was wicked. "A place where a god can do no wrong. That sounds lovely."

"What about you?" I asked the god within me. "Perhaps some of your brethren are there. The other Nameless Ones."

The Ravager eked out of me now, at first a bunch of dark mist. Darker than aether, but still the same shade. It took form, solidifying a little. It was a nereid—a creature of legend—with gills in its neck, a delicate flat nose, and luminous dark eyes; with hair like seaweed and an incredibly long tail that moved like an eel and fluttered like a fancy goldfish. She was beautiful and menacing at the same time. I aspired to be as wonderful as the Ravager in her nereid form.

"So you know who I am," she said.

I nodded. "I saw you here in a vision—at the beginning—with your siblings. This is where it all started, isn't it? When this place was a part of Citadel?"

The nereid nodded. "Yes, this is where it all began. And it is where it must end for me, though you must go on. If you see my sister again, tell her I am sorry."

"I will," I whispered.

She came forward towards me, her sharp teeth showing as she opened her mouth to speak. Ash tensed, but I held up a hand. The nereid bent towards me, lifting Helene's necklace from my chest. "My sister is not the only one who can bestow gifts," she said, her smile a mix of sinister and sweet. "May your pain be alchemized into more power than you ever could have imagined."

Ash's eyes widened as the Ravager sent another wisp of liquid shadow into Helene's necklace. I looked into the nereid's dark eyes, wondering how long she'd been sneaking parts of herself into the necklace.

"Can it hurt me?" I asked.

"All power can cause pain, Mina," the nereid reasoned.

Exhaustion threatened to bowl me over as she placed the golden necklace in my outstretched palm. When my fingers closed around it, I saw what the dark stone contained: a firedrake, like Helene's. Something inside me sprang forth as a tight bud that would someday be a bloom—a sign that even now, with winter coming, that spring would come again.

The nereid smiled. "I thought you might like to keep part of her, though he is wholly yours."

I inclined my head as the god that was once a Ravager went through the gate to the divine realm. As she disappeared, I felt nothing but peace, and was nearly bowled over by the relief of it. The entire time I had planned for this, I had not been sure it would work.

This had been a test of my trust in myself, greater than any I'd ever experienced. With no one to tell my plans to, for fear that the Ravager might know and refuse to cooperate, I'd had to go on faith in what I'd seen in my puzzle pieces.

I had been right. Right to trust Ash to understand me when the time came. And right to trust myself. A sob wracked through me. Ash's arms went around me and we sank to the mirrored, liquid ground. He rocked me back and forth, feeling my need for the movement.

"You did it," he murmured into my hair. "I knew you had a plan."

"I didn't know if I was right," I sobbed into his bare chest. "I wanted to tell you."

"I know," he said. "I know. You did everything right."

The way he held and rocked me was so instinctive, so perfect. I closed my eyes and let him help me as I screamed, letting out the built up emotions that had been penned inside me for far too long. I felt the shudder in his chest. He was crying too.

I wasn't alone. I might need solitude from time to time, but I would never be alone again. Ash was with me, always. Poe, Skye,

Morpheus, Muse and Arcturus. Even the Aestras and the Chevaliers, Edith and Karnon and the Syndicate. I had people now. The elementals. A whole world of magic and wonder to protect.

My sobs quieted. We had solved the problems of the Ravagers and Boreas, but our people still needed us. I pulled away from Ash. "We have to go."

He wiped my tears with his thumbs, then nodded, helping me to my feet.

"What will happen to Boreas' army?" I asked the guardian, as I remembered what my father came here for. "Does someone need to do something about that?"

Nothing can be done by you that will not be done by another, the guardian replied, still incredibly cryptic. *I believe you are needed elsewhere.*

The view through the gateway shifted. It was the conservatory. Sounds of fighting became apparent as the image clarified. *Go,* the elemental soldier said. *Go and help your friends.*

I looked at Ashbourne's naked body as we stepped through. "I guess Sirin is just going to have to get used to you this way."

CHAPTER 51

MINA

The conservatory was chaos. Someone had set the building on fire, and there were screams in the distance. As we stepped through the gateway, a masked assailant dove towards us. Ash ducked, pushing me out of the way.

"Aeros," I called, knowing the firedrake's name without having to be told. He sprang from the necklace, but came from within me. The Ravager had carved out a space inside me that the firedrake would occupy for the rest of my days. Joy filled me as the last piece of the puzzle clicked into place.

I was whole in a way I never expected to be.

Aeros was a magnificent creature of shadow, flame, and aether, and as it loosed its flame at Ash's attacker, the assailant screamed. Ash smiled that wicked Thuellos smile at me as he sprang to his feet.

"That's a good trick," he said as two curved knives, made from pure empyrae, sprang to life in his hands. In two elegant motions, he slit the burning attacker's throat and intestines.

Two more followed, and he cut through them as though they were nothing more than butter, and he a hot knife. Two Oscarovi stepped out from behind thick foliage. Their familiars, a pair of swans, were instantly recognizable. So, Caralee Ellis-Whitely and Rebecca Smytheson had been a part of this all along.

"My father is dead," I explained. "Surrender."

Caralee frowned. "I think we'd know if the Emperor was dead."

They were calling him the Emperor. I had to suppress a groan of utter disgust.

Rebecca nodded. "I agree. We would know. She's clearly working against him, though. Get her."

The swans took to the air. Aeros was still helping Ash. I whispered for aid. Huge, aethereal serpents appeared, wrapping around Caralee and Rebecca's feet, holding them in place. I whispered again, calling for aid from the air as the swans dove toward me. Two gryphon vultures swept out of the darkness, manifesting out of thin air, their heavy talons sinking effortlessly into the swans.

Caralee screamed as her familiar disappeared. "You little bitch. Your father will punish you for that—I can promise you that much."

The way she said it turned my stomach. "Do you think my father is going to…"

"Marry her, make her Empress," Rebecca said, smug. "*Yes*. Caralee is *special*, Mina. And he is going to beat you silly when he finds out what you did." The whine in her voice was enough to make me slit her throat then and there, but I thought of Poe and restrained myself.

The vultures snuffed out Rebecca's swan next, and she snarled when it disappeared.

They've killed nearly a dozen people tonight, the serpent that held Caralee said. *I see it in this one's mind. She enjoyed it.*

I stepped towards the two of them, sighing. My father never ceased to disgust me, even after his death. But these two were too much. I glanced over my shoulder, to make sure Ash was all right.

He was trading barbs with his assailant, though I could not hear what they said to one another. Aeros returned to me, curling around my shoulders. *He does well on his own and does not need me.*

The firedrake glowed with both aether's dark light and empyrae. Caralee's eyes widened with fear as I approached her. I took her chin in my grip. "How do you think my father will punish me for killing you, Caralee?"

She glared at me. "I don't care to think about such things."

The snake tightened around her legs and arms. *She would like to watch him torture you.*

I shook my head. "Torture, Caralee? I am sorry to disappoint you both, but Daddy is dead." I conjured an empyraeic knife and slit Caralee's throat, cutting all the way to her spine, then pushed her over. "And so are you."

Rebecca swallowed a scream. "Keep her still until this is over," I said to the snakes. "She knows everything that Caralee and the others have done, and if she doesn't want to meet a much slower end than Caralee, she will tell us all she knows."

Rebecca's eyes fell to the ground, but I stepped towards her, wrapping my bloody fingers around her chin, just as I had with Caralee, lifting her eyes to mine. "Won't you, love?"

"Yes," she sputtered. "Please don't hurt me."

Aeros hissed in her face, spitting little sparks at her. A crowd of Karnon Archambeau's Oscarovi and Chevaliers came running, elemental spirits at their sides. As they reached me, Ash cut down the last of his assailants.

I nodded towards Rebecca. "Take her somewhere for questioning. The serpents will help." Perhaps we would learn more about what Maman and Boreas had been planning. We would have to ferret out their cohort in the coming days. I searched myself for guilt or sadness at killing Caralee, but found none.

She was a vile creature, Aeros reasoned. *There is no reason for guilt or sorrow. She killed many, and planned to kill many more.*

I nodded, stroking his scales. They were smooth and almost soft now that he was fully corporeal.

"The queen would like to see you," one of the Chevaliers said. "If the two of you don't mind."

Ash nodded, his naked body splattered with blood. "In a moment, friend." He swept me into his arms, pinning me hard against him as Aeros disappeared within me. "I need to kiss my wife first."

His wife. I loved the sound of that. I laughed, tears in my eyes. It was all right to cry now. I was allowed to have emotions. Ash smiled down at me. "That was some high grade murder right there. Very impressive." He growled a little over the word impressive.

One of the Chevaliers let out a low whistle, and the Syndicate Oscarovi snickered. I heard one of them say, "C'mon, her royal highness will understand."

Another said, "The two of 'em'll probably fuck right there from the looks of things," as they disappeared with Rebecca.

"Well, wife," Ash said, pulling me closer. The hard length of him pressed into me. "What do you think? Should I fuck you right here?"

I wound my arms around Ash's neck, heat pooling in my belly. "I think you should."

"Lady take the two of you," Skye cried from the path. "Here?"

I sighed, looking up into Ash's golden eyes. "They are just going to keep coming."

He smiled. "We could make them watch."

Skye made a mock gagging noise. "Some propriety, please!"

"Propriety, she says." I brushed a kiss to Ash's cheek, before slipping behind him, slapping his bare, blue ass. "Msr Claymore! Propriety."

He laughed, running towards Skye. "Was this the propriety you were looking for?" He grabbed her up, kissing both her cheeks.

"The two of you should not be allowed to influence one another further," she said. "You've made each other worse somehow."

I smirked at her as I passed them, Ash throwing his best friend over his shoulder. "Do you think this form makes my arse look good?"

"Put me down," Skye shrieked.

"Her dignity must be considered!" I said as we made our way through the conservatory. Skye's laughter was a balm to my soul.

The bodies of our enemies lay everywhere. Only a few of our own littered the conservatory floor. Inside the atrium of the conservatory, a small group of Oscarovi and Vilhari gathered around Poe. A Corvidae healer sewed up a small cut on her shoulder.

I rushed forward. The healer squawked at me, warning me to stay back. "Let me finish," she said.

Poe raised an eyebrow. "Is he dead?"

I nodded. "And the Ravager is gone."

Her eyes fell closed for a brief moment while the healer finished.

"Try to keep your arm quiet for a few hours. The stitches will fall out on their own when it heals."

Poe took the Corvidae's bare hand. "Thank you, friend."

"Your Highness," the healer said as she backed away.

We collided in a tangle of arms and hair. Though Poe looked calm on the outside, when I hugged her, she shook. "It's over," I whispered.

"No," she said as she pushed me back. "It's just the start."

She was right, of course. I took her hand, holding it tight as we leaned against one another. "Where will we go now?" I asked.

"I suppose we have to find home again, don't we?" she said as we watched Ash dump Skye off his back. Morpheus materialized out of nowhere, rubbing his face against their legs.

Muse rushed in, Arcturus not far behind him. "Poe," he gasped. "Viridian has returned. You must come."

"It's your cousin," Arcturus added, when none of us reacted quickly enough. "Viridian's brought your cousin from Ismit, Poe."

Poe's grip on my hand tightened. "Well," I said softly. "I suppose we should go meet them."

Poe nodded, then whispered, "Could Ash put some clothes on first, please?"

The sun crept high enough in the sky to bring on the gray light of a winter morning. I looked back over my shoulder as I followed Poe. "You heard the queen, Claymore. Your nakedness shall no longer be tolerated."

The roar of his laughter rang in my ears like music as I followed Poe into a new day.

CHAPTER 52

ASHBOURNE

A *month later*

Endymion Feriant was one handsome, charismatic person. They were the talk of Pravhna, invited to every party as the Grand Exhibition got underway, which was wonderful, as none of us wanted the city at large to know just how close we'd come to utter destruction.

The papers all ran stories about Poe's cousin returning to her, after long years hidden in Brektos, on their front pages. The story that the Chevaliers had dispensed with the arsonist responsible for all the fires and explosions in the city for the past year wasn't even page three news. Pravhna was nothing if not the same as ever, despite all we'd seen.

I folded my newspaper and checked the time. If I left now, I could still make it without being late. Mina had asked me to rest and recuperate, but I was struggling with the task. Upstairs, the sound of construction was nearly unbearable, and yet I was supposed to just sit here sipping tea and reading the paper.

The architect, a young Strix woman recommended to us by Karnon Archambeau, came downstairs gasping at her pocket watch as she reached the last step. "Sir, you'll be late. Don't keep the Lady waiting."

The people of Pravhna had started calling Mina "the Lady" and Poe "Highness" as terms of endearment. The epithets felt as evergreen as the way everyone knew Edith Braithwaite was "Herself." Not to be left out, I was "the Lady's husband," and Skye "Highness' wife." I couldn't help but smile whenever I heard them.

"I'm going, I'm going," I said. "Do you need anything?"

The architect shook her feathered head. "No, the contractor will be here in an hour, and we'll have the tile finished today. Another week and you and the Lady will be able to move in."

That too made me smile. I pulled my overcoat from the hook by what was once the door to my office with Skye, and was now the front hallway to what would soon be my home with Mina. Outside, the streets were bustling with energy. The Grand Exhibition had the city packed to the gills. It was the perfect time for a store opening.

As I walked, the smell of roasting chestnuts and toasted marshmallows filled my nose. A Vilhari street vendor on the corner was accompanied by an Oscarovi guitarist who sang an old folk ballad. My boots crunched on the freshly fallen snow. Soon, Pravhna would be heavily blanketed with the stuff, and the season would begin in earnest.

A social season with the Grand Exhibition going on sounded exhausting more than anything else, but Poe and Skye were looking forward to it. Footsteps fell in time with mine, just a few feet behind me. I slowed, trying to calm my frayed nerves. I understood now why Mina often did not like for others to stand behind her. It made me uncomfortable as well.

"Hi, Ash," a soft voice said.

I looked to my left and found the young Morgaine Yarlo walking next to me, her greymalkin companion Bayun trotting alongside us. The auburn lynxcat was massive and moved more like a lyon than a housecat. "I wondered if we'd see you again," I said.

She smiled, pushing her short dark hair away from her face. "I had lots to do here. But you took care of your Ravager, I see."

I nodded. "Mina did."

Morgaine nodded. "You found out what they are?"

Again, I nodded. "Yes."

Her pretty brow furrowed. She kept pace with me, but she bent to pick up Bayun, sweeping him onto her shoulders like he was a fur stole. "We have to go today, but I wanted to stop and see you and Mina first."

"I am going to meet her now," I said. "We're nearly there."

Morgaine nodded, but her face was serious, as was the greymalkin's. We walked in silence for a few blocks, uphill toward the medial district. There was a crowd out front of our destination I could see from a block away.

"Come this way," I said, ducking into the alley behind our building. "Mina is likely in our new office."

Morgaine followed, Bayun jumping down from her shoulders. I unlocked the back door and called out to my wife. "Darling, I'm here. With friends."

Mina's head popped out of the storeroom. She wore a lovely wool suit in a deep eggplant shade that set off her rosy cheeks. "Morgaine Yarlo," she breathed. "I am so glad to see you."

Morgaine shook her head. "You look so much like my Echo. Not exactly like her, but there's something about you."

Mina smiled. "Are you going home to her soon?"

Morgaine's chin quivered a bit and she nodded. She seemed so young. "Yes. But I have to return this to your sister first, and I thought you might like to see her."

My heart almost stopped as Mina's eyes widened, filling with tears. "Ouriel? I could see her?"

Morgaine nodded. "For a moment."

Mina looked to me, not for permission, but for grounding. I nodded to reassure her. She refocused on Morgaine. "Thank you. I would take even the briefest of glances just to see her again."

Morgaine smiled, then pushed her jacket up above her forearm and pressed her finger into the tattoo of the compass there. A blade of empyrae appeared in her hand. It burned white-hot, the most powerful empyrae of all, starfire. She made a long slice in the fabric of the universe.

"Morgaine?" a familiar voice said through the cut. "Is that you?"

"Yes," Morgaine called through. "I have Lumina with me."

A curvaceous woman, pale like Mina, with flaming auburn hair stepped through the cut Morgaine had made, her own power opening it further. She looked around the office, taking in the aetheric lights, the beautiful wood-paneled walls, the lush velvet curtains that were currently drawn over our front windows and doors. Mina had done all this herself in the past weeks, getting us ready for the grand opening today, though our office would not be the main focus of the event.

"Is this yours?" Ouriel breathed.

Mina nodded. "Yes, Ashbourne and I are private investigators."

Ouriel smiled as she gazed at her sister, her pale freckled cheeks flushing prettily, the same way Mina's did sometimes when she was overwhelmed with emotion. "It is so good to see you."

She wore strange clothing—pants made from stretchy, tight fabric and a cropped top that was short-sleeved, along with the same odd white shoes that Morgaine wore. Her nails were long, lacquered with opalescent white paint that glimmered in the lamplight.

"I thought we might never see one another again," Mina said, touching Ouriel's freckled face.

They fell into each other's arms, whispering things I could not hear. Nor did I try to. She would tell me, eventually. Morgaine and I stood awkwardly waiting for a few minutes.

"Thank you," I whispered to her. "She has been thinking about Ouriel a lot."

Morgaine nodded. "I can understand that. It is horrible to be separated from the ones you love." She placed a hand on my arm. "I am so glad you finally found her, Ash."

I remembered now, telling Morgaine about Lumina, back when I traveled with her in the limen. With Finn and Larkin. "Will you ever see my nephew again?"

She shook her head. "No, the door to Okairos is closed, and must remain so. I'm sorry. But you would be proud of him."

"I would?" I asked, a grin lighting my face.

Morgaine smiled. "Yes. My sources tell me he is very like you."

I didn't have time to ask who her sources were, but the grey-malkin seemed to wink at me. I resisted the urge to pick him up and squeeze him. Morpheus hated such things, and I assumed the little lyon would as well.

"I'm sorry it isn't more," Mina said as she pulled back from Ouriel. "There is still so much we don't know."

So, she'd told her sister that we still didn't know the full scope of Boreas' plans. That we might never know. That his followers all died suddenly when questioned too aggressively—right as they broke, and seemed willing to tell all. Whatever magic Boreas had done, he'd kept many of his secrets, even in death.

"That's all right," Ouriel said. "You did the most important part."

Mina nodded. "Will I ever see you again?"

Tears filled Ouriel's eyes. "I don't think so."

A tear slipped down Morgaine's cheek. She smiled up at me. "I just know… I know how much Lumina means to her. This is hard."

I nodded. It was hard to watch them say goodbye to one another.

"Thank you," Mina said. "For making the bargain with the Ravager on my behalf. It saved my life."

Ouriel smiled. "I wish we had more time."

"Babe," a deep voice called from beyond the cut in the universe. "It's closing."

"Go," Ouriel said to Bayun and Morgaine. "I'll be right there."

She hugged Mina again. Morgaine held out a hand to me. I took it and shook. "Thank you for everything," I said. "Best of luck."

She smiled and waved as she and the greymalkin disappeared. Mina and Ouriel hugged again, this time longer and harder than before. I had to look away; the bittersweet expression on Mina's face was too much to bear.

A pale man who had a few inches and at least seventy-five pounds on me poked his head through the slit. He wore a tight short-sleeve shirt that showed off the massive muscles in his tattooed arms. His fair hair was pulled away from his rugged face. "Babe," he said again, softly. "There's no more time."

He looked to me and nodded. There was something familiar about him. "Torbjorn?" I breathed. "Torbjorn Greystone?"

"Good to see I'm remembered," he said. "And you're Ashbourne Thuellos."

I nodded, flabbergasted by the Wolf's presence. He had been one of Interra's most legendary fighters, but had disappeared when

Ouriel was a young woman. Ouriel smiled at him. "That's him," she whispered to Mina. "Twelve years."

Mina smiled and rushed forward, kissing the Wolf on each cheek. "Take care of her."

He smiled as Ouriel took his hand. "I will."

They disappeared through the slit between worlds and Ouriel's voice was the last thing I heard as it closed. "I love you," she said.

"I love you too," Mina called back as the world was put back to rights. I rushed to her side, and she leaned against me, her head resting on my shoulder as naturally as if it was made to fit there.

"I don't know how they found one another," she said. "But they've been married for twelve years. She's happy, Ash. My little sister is happy."

She burst into tears, and I couldn't tell if they were joyful tears or sad ones, knowing she would never see Ouriel live out that happiness. I didn't need to know. All I needed was to hold her. I scooped her into my arms and sat down on one of the overstuffed chairs near the hearth, which crackled merrily.

There were footsteps in the back hall, and I assumed Poe or Skye, or even Morpheus, might be along to tell us it was almost time for the grand opening, but to my surprise it was an owlet with the visage of a snowy owl. In fact, it was an owlet that was very familiar to me. The littling I'd rescued the day this all began. I couldn't believe my eyes.

"Hullo, sir," the owlet said. "Pleased to tell you I'm alive."

I shook my head in surprise. "But… the fire?"

Mina raised her head. "They escaped. Like Brigitte did at the cabin. Did you know some Strix can slip between?"

I grinned, slapping my thigh with delight. "I did not know that."

"Highness says they're going to open in five, whether you're there or not, m'Lady," the owlet said, disappearing into the back hallway, through a strategically placed door that connected our office and the bookstore next door.

Mina pulled a hanky from my jacket pocket and dried her tears, patting her nose a few times. "Do I look as though I've been sobbing?" she asked.

"Not at all," I lied. Her nose was a little red, as were her cheeks, but it was nothing more than adorable in my view.

She slid off my lap, pulling me out of my chair. "Let's go," she said.

We walked down the hall together, and opened the door. The store smelled like books, both new and old, and tea and coffee. The ceilings were high, tiled with beautiful mosaics that depicted different elementals. Poe's staff chatted excitedly to one another. All our friends were here to help celebrate.

The bookstore had been Skye's idea. There was no real role for an Aethereal queen in the modern world. The way politics were turning, it was obvious that the time for monarchy was long, long past us. But Poe had wanted to be a part of life, in touch with the people who still looked up to her as a public figure.

And, I suspected she and Mina had some plan they hadn't yet decided to reveal to Skye and myself. The two of us had to make peace with the fact that our wives were as close to one another as they were to us, and that they were forever scheming. My best friend spotted me from across the store and grinned. No matter what the Lady and Highness were planning, it was fine with us.

This was their world, and we were just happy to live in it. When this building, right on the line between the upper echelons and the undercity, went up for sale, the four of us pooled our money and bought it and the old office outright. Poe and Skye would live in the space above the shop, and we in the undercity. But every day, we would come to work in the same building. It wasn't the life I thought we might have. It was better.

Poe smiled when she saw Mina, grabbing her hands and kissing them. "It's time."

When she released them to me, Mina smiled back. "Congratulations. Is it everything you hoped it would be?"

I took my wife's hand back, reveling in the feeling that, at least for a little while, we were going to live an average life. We had not heard from the god once since killing Boreas, and that was fine with me. We deserved this rest.

Poe looked around at Skye making coffee and tea with Viridian, Muse, Arcturus, and her cousin Endymion. At Morpheus sleeping on a pile of books. At me, holding her best friend's hand. She nodded. "It is. It will be."

Mina let go of my hand and followed Poe to the front door. A sign in the window read "The Lost Court." Skye put four cups of coffee on the counter, and shouted out, "Order up for her Royal Highness."

Poe grinned, turning the sign on the door from "Closed" to "Open" and looked back over her shoulder at us. "It's time for a new chapter," she said as she opened the door. Light flooded in with the customers that waited outside.

Mina smiled back at me as they came inside. A new chapter, indeed. "Show me to the romance section," I said, joining my family at the coffee bar. "I desperately need something new to read."

EPILOGUE - MINA

MANY YEARS LATER. SUMMERTIME, JUST OFF THE COAST OF VAIA MAR

The glittering lights onshore sparkled in the night as the yacht glided into the dark waters of the bay. The silver lamé fabric of my dress swished around my calves, cool against my skin. The chill of the fabric was a balm in the warm night. I twisted my hips a little, watching the skirt twist around me.

Poe laughed, a breeze touching the feathered layers of her dark hair as she leaned against the railing. Pink dolphins played in the wake of the yacht. "I love that dress on you."

I smiled back at her, pleased that she liked it. The modistes had brought out an entire season of sequins and lamé to accommodate the wave of discotheques opening all over Cerne this summer, and I was mesmerized by all the metallic fabrics.

Skye and Ash were inside getting drinks for us. I turned to stand next to my best friend, leaning on the railing so my shoulder bumped into hers. "I'm glad we're doing this."

She nodded, her warm skin pressing back against mine. Her weight against me was a comfort. We'd waited years for tonight, playing a long game. We had to be sure we'd dealt with all of Boreas and Vaness' people before we made our next move. It had taken decades to get here, of watching power rise and fall in the city. Of making sure Pravhna's upper echelons were on the right track.

Of letting the city get used to their lost heir. Of watching her fame fade into something more mundane as the years passed. Of living and enjoying one another. It had been wonderful, there was no denying it. But as things went, trouble rumbled through the under-city, and it was time for us to meet it. From deep within me, Aeros beat his wings. He was as excited for what came next as I was apprehensive.

Poe sighed, watching Muse and Arcturus join Skye and Ash at the bar over her shoulder. "I wish Morpheus was here tonight."

I rolled my eyes. The feline stubbornly would not set foot on the boat. Apparently, he got seasick. All this planning and the fey beast wasn't even going to be here. "He's busy sleeping on all the new furniture, I'm sure."

The townhouse in Halcyon Gate was cozy, finally finished after nearly a decade of remodeling. It was perfect timing, really. I smiled at the sequined-covered bump. "How is Elurin doing?"

Poe grinned, running a protective hand over her belly. She had decided to name the baby after her ancient ancestor, the first ruler of her bloodline in House Feriant. "They are well. Already so wise."

It was still bizarre to me that the baby spoke to her. Ventyr reproduction was much different than that of the Vilhari, I'd learned in the past few months. I'd never paid much attention until now.

"Good," I murmured. "And you're certain you want to do this? We could wait until after the little one is born."

Poe shook her head. "I feel fine, Mina. I can do both."

We'd had this discussion a thousand times. The pregnancy had been a surprise for us all, but Poe wasn't letting it stop her. We'd planned for this for far too long. Besides, babies were a blessing.

I didn't want any of my own, but Elurin was a blessing beyond what I could articulate. Nothing could make me happier than my two best friends having a child together. A muscular Strix with the visage of a snowy owl stuck their head out from the doors that led inside. Our little hatchling had grown so much over the years.

"Viridian and Gerard say it's time," Flox said, extending a gloved hand to Poe. She took it, letting herself be guided inside. Flox brushed a kiss to her hair as he passed her off to Skye. "I love you, Ma."

Her eyes sparkled up at her adoptive child. "And I love you."

Skye smiled down at her. "Ready, Highness?"

She nodded, glancing back at me for reassurance. I nodded once, then whispered for Aeros. He slid from between, curling around my neck, his bright eyes glowing with empyrae as he chortled with gleeful anticipation. I shook my head as Ash took my hand.

We fell into formation behind Skye and Poe. Muse and Arcturus came next. Flox pushed open the doors to the yacht's ballroom. Endymion Feriant had done well in the preceding years. The two story space was full of familiar faces.

Edith Braithwaite stood at the center of the crowd, flanked by Vionette and Karnon. Syndicate representatives from every quarter of Pravhna and the other Pevkan cities were here tonight. There were even a few leaders from Cerne and Silvri, and quite a few from Brektos, of course. Those who were connected to Endymion Feriant, the Syndicate's now-universally recognized global leader.

A level above us, Endymion stepped forward, a glass of sparkling wine in their hand. They raised the glass and the room quieted. "All hail the queen of the lost court."

Everyone in the room raised their glass. "All hail the queen."

"Welcome to the Syndicate, cousin," they said with a nod, dark hair falling into their eyes. As it always did where Endymion was concerned, suspicion tickled at the back of my mind.

They'd acted as head of the lost court for too long, and the rumors of corruption within the Syndicate seemed to be traced back to them. We'd spent years watching, waiting, becoming so domestic as to appear harmless.

Tonight, we made the first move of what would be a very long game. The crowd raised their glasses to their lips and sipped. A toast to the new Syndicate leader of Halcyon Gate. Music started and people around us began dancing as the lights in the ballroom lowered. Edith and Vionette rushed forward to embrace Poe and Skye, already talking about plans. Karnon held back until Ash and I approached.

He gave Aeros an approving nod, then swept past us to ask one of the Corvidae leaders from Ismit to dance. He was understandably suspicious of our motives. Muse and Arcturus were next to break off from us. Flox stayed at the edges of the crowd, watching things carefully. Our little owlet had grown into a fierce protector.

"Well, my love?" Ash asked as he took my waist. "Shall we dance?"

I nodded, letting him pull me onto the dance floor. The notes from the music swelled as his grip on my waist tightened. The new way people danced was fascinating to both of us. I rolled back in Ash's arms as the music rose.

Aeros dove back within me to absorb some of the pain from my movements. My familiar and I had worked out a way that I could enjoy myself more fully. Every movement, at least for a few minutes, could just be pleasure for me with Aeros taking my pain the way the Ravager had.

As I turned in Ash's arms, I took hold of his hand, letting him spin me out away from him, as my feet moved to the beat of the music, my dress twirling out around me. A wolf-whistle sounded from across the dance floor. Flox.

I shook my head, but Ash grinned. In the dim light of the yacht ballroom, every muscle in his chest was visible through the tight fit of his collared shirt. He was handsomer than ever, in my opinion, and heat built in me as he spun me back into him. He held me close for a moment, before sending me away as we flowed through the familiar footwork. The beat in the music picked up in tempo, and there were more whistles as Ash spun me, the choreography of the dance more complicated now.

Every touch was exhilarating as this new world we stepped into. The past years had been peaceful. That peace had been healing. Now we both grew restless, feeling the churn of time. Poe and I had always guessed this might happen. That while one set of problems were solved, another would brew in the background.

This is why we prepared. And though we hadn't let Ash and Skye in at first, we'd brought them in as soon as we knew the direction the winds of power blew in. Poe had been suspicious of her cousin from the start, but both of us were too wise to make waves.

Skye and Poe were older now, and though they were about to start a family, they were more fiercely devoted to Sirin than ever. Now wasn't the time to disappear into domestic bliss. I agreed with Poe on that count. She was more powerful than she'd ever been, and her influence would only continue to grow.

The music swelled one more time and Ash lifted me off the floor. As I slid down his lithe, muscular body, his mouth met mine. Our tongues danced as his fingers tangled in my long hair.

"Gods, you are beautiful," he breathed against my mouth. "Do you think Endymion has any idea what's coming for them?"

I smiled my most menacing smile. "Not a clue."

The Syndicate was dangerous, but so were we. Somewhere in the aether, I thought I heard She of the Dark Places laughing. Perhaps it was fanciful to think so, but the god chose me for a reason. I wrapped my arms around Ash's neck and leaned back to stare into his golden eyes. This is exactly where I was meant to be.

CHEVALIER, FIRST CLASS

A Prequel Story

S KYE AESTRA WAS outrageously plastered. She was, in fact, so intoxicated on Oblivion that the aetheric lights had a telltale green sparkle to them. *Le fey verte* twisted its devotees' perception of the world, causing everything from true dreams to mild hallucinations. This was Skye's first time with the emerald drink, and she hoped it would be her last. Being this drunk in Pravhna would be dangerous in any situation, let alone in the infamous Merc, seat of the Halcyon Gate Syndicate.

The four-story pleasure house was legendary for its shabby glamour and the dangerous undercity element that frequented it. It was the kind of place everyone knew about but few from the upper echelons ever actually went—unless they wanted to end up in the next day's gossip rags. This was, of course, exactly the reason she was here. Or half of it anyway. She *wanted* her family to know what she'd done after they'd exiled her. It would serve them right to read about her further betrayal to House Aestra's honor over breakfast.

But more than petty revenge, she needed the undercity to know the rumors they'd hear in the coming days were true. She was a free agent, whether she liked it or not, and being seen here tonight was as much about getting out in front of the tittle-tattle as it was for her own safety. As a chevalier, first class of one of the high Vilhari houses, even in exile, she would be hated in the undercity, a target all her days if she showed fear tonight.

So she made a point of following *le fey verte* down whatever rabbit hole the emerald green liquid took her on, keeping her shoulders relaxed and her expression calm. If all went well, she'd establish enough of a reputation to make her presence known to the Syndicate and then fade into the undercity unbothered. The Strix working the bar inclined his feathered head at the bottle of Oblivion that sat just out of Skye's reach. She nodded to him, and he sat up the contraption that filtered the green spirit through a sugar cube that sat atop a metal grate, into her glass. The light, floral scent of anise and hyssop filled her nostrils, as the bartender's barn owl visage turned her way.

"Watch how much of that you put down," he warned, his obsidian eyes honing in on her. "Pace yourself, chevalier."

Skye nodded as he pushed her glass out from under the contraption. The Strix obviously knew who she was and guessed what she was about, as his onyx eyes flicked to the party happening on the second-floor mezzanine.

The four leaders of the Halcyon Gate Syndicate held court at the Merc once a month, displaying their power in a dazzling spectacle. The music alone was far superior to any they got in the upper city, and Skye sensed pure aether in the air. A herd of transparent elk thundered through the glass-domed atrium at the center of the building, a show of power from Karnon Archambeau, the First Quarter Syndicate boss. The Syndicate was considered a scourge in the upper city, but Skye knew better. Halcyon Gate was corrupt, but they kept the upper city at bay and the undercity profitable.

Skye spotted Archambeau by the balcony. The Oscarovi was seated next to one of the most beautiful women Skye had ever seen. Petite and curvaceous, the woman's mahogany hair fell in waves around her bare shoulders. Skye watched her finely boned face as she conversed with Archambeau—she had to be the only person in Merc tonight who was unaffected by the heat. Not even an attractive glow of sweat graced the woman's perfectly sculpted brow.

By contrast, to avoid sweating out Oblivion, Skye had already shed her wool jacket, and the back of her linen camisole clung to the tightly clenched muscles of her back. She caught her reflection in the mercury glass mirror behind the bar. She'd rubbed her eyes earlier, forgetting that she'd lined them with kohl, and the effect now was more that of a feral warrior, rather than the understated glamour she'd been going for.

Just as well, she thought.

She didn't want the Syndicate thinking she was an easy mark. A cloud of poppy smoke drifted her way and she resisted the urge to cough as it burned her nose and eyes. She didn't need it adding to the effect of the Oblivion. Somehow, she had to stay sharp. Skye's only goals tonight were to show no fear and get in touch with Muse. The seer would have a line on where she might set up shop and a place to stay for the night. She had a little money of her own—just enough, she hoped, to spin her skills as a chevalier into a new life—a quiet, anonymous one.

On the mezzanine, the tiny brunette appeared to be saying her farewells. Skye was a bit surprised when Karnon merely kissed her hand. The man was a notorious flirt, and this development made him more interesting. She sought out the other Syndicate leaders amongst the glittering crowd of supplicants on the mezzanine. It would be good to put their names to faces so she didn't make foolish mistakes. A brown tweed suit caught her eye first. That had to be Edith Braithwaite, a Strix with a barn owl visage so similar to the bartender's that Skye assumed they were related. She was the Merc's owner, after all. No magic there, as the Strix were talentless, but plenty of money, charm and power. Vionette Celestine was the only Vilhar atop the Halcyon Gate hierarchy, but where was she?

A sheen of ebony hair met the tiny brunette's as Skye located Celestine. The Vilhar had to bend to kiss the brunette's cheeks, her faint smile widening as she tucked her hair behind a pointed ear. The brunette was saying something amusing, apparently, her pretty hands fluttering as she gazed up at the Vilhar. Skye couldn't place Vionette Celestine's heritage by simply looking at her, of course. She'd have to use aether for that. Talent was the only reliable determinant of power in Pravhna these days. Even the undercity ran on the same suffocating dynamics as the upper city.

The brunette held one of Celestine's hands in her own, admiring a ring on the Vilhar's index finger. Celestine dressed like a Vilhari aristocrat, in a perfectly tailored wine-colored gown. The lacework on the closely fitted, high-necked garment was stunning, sparkling with tiny jewels. Skye wasn't sure how Celestine managed to move so gracefully with such a tight fit, but it was certainly expensive looking.

By contrast, the brunette's seafoam green gown had some light boning that nipped her waist in, but the rest of the fabric fell sumptuously over the curve of her hips, leaving Skye to wonder about the shape of her legs. The dress exposed her shoulders and a pair of soft, luscious arms—and the color. The seafoam contrasted perfectly with the brunette's deep bronze skin. She practically glowed as she talked with Vionette Celestine.

Something in Skye ached powerfully. She shook her head; the Oblivion was getting to her. Celestine's narrow eyes flicked down to the first floor for a moment, sliding over the bar, as though she'd sensed someone watching. Skye's gaze fell into her drink before she could locate the fourth Syndicate leader—not that she would have anyway. No one knew who he was. He was known only as Chopard, and to her knowledge, no one knew whether he was Oscarovi or Vilhari.

When she glanced back at the mezzanine, Celestine had disappeared into the crowd, and Skye couldn't pretend she was watching anyone but the brunette, who had moved on to speaking with Edith Braithwaite. Did she know all the Syndicate leaders personally? The woman pressed her hand into Edith's, as though in farewell, the two of them nodding to one another politely. But Skye's keen eyes caught the merest hint of something passing between them. Had the Strix passed something to the brunette, or the brunette to the Syndicate boss? Skye blinked a few times, her vision blurring around the edges. She was losing control.

The black linen camisole she wore clung to the sweat beading down her muscular back. Even the single plait of her silver hair was heavy and damp, seeming to generate its own humidity in combination with the heat of the air and her body. She stood and the room spun. By instinct, her hand went to the rapier at her waist. She took her jacket from the chair, fishing out enough coin to pay for her drink and a generous tip.

The Merc's lavatory was unforgivably far from the atrium bar and painted a dizzying shade of bright green that was chipped in certain places to reveal layers of cream and pink paint underneath, giving the room the effect of a pastel, layered dessert. Or maybe that was the Oblivion talking. Skye couldn't be sure. She unbuttoned her pants and dropped onto a toilet to relieve herself. The door of the stall she'd stumbled into banged into her knees.

"Occupied," she roared.

"Apologies," a soft voice said from the other side. Footsteps retreated into the next stall, and Skye pushed the door shut, remembering to lock it this time.

She fumbled in her pockets, searching for the little vial of allheal she'd brought with her. It was lucky she'd thought to snatch it from Mother's studio before she'd left the estate; the stuff was worth a small fortune. Skye was as careful as she could be, using the tiny dropper in the vial to squeeze one drop of the substance under her tongue.

She waited for the tincture to take effect. Next to her, the person who'd almost barged in on her flushed, then exited the stall to wash her hands in the brass sink. Between the crack of the stall door, Skye could see the sparkling back of the woman's seafoam dress. It was the brunette. She nearly groaned aloud, thinking of the way she'd shouted at her.

By the time she was certain the woman had gone, Skye's head had cleared, the allheal having done its work. She put herself back together, pausing at the sink to wash her hands and splash water on her face, cleaning the rest of the kohl off her eyes and cooling her at the same time. A pit of unease formed in her stomach, as though the hot, close air in the Merc had changed somehow.

Skye paused—she'd always had a nose for trouble—a sense for when things were about to go sideways. It wasn't quite the Sight, she was nothing like Muse, but it had always served her well. The feeling didn't have the sharp flavor of society machinations, nor the sourness of violence—but instead, the metallic undertone of something more personal. A quick flash of pale green fabric falling over a curved hip crossed Skye's mind. The impression of unwanted pursuit followed quickly.

Skye's intuition had never manifested as a vision before, but she'd known Muse long enough not to question it. He'd told her it might come to this, that at some point her odd feelings might shift into something more. She slung her jacket over her shoulder—she had to leave the Merc. The tiny flash of true sight she'd received had the distinct smell of wisteria attached to it.

The brunette was outside, and she was in trouble. If there was one thing Skye was good at, it was managing trouble, and what better way to meet a beautiful woman than to save her from a dire situation? A smile tugged at the corner of her mouth as she exited the lavatory, taking long strides down the back hallway clouded with poppy smoke.

The glass doors to the Merc opened, and though the night air wasn't much cooler than inside the pleasure house, it was certainly fresher. She breathed in the rich scent of night-blooming flora, searching for wisteria more specifically. Skye stepped out into the night, appreciating the way the din of the Merc died as the door closed behind her. She hadn't realized how much the sound of all those people had been grating at her nerves. No wonder she'd downed too much Oblivion far too fast. She took a few steps onto the street, mist curling around her tall, black leather boots. The mist dampened sound and cast the acidic light of the aetheric lamps into eerie, billowing shapes.

The quiet made it easier to focus. Skye let her senses reach out around her, searching for any sign of the brunette or wisteria. She let out a brief string of curses. The smell of the wisteria that clung to every door frame and alley-bower filled her nose, the stuff was ubiquitous. That wouldn't help her, but the brunette couldn't have gotten far.

She calmed herself—left or right? More like higher or lower. The Merc sat on one of the steepest hills in the undercity, near the actual Halcyon Gate, for which the Syndicate was named. The gate between upper Pravhna and its lower half curved over the cobbled street to her left in all its wrought iron glory. It was not a working gate, but a symbol of a clear divide in cultures. To her right, the street curved down and away from her, ancient trees growing up amongst the townhouses as though the undercity's architecture was part of Pravhna's great forest. The ominous feeling she had about the brunette intensified as she stared into the deepest parts of the undercity below, cold dread taking hold of her.

That was where the brunette was: deeper in. The intoxicating effects of the Oblivion had gone, but some of its ability to lower inhibitions lingered. Skye, who was known in the first class for her devotion to examining potential outcomes before acting, walked towards whatever Lady Fate had in store for her this evening. Around her, lightning-flies that couldn't survive in upper Pravhna winked, their green-gold abdomens phantoms in the mist. This far down in the city, elemental spirits lurked around every corner, iridescent indigo wisps that she could only see in her peripheral vision, knowing that if she turned to face them head-on, they'd disappear.

A howler sat atop a crumbling stone obelisk in an overgrown garden, its dark eyes peering down at her. The little fey birds looked like a cross between a cat and a falcon, adorable and dangerous at the same time. Its head swiveled and it let out a soft "two-woo," as though in greeting.

Skye tipped her head to the bird. It was kin of a sort, after all. "Good evening, little one."

The bird narrowed its eyes at her as she passed. A block or so away, sounds of an argument floated out from a dark alley. The howler hooted again, louder this time. One side of the argument quieted immediately at the noise. The other grew louder. Skye's pace quickened, her hand moving instinctively to her rapier. Had she found the brunette? The hot night air tensed, and as she softened her footsteps, she could make out snippets of the conversation now.

". . . who you think you're fooling, but I'm on to you."

Skye paused, her heart thumping in its slow, even way despite the tension gathering in her shoulders. She was sure of it now. It was definitely the brunette. Something deeply protective stirred in her at the fierce note in the woman's voice.

"You're on to nothing, you fool," a second voice responded.

This one was harsh, with the cultured accent of the Citadel echelon—and it was *familiar*. Inwardly, Skye tensed. She would have to proceed carefully if a Vilhar of her own class was involved, more so if it was someone she knew.

The second speaker spoke again. "Where did you get *this*?" There was absolute fury in his voice.

Sounds of a scuffle ensued, with the first speaker hissing, "Get your hands off me, Viridian."

Skye unsheathed her rapier at the sound of the name and rounded the corner of the alley. A large Vilhar held onto the brunette. A sliver of moonlight shone down on them, hitting the brunette directly in the eyes. One fist was clenched at her side. She held something in it that she was keeping away from Viridian.

She kept her voice low and steady. "Viridian Montclair. What in the Lady's name are you doing?"

The Vilhar spun, his lip curling. He was a lord and she a mere chevalier, though she wasn't even that anymore. She was out of line, and they both knew it. "Mind your business, Aestra."

"Oh, but I can't," Skye said with a casual grin. The expression was foreign to her and thus fell off as quickly as it had arrived. "Let go of her."

The brunette's eyes rolled in exasperation as she tried again to pull out of Viridian's grip. The object she'd been keeping away from Viridian disappeared. She was using Skye's appearance to distract him. Clever girl. "I don't need your help, whoever you are. Thank you."

Viridian glared at the brunette and then at Skye. "I'm warning you, chevalier. Leave us."

Skye sheathed her sword. She could beat Viridian in a fight, but she didn't want the trouble killing him would rain down on her. She leaned against the wall of the alley, the cool limestone a balm as she racked the annals of Vilhari custom in the back of her mind. Surely, there was a loophole that would get rid of Viridian without bloodshed.

A slow, genuine smile spread over her face. She stared directly into the brunette's warm hazel eyes as she spoke. "She owes me coin."

As expected, Viridian visibly cringed. To speak of finances was vulgar, and the thought of someone owing someone else something as low as coin offended his sense of propriety.

The brunette's mouth fell open. The sight of her luscious, full lips sent heat through Skye. Every angle and curve on the woman was precise, as though she'd been carved from bronze. Skye kept her face still as stone, though her insides had already gone to molten lava for the brunette.

Viridian Montclair glared, a snarl on his lips. "Hand over the money you owe her and be done with it."

The brunette looked momentarily annoyed, then a gleam shone in her large eyes. She'd play along then. Skye was pleased; the brunette was sharp. She loved sharp women. Her blood sang, flooding every part of her, lighting her up from within.

"I don't have what I owe you," the brunette said. Her voice was like smoke now, smooth and husky at the same time, with a hint of an accent that suggested northern shores and seaside forests. "And we agreed I'd pay you in jewels this time, not coin."

Smart. If they were trading in jewels, only specific ones would do, especially if Skye was planning to sell to the Oscarovi. Not just any jewel would harness spirit power. "So we did," Skye purred. "But you've been avoiding me, and it's time to pay up. My buyer has been waiting far too long as it is."

Viridian's eyes narrowed. "When did House Aestra fall low enough to broker jewels to Oscarovi?"

Skye shook her head, as though Viridian was sorely behind the times. "Mother cut me out. I'd have thought you'd have heard something like that already, Montclair."

That got Viridian Montclair thinking, and his grip on the woman loosened enough for her to shy away from him. He was the type that liked to think he knew the inner workings of the high echelons. No matter that few outside her own family would know this yet and she was giving him valuable intelligence. It was worth it if Skye could get this brilliant woman away from him. Viridian Montclair had a reputation for being involved in unsavory business, and Skye wouldn't leave the brunette with him for anything.

The little howler glided down, as if out of nowhere, landing on the brunette's bare shoulder, rubbing its face along her soft jawline. The brunette took one step towards Skye, then another, as Viridian seemed to be chewing over the news that Skye Aestra, chevalier, first class, had been exiled from Vilhari society.

The brunette took her arm, her bare skin sliding against Skye in a way that sent chills down her spine. "I apologize, Viridian. I'm afraid we'll have to continue our conversation another time."

He startled, his silver eyes ablaze with fury, but he merely nodded. "Fine then."

The two of them watched as he stalked down the alleyway and onto the opposite street, listening as his footsteps disappeared, replaced by wing beats. The little howler took off after him.

"Rue will track him—make sure he's gone, not circling back," the brunette explained as she maneuvered them out of the alley. They were quiet as they went, both obviously worried that Viridian Montclair might make his way back. The brunette led Skye a few blocks deeper into the lower city then stopped in front of a pretty limestone townhouse. The building was covered in wisteria, with a large, round leaded glass window on the top floor that reminded Skye of a clock.

The brunette let go of Skye's arm and took one step up, then another. "Thank you for your assistance. Though, I didn't need your help."

"Didn't you?" Skye asked, stepping forward. "What did you hide from Viridian?"

The brunette frowned. "Nothing."

Skye's interest piqued. "I *saw* you. You hid something from him."

The brunette's dark eyes narrowed, and her full lips twisted a bit, as though she were thinking carefully. "He tried to take something from me. Something that is mine."

"It sounded like you were blackmailing him," Skye mused, her head tilting to the side.

"Is this some kind of interrogation?" the brunette said, recoiling from Skye, fear and defiance in her eyes. "Viridian called you chevalier. Are you going to arrest me for accosting him?"

Surprise gripped Skye's chest, stealing the breath from her lungs. "No," she breathed. "I was just curious about what got Viridian Montclair into such a tizz. He is the absolute worst."

A smile curved at the edges of the brunette's pretty mouth. "That he is."

Her arm extended towards Skye, her fingers uncurling to reveal a simple stick pin. In the shadows, Skye couldn't quite make out what the figure on it depicted.

The brunette's fingers closed around it before Skye could make out anything clearly. "He tried to take this from me. It was my mother's. I shouldn't have worn it this evening."

Odd that Viridian Montclair, whose House was one of the richest on Sirin, would have attempted to steal what had appeared to be a relatively simple stick pin. Everything about the brunette was mysterious, compelling even.

Mist curled around Skye's boots and the wisteria smelled like heaven, while the brunette smelled like something else, roses, but also something peppery and warm. She smelled like an expensive atelier and a wild garden all at once. Skye stepped closer—there was something else there. She'd assumed the woman was Oscarovi, but upon closer examination, she smelled her mistake.

"You're Vilhari?" Skye asked, letting out a breath.

The tiny, curvaceous brunette gritted her teeth. "That is none of your godsdamn business."

Some women were instantly ugly when they were angry. The brunette was even more beautiful. Everything about her drew Skye in. She hadn't meant to lean forward the way she was, their faces level now that the brunette was standing on the steps. Her soft, for they *must* be soft, rosy lips parted, and it was as though some preternatural force drew them together.

Skye's eyes fell closed. A tiny hand pushed her shoulder sharply. "What in the Lady's name do you think I'm about?"

Skye's eyes flew open. What *had* she thought the brunette was about? Why had she thought she was about to kiss her? If Skye were one to chuckle at her own expense, she would. But as she wasn't, she refrained.

The brunette looked around. The street was empty. Most people were out reveling or already abed this time of night. During Pravhna's six short weeks of true summer, most enjoyed the sweltering heat to their maximum ability. Skye happened to hate every second of it.

"Fate curse you," the brunette swore, running the back of one of her graceful hands across her damp forehead. "You've seen me with Viridian . . . Best you come up and talk for a few."

"To your flat?" Skye asked, somewhat amazed at her luck.

"No," the brunette retorted sharply. Her expression softened a measure. "To my garden."

She turned to unlock the door, giving Skye a full view of the back of her dress. It was intricately beaded and translucent, revealing the soft, generous curves of the brunette's lovely figure. Skye nearly fell to her knees in worship, summer's heat suddenly a welcome boon rather than a hideous burden.

The brunette's voice was low and sultry as she turned. "Are you coming?"

Heat coursed through Skye, pooling in her abdomen, slinking lower as the brunette's long lashes touched her flushed cheeks. Skye reached out and caught her bare hand. It was far too hot for gloves, so their skin met, the touch electric.

"I—" Skye couldn't form words.

She'd never been so affected by a woman before. Certainly, she'd felt immeasurable desire, pleasure, and all the rest for several women in her lifetime. But this was something different. The brunette had utterly captivated her in just a few hours. Going upstairs with her now felt dangerous, as though she might topple over the precipice of a cliff, never to return. It had already been a difficult day, and Skye was not accustomed to allowing her emotions so much leverage over her actions. She pressed as chaste a kiss as she could manage to the back of the brunette's hand.

"I'm afraid I cannot come up."

The brunette turned, her hazel eyes glinting with irritation. "And why not?"

The corner of Skye's mouth twitched. It had been so long since she smiled this much, she'd forgotten what it felt like. "You are far too beautiful to be alone with."

The brunette rolled her eyes, but Skye saw the bloom in her cheeks and the way her shoulder blades drew together ever so slightly as her back arched with arousal. Her mouth fell open, giving Skye the briefest glimpse of her soft, wet tongue. Skye stepped back, knowing she was practically panting.

The laugh that came out of her then was full throated and joyful. The first in months, maybe years. She shook her head, fishing a calling card out of her jacket pocket. It was her last one, and she'd meant to use it to reach Muse.

She handed it to the brunette, who took it with graceful fingers, reading Skye's name and rank. "Ring me up in daylight if you'd like to talk." Still, she needed a room for the night. "Do you know Muse?"

The brunette nodded. "Who doesn't know Muse?"

Skye laughed again. This was becoming a habit—Mother always accused her of being taciturn, but something about the brunette brought it out of her. "Can you point me in the direction of his current abode?"

"Yes," the brunette said, taking a step down. "He's just around the corner, as it happens."

"Thank you," Skye replied, hardly able to breathe the same air as the beauty in front of her. "Would you care to join me for breakfast tomorrow?"

"Perhaps," the brunette said, her lips curving into a smile.

Skye shook her head. She'd always been able to spot a liar. "You won't, will you?"

The brunette went up on her tiptoes, as though in slow motion. "I won't, but I'll want to. Probably more than you could guess."

Her lips met Skye's in a press of soft heat, her tongue silken, tasting of lilac wine. The brunette's soft body went languid against hers. Skye was almost afraid to touch her, lest the kiss end too soon, but she couldn't pass up the chance she was being given. She'd been starved of joy and affection for far too long, so she allowed herself this. Her hands skimmed the brunette's sides ever so lightly, over the curve of her hip.

If she pressed harder, she'd get a handful of the gorgeous woman's soft flesh and she wouldn't stop until she had her flat on her back. Skye was wont to take her right here on the steps, but she was a chevalier. First class. So she kept her touch light, eliciting a gasp of delight from the woman.

"Come up," the brunette breathed against her lips. "Spend the night with me."

Skye's breath came in hard gasps now as the brunette pulled on her braid, exposing her neck. She would cut the plait off tomorrow, foregoing the history of her family, signifying that she was no longer a member of House Aestra. Couldn't she give herself this one night of pleasure?

"What will happen after that?" Skye asked, knowing her heart was already too invested—and she didn't even know the woman's name.

Her card was still in the brunette's free hand, which she looked at now. "Chevalier, first class?"

Skye shook her head. "Not anymore. In name only, just like I told Montclair."

Regret filled the brunette's eyes. "I'm afraid that doesn't suit my purposes. I have a plan, you see."

Skye swallowed hard. The rejection stung deeper than she liked. "Say no more."

"We will meet again, Skye Aestra," the brunette said with a smile. The look in her eyes was one of clarity, but also the kind of soft longing that told Skye she hadn't wanted her to retreat. Not really. Something more complicated was at play here. "I'm keeping your card."

Skye made a little bow, her heart beating faster. So all wasn't lost. Perhaps the brunette's plan, whatever it was, had little bearing on her romantic prospects. It would be better not to be used for her position, after all.

"And whose name shall I read when I receive your call?"

The brunette sighed, gazing heavenward. "Hippolyta Endymion." Endymion. The surname was familiar, but Skye couldn't quite place it. "But you can call me Poe. Everyone does. In fact, I'd much prefer it if you didn't mention my full name to anyone else. Can I trust you?"

Skye nodded. "I'm a vault."

Poe slipped Skye's card into the bodice of her dress, and she nearly lost her resolve not to make a one-night affair of Poe Endymion.

The beauty's words shored it up, though. "I sense that about you," she said thoughtfully, taking a step backwards, one perfectly groomed eyebrow raised. "Yes, you're one to trust. What a rarity in this city. A chevalier with honor."

Skye inclined her head. It was true, for all the good honor had ever done her. "Please call on me."

She waited as Poe unlocked her door and went inside. When the light came on in the round window on the top floor, Skye set about her business, her heart thrumming with anticipation. Even if she never saw Poe Endymion again, it was a beautiful start to her new life —but she had a feeling she *would* see her again. She only hoped it would be soon.

The Aethereals Duology is complete. Thank you so much for reading.

If you would like to know more about Ashbourne's nephew Finn McKay and to see more of Morgaine Yarlo's mysterious journey through the world of The Tapestry, *The Immortal Orders* is a complete trilogy that starts with *Dark Night Golden Dawn*.

ACKNOWLEDGMENTS

This duology was written during one of the hardest periods of my entire life. Nobody tells you when your partner gets cancer that your whole life will change too. Mine sure did.

So thank you to everyone who made this book possible to publish the first time around. Thank you to Victoria and Kenna for always having my back with the words. Thank you to all the early readers. Thank you to the Rogue Order, always.

And most of all, thank you to you, the readers. None of this is possible without you.

Thank you endlessly for letting me be your author.

Allison

ABOUT THE AUTHOR

Allison Carr Waechter is probably feeding a monster cat right now. She lives in Minnesota with two enormous felines and one very supportive Book Daddy. She is a former college writing instructor, has some degrees in in English Literature, and loves books with magic and romance.

LET'S CONNECT

Join Allison's newsletter at www.allisoncarrwaechter.com for things like:

- Exclusive access to a library of bonus content for all of Allison's books
- Exclusive access to sneak peeks at character art, covers, etc.
- News about new books, special editions, and translations
- The latest news about works in progress
- Priority access to Allison's limited eARCs

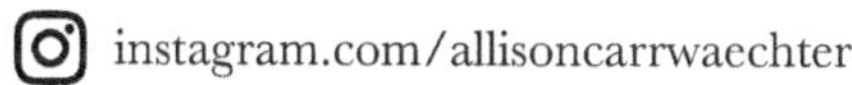 instagram.com/allisoncarrwaechter

ALSO BY
ALLISON CARR WAECHTER

THE TAPESTRY BOOKS

These series all exist in the same universe and timeline, and have some overlapping characters.

THE IMMORTAL ORDERS

Dark Night Golden Dawn

Beneath the Alabaster Spire

Awaken the Fifth Order

At the White Wolf (novella)

Behind the Iron Gate (standalone, sequel, FALL 2025)

THE AETHEREALS

The Hollow Plane

The Ravaged Dark

THE WORLD OF THE ORPHIUM MAERE

The Consulate

The Swan

The Angel (coming 2026)

BLACKBIRD HOLLOW

Co-written with Victoria Mier

Welcome to Blackbird Hollow